First Edition

I would like to thank the following people whose assistance has been integral to the creation of this work:
Julia, for her invaluable help and guidance with the text.
Dr Kaveh Farrokh, for his great knowledge of the Parthian Empire.
'Big John', for designing the cover.
Holly Martin, for the cover image.
Ardeshir Radpour, for his help regarding sourcing the cover image.

List of principal characters
Those marked with an asterisk * are Companions – individuals who fought with Spartacus in Italy and who travelled back to Parthia with Pacorus.
Those marked with a dagger † are known to history.

The Kingdom of Dura

*Alcaeus: Greek physician in the army of Dura

*Byrd: Cappodocian scout in the army of Dura

Dobbai: Scythian mystic, formerly the sorceress of King of Kings Sinatruces, now resident at Dura

*Drenis: Thracian, former gladiator in Italy and now a senior officer in the army of Dura

*Gallia: Gaul, Queen of Dura Europos

Kronos: soldier from Pontus, commander of the Exiles in the army of Dura

*Lucius Domitus: Roman soldier and former slave. Commander of the army of Dura

Marcus Sutonius: Roman soldier captured by Pacorus, now the quartermaster general of Dura's Army

*Pacorus: Parthian King of Dura Europos

Rsan: Parthian governor of Dura Europos

Spandarat: Parthian lord in the Kingdom of Dura

Surena: a native of the Ma'adan and the King of Gordyene

*Thumelicus: German soldier in the army of Dura

*Vagharsh: Parthian soldier who carries the banner of Pacorus in the army of Dura

The Kingdom of Hatra

Adeleh: Parthian princess, youngest sister of Pacorus and wife of Vata

Aliyeh: Younger sister of Pacorus and Queen of Media

†Apollonius: Governor of western Hatra

3

Assur: High priest of the Great Temple at Hatra

*Diana: former Roman slave, now the wife of Gafarn and Queen of Hatra

*Gafarn: former Bedouin slave of Pacorus, now King of Hatra

Herneus: Governor of eastern Hatra

Kogan: Parthian soldier, commander of the garrison of Hatra

Mihri: Parthian Queen of Hatra and mother of Pacorus

Spartacus: Prince of Hatra

Vata: boyhood friend of Pacorus, governor of northern Hatra

Vistaspa: Parthian commander of Hatra's Royal Bodyguard and general of Hatra's army

Other Parthians
Aschek: King of Atropaiene

Atrax: King of Media

Axsen: Queen of Babylon

†Mithridates: former king of kings, now an exile in Syria

*Nergal: Hatran soldier and formerly commander of Dura's horse archers, now the King of Mesene

Nicetas: Prince of Persis, son of Narses

†Orodes: King of Kings of the Parthian Empire

Peroz: Prince of Carmania

Phriapatius: King of Carmania

*Praxima: Spaniard, former Roman slave and now the wife of Nergal and Queen of Mesene

Silaces: soldier of the Kingdom of Elymais

Chapter 1

'Miserable Armenian bastards.'

I kicked at the ground in frustration, stubbing my toe painfully as I did so. Having just returned from a costly campaign the last thing the army needed was another war. I kicked at another flagstone.

'Treacherous Armenian bastards.'

Gallia, my wife, handed me back the letter from my brother King Gafarn, ruler of the Kingdom of Hatra, and raised an eyebrow at me while stable hands and the courier who had brought the bad news stared at me and then at each other.

'Bastards!'

For some reason that was the only word I could think of. I saw Dobbai descending the palace steps and begin to amble towards me. She was the old witch who had been the sorceress of King of Kings Sinatruces, ruler of the whole Parthian Empire. Dobbai now resided in the palace with my family. She was coming to gloat no doubt. Marvellous!

'Are you going to stand there kicking the ground all day long?' asked Gallia. 'Gafarn is requesting your aid.'

'What?'

'Did you read the entire letter?' I had not, so incensed had I been by the first few lines informing me that the Armenians had declared war on the Parthian Empire. I quickly read all the words.

'Problems, son of Hatra?' Dobbai stood in front of me, a knowing expression on her face.

'The Armenians have declared war on Parthia,' Gallia answered for me. 'Hatra is in peril.' Armenia, now a client state of Rome, lay to the northeast of Parthian territory and directly north of Hatra.

Dobbai nodded as though this information was no surprise to her.

'Why does this come as a shock to you? You are, after all, a warlord. Would you not seek to strike at your enemies when they were at their weakest?'

We were certainly that. The recent Battle of Susa that had finally ended Parthia's civil war had been a draining three-day affair resulting in Dura's army suffering heavy casualties. That was bad enough, but the armies of the other kings of our great alliance had also suffered substantial losses in the battle, none more so than the Kingdom of Hatra. It had lost its king, my father. And now Hatra was in danger from an Armenian invasion.

I looked at Dobbai, fixing her black eyes with my own. Sometimes I disliked intensely her ability to state the blindingly obvious.

'You should have dealt with the Armenians two years ago when you had the chance,' she continued. 'Your failure to kill Tigranes now returns to haunt you.'

'First of all,' I said loudly enough for most people in the courtyard to hear me, 'I did not fail to kill Tigranes. I was invited to support my father, may Shamash bless his memory, in his discussions with Tigranes. I was but one of the kings present that day.'

'But it is common knowledge that you begged your father to launch an attack against the Armenians,' she replied calmly. 'You knew that not to fight them that day was merely postponing the inevitable. And so it is.'

'Armenian bastards,' I muttered.

'I wish you would stop using such language, Pacorus,' said Gallia. 'Remember you are a king.'

'What are you going to do?' asked Dobbai.

That was a very good question to which I had no immediate reply.

'There will be a council meeting in one hour,' I announced.

As usual the meeting took place in the headquarters building standing opposite the palace inside the Citadel. This stronghold was perched on a high rock escarpment inside my capital city of Dura. On this occasion I had asked Strabo to attend in his capacity as quartermaster responsible for the army's horses, camels and mules. He positioned himself in a chair opposite Gallia where he could spend the meeting leering at her lithe figure. I asked Rsan, the city's governor, to start the proceedings. As usual he had brought two fresh-faced young clerks along to take notes of any decisions made. The offices of the building were stuffed full of parchments recording the details of every meeting since I had become King of Dura. To what end I never understood, aside from keeping the city's parchment makers in business. Because the room was fuller than normal the air was stuffy and oppressive, made worse by the lack of any wind outside. Everyone drank copious amounts of water from the jugs on the table to quench their thirsts.

Rsan cleared his throat.

'The king has called this meeting due to the unexpected news we have received from Hatra concerning the Armenian decision to commence hostilities against the empire.'

The two clerks scribbled furiously to write down Rsan's exact words. Why did he have to have two sets of records? I smiled – no doubt to have a spare set in case one got destroyed!

'King Tigranes is seeking to take advantage of the state of exhaustion the empire finds itself in following the toppling of Mithridates and Narses. He believes he has an excellent chance of seizing large chunks of the empire, specifically the Kingdoms of Hatra and Gordyene.'

'I would say their chances of doing so are excellent,' remarked Lucius Domitus, the army's general.

'We should have fought them when we had the chance,' added Kronos, commander of the Exiles, one of the two legions of foot soldiers I had raised. Both legions, Exiles and Durans, were trained and equipped in the same way as their Roman equivalents. Dobbai smirked at his comment.

'You are so right, Kronos,' I agreed, frowning at Dobbai, 'but we did not and nothing can alter the past. The Armenians will attack the Kingdoms of Hatra and Gordyene with the intention of conquering them. Gafarn has asked me for help and I expect Surena to do the same. The question is: can the army march north to reinforce and assist both Hatra and Gordyene?'

7

'Not a chance in hell,' remarked Domitus bluntly. 'It will be at least three months before it is ready to march anywhere, and even then it will be under strength. We lost a thousand legionaries, a hundred cataphracts, six hundred horse archers and a hundred and fifty squires. All dead.'

'And seventeen Amazons,' added Gallia gravely.

'Indeed,' said Domitus, 'and then there are the wounded.'

I looked at Alcaeus, our Greek chief physician who headed the army's medical corps. He frowned.

'I'm afraid it is not good news. Over two thousand legionaries have been treated for wounds received at Susa. Of those, around half have injuries that will take two months or more to heal properly, broken arms and wrists mostly. As for the horsemen, two hundred cataphracts were wounded in the battle, and of those over fifty require bed rest for a further month at least. Six hundred horse archers were also injured and around a hundred will not be back in the saddle for a minimum of five or six weeks.'

It was a most depressing summary and the only sound that filled the room after Alcaeus had finished speaking was the scribbling of the clerks as they noted everything down. The rest of us sat in silence, Domitus as ever toying with his dagger.

It was Gallia who spoke first. 'What will the Armenians do?'

'They will try to take Gordyene back first, no doubt,' I surmised, 'followed by an invasion of Gafarn's kingdom to seize the whole of northern Hatra, which means Vata at Nisibus will feel the full force of their wrath first.'

The Kingdom of Gordyene had been lost to Parthia when the Armenians had occupied it. It had subsequently been repossessed by Surena, formerly my squire who had been tutored in the arts of war at Dura. He had matured into a fine commander and so I sent him into Gordyene with an expeditionary force to wage war against its Armenian occupiers. But his martial brilliance had resulted in the Armenians being expelled from the kingdom altogether, earning him Gordyene's crown from a grateful King of Kings Orodes.

'Why did they declare war?' asked Kronos. 'Why not just launch an offensive? Seems odd.'

I thought of the Armenian King Tigranes, named 'Great' in some quarters, and his pompous son Prince Artavasdes.

'I assume Tigranes is making a grand gesture to illustrate to the world how powerful Armenia is.'

Dobbai let out a low cackle. 'You are wrong, son of Hatra. The Armenians wish to attract all attention to themselves so the empire's eyes are diverted from another source of danger.'

'What danger?' I asked.

'I see the eagles spreading their wings,' she replied casually.

Rsan was both confused and alarmed. 'Eagles? I do not understand.'

Domitus pointed his dagger at Dobbai. 'She means the Romans.'

'We have no reports of movements in Syria,' I replied.

Dobbai looked at me with a self-satisfied expression. 'You will. Like the Armenians they will have observed the empire tearing itself apart and will also conclude that it is the right time to strike, while it is weak.'

'Crassus will not arrive in Syria for many more weeks,' I assured her. 'Byrd has kept us fully abreast of the situation in the Roman province.'

Byrd, the army's chief scout, was also a successful businessman who lived in the great tent city of Palmyra. His offices in Syria supplied him with intelligence regarding Roman plans. We all knew that Marcus Licinius Crassus, Rome's richest man, was on his way from Italy with an army to assume the governorship of Syria but he was marching overland and the journey was long and arduous.

She looked away to stare out of the window at the courtyard. 'Have it your own way, son of Hatra.'

'What are you going to do about Gafarn's plea?' asked Domitus.

'Wait until I have heard from Orodes.'

Gallia looked most surprised. 'You will not aid your brother?'

'The Armenians will try to capture Nisibus first, but the city has strong defences and in Vata the region has a very able commander. Hopefully that will give us time to organise a coordinated response. It is better to wait until Orodes forms an alliance that we can join.'

'He's right, Gallia,' said Domitus. 'Dura's army would be more effective as part of a larger force that can march north to confront the Armenians.'

'Time is what we need to create a force large enough to defeat the Armenians,' I said. 'Vata will buy us time, and let us not forget that Surena in Gordyene will also be in peril.'

'I wouldn't worry about him,' said Domitus, 'he liberated the kingdom and he's more than capable of keeping hold of it.'

'You have changed your tune about him,' remarked Gallia. 'It was not long ago that you were calling him a puppy.'

Domitus nodded. 'True enough. But the puppy has grown into a cunning dog with sharp fangs.'

'Be that as it may,' I replied, 'he too will need assistance to battle a full-scale Armenian invasion, though I am sure Media and Atropaiene will send him help.'

'We can always take the lords north with us,' remarked Gallia. 'They were most unhappy that they were left behind when we fought Narses and Mithridates.'

Domitus and Kronos nodded in agreement and in truth the addition of twenty thousand horse archers would certainly stiffen the army. Unlike most Parthian kingdoms Dura had a standing army. But like every Parthian domain it had lords who in times of war could raise their own troops from those who worked on their lands. These were mostly horse archers.

'In fact,' continued Gallia, 'with the lords and their men we would not need to wait for Orodes.'

'Do not leave the kingdom undefended,' said Dobbai with force, 'unless you want the Romans to pluck it like a ripe fruit.'

I frowned at her. 'You keep going on about the Romans but as far as I know the border with Syria is quiet.'

Dobbai rose unsteadily to her feet and shuffled towards the door. 'Did I say anything about the Syrian border? The army must remain here if the city is to stay safe.'

Domitus winked at Kronos and then tried to be clever. 'I thought you said that as long as the stone griffin stood at the Palmyrene Gate Dura would never fall.'

The Palmyrene Gate was the main entrance to the city and above it stood a stone griffin statue that Dobbai had commissioned to safeguard Dura.

Dobbai spun round and pointed a bony finger at him. 'Even though you have been in Parthia for many years you still retain the arrogance of your race, Roman. If the city is left undefended then it will fall.'

'Then your words concerning the griffin were false,' Domitus shot back at her.

She curled her lip. 'Even the most simple-minded person knows that city walls need to be defended. Why would the gods help those who refuse to help themselves? Would you go into battle without your sword, Roman?'

Domitus looked around and smiled. 'Of course not.'

Dobbai regarded him coolly. 'Then Dura must remain protected at all times.'

'And what of the Armenians?' I asked.

She shrugged. 'What of them? The old fool Tigranes believes that the empire is weak and will fall into his lap. He will soon be disabused of that notion.'

But the empire was weak, and even though I concluded the meeting by informing all present that we would wait until we received word from Orodes I worried that the Armenians would flood into Hatra and Gordyene with ease. Following the Battle of Susa the victorious kings badly needed a period of rest in which to rebuild their forces. The Kingdoms of Hatra, Gordyene, Babylon and Media, to say nothing of Dura, had suffered substantial losses, especially among their heavy horsemen. To wage another war would sap their depleted resources further. My spirits were not improved when I received a letter from Orodes at Ctesiphon, the palace of the high king, informing me that aside from royal bodyguards the Kingdom of Babylon would be able to field a mere ten thousand horse archers, two hundred mounted spearmen and no foot soldiers to counter the Armenian threat. Those few foot soldiers the kingdom possessed – five thousand – were needed to garrison the cities of Babylon, Kish and Seleucia and the royal compound of Ctesiphon itself. Just as I could not leave the walls of Dura undefended, so Orodes could not denude the cities of his wife's kingdom of soldiers lest civil disorder broke out. The temples and palaces were a tempting target for organised bands of thieves and other undesirables who infested every city on earth.

'He's king of kings now,' said Domitus, 'so he can summon the forces of all the kingdoms in Parthia.'

The day after the meeting I had made an evening visit to his tent in the legionary camp located half a mile west of the city. Now that he had a wife – Miriam – and a residence in the city he usually spent the evenings inside the city walls, but he was sleeping in his tent as the army made ready to embark on a field exercise.

I poured myself a cup of wine and sat facing him at the table.

'There are only two kingdoms that have been largely untouched by the recent civil war,' I replied. 'Carmania in the southeast corner of the empire and Nergal's Kingdom of Mesene to the south. Carmania is around twelve hundred miles from Hatra and even if its king, Phriapatius, has been summoned it will take his army ten weeks to travel the length of the empire before it is any use.'

'Nergal will come,' Domitus assured me. Nergal was a Companion, one of those who like Domitus had returned with me from Italy following our time fighting by the side of Spartacus.

'Nergal will come,' I agreed, 'and will join with Orodes and then we will join with them. Let us hope it will be enough.'

'And the other kingdoms?'

I sipped at the wine. 'Exhausted by years of strife they will be reluctant to send troops to the west and leave their own lands vulnerable to attack. The nomads of the northern steppes and the Indians would exploit any weakness along the empire's northern and eastern borders.'

He leaned back in his chair. 'It is down to us, then.'

I tried to smile. 'It has always been down to us, my friend.'

'It won't take long to build up the army,' he reassured me. 'There is always an endless supply of young men presenting themselves at the gates of the Citadel to volunteer their services.'

Service in Dura's army was open to anyone and advancement was dependent on merit alone. That said, there were certain qualifications that Domitus as its general had insisted on, which were the same as those applied in the Roman Army. These were: a healthy body with all limbs intact (it never ceased to amaze me the number of one-legged individuals who tried to enlist on the grounds that sitting in the saddle did not require the use of two legs!), unmarried, no dwarfs, good eyesight and a good character. All those initially accepted were inducted into the replacement cohort where a further weeding-out process began to determine their suitability for a life in the military.

'It takes a year to turn a recruit into a fully trained legionary Domitus, and we do not have that length of time.'

'Perhaps we could speed up the process,' he mused, 'seeing as a lot of those presenting themselves at the Citadel are runaways from Syria and have probably seen some sort of military service.'

11

I thought of the long line of scrawny individuals in threadbare clothing I had seen that very morning, some of them bearing brands on their foreheads signifying they had been Roman slaves – FUG, *fugitivus* – runaway; KAL, *kalumniator* – liar; and FUR, *fur* – thief. Others had ears that had been bored – the mark of a Mesopotamian slave, no doubt having fled from other Parthian kingdoms, perhaps even from Hatra that lay just across the River Euphrates. Others had made the journey from Egypt, runaway slaves who had worked in the pharaoh's gold and copper mines.

'No,' I replied. 'We stick to the system that has made Dura strong.'

'Well,' he replied, 'that means the legions will be two thousand men down when we march.'

I finished my wine. 'Can't help that.'

'And the horsemen?'

I stood up and walked over to the entrance of the tent. As it was summer and it was hot the flaps were tied back to allow what was now only a whisper of wind to enter. Outside was the parade ground and beyond it the camp's central avenue that led to the main entrance flanked by neat rows of tents.

'The older squires can be promoted to make up the losses among the cataphracts and Vagises will send messages to the lords asking that they spread the word among their retainers that I am looking for new horse archers. We should be able to replace the losses we suffered at Susa in three months.'

'You think we have that long?'

The sky was pink as a yellow sun descended in the western sky to signal the end of another day.

'I hope so. I sincerely hope so.'

I turned and walked back to the table.

'The one thing in our favour, the only thing thus far,' I said, 'is that we have time to defeat the Armenians before Crassus arrives.'

The next day I sat in the throne room and dictated letters to Orodes, Surena, Atrax and Gafarn. Rsan fussed over the scribes like a mother hen while Gallia, sitting next to me, observed the proceedings.

I informed Orodes that Dura's army would prepare to march north but would wait until he arrived with what forces he could muster from Babylon and Susiana. The latter kingdom was his own and ordinarily would have supplied a great many soldiers, but most of them had been slaughtered at Susa when we had defeated Narses and Mithridates. Those still alive would be needed for garrison duties, for to leave the kingdom's towns and cities undefended would be to invite the hill men who infested the nearby Zagros Mountains to pillage them at will.

I pledged aid to both Surena and Atrax, King of Media. Media lay to the east of Hatra and south of Gordyene. But I informed them both that at present I was unable to offer any assistance, but hoped that they could assist each other. They could also call upon King Aschek of Atropaiene. The latter was always reluctant to embroil his kingdom in conflict but as his realm was positioned directly east of Gordyene he knew that if Surena fell then his lands would be open to an Armenian invasion. I also knew that Orodes would request the assistance of Nergal and so I also sent a letter to Uruk stating that I looked forward to linking up with him and his men when we assembled our joint forces.

As a scribe sitting at a desk in front of me completed each letter, the parchment was folded and then Rsan sealed it with hot wax, into which was pressed my griffin symbol. Then it was given to a waiting courier whose horse stood ready in the courtyard.

'What are you going to say to Gafarn?' asked Gallia.

'That I will wait until I receive word from Orodes,' I replied, and then pointed to a scribe waiting for instructions.

'He will expect you to reply that you are marching to Hatra straight away.'

'It would be better to wait for Orodes and Nergal,' I reiterated. 'Our combined forces joined with Hatra's will be more than a match for the Armenians, who have yet to make any moves aside from declaring war on the empire.'

I again indicated to the scribe that I was ready to begin dictating when Dobbai ambled into the room, and proceeding to ignore us walked over to the table Rsan was standing by, a rolled parchment in her hand. Ignoring him she picked up the crucible of wax that was being heated over an oil lamp and poured some on the parchment to seal it, then took the wax stamp and pressed it into the hot substance. By now everyone in the room was looking at her as she went about her business seemingly oblivious to our presence.

I cleared my throat. 'In case you had not noticed I am in the middle of important business.'

Dobbai gestured to one of the waiting couriers, who looked at Rsan in confusion.

'Come here, boy,' she snapped. 'Take no notice of the tallyman.'

Rsan glowered at her then turned to face me. 'Majesty, I really must protest.'

I held up a palm to the courier. 'These riders carry letters that concern the affairs of the empire, Dobbai.'

She looked at me with pursed lips and held up the parchment. '*This* is also important, son of Hatra, and must reach its destination speedily.'

Rsan was now beside himself with anger at being treated so disrespectfully in front of everyone and gestured to the two guards standing by the closed doors to the chamber to come forward. He pointed at Dobbai.

'Escort her to the palace's private wing.'

Dobbai spun on her heels to face the approaching legionaries.

'Touch me,' she said, 'and your balls will wither to nothing and maggots will grow in your bellies.'

The two men, veterans of many battles, froze and looked at each other and then at me in alarm, while beside me Gallia suppressed a giggle. I frowned at her before waving the guards back to their posts.

13

'May I enquire the nature of the important business that is contained in the despatch you are holding?'

Dobbai turned to face me, a self-satisfied smug look on her face. 'You may enquire and I may choose to ignore you. But suffice to say that it will be to your advantage in the coming struggle with your enemies.'

She again waved forward one of the couriers and I shook my head at Rsan who was about to protest. Dobbai handed the man the parchment and leaned towards him to whisper something in his ear.

'The post station in Neh will know where to send it once it has reached there.'

'Neh!' I said loudly. 'That is at the other end of the empire. What possible business can you have in Neh?'

Dobbai ignored me and continued speaking to the courier. 'Go now and may the gods protect you.'

He bowed his head to her and then walked from the hall, the guards closing the doors behind him as he left. Dobbai grimaced at Rsan and wandered back towards the private wing of the palace.

'Are you going to say anything further on this matter?' I asked.

'I would,' she replied, 'only you have more pressing matters to attend to.'

I looked at Gallia and shook my head. Dobbai disappeared behind the door at the rear of the throne room leading to the wing that contained our sleeping quarters just as muffled voices came from behind the closed doors of the main entrance. They swung open to reveal the figure of Byrd.

Rsan looked nonplussed as my chief scout strode towards the dais and halted before me. His swarthy face and slovenly attire were covered in dust and it was obvious he had been in the saddle for hours. He nodded at Gallia and then me.

'Romani are going to invade Haytham's kingdom,' he announced without emotion.

I stood up and gestured for him to sit on my throne.

'When?' I asked.

He slumped down into the high-backed chair.

'Two weeks,' he replied. 'My office in Antioch told me of this and I inform Haytham. He gathers his forces to meet Romani at the border.'

I pointed at the guards by the doors.

'Go and find General Domitus and request his presence here, Lord Kronos as well. Rsan, where is Aaron?'

'In the treasury, majesty,' he answered.

'Get him too.'

I ordered water to be fetched for Byrd as we waited for Domitus and the others to arrive. The scribes sat at their desks looking at each other in confusion as I began pacing in front of the dais mulling over this most unfortunate development. Gallia brought me back to the present.

'Are you going to answer Gafarn's plea for help, Pacorus?'

I stopped pacing. 'Hatra will have to look to its own means for the present, my sweet.'

14

However, while I waited I did dictate a letter to Gafarn and another to Orodes informing them of Byrd's news and that it would now be impossible for Hatra's army to march north until the threat that had appeared in the west had been dealt with. Rsan returned with Aaron ten minutes later and twenty minutes after that Domitus and Kronos appeared. Byrd was still seated in my chair as the clerks and couriers filed out of the chamber and the doors were closed behind them. Domitus nodded to Byrd.

'I take it you have not summoned us here to announce that you have renounced your throne and Byrd is now king.'

'The Romans are about to invade Haytham's lands,' I said.

Domitus nodded thoughtfully. 'How many men?'

'Two legions,' replied Byrd, 'plus light troops and horsemen. They will cross border in two weeks.'

Byrd told us that Haytham had summoned his lords and their followers to join him at the border.

'Which is where?' asked Kronos.

'Around a hundred miles west of Palmyra.'

Domitus looked alarmed. 'Haytham intends to engage the Romans in battle?'

Byrd nodded then shrugged. 'He is Agraci king. He cannot look weak to his people.'

Domitus ran a hand over his cropped scalp then looked at me. I knew what he was thinking. Brave though Haytham's warriors were, they would be no match for trained Roman legions. It could be a bloodbath.

'I tried to tell Haytham that Romani are fearsome soldiers,' said Byrd despairingly, 'but he no listen.'

'Unless he gets lucky he will fail,' remarked Domitus.

'Haytham did not send me, Pacorus,' said Byrd, 'but I ask you to support him in this war.'

I looked at him and then Gallia and remembered the first time that we had met the Agraci king, when we had taken his daughter Rasha back to her father following her incarceration at Dura. There had been only four of us on that journey – Gallia, Byrd, Haytham's daughter and myself – that had taken us deep into Agraci territory lying to the west of Dura. He could easily have killed us all, especially me, a Parthian, one of the implacable enemies of his people. But he had allowed us to live and from that time friendship had grown between Dura and the Agraci. Since then Haytham had come to my aid twice: once when I had faced the Roman Pompey and a second time when Narses and Mithridates had me cornered like a rat. What's more Malik, Haytham's son, was a close friend who had accompanied me on many campaigns and Rasha was like a daughter to me. Haytham was my friend and ally and I would not desert him.

'Dura will assist Haytham, Byrd, have no fear.'

Gallia smiled at me approvingly.

'Is that wise, majesty?' queried Rsan.

'Haytham is Dura's friend, Rsan,' I answered. 'He has come to my aid more than once. What sort of man would I be if I deserted him now?'

My governor brought his hands together in front of his chest.

'Indeed, majesty, but with Hatra in peril is not your first duty to your brother, a family member and a fellow Parthian?'

'Hatra's army is strong, Rsan,' I assured him, 'but Dura cannot tolerate the Romans occupying Palmyra, which is only seven days' march from this very chamber.'

But Rsan was not thinking about strategy or the Romans.

'There may be some who might criticise your decision to favour the Agraci over your own people, majesty.'

Gallia crossed her arms and fixed Rsan with her unblinking eyes. 'And who would they be, Rsan?'

My governor suddenly looked most uncomfortable. 'Not I, majesty, of course not.'

'Of course not,' remarked Domitus dryly.

'But the courts of other Parthian kings may be surprised that you would support Haytham instead of your brother.'

'I have never been interested in the opinions of other courts, Rsan,' I replied, 'especially as a good number of them have spent the past few years trying to destroy me. As for Gafarn, the walls of both Nisibus and Hatra are strong and Gafarn can muster tens of thousands to fight the Armenians. It will avail us little if we defeat the Armenians only to see Dura captured by the Romans, who will then use this city to launch a full-scale invasion of the empire.'

Byrd stood up, walked from the dais and embraced me. 'Then I can tell Haytham that the army of Dura will be marching to reinforce him, Pacorus?'

I smiled at him. 'Yes, my friend, you can tell him that we are on our way.'

Rsan was shaking his head but my mind was made up.

'It will take us a week to get to Palmyra,' said Domitus. 'How long did it take you to get here, Byrd?'

'Just under four days.'

Domitus was most concerned. 'Which means that Haytham will leave Palmyra in two days if he is going to give battle at the border. We will never catch him up.'

'We might,' I answered, 'if we take horse archers only.'

All this time Aaron had been standing near Rsan observing the proceedings and probably wondering why he had been summoned. But now I turned to him.

'Aaron, what news have you heard from Alexander and his Jewish fighters?'

Dura had been instrumental in providing weapons to Jewish fighters in Roman-occupied Judea, for which we had been paid handsomely in gold. They were led by a prince named Alexander Maccabeus, a man who dreamed of freeing his homeland from Roman oppression but who had been heavily defeated last year and his men scattered. He himself still lived, though, and while he did so the flame of rebellion still burned in Judea.

'I heard from him three months ago, majesty,' said Aaron. 'He is holding out in the hills of eastern Judea.'

'Good,' I said, 'please write to him again today, asking that he attack the Romans in Judea with all the strength he has. Anything to divert Roman eyes from Palmyra.'

After resting and taking refreshments Byrd rode back to Palmyra on a fresh horse and I sat down with Gallia, Domitus and Kronos to work out a plan. Despite their protests I decided to take Vagises and his horse archers, who could ride at a moment's notice. Gallia wanted to accompany me but I told her to muster the lords and their men and to follow me to Haytham's capital after she had done so. The legions and cataphracts would remain at Dura. Taking the horse archers would enable us to cover thirty miles a day at least, meaning we would reach Palmyra in five days.

I set off the next day with two and a half thousand horse archers and a thousand camels carrying spare arrows. Gallia sent a summons to all the lords to attend her at the Citadel with every horse archer they could raise. In this way I hoped to muster an additional twenty thousand riders to support Haytham. In addition to spare quivers the camels carried waterskins, food and fodder for the horses, the humped beasts themselves being quite able to subsist on their bodies' reserves until we reached Palmyra.

We rode over thirty miles the first day and nearly forty on the second, camping at night under the stars with only our cloaks to sleep in. It felt strange not resting for the night behind a ditch and rampart surmounted by stakes as was the custom in Dura's army, but we posted guards every ten paces and at any one time half the men were standing to arms, being relieved every two hours. The days were hot and dry, particularly on the third morning when we broke camp before dawn and rode for five hours before resting the horses for three hours, then commencing our journey once again for another three hours. As we neared Palmyra I noticed the reduced amount of traffic on the road, a sure sign that conflict was imminent. The trade caravans of the Silk Road had a sixth sense when it came to discerning trouble and acted accordingly. Thus the number of caravans travelling through Dura on their way to Palmyra and then on to Syria and Egypt would diminish to nothing until after hostilities had ceased. They would travel north to Hatra instead, though as that kingdom was soon to be embroiled in war traffic might cease altogether.

On the fifth morning we spotted the Jabal Abu Rujmayn, the imposing mountain range located due north of Palmyra, and two hours later ran into an Agraci patrol five miles east of the great oasis settlement. It comprised half a dozen elderly men wrapped in black robes, their black face tattoos faded on their leather-like tanned skin. Their commander, a tall, gangly individual with piercing hazel eyes, bowed his head to me.

'Greetings, lord. We were expecting you.'

Byrd had obviously arrived before us. 'Where is your king?'

'He has taken a great host of warriors west, lord, to fight the invaders.'

I closed my eyes. We had arrived too late. I prayed to Shamash that Haytham would not engage the Romans until we reached him. Perhaps there was still time.

'Prince Malik accompanies his father?'

He smiled to reveal a set of perfect white teeth. 'Yes, lord. He hopes to slaughter his father's enemies.'

Hopefully Malik would temper his father's eagerness to immediately attack the Romans.

'We are to escort you to the governor's tent, lord.'

'The governor?'

He nodded. 'Yes, lord, the king left Byrd as chief of Palmyra in his absence.'

Vagises took the companies to one of Palmyra's great watering holes that were filled by springs bringing the precious liquid from deep in the earth, making the surrounding desert bloom. I accompanied the grizzled old Agraci warrior to the middle of the settlement where Byrd's tent was pitched, riding through a multitude of canopies and a site that was seething with activity. At least Haytham had not ordered the evacuation of Palmyra. Not yet.

My escort left me at the entrance to Byrd's tent where a servant took Remus, my stallion, from me and another escorted me inside the expansive goat hair structure. I waited for my presence to be announced and then Noora, Byrd's wife, appeared, embracing me and welcoming me to her 'modest' home, which in truth was grander than Haytham's own tent.

'Byrd is most unhappy, lord,' she said to me in hushed tones as we entered the main compartment where my friend was seated on a heap of cushions on the carpeted floor. 'He wanted to go with Haytham and Malik but the king insisted that he stay here to rule Palmyra in his absence.'

He rose and we embraced.

'It is a great honour that Haytham has bestowed on you,' I said.

'I no governor,' he sniffed, 'I should be with him and Malik.'

While the small army of servants that he and Noora had amassed served us refreshments Byrd told me that Haytham had departed with his warriors two days ago, intent on stopping the Romans at the border.

'I told him that you were coming but he would not wait. Yasser and Vehrka said it was dishonourable to remain idle in face of enemy invasion.'

Yasser and Vehrka were two of Haytham's lords and the latter was Malik's father-in-law.

'I can understand that,' I replied, 'especially as it is Vehrka's lands that the Romans are marching across.'

'Not only Romani,' said Byrd.

'Who else?' I asked in alarm.

'King Sampsiceramus of Emesa.'

He may have had a ridiculously long name but Sampsiceramus ruled a prosperous kingdom, made rich by the profits of the Silk Road. When Pompey had conquered Syria and Judea the ruler of Emesa had thrown in his lot with the Romans, becoming their client king. Located on the eastern bank of the River Orontes and close to the Mediterranean coast, the city of Emesa was around a hundred miles west of where I was sitting and the destination of the trade caravans once they had passed through Palmyra. From there they travelled either north to Roman Syria or south to Egypt.

'He provides slingers, archers and spearmen for Romani,' continued Byrd. 'Haytham should have waited for your archers,' he finished glumly.

If Haytham engaged the Romans and their allies before I reached him then he would be at a great disadvantage when it came to missile power for the Agraci horsemen had few archers and no slingers.

'Who else is with the Romans?' I asked, hoping the answer would be Mithridates.

Byrd knew what I was alluding to and smiled. 'He and his mother still at Antioch, so my spies tell me.'

I heard horses' hooves outside and moments later Rasha burst into our company. She was now on the verge of womanhood and her body had become more curvy and her face more attractive. Gone was the young girl I had first encountered when I arrived at Dura. In her place was a raven-haired beauty. I stood and was nearly toppled over as she threw her arms around me and kissed me on the cheek.

'Greetings little princess,' I said, though she was nearly as tall as me now and in a couple of years would no doubt surpass my height.

'Where's Gallia?' she asked, looking around before kissing Noora and then Byrd.

'She will be here soon.'

'And then we will go and fight the enemy,' she beamed.

'And then you will stay here,' commanded Byrd. 'Your father has enough to worry about without his daughter getting into trouble.'

Rasha stuck her tongue out at him and Noora laughed. How great was Byrd's influence among the Agraci that Haytham himself would trust him with the life of his daughter and the safekeeping of his city.

The next day Rasha was thrilled when Gallia rode into Palmyra at the head of the Amazons and twenty thousand horse archers. As usual the latter were led by the old brawler Spandarat, who was itching for a fight. Byrd wanted to give a great feast to celebrate the arrival of Gallia and my lords but I declined the offer. For one thing I did not want Spandarat and his fellow nobles getting roaring drunk and being unfit for duty the next day. So he went to bed an unhappy man but at least woke without a hangover and was in the saddle before dawn to ride alongside Gallia, Vagises and me as we headed west into the desert across the rock and

19

gravel steppe. It was already hot and everyone was wearing either floppy hats or head cloths, their helmets dangling from the horns of their saddles.

Five hours after leaving Palmyra I saw a great dust cloud on the horizon and ordered a halt.

'Is it a sandstorm?' asked Vagises.

I shook my head. I had seen many sandstorms during my life, had observed the terrifying orange-brown wall of sand come out of the desert, the bottom of which appeared to contain millions of desert flies. The wall of sand could be up to a mile high and swallow whole towns and cities in its path. The storms could last for hours, days or even weeks but this was not one. This dust cloud was too sparse and immobile: the particles were being kicked up by thousands of horses and men. We had found Haytham and the Romans.

I gave the order to deploy into battle formation: a thousand of Dura's archers on the left wing, another thousand on the right and the remainder in the centre with the Amazons. The lords were deployed behind the centre – twenty blocks of horsemen numbering a thousand riders each. And behind them were the camels carrying spare arrows. Vagises sent a score of horsemen to scout ahead while we advanced at a trot towards the battle on the horizon.

They returned to report that the Romans and their allies were advancing towards us in a long line, having apparently routed the Agraci. The latter were still launching attacks against the enemy but their efforts were uncoordinated and haphazard. I turned to Vagharsh and told him to unfurl the standard, then ordered a general advance.

Ahead I could see a mass of black riders – Haytham's warriors – and could hear shouts and screams as men fought and killed each other. We broke into a canter as we headed towards the battle and then I saw a party of Agraci galloping towards me. I ordered a halt as Malik and fifty of his men pulled up their horses. The prince looked tired and angry.

He nodded at me. 'Greetings, Pacorus, you are a sight for sore eyes.'

He noticed Gallia and bowed his head at her.

'I am glad to see that you are unhurt, Malik,' she said.

He glanced back at the battle raging around a thousand paces in front of us. 'The same cannot be said for many of my people.'

'What happened?' I asked.

'The Romans and their treacherous allies from Emesa appeared two hours after dawn and my father ordered an immediate assault on them. I have ridden with you too long, my friend, not to know that our horsemen would not be able to break their formation but he would have none of it. So we attacked and their archers and slingers positioned among the legionaries cut down many of our riders before they could get close to their ranks.'

'They deployed into a square?' I asked.

He nodded. 'A great hollow square that we attacked on all sides and inside it they hid their horsemen, and when our losses mounted and we tired they formed into line and then their horsemen attacked us.'

20

'Where is your father now, Malik?' asked Gallia.

'Desperately trying to halt the Romans.' He turned to me. 'He needs your help, Pacorus.'

'We will halt the enemy's advance, my friend,' I replied. 'But the first thing you must do is to ride to your father and convince him to pull his warriors back, to disengage from the enemy.'

Malik shook his head. 'He will never agree to that.'

I leaned over and grabbed his arm. 'You must convince him to do so, otherwise the Romans will be in Palmyra this time tomorrow.'

He turned from me and made to kick his horse forward then swung in his saddle.

'Lord Vehrka is dead.'

I was shocked. 'How?'

'Killed by the Roman horsemen. They are very good, Pacorus, well led.'

He urged his horse forward and then he and his escort were galloping back to the battle line.

The Agraci did not fight as part of an organised army but as individuals grouped round their lords, much like the retainers of my own lords, and though brave and fearless were no match for the discipline and fighting skills of the Roman Army. Now they fell back in dispirited and angry groups, passing through my men as Haytham and his son rode up to where Gallia and I waited on our horses. With them were Yasser and a dozen other Agraci lords. Haytham wore a livid expression. He bowed his head to Gallia and nodded at me.

'I thank you on behalf of the Agraci people for coming to our aid, Pacorus. Byrd exceeds his authority, I think.'

'We are happy to help our friends and allies, lord king,' said Gallia.

'We are glad to fight alongside you, lord,' I said.

'These Romans are like cockroaches, difficult to kill,' he spat.

I looked beyond Haytham to see long lines of red shields advancing towards us with horsemen on their flanks.

'There are slingers and archers interspersed among those legionaries,' warned Malik.

'If your men form up behind my own,' I said to Haytham, 'then we will first bring the enemy to a halt.'

By now the vast majority of the Agraci had passed through the gaps between the lords and their men in the centre and Vagises' horse archers on the wings. The latter now moved to position themselves directly opposite the Roman horsemen on the flanks of the legion and a phalanx of Emesian spearmen that were moving forward at a steady pace. I turned in the saddle and waved Spandarat forward.

I pointed at the enemy troops approaching. 'Spandarat, we must halt those troops opposite. Therefore if you and the other lords would assault them I would be eternally grateful.'

He rubbed his hands together and grinned. 'Lovely.'

21

He withdrew to where his fellow noblemen waited on their horses and imparted my wishes to them. Moments later they were galloping to take up position in front of their men and then led them forward.

Within minutes twenty thousand horse archers were unleashed against the ranks of the enemy. They charged in twenty great columns, each one grouped behind their lord and began shooting their arrows at a range of seven hundred paces from their foes. The missiles arched high into the sky and then fell onto the heads of the Romans and their Emesian allies, the latter in their great phalanx were not able to lock their shields above their heads like the men of the Tiber. The slingers and archers interspersed among the Romans suffered the most casualties, being struck by dozens of arrows that suddenly fell among them.

My lords may not have led the most disciplined or well-equipped soldiers in the world but they knew how to conduct themselves in battle. They knew that if they moved at speed and kept out of range of the enemy they would improve their effectiveness and reduce their own casualties. And so at a distance of four hundred paces from the front ranks of the enemy their men wheeled their horses right and right again to ride back to their starting position, twisting in the saddle to shoot a parting arrow at the opposition over the hindquarters of their horses as they did so.

While the enemy's centre was being subjected to this arrow storm Vagises' horse archers on either wing held their positions, while behind where I watched the drama beside Gallia, Haytham and his warriors reformed and strained to be unleashed once more. To our front the lords' men were shooting around five arrows a minute, meaning their would empty their quivers in six minutes, but in that short space of time they managed to halt the advance of the enemy. As the lords led their men to the rear to replenish their quivers from the camel train a dust-covered Spandarat rode up to me with a big grin on his face.

'Soon as we've stocked up on arrows we'll go back and finish them off.'

I peered past him at the wall of locked Roman shields.

'You have halted them, well done,' I said. 'But for the moment we wait to see what the enemy will do.'

His grin disappeared.

'Time to finish them off, otherwise they will crawl back to Emesa.'

'That is for Haytham to decide,' I reminded him.

The attack by Dura's lords had taken the enemy by surprise. Believing that Haytham's warriors were assaulting them, they had once more prepared to fend them off with slingers and archers. Instead they had been subjected to a missile storm that had felled many of their own missile troops, who carried no shields and wore no body armour. Their own bows had a shorter range than our own recurve models and though their slings could shoot as far, our initial volley had been such a surprise that they had failed to shoot any missiles in return.

Malik and Haytham now rode forward to join out little group as silence descended over the battlefield and the choking dust that had hung over it mercifully began to slowly dissipate.

'They have been halted, lord king,' I said to Haytham.

'But they still stand on my land,' he growled.

I knew he would launch another general attack that would achieve little apart from reaping another harvest of Agraci dead, but it was not my place to tell him what to do in his own kingdom. Nevertheless, I felt honour bound to point out that it would be rash to launch a frontal assault and was just about to say so when Malik spoke.

'Their horsemen are advancing.'

We all looked to where he was pointing at the enemy's right wing, from where a group of horsemen were advancing against Dura's horse archers.

'Roman horsemen,' he sneered, 'the same ones who inflicted many losses on us earlier.'

'Vagises will deal with them,' I assured him.

'What about those?' I heard Haytham say.

I turned in the saddle to stare at the enemy's other wing, which consisted of a great mass of spearmen wearing white tops and silver helmets.

'The horsemen of King Sampsiceramus,' spat Malik.

There appeared to be around a thousand Roman horsemen but many times that number of Emesian riders who were now advancing with spears levelled towards the thousand Durans facing them. I turned to Spandarat.

'You and the lords must assist our horse archers on the right, Spandarat, otherwise they will be forced back' I looked sheepishly at Haytham. 'With your permission, lord king.'

He smiled savagely. 'You have done more in twenty minutes than I did in a whole morning, Pacorus, so please carry on.'

'Go, Spandarat,' I ordered.

He whooped with delight, dug his knees into his rough old mare and galloped away to his fellow nobles.

'I will assist Spandarat,' announced Gallia, who turned and raised her bow. 'Amazons!'

Her warriors raised their bows in acknowledgment and moments later were riding behind their queen as she accompanied Spandarat towards the seething mass of enemy horsemen. It was the first time Haytham had seen Gallia on the battlefield. Formerly she had always been charm and beauty in his presence, not the fearless killer he now saw.

'You do not fear for her safety, Pacorus?'

'Shamash will protect her,' I replied, hoping that my god would wrap her in a cloak of invulnerability.

I turned and signalled to the commander of the six companies of Duran horse archers who were grouped immediately behind me.

'We go to aid Lord Vagises, follow me with your men.'

23

He saluted and rode back to his companies as Malik's bodyguard – a hundred black-clad warriors – closed around him.

'I am coming with you, Pacorus.'

I smiled at him. 'It would be an honour, my friend.'

'Are we going or not?' grumbled Vagharsh as his horse scraped impatiently at the earth.

'I would ask you to be patient a little longer, lord king,' I said to Haytham, 'and the day will be yours.'

He raised his hand as I bellowed at Remus to move. He reared up on his hind legs and bolted forward as I headed for the left flank, followed by Vagharsh, Malik, a hundred Agraci warriors and six hundred horse archers. In front of us Vagises had withdrawn in the face of the Roman onslaught, enticing their horsemen forward in expectation of an easy victory against the lightly armed horse archers they faced. The Romans, maintaining a tight, disciplined formation, were charging now, their large, tan-coloured shields tight to their left sides and their spears levelled. I pulled my bow from its case and then extracted an arrow from my quiver as we rode across the front of the densely packed ranks of Haytham's warriors towards the Romans. The Agraci cheered us as we passed, though they were probably acclaiming their prince who was accompanying us rather than me or my men.

I nocked the arrow in the bowstring and leaned forward in the saddle as Remus thundered across the ground made bone-dry by a merciless sun. The Romans were cheering now as they chased Vagises' apparently fleeing horsemen. Signallers in the horse archers accompanying me blew their horns to indicate the charge as we broke into a fast gallop.

We were closing on the left rear of the Roman formation as I released my first arrow and reached into my quiver to nock another. Behind me six companies of horse archers deployed into line as their members released arrow after arrow at the Romans, tearing gaps in their ranks as the missiles struck animals and riders, the bronze arrowheads piercing flesh and smashing bones. Above me the air was thick with shafts as six hundred men loosed around three and half thousand arrows a minute at the enemy.

The Romans in the rear ranks, thinned by my archers, halted and desperately tried to reform to meet the new threat. But stationary targets meant my men could now aim more accurately as the companies slowed their pace and then wheeled right so they could ride parallel to the Roman line, raking them with arrows as they did so. And then Vagises' men began their own shooting, at first releasing their bowstrings over the hindquarters of their horses and then halting to about-face to shoot volley after volley so the front ranks of the Romans literally rode into a wall of arrows. This first halted them and then forced them back as saddles were emptied and horses were struck multiple times by missiles.

We kept our distance from the Roman horsemen as they were armed with spears and shields and to fight them at close quarters would be to invite our destruction. Our advantage lay in archery from a safe distance, using the power and range of our bows to shoot them to pieces. The Roman commander also realised this for I heard trumpet blasts and then saw the horsemen change direction.

Their discipline was magnificent as they about-faced as on the parade ground and withdrew to the safety of their own lines. I saw a figure on a brown horse, a man sitting tall in the saddle, his stature increased by a great red crest in his helmet. He remained at the rear of his horsemen so all could see that he did not fear us. He was undoubtedly their commander.

I dug my knees into Remus' sides and he shot forward to pursue the fleeing Romans, Vagharsh, Malik and his warriors immediately behind me. The Roman with the great crest saw us and about-faced to meet us, a sword in his hand and a shield held close to his body. The rearmost company of his men – a hundred riders – likewise turned and closed up on their leader. I slipped my bow back in its case and drew my sword as the two groups of riders collided. Like their Roman opponents Malik's men were equipped with spears and shields in addition to their swords and there was a rapid succession of dull thuds as spearmen tried to drive their points into an opponent's torso, only to see their lances either miss their target or glance off a shield.

I swung my sword at the Roman commander's head but he saw my weapon and met the blade with his own, then used his own sword to chop at my head and strike at my body, blows that I parried with difficulty. Whoever he was this Roman knew how to use a sword. I tried to thrust my *spatha* at his mail-covered chest but he brought his shield in front of him to block the strike, before trying to lop off my head with a great scything attack with his own blade. I instinctively leaned back in the saddle and his blade missed my flesh by a hair's breadth. As our horses did their own intricate dances around each other we continued to hack and thrust with our swords, but he countered every strike I made, seemingly without effort, while I had difficulty in fending off his expert sword strokes. Perhaps it would be better to kill him with an arrow!

I pulled Remus back a few feet and then Malik was at my side, pointing his bloodied sword at my opponent.

'Time to die, Roman. You are alone and surrounded.'

I looked around and saw that he was indeed the only Roman in the immediate vicinity. Behind him, on each side and to his front was a host of Agraci warriors in their saddles with their spears pointed at him. And beside Malik was Vagises, whose horsemen must have either killed or chased away the remaining Romans. As more and more Agraci and Parthian riders gathered round the Roman rested his sword on his right shoulder, his shield still tucked tight to his left side, seemingly unconcerned that he was surrounded by many enemy soldiers intent on killing him.

'Are you hurt, Pacorus?' asked Malik with concern.

I shook my head, rivulets of sweat running down my face for it was still very warm.

25

'No, my pride is a little dented, that is all.'

The Roman sheathed his sword and slowly removed his helmet to reveal a round face topped by thick curly hair, a square, clean-shaven jaw and a large forehead. He also had a thickset neck. I estimated him to be in his mid-twenties.

'So you are King Pacorus of Dura. I have heard much about you,' he said to me in Greek.

His stare was determined, his voice firm.

'Kill him,' commanded Malik.

'Stop,' I shouted as a dozen Agraci prepared to skewer the Roman with their spears. Malik turned to me with a quizzical expression on his face.

'My apologies, Malik, but he appears to know me and I would know his identity before you kill him.'

'You are a famous warlord, Pacorus, it should not surprise you that many have heard of your name.'

'Indeed you are,' said the Roman in Agraci. Whoever he was he clearly had knowledge of languages as well as the arts of war. I must confess that I was becoming more intrigued by this individual by the minute.

I turned to Vagises. 'What is the situation?'

'We have pushed back the Roman horsemen. I sent five companies to shadow them to ensure they do not return.'

'Your men are well trained,' said the Roman, now speaking in Parthian.

'We've had a lot of practice killing Romans,' sneered Vagises.

Malik smiled. 'Are you afraid, Roman?'

'Everyone dies, Prince Malik, therefore it would be foolish and a waste of time to fear that which is inevitable.'

'As you appear to know all of our identities,' I said, 'it would be courteous if you could at least furnish us with your name.'

He smiled. 'I am *Praefectus Alae* Mark Antony, deputy commander of the army of Syria.'

The deputy commander of the Roman Army in the east was worth more alive than dead and would command a large ransom, in addition to being a useful bargaining tool in any discussions with the enemy.

'I think this Roman should be kept alive,' I whispered to Malik, 'at least for the time being.'

He looked most unhappy but allowed logic to suppress his bloodlust, slamming his sword back in its scabbard. He pointed at Mark Antony.

'You are to be taken to my father, the king, who may not be as merciful as his son.'

So our prisoner rode between Malik and myself as we trotted back to the centre of the Agraci battle line, past thousands of Agraci warriors as once more Vagises' horse archers formed up on the left wing to face what was left of the Roman horsemen. When we arrived at the spot where Haytham's great black banner hung limply from its flag staff with his lords gathered behind it, we also found Gallia and a grinning Spandarat.

26

Both of them were covered in dust but as far as I could tell there was not a scratch on either of them. As we halted Haytham's stare settled on the bold figure of Mark Antony.

'A gift for you, father,' announced Malik, holding out his arm towards the Roman captive. 'This is the deputy commander of the Roman army.'

'Has Agraci custom changed, lord king?' asked one of Haytham lords. 'Do we now take prisoners?'

'Silence!' barked Haytham, before looking at his son. 'We do not treat with invaders, Malik, you have made a mistake.'

'The mistake was mine, lord king,' I said. 'I thought you might have a use for such a high-ranking prisoner.'

Haytham nudged his horse forward to take a closer look at this Mark Antony. The latter still maintained an air of calm but averted Haytham's eyes. He had obviously heard of the king's ruthlessness and his indifference to suffering. Haytham rode slowly round the captive.

'Queen Gallia has destroyed the enemy horsemen on their left wing, Pacorus.' He was talking to me but staring unblinking at Mark Antony. 'There were thousands of Emesian horsemen and now there are none, is that not so, Gallia?'

'It is as you say, lord king,' replied Gallia with pride. I smiled at her.

Haytham continued to circle the prisoner, who was now looking decidedly perturbed. 'The Romans and their allies think the peoples who inhabit these parts are weak and can be crushed and enslaved with ease. Imagine what they will say when they learn that a woman has beaten them. What will they say in Rome, Roman?'

Haytham halted his horse directly in front of Mark Antony.

'Rome will be disturbed to hear of such a thing, lord king,' Antony replied. 'Tinged with admiration.' He glanced at Gallia who still wore her helmet, its cheekguards fastened shut. 'For Queen Gallia's name is known throughout the world.'

'What use can I have for this Roman, Pacorus?' Haytham asked me.

'To ransom him for a great sum, lord king,' I answered, 'for the proconsul of Syria will give you much gold for his safe return.'

'I have enough gold,' snarled Haytham. 'Gallia, it is for you to decide this Roman's fate.'

Haytham wheeled his horse around and returned to the head of his lords. Mark Antony looked at the mail-clad figure of my wife whose face was still hidden by her helmet's cheekguards. I looked at Malik who smiled maliciously. He knew as well as me that Gallia hated the Romans and would probably kill him herself.

'That's you done for,' remarked Spandarat to Mark Antony casually as Gallia slowly pulled her bow from its hide case behind her. I made to protest but Malik laid a hand on my arm.

'No, Pacorus. His life is Gallia's now.'

A sudden commotion in the rear interrupted her role as Haytham's executioner as a group of Agraci riders came through the ranks to present themselves to their king. After they had halted I saw that half a dozen had been escorting one man, who now dismounted, pulled aside his black face veil and went down on his knees before Haytham.

'Princess Rasha has been captured by the enemy, majesty.'

There was a murmur from behind and the king spun in his saddle. 'Silence!'

He looked down at the prostrate figure before him. 'Get up.'

The man slowly rose to his feet as I thought of the ramifications of what he had said. If Rasha had been captured then that could only mean that the other Roman legion had captured Palmyra. I closed my eyes and thought of Byrd and Noora. Had they been taken, too, or were their corpses lying on the earth?

'Have the Romans taken Palmyra?' asked Haytham.

'No majesty,' replied the man. He glanced at me. 'After King Pacorus left Palmyra the princess insisted that we, that is she and her bodyguard, follow the king and that is what we did. We stayed hidden and then joined the riders that Dura's lords brought with them. The princess joined the charge against the Emesians but became separated from us at the height of the battle.'

'Is she dead?' asked Haytham without emotion.

'No, majesty. I saw her being led away by a group of their horsemen. As far as I know she is still alive.'

'And the rest of her bodyguard?'

The man cast down his eyes. 'All dead, majesty,' he replied softly.

Haytham pulled on his horse's reins to wheel him left, and in a lightning-fast movement drew his sword and slashed it across the man's neck. Blood sheeted in all directions as the man clutched his neck and then fell to the ground, gurgling for a few seconds and then falling silent as his lifeless corpse lay on its back, blood oozing onto the parched ground.

'We attack the enemy at once,' Haytham shouted to great cheers from his lords.

I looked across the corpse-strewn no-man's land that separated the two armies and saw the unbroken line of shields of the Roman legion directly opposite, and then squinted before making out horsemen deployed on its right. Granted there were no longer any horsemen on the enemy's left wing but next to the legion there was still a large phalanx of Emesian spearmen and no doubt many slingers and archers standing among the enemy's ranks. To charge an unbroken army of enemy foot was to invite disaster.

'Lord king,' I shouted to Haytham.

Haytham turned his horse to face me. 'What?'

'We can get Rasha back without the spilling of any more Agraci blood.'

'Did you bring your sorceress, Pacorus, so she could weave a spell to return my daughter to me?'

'No, lord,' I answered, 'but will you give me a chance to prove my words.'

28

He looked at me with his cold black eyes. I knew that he desired more blood but I also knew that if he launched an attack his daughter, if she still lived, would have her throat slit before his warriors even got close to the enemy. All eyes were on Haytham as thirty thousand Agraci warriors and over twenty-three thousand Duran horse archers steeled themselves for another fight.

'You have one hour,' he snapped, pointing at Mark Antony. 'If you fail he dies and I attack.'

I thanked Haytham and then sent an emissary to the enemy requesting a parley, stating that we had captured their Roman commander and wished to trade him for a young woman that had fallen into their hands, further insisting that she was not to be harmed or violated in any way. I prayed that her captives had not already raped her, if she still lived. While we waited for a reply I suggested to Haytham that we should extend our line greatly to impress the enemy with our numbers. He and his lords thought this a waste of time but he indulged me, and so the horizon was slowly filled with Agraci and Durans as we waited for an answer.

It came only minutes before the hour was up and was good news. The enemy agreed to a parley but insisted that it take place an hour after dawn the next morning. The people of Emesa worshipped the sun god El Gabal and thus thought any important negotiations should take place when their deity was looking favourably upon them. I too believed this, but knew that only Shamash was the god of the sun. Haytham looked sullen and his lords were most unhappy that they had been denied the opportunity to again dip their swords in the enemy's blood, but I was delighted that Rasha was alive and that we stood a good chance of getting her back. Haytham wanted our prisoner to be staked out on the ground for the night but I requested that he be released to me.

'Why are you so interested in this man?' he asked as his warriors were stood down and cooking fires began to cover the plain.

'I wish to know more about Roman plans, lord.'

He laughed. 'They plan to conquer the whole world, Pacorus. You above all should know that.'

Gallia wanted nothing to do with the Roman and declared that she would be spending the night in the company of the Amazons. As we had no entrenching tools with us we could not dig a ditch and erect a palisade to surround our tents I ordered Vagises to mount patrols far and wide throughout the night. I did not trust the Romans not to launch a night assault to free their commander. The Agraci pitched their tents over many square miles, though Haytham also sent out patrols to ensure his sleep was not disturbed. As for the enemy, Vagises reported back to my command tent just before midnight that they were inside their Roman camp and showed no signs of leaving it.

'Your men did well today,' I said as he settled himself into a chair at the opposite end of the table to where Mark Antony was sitting.

'Thank you, Pacorus. Nergal trained us well.'

I poured wine into a cup and gave it to him as he watched the Roman with suspicion.

I took the jug and refilled Mark Antony's cup. He nodded and held the cup up to me.

'To noble adversaries.'

I drank some wine in acknowledgement of his toast and sat at the table. Vagises rose, held his cup up to me and drained it before slamming it down on the table.

'By your leave, Pacorus, I have patrols to organise.' His eyes never left Mark Antony. 'To make sure the Romans do no not slit our throats while we sleep.'

He curled his lip at Mark Antony and left us.

'Your commander does not like me,' observed Antony.

'Do not take it personally, he has a low opinion of all Romans.'

Antony leaned forward. 'Tell me, was he a slave, for I have heard that you only enlist slaves in your army? Men say that is the reason it fights so fiercely.'

I nodded at the closed tent flaps. 'That man, Vagises, is a Parthian who was taken captive with me in Cappadocia before we were transported to Italy as spoils of war. He has little reason to regard Rome or the Romans with affection.'

He leaned back in his chair. 'And you?'

'I do not hate my enemies, because to do so would cloud my judgement at a time when clarity of thought is essential.'

He nodded approvingly. 'A most philosophical answer.'

I poured him some more wine. 'Now it is your turn to answer some questions. Where is the other legion that your proconsul commands in Syria, for I know that only one was present today? You and your allies underestimated the fighting abilities of the Agraci, I think.'

He laughed mockingly. 'The Agraci have no fighting abilities. We were more than capable of dealing with them before...'

I smiled. 'Before I arrived, you mean. You honour me, commander.'

He stiffened. 'My title is *Praefectus Alae*.'

'It is a great pity that so many of your fine horsemen now lie dead on the desert floor. That is the price invaders pay for their aggression.'

'That is the price Rome pays for civilising the world,' he tried to correct me.

How many times had I heard that argument before? 'Roman civilisation is built on the corpses of vanquished peoples.'

'Only the strong deserve to live,' he said casually.

'And the weak deserve only slavery or death, I suppose?'

'The gods have charged Rome with civilising the world. If our mission was not a divine one, how else can you explain Rome's victories over the other tribes of Italy hundreds of years ago, her conquest of Carthage, Greece, Pontus, Armenia and Syria?'

I sipped my wine. 'And now Rome seeks to add Parthia to that list.'

He was momentarily nonplussed. 'I am a soldier, sir. I obey orders.'

30

I laughed. 'And a member of one of Rome's most prominent families, I'll hazard.'

He blushed. 'I have been fortunate to have been born into a noble family, I admit, though everything I have achieved has been by my own hand.'

'You are to be congratulated. I hope being exchanged for a young girl does not harm your reputation.'

'There will be other battles to fight,' he replied flatly.

'I am curious about one thing,' I continued. 'Why did you not wait until Crassus had arrived in Syria before commencing hostilities again the Agraci and Parthia?'

'You are very well informed,' he said.

'When you rule a frontier kingdom it is wise to know what is happening in adjacent lands. So, why not wait for Crassus?'

'As I said, I am a soldier and take orders,' he replied evasively.

'Have it your own way. I am sure all will be revealed when he arrives. If I was a gambling man I would wager that your commander, Proconsul Aulus Gabinius, desired to make his name great before Crassus arrived in Syria.'

He placed his cup on the table. 'King Pacorus, as you have saved my life it is only proper that I return the courtesy. If you would be prepared to submit to Roman rule then I can use whatever influence I enjoy to have you exonerated from your crimes.'

'My crimes?'

'We know that you have been supplying the rebels in Judea with weapons. That in itself is enough to earn you a death sentence. Would it not be better for you and your kingdom to live in peace under the protection of Rome?'

I tilted my cup at him. 'Under the heel of Rome would be a more accurate description, I think. I must decline your kind offer.'

His mouth creased in disapproval. 'When Crassus arrives he will sweep aside all opposition. We know that Parthia is weak through years of civil strife and is in no position to repel a Roman army. To oppose us is to invite death and destruction. I am merely suggesting that a logical course of action would be to accept the inevitable and act accordingly.'

'A very Roman way of thinking,' I replied.

Frustration was etched on his handsome features. 'You must know that you cannot defeat us.'

'If I knew such a thing, Mark Antony, then I would not be sitting here at this table but would be sleeping in my palace as a client king of Rome.'

'No rival has defeated Rome, King Pacorus, and none will. You yourself have endeavoured to copy Rome, for is not your army modelled on our own?'

'It is true that I have adopted some Roman practices,' I agreed, 'but my army is Parthian, Mark Antony, not Roman.'

'If you agree to be an ally of Rome,' he persisted, 'then your kingdom will be safe from any harm. But I have to tell you that if you are still in arms against Rome when Crassus arrives he will show no mercy.'

'Is that what you told Mithridates?'

His eyes averted mine. 'Mithridates?'

'I know that he has taken refuge in Antioch with his venomous mother. Does your proconsul plan to make him the puppet ruler of Parthia?'

Mark Antony said nothing but turned the cup in his hand.

'Your silence speaks volumes.'

I did not press him further on the subject of Mithridates. It had been an agreeable evening and I knew the character of the former king of kings better than he did. It was plain that the Romans would use Mithridates if they could and were probably already thinking of installing him as a puppet ruler of the empire, though how they would do so with only two legions remained a mystery. Perhaps they believed that Parthia had been so weakened by civil war that it was like a wooden house riddled with woodworm, and required only one good kick to bring the rotten structure crashing to the ground.

Chapter 2

The new dawn came soon enough and with it the familiar sounds of soldiers complaining and their officers barking orders, the grunts of irritable camels and the reassuring clank and clatter of cooking utensils as men prepared breakfast. I had fallen asleep at the table and woke with an aching neck after what had been perhaps two hours of slumber. I went outside to stretch my legs as Mark Antony still dozed in the tent. Around me the neat rows of the horse archers' tents were already being dismantled prior to being packed onto the camel train. Normally the tents would be stashed on wagons but these had been left at Dura.

Horns sounded assembly and then each company of horse archers paraded for roll call. The lords and their men were probably still sleeping but in Dura's army soldiers rose before dawn. As I stretched out my arms I noticed that my tent was ringed with guards, twenty in all, all facing inwards. As I rubbed the stubble on my chin I saw Gallia and Vagises walking towards me. The commander of my horse archers saluted.

'Why all the guards?' I asked.

'To make sure the Roman did not escape,' he replied.

'You look terrible,' said Gallia looking remarkably fresh, her hair hanging loose around her shoulders.

'Too little sleep, my love, as a consequence of debating with our Roman friend.'

'He is no friend of mine,' she sniffed. 'Where is he?'

'Still sleeping,' I answered.

Vagises nodded. 'Pity he didn't try to escape, then we could have put a few arrows into him.'

'And then we would not get Rasha back.'

At that moment a tent flap opened and Mark Antony appeared, dressed in his silver muscled cuirass and wearing his helmet adorned with its large red crest. He tipped his head at me and then strode over to our little group, removed his helmet and bowed his head to Gallia. His eyes were alight with glee as he admired her.

'It is an honour to meet you, majesty,' he beamed. 'I have heard much about the beauty of the famed Queen Gallia of Dura and I have to say that I never knew such elegance and allure existed among the Gauls.'

Gallia regarded him coolly, this Roman noble who strutted like a rutting peacock even among his enemies.

'Remember, Roman' she said slowly, 'your life is still mine until Princess Rasha is freed by the enemy.'

'Well,' I said, desirous to dissipate the mood of gathering threat, 'perhaps you would like something to eat, Antony, before you are exchanged.'

I ordered food to be brought to the tent but could not persuade Gallia and Vagises to join us for breakfast. So after a meal of dates, biscuit and water I rode with my wife, the Amazons, a hundred horse archers and our captive to the camp of Haytham. Despite the early hour the day was already hot and airless and we sweated in our armour and helmets. Once

33

more Dura's horse archers were posted to the wings as thousands of Agraci warriors mounted their horses and camels and rode forward to face the enemy, whose camp lay five miles to the west.

The Agraci king was waiting on his horse at the head of his lords when we arrived at his tent, Malik beside him.

'Greetings, lord king,' I said, bowing my head to him and then smiling at Malik. 'Shall we go and get your daughter back?'

He nodded at me, then Gallia and ignored Mark Antony as he nudged his horse forward and we followed him out of camp. Malik rode beside me as a great column of Agraci trotted behind us.

'My father still desires to destroy the enemy, Pacorus, if we get Rasha back or not. More warriors arrived during the night. He believes he can defeat them easily.'

I thought of the disciplined ranks of the Romans and the ease with which they had defeated the Agraci yesterday.

'I think it would be better to convince the enemy to retreat, Malik, at least until Domitus can bring the rest of the army. You yourself know that horsemen cannot break disciplined foot.'

'I may know that, Pacorus, but trying to convince my father that talking is preferable to fighting is another matter.'

Half an hour later we watched as a delegation rode out of the enemy camp and threaded its way between the corpses and dead animals littering the ground from yesterday's battle. Most of them were Agraci and I could understand Haytham's desire to avenge their deaths. There must have been upwards of thirty-five thousand Agraci deployed behind Haytham, stretching left and right for around two miles. Beyond them was a dragon of Duran horse archers on each flank. Vagises had divided the lords into two bodies and had allocated one to each wing, deployed behind his horse archers. In this way nearly sixty thousand men faced the Romans and their Emesian allies. How many the latter numbered I did not know but Gallia had told me that she and the lords had scattered around ten thousand of their horse the previous day. If most of those horsemen had subsequently made it back to camp then I estimated the enemy to number around thirty-five thousand men, unless they too had received reinforcements during the night.

The party of enemy horsemen met a score of Agraci riders in the middle of no-man's land as I waited with Haytham. The king was in a sullen mood and spoke only to Gallia, reminding her that she was to kill Mark Antony if Rasha had been murdered. Any ebullience or bravado Mark Antony may have had evaporated as we waited for the king's men to return to our position. He waited on his horse looking ahead, unblinking, small rivulets of sweat running down his noble face. The riders returned to report that King Sampsiceramus himself would meet with Haytham to ensure that the exchange of prisoners went smoothly, but could the meeting be held away from the stench of dead bodies as the king had had a full breakfast and the aroma of decomposing flesh would be offensive to his nose?

I noticed that Haytham's grip on his horse's reins tightened as he was informed of this request and for at least a minute afterwards he said nothing. I looked at Malik who wore a stony expression, and when I caught Yasser's eye he merely shrugged. The rider looked at his king in confusion and then at the group of Agraci and Emesians who waited for an answer.

At last Haytham spoke. 'He comes into my kingdom uninvited, he kills my warriors and now he complains that their rotting flesh offends him. Perhaps I should slaughter his army so that the stench is so great that it will deter him from entering Agraci territory ever again.'

His lords behind him murmured their approval and several drew their swords. Though it was not my place to do so, I spoke.

'Lord King, let me parley with Sampsiceramus on your behalf.'

Haytham looked at me. 'You?'

'I would consider it an honour.'

Yasser and the other lords looked at each other in confusion, and even Malik looked perplexed.

'Why should you care if the King of Emesa lives or dies?' asked Haytham.

'I do not,' I replied, 'but I do care about the life of Rasha who is like a daughter to me.'

'Why do you, a great warlord, go out of your way to avoid bloodshed?'

I did not dare tell him that it was because I believed that he might lose. 'Because I value your daughter's life over my quest for glory.'

Haytham considered for a moment.

'Very well, for my daughter's sake and the friendship between Palmyra and Dura I will grant you your wish.'

The rider was sent back to the Emesians and an hour later I was riding with Gallia, Vagises, the Amazons and a hundred other horse archers to meet with the enemy. The venue was two miles to the north, well away from yesterday's battlefield where ravens and flies were already feasting on dead flesh. Mark Antony rode behind Gallia and me and in front of Vagises, who had his drawn sword resting on his shoulder for the entire journey. We slowed when we saw the enemy party approaching us and then halted as we awaited our guests, the Amazons forming into line behind us and the other horse archers on either side of them. It was now blisteringly hot and windless and I wanted negotiations to be concluded as quickly as possible.

That was a remote hope as the Emesian party inched its way towards us, preceded by at least fifty members of what I assumed were some sort of royal foot guard. Each man was wearing a cuirass of silver scales that shimmered in the sunlight, a bronze helmet adorned with twin silver feathers, his features obscured by a mail face mask. On his left side he carried an oval shield faced in burnished bronze and in his right hand was a javelin. Silver greaves, red tunic and leggings and a long sword completed his appearance.

Behind these sparkling soldiers came a large chariot pulled by four black horses carrying the King of Emesa himself, a huge fat man in a great silver robe that covered his massive bulk. As the chariot edged closer I saw that Sampsiceramus was almost bald aside from two clumps of hair just above his ears. His robe was the size of the eight-man tents used by Dura's army and there was hardly enough room to accommodate the chariot's driver.

Beside the chariot walked a muscular black man in his early twenties I estimated, who carried a large silver parasol on the end of a long pole that he held over the chariot so the corpulent king was shaded from the sun. Behind the barefoot black man walked a member of the royal guard holding a great whip in his hand, while on the other side of the chariot walked a tall, wiry man in a white robe with white sandals on his feet. Behind them all tramped an additional two hundred members of the royal guard. The entourage halted around fifty paces from us. Then the man in the white robe moved closer to the chariot where he was spoken to by the king. Moments later he shuffled over to us and stopped in front of me. His long face wore a serious expression and his brown eyes darted from me to Gallia and then Mark Antony. He looked back at me in confusion.

'I am Harrise, chancellor to the great King Sampsiceramus. We were led to believe that King Haytham himself would be present for the exchange.'

'He sent me instead,' I answered.

The chancellor clasped his hands together in front of his chest.

'And you are?'

'Pacorus, King of Dura, friend and ally of King Haytham.'

'And godfather to his daughter, Princess Rasha, whom your king now holds captive,' added Gallia.

Harrise's eyes opened wide and his jaw dropped in surprise.

'King Pacorus, of course. If your majesty would wait for a few moments while I announce your presence.'

'Be quick about it, then,' I said.

He bowed his head then scuttled back to his monarch. I looked at Gallia.

'Godfather?'

'A nice touch, I thought,' she replied.

The reed-thin chancellor returned, sweat running down his wrinkled face.

'The great King Sampsiceramus would speak to you personally, King Pacorus.'

'Not until we have seen that Princes Rasha is safe,' said Gallia forcefully.

Harrise's brow creased in consternation at the continual interruptions from the helmeted individual sitting on my right.

I smiled at him. 'This is my queen, Gallia, who is like a mother to the princess. Like her I desire to see that she is alive before I speak to your king.' I pointed at Mark Antony. 'As you can see, our prisoner is alive and unharmed.'

So he scurried back to his king once more as the sun rose in the sky and roasted our backs. When he returned his robe was soaked with sweat for the temperature was almost unbearable.

'The great King Sampsiceramus would be delighted to meet with you, majesty.' He then bowed his head to Gallia. 'And you, highness.'

Gallia turned to Vagises. 'If they try anything, kill him.'

'Kings do not "try anything", my sweet,' I said, 'it is considered ill manners.'

'My father was a king,' she growled, 'and he sold his own daughter into slavery. I have little respect for royalty.'

We walked our horses ahead as the king's chariot edged forward, and from the ranks of the royal guard behind it came the familiar figure of Rasha, who was escorted by a great brute in scale armour, helmet, face veil and carrying a huge double-bladed axe, no doubt to kill her if any mischief was attempted. She trudged disconsolately behind the chariot until she saw Gallia coming towards her mounted upon Epona.

'Gallia!' she shouted and raised her arm.

'Have no fear, Rasha,' my wife answered back. 'We are here to take you home.'

The phalanx of guards behind her moved forward slowly to be near their king, while behind me the Amazons and the other horse archers pulled their bows from their cases and edged their horses forward, but in truth the atmosphere was not threatening. My initial impression was that the enemy wished to avoid further bloodshed.

I halted Remus around ten paces from the king's chariot. He really was an enormous man, with a massive fat neck and a bulbous nose. His eyes were very large and protruded from his fat face so that he resembled one of the goldfish that swam in the royal ponds at Hatra. He seemed to be a rather short man until I realised that he was sitting on a chair to relieve his legs of the great strain in supporting such an enormous weight. Directly behind the chariot were half a dozen slaves, all teenage boys, carrying towels and jugs.

'Greetings King Pacorus,' said Sampsiceramus in a slightly quivering voice.

I raised my hand to him. 'Greetings King Sampsiceramus.'

Gallia removed her helmet and shook her hair free. The king's eyes bulged even more as he examined my wife.

'And greetings to you, Queen Gallia,' he slavered.

I could tell that Gallia was disgusted by his appearance and manner but she played the queen and gave him a dazzling smile and bowed her head, causing his heavy breathing to increase. I hoped he would not have a heart attack before our negotiations were concluded.

He nodded to Harrise who waved forward Rasha. Haytham's daughter looked sullen as she halted next to the gilded chariot.

'Did they mistreat you, Rasha?' I asked.

37

'No, but they stole *Asad* from me.'

Asad was a fine young stallion that had been given to her by her father. I pointed at Mark Antony sitting on his horse.

'You see that we have allowed our prisoner to retain his horse, lord king. I would ask you to reciprocate the courtesy with regard to your captive.'

The king screwed up his giant nose but ordered Harrise to get Rasha's horse. While we waited one of his slave attendants rushed forward and dabbed the sweat-covered royal forehead with a towel.

The king smiled at me. 'This heat is intolerable.'

'Indeed, lord king. Far better for all of us to be relaxing in our palaces rather than fighting each other in this bleak desert.'

My words made him uncomfortable and he fidgeted with his plump, ring-adorned fingers while what seemed like an eternity passed before one of his horseman came trotting up with *Asad* in tow. Rasha whooped with delight as he was brought to her and she vaulted into the saddle, though her guard stood before the horse gripping its reins to deter her from riding away. I waved Mark Antony forward and the guard stood aside. Rasha nudged *Asad* as the Roman commander halted beside me.

He offered his hand. 'Thank you for your hospitality, King Pacorus.'

I shook his hand, much to the disgust of Gallia. 'The pleasure has been mine. I pray that you will return to Rome safely, Mark Antony.'

He walked his horse forward, passing Rasha who rode to Gallia's side to embrace my wife.

Sampsiceramus clapped his hands. 'All's well that ends well.' He gave Mark Antony a sideways glance. 'You may retire to the rear, out of our presence.'

Antony gave him a disparaging look before riding away, while Sampsiceramus tapped his driver on the shoulder to follow him.

'Just a moment, lord king,' I called.

Harrise frowned and the king registered surprise.

'Have not the terms of the exchange been met, King Pacorus?'

'They have, lord king, but there is another matter I wish to raise.'

'Oh?'

'The withdrawal of your army from King Haytham's territory.'

'That is between me and Haytham,' he replied haughtily.

'I am a friend and ally of King Haytham. I consider any aggression against him to also be an assault against me.'

Sampsiceramus became flustered. 'I make no war upon Dura, not at all.'

'By marching your army into my friend's kingdom you do so.'

'I have returned Haytham's daughter as I agreed to do.'

'If I ride back to Haytham without your promise to return back to Emesa he will recommence hostilities. You can see the great advantage he has in numbers, and tomorrow these will increase when Dura's army arrives.'

His eyes bulged and he swallowed and I knew I had him. 'Dura's army?'

'Yes, lord king, for I am pledged to fight alongside my ally. As we speak,' I bluffed, 'my legions and heavy horsemen are marching towards this place, fresh from their victories in the east and eager to add more glory to their already fearsome reputation.'

The gossip that was carried by the trade caravans would have told of our great victory at Susa, of the death of Narses and the toppling of Mithridates, who anyhow was at Antioch as a guest of the Romans. As he fidgeted with his hands once more I could tell that he was very agitated. As he looked at me and then at Harrise, the parasol above his head moved slightly, allowing the sun's rays to fall on part of the king's head. Sampsiceramus looked daggers at the black slave who held the sunshade and then smiled devilishly as the guard lashed his back with the whip. The slave flinched in agony as the leather cut into his flesh and again the parasol moved to expose the crown of the king's head to the sun. The guard struck the slave's back again with his whip, making a loud crack on impact. Behind me came angry murmurs from the Amazons, many of them former slaves who had been subjected to such cruelty. The guard flogged the slave a third time, causing him to collapse to his knees and drop the parasol.

'Kill him,' ordered Sampsiceramus.

The guard dropped the whip and drew his sword, grasped it with both hands and hoisted it above his head to deliver a fatal blow to the slave. The arrow hit him square in the neck, just under his mail face veil, and caused blood to flood in great spurts from the wound. He collapsed on the ground while behind him the other royal guards raced forward to protect their king.

Gallia strung another arrow in her bowstring as her Amazons and other horse archers brought up their bows and aimed their arrows at Sampsiceramus' bulk.

'Order your men to stand down,' I shouted, 'otherwise you will be turned into a pin-cushion.'

The king flipped up a fleshy hand to stop his soldiers as he stared in terror at me. This was not how negotiations between kings should be conducted, not at all, made worse by him no longer having any protection from the sun that was now cooking his pink flesh.

The royal guards had locked shields and the front rank stood ready to hurl their javelins, but their king knew that he would be the first to die and so commanded Harrise to order his guards to stay where they were.

I pointed at the slave struggling to his feet. 'He will be coming with me. What is his name?'

The king blinked, his head beaded with sweat. 'Name?'

'Yes,' I bellowed. 'His name, what is it?'

'Slave, er, Scarab,' he gibbered.

'Scarab,' I shouted, 'come here.'

The slave looked behind him at the dead soldier whose blood was still spurting from his neck, then at the king.

'Now!' I shouted.

He walked briskly over to me and bowed his head. I held out my right hand.

'Take my arm.'

His grip was strong as I pulled him up onto Remus' back behind me.

'Take your army back to Emesa, lord king,' I said to Sampsiceramus, 'otherwise you and it will be destroyed in this barren place.'

Gallia replaced her helmet on her head as we rode back to Haytham with his daughter, Vagises and his horse archers forming a rear guard to ensure the Emesians did not attack us.

'Scarab is an unusual name,' I said to the slave behind me.

'All Egyptian slaves are named so, highness,' he said. 'It means "dung beetle", the lowest of creatures. That is what the Emesians think of Egyptian slaves.'

'You are a slave no longer,' I told him.

Rasha hugged her father when we reached Agraci lines where we also found Spandarat. I ordered Vagises to find our new friend a horse, not knowing if he could ride or not. Haytham ordered that Rasha was to return to Palmyra at once and to ensure she did assigned a score of warriors as her escort, telling their commander that upon arrival she was to be confined to his tent under armed guard. When she began to protest he erupted like an angry volcano and threatened to have her banished if she said another word. So she went back to Palmyra and we waited for the Emesians to make their move.

They did so an hour later when scouts informed Haytham that a long line of foot and horse was exiting the enemy camp from the western entrance back towards the city of Emesa. Roman horsemen led by a commander with a red-crested helmet were providing a rear guard for their allies. Haytham may have felt cheated of a victory but I was relieved. Palmyra was saved, albeit temporarily, and I could now concentrate on affairs to the north, specifically the Armenians.

We stayed for two days at Palmyra, long enough for Scarab to get his back cleaned and bandaged and for me to convince Haytham that it would be wise not to raid Emesa. I sent Spandarat and the nobles back to Dura while Haytham ordered his lords and their men back to their territories but sent Malik west to keep watch on the enemy. I knew that he was thirsting for vengeance, not only to avenge the death of Vehrka but also to appear strong to his people. I believed that forcing the Romans to retreat was a victory but the king of the Agraci did not agree.

'They will be back,' he complained as we sat cross-legged in a circle on the floor of his tent.

'And when they do we will once more stand together,' I reassured him.

He was not convinced. 'We should have destroyed them when we had the chance. Vehrka must be avenged.'

He looked at Gallia.

'You should have killed that fat king when you had the chance.'

'Sampsiceramus may prove useful to you yet, lord,' I said.

Haytham picked up a piece of flatbread and dipped it in yoghurt.

'How so?'

I shoved a date in my mouth. 'A weakling client king will think twice before invading Agraci territory again in a hurry. The Romans promised him an easy victory, no doubt. But he will be reluctant to venture east again, notwithstanding their promises.'

He was still sceptical. 'What will you do now?'

'Return to Dura and await Orodes' instructions.'

Haytham smiled. 'The prince is now the high king of the Parthian Empire?'

'He is, lord,' answered Gallia.

'He will make a good king of kings,' I said.

Haytham studied me for a few seconds. 'I heard that the crown was first offered to you, Pacorus.'

'It was, lord, and I turned it down.'

'Or rather Dobbai turned it down for you,' Gallia corrected me.

Haytham's eyes opened wide in surprise. 'What business was it of your sorceress?'

I shrugged. 'She said it was not my destiny to be high king. Besides, in truth I had no appetite to try to keep the kings of the empire happy, to listen to their interminable squabbles and grievances and try to appease them. Orodes has a thoughtful nature and the tongue of a diplomat.'

'He will make a great king,' said Rasha.

Gallia laughed and placed an arm round her shoulders.

Haytham looked at them both. 'Yes, he will. Perhaps I should send you to him, Rasha, so you can learn to be a good princess.'

Rasha clapped her hands with excitement. 'That would be a great honour, father.'

He pointed a finger at her. 'You are still in disgrace for disobeying my orders and will remain here until I can find a husband for you.'

A veil of sadness descended over Rasha's face and she said no more. Poor Rasha, she so wanted to see the world and all the mysteries in it, but her father desired her to be married as quickly as possible to tame her wild spirit.

On the trip back to Dura I got to know more about Scarab, the latest addition to my royal household. Now swathed in black Agraci robes, his black face made him look like a demon from the underworld, though I was pleased to discover that he had an amiable and thoughtful nature. He told us that he was the son and grandson of slaves and had been purchased from his Egyptian lord for a great sum when the latter had been visiting Emesa on business. It transpired that Sampsiceramus wished to surround himself with Egyptian slaves after having been told that they were more intelligent and hard working than Jewish or Syrian slaves. Scarab's ancestors were originally from a place called Nubia, which is on Egypt's southern border, though he himself had been born in Egypt. He

41

had a certain amount of education, being able to speak Egyptian and Greek and had picked up some Latin from the frequent visits of the Romans to the palace in Emesa.

He rode behind Gallia and me and next to Vagises as our long column made its way back east, the road almost devoid of other traffic as a consequence of the recent fighting. Any whiff of trouble had the effect of making the caravans that usually plied this route disappear. Nothing interrupts trade so much as war. Hopefully the restoration of peace, albeit fragile, would restore commercial activity.

'What will you do now, Scarab?' I asked after we had dismounted to walk alongside our animals to conserve their strength.

Throughout the journey his eyes had always been cast down to avoid our gazes, and it was so now as we walked along the dusty track.

'I am your slave, divinity,' he replied, 'it is for you to decide.'

'You are a free man, Scarab,' said Gallia, 'you may go where you will.'

Scarab looked at her in confusion, then cast his eyes down when she smiled at him.

'I do not understand, divinity.'

'It is as my queen says,' I replied. 'You are no longer a slave and are free to decide your own destiny.'

'There no slaves in our palace,' said Gallia.

Scarab was even more confused. 'No slaves?'

'It is true,' I assured him.

'But who prepares your food and serves it to you, divinity?'

Gallia smiled. 'We have servants, it is true, but they are free and are paid for their work.'

'They are paid?' he said incredulously.

'Of course,' I replied. 'Why else would they work for me? Perhaps you would like to work for me?'

'I would consider it a great honour, divinity,' he replied.

'You could do with a squire,' suggested Gallia.

I had not had a squire since I had found Surena among the marsh people, the Ma'adan, all those years ago and he had gone on to become a king himself. I doubted Scarab would follow the same path but he was young, strong and rode a horse well enough. He would do.

Our leisurely ride back to Dura was interrupted a day out from the city when we were met on the road by Domitus leading a party of cataphracts. Even before I spoke to him I knew that something was wrong and my stomach tightened. Gallia and Vagises sensed it too as the commander of the army brought his horse to a halt in front of me and raised his hand in salute.

'You had better hurry back to Dura,' he said. 'There has been a great battle in the north of the Kingdom of Hatra.'

The knot in my stomach tightened some more and my heart began racing. 'Battle?'

42

'Vata engaged Tigranes and a great host of Armenians near Nisibus. We heard the news yesterday and I thought I should convey it to you myself.'

I sighed. 'What happened?'

'Vata was killed and his army scattered. Nisibus has fallen to the Armenians who now hold the whole of northern Hatra.'

'What of Adeleh?' asked a shaken Gallia.

Adeleh was my youngest sister and the wife of Vata. Domitus shook his head.

'I do not know.'

We rode the rest of the day and through the night to arrive back in Dura as the new dawn was breaking. Tired, unwashed, our clothes covered in dust, I immediately convened a meeting of the council to decide our next course of action. After a wash and a change of clothes I went to the barracks in the Citadel and sought out the officer in charge. This long building located in front of the southern wall housed a century of legionaries, a company of horse archers and another company of cataphracts. Companies and centuries were continually rotated through the Citadel and city to undertake guard duty, which usually meant nothing more than standing sentry in the palace and treasury and manning the walls and gates of the Citadel and Dura, the horsemen providing escorts for myself and Gallia when we left the palace.

The commander, who fortunately spoke Greek, was ordered to allocate our Nubian recruit a bed and find him leggings, tunic and a pair of boots and then get a meal inside him.

Two hours after riding into the city I was seated in the headquarters building staring at the hide map of the empire hanging on the wall of the room we used for these meetings. It made depressing viewing as Domitus stood by the side of it with letters that had been arriving at the city.

'We know that three Armenian armies have invaded Parthia,' he said, 'one under Tigranes that defeated Vata and captured Nisibus, another led by his son Artavasdes that moved into Gordyene. We have no details as to the size of these armies. We have also received news from Aschek that another Armenian force has attacked his kingdom from the north.'

'Three armies?' I was astounded. 'I did not realise the Armenians had so many soldiers.'

'Tigranes has prepared well,' muttered Dobbai. 'He is not called "Great" for no reason. He has watched the empire tear itself apart these last few years and now he makes his move.'

'Supported by the Romans, who pull his strings,' said Aaron bitterly.

'Speaking of whom,' I said. 'Do we know the whereabouts of the second Roman legion in Syria?'

'Byrd sent word that his spies in Antioch have informed him that it remains in the city.'

I frowned. 'That is most odd. I expected it to be with the fat king of Emesa, but it just sits in Antioch.'

'Will the Armenians march on the city of Hatra?' asked Gallia with concern.

I shook my head. 'Hatra has strong walls and, more importantly, is positioned in the middle of a desert. There is no water outside the walls to support a besieging army.'

'Unless your brother decides to march outside the city walls and fight Tigranes, just as that fool Vata did,' remarked Dobbai.

'He would not do that,' I snapped, 'and Vata was not a fool. He was my friend.'

'He lost the whole of the north of your brother's kingdom,' retorted Dobbai, 'that makes him careless at the very least.'

'The greater danger lies to the east,' continued Domitus, looking at the map. 'If the Armenians conquer Gordyene they will push on into Media, which lies on Hatra's eastern border. If Atrax's kingdom falls then the Armenians will be able to pour into Hatra from the east.'

'The Roman speaks with wisdom,' said Dobbai. 'We live in strange times indeed.'

'Gordyene is held by Surena,' I stated, 'it will not fall. Have we had any news from him?'

Rsan shook his head. 'None, majesty.'

'Let us hope that he has not been killed by the Armenians also,' added Kronos glumly.

'Any news from Orodes?' I asked.

'None' replied Domitus, 'though he will have received news of Vata's death at the same time we did.'

'Very well, prepare the cataphracts and horse archers to march to Hatra,' I ordered. 'There is little point in waiting here for the Armenians to conquer the northern half of the empire.'

'What about the legions?' queried Domitus.

'With two legions still in Syria they must remain here to counter the Romans. I will also leave the lords here.'

'That means only four thousand horsemen will be riding to Hatra with you, Pacorus,' said Domitus.

Fortunately the army had had nearly six months in which to recuperate its strength following our victory at Susa, and in that time the legions and horse archers had been brought back up to strength. The loss of a hundred cataphracts had been most grievous, but with the promotion of the most promising squires their numbers had been restored to a thousand. Dura was fortunate to lie on the Silk Road for the caravans always brought with them adventurous young men who fancied a life of soldiering rather than trade. Then there were the runaway slaves who came from Syria, Armenia and other kingdoms in the empire. But as long as they passed the induction process all were welcomed into the army's ranks, specifically the legions. Recruits for the horse archers and cataphracts were drawn largely from the families of Dura's lords and their farmers. Despite the years of civil strife within the empire Dura's lands had been spared devastation and had prospered, which meant farmers not only produced abundant crops but also large families, from which Domitus enlisted many young recruits.

That evening I relaxed on the palace terrace in the company of Gallia and my daughters. Claudia was now nine and resembled her mother in appearance with her high cheekbones and thick hair, which was light brown instead of blonde. Isabella was six and had a more olive complexion than her older sister, whereas Eszter, now five, looked like one of the Agraci with her mop of unruly hair, dark brown eyes and brown complexion. As usual Dobbai joined us; sitting huddled in her cushion-stuffed chair. Claudia fussed round her bringing sweet meats, fruit juice and pastries from a table piled high with food and drink, though Dobbai ate little. Ever since she had assisted in bringing Claudia into the world Dobbai had had a special bond with my eldest daughter, who now knew more about the gods, spells and magic herbs than many of the empire's most learned holy men. Isabella, named after the wife of King Balas of Gordyene who had made such an impression on Gallia when we had been married, was a thoughtful and kind-hearted child, whereas Eszter was a wild thing, fearless like her mother and with a similar temper. A sand storm had been battering Dura when she had been born and Dobbai had told me that it was a sign my daughter would be fierce and uncontrollable like the wind that had brought her into the world.

She now raced round the terrace squealing at the top of her voice as she did so. Then she stopped and squealed with fear before throwing herself into my lap, knocking my plate of food on the floor. Claudia and Isabella also cried out in alarm and retreated to stand behind Dobbai who opened her eyes at the commotion. I turned and saw the strapping figure of Scarab standing beside the officer I had handed him over to earlier. The Egyptian had swapped his Agraci robes for a spotless short-sleeved white tunic, baggy white leggings and leather boots. The white of his clothing accentuated the dark colour of his skin and gave him a somewhat ominous appearance. It had certainly frightened my children and Scarab looked most upset that he had alarmed them.

'It is quite all right,' I reassured Eszter, before helping her onto her feet and getting out of my chair. I waved Scarab forward.

'Welcome, Scarab, please come over.'

The officer nodded to him and our Egyptian friend took two steps forward to prostrate himself before me.

'Thank you, divinity,' he said.

Gallia rolled her eyes and Dobbai laughed.

'He's no god, boy, though sometimes he thinks he is.'

I walked forward to stand before Scarab. 'Get up.'

He did so and the officer smiled at him.

'He's eager to please, majesty.'

'Yes,' I said, 'I can see that.'

My daughters stood in silence as I introduced each of them to Scarab, who smiled to reveal perfect white teeth. I told them he was going to be my new squire and came from a land far away called Nubia. Eventually

Eszter stepped forward and touched Scarab's muscular arm and then looked at her fingers.

'It does not come off,' she said in surprise.

Gallia frowned but Dobbai laughed. 'That is the colour of his skin, child, not paint.'

She gestured to Scarab to approach her. He looked at me and I nodded.

Despite his size he was obviously nervous at being in the presence of this old woman with the severe countenance.

'You know of me, boy?'

He nodded. 'You are the sorceress of the king. Your name is held in awe by many.'

'How ridiculous,' she scoffed. 'Give me your hand.'

He held out his right arm and she grabbed his wrist to look closely at his palm.

'You chose wisely, son of Hatra. The gods send you a guardian.'

'I think we have alarmed Scarab enough,' I said. 'Go and get some rest. Your training begins tomorrow.'

While Scarab began to receive instructions on the duties required of a royal squire a courier arrived from Babylon with a letter from Orodes. I assembled the council and then read its contents to everyone. It did not make heartening reading and indicated just how weak the empire was at this present juncture. Orodes was waiting for Nergal to arrive from Uruk at the head of ten thousand horse archers, to which he would be adding five hundred heavy horsemen and a further five thousand horse archers. He could spare no foot soldiers as those he had were spread across three kingdoms – Babylon, Susiana and Elymais – undertaking garrison duties. He had called on the help of King Phriapatius of Carmania but his troops would not be available for many weeks due to the great distance they had to cover.

'Twenty thousand horsemen won't be able to defeat the Armenians,' remarked Domitus glumly.

'The legions should march with you,' agreed Kronos.

'No,' I replied. 'If we strip Dura of men the Romans will march straight in. The frontier with Syria is quiet for the moment, but to denude this kingdom of troops is to invite the Romans to invade.'

'What of the lords and their men?' asked Domitus.

'They will stay here with you, my friend,' I answered, 'to deter the Romans. Remember, sometime next year Crassus and his army will be arriving in Syria. Dura has to remain strong.'

'What of Media and Atropaiene?' asked Vagises.

'Aschek has his own Armenian invasion to deal with and Atrax will hopefully be assisting Surena in Gordyene. He will not be able to spare any troops to reinforce Orodes.'

The room fell silent. Domitus adopted his usual habit of toying with his dagger while Kronos and Vagises stared at the tabletop. Rsan looked very concerned and Aaron thoughtful. Dobbai for once appeared lost for words. Afterwards, somewhat deflated, I wandered back to the palace where one of the young apprentices from the armouries was waiting for me with an invitation from Arsam, the chief armourer, to attend him in his workplace. The latter was a collection of buildings in the northwest corner of the city, beyond the Citadel's walls, home to hundreds of armourers and their apprentices where the weapons, armour, shields and horse furniture for the army were produced.

I took Scarab with me. He had spent the morning at the stables mucking out stalls and grooming horses. I had taken Remus out for his daily exercise, and when I returned Scarab assisted me in unsaddling and ungirthing my horse and then rubbing him down, all the time asking me questions about Dura and its army. He certainly had an inquisitive mind. He still called me 'divinity', much to the amusement of the stable hands, and for the moment still believed that he was a slave. But then, all he had ever known was bondage and cruelty. As the time passed he would hopefully get used to his new position.

Ever since the murder of Godarz, the city governor, Domitus had insisted that I should have an escort wherever I went, even on the shortest journeys, and so it was today as I walked from the Citadel to the armouries. A score of legionaries flanked Scarab and me as we strolled out of the gates and turned right. Thumelicus, a big German who was a Companion and one of the army's most formidable soldiers, happened to be on guard duty in the Citadel that week so commanded the detail.

'When do we march north to fight the Armenians?'

'You don't,' I told him. 'The legions are staying here just in case the Romans invade.'

A look of disappointment spread across his big face. 'More marching and guard duty, then. Can't wait. We should have fought them all those months ago when we had the chance.'

'Well we didn't so there is no point agonising over what might have been.'

Thumelicus looked at Scarab. 'Who's this?'

'My new squire. He was a slave in the city of Emesa.'

Thumelicus grinned at Scarab. 'So this is the one that prompted Gallia to put an arrow in one of the enemy's soldiers.'

I nodded.

'He doesn't say much. Did they cut out his tongue?'

'No,' I answered. 'He does not yet speak Parthian.'

We arrived at the gates that led to the armouries, the sentries on duty snapping to attention as we passed them. The wall was a fairly recent addition but was deemed necessary to deter thieves. Dura's weapons were among the finest in the empire and commanded a high price. The man responsible for equipping Dura's army with the implements of war was a stocky Parthian who had learnt his craft in the armouries at Antioch and Hatra before taking up residence at Dura. That had been nearly fifteen years ago and in that time he had established a large group of talented sword smiths and armourers. Because Dura was a frontier city he knew that its rulers would always place a high premium on having first-class weapons to equip its army.

I had purposely increased the capacity of the city's armouries, which meant hundreds of workers and apprentices, who produced a steady stream of weapons and armour. Such a large pool of labour and high production was expensive and a drain on the treasury, but it was money well spent because it resulted in Dura's army being one of the most well equipped in the empire.

Arsam stood with his thick arms folded across his barrel chest in front of one of his workshops, a high and long single-storey building with a tiled roof. From within I could hear hammers beating metal and chisels being struck, and then the smell of burning charcoal reached my nostrils. Thumelicus put his arm round my shoulder.

'Here you are. We will be waiting for you when you have finished.'

'There is no need,' I told him.

He shook his head. 'I beg to differ. Even since Godarz's murder Domitus has been adamant that you have a guard at all times. Besides, I heard that bastard Mithridates is at Antioch and that is not that far away.'

He tilted his head at Scarab.

'You sure he isn't an assassin? He's as big as that boyfriend of the killer with the big breasts sent to murder you.'

I held up my hand. 'Thank you, Thumelicus, but much as I would like to stand here and gossip I have business with Arsam.'

I left Thumelicus and his men and joined Arsam at the entrance to the armoury.

'Is that man your brother, divinity?' asked Scarab, glancing back at Thumelicus.

'No, not at all.'

He looked confused. 'Then why is he allowed such familiarity, for it is death in Egypt and Emesa to touch the body of the king.'

'It is a long story,' I replied. 'I will tell you one day.'

Arsam bowed his head, frowned at Scarab and went inside the workshop. My ears were assaulted by a cacophony of noise as dozens of men wearing leather aprons stood working at anvils, benches and forges shaping, beating and cutting metal. The building was light and airy with many open windows, a high arched roof and a dirt floor to minimise the effects of molten metal spills. Good light is essential when working with metals and leather protection and ventilation even more so when beating and shaping hot iron. Nevertheless, the air was full of dust and fumes and the smiths and apprentices were covered in sweat and grime. The heat produced by the forges was intense and I too began to sweat as we made our way through the rows of benches and tool racks. There was an endless number of pliers, end nippers, hammers, metal cutters, hack saws, hand saws, hole punches, knives, razors, bevellers, awls, chisels and vices. And at the far end of the building were half a dozen forges that resembled the red-hot fires of the underworld.

We passed through the small army of workers to exit the rear of the workshop and enter an open space leading to a second workshop.

'Take a look at this,' said Arsam, walking over to a table positioned along the wall of the workshop we had just left.

He picked up an arrow and handed it to me.

'We have been experimenting with different types of arrowheads. The one you are holding is made of steel and will go straight through mail armour.'

I looked at the arrowhead, which was long and thin and tapered to a point, like a needle. I turned the cedar shaft in my hand. There was also a recurve bow, similar to my own and the ones used throughout the empire, lying on the table.

'Take a shot at that target,' said Arsam, pointing to a straw dummy forty yards away, over which had been placed a mail shirt that was the same as that worn by the army's legionaries.

I took the bow, nocked the arrow and shot it at the dummy. The arrow hissed through the air and struck the target. I walked over to the dummy with Arsam and saw that the missile had gone straight through the mail shirt.

'Just as our legionaries wear mail shirts, so do the Romans,' he said, yanking the arrow from the target.

'And like Dura's soldiers,' I said, 'the Romans also have shields.'

Arsam smiled knowingly at me. 'Wait here.'

He dashed back inside the workshop and re-emerged moments later carrying a shield sporting the Duran markings of griffin wings. He carried it to a wooden stand positioned next to the dummy and walked over to the table, picking up another arrow.

He held it out to me. 'Take another shot.'

I walked back to my shooting position and knocked the arrow in the bowstring. I raised the bow and pulled back the bowstring so the three goose flight feathers were adjacent to my face, then released the string. The arrow flew straight and true and slammed into the shield, just above the central steel boss. Arsam was grinning like an idiot.

'Now go and take a look at the shield, majesty.'

I handed the bow to Scarab and told him to follow me as I walked over to the target. When I reached the shield I saw that the arrow had pierced the layers of wood and one of the reinforcing strips attached to its rear and had exited the other side to a length of six inches.

'If it will go through our shields then it will also pierce Roman ones,' said Arsam with satisfaction. 'We've tested them on helmets as well. They go through them like a knife through parchment.'

Most of the arrowheads used by my horse archers were three winged and cast from bronze. As such they were relatively cheap and hundreds could be produced on a weekly basis.

'These new arrowheads are steel?' I asked.

Arsam nodded. 'Heated in the fire and then shaped on an anvil.'

'Which means they are more expensive and will take longer to make than bronze arrowheads.'

'But are more effective,' he replied. 'With Crassus' legions on the way it would be advantageous to have the armoury well stocked with these little beauties. Marcus thinks it is a good idea.'

'Very well,' I said, 'begin production of the new arrows, though you cannot recruit any more armourers. Four hundred plus their apprentices is quite sufficient.'

'But I have your permission to offer overtime, majesty?' he quizzed me.

I jabbed a finger in his broad chest. 'Just make sure that this new venture does not turn into a way of making your armourers richer than they already are. Aaron has shown me the expenses incurred by your workshops and they are already prohibitive.'

He looked hurt. 'Your soldiers are equipped with the finest weapons and armour that men can make, majesty, and I have assembled the most skilled smiths in the world. But they don't come cheap.'

He had a point, but my treasury was not a bottomless pit. 'Just keep costs under control, that is all I ask.'

Afterwards I went to see Marcus Sutonius, a former Roman captive and now my quartermaster general. He still lived in the walled residence where he and his fellow Romans had been held following their capture after I had defeated Lucius Furius before the walls of Dura. Then they had been surly prisoners but now they were enthusiastic members of the army. Many had married Parthian women and lived in the city with their wives and children, but Marcus, a confirmed bachelor, had remained where he had first been confined. The building was now full of studies, archives and workshops and he had a small team of young men that he was training to be future engineers of the army. He was now almost completely bald and rather portly, but his mind was as sharp as ever.

I found him pouring over notes at his desk in his study. The walls of which were filled with pigeonholes holding a multitude of scrolls. He waved me in when he saw me and looked surprised when Scarab followed behind.

'This is Scarab, Marcus, my new squire.'

He smiled thinly at him and then pointed at a chair on the other side of the desk. I removed some notes that lay on it and sat myself down.

'I have just been to the armouries where Arsam showed me his new arrows.'

Marcus looked up and smiled. 'Very efficient, aren't they? You should equip all your horse archers with them.'

'That is what Arsam said and as I told him, the treasury does not hold an inexhaustible amount of gold.'

He leant back in his chair and placed his hands behind his head. 'It would be a wise investment.'

'Mm. Well, let's see. Three thousand horse archers each with a quiver of thirty arrows. That equates to ninety thousand arrows. Then there is the camel train carrying spare quivers: a thousand camels, each one carrying fifty full quivers. A further...'

I tried to do the sums in my head.

'One and a half million arrows,' Marcus answered for me.

'Quite impossible,' I said. 'The cost would be ruinous.'

'You sound just like Rsan,' he smiled. 'The city's finances are in a healthy state, are they not, majesty?'

'They are,' I agreed. We still had much of the Jewish gold that we had received in return for arming Alexander's soldiers in Judea.

He leaned forward, his visage serious. 'Then I would strongly advise you to begin equipping your archers with these new arrows. It will pay dividends.'

I had always heeded the advice of Marcus and I did so now, though I still had serious reservations about such a large outlay of money.

'As your quartermaster general, majesty, it is my task to ensure that your army is equipped with the most effective weapons and armour.'

'That is just what Arsam said,' I replied.

'He is a wise man.'

I had a feeling that they had worked out their strategy before they brought this matter to my attention. They had conspired to outmanoeuvre me and had succeeded so I gave in gracefully.

'You are authorised to begin equipping the horse archers with these new arrows, Marcus, though I have told Arsam he will have no extra staff to produce them. That being the case, how long will it take?'

Marcus rose from his chair and walked over to the pigeonholes facing his desk and pulled out a parchment. He unrolled it and handed it to me.

'Six months should suffice.'

He had compiled a most detailed production schedule, though I noticed there were no details of costs.

'Very comprehensive, Marcus, my congratulations, though costs are conspicuous by their absence.'

'No expense is too great if it safeguards the kingdom, majesty.'

I left his office a happy man, content in the knowledge that he and Arsam had the best interests of my kingdom at heart.

On the way back to the Citadel Scarab questioned me about the armouries, wanting to know whether those who worked in them were slaves.

'No,' I told him, 'they are all free men who are paid for their services, very well paid in some cases.'

'Then what is to stop them running away, divinity?'

I laughed. 'Nothing. If they do not wish to work for me then they are free to seek employment elsewhere.'

'But the work they perform is important to you, divinity?'

'Invaluable,' I replied.

He looked thoughtful. 'Then would it not be better for you to employ slaves to do this most crucial work, knowing that they cannot leave your city?'

'I do not keep slaves, Scarab, and never will. Besides, I have found that men work better if they have a choice in the matter, and toil harder if their backs are not lashed by the whip.'

When we reached the gates of the Citadel I stopped and pointed down the main street of the city that led to the Palmyrene Gate. I dismissed Thumelicus and his escort and stood with Scarab observing the crowd of people that filled the thoroughfare, along with their carts, camels and mules.

'There are no slave markets in Dura, Scarab, and the city is all the better for it. Slavery brings nothing but misery and I will not tolerate it.'

When we walked into the Citadel I saw Dobbai standing at the top of the palace steps. She beckoned me over. I told Scarab to go and find the chief stable hand, whom I had spoken to earlier concerning finding a suitable mount for my squire. As we walked through the porch and entrance hall I told Dobbai about the new arrows that Arsam and Marcus had been developing. She was underwhelmed to say the least.

'It will take more than a few arrows to defeat the Armenians and Romans. The empire is in great danger. Its enemies grow stronger while Parthia grows weaker. I have underestimated the threat it faces.'

'When Orodes arrives our combined forces will march north to deal with the Armenians before Crassus comes.'

She shook her head. 'The Romans in Syria will join with the Armenians before then to make a great army that neither you nor Orodes will be able to defeat.'

'It is comforting to know that you have so much confidence in me.'

We had reached the throne room by now, my griffin banner hanging behind the two thrones at the far end. Aside from guards at the doors the room was empty and my footsteps echoed around the chamber as I walked towards the door that led to our private quarters, Dobbai trailing after me.

'I want you to send Gallia and the children away,' she said suddenly.

I stopped and turned to face her.

'Away, why?'

'Send them to stay with one of your lords for a few days. The one-eyed one, he will do.'

'Spandarat? Why?'

'You must trust me. But you should know that if they stay here they may be in danger for there will be a price to pay.'

I wondered if she had been out in the sun too long and was suffering delirium, but her face was a mask of steely determination and I knew that she was deadly serious.

'They should leave tomorrow morning and must not return until I decide that it is safe for them to do so.'

I was both confused and bemused. 'What is the nature of the danger you allude to?'

An evil smile crept over her face. 'Of a divine kind. You wish to save the empire, son of Hatra?'

'Of course.'

'Then you must assist me in enlisting the aid of the gods.'

Gallia was most unhappy when I informed her that she had to leave the city with our daughters the next day and at first refused. However, following a discussion behind closed doors with Dobbai she reluctantly acceded to the old woman's wishes. Spandarat's large stronghold was located only twenty miles northeast of Dura so the journey would not be long and I knew that she and my daughters would receive a warm welcome.

'What a ridiculously sentimental person you are,' Dobbai scolded as she stood with me at the top of the palace steps watching Gallia, my daughters and her Amazon escort ride from the Citadel the next morning.

'She is the Queen of Dura, son of Hatra, and has the power of life and death over the kingdom's subjects, not some landless vagrant who goes in search of people's charity.'

After they had left Dobbai sent the palace's chief steward into the city to purchase the wood of a tamarisk, or salt cedar as it is sometimes known, an evergreen tree with grey-green foliage and revered in many lands as the tree of life. When he returned she ordered half a dozen carpenters from the palace to cut the trunk into six equal portions and gave one to each of the craftsmen. She was seated on Gallia's throne beside me as she gave each carpenter a scroll that contained a name that he was to carve on each piece of his tamarisk. They were told to return to her the next morning with the carved pieces.

She sent a guard to the treasury to bring Aaron to the throne room with a pouch of gold coins, which was given to the chief steward with instructions to go back into the city and bring back six sculptors who worked with clay. Aaron quite reasonably asked what the money was for and was given short shrift by Dobbai, who waved him away. When he said that he was not accustomed to giving money away freely she reminded him that had it not been for me he would have been nailed to a cross by the Romans, which meant that I owned his soul and he should do as he was told. Aaron took umbrage at this and stood before her with his arms folded.

'Any expenditure should be ratified at the council meeting, majesty,' he protested.

'He is the king,' snapped Dobbai, jerking a thumb at me, 'and can do what he wants with his own money.'

'The contents of the treasury belong to the king, of course,' riposted Aaron, 'but he has charged me with its safekeeping to ensure it is not frittered away on frivolities.'

Dobbai glared at him. 'Frivolities! The safety of the empire is not a frivolity, Jew. The matter that concerns me is of the greatest import.'

Aaron laughed. 'I hardly think a pouch of coins is going to change the course of history.'

Dobbai's eyes burned with anger. 'Get out! Before I weave a spell to turn you into a frog that will be eaten up by a cobra.'

Aaron pointed a finger at her. 'You are an abomination in the eyes of god.'

Dobbai laughed. 'What god is that, Jew?'

'The god of Abraham who created the world and everything in it.'

'Your god is weak and helpless,' she sneered, 'and has no power here. What sort of god lets his people be turned into slaves without raising a finger to help them?'

Aaron looked at me, shaking with rage. 'What she says is blasphemy, majesty. I must protest in the strongest terms. If this was Judea she would be stoned for saying such things.'

Dobbai laughed even louder. 'Judea? The last I heard it was a Roman province. And whereas your god does nothing while its people are crushed I intend to enlist the aid of our gods to turn back the invaders.'

Aaron was going to reply but I held up my hands to call a halt to their bickering. I placed an arm around Aaron's shoulder and thanked him for his diligence and loyalty and asked him if he would liaise with Marcus and Arsam concerning the production of the new arrows for the army's horse archers. Dobbai watched him go contemptuously.

'The Jews are a most tiresome people,' she muttered, making herself comfortable on Gallia's throne.

'Aaron is a good man,' I said. 'You should treat him with respect.'

She waved a hand at me. 'Why, because he can count beyond one hundred? He has proved useful in filling your treasury with gold but now his usefulness has come to an end. You should get rid of him.'

'I will do no such thing,' I replied. 'He is loyal, hard working and diligent.'

'So is a mule,' she retorted, 'but you would not make one your treasurer. You should have a man who worships our gods instead of a foreign heathen.'

Now it was my turn to laugh. 'Look around you, Dobbai, this city is full of foreign heathens. Men and women from the four corners of the earth have made Dura their home, that is what makes it strong.'

She curled a lip at me, reached into her robe and pulled out a folded papyrus sheet. She unfolded it and handed it to me.

'Here. Go and collect these.'

I took it and saw six names written on it: Domitus, Kronos, Drenis, Vagises, Vagharsh and Thumelicus.

'Go and collect them and bring them here,' she ordered.

I waved over one of the guards but she held up a hand to him.

'No, you must be the one who gathers them, son of Hatra.'

And so I left her in the throne room as I went to the stables to collect Remus, on the way passing the chief steward who was ushering the sculptors through the reception hall. I also encountered Thumelicus and told him to attend Dobbai in the palace, ignoring his probing questions and ordering him to change the habit of a lifetime and obey commands without question. I rode to the headquarters tent in the legionary camp where Domitus and Kronos were planning a large-scale exercise involving both legions in the desert. When I told them that they were both to report to the palace immediately they asked why. I told them that I knew as much as they did.

'And who are we reporting to?' queried Domitus.

'To Dobbai,' I answered.

He rolled his eyes. 'I sometimes wonder who rules this kingdom.'

'I do,' I snapped, 'now kindly go to the palace. Where is Drenis?'

'At the training posts,' said Kronos.

'Very well, I will see you both at the palace.'

I left them both perplexed and rode outside the camp, beyond the western gate, to where rows of wooden posts had been sunk into the ground, against which legionaries could hone their swordsmanship. I saw Drenis standing watching dozens of men practising stabs, feints, thrusts and lunges with wooden swords and holding dummy shields, the practise swords and shields weighing more than the standard-issue items to strengthen each man's arms. Drenis was tapping his vine cane against his leg, occasionally bellowing at the men to hack harder and keep the shields tighter to their bodies. I slid off Remus' back and stood beside him.

'Come to work on your sword skills, Pacorus?'

'No, I require you at the palace.'

He raised an eyebrow. 'Problems?'

'I hope not. If you could come immediately I would appreciate it.'

He handed over command of the men to a centurion from the Durans and began marching to the city as I left him and galloped away to find Vagises and Vagharsh. Fortunately they were both in the city and so I rode with them back to the Citadel and waited for the others to arrive. Dobbai asked us to gather on the palace terrace where we were served cool fruit juice in the shade of the pergola. Even though it was late afternoon it was still hot and there was no wind to cool us.

Thumelicus, on duty at the Citadel, had already made himself comfortable, his great frame occupying a large wicker chair as young servant girls brought him an endless supply of fruit and pastries. Domitus and Kronos arrived soon after and also emptied several cups of fruit juice to slake their thirsts, servants handing them towels to wipe their sweaty faces and necks. The last to arrive was Drenis, who unlike Domitus and Kronos had never learnt to ride and so walked everywhere. When all had assembled and refreshed themselves Dobbai dismissed the servants and ordered the doors that led to the terrace to be closed, before standing before us all – a frail old woman dressed in aged robes who drew herself up and looked at us each in turn with her black eyes.

'So, we come to it, the decisive moment in the life of the empire. Parthia is like an injured lion that needs time to recover from its wounds, but there is no time. No time before the Armenians and Romans gorge on its weakened body. If they do then it is all over and Parthia will be no more. The Armenians will take the north and the Romans will conquer the lands between the Tigris and Euphrates, and afterwards those kingdoms that lie between the Tigris and the Indus. This I have seen.'

I felt a sense of dread shoot through me and looked at Domitus who was staring ahead with a stony, emotionless expression.

'Dura cannot defeat these mighty enemies on its own,' she continued, 'even with the assistance of the Agraci.'

'We are not on our own,' I said. 'We have a new king of kings who leads a united empire.'

Dobbai shook her head. 'You are wrong, son of Hatra. Only Dura among the kingdoms is strong. The eastern realms have been bled white; you should know, you yourself killed most of their soldiers. To the north, Margiana and Hyrcania have been exhausted fighting the numberless nomads of the great steppes. Persis, the former kingdom of Narses, is a shell and Susiana and Elymais are in a similar state. Nergal's Mesene has not been ravaged by war but is a poor kingdom that can raise few soldiers. You all know the dreadful state that the Kingdom of Babylon has been reduced to, and Media and Atropaiene have also suffered grievously these past few years.'

'Hatra is still strong,' said Domitus.

'Hatra is perhaps the weakest of all,' replied Dobbai, 'for it has lost its greatest son. Without King Varaz there is no one to halt the Armenian flood.'

'What of Surena in Gordyene?' asked Vagises.

Dobbai shrugged. 'He is capable but has to deal with an Armenian invasion before he can provide help elsewhere. But by then the Armenians will have conquered Hatra and the Romans will have invaded the empire. So you see there is only Dura and its army.'

'Well, then,' said Kronos, 'what are we waiting for? We must march north to fight the Armenians at once.'

Dobbai chuckled. 'And if you did, then you and your men would be carrion for crows. You cannot defeat the empire's foes without assistance.'

'Who will aid us, old woman?' asked Thumelicus, a leg hanging over his chair's arm.

'The Agraci?' offered Vagharsh.

'The Agraci?' she said derisively. 'They can barely defend their own patch of scorpion-infested desert.'

'Then who?' asked an exasperated Domitus.

'The gods,' I said, thinking aloud.

Dobbai nodded her head. 'The gods, exactly. I intend to call upon the divine ones for their help.'

Drenis looked at Thumelicus who burst out laughing.

'There may be some among you,' continued Dobbai, observing Thumelicus with an icy stare, 'who believe the gods do not exist. More fool them. Only the gods can help the empire, and only you can help me summon them.

'All of you have fought by the side of the king for many years and are his most trusted and loyal companions.'

Thumelicus winked at me and smiled. Dobbai saw him.

'Though the gods have blessed some of you with a surfeit of brawn at the expense of a deficit of brains.

'I therefore ask each of you to support your friend and king by taking part in a ritual to summon the help of the gods. I ask this of you but do not command, for each of you may face danger.'

'What danger?' asked Thumelicus. 'We don't have to jump over a pit full of snakes or sharpened stakes do we?'

'Don't worry, Thumelicus,' said Drenis. 'No self-respecting snake would ever sink his fangs into your sour-tasting German flesh.'

'The gods are cruel and vengeful,' continued Dobbai. 'They often demand a high price for their help. They might demand each of your lives. So think carefully before you make your choice.'

She fell silent and looked at me first. I had to admit that I felt nervous, not for myself but for my friends gathered round me.

'For myself, I have always desired the empire to be strong and free, therefore I will assist you. But do you need all of us?'

'Yes,' she shot back. 'Six of your best men who have stood beside you in battle.'

'Count me in,' said Thumelicus casually. 'Anything other than standing guard duty.'

'I will assist you,' said Domitus.

'And I,' added Kronos.

Drenis nodded at Dobbai, as did Vagises.

'Me too,' said Vagharsh.

Dobbai nodded approvingly. 'Good. You are all to assemble in the throne room tomorrow, just before sunset.'

She walked across the terrace, opened the doors and disappeared, leaving us all none the wiser. Thumelicus rose from his chair, belched and followed her as the rest of us trooped after him in silence. We had known Dobbai long enough to know that her warnings and prophecies were not to be dismissed lightly, and I think all of us were a little apprehensive about what the following evening would bring.

The next day, after my early morning ride, with Scarab accompanying me I joined a company of horse archers on their way to the shooting ranges. These were located south of the city and comprised rows of targets at differing heights and angles, which horsemen shot at as they rode past. Scarab had never shot a bow in his life and so practised on foot as I emptied my quiver from the saddle. Afterwards we extracted the arrows from the targets and returned those that were undamaged to our quivers and took the broken ones back to the armouries to get replacements. Aaron was always complaining about the amount of arrows that were lost on the ranges but as I had told Rsan when he had been treasurer, a pint of sweat saves a bucketful of blood. Train hard, fight easy.

Scarab's horse was a dapple-grey mare that had a dependable and steady temperament the chief stable hand assured me. She had a sturdy frame and powerful legs to carry the strapping Scarab. I thought they matched each other well.

'I shall call her *Panhsj*, divinity,' announced Scarab.

'An unusual name,' I said.

'It is the Egyptian word for "Nubian", divinity.'

'An excellent choice,' I agreed.

The evening came soon enough and with it a flurry of activity in the palace as Dobbai ordered the servants to leave their quarters and the guards to return to barracks. The sculptors had arrived mid-afternoon with their work and had been ushered into the throne room, the doors of which were locked after they had deposited their handiwork and departed. As the sun began to dip in the west the whole palace was empty apart from Dobbai, who stood at the top of its steps with her arms folded.

After I had left Remus at the stables I dismissed Scarab and walked into the Citadel's empty courtyard, the only individuals on view were the guards at the gates and on the walls. I saw Thumelicus exit the barracks and walk towards me, followed by Vagises and Vagharsh. They all nodded to me as we gathered at the foot of the steps. Minutes later Domitus, Drenis and Kronos strode through the Citadel's gates, all of them dressed in full war gear. Indeed, I noticed that all of them were attired as if for battle whereas I only carried my sword and dagger. Perhaps they knew something I did not.

When all seven of us had assembled Dobbai waved us up the steps and led us through the porch and reception hall to the closed doors leading to the throne room. It seemed odd to see no guards posted at the columns and either side of the doors, and odder still to discern the absolute silence all around.

'Open the doors, son of Hatra.' Dobbai's words made me jump as she held out a large iron key to unlock the doors.

I took it from her, walked to the doors and turned it in the lock. I made to enter but she laid a bony hand on my arm.

'Me first.'

She pushed open the doors and ordered us to follow her. Our footsteps on the tiles echoed round the empty chamber lit by oil lamps. I saw six statues of what appeared to be sitting animals of some kind arranged in a line in front of the dais and also cages containing chickens. Dobbai turned and held a hand up to us to stop our progression as she walked onto the dais and faced us.

'Each of these clay figures represents a divine one whose aid I wish to summon. These figures will act as vessels through which the gods will send their assistance. Each of you will bear a figure and by doing so you will reveal yourself to that god. He will then know you, for good or ill.'

She pointed at me.

'Stand beside me, son of Hatra, for I will summon the gods on your behalf and you must be visible to all of them.'

I walked forward and stepped onto the dais and faced the others. I saw that each statue resembled a sitting hound, though the facial features were more like those of a demon, with bulging eyes, large fangs and a snarling visage. They looked hideous. Each one was also painted a different colour and had a chain around its neck, to which was attached a piece of tamarisk into which had been carved the name of a god.

Dobbai pointed at Kronos and then at the yellow-painted statue on the right-hand end of the row of clay dogs.

'Stand behind the statue and place your right hand on its head to call Shamash.'

Kronos did as he was told.

'Speak these words,' she barked. 'I call upon you, O Shamash, great lord, to look with favour upon my handiwork. Through thy righteous power may I have abundance of strength. With strong weapons for the fray, protect my soldiers. May my weapons advance and strike and overthrow the weapons of the enemies.'

Kronos repeated the words. Dobbai pointed at Domitus and instructed him to stand next to Kronos and place his right hand on the orange-painted statue, and then to recite the words she spoke, which this time called upon Adad, the god of storms, for his aid. Drenis laid his hand on the next statue in the line, this one painted blue and representing Anu, the sky god who is in charge of the Bull of Heaven sent to earth to avenge the gods. After Drenis had finished his speech to Anu, Vagises stepped forward to stand behind the purple dog that represented Marduk, the supreme god. Vagises recited the summons with solemnity, as did Vagharsh who laid his hand on the head of the green hound, representing Ninurta, the god of war who fights with a bow and arrow and a sickle sword. Last came Thumelicus who recited Dobbai's words to summon the demon Pazuzu who protects humans against plague and evil forces. This hound was painted red and had a particularly gruesome face for Pazuzu had the head of a monster.

Dobbai stepped off the dais to the cages containing the chickens, opened one and removed its captive. She walked over to where Kronos stood with his hand on the statue dedicated to Shamash; slit the chicken's throat with a knife allowing the blood to gush over his hand, arm and the statue. She held her arms aloft, the dead chicken in one hand, the bloody knife in the other, and called upon Shamash.

'Expel the malevolent ones God of the Sun.'

She fetched a second chicken and sacrificed it over Domitus' hand, calling upon Adad.

'Consume their lives fierce one.'

The statues of Anu, Marduk, Ninurta and Pazuzu were likewise doused with chicken blood. With each slash of her knife Dobbai implored the deities to kill and put the empire's enemies to flight. By the time it was over the floor was covered in blood, feathers and dead chickens.

Thumelicus must have muttered something to Vagharsh because Dobbai spun on her heels and glowered at him.

'Silence! The gods are close and none of you may speak in their presence.' She looked at me. 'Not even you, son of Hatra.'

59

She walked back to the now empty cages and picked up two small earthenware containers and waved me over. She handed them to me and then bent down to pick up another, then turned to face my comrades.

'Time to unleash the gods,' she said. 'Each of you must carry your sculpture from the palace to the riverbank. Do not talk; keep your eyes ahead. Above all keep a tight hold of your statues. You must walk behind me, son of Hatra.'

She walked over to the doors and opened them as I trailed after her and the others picked up their gore-covered clay statues and filed after us. At the doorway she stopped and pointed to me.

'Pour the contents of the containers you hold on the threshold.'

I removed the cork from one and poured the contents, which was milk, across the threshold as instructed, then did the same with the contents of the other container, which was honey.

Dobbai bowed her head. 'By milk and honey I ensure peace and prosperity within this palace.'

We walked through the reception hall and into the porch and I saw that the courtyard below was ringed with guards, though each legionary was facing the walls.

'Avert your eyes,' bellowed Dobbai, 'any man who looks round will be struck dead at once by the divine ones.'

We followed her across the courtyard to the gates where she poured oil across the entrance from her container, spreading her arms and looking to the heavens.

'With oil I seal this portal and protect all within.'

The route from the Citadel to the Palmyrene Gate was lined with soldiers, all of them likewise facing away from the street along which we now walked. At regular intervals along the route legionaries held torches to illuminate our journey, while in front of us Dobbai recited chants and prayers in a language I had never heard before.

On we walked, through the Palmyrene Gate and then north along the western wall of the city, more legionaries lining our route as we moved beyond the city walls to change course towards the banks of the Euphrates. It was night now but the land was illuminated by a full moon that cast everything in a ghostly pale grey glow. There was no wind and the air was warm and dry.

At the river we left the guards and at the water's edge were told to halt by Dobbai, who hissed that none of us was to say a word until we had returned to the Citadel. She scurried back to the centurion commanding the final detachment of guards and instructed him to take his men back to camp.

She led us to the riverbank directly below the escarpment upon which the Citadel stood and instructed that the statues be placed on the ground, facing east across the river.

'Stand back, all of you,' she commanded, before walking to the water's edge where she once more raised her arms to heaven.

'O Shamash, great lord, exalted judge,' she called, 'the one who supervises the regions of heaven and earth, the one who directs the dead and the living, give life to these statues for the overthrow of those who desire to destroy your subjects. We bow before you and pledge our lives to you and the other gods who have blessed us.'

She let her arms drop to her sides and stood facing the water for a few moments, then turned and looked at us.

'It is done. We must leave this place. And stay silent.'

I looked at Domitus who appeared completely bemused by it all while Vagharsh looked bored. Drenis caught my eye and shook his head. Kronos was looking at his blood-splattered arm with disgust. Vagises appeared somewhat awed by it all while Thumelicus looked disinterested. The night was completely silent and still as we followed Dobbai back to the city. I looked at the marble-smooth black surface of the Euphrates and then at the far bank. Everything was calm and unruffled. Last in line, I glanced back at the statues standing motionless a few feet from the water's edge and then saw, to the south, what appeared to be a mist over the river.

As the seconds passed the mist seemed to be getting closer, a thick wall of whitish-grey that covered not only the water but also the riverbanks. How could this be? There was no wind to move it and yet the mist was rolling towards me. I stood transfixed by this celestial wall and then felt a tug on my shirt.

'Hurry, son of Hatra,' hissed Dobbai, 'you will die if you remain here.'

I walked briskly beside her as we tried to catch up with the others, occasionally glancing back at the mist that was now not only behind us but had also enveloped the far riverbank. We caught up with my comrades and walked with them in silence along the city's western wall to reach the Palmyrene Gate. The atmosphere had now changed from hot and airless to cold and clammy and I began to shiver. Then, suddenly, the acrid scent of sulphur entered my nostrils to make me retch.

We reached the entrance coughing and Dobbai ordered the great wood and iron gates to be closed. She ordered the guards to lock themselves in the gatehouse. By now the legionaries who had lined our route had dispersed back to barracks or camp and as Rsan, under orders from Dobbai, had ordered a city wide curfew, only eight of us remained on the main street of Dura as the temperature continued to drop.

Thumelicus rubbed his hands and breathed on them and I noticed that his breath misted.

'We must get back to the Citadel quickly,' hissed Dobbai.

We retraced our steps up the main street as the citizens of Dura hid in their homes and prayed to the gods that had been unleashed on the world. We quickened our pace to the Citadel, though Dobbai's old and frail legs meant she quickly fell behind. Thumelicus stopped, turned and ran back to her and then scooped her up in his great arms and began running towards the Citadel. Dobbai did not protest as I looked back to see a great wave of mist rise up above the Palmyrene Gate.

61

We sprinted the last hundred paces to the Citadel and then, after Thumelicus had put her down, Dobbai ordered the gates to be closed and sent the guards back to barracks. She also shouted at those on the walls to return to their quarters. We stood gasping for air in the empty courtyard, the air now chill and burning our lungs as we gulped it in.

'We are safe now,' said Dobbai calmly, 'they cannot enter. You may speak.'

Thumelicus rubbed his arms. 'I've never known it to be so cold.'

'That is what happens when the veil that separates two worlds, the one of mortals, the other of deities, is temporarily torn,' remarked Dobbai.

'Let us get some warm wine inside us,' I said.

'What is that?' asked Kronos, cupping a hand to his ear.

We stood and looked around and then I heard a low growl and then a snarl. The noises seemed to be coming from the shadows next to the palace.

'A stray dog, that is all,' said Domitus.

Then there was a louder growl and a thunderous unholy bark that sent shivers down my spine.

'If it's a dog it must be the size of a bull judging by that noise,' remarked Thumelicus.

We heard frenzied barking and snarling all around and we huddled together in fear of our lives. The noises were not coming from the Citadel but from outside, from the foot of the escarpment. The angry, demonic growling, barking and snarling grew louder and louder until we were forced to cover our ears. Then it suddenly changed into a chorus of savage howls that filled the air and pierced our brains like red-hot needles. I fell to my knees and screamed in pain as the howls became higher pitched until I could take it no longer, and was on the verge of passing out. Then suddenly there was silence.

Dobbai, looking pale and exhausted, nodded at me. 'It is over. The gods have answered my plea and have unleashed the ageless ones upon the world. Now the veil has been restored.'

'What about that mist?' asked Vagises. 'I have never seen anything like it.'

'We can see it from the palace terrace,' I said.

We raced up the palace steps, through the porch and reception hall into the throne room, through the door at the rear that led to the private wing and the terrace. We ran onto the terrace and raced over to the balustrade to peer at the mist, except there was no mist, not a trace of it. The moonlight illuminated the still waters of the Euphrates and the surrounding terrain. There was no wind, no unworldly noises and no cold, clammy air. The temperature was once more warm and pleasant. Had it all been a monstrous dream?

We looked at each other in confusion as Dobbai wandered out onto the terrace and announced that she was going to bed and advised us to do the same. But we each pulled up a chair so we could sit and stare through the stone columns of the balustrade at the river below, intent on seeing any other divine apparitions. We said nothing to each other as we waited for the gods to reveal themselves once more, but gradually we all drifted into a deep sleep.

When I awoke it was morning and the sun was shining in my eyes. My mouth felt parched and my limbs ached. Around me the others slowly roused from their slumber and also began complaining of aches and pains. The guards had returned to their positions in the palace and I ordered one to go to the kitchens to fetch us all some breakfast. I left my complaining companions and went to the barracks to find the officer commanding the garrison's horse archers. I ordered him to send a detachment to the base of the escarpment to bring back the clay statues that we had left there before returning to the terrace.

The others were being served fruit, bread, cheese, wafers and yoghurt to fill their empty bellies, and water and fruit juice to satisfy their thirsts. I joined them and ate a great chunk of cheese and then a large portion of freshly baked bread, then gulped down two cups of water. The servants had also brought silver bowls so we could fill them with water and wash our faces and cleanse the blood from our hands and arms.

The flustered chief steward came to inform me that the dead chickens and their cages had been removed from the throne room and the floor had been cleaned. After he had left the officer from the horse archers arrived, holding his helmet in the crook of his arm and bowing his head.

'Did your men bring back the statues?' I asked him, cutting off a slice of watermelon with my dagger.

'No, majesty, there were no statues.'

The others stopped their eating and looked at him.

'Are you sure?' questioned Vagises.

'Quite sure, sir,' he replied, 'there were only...'

He glanced at Vagises and then at me.

'Go on,' I ordered.

'We found only six sets of scratch marks in the ground by the waters' edge.'

Domitus raised an eyebrow. 'Scratch marks?'

'More like deep gouge marks, sir, as though someone had been hacking at the earth with an entrenching tool.'

Chapter 3

Three days later Gallia and the children were allowed to return to the palace. Dobbai had confined herself to her bedroom and had asked not to be disturbed, saying that the ritual had exhausted her and she needed time and isolation to recuperate. The children were disappointed but I explained to them that she was now an old woman who needed lots of rest. Claudia was not fooled, though, and said that Dobbai had told her before she had left the palace that she was going to use strong magic. I shuddered to think what else she had imparted to my daughter over the years.

'And did it work?' asked Gallia as she brushed her hair in our bedroom that evening, a slight wind ruffling the net curtains at the entrance to the balcony.

I smiled. 'Well, as far as I know the Romans and Armenians have not disappeared.'

She turned and frowned at me. 'Don't be flippant, it does not suit you.'

I rose from the bed and stood behind her to kiss her on top of her head. I told her about the clay statues, the cold mist that came from nowhere, the chilling growls and howls that filled the air and the disappearance of the statues the next morning. I did not tell her that all those who had taken part might be in danger of divine retribution.

She placed her brush on the table and looked up at me. 'I hope you are wearing a charm to ward off evil.'

'Evil?'

She stood and ran a finger down my scarred cheek. 'I am not a fool, Pacorus. I know that Dobbai sent the children and me away because the spell she was going to weave was potentially dangerous to those taking part.'

I reached inside my shirt and pulled out the lock of her hair I always wore round my neck. 'This is the only charm I need. Besides, Dobbai called on the gods to protect the empire and since I fight to protect Parthia I don't have anything to worry about.'

She looked at me with her beautiful blue eyes. 'Perhaps. Let us hope the gods see things the way you do.'

'We should have held the ceremony weeks ago. Perhaps then Vata might still be alive and the Armenians would not hold half of my brother's kingdom.'

She shook her head. 'Vata took the decision to fight the Armenians, no one else.'

I turned away from her and walked to the balcony entrance, parting the curtains to stare at the night sky.

'It is my fault he is dead.'

'What?'

'When the kings faced the Armenians all those months ago I urged my father to attack them. I knew we could have beaten them that day but he declined to fight. When they returned Vata must have believed that he alone could defeat them.'

She walked over and placed her arms round me. 'Then he was a fool and paid for his foolishness with his life.'

'And half my father's kingdom,' I added.

Orodes and Nergal arrived at Dura five days later with their combined forces, their men pitching tents on the east bank of the Euphrates, directly opposite the Citadel. It was the first time Orodes had been back to the city since his coronation as king of kings and he received a rapturous reception from the citizens. He had always been a popular figure and now was even more so. People believed that the empire was in a pair of safe and just hands after the tyranny of Mithridates. Gallia and I rode out to greet him, Nergal and Praxima and escorted them through the city to the Citadel, along a route thronged with cheering crowds.

'If they only knew the peril the empire faced,' Orodes said to me, smiling and waving at the people as young girls tossed rose petals at him.

'Sometimes it is better to live in ignorance, my friend.'

That night we gave a great feast in the banqueting hall to celebrate the arrival of our friends and their senior officers. It was an opportunity for old friends to meet again for Orodes and his bodyguard had once lived in the city and had fought as part of Dura's army. He insisted on ignoring protocol and sat with Alcaeus, Domitus, Kronos, Vagises and other senior officers from my army, men he had shared many dangers with. Gallia and I occupied the top table with Nergal, Praxima and Dobbai, who seemed to have regained her old vigour and appeared to be pleased that we were all together again.

I was especially delighted to have Nergal and Praxima back at Dura. Nergal had been my second-in-command in Italy when we had fought for Spartacus and although Vagises was an excellent leader it had been Nergal who had forged my horse archers into a fearsome weapon. I had no regrets about making them rulers of their own kingdom but sometimes I yearned for the old times when we had been all together.

Dobbai must have noticed that I was in a reflective mood as she remained beside me when Nergal left the table to speak with some of the men he used to command.

'The years pass and yet we do not notice until it is too late,' she said.

'I did not know you were a philosopher,' I replied.

I pointed at Nergal who was in fits of laughter among a group of Duran horse archers. 'Nineteen years ago Nergal and I were captured by the Romans and taken to Italy. It seems like yesterday and yet it is also another world. So much has happened since that time, and yet here we are on the verge of another campaign. After Susa I just yearned for peace and yet that is the one thing that seems to elude me.'

I looked at her haggard face. 'Will I ever know peace?'

'Alas, son of Hatra, it is both your fate and doom to be a great warlord. You cannot stray from the path the gods have chosen for you. You cannot change your destiny.'

Her words gave me scant comfort but the company of my friends made it an enjoyable evening and the next day I rode with Orodes and Nergal to the legionary camp. Domitus and Kronos arranged a parade of the Durans and Exiles to honour our royal guests and afterwards we retired to Domitus' command tent. Orodes was still the same amiable character I had known for years but I noticed that there were now some worry lines on his face. I suspected the onerous office of king of kings was already taking its toll.

'Axsen refuses to stay at Ctesiphon when I am not there,' he told us, 'she dislikes its atmosphere and associates it with Mithridates. She has moved back to Babylon.'

'Babylon is her home,' I said. 'Besides, it is only a short distance from Ctesiphon.'

'Who is in charge of the royal treasury?' asked Domitus.

A wry smile crept over Orodes' face. 'Alas it is not as full as it should be. Mithridates took a sizeable quantity of gold with him when he fled to Syria.' He smiled at me. 'There were also a number of kingdoms who refused to pay the annual tribute. What gold remains is under the protection of Mardonius who provides troops from Seleucia to garrison Ctesiphon.'

'You will use it to rebuild Babylonia?' asked Nergal.

Orodes nodded. 'I promised Axsen that I would assist in the rebuilding of her kingdom, which suffered grievously at the hands of Narses and Mithridates. So you see, my friends, I am an impoverished high king.'

Poor Orodes. He had once been banished by his stepbrother Mithridates because of his support for me and had spent years at Dura as a landless prince. Now he ruled an empire that was exhausted by civil strife and beset by foreign invaders.

Horses' hooves on the baked earth outside the tent interrupted our musings and seconds later a dust-covered Byrd and Malik stepped inside the tent.

'So,' beamed Malik to Orodes, 'this is where you're skulking.'

Orodes rose from his chair and the two of them embraced, dust coming from Malik's robes as they did so.

'It is good to see you, old friend,' said Orodes, as he hugged Malik again. He then embraced Byrd.

'And you too, Byrd.'

'Help yourself to some water,' I said to the pair as the others greeted them, 'you look as though you have had a hard ride.'

'Bring news of Romani,' said Byrd, taking a cup of water from Malik and sinking into a chair.

'My contacts in Antioch report Romani legion moving to Zeugma. Governor and Mithridates go with it.'

Zeugma was a former Parthian city that was ruled by the aged King Darius, a child molester who had defected to Rome nearly twenty years ago. Built on the banks of the northern Euphrates, a hostile Zeugma meant enemy troops could pour into northwest Hatra.

'So the Romans intend to link up with the Armenians and march south to put my stepbrother back on Ctesiphon's throne,' remarked Orodes bitterly.

'The other Roman legion is still licking its wounds at Emesa,' added Malik. He looked at me. 'Surely one legion can be dealt with easily enough?'

'One legion, yes,' I replied. 'But one legion plus one hundred thousand Armenians is another matter. Our only hope is to link up with Gafarn at Hatra and meet the enemy north of the city with our combined forces.'

'How many men do you think we can field against the Armenians, Pacorus?' asked Orodes.

'After combining our forces with those at Hatra, perhaps fifty thousand men,' I answered.

Orodes looked concerned. 'So few? I thought Hatra alone could muster over sixty thousand men.'

'That was before Vata's defeat and the loss of the north. The towns in the northwestern part of the kingdom are still holding out as far as I know and Lord Herneus remains in charge at Assur in the east, but the loss of Nisibus and the surrounding lands is a heavy blow.'

'And remember Hatra's army also suffered losses at Susa,' added Domitus.

'We all suffered losses in that battle,' remarked Orodes grimly.

I tried to raise their morale. 'Gafarn will wait until we arrive and then we can launch a counterattack against the Armenians. Thus far they have tasted only victory and will be over-confident, expecting an unopposed march to the walls of Hatra. In adversity the seeds of our triumph may have been planted.'

I was not sure whom I was trying to convince, myself or them, but I knew that we stood a chance of at least halting the Armenians if Gafarn waited for us to arrive at Hatra.

Except that he did not wait and the next day a courier arrived from Hatra telling of a battle with the Armenians fifty miles north of the city in which Gafarn had been soundly beaten and his forces scattered. He himself had escaped back to the city with the remnants of his army, but Tigranes had now inflicted two major defeats on Hatra's army in a matter of weeks and the kingdom stood on the brink of calamity.

I showed the letter to Orodes who read it and passed it to Nergal. We stood on the palace terrace in stunned silence as Gallia and Praxima also digested the grim news.

'Why?' I heard myself saying. 'Why would he give battle before we arrived?'

I sat down and stared at the floor. Tigranes would surely now lay siege to Hatra itself. He was probably only one or two days' march from the city. It was now imperative to get to Hatra as quickly as possible. I looked at Orodes and knew he was thinking the same.

'We leave at dawn tomorrow,' he said.

I saw Dobbai wander onto the terrace and walk over to her chair. She smiled at Orodes and ignored the rest of us before easing herself into her nest of cushions. She looked at our glum faces.

'Did you all eat something disagreeable at breakfast?'

'We have received ill tidings from Hatra,' I snapped. 'Gafarn gave battle to Tigranes and lost.'

'Naturally,' she said casually. 'They do not call the Armenian king "great" for nothing, and who is Gafarn but a low-born slave who has gained a throne by chance?'

I was fuming at her casual attitude to this fresh calamity that had beset the empire and stomped over to face her.

'I hope that ritual we all took part in was not in vain,' I seethed.

Her eyes blazed with fury. 'Do not blame the gods for the vanity of Vata or the idiocy of your brother.'

Orodes and the others looked at us in confusion as Dobbai rose from her chair and pointed at Orodes.

'You must beware of your brother, high king, for your failure to kill him at Susa will return to haunt you err long.'

'Mithridates is with the Romans in northern Hatra,' he replied.

'He has left them,' she replied with conviction.

'Where is he?' I asked.

She looked indifferent. 'How should I know? But I would advise you to find him quickly.'

She sat back down in her chair and closed her eyes. I was still fuming and Orodes was shaking his head in confusion.

We left Dura at dawn the next morning; horse archers, cataphracts, squires and camels carrying spare arrows in a great column heading east to Hatra. Domitus and the two legions were left behind with the lords and their men in case the Romans at Emesa and their fat ally decided to try another assault against Palmyra. To this end I sent a message to Haytham with Malik who went back to Palmyra with Byrd, that he was to summon Domitus immediately if the enemy left Emesa, but asked him not to initiate hostilities until my men had reinforced him.

Gallia and Praxima rode together at the head of the Amazons whose numbers had once more been restored to one hundred women following their losses at Susa. The number of my cataphracts had also been made up to a thousand by promoting the eldest among the squires and inducting youngsters to take their places. The horse archers were once more up to three thousand by undertaking a recruiting drive within the kingdom.

We covered at least thirty-five miles each day so that it took us just over four days to reach Hatra. Mercifully, though it was still hot, the fierce heat of high summer was behind us. That said it was still very warm and so riders and horses sweated as we travelled across the sun-blasted sandy ground. The thousands of animals kicked up a huge dust cloud that was our faithful companion each day, covering us in a fine layer of grime that stuck to our clothes and sweaty flesh. It also made us cough as the particles entered our mouths and nostrils until we were forced to cover our faces like the Agraci do.

At the end of the fourth day we camped ten miles southwest of the city and Orodes sent a company of horse archers ahead to make contact with the garrison. I prayed that the city of my ancestors had not already fallen to Tigranes as I watched them disappear with the sun on their backs as it dropped into the western sky. Around me exhausted men and boys unsaddled their horses and let them drink from waterskins before they were corralled in temporary stables made from poles and canvas sheets, while the camels spat and growled as they were relieved of their heavy cargoes.

There were no campfires that night as the sky was devoid of clouds and the glow of any flames would be seen from afar, especially by any Armenian patrols that might be near. As a precaution we posted a heavy guard in all directions and enforced strict noise discipline.

The Durans arranged their eight-man oilskin tents in neat rows as they had done many times before on exercise and on campaign. The horse archers of Mesene did likewise. Only the horsemen from Babylon and Susiana pitched their tents in ever-widening circles around the canopy of the king of kings.

I sat on the ground in front of the tent I would share with Gallia as Scarab cleaned my helmet and cuirass a few paces away. After he had pitched our tent he smeared cedar oil around its base to repel any snakes that might be lurking nearby, while we all scoured the ground to kill any insects in an effort to deter camel spiders approaching us. Though they were not poisonous these giant eight-legged monsters could inflict a nasty bite that could easily become infected in the heat of the day.

Gallia watched Scarab go about his duties.

'I hope you are not treating him like a slave.'

I was most hurt. 'Of course not! He knows he is a free man and is with me of his own volition.'

'He must be the oldest squire in the army.'

'Yes,' I replied, 'but he joined us under exceptional circumstances and will just have to catch up.'

Scarab came over and bowed deeply. 'Would you like me to clean your sword, divinity?'

Gallia burst out laughing. 'Divinity? You should put a stop to that nonsense straight away!'

I ignored her chiding. 'Thank you, Scarab, but I like to clean it myself.'

Gallia whipped the dagger from her boot and stabbed it down to impale a large scorpion that was scuttling past her. She held up the wriggling creature on the end of her blade.

'Mithridates would be an idiot to return to Parthia. Death awaits him if he does.'

Scarab looked at her in alarm; this foreign woman who was both beautiful and fearsome. He did not know what to make of her. Then again, neither did most of the empire.

She looked at him. 'Where is your family, Scarab?'

'I lived with my parents, who were also slaves, in the house of their master in Egypt before I was sold to a merchant from Emesa. That was many years ago, highborn.'

She observed the still wriggling scorpion on the end of her dagger. 'Perhaps one day you will return to Egypt, to free them from bondage.'

She rammed the dagger into the ground, cutting the scorpion in two.

'I prefer to stay in Parthia, holiness.'

The next morning the company that Orodes had sent to Hatra returned with news that the Armenians were not laying siege to the city and that King Atrax and a force of Medians had arrived to strengthen the garrison. A wave of relief swept through me and I hugged Gallia because it also meant that Surena in Gordyene, to the north of Atrax's kingdom, must have halted the Armenian invasion of his land. And Atrax would never have left his kingdom if neighbouring Atropaiene was still under threat, which meant that Aschek must have at least halted the enemy forces threatening his realm.

It took us just over two hours to reach Hatra, a detachment of cataphracts sent by Gafarn linking up with us a mile from the city walls. I was surprised that it was not Vistaspa who commanded these men but was informed by the officer in charge that the leg wound he had suffered at the Battle of Susa had still not fully healed.

If I had been heartened by the news of Atrax's arrival in the city I was shocked when we reached Hatra and rode from its southern gates to the royal quarter in the north. The city had always been a bustling, thriving place but now it was filled with refugees with fear in their eyes. With listless expressions they huddled in doorways or gathered in cowering groups on the streets as they observed us ride past. I hardly recognised this place that had once been the western shield of the empire.

'How long have these people been here?' I asked the commander of our escort.

'They arrived following the loss of Nisibus, majesty,' he answered. 'For a week the road to the north was filled with refugees fleeing the Armenians.'

'How many?'

'Thousands, majesty. The king has established makeshift camps in the city's squares but as you can see, others are living on the streets.'

Hatra was watered by springs supplying sweet water from the earth so its citizens would never die of thirst, but its one hundred thousand inhabitants required large amounts of food each day to subsist, and thousands more mouths to feed would quickly exhaust the city's food supplies. By the time we reached the palace in the north of the city my spirits had been deflated.

Our horses were taken from us at the palace steps and we were immediately taken to the throne room where Gafarn awaited us. If the city had appeared downcast the atmosphere in the throne room was close to despair.

The cavernous chamber had been cleared of courtiers and slaves and only a few guards remained along the walls and at the doors. The latter were closed as we paced across the marble tiles, our footsteps echoing around the room as we approached the dais. Ahead a downcast Gafarn and a pale Diana were seated on their thrones, while standing to their right were Atrax, Aliyeh and Adeleh, who looked forlorn and lost. On the other side stood the gaunt and frail Assur, chief priest at the Great Temple; Kogan, commander of the city garrison, now in his late sixties; and Addu, the city treasurer. Next to him stood a grim-faced Herneus, governor of the eastern city of Assur who nodded to me, and another, slimmer man with a thick black beard and long black hair. He was dressed in a rich scale armour cuirass, long-sleeved white shirt, brown leggings and boots. I had never seen him before.

When we reached the dais Gafarn and Diana stood and with the others bowed to Orodes, their high king. Gafarn then nodded to Kogan who ordered chairs and refreshments to be brought for us, Diana giving up her throne so that Orodes could sit on it as befitting his status. She sat in a simple wicker chair that was placed beside Gafarn while the rest of us settled into our chairs in front of the dais, though not before we had embraced both Gafarn and Diana. Nergal and I also embraced our friend and companion-in-arms Atrax. I also hugged Adeleh and tried to be warm towards Aliyeh but she waved me away. Always aloof and serious, my sister had turned into a calculating and icy queen who forgot little and forgave nothing. She had never forgiven me for the fact that her husband, the King of Media, had a permanent limp, a disability she blamed on me for supposedly encouraging Atrax to fight the Romans. The result had been his defeat and impediment.

Slaves brought us cool water to slake our thirsts as Gafarn began by thanking us for coming to his aid. He appeared withdrawn, weighed down by the burden of ruling such a great city and I wondered if he was finding it all too much. He smiled thinly at Assur who stepped forward and asked us all to rise and bow our heads.

'Great Shamash, Lord of the Sun,' the high priest began, 'smile down on this Your city, and those who protect it and Your great temple. Unworthy though we are, grant us the wisdom and the means to drive back the godless heathens who have invaded Your lands and threaten those who love and fear You. In this time of strife we ask for Your divine help and deliverance. For only You can give us the strength to repel the foreign invaders.'

He turned, bowed his head to his king and returned to his position as we resumed our seats.

'Hatra is in great danger,' stated Gafarn flatly. 'We lost ten thousand men at Nisibus when Prince Vata was most tragically killed.' He smiled sympathetically at Adeleh. 'And a further five thousand when we engaged Tigranes only a few days ago to the north. Now the hordes of Tigranes stand ready to assault this great city. Had it not been for your arrival, my lords, his soldiers might already be scaling its walls.'

'Where is Tigranes now?' enquired Orodes.

'He has pulled his army back to the northeast, towards the Tigris,' answered Gafarn.

'He needs to be near a water source to maintain his multitude of men and animals,' added Atrax.

'He has requested a meeting with me,' said Gafarn bitterly.

I looked up. 'Meeting, why?'

'To dictate surrender terms, no doubt,' he replied.

'You must never surrender, brother,' spat Adeleh. 'You must crush this Armenian upstart, this mountain dweller whose presence in our lands defies our father's memory.'

'We will not surrender, of course not,' said Gafarn.

'You should march against him again, brother,' said Adeleh, 'and this time you will have other kings beside you.'

I looked at Adeleh and suddenly it all made sense. I wondered why Gafarn had not waited until we had arrived and now I knew: Adeleh had obviously pestered him into attacking Tigranes to exact revenge for Vata and the result had been a cheap victory for the Armenians.

'If only some had come earlier,' said Aliyeh, looking at me, 'then Prince Vata might still be alive and northern Hatra still free.'

I bristled at her insinuation. 'If you have something to say, *dear* sister, then say it.'

'When the Armenians invaded Hatra, you chose to help the Agraci filth first ahead of your own family. And now my sister is a widow and the enemy are nearly at the gates of this city, all because of you.'

Orodes and Atrax were aghast at her words and Gallia was fuming, while Nergal and Praxima looked distinctly uncomfortable.

'You should have come sooner, Pacorus,' said Adeleh. 'Vata was your childhood friend.'

'You waste your words, sister,' hissed Aliyeh. 'Our brother has become Haytham's pet and takes orders from Palmyra, not Ctesiphon.'

At a stroke she insulted both Orodes and me by insinuating he was a weak high king who had no control over his empire. I jumped up.

'Enough! I did not come here to be insulted by you. One day you will talk your head off your shoulders.'

Atrax then rose slowly from his chair. 'You forget yourself, Pacorus. Aliyeh is a queen and should be treated as such.'

Aliyeh smiled maliciously at me. 'It is quite all right, Atrax. Pacorus has spent too long in the company of the Agraci and has adopted their manners and customs, it seems.'

Gallia leapt up and pointed at Aliyeh. 'And you need to learn some manners.'

Aliyeh looked at Gafarn, a hurt expression on her face. 'Are you going to allow me to be spoken to thus in the palace where I grew up? My father would not have allowed such a thing.'

'Do not speak of my father,' I warned her.

Gafarn raised his hand. 'Can you all please compose yourselves and sit down. This is no time for a family squabble.'

Aliyeh regarded me contemptuously. 'Is he a member of our family? I sometimes wonder.'

'And I often wonder how such a spiteful, mean and nasty woman could be the daughter of my parents.'

'If you insult my wife once more,' said Atrax, 'I will have no choice but to draw my sword against you, Pacorus, though I would rather die a thousand times before I did so.'

'You are a true friend and man of honour, Atrax,' I said, 'and because of that I will withdraw from this assembly since I can see that my presence offends some among it. For I would rather cut off my own sword arm than raise it against you.'

I bowed my head to him and then Orodes, turned on my heels and walked towards the doors. Orodes and Gafarn called after me to stop but I ignored their pleas. Gallia likewise took her leave and came to my side.

After we had left the throne room we went to search for my mother, finding her in the garden she had tended so lovingly for years. She was kneeling in front of a bed of red chrysanthemums when we walked slowly up to her and halted. Sensing our presence, she stopped her digging and turned and smiled. I was shocked by her appearance. Her long black curly hair was now streaked with grey and she had lost a lot of weight so that her arms were thin and her face somewhat gaunt. Her brown eyes were full of pain and sorrow and my own eyes misted as I ran over to her and held her tight. She began to cry but then stiffened and released me, composing herself before she walked over to Gallia and embraced her.

'How are you, mother?' I asked.

'Worked off my feet, Pacorus. I have been trying to bed in these chrysanthemums but there are never enough hours in the day.'

I smiled. 'You have a small army of gardeners to help you.'

'Oh, they are competent enough but flowers require loving care for them to flourish. Your father is always telling me...'

She stopped and held a hand to her mouth, then turned away from us and went back to her digging. I knelt beside her.

'I am sorry about father. I wish it had been me in his place.'

She cupped my face with her hand. 'No, Pacorus. It was his time. He died fighting for what he believed was proper and just and I think events have proved him right. Orodes is a good man.'

'Yes he is,' I agreed. 'And Gafarn is a good king.'

'Your brother thinks that you should be King of Hatra but I told him many years ago that the gods decided you should take a different path.'

She put down her trowel and stood.

73

'Gallia, dear, you are looking very well. Did you bring my grandchildren?'

Gallia looked at me in alarm. It was as if nothing existed to my mother beyond this garden and the Armenians and Romans were mere figments of our imagination.

'We left them in Dura, mother,' replied Gallia, linking her arm in hers, 'but we will bring them very soon.'

And so we walked with her under cypress trees, willow and date palms; along paths between ponds filled with carp and goldfish; the sweet fragrance of jasmine and myrtle filling the air. White doves flew around us and peacocks displayed their plumage. It was a place of serenity and beauty where one could forget the horrors of the outside world and the creeping doom that was approaching Hatra; a sanctuary that my mother had escaped to and in her mind would never leave.

The armies of the kings had made their camp to the north of the city and that was where Gallia and I slept that night, happy to be away from the poisonous barbs of my sisters. Adeleh I could forgive because of her grief but Aliyeh had incensed me.

'I have a mind to ride back to Dura in the morning,' I said to Gallia as we sat outside our tent waiting for Scarab to return from the field kitchens with our evening meal.

'Orodes and Gafarn need you. We must present a united front against the Armenians.'

I scraped at the earth with the heel of my boot. 'She never used to be like that, Aliyeh I mean. She was always serious and somewhat aloof but never scheming or malicious.'

'Power has corrupted her,' mused Gallia.

'No doubt she has been bending Atrax's ear about launching an attack against the Armenians to avenge Vata.'

'You do not think we can defeat the Armenians?'

I shrugged. 'If we fight them it must be on our own terms, not theirs. At the moment Tigranes is strong and has inflicted two successive defeats on us. He and his army will be confident that they can do so again. On the other hand, if we wait his strength will only increase when the Romans reinforce him. The next few days will be crucial.'

Scarab returned with freshly roasted goat and chicken, plus wine that Gafarn had sent from the city earlier. I told him to eat with us but I could tell he was most uncomfortable because he hardly ate anything and watched both of us all the time, offering to refill our cups after we had sipped from them and generally acting like a slave. Old habits die hard and it would take him a while to adjust to his new life.

The ending of the day was far more agreeable than its earlier part when Nergal and Praxima arrived with a hundred of their horse archers dressed in red kaftans, over which they wore scale armour cuirasses and helmets on their heads. Scarab fetched two more stools so our friends could sit with us while their men dismounted and I told them to go and get themselves something to eat.

The sun was casting long shadows and the sky was now turning orange and purple as the day waned and evening approached. Scarab threw more sticks on the fire and served our guests wine. Praxima found it difficult not to laugh as he bowed and called her 'divinity'.

'Actually,' I said, 'you are correct to address them so, for to the people of Mesene they are gods.'

Scarab looked most impressed by this news and bowed even lower, averting his eyes from theirs as he retreated from our presence.

'Where did you get him from?' asked Nergal.

'We picked him up during our recent meeting with the Romans,' I said. 'He was a slave and now he's my squire.'

'There is a meeting in the palace tomorrow, Pacorus,' said Nergal, changing the subject, 'to discuss how we are going to deal with the Armenians.'

'Sending my eldest sister to batter them with her tongue would be a good start,' I suggested.

'The Armenians need to be stopped,' said Praxima, 'else they will swallow up all the lands between the Tigris and Euphrates.'

She was right. Tigranes stood on the verge of victory and there appeared very little that we could do about it. I thought back to that night when Dobbai had performed her ritual. Where were the gods; had it all been in vain? Perhaps I had been wrong to put any faith in a rambling old woman.

I smiled at Praxima. 'Tigranes thinks he has already won, no doubt, but that may be his undoing. His aim is to march south beyond Hatra but cannot while the city is still Parthian, for to do so would leave a mighty hostile citadel in his rear. He must take the city if he is to advance further.'

'The Armenians have no siege engines,' said Nergal.

'But the Romans do,' added Gallia, 'and if they join with Tigranes then Hatra will be in great danger.'

'Not necessarily, my sweet,' I replied. 'Hatra's walls are strong and high and the nearest water supply is over fifty miles away, at the Tigris. Not only that, a besieging army would have to fend off forces sent from Media, Dura and Babylon. What Tigranes needs to achieve is to crush us in battle in the hope that a demoralised Hatra opens its gates to him in submission.'

'That will never happen,' growled Praxima.

I stood and went over to her and kissed her on the cheek.

'Perhaps we should make you the city governor, then Hatra could hold out for a hundred years.'

She threw back her head and laughed, shaking her mass of long red hair, then instinctively sprang to her feet and clutched the hilt of her sword, as the calm of the night was interrupted by shouting. I turned to see three of my horse archers approaching on foot, two of them holding the arms of a tall, well-built youth with long black hair.

75

'Let go of me, barbarians. I am a prince and will have you flogged for your insolence.'

'And I'm the King of Babylon. Now be quiet,' said the unimpressed officer in charge.

We all stood as the group approached and the officer saluted, holding a sword in a scabbard in his right hand.

'Apologies for the interruption, majesty,' he said to me, jerking a thumb at the boy. 'A patrol found this one trying to enter our camp. He says you are his uncle.'

I looked at Gallia and smiled at Nergal and Praxima and then waved the two guards holding the youth forward. The fire illuminated his square jaw and thick neck and the fire in his eyes reminded me of his mother.

'You can let him go,' I said to the guards, 'he is family.'

He yanked his arms free and then glared at the officer holding his sword.

'That's mine,' he snapped.

I held out my hand to the officer who passed me the sword. He bowed then he and his men left us. I drew the sword from its scabbard. It was a beautiful piece, finely balanced and exquisitely made. The long, straight blade was double edged and the hilt comprised a steel cross-guard, a grip wrapped in leather strips and a silver pommel in the shape of a horse's head.

'A fine sword, young Spartacus,' I said.

I slid it back in the scabbard and handed it back to its owner. We retook our seats as he buckled his sword belt round his waist.

'You should not try to enter my camp unannounced,' I reprimanded him. 'It may be your father's land but my men will still put an arrow in you if you try to sneak past them.'

'I wished to see you, uncle,' he protested. 'Mother told me that you had decided not to stay in the palace. Have you come to fight the Armenians?'

'I have come to support your father,' I corrected him. 'This is King Nergal and Queen Praxima of Mesene, who have also come to support your father.'

He bowed his head to them as Scarab brought a stool for him to sit on and offered him a cup of water.

Spartacus watched him go.

'Is he your slave?'

'We do not keep slaves,' said Gallia.

'I have heard this. In the palace we have many slaves. They are treated well,' he said firmly.

'Not all slaves are treated kindly,' said Praxima with bitterness.

'I have heard that your army is made up of former slaves, uncle.'

'Not all of it,' I replied, 'but there are many who have escaped from bondage.'

'My aunts do not approve of it,' he said.

'I can imagine,' I smiled.

76

'They do not approve of me,' he said softly.

Gallia looked at me and then at Praxima.

'Why?' she asked.

'Because my father, my blood father, was a slave. And my current parents were also slaves. I may be a prince but it makes no difference. The other squires call me *servus*, which is Latin for slave. By doing so they insult me twice, by reminding me that I was born to slave parents and that they were both killed by the Romans. The gossip in the city is that because the present king and queen were slaves Shamash has abandoned us and will continue to do so until a Parthian noble sits on the throne.'

'You should be proud of your real father and the parents who have adopted you,' said Nergal.

'They say that he was a great leader, the man I am named after.'

'Perhaps one of the greatest who has ever lived,' I said.

We spent the rest of the evening regaling him with tales of Italy and Spartacus. I am sure that he had heard them a hundred times before but never from our mouths. So Gallia told him of the founding of the Amazons and how she had maintained their numbers at one hundred ever since, of how she had rescued me on a beach near Thurii and how I had returned the favour later when her father had kidnapped her. He sat open mouthed as Praxima told him about the Battle of Mutina and how we slaughtered the Gauls and Romans and then afterwards marched south instead of north over the Alps. We told him of Domitus, Thumelicus, Drenis and Vagises. He want to bed happy, while I made a promise to myself that I would do everything I could to turn back the Armenian tide.

To that end we rode with young Spartacus back into Hatra the next morning to attend the council of war. It was held in the office next to the throne room, a great hide map of the empire hanging on the wall. Waiting for us was Orodes, Gafarn, Vistaspa, Kogan, Herneus, the man with the black beard and Atrax, the latter shaking my hand and saying nothing of what had happened the day before. I walked over to Vistaspa and clasped his forearm. He tried to get up but his injured leg was still in splints so I told him to stay seated. He looked pale and in pain and I wondered if he would see the new year.

The doors were closed and the meeting got under way with Gafarn introducing the severe-looking man with the beard as Lord Apollonius, the governor of western Hatra who held the towns of Ichnae, Nicephorium, Carrhae and Zenodotium; all of which were under threat of being assaulted by the Romans. No wonder he looked serious!

'What strength can the Kingdom of Hatra muster?' asked Orodes.

A grim-faced Gafarn pointed at Apollonius first, who stood and cleared his throat.

'If I brought all the garrisons of the towns together the number would total two thousand foot and five thousand horsemen, majesty.'

'And you, Herneus?' asked Gafarn.

'There is at Assur ten thousand horse archers and a thousand foot soldiers.'

Gafarn smiled at Vistaspa. 'There is in this city a thousand cataphracts, twenty thousand horse archers and the garrison of two thousand foot soldiers.'

'Twenty-one thousand horsemen,' I said, 'plus those who have arrived from Media, Dura, Mesene and Babylon.'

These amounted to an additional two thousand heavy horsemen and twenty-two thousand horse archers.

'Forty-five thousand men in all,' remarked Orodes with satisfaction. 'Enough to convince Tigranes not to provoke us, I think.'

'When we last encountered Tigranes at Nisibus,' I said, 'his army was deficient in heavy horsemen so we need to increase the number of our cataphracts to impress him.'

Vistaspa winced as pain shot through his leg and there were beads of sweat on his forehead.

'Hatra and Dura can muster a thousand each, while Babylon and Media have five hundred apiece. Three thousand men,' he said. 'There are no more.'

'There are another six thousand we can put into the field,' I replied.

They all looked at me in confusion.

'It is quite simple,' I continued. 'We arm every squire and attire him in scale armour. We can place them behind their masters to stiffen their resolve so Tigranes sees nine thousand *kontus* points arrayed against him.'

'If the Armenians attack, majesty,' said a concerned Kogan, 'then those boys will be the first to fall.'

'It is a risk,' I agreed, 'but desperate times call for desperate measures and these are desperate times, my friends.'

I looked at Orodes. 'The decision rests with you.'

He looked at Gafarn and then Atrax, who both nodded at him.

'Very well, we will try what Pacorus suggests.'

The rest of the meeting addressed matters in Gordyene and Atropaiene. Atrax reported receiving regular updates from Surena who was more than holding his own against Prince Artavasdes and his Armenians. True to form, Surena had initially avoided the invaders, being content to launch raids against their flanks and rear. These had proved so effective that Artavasdes had halted his advance. Intercepted messages had revealed that he had appealed to his father for reinforcements, without which capturing Vanadzor, Gordyene's capital city, would be impossible. As for Atropaiene, the Armenian force that had invaded the north of that kingdom had been nothing more than a large-scale raid and had quickly retreated after burning and looting a few dozen villages and carrying off their inhabitants as slaves.

As two squires and two camels loaded with spare armour and weapons attended every cataphract, it was relatively easy to create another six thousand heavy horsemen. And while we waited for Tigranes to inform us of the time and place of the meeting the squires practised riding in formation. It was decided that the squires from each kingdom should deploy immediately behind their masters in the front rank. Thus Dura's cataphracts would deploy in two ranks: five hundred men in the first rank, another five hundred in the second. And behind them would be two thousand squires in four ranks.

This formation was copied by the heavy horsemen of Media, Hatra and Babylon and made for an impressive sight on the arid plain north of the city.

'That should deter the old man,' I said smugly as we admired the thousands of horses, men and boys covered in scale armour, a forest of *kontus* points stretching right and left.

'Let us hope so, Pacorus,' said Orodes, not wholly convinced.

'One more thing,' I said. 'If negotiations fail then we must launch an immediate attack against the Armenians. We should not repeat the mistake made at Nisibus.'

'I agree,' said Atrax. 'I was there that day and we could have destroyed Tigranes and his army.'

'I am with you, Pacorus,' added Nergal.

'And I,' said Gafarn.

'And you, high king?' I asked Orodes.

I knew that I was forcing his hand but I feared that Orodes' sense of fair play and high honour would preclude any talk of fighting before negotiations had failed, but I did not trust Tigranes, who had already seized the northern part of my brother's kingdom and threatened the rest. For all I knew he was demanding this meeting to gather us all in one place so he could slaughter us.

'Very well,' said Orodes with reluctance.

Two days later a messenger arrived from Tigranes saying that he would meet us forty miles north of Hatra, which I found most curious. As he and his army were near the Tigris to the northeast I wondered why he would travel west into the desert to meet with us. It made no sense. But if Tigranes liked to undertake futile marches in the desert, so be it. All I was concerned about was the safety of Hatra.

On the first day out from the city we covered twenty-five miles before making camp in the vast emptiness of the flat desert plain. In this desolate place a city such as Hatra, which drew its water from underground springs that supplied the precious liquid all-year round, was worth is weight in gold. If Hatra fell then foreign armies could pour south into Babylon and Mesene and conquer all the lands between the Euphrates and Tigris with ease. From Hatra an enemy could also strike east towards Media and Atropaiene and west to Dura. It was no exaggeration to state that if Hatra fell then the whole of the western half of the Parthian Empire would crumble.

These thoughts swirled in my mind the next day when we broke camp and headed north to meet with Tigranes. When we reached the designated spot there was no sign of the Armenians and I began to wonder that it may have been a ruse to lure us out of Hatra so Tigranes could assault the city, but as the city garrison would be manning the walls, the gates would be shut and the surrounding moat full I discounted this possibility. My fears were then dispelled when parties of horse archers began to appear on the horizon, and behind them columns of foot soldiers tramping across the dusty plain.

Our own horsemen were already moving into their battle positions – cataphracts in the centre and horse archers on the wings. We extended our line as far as possible to create an impression of strength that would hopefully awe the Armenians. The six thousand heavy horsemen in the centre looked very imposing, pennants fluttering in the easterly breeze and the sun's rays glinting off steel leg and arm armour and the silver scales of Hatra's royal bodyguard. The latter were placed in the centre of the line, with my Durans to their left and Orodes' bodyguard on their right. Atrax's heavy horsemen were deployed to the right of Orodes' men. I had to admit that the sight of nine thousand cataphracts was a wonder to behold, even if two-thirds of them were only nervous boys.

On our right wing were deployed the horse archers of Babylon, Mesene and Media – a total of nineteen thousand men – while our left comprised my own horse archers – three thousand under Vagises – and Hatra's twenty thousand extending far into the distance. Thus did we muster fifty-one thousand soldiers on this barren stretch of earth. In addition, stocked with spare arrows and deployed in the rear of both wings, were the camel trains of Hatra, Media, Dura and Mesene.

As they had both foot and horse the Armenians placed the former in the centre and the latter on the wings. The great majority of the foot soldiers were élite spearmen equipped with large rectangular shields faced with iron and protected by bronze helmets and thick leather armour. They held their long spears with both hands and so their shields had to be strapped to their forearms. Deployed in one huge phalanx, they stood directly opposite our cataphracts and numbered around twenty thousand men. Either side of them were groups of foot archers and slingers to provide missile support for the spearmen. These numbered between five and seven thousand.

On the wings the Armenians grouped their horse archers interspersed with blocks of mounted spearmen, though I noted that they either did not have enough horsemen to match our frontage or were keeping some back in reserve as both our wings outflanked theirs to a considerable extent. I estimated each Armenian wing to number around ten thousand men, which meant on sight we matched the size of the Armenian army, though there may have been a substantial reserve in their rear.

After the Armenians had deployed into position Tigranes himself appeared, riding from behind the phalanx of spearmen and escorted by around two thousand heavy horsemen, his personal bodyguard. The latter were magnificently attired in black leggings and blue tunics, over which they wore short-sleeved mail shirts. Their heads helmets sported purple plumes and mail face veils. They carried long spears and their horses were protected by scale armour covering their bodies but not their heads or necks.

As he had been at Nisibus, the king was dressed in a purple and white striped tunic and had a rich purple cloak around his shoulders. A tall, imposing man, the conical jewel-encrusted hat he wore made him appear even taller.

As I sat next to Orodes watching Tigranes walk his horse into the middle of no-man's land the other kings came to our side. Nergal and Praxima galloped across the front ranks of the cataphracts with a huge yellow banner carrying a double-headed lion sceptre crossed with a sword billowing behind them. Atrax brought Media's banner of a white dragon on a black background to stand beside that of Mesene and the horned bull of Babylon and the eagle with a snake in its talons that was the emblem of Susiana, both of these kingdoms being ruled by Orodes. Behind me the brave and loyal Vagharsh held Dura's banner of a red griffin on a white background. The last banner to arrive was that of Hatra – a white horse's head on a red background – carried behind Gafarn who had been with the officers of his horse archers on the left wing.

The Armenian ranks were dotted with red, yellow, purple and blue flags and dragon windsocks, while behind Tigranes was carried a huge white flag upon which was a purple six-pointed star, the symbol of Armenia. Tigranes halted his horsemen around five hundred paces from our position as the breeze stiffened and gave life to the hundreds of flags among the Armenian ranks. A lone rider came from behind Tigranes and headed towards us. Orodes turned in the saddle and pointed to one of his own officers, who spurred his horse forward to meet the Armenian rider. This was normal protocol for determining the size of each party in the discussions to guarantee equal numbers.

'At least we are not outnumbered,' remarked Gafarn.

'They may have a reserve behind that phalanx of spearmen,' I said. 'We should not underestimate Tigranes.'

'Speaking of Tigranes, it would be to our advantage, I think, not to provoke him,' Orodes cautioned me.

No doubt he was thinking back to the meeting between my father and Tigranes outside Nisibus when I had goaded the Armenian king and had been rebuked for doing so by my father. Orodes had been a prince that day and had not been part of the negotiations, but I told him what had happened afterwards. That day I was confident we could defeat the Armenians. Today I was not so sure.

'Have no fear, my friend,' I replied, 'it is you who will do all the talking, not I.'

However, when we finally met Tigranes it was he who was intent on goading me. He was at least eighty years old now and though he had plenty of wrinkles his cheeks were no longer sunken and his eyes sparkled with vigour. War and conquest clearly suited his constitution. It was the first time he had met Orodes, the honest and honourable high king of the empire, and though he did not insult my friend he made it plain that he was bargaining from a position of strength. Orodes chose his words carefully not to give offence to Tigranes.

'Parthia does not want war with Armenia, King Tigranes, but I must demand your withdrawal from all the lands of the empire that you have invaded.'

Tigranes smiled mischievously. 'King Orodes, Armenia did not start this war but has merely responded to aggression initiated by one of your own kings.'

I stifled a laugh as Orodes' brow furrowed.

'I do not understand.'

'Do you not? Then let me explain,' he replied, his eyes on me all the time. 'Gordyene was an Armenian province until Parthia saw fit to send a murdering upstart to wreak destruction upon it. Such an outrage cannot go unaltered.'

Orodes nodded solemnly. 'I can understand your anger with regard to the shedding of Armenian blood, lord king, but you would agree that Gordyene is a Parthian kingdom.'

Tigranes looked disinterested. 'I do not know the history of Gordyene,' that was a lie, 'only that my Roman allies gave it over to my safekeeping after they had conquered it.'

This was particularly galling because King Balas, the ruler of Gordyene, had supported Tigranes against the Romans when he had been their foe. Balas had been killed fighting the Romans and his former friend had ended up inheriting his kingdom.

'But I believe I am right in saying,' continued Orodes, 'that Hatra has never been part of Armenia and yet your soldiers occupy the northern part of this kingdom.'

Tigranes looked thoughtful. 'If the upstart king who rules Gordyene leaves that kingdom then I will consider doing the same in Hatra.'

I could no longer hold my tongue. 'Impossible!'

Tigranes laughed. 'King Pacorus! I wondered how long it would be before you graced us with your opinions.'

'I am here at the request of King of Kings Orodes,' I spat at him.

'Tell me,' Tigranes said to me. 'Are Hatra's problems still your problems, and are its wars still your wars?'

I tightened my grip on Remus' reins. 'They are.'

'The affairs of Hatra concern all the kings of the empire,' interrupted Orodes.

Tigranes looked past us to where our horsemen were drawn up.

'Where are your famed legions, King Pacorus, the men who have spread death and fear throughout Parthia?'

'I did not think it worthwhile to bring them,' I answered, 'such is the mediocrity of the opposition we face.'

Gafarn and Atrax laughed but Tigranes looked at me with hateful eyes.

'Perhaps you wish for things to be settled here, today, just as you did at Nisibus all those months ago?'

He was right, I did. But I kept my tongue and refused to take his bait.

'High King Orodes decides the actions that will be taken this day,' I replied.

Orodes looked relieved while Tigranes looked smug.

'These are my terms, King Orodes,' he declared. 'I am prepared to suspend hostilities in Hatra on condition that all the territory I currently hold up to Mount Sinjar becomes part of Greater Armenia in perpetuity. In addition, once my son has completed the conquest of Gordyene that kingdom will also revert to being Armenian.'

Mount Sinjar was a low limestone ridge that was only just over sixty miles north of the city of Hatra. I could see it now on the northern horizon, a long white strip of high land in the otherwise slightly undulating plain.

'The alternative,' threatened Tigranes, 'is to continue hostilities.'

Tigranes knew that we also faced a Roman invasion in the northwest, to say nothing of the army under Crassus that he surely knew was on its way. I had little doubt that the two wings of our army would be able to shoot the enemy's flanks to pieces with their bows, but the Armenians also had horse archers and mounted spearmen that could inflict heavy losses on us. And in the centre two-thirds of our heavy horsemen were boys who had never fought in a battle.

'As a show of good faith,' said Tigranes, 'I am prepared to withdraw my forces to the city of Nisibus.'

That was about a hundred and fifty miles north of Hatra, which would at least give Gafarn some respite, though at the cost of losing half his kingdom. It also meant that the city of Assur would no longer be threatened with an immediate assault and, as Surena was still more than holding his own in Gordyene, that kingdom was safe for the time being. Orodes caught my eye and I nodded ever so slightly at him. Orodes then looked at Gafarn and sighed.

'In the interests of peace, lord king,' he said to Tigranes, 'I accept these terms on condition that you immediately pull back to Nisibus.'

Tigranes could barely conceal his delight. 'Consider it done, King Orodes,' he replied. 'I look forward to continual fruitful relations between us.'

Orodes nodded curtly and then wheeled his horse away, followed by Gafarn, Nergal and Atrax. I was about to tug on Remus' reins when I heard Tigranes' voice.

'Do you still think I am a Roman puppet?'

'I think,' I replied slowly, 'that your son will never conquer Gordyene and you should enjoy your stay in Hatra. It will be brief.'

Gafarn was very downcast during the journey back to Hatra despite Orodes' attempts to cheer him.

'I have let our father down,' he said to me as he sank in his saddle.

'Father would have been proud of you, Gafarn. Had I been on the throne no doubt the whole of Hatra would have been lost by now. At least we have bought some time.'

'Time for what?' he said disconsolately.

'Time to organise,' I replied.

Two days later we were back in Hatra, whose inhabitants appeared relieved when news spread that the Armenians were pulling back north. On the second morning following our arrival back in the city we gathered in the throne room to say our farewells. Diana was as warm-hearted and generous as ever and I was glad that we had saved her city, at least for the moment. My sisters ignored me but I did not care. What were their opinions to me?

'We will recover those lands that have been lost,' promised Orodes, standing next to the dais, 'that I promise. But first we must assist Surena in Gordyene. To this end I have asked King Atrax to send him reinforcements, which he has agreed to do.'

Atrax smiled at Orodes while Aliyeh shook her head.

I saw Gafarn look up and beckon over a dust-covered courier who had entered the room. Gafarn stood as the man walked to the dais, bowed his head and handed him a letter. We watched as my brother returned to his throne, broke the letter's seal and read the contents. He seemed to visibly wilt as he handed it to Diana and held his head in his hands.

'What is it, brother? I asked.

A pale Diana handed the latter to Orodes.

'We have been duped,' he said softly. 'This is from Herneus at Assur. While we were engaged in polite conversation with Tigranes it appears that a great host of horse and foot advanced south past Assur towards Seleucia.'

'Armenians?' I asked with concern.

'It appears not,' replied Orodes. 'Herneus' scouts reported that they saw a great banner depicting an eagle clutching a snake in its talons.'

'It cannot be,' I said, dumbfounded.

'It would appear,' remarked Orodes bitterly, 'that Mithridates has returned to Parthia.'

Chapter 4

The office was empty and I was alone with my thoughts staring at the map of the empire. They were not good company. I glanced to my right, at the chair that my father had always occupied at the meetings of Hatra's council. How we needed him now. I looked back at the map. The Armenians controlled the whole of northern Hatra; there was a Roman legion at Zeugma poised to join with their Armenian allies. There were Armenian troops in Gordyene. Roman cavalry and another legion at Emesa still threatened Palmyra, and now Mithridates was marching with an army towards Seleucia. Orodes had sent a courier to the city to warn its governor, the aged General Mardonius, of the approaching threat. His small garrison of a thousand men would not be able to withstand a determined assault, especially as the city's defences were in a state of disrepair.

I looked at the empty chair. What would you do, father?

'I'm glad he is not here to witness our misfortune.'

I turned to see Gafarn standing behind me, his slim frame silhouetted in the doorway.

'Hatra was the strongest kingdom in the empire once, a bulwark against external foes and a stabilising factor in Parthia's internal affairs, and now it lies prostrate and helpless like a new-born lamb.'

I walked over and placed a hand on his shoulder. 'We are not beaten yet, brother. Remember Rhegium.'

He looked perplexed. 'Rhegium?'

'Yes, when Crassus had Spartacus and his army penned in like cattle ready for slaughter with their backs against the sea. Well, we turned the tables on Crassus and can do the same again.'

He smiled. 'Same old Pacorus – defiant in the face of impending doom. You should rule Hatra; it is your birthright.'

He looked directly at me. 'I would gladly relinquish the throne if it meant that this city and its kingdom were saved.'

I grabbed his shoulders with both hands. 'You are Hatra's king, Gafarn, no one else. It is your destiny, just as it is mine never to wear its crown. You have suffered a setback, that is all, but if I have learned anything from the Romans it is not to sit and wait for an enemy but to take the fight to them.'

'What are you thinking?'

I smiled slyly. 'That the time for talking is over.'

An hour later everyone was assembled in the office as I stood before them in front of the map. Couriers had arrived from Babylon, Seleucia and Assur with news of the army of Mithridates and its progress. It was marching down the west bank of the River Tigris towards Seleucia, which it would reach in around nine days.

I began pacing up and down. 'The immediate threat is Mithridates, he obviously intends to capture Seleucia and use it both as a base and a rallying point to mount a challenge against Orodes.'

I nodded at my friend.

'He seeks to take advantage of our current predicament to become high king once more.'

'He has no support,' said Atrax. 'How then does he intend to capture the high crown?'

'With the help of his Roman and Armenian allies,' replied Orodes, his face a mask of anger.

'That is correct, lord king,' I continued. 'We now know that the meeting with Tigranes was a decoy so Mithridates could sneak past us. But we may yet prevail if we act quickly.'

'What do you have in mind?' asked Orodes.

I suddenly became aware that I was no longer speaking to my friend, Prince Orodes, but the king of kings of the empire, and that it was not my place to lecture him.

'It is only an idea, lord king,' I started to say.

His brow furrowed with annoyance. 'This is not the time to be standing on ceremony, Pacorus. What use is protocol if there is no Parthian Empire left? Please speak your mind.'

Atrax, Gafarn, Nergal and Praxima nodded in agreement while Gallia looked at me in exasperation.

'Very well. My plan is to bring the legions from Dura to link up with my horsemen west of this city and then march to Seleucia to fight Mithridates. Hopefully Mardonius will be able to hold the city, but if it falls then I will use Marcus' engines to batter my way in. Either way, I intend to hunt down and kill Mithridates once and for all.'

'If you withdraw the legions from Dura,' said Gallia, 'you will leave the city undefended. There are still Roman troops at Emesa.'

I looked at Nergal. 'Not if the King of Mesene takes his army to the city.'

Nergal looked surprised.

'You were my second-in-command, Nergal,' I continued. 'You have also fought beside Malik and Spandarat. They know you and trust you. Who better to be in charge of Dura in my absence? And who better to be the guardian of my family?'

Praxima smiled and Nergal nodded. 'I accept this responsibility, Pacorus. But what of Hatra? You will be stripping it of the troops we have brought here.'

I tilted my head at Kogan. 'The garrison can be reinforced by Hatra's own horse archers, but there is no point in other horsemen being cooped up inside a city. Therefore I propose that Atrax and Orodes concentrate at Assur, which is only two day's ride from Hatra, but which has ample grazing for horses and camels. Orodes should also assume command of Hatra's heavy horsemen. They are wasted here. If the Armenians assault the city a relief force can be hastily assembled at Assur, and once I have dealt with Mithridates I will bring Dura's army back north.'

'I wish to accompany you south, Pacorus,' declared Atrax. 'I have no interest in idling away at Assur while you fight Mithridates.'

I smiled at him as Gallia rolled her eyes.

'We need you here, my friend,' I said to him. 'The Armenians pose the greatest threat to the empire, notwithstanding Mithridates' inconvenient appearance.'

'What about the Romans?' asked Nergal.

'At the moment there is only one legion at Zeugma and another at Emesa,' I said. 'They have already been frustrated in their attempts to capture Palmyra. I see no reason why we cannot do the same with their desire to seize the lands between the Tigris and Euphrates.'

'So,' said Orodes, 'are we all agreed on Pacorus' plan?'

Atrax nodded, as did Nergal and Gafarn.

'It is settled then,' he said. 'One more thing, Pacorus. You are henceforth lord high general of the empire.'

I went to protest but he held up a hand to me. 'It is not a request it is a command, unless you would defy your king of kings.'

I bowed my head. 'As you desire, lord king.'

Though I was pleased that my plan had been adopted I was less so by my new appointment. I had held the post before when the father of Orodes, Phraates, had been king of kings and had not particularly enjoyed it. Still, it gave me control over all the armies that Parthia could put in the field, theoretically at least. Orodes had my appointment proclaimed to the whole city and despatched couriers to the far corners of the empire to spread the news. No doubt it would be received coolly by the empire's eastern kings whose armies had been worsted at my hands in the past. That did not matter. What did was to stop them thinking that there was any merit in supporting the returned Mithridates.

I said my farewells to an emotional Diana that afternoon in her private chambers in the palace, young Pacorus in attendance. The son they had named after me was seven years old now and had inherited his father's slender frame and his mother's amiable disposition. We were soon joined by Gafarn, Nergal, Praxima and Gallia, the latter embracing her friend and telling her not to worry.

'Now that Pacorus is lord high general I will not worry,' she said.

'I hope I will be able to repay your faith in me,' I replied.

'I wish I was coming with you,' remarked Praxima, 'to kill Mithridates, I mean.'

'Do not worry,' I assured her, 'there will be enough killing to go round before long.'

'Will you see your sisters before you leave?' queried Diana. Ever the peacemaker.

'No,' I stated flatly. 'But I would advise you to encourage Adeleh to join Aliyeh when she goes back to Irbil to get them both out of the way.'

'Adeleh would never leave her mother and Hatra,' said a horrified Diana. 'This is her home.'

I sighed. 'Her home was Nisibus, but she lost that when she encouraged Vata to fight the Armenians, and am I right in thinking, Gafarn, that she pestered you to march against Tigranes as well?'

Gafarn looked uncomfortable but said nothing.

'I will take your silence as confirmation of this. Clear heads and hard hearts are what are needed at this time. Sentimentality will get us all killed.'

'Thank you Pacorus,' said Gallia, 'we are not a group of your officers.'

'More's the pity,' I mumbled.

Later I sent a courier to Dura to alert Domitus to my intentions and to order him to bring the legions over the Euphrates and head for Seleucia. I also told him that Nergal was marching to the city to reinforce Haytham in the event of the Romans once more advancing from Emesa. Gallia informed me that she and the Amazons would also be travelling back to Dura with Nergal and Praxima.

'You could stay here,' I said as I finished a letter to Surena informing him of the decisions taken at Hatra.

'I would only come to blows with your sisters if I did and that would upset your mother and Diana, so it is best I return home to be with the children.'

That afternoon we both went to see my mother in her garden. We found her sitting in the pagoda with a ghost from another time. My mother, dressed in a simple white gown with her hair gathered behind her head held in place by a large gold clip, was cleaning the fingernails of a woman we had brought back with us from Italy.

'Rubi?' Gallia scarcely believed her eyes as the ghost turned to look at the strangers who approached her.

She had been a slave whom we had rescued near the town of Rubi in Italy, after which Gallia had named her. The Roman slave catchers had cut out her tongue and so the only sounds she could make were grunts and hisses. She recognised Gallia instantly, jumped out of her seat and threw her arms round my wife.

'Hello Rubi. It is good to see you.'

'Rubi,' snapped my mother, 'please come and sit down.'

Rubi looked at my mother with a hurt expression and then slunk back to her chair and held out her hand to my mother.

'How are you Rubi?' I enquired.

She saw me and hissed, baring her teeth.

'Don't upset her, Pacorus,' said my mother.

Slaves standing at the edge of the pagoda positioned two chairs near my mother for us to sit in as others brought fruit juice and pastries.

'How has she been?' Gallia asked my mother, smiling at Rubi.

'She likes it here, among the flowers and trees. I have the Sisters of Shamash bring her here as much as possible.'

The Sisters of Shamash were an order of virgins who had pledged their lives to the Sun God. In addition to their religious duties they cared for the mad, orphans and cripples who were brought to the gates of their walled sanctuary positioned behind the Great Temple.

'You are leaving, then?' said my mother.

'The affairs of the empire demand my attention, mother.'

She smiled at Rubi. 'Well, when you return you must bring my grandchildren. I have not seen them in an age.'

'We will bring them soon,' promised Gallia.

We sat with them both as my mother finished cleaning Rubi's fingernails. She immediately went back to the flowerbeds and began pawing at the earth with her hands. My mother shook her head.

'Poor Rubi, she doesn't understand.' She sighed. 'It seems like yesterday when you brought her here. So much has happened since then. Things have never been the same since Sinatruces died.'

'Sinatruces?' I asked.

'Yes,' she rebuked me, 'he was the king of kings and since his death things have taken a turn for the worse.'

'I hope things will return to as they were, mother.'

She frowned at me. 'Don't be absurd. Things can never be as they were. I hope you have not brought any more Agraci here. People took a very dim view of it.'

We left her in the company of Rubi and returned with sad hearts to our quarters. The death of my father had affected her deeply and I worried that she was losing her mind. She was like a lost soul and there was nothing I could do.

We left Hatra the next day, Gallia and the Amazons riding west with Nergal and Praxima towards Dura while I journeyed south with my horsemen to rendezvous with Domitus in southern Hatra, at a spot on the Euphrates some one hundred miles southwest of Dura and around eighty miles from Seleucia. We had heard from Babylon that Axsen was safe in the city and had sent troops of the garrison to reinforce Mardonius at Seleucia. I was not unduly worried about Orodes' wife – Babylon's walls were high and were surrounded by a deep moat. Narses himself had twice tried to storm the city and had failed. Seleucia was a different matter, though. Its defences were average at best and Marcus' machines had done much damage to them during our recent assault on them.

The road was devoid of caravans and the small mud-brick forts that my father had established throughout his kingdom were also standing empty. Their garrisons had been sent north to the city. Just as the old year was dying so the Kingdom of Hatra appeared to be ailing – an indication that the empire itself was in a fragile state.

I rode at the head of our column of horses and camels in the company of Vagises, Scarab and Vagharsh, who carried my griffin banner in its wax sleeve. Ahead and on our flanks rode parties of horse archers to ensure we did not run into any of Mithridates' soldiers, who were no doubt plundering far and wide anything of value. Beyond them Byrd's men scouted our route. In his and Malik's absence they became even more elusive and distant. Their commander, a gruff Agraci warrior with a thick black beard, rode in every night to report to me. He told me that that the land was empty and there was no sign of the enemy. Hardly surprising: we were moving in a southwesterly direction towards the Euphrates.

89

I had been tempted to strike southeast with just my horsemen to try and catch Mithridates before he reached Seleucia but the reports sent by Herneus at Assur estimated Mithridates' army to be around fifty thousand strong – too many for four thousand horsemen to fight.

'We should have killed Mithridates at Susa,' complained Vagharsh bitterly. 'We march to deal with him instead of fighting the Armenians.'

'Mithridates is the biggest immediate threat,' I said. 'His return to the empire may encourage the eastern kings to waver in their allegiance to Orodes.'

'He may flee to the east anyway,' remarked Vagises, 'to be among his allies.'

'He may,' I agreed, 'but I believe he will wish to stay close to the Romans and Armenians. If the Armenians and Romans defeat Orodes they will sweep into Hatra and Babylonia to link up with him. Then the Romans will have another client king and Parthia will be no more. No wonder they provided him with a substantial army. The costs of furnishing him with so many men are as nothing compared to the riches they will gain if they seize the empire.'

'One thing I do not understand,' said Vagises. 'Why didn't they wait until Crassus arrived with his army to improve their chances of victory?'

'Roman vanity,' I replied. 'I remember Byrd telling me that the Roman governor of Syria, Aulus Gabinius, is an avaricious man. Therefore he wishes to achieve glory and riches before Crassus arrives.'

'Scarab, did you ever see the Roman governor of Syria?' I asked him in Greek.

'He visited the king at Emesa a number of times, lord.'

At least he had stopped calling me 'divinity'!

'He is a man who likes rich living.'

'Which is why he wants control of the Silk Road,' I said. 'I should thank him, really.'

Vagises and Vagharsh, who both understood Greek, looked at each other in confusion.

'That's right,' I continued, 'for if Aulus Gabinius was a rational and modest man he would have waited for Crassus to arrive so the Romans would have his troops in addition to his two legions.'

'You will be visiting Antioch in person, then, to convey your thanks?' joked Vagises.

On the fourth night we made camp eight miles north of the Euphrates. Though the men pitched their tents in neat rows we did not have any entrenching tools with us and so were unable to dig a surrounding ditch and build a rampart. Though we were in Hatran territory it felt odd not to be surrounded by a wall of earth and so every third man was always on guard duty. The squires and veterinaries attended to the horses and camels and Strabo's small logistical corps allocated fodder for the beasts.

It had been another uneventful day and at the end of it I was sitting in my tent in the company of Vagises while Scarab was in a corner rubbing lanolin into my leather cuirass to preserve it. Though the climate of

Mesopotamia is generally hot and dry, the sweat from my body and the dust in the air meant it had to be cleaned every night to stop it rotting.

'I never thought we would be fighting Crassus again,' mused Vagises, staring into his cup of water.

'Nor me. But at least we will be fighting him on our own ground instead of in Italy.'

'He's a cruel bastard,' spat Vagises. 'He had six thousand crucified after Spartacus was killed.'

'Afranius!'

He looked at me quizzically. 'What?'

'Afranius,' I replied. 'There's a name that has come tumbling from the past. You must remember him, surely? A fierce Spaniard who dreamt of marching on Rome and took command of the remnants of the army after Spartacus' death in the Silarus Valley.'

Vagises racked his brains for a few moments and then nodded. 'I remember him – hair cropped, stocky, full of anger.'

'I hope he died with a sword in his hand and not nailed to a cross.'

'We all hope for that,' said Vagises darkly.

Outside I heard hooves on the ground and horses snorting and then the guards opened the tent's flap to allow two dust-covered individuals to enter. We stood up as they pulled aside the head cloths covering their faces and smiled.

'You didn't think we would let you fight Mithridates on your own, did you?' smiled Malik.

I laughed and embraced him, then Byrd, and told Scarab to serve them water as they took the weight off their feet. They took off their headdresses and stretched out their limbs.

'Hard ride?' I enquired.

'Byrd has some welcome news,' said Malik.

Byrd took a gulp of water. 'Romani not invade Parthia. Aulus Gabinius is heading for Egypt.'

I looked at him and then Malik in disbelief.

'It is true,' said Malik. 'The Romans are invading Egypt instead of Parthia.'

I could not believe it. 'Why?' was all I could utter.

Byrd smiled. 'Gold. Egyptian pharaoh offered Romani governor ten thousand talents to put him back on his throne. My sources in Antioch report Aulus Gabinius has forsaken Mithridates and hurries south.'

I slapped Vagises on the arm and then remembered Dobbai's ritual at Dura. Pure coincidence I told myself. And yet...

'What about the legion at Emesa?' I asked.

'Already marching towards Egypt,' said Byrd. 'Pharaoh Ptolemy friend of Pompey and Romani. A few years ago he was forced into exile in Rome after his people rebel. Now he bribe Aulus Gabinius to get back his throne.'

Ten thousand talents was a huge amount of gold. I had heard stories of the fabulous wealth of Egypt and how its rulers covered their pyramids with gold, but I thought they were myths. Clearly not. But whatever the truth, Egypt's pharaoh had unwittingly done Parthia a great favour.

'Dura already knows the news,' reported Malik, 'so Nergal and his army are also marching with Domitus.'

With the Roman threat to Palmyra and Dura removed there was no need for Nergal to remain in my city. His additional numbers would be welcome in the fight against Mithridates.

Four days later, having arrived at the Euphrates, we linked up with Domitus, the King of Mesene and the Amazons. Our combined forces now totalled twenty-four thousand fighting men as we struck west towards Seleucia. The army marched at a rate of twenty miles a day since we had Marcus' machines with us in case we needed to storm the city. They were loaded on slow-moving wagons pulled by oxen. I prayed that Mardonius still held out.

I had tried to dismiss from my mind the notion that Dobbai's ritual was responsible for the Roman withdrawal from Parthia but Domitus was having none of it. The day was hot and windless and in the early afternoon we had dismounted to save the horses' stamina. We had made good progress during the morning but now our pace slowed as the sun beat down on us from a clear blue sky. As usual a pall of dust hung over our long column as we trudged towards Seleucia.

'Looks like that old witch Dobbai has used her magic to good effect,' said Domitus, sweating in his helmet.

'You really think that, Domitus?' I asked.

'Of course, how else can you explain the Romans withdrawing?'

'It is a coincidence,' I assured him, 'nothing more.'

'A very convenient one,' said Gallia.

'What did Dobbai say about it?' queried Domitus.

'She said that the gods give but they also take and that we should have a care,' replied Gallia.

'Strange about those statues, though,' reflected Kronos.

'What statues?' asked Nergal.

So an eager Domitus told him and Praxima about the night we carried the clay statues down to the banks of the Euphrates, the cold mist that appeared from nowhere and the mystery the next morning when the statues had disappeared.

'They were probably stolen,' I said. 'Someone at the caravan park probably spotted us and waited until we had returned to the palace before taking them.'

'And made all those scratch marks in the ground?' retorted Domitus. 'I don't think so.'

I looked at him. 'I thought Romans were a practical people and didn't believe in myths and monsters.'

'So we are,' he said, 'but like all peoples we like to have the gods on our side.'

'How many gods do the Romans have?' asked Kronos.

Domitus put a hand to his chin. 'Let's see. Around twenty major gods and fifty minor ones.'

'Is that all?' remarked Gallia dryly.

I looked up at the cloudless sky. 'It is appropriate that the sky is so vast, otherwise there would not be room to accommodate all the gods that people worship.'

'Aaron's people believe that there is only one god,' said Gallia.

'Aaron?' said Nergal.

'My treasurer,' I replied, 'and a Jew.'

'Domitus is a Jew as well,' added Gallia.

Everyone turned and looked askance at him.

'I am not!' he protested. 'I am married to a Jew, that is all. I have prayed to Mars all my life and I don't see any reason to change now. It is a ridiculous idea that there is only one god.'

'When we have to fight Crassus,' said Nergal, 'who will your god Mars decide to help, Domitus, us or him?'

'Us of course,' he replied without hesitation.

'You sound very certain,' I said.

'In ancient mythology Mars laid with a nymph named Harmony and fathered a race of warrior women called Amazons. So you see, Mars will protect his children in the coming war.'

But before that war we had to deal with a more pressing conflict, so I asked Byrd to acquaint me with the composition of Mithridates' army. Byrd, the Cappadocian pot seller and once a penniless Roman slave, was now the owner of a transport guild that operated in Syria, Judea, western Parthia, Cilicia and Cappadocia. His close bond with Malik had made him a friend of the Agraci. His marriage to Noora and the gold that Dura paid to a faithful servant provided him with the funds to procure a great number of camels. And the esteem in which he was held in Dura and among the Agraci ensured that his beasts could travel freely throughout the Arabian Peninsula and along the Silk Road in the Parthian Empire. It was not long before his camels were being hired by merchants in Syria and Judea to transport goods from Mesopotamia and Agraci lands to the ports along the Mediterranean coast. Soon Byrd had set up offices in Antioch, Damascus and Emesa as his transportation empire expanded. And now he had opened a further two offices, in Tyrus in Cilicia and in Caesarea in Cappadocia. His camels were always in demand to transport timber, textiles, silver, wine, bitumen and lead, much of which was then transported by ship to Italy. I often wondered what the Roman authorities in Syria and Judea would have thought if they knew that the man who controlled this vast transport network had been Spartacus' chief scout. Now he was sitting with us all in my command tent after another day's march at the head of his ragged band of scouts. His swarthy features and dirty Agraci robes gave him the appearance of a penniless vagrant, an individual you would pass in the street without giving him a second glance. But this 'vagrant' probably possessed more gold than Dura had in its treasury.

We were just over ten miles west of Seleucia and had yet to encounter any opposition.

'We rode to within two miles of the city today,' said Malik. 'We saw nothing on the roads and no patrols, enemy or Babylonian.'

'How many troops does Mithridates have?' I asked Byrd, eager to know if Herneus had exaggerated.

'My office in Tarsus tell me that for foot soldiers Mithridates has over twenty thousand Cilician warriors and a further twenty thousand Thracian mercenaries. He also has over ten thousand Sarmatian horsemen.'

'Where did he get the money to raise that many troops?' asked Domitus, who had taken to his usual habit of playing with his dagger.

'Loans secured on seizing Parthia,' replied Byrd.

'Who are the Sarmatians?' asked Gallia.

'A wild people who live north of the Caucasus Mountains,' I replied. 'I see the hand of Tigranes in this. He must have suggested bringing these heathens into the empire.'

'Perhaps Mithridates has crossed the Tigris,' suggested Nergal, 'and is heading for Susa.'

Susa was the capital of the Kingdom of Susiana and his homeland, but Susa was garrisoned by troops loyal to Orodes and after our great victory there the gold that remained after Mithridates had fled to Syria was conveyed back to Ctesiphon.

'No,' I said, 'his objective would have been Seleucia and Ctesiphon just across the river where the gold is stored. Besides, the further east he goes the greater distance between him and his new friends, the Armenians and Romans.'

'And his mother,' quipped Domitus, 'unless the old hag is with him.'

I looked at Byrd. He shook his head.

'Queen Aruna stay at Antioch with her ladies and courtiers. Palace there very grand.'

'I cannot believe that Mithridates is commanding the army,' remarked Nergal. 'He must have a Roman general with him.'

'No Romani general with him,' said Byrd with certainty.

'Mithridates is no commander,' said Domitus, 'notwithstanding how many men he has.'

'The question is,' interrupted Kronos, 'where are they?'

No one had an answer to that question and when the army broke camp the next morning, the first day of the new year, Byrd, Malik and their scouts were already looking for the enemy, having left in the darkness of the early hours. As soon as the legionaries filed out of the camp's eastern entrance they adopted their battle positions: the Durans on the left, the Exiles on the right, each of them in three lines. While ten thousand hobnailed sandals tramped towards Seleucia the squires helped their masters and their horses into their scale armour and then a dragon of cataphracts rode out to take up position on the left flank of the Durans.

Nergal and his horse archers followed the cataphracts, riding south to deploy on the right wing, next to the Exiles. So ten thousand horsemen were arranged in two great blocks, fifty companies in each.

Vagises and his three thousand Duran horse archers galloped north to deploy on the left wing of the army, adjacent to the cataphracts. The latter had their full-face helmets pushed back on their heads as the temperature was already rising, though today at least there was a pleasant northerly breeze to abate the stifling heat.

The last to leave camp were the camel trains of Dura and Mesene, each one composed of a thousand beasts carrying spare arrows. Behind them the squires, veterinaries, farriers, physicians, the Roman engineers and their machines remained in camp under the command of Marcus Sutonius. The camp was not disassembled and in our absence the squires manned the ramparts with their bows – I would not put it past Mithridates and his men to spring from the desert to attack us from behind.

I rode a hundred paces in front of the army in the company of Gallia, Nergal, Praxima, Vagises, Domitus and Kronos, the latter two on foot. The pace of our march was slow to reflect our caution as we headed towards Seleucia. Behind us the banners of Dura and Mesene fluttered in the breeze and behind them came the Amazons holding their bows with arrows nocked. After an hour the yellow mud-brick walls of Seleucia loomed into view.

Now two hundred and fifty years old, Seleucus I Nicator, one of Alexander of Macedon's generals, who had founded the Seleucid Empire, had originally established the city. Seleucia had been the first capital of that empire and its walls encompassed the city in the shape of an eagle with outstretched wings. Those walls had originally been strong but now they were in a state of dilapidation after years of neglect. They had been made more derelict by our recent assault in which the gatehouse had been demolished along with several of the adjoining towers dotting the perimeter at regular intervals. As we got nearer to the city I saw that there were additional great gaps in the wall where the masonry had been demolished. I signalled a halt. We were now some seven hundred paces from the city's gatehouse.

'Something is wrong.'

Domitus looked up at me. 'Those breaches in the wall are new.'

'Curious that there is no rubble where sections of the wall have collapsed,' pondered Kronos.

'Or were knocked down,' suggested Domitus.

'Why would Mardonius knock down sections of the wall?' asked a confused Gallia.

'He wouldn't,' I replied.

And where was Mardonius? As I scanned the surviving sections of the wall and towers the second-line cohorts of the Durans and Exiles moved forward to form an unbroken first line, while behind them the third lines moved forward to provide support. Either side of the shattered remains of the gatehouse were two demolished sections of wall, each one roughly a hundred paces wide. Aside from the standards fluttering and horses chomping on bits there was no noise. Seleucia was supposed to have a population of eighty thousand citizens but today it appeared to be a ghost city. There were no guards at the city's main entrance and none on the walls. By now the appearance of twenty-four thousand soldiers standing in front of the city would have been noticed by even the most short-sighted sentry but still there was no activity.

'I have a feeling that Mardonius no longer commands here,' said Gallia.

Before anyone could answer a rider appeared at the city entrance, a man in a helmet mounted on a large light bay horse that suddenly galloped towards our position.

'Amazons!' shouted Gallia and her warriors flanked left and right and brought their bows up, ready to shoot at the approaching horseman. Gallia and Praxima pulled their bows from their hide cases and nocked arrows. When he got to within two hundred paces from us the rider slowed his horse to a trot and then a walk as he held out his arms to indicate he held no weapons. He wore a short-sleeved suit of leather lamellar armour over a blue shirt edge with yellow. He halted his horse a hundred paces from us.

'My lord high general wishes to meet with King Pacorus of Dura,' he shouted.

'Does he mean Mithridates?' asked Domitus.

I nudged Remus forward a few feet.

'Careful, Pacorus,' said Gallia, 'it may be a trap.'

I looked at the man who still had his hands spread wide and his palms open.

'I am confident that the Amazons will drop him before he can try anything.'

'We may drop him anyway,' added Praxima menacingly.

'I thought you were the lord high general of the empire?' said Domitus.

'It appears I have a rival,' I replied. 'I am King Pacorus,' I cried out. 'Who is your lord high general?'

'King Nicetas,' he shouted back.

I looked back at the others who stared back at me with blank faces. I had never heard the name and neither had they.

'If you assent, majesty,' the soldier continued, 'he will meet you alone at the midpoint between your army and the city walls.'

'Do you want me to kill him, Pacorus?' offered Praxima.

'No thank you,' I replied.

I had to admit I was curious to know the identity of the man who claimed the title I held.

'Very well,' I called back. 'Go and tell your general to show himself.'

The soldier bowed his head and then turned his mount to gallop back to the city. The Amazons lowered their bows as Gallia rode up to me. Meanwhile, the walls of Seleucia still appeared devoid of any life.

'Mithridates has captured the city,' she said sternly.

I nodded. 'It would appear so. Whoever this Nicetas is I assume he is in his service.'

Behind us Byrd and Malik brought their horses to a halt and then walked them forward.

'No enemy within twenty miles,' said Byrd.

'The land is empty of all life,' added Malik.

I kept looking at the city. Had Mithridates massacred the population? The absence of any crows or buzzards circling overhead suggested that the streets were not piled high with corpses. The mystery deepened.

'Not quite empty,' remarked Domitus, pointing at the walls.

I looked to see that another figure had appeared at the remains of the gatehouse, a man mounted on a black horse wearing what appeared to be a silver cuirass over a bright yellow tunic.

'That must be Nicetas, whoever he is,' said Nergal.

'Time to solve the mystery,' I said, nudging Remus forward as the individual who apparently had the same title as me approached.

'Do not go, Pacorus,' called Gallia, 'it is obviously a trap.'

'She is right,' added Domitus, but I merely raised my hand at them. I was too curious to see this man up close and solve the riddle we faced.

As Remus walked forward I heard footsteps behind me and turned to see Domitus and Kronos hurrying back to their men. The hairs on the back of my neck stood up and I suddenly felt tense, and yet there were no soldiers on the walls and silence still enveloped Seleucia. Ahead the man in the silver armour continued to move towards me, his left hand holding his horse's reins and his right arm hanging by his side.

We were now less than a hundred paces apart and I saw that his cuirass was made up of dozens of overlapping rectangular silver scales that shimmered when he moved. His head was encased in a gilded helmet with large cheekguards hiding some of his features. And yet, as he came closer, there was something about his fair skin, powerful frame and neatly trimmed beard that was familiar. He halted a few feet from me, his magnificent stallion flicking its long black tail.

'King Pacorus of Dura.' His tone was both aggressive and slightly condescending.

'And you must be Nicetas,' I replied, 'though your name was previously unknown to me before today.'

'*King* Nicetas, and it is known to you now,' he growled. I kept looking at his young face and saw in it a resemblance to someone I had known. But who?

His brown eyes burned with contempt as he looked past me. 'So this is the famed army of Dura, the instrument by which Orodes has usurped the throne of the rightful king of kings.'

He looked back at me. 'Men say that it is invincible, that it is protected by the magic of a sorceress. And yet it seems ordinary enough. Perhaps the stories have been exaggerated.'

He really was full of his own self-importance.

97

I had no time for his strutting. 'You are here at the behest of Mithridates, so state what you have to say.'

He was momentarily nonplussed by my manner but then his insolence returned.

'*King of Kings* Mithridates demands that you and the rabble of Dura leave this place and withdraw back across the Euphrates. The army of Mesene will likewise withdraw to Uruk, there to await the high king's pleasure.'

I was beginning to lose my patience. 'First of all, boy, you will answer my questions rather than dictate terms. Firstly you will inform me what has happened to Lord Mardonius, whose city this is. And secondly you will reveal the whereabouts of Mithridates so that justice can be served upon him.'

Nicetas smiled evilly to reveal a row of perfect white teeth, fixing me with his stare before raising his right arm. The walls beyond the left of what had been the gatehouse were suddenly lined with soldiers, two of them holding an elderly man – Mardonius. I looked on in horror as they hurled him over the battlements and then saw his body jerk violently as the noose around his throat snapped his neck.

'Lord Mardonius was judged, found guilty of aiding traitors and sentenced to death,' said Nicetas without emotion.

I was stunned by what I had just seen and still staring at the dead body of Mardonius when I caught a grey blur out of the corner of my eye.

'King Mithridates wishes you to withdraw but I suggested to him that your death and the destruction of your army would serve our interests better and he agreed.'

He had hoisted his sword above his head and now dug his knees into his horse, which bolted forward. I instinctively yanked on Remus' reins and he turned to the right as Nicetas came alongside and swung his sword at me, the blade cutting deep into my left arm. I screamed in pain and drew my own sword, wheeling Remus away from him as he turned his own horse to face me once more.

'I am the rightful King of Persis and the son of King Narses who was murdered by your own hand at Susa, and I will have my revenge.'

He raised his sword and I prepared to meet his attack, but instead there was a blast of noise as thousands of men suddenly charged from the city. From the remains of the gatehouse and from the two breaches in the walls on either side they flooded out – a great mob of warriors on foot wielding axes, javelins and small wicker shields. They had no organisation or discipline but headed for the legions like a great herd of maddened animals, piercing the air with their feral screams. There were thousands of them.

Nicetas shouted in triumph and raised his sword once more, before letting out a groan when the arrow slammed into his shoulder. He grimaced in pain and then wheeled his horse away as the unstoppable wave of oncoming warriors threatened to engulf me.

'Move, Pacorus!' screamed Gallia as she rode to my side with the Amazons forming a screen in front of us. She grabbed Remus' reins and then shouted at Epona to move as we galloped back to the Durans, the Amazons turning in the saddle and shooting arrows at the oncoming enemy over the hindquarters of their horses.

'Let them through,' I heard a voice in front of me shout as the ranks of the legionaries opened to allow us to pass through them. We halted in the space between the first and second lines of cohorts as a loud scraping noise filled our ears. The enemy wave had hit the breakwater that was the legions. The air was thick with javelins as the Cilician warriors hurled their missiles at the locked shields of the Durans and Exiles, then they went to work with their axes, literally trying to hack the legionaries' shields to pieces.

The wild charge buckled and bent the front line of the legionaries but did not break it, and as the Cilicians spat and cursed and hacked with their axes, the rear ranks of the first-line centuries hurled their javelins forward into the stinking, seething mass of enemy warriors.

The Cilicians wore no armour or helmets and so every javelin found flesh and bone, felling hundreds in the densely packed press. The line had held.

I rode north along the rear of the Duran first line to where the cataphracts were deployed in two lines, each one of two ranks.

Vagises galloped over as the Amazons deployed in three ranks behind us.

'You should let Alcaeus see to that arm,' said Gallia. 'I told you it was a trap.'

But my attention was focused on what was happening directly ahead as horsemen began pouring through the gaps in the city walls – Sarmatian horse archers wearing ox-hide corselets and helmets – grouped round their chiefs and their dragon windsocks.

I pointed at them. 'Destroy them, Vagises.'

He saluted and galloped back to his horsemen. Moments later three thousand horse archers had deployed into thirty columns as companies charged at the disorganised mass of Sarmatian horsemen and began discharging arrows, the men at the front of the columns shooting their bows and then wheeling right to gallop to the rear of the formation as their comrades behind shot their bows in turn and likewise rode to the rear of the column.

Vagises' men were outnumbered by the Sarmatians but the latter lacked discipline and cohesion and never recovered from being assaulted by horsemen who directed a withering arrow storm against them. A few loosed their bows and attempted to charge but too many of their comrades had been hit by missiles and so they began to disperse, most back to the city. A few fled north into the desert.

To my right the Cilicians were still hacking at the Durans and Exiles but were suffering fearful casualties as the legionaries went to work with their short swords and began pushing them back towards the city. In the ever-increasing cloud of dust that was being kicked up by thousands of men and horses' hooves I could not discern what was happening beyond the Exiles, on the army's right wing, but felt certain that Nergal's men would be holding their own at least.

I felt a surge of pain shoot through my left arm and looked down to see the whole of my ripped lower sleeve was covered in blood that had dripped onto my leggings.

'Get that wound seen to,' commanded Gallia as arrows thudded into the ground a few paces from her – the parting shots of the Sarmatian archers.

'I'm fine,' I insisted, wincing from the pain coming from my arm.

She reached over, grabbed my reins and led me to the rear.

'Take command of the Amazons,' she said to Zenobia, leading me through the cataphracts and then behind the battling Durans. The men of the second line stood with their javelins in their right hands and their shields on their left sides, ready to reinforce their comrades in the first line. Men ferried the wounded on stretchers to the rear where Alcaeus and his physicians were waiting to treat them. Gallia led me over to our Greek friend. He was standing with his canvas bag slung over his shoulder, running a hand through his black wiry hair. Gallia called to him.

I slid off Remus' back as he approached and saw my bloody arm.

'Sword cut,' said Gallia.

'It's nothing,' I protested.

Alcaeus reached into his bag and pulled out a pair of sprung scissors to cut away the bloodied sleeve of my shirt just below the shoulder.

'It doesn't look like nothing,' he scolded me as he put the scissors back into his bag and examined the wound.

'Fortunately for you your opponent chose to slash instead of stab. Looks worse than it is, though you appear to have lost a deal of blood.'

He pulled a small clay pot from his bag and removed the cork, then poured some of the watery contents onto my arm. It felt as though he had laid a red-hot iron on my flesh. I winced.

'Acetum to clean the wound,' he said.

He took another pot from his bag of wonders, this one containing honey, which he applied to the wound before binding it with a bandage.

'You should go back to camp, really,' he remarked, 'but I suppose there is little chance of that.'

'Thank you, and no, I will not be going back to camp.'

I hoisted myself back into the saddle and went to find Domitus. I discovered him standing behind the first-line cohorts with Kronos and a group of their senior officers. He saw my bandaged bare arm.

'You and the other lord high general ran out of words, then?'

'What's happening?' I asked.

'What's left of them are falling back to the city. Do you want us to pursue them?'

'Not yet,' I replied. 'Casualties?'

'Very light. They gambled on their mad charge breaking us but we stopped that easily enough.'

'Nergal sent a rider over to report that he had thrown back the horsemen that had assaulted his wing,' added Kronos.

I looked up at the sun and judged the time to be midday. It was now very warm and legionaries were drinking from their water bottles to quench their thirst.

'Are we going to storm the city?' asked Domitus.

'Yes,' I replied, 'but send for Marcus and his machines. I think we will need them.'

A lull descended over the battlefield as the fighting petered out and the remnants of the Cilicians withdrew to the relative safety of Seleucia. With Gallia I rode back to where my heavy horsemen remained in their initial positions, having been nothing more than front-row spectators to the carnage. As usual the Durans and Exiles had been very efficient in their work, the ground in front of their positions carpeted with Cilician corpses and the badly wounded. Already parties of legionaries were going among the fallen looking for those still alive, slitting their throats when they found them to put them out of their misery.

The shrill blast of whistles followed by trumpets called them back as fresh troops marched from Seleucia. There was a rapid reorganisation among the Durans and Exiles as the rear centuries in each front-line cohort swapped places so that fresh legionaries stood ready to receive a new enemy. Whereas the Cilicians had hurled themselves against the legions in a disorganised, feral rush, these soldiers – Thracian mercenaries – emerged from the city and deployed into battle formation before they advanced.

The assault of the Cilician foot and horse had been designed to soften us up before the Thracian attack, to thin our ranks and shake our morale to make the task of the more heavily armed soldiers who now flooded the ground in front of the city easier. If that was the plan of Nicetas then it had failed as our losses had been light and he had greatly underestimated the professionalism of Dura's army. But then this was hardly surprising if Mithridates had been whispering in his ear about my army of slaves.

In the vanguard of the Thracian contingent were élite troops equipped with the fearsome *rhomphaia*, a weapon that had a long, slightly curved, single-edged blade attached to a much shorter pole. Held with both hands, it was essentially a battle scythe that could slice through helmets and armour and was also used to chop through horses' legs if cavalry got too close to their users. These men wore helmets, bronze breastplates and metal greaves.

Behind these élite troops came more Thracian foot armed with the shorter, one-handed *rhomphaia* and carrying large oval shields called *thureos*. Like our own shields they were made of wood, faced with leather and had a metal boss over a central handgrip. They also wore helmets and studded leather armour vests.

I sent a rider to our right flank to ask Nergal to direct his horse archers against these Thracians before they had a chance to attack our own foot soldiers.

More and more Thracians were coming from the city until there must have been upwards of twenty thousand of them arrayed in front of the legions, and then they began to move forward. Domitus had pulled the Durans and Exiles back around a hundred paces so that our wings of horsemen were advanced of the centre, and from the flanks companies of horse archers rode forward and inwards to shoot volleys of arrows against the Thracians, who suddenly charged.

They covered the seven hundred paces of ground between them and the front ranks of legionaries in around two and a half minutes, the first four ranks of élite troops sprinting forward and becoming separated from those behind who tried to retain their cohesion. But all of them ran into the hail of arrows that was shot at them from both flanks. This not only killed and wounded hundreds but also disrupted their momentum. And as the survivors got to within fifty paces of the legions the first five ranks of legionaries ran forward and hurled their javelins.

From our first line of fourteen cohorts standing shoulder to shoulder came sixteen hundred javelins thrown at the oncoming enemy. Hundreds of iron points found their target and cut down most of the front rank of Thracians, those behind tripping and stumbling as they tried to pick their way through the newly laid field of carrion.

Those Thracians following behind hauled their shields above their heads as protection against the arrows being shot at them. However they were moving too quickly and their ranks were too ragged to form an unbroken roof of leather and wood. So arrows plunged from the sky to hit arms and legs and pierce sandal-clad feet.

There was an ear-piercing crack as the élite Thracian troops collided with the front ranks of the legionaries and began wielding their fearsome *rhomphaias*, slashing and hacking at shields and helmets. I was thankful that the legionaries in Dura's army had their helmets strengthened with forehead cross-braces designed to offer additional protection against men on horseback wielding swords. They were just as effective against a Thracian *rhomphaia*.

As the shouts and screams of thousands of men locked in combat echoed across the battlefield, I heard fresh trumpet blasts and then saw a volley of javelins coming from the rear ranks of our front-line centuries to land among the great press of Thracians. Hundreds more of the latter were killed and wounded but still they pressed on, hacking and thrusting with grim determination, actually forcing the cohorts back.

I sent a courier to the cataphracts to order them to wheel inwards to their right to attack the rear ranks of the Thracian foot, at the same time ordering Vagises to deploy his horse archers forward to give protection to the cataphracts. I had no idea what was happening on the right flank but knew that Nergal would have his men under tight control.

I could see the unbroken line of the cohorts being forced back under the ferocious pressure that the enemy was subjecting it to. But it did not break. Then the cataphracts launched their charge. They drove deep into the rear ranks of the enemy, spearing dozens on the end of *kontus* points before hacking at men on foot with their swords and maces. As they had been trained to do the hundred-man companies darted into groups of the enemy, killed as many as they could and then withdrew quickly to reform out of harm's way. Their horses may have been covered in scale armour but the animals' lower legs were still vulnerable to scything *rhomphaia* strikes.

The cataphract action lasted for perhaps ten minutes at most but it shattered the Thracians' morale. Attacked from the rear by armoured horsemen, the rear ranks began to disengage and retreat back towards the city. And like an invisible wave the faltering morale rippled through the enemy soldiers. Small groups initially peeled off the main body to scurry back to Seleucia, running a gauntlet of arrows as they did so, then more and more Thracians locked shields over their heads and shuffled back to the city.

In the mêlée, meanwhile, the legionaries gained the upper hand. The hate-filled men in front of them began to tire as the legionaries they had been battling were replaced by soldiers from the rear ranks, matching their frenzy with their close-quarter weapons. And volley after volley of javelins was launched against the Thracians as fresh missiles were ferried from the cohorts in the second line. Then the Durans and Exiles began to press forward.

I leaned across to grab Gallia and kissed her as I heard a chant resonate across the battlefield – 'Dura, Dura' – and knew that the fight had been won. Then, suddenly, like a dam bursting, the Thracians gave way and ran for their lives. Many were cut down by a withering rain of arrows as they turned tail and fled back to the city, hundreds discarding their shields and weapons as they did so. The Durans and Exiles did not follow.

Hundreds of satisfied cataphracts rode past me to deploy once again to the left of the Durans. I rode with Gallia and the Amazons to find Domitus to congratulate him on his victory.

We cantered past members of Alcaeus' medical corps tending to the wounded and organising their transport on wagons back to camp. I saw the colour party of the Durans guarding the golden griffin and caught sight of a white transverse crest on a helmet nearby and headed towards it. I saw also saw a helmetless Thumelicus shaking his head and knew that something was wrong.

I jumped from the saddle and pushed my way through a throng of soldiers who had gathered around Domitus, most of them stepping aside when they recognised me. Thumelicus said nothing as he walked away, holding his head in his hands. I froze when I looked down to see Domitus cradling the head of Drenis in his arms, tears running down his cheeks. Drenis, a Thracian and former gladiator who had shared the same *ludus* in Capua as Spartacus, a Companion whom I had fought beside for nearly twenty years, a man who had helped to turn Dura's army into one of the most fearsome fighting machines in the world, was dead.

He had been killed fighting in the front rank where he could always be found, cut down by a plethora of *rhomphaia* blades but slaying many of the enemy before he fell. I could not believe what my eyes were revealing to me as Domitus stood up and wiped away his tears.

'Take his body to the rear,' he commanded, his voice firm and deep, 'we will burn it tonight.'

I stood, numb, as a stretcher was brought and the gashed body was placed upon it, before being covered with a white cloak. Domitus laid a hand on his dead friend.

'We will meet again, my brother.'

His face was a mask of grim determination as he came over to me.

'They will regroup in the city. We need to get inside before they have a chance to reorganise.'

'We can get in using those breaches they have made in the walls. It won't take long.'

There was no emotion in his eyes just a cold anger. He said nothing about Drenis and neither did I. What was there to say? There was still enough of the day left to take out our hurt and anger on the enemy.

As Marcus and his men unloaded their machines from carts pulled by oxen the Durans and Exiles lent on their shields or lay on the ground. Nergal and Praxima came from the right flank and I told them about Drenis. We stood in a circle drinking water and holding the reins of our horses while the Amazons rested on the ground behind us. It was now mid-afternoon and there were still a few hours of daylight left.

'Will you wait for the new day before you assault the city, Pacorus?' asked Nergal.

'No,' I answered. 'The attack will commence as soon as Marcus has set up his machines.'

'What if Mithridates escapes across the Tigris into the east of the empire?' said Praxima.

I had also considered that possibility, and in truth that is what he would probably do. He might have already fled Seleucia as far as I knew. It did not matter.

'We will take Seleucia,' I said, 'and then we will hunt down Mithridates no matter how long it takes or how far he runs. This time he will not escape.'

An hour elapsed before Marcus' machines were ready to commence their deadly work, by which time the wall breaches and gap where the gatehouse had been had all been sealed by locked Thracian shields. In addition, the surviving sections of the walls had been lined with archers, no doubt the survivors of the Cilician horsemen who had been dispersed earlier. Ordinarily an attacker would suffer heavy casualties crossing open ground under arrow fire to force an entry to the city, though a *testudo* formation would be largely immune from enemy missiles. Nevertheless the enemy would also throw rocks from the walls when my men were within range, which would inflict casualties. But I had no intention of exposing my men to enemy missiles.

Marcus had positioned one of his larger ballistae opposite each of the breaches in the walls, at a distance of six hundred paces away, a century of legionaries providing cover while his engineers set up and sighted their pieces. But the enemy were content to stand and watch as the strange machines that resembled giant bows laid horizontally on wooden frames were assembled. Marcus also had fifty smaller ballistae, each one operated by two men, which were positioned between the larger ones, ready to shoot at the men on the walls.

While Marcus and his men laboured to get their machines ready legionaries and horsemen withdrew out of the range of the archers on the walls. The city defenders took this as a sign that we were withdrawing for the night and started jeering and whistling and congratulating each other. Below them the Thracians who were defending the wall breaches remained immobile and silent. And in no-man's land between the walls and our forces lay thousands of corpses, either cut down by Dura's heavy horsemen or killed by arrows. But not all were dead: there were many injured whose bodies had been slashed and hacked by swords and maces or hit by arrows. The badly injured lay on the ground and moaned and sobbed, some crying out pitifully to their gods to save them, though most just called for their mothers.

Those who were able either staggered unsteadily to their feet to attempt to get back to the city, or crawled on the ground to try and reach safety. Seeing this, Gallia and the Amazons stood up and began shooting at these poor wretches. As they were using their bows at long range and the light was beginning to fail it required considerable skill to hit their targets. But my wife's warriors were nothing if they were not accomplished archers. Soon they were joined by Vagises, Nergal, Praxima and several of the officers of Dura's horse archers, their men sitting on their horses and cheering when one of the wounded was hit.

The jeering and whistling coming from the walls soon changed to cries of rage as they watched their wounded comrades being slaughtered. I wondered if it might provoke an assault by the Thracians who stood in the wall breaches, but they retained their discipline and kept their anger in check as Gallia hit a hobbling figure who spun round before collapsing on the ground. Arrows hitting targets at the furthest extent of their range would rarely inflict a fatal wound but would only add to the victim's pain and misery, but this thought suited my mood at that moment as I watched my wife and her Amazons empty their quivers.

The sun was falling in the western sky behind us by the time Marcus ambled over to where I waited on Remus observing the walls.

'We are ready, Pacorus,' he said.

'Begin,' I ordered, 'and do not stop until I tell you.'

He saluted then trotted back to the first large ballista that was pointing at the breach to the left of where the gatehouse had been. It was completely filled with locked shields, behind which I could see rows of helmets. I smiled.

'This is for you, Drenis,' I muttered as a loud crack announced the shooting of the first projectiles.

The ballistae were remarkable weapons of war, their projectiles shot by torsion produced by two thick skeins of twisted cords through which were thrust two separate wooden arms joined at their ends by the cord that propelled the missile forward. The large ballista could fire one missile a minute up to rage of around thirteen hundred feet, the smaller ones around four shots a minute up to range of around a thousand feet.

The first projectiles fired by the larger models were clay pots filled with the thick white liquid that came from China, though Marcus and Arsam had been perfecting their own variety at Dura for a number of years now. They kept the exact composition a closely guarded secret, but did tell me that the ingredients included naphtha, the thick black liquid that seeps from the earth throughout the Arabian peninsula and Mesopotamia, soap and oil derived from palm trees.

The pots were sealed and then coated with pitch, which had been 'cooking' over a brazier nearby, before being placed on the ballista and then set alight. On the ballista it sat in a cradle of chrysotile, the wondrous material that does not burn, so the flames would not incinerate the propelling cord, before it was shot towards the enemy.

We watched the flaming pot hurtle through the air and smash into the shield wall to produce a huge yellow and orange fireball as the contents ignited. We heard high-pitched screams as the burning liquid splashed faces, necks and arms. It burned fiercely and was almost impossible to extinguish and so the previously disciplined formation of soldiers dissolved as individuals' flesh melted.

A minute later the ballista shot a solid stone ball weighing fifty pounds that smashed through torsos and skulls as it careered through the now faltering Thracian ranks. Then another volley of fireballs was launched at the wall breaches to inflict further horrendous casualties as men were tuned into human torches. The Thracians were beginning to melt away, many literally as their flesh was coated with the burning liquid that could not be put out.

And while the Thracians were being subjected to this torment the smaller ballistae were sweeping the walls with more diminutive missiles, mostly stones and iron-tipped projectiles that speared archers and crushed skulls with ease. Soon the walls were devoid of enemy soldiers.

Marcus' machines kept shooting for nearly an hour until there were no longer any Thracians left guarding the wall breaches. It was early evening and what was left of the enemy had retreated from the city walls to the palace next to the Tigris, or perhaps across the stone bridge that spanned the river to seek refuge in Ctesiphon. Or perhaps they had only retreated a short distance from the city walls and were waiting for us to enter Seleucia. It was time to find out.

106

Domitus formed his men into four huge columns, two of Durans and two of Exiles, each one ten men across, and then directed them into the city via the breaches in the wall. I dismounted, acquired a shield and joined one of them with Domitus standing beside me in the front rank. News of the death of Drenis had spread through the army to produce a mood of grim determination among the men.

As soon as the ballistae had stopped shooting the columns advanced across no-man's land, the men in the first five ranks with their swords drawn and those following clutching fresh javelins brought from camp. The columns had been issued with torches but the flames in and around the breaches made by the fireballs cast the corpse-filled ground in a red glow and allowed us to pick our way through the bodies. When we reached the walls our eyes beheld fresh horrors and our nostrils filled with the nauseating aroma of roasting flesh as we stepped over dead Thracians.

We moved into the city, past charred and disfigured bodies, to find that the enemy had fled. Seleucia is divided into two halves: north of the main street that runs from west to east is where the palace, temple district and government officers are located; to the south is where the crowded dwellings of the citizens are sited. After a quick assembly of senior officers half the Durans secured the area around the gatehouse while the rest undertook a sweep of the population's homes to search for enemy soldiers. The Exiles pushed on towards the palace that overlooked the Tigris and the harbour area at the river.

The stone bridge across the river was secured easily enough, Domitus deploying men on both sides of the structure to ensure no one escaped the city. Ctesiphon was within striking distance but I decided to wait until Seleucia had been thoroughly searched before we captured the court of the king of kings and its treasury. I stood with Domitus on the western side of the bridge staring at the black waters below.

'Mithridates is not here,' he said. 'He probably ran away as soon as the fighting started.'

He looked across the river.

'He won't be at Ctesiphon either.'

'It doesn't matter,' I said, 'we will organise a pursuit in the morning.'

But I was troubled by the thought that we would not be able to follow Mithridates, especially if Tigranes launched an assault against Hatra. If that happened I would have to take the army back north and Mithridates would be free to create mischief in the eastern half of the empire once more.

At that moment a legionary, a member of the Exiles, arrived with news that Kronos' men were being shot at from the palace. I slapped Domitus on the arm.

'Or perhaps Mithridates is trapped in the palace.'

Though I had been in the saddle since the early morning and had fought a battle during the day, any tiredness left me instantly at the prospect of cornering Mithridates. The messenger escorted us to where the Exiles were taking up positions around the palace prior to an assault.

Seleucia's palace was built in the Greek style reflecting its heritage. A large, square building, it was enclosed within a strong circuit wall that had square towers at regular intervals along its length. These towers had tiled roofs and square windows fronted by wooden shutters, from which archers, slingers and spearmen could launch missiles at an attacker. The large and impressive gatehouse on the south side of the wall also had wooden shutters on each of its two storeys above the huge twin gates to rain down missiles upon a foe.

Though Ctesiphon was thought of as the greatest palace complex in the empire, Seleucia's royal residence was also an impressive structure. Its east wing housed the vaulted throne room, the south wing the royal suites whose floors were decorated with rich floor mosaics and columned courtyards. The banqueting hall was located in the west wing, while in the north wing there was a high, open veranda that gave spectacular views of the Tigris to the north of the city. Around the palace were granaries, barracks, stables, armouries and storerooms.

We found Kronos three hundred paces from the gatehouse giving directions to his senior officers. His men were deployed in their centuries all around the wall beyond the range of enemy missiles. They carried no torches now so as to deny the foe any aiming points but they were still visible in their white tunics and carrying white shields sporting griffin wings. Kronos dismissed his officers before we reached him.

I looked at the walls that appeared empty of any soldiers. In fact I could see no torches on the walls and no lights beyond them.

Domitus read my thoughts.

'Looks deserted.'

'It is not,' replied Kronos. 'I sent a couple of centuries forward to the gates but they were shot at before they got near them. The enemy are behind those shutters.'

'Did you lose any men?' I asked.

Kronos shook his head 'They were in *testudo* formation. One man broke an ankle when they fell back. I have sent for the ram to smash those gates open.'

In addition to the ballistae that Dura's army had gained when I had defeated a Roman army before the walls of my city, at the same time it had also captured a battering ram. This ram comprised a large tree trunk that hung from chains fixed to the top of a sturdy arched frame. Over this frame were fitted wooden boards, protected by hide, clay and finally iron plates. The thick roof was designed to defeat enemy missiles and the clay was a fireproof barrier. The ram was mounted on four large wooden wheels to allow it to be pushed forwards and backwards. On the end of the tree trunk was a massive iron head cast in the shape of a snarling ram that the troops had nicknamed 'Pacorus'.

Men standing either side of the log operated the ram, which had leather straps fixed to it that allowed them to pull it back and then hurl it forward to smash the iron head against the target.

After their experience at the walls, what was left of the enemy was clearly weary of our machines and so had hidden themselves in the gatehouse and in the towers. It was suddenly eerily quiet as we waited for Marcus and his ram.

'Do you think Mithridates is in there?' asked Kronos, tilting his head towards the palace.

'I hope so,' I replied, though I did not think so. In addition to being a murdering wretch the stepbrother of Orodes was also a coward and my gut told me that he was long gone.

I heard a crack and felt a slight breeze on my face, which was then showered with liquid. I heard a groan and saw with horror that an arrow was stuck in Kronos' neck. He collapsed to the ground.

'Shields, shields!' screamed Domitus as he grabbed Kronos' right arm and began to haul him away from the walls. I took his other arm and we pulled him across the ground as a century of men rushed forward and formed a wall of shields around us.

Blood was spurting from the arrow wound as Kronos looked up at me and tried to smile.

'Don't talk, keep still,' I told him.

A medical orderly knelt beside him, took a bandage from his bag and applied it to the wound in an effort to staunch the flow of blood, but the arrow had penetrated too deeply into his neck and Kronos was dead within seconds. The fountain of blood subsided as life left the commander of the Exiles and I stared in disbelief at my dead comrade. This was the man who had marched all the way from Pontus when that kingdom had fallen to the Romans; who had helped me raise a legion of his exiled countrymen and forged them into an élite fighting formation. He had fought beside me at Dura, the Tigris, Babylon, Makhmur and Susa and had not suffered a scratch. And now a single archer had killed him.

Domitus commanded the orderly to remove the arrow from the wound and then had the body covered with a white cloak and taken to the rear where it would be cremated alongside Drenis when the fighting was over. They would burn with Mardonius, whose body I had ordered to be removed from the walls. My hatred for Mithridates burned with a white-hot intensity for what he had been responsible for at this place. I vowed to hunt him down even if it meant going to the end of the world to find him.

The ram arrived shortly after we lost Kronos and its iron head was soon smashing in the two gates. The soldiers in the gatehouse above tried to halt its progress by hurling spears and rocks against it but Marcus had also brought his smaller ballistae with him and they shot iron and stone balls to splinter the wooden shutters, and then dismounted companies of Vagises' horse archers poured volley after volley of arrows at the firing positions. Very soon no missiles were coming from the gatehouse.

Like most of Seleucia's defences the palace gates had not been maintained and though they looked impressive they were very old, over two hundred years at least, and when they were subjected to a fierce pounding they gave way easily enough. The defenders had had no time to reinforce them with braces or rubble and so, after twenty minutes of being battered, they were forced open.

The same orderly who had tried to save Kronos re-bandaged my wounded arm as the first of the Exiles forced their way through the gates and into the palace compound. Domitus had wanted to lead them but I had forbidden him to do so – I did not want to lose any more friends this day. So as the first shards of light appeared in the east we stood and watched as century after century raced into the palace to exact revenge for the death of their commander. Most of the Thracians and Cilicians were butchered without mercy whether they threw down their weapons and tried to surrender or not. A few Sarmatian horsemen attempted to mount their horses and cut their way through the mass of Exiles who flooded into the palace, but their horses panicked in the face of the dense ranks of the legionaries and their riders were soon dragged from their saddles and stabbed to death.

After the brief, violent battle was over I walked with Vagises and Domitus, escorted by a century of Exiles and a hundred horse archers, through the smashed gates and into the palace compound. The ground was sprinkled with enemy dead all around, mostly Thracians and Sarmatians but a few bodies attired in short-sleeved red tunics marking them out as Cilicians. There were some shouts and screams coming from inside the palace but most of the fighting was over. The gatehouse and all the towers had been cleared of enemy soldiers and groups of Exiles were standing guard on the walls, at the gatehouse and at the entrance to the palace itself.

We stood in the middle of the square in front of the palace as parties of Exiles began dumping enemy swords, bows, spears and armour in separate piles that would be examined by Marcus to see if any could be salvaged for further use. All the weapons and armour for Dura's army were produced in Arsam's armouries to ensure their quality, but captured stocks could always be sold on to third parties such as Alexander's Jewish insurgents. His fighters had originally been armed with weapons produced at Dura but since then he had suffered a series of crushing defeats and he had used up all of his gold reserves. Perhaps I would send him the weapons that were being stockpiled in front of me free of charge. They would, after all, be used to kill Romans and the fewer Romans there were in the world would be of benefit to the empire.

Marcus sauntered over to where we stood and raised his right arm in a Roman salute. Dressed in simple beige tunic, sandals, leather belt and wide-brimmed hat, he looked like a gardener rather than a quartermaster. But he had one of the keenest minds in the empire and his organisational skills were second to none.

'Terrible business about Drenis and Kronos,' he said. 'My commiserations.'

I nodded and Domitus stood by impassively.

'Your engines did good work, Marcus,' I told him.

'Seleucia's walls will need rebuilding and strengthening,' he replied.

'That is not our concern,' I replied. 'Once Mithridates has been captured Orodes can rebuild them at his leisure for there will no longer be any traitors to hide behind them.'

But a thorough search of the palace revealed that, just as I had feared, he had fled the city before we entered it. Some prisoners were taken, however, when a group of the enemy had barricaded themselves on the veranda in the north wing of the palace. They had shouted to the legionaries who were battering down the doors that they were men of importance who would command a great ransom and were known to the King of Dura. The latter declaration probably saved their lives as they were ordered to open the doors and surrender themselves immediately.

There were five of them: two Thracians, a bearded Sarmatian officer dressed in a magnificent scale armour cuirass, an unconscious and pale Nicetas whose shoulder wound had been bandaged but who had obviously lost much blood, and an individual whom I had met before.

'Udall,' I said to the man with the scruffy long hair who stood before me.

I had first encountered him when he had been a junior officer in a force of foot soldiers sent by Narses to intercept my army near Seleucia. Vagises' horse archers had destroyed most of that force and Udall had been taken prisoner. I had let him and the rest of those men who had surrendered with him march away, after which he had spun a tale to his king about how he had slowed down Dura's army. As a reward he had been made governor of Seleucia and was in that post when I had stormed the city as part of an alliance of kings led by my father determined to remove Mithridates and replace him with Orodes. After the city had fallen I had once again let Udall go free, and now here he was before me a prisoner for a third time.

'I submit to your mercy, majesty,' he said, bowing deeply, his hands bound behind his back like the others standing in a line in front of me.

I said nothing to him as I moved to stand before the Sarmatian. These people spoke Scythian, a coarse, harsh language that was spoken by the savage nomadic peoples who occupied the great northern steppes. As part of my boyhood education I had been tutored to speak and write it but had not spoken it in an age.

'You are far from your homeland, Sarmatian.'

'I go where there is work,' he replied indifferently.

'Where is Mithridates?'

'Long gone,' he smiled. 'He has escaped you.'

I moved along the line to look at the Cilicians, both of whom were swarthy wretches who looked at me with hateful eyes.

'What is your story?' I asked one of them, to which he replied by spitting in my face.

Domitus standing beside me drew his *gladius* and thrust it through the man's neck, after which my face was once more showered with gore as blood spurted from the wound. The Cilician collapsed as Domitus stepped over his body and rammed his sword into the side of his comrade, driving

111

the blade up under the man's rib cage to pierce his heart. He too collapsed to the ground. Domitus pointed at Udall.

'This is the consequence of letting people go free instead of killing them, a mistake that Mithridates would not have made.'

I ordered the surviving prisoners to be taken back to the palace until I decided their fate and walked over to a water trough to wash my face. Domitus followed me.

'What are you going to do with them?' he asked.

I rubbed the stubble on my chin and saw that blood was seeping through the fresh bandage on my arm.

'You cannot let them live,' he continued before I could answer. I could tell that he was seething with rage over the deaths of Kronos and Drenis.

'You are right,' I said, 'but first we have to attend to our dead.'

That afternoon, after Alcaeus had dressed my arm again and I had changed into a fresh tunic, most of the army was drawn up on parade to the west of the city wall. Two cohorts, one from the Durans, one from the Exiles, were left in the city to man what was left of the walls, guard the palace and the bridge over the Tigris and patrol Seleucia. The rest, including the squires, farriers, armourers, veterinaries, physicians and civilian drivers, plus the legions' golden griffin and silver eagle standards, were drawn up to witness the cremation of our dead. We had lost only a hundred and fifty killed during the capture of Seleucia but it did not feel like a great victory, not with the bodies of Drenis and Kronos lying on their funeral pyres.

The shields of the Cilicians and Thracians had been collected to make individual pyres that had been soaked in oil, and now they were lit to consume the bodies on top of them. Thumelicus, tears streaming down his face, lit the pyre of Drenis while Domitus did the same for that of Kronos. I held a torch and lit the heaped shields beneath the body of Mardonius and then watched as the flames took hold and black smoke ascended into a clear blue sky as the souls of our comrades were welcomed into heaven.

Afterwards we marched back to camp to ponder our next move. The spirits of the army were downcast as both Drenis and Kronos had been popular figures. Nergal and Praxima were similarly dejected as they had both known Drenis from our time in Italy. Our mood was not improved when Byrd and Malik rode into camp just before sunset to report that an army was on the other side of the Tigris and was heading for Seleucia.

'Our scouts ran into its vanguard earlier,' reported Malik as we relaxed in my tent.

'They come from the direction of Susa,' added Byrd.

'Did you see any banners?' I asked.

Malik shook his head. 'Only horse archers who shot at us from a distance.'

'Does Mithridates have another army?' queried Nergal.

'Perhaps the eastern kings have renounced Orodes and are marching to put his stepbrother back on the throne of Ctesiphon,' added a concerned Praxima.

I tried to allay their fears. 'The eastern kings are as weary of war as we are. In any case we would have heard something from Khosrou if the eastern kingdoms were rebelling against Orodes.'

Their stern-looking faces told me that I had failed to reassure them and in truth I too was full of doubts. Why would they plunge the empire into another civil war, especially as both the Armenians and the Romans threatened Parthia? But then, the western kingdoms, my own included, had slaughtered many of their men over the past few years. Perhaps their only desire was revenge.

'The only way to end our doubts,' said Domitus, 'is to march east to meet this new army and defeat it. I suggest we all get some rest. Tomorrow might be a long day.'

With that he rose, nodded to everyone and then took his leave of us. Looking at the tired faces and puffy eyes around me I realised he was right. We had not slept for two days and I suddenly felt very tired. I yawned and stretched out my arms, wincing as pain shot through my left arm.

'Does it hurt?' asked Gallia.

'No,' I lied, though at least the wound had finally stopped bleeding.

Nergal and Praxima rose and embraced us before they too left and rode back to their camp with their escort. Gallia kissed me and withdrew to the sleeping area, leaving me alone with Scarab who was clearing the table of cups and jugs.

'You were victorious today, highness,' he said, flashing a row of white teeth at me.

'Yes,' I replied, 'though victory was bought at a heavy price.'

He looked concerned. 'You lost many men, highness?'

'Our casualties were light, but among them were two men for whom I would swap all my victories to have back.'

'They were your friends, highness?'

'Yes, they were my friends.'

'Perhaps you will meet them again, highness, in the next life.'

I looked at him. 'You believe that we all go on to another life?'

He stopped his cleaning and pondered for a moment. 'When you are a slave, highness, the only thing that gets you through each day of torment is the thought that there is a better life after this one.'

I rose from my chair and picked up my sword that was leaning against it.

'Let us hope you are right, Scarab.'

Chapter 5

The army marched two hours after dawn. I left Marcus and his machines behind and appointed him temporary governor of Seleucia in our absence, leaving him two cohorts of Durans to back up his authority. Nergal and his horse archers had left earlier with Malik, Byrd and their scouts, crossing the Tigris and striking southeast to intercept the army that had mysteriously appeared seemingly from nowhere. Vagises then led Dura's horse archers across the bridge over the river followed by the legions. Finally the cataphracts in their scale armour, followed by their squires, the camel train carrying spare arrows, and wagons filled with supplies crossed the bridge.

It was another glorious day and many of Seleucia's citizens had turned out to line the streets to see the army pass through their city. The legionaries marching six abreast and the cataphracts fully encased in their armour presented a magnificent sight, griffin pennants fluttering from every *kontus* and white plumes fixed to every legionary's helmet. It was at times like these that I realised what a formidable machine Dura's army was and it filled me with hope that we would be able to defeat the new threat that had appeared in the east.

After leaving the city and crossing the Tigris we headed in a southeasterly direction, following the churned-up ground made by the thousands of Nergal's riders. Three hours later the King of Mesene returned with his horsemen in the company of Byrd and Malik and I halted the army.

'It is Phriapatius and the army of Carmania,' said Nergal.

'So the mystery is solved,' I replied. 'How many men does he bring with him?'

'Thirty thousand, perhaps more,' said Byrd.

'All horsemen,' added Malik.

We marched towards Phriapatius for another hour and then deployed into battle order, the legions in the centre and the horse archers on the wings. Nergal's men formed our right flank and Vagises' men deployed on the left. In between the legions and Dura's horse archers were my cataphracts arrayed in two ranks. To give the illusion of strength the legions were deployed in two lines, while on both flanks the horse archers were drawn up in their companies side by side. In this way our battle line had a width of over five miles. The camels carrying the spare arrows were deployed immediately behind the horse archers and the wagons holding spare shields, armour, helmets and javelins were sited to the rear of the legions.

I rode with Gallia, Vagharsh and the Amazons to the centre of the line, a hundred paces in front of the legions, and there we waited for Nergal and Praxima. Gallia and Praxima were dressed for battle like the Amazons: mail shirts, helmets with closed cheekguards and full quivers slung over their shoulders. The banner of Mesene fluttered behind Nergal and Praxima as Mesene's king halted beside me. His wife took up her position next to Gallia. The Amazons raised their bows to salute their former second-in-command, now a god in Uruk.

The stoical Vagharsh held my griffin banner behind me as ahead a group of horsemen galloped towards us, their mounts kicking up a great cloud of dust as they hurtled across the parched earth. I looked into the cloudless sky and felt a trickle of sweat run down my neck. It was going to be another hot and bloody day.

'It would appear that Byrd and Malik have found the enemy judging by the way they are riding.' I looked down to see Domitus standing beside Remus, vine cane in his hand.

He nodded towards the black-clad riders who suddenly veered to the right while two of their number continued to head towards us, slowing their horses as they got nearer.

'You and your scouts didn't fancy fighting them, then?' shouted Domitus.

Malik raised his hand in recognition of his friend while Byrd ignored him as they both pulled up their horses in front of me.

Byrd turned in the saddle and pointed ahead. 'Phriapatius and his army draw near.'

'About half an hour away,' added Malik.

'Will you attack first or fight a defensive battle?' Domitus asked me.

'We are not here to fight, Domitus,' I told him.

He looked at me wryly. 'Has anyone told the Carmanians?'

Nergal smiled at him nervously though none of us knew what the intentions of Phriapatius were. Nestled in the southeast corner of the empire, Carmania had been untouched by the recent civil war and though its army had been forced to retreat after it had invaded Nergal's kingdom as part of the alliance of Narses and Mithridates, Phriapatius could still muster a substantial number of soldiers. Perhaps he desired no less than the high crown itself and sought to take advantage of our difficulties with the Romans and Armenians to seize Ctesiphon and Seleucia. I smiled to myself. Soon Seleucia would be nothing but a pile of rubble if it had to endure any more assaults.

Byrd and Malik stayed with us as their scouts went to the rear of the army to rest themselves and their mounts. I saw Byrd put a hand on his lower back and rub it.

'Are you hurt?' I asked.

Gallia and Praxima looked at him with concern. He arched his back and then rubbed it again.

'No. Getting old. Cannot sit in saddle for hours like I used to.'

I had never thought of Byrd as old before. In fact I had never even considered his age. He was just Byrd: ageless, withdrawn and scruffy, someone who was always there when I had need of him. But now, looking at him, I could see that the lines on his face were deeper and more numerous and it made me ponder. I had known him for nearly twenty years and they had passed in the blink of an eye.

115

My daydreaming was interrupted by the appearance of the Carmanians who at first resembled a thin black shimmering line on the horizon. After a few minutes the line increased in height as thousands of horsemen approached our position, and then I could make out the different troop types as they trotted forward. In the centre of their long line was a formation of cataphracts – men in scale armour wearing helmets, carrying long lances and riding horses that wore half-armour covering their bodies but not their necks or heads.

Either side of these heavy horsemen were dense blocks of mounted spearmen, soldiers armed with lances and carrying large round shields painted red on their left sides. They were equipped with helmets but wore no armour on their legs or arms. They were probably wearing some sort of body armour – leather most likely – though I could not tell at this range. On the wings Phriapatius had placed his horse archers to match our own mounted bowmen.

The Carmanians halted around five hundred paces in front of us and after a tense few minutes in which neither side made any movement a solitary rider emerged from where Phriapatius was mounted on his horse in front of his banner: a huge golden peacock on a red background. The horseman galloped towards us as an officer of my cataphracts similarly left his position to meet him. This was standard protocol and indicated that Phriapatius wished to talk, which was a good sign at least.

The riders halted before each other in the middle of the space between the two armies, and following the briefest of discourses my officer returned to state that Phriapatius wished to talk with me.

'How many in his party?' I asked.

'Four, majesty, including the king.'

I turned to Nergal. 'I would consider it an honour if you and Praxima would accompany me,' then I laid a hand on Gallia's arm. 'You too.'

We nudged our horses forward and walked them slowly into no-man's land, our hands clutching our reins and well away from our sword hilts. There was little danger of violence between us but such gestures showed good faith when meeting with potential enemies. I looked behind me to see the lone figure of Domitus, white crest atop his helmet, standing a hundred paces beyond the front rank of the Durans. I felt a pang of sorrow when I looked across at the Exiles where there was no Kronos present.

'I will find you, Mithridates,' I heard myself say, 'and you will pay for all your crimes.'

'What?' Gallia was looking at me quizzically.

'Nothing.'

We brought our horses to a halt ten paces from Phriapatius' party. He looked much the same as the last time I had met him at the Tigris where he had professed his reluctance at being part of the alliance forged by Narses and Mithridates. Now Narses was dead and Mithridates a fugitive. Their alliance was smashed, which begged the question: now neighbouring Persis and Sakastan no longer threatened Carmania, what action was Phriapatius taking?

Not a particularly imposing figure, the King of Carmania was of medium height with broad shoulders, a thick black beard and a large nose. Like many of the people who inhabited the lands near the Arabian Sea his skin and eyes were a dark brown. He regarded me with those eyes before his mouth broke into a broad grin.

'We got here as fast as we could,' he said. 'As lord high general I thought you might appreciate some assistance.'

I have to confess that relief swept through me. 'You are most welcome, lord. But I made no demand on your presence in these parts.'

'When I heard that Mithridates had returned to haunt Parthia I suspected that you might need all the help you could muster, especially with the Romans and Armenians threatening the empire as well.'

'You thought right,' I answered.

Phriapatius spread his arms wide. 'But I am forgetting my manners.' He bowed his head to Nergal and Praxima. 'I am pleased that we are meeting under happier circumstances and would welcome closer relations between the Kingdoms of Carmania and Mesene.'

This was an interesting moment as the last time Nergal and Praxima had met with Phriapatius had been after they had chased him and his army out of Mesene and back across the Tigris. He had invaded their kingdom and for an anxious moment I thought that Nergal might throw his peaceful overtures back in his face.

Nergal nodded at Phriapatius. 'We would like that also.'

Phriapatius looked relieved and grinned once more. He held out a hand to the two younger men sitting behind him. Like him they were dressed in open-faced bronze helmets, short-sleeved silver scale armour cuirasses with sculptured bronze plates bearing peacock motifs on their shoulders, red silk shirts and expensive red boots on their feet. They had been present at our previous meeting.

'These are my sons,' said Phriapatius, 'Phanes and Peroz.' He looked at the fourth member of his party, an older man in a simple iron scale-armour cuirass with a rather battered helmet on his head. Grey hair showed beneath his headdress but his eyes were clear and alert.

'And this is Lord Nazir, the commander of my army.'

Nazir gave the slightest nod but his eyes never left Gallia, whose identity was as yet unknown to the Carmanians. Phriapatius also looked curiously at the helmeted figure of my wife.

'Lord king,' I said, 'you are already acquainted with me and the rulers of Mesene, but may I introduce my wife, Queen Gallia of Dura?'

Gallia removed her helmet and bowed her head at a clearly delighted Phriapatius. 'So, at long last I meet Dura's warrior queen whose name and fame has spread to the furthest extent of the empire and beyond. I am delighted to make your acquaintance, lady.'

Gallia gave him a dazzling smile. 'You honour me, lord.'

117

Phriapatius slapped his hands together. 'This has been a most excellent meeting. You must all dine with me tonight in my tent before we all journey together to Seleucia.'

'Alas, lord king,' I said, 'we are on urgent business that takes us into the east.'

Phriapatius raised his eyebrows knowingly at me. 'But perhaps not.'

He turned and raised his hand and I saw three riders emerge from the Carmanian ranks. Gallia and Praxima, suspecting treachery, reached behind them to pull their bows from their cases.

Phriapatius held up his hands. 'It is no trick I promise. Rather it is a gift for you, King Pacorus.'

Intrigued, I watched as the three horsemen approached in a line and saw that the two on the outside were soldiers escorting the one in the middle, whose reins were being held by the horsemen on his left. The middle rider had what appeared to be a sack over his head and his hands were pinioned behind his back. As they drew alongside Phriapatius I also saw that the feet of the covered rider were tied together under the belly of his horse. He was obviously a prisoner of some sort. Most odd.

The soldier who had been holding the prisoner's reins continued to keep a tight grip on them as Phriapatius manoeuvred his horse to bring him to the left-hand side of the prisoner.

'We encountered him two days ago. He rode boldly into my camp with a score of horsemen and demanded my allegiance.' He reached over and pulled the sack off the prisoner's head. 'Imagine that. Insolent wretch.'

They had gagged Mithridates so he could not speak but he looked with wide, terror-filled eyes at his mortal enemies before him.

'He took my two youngest sons as hostages when he was high king,' continued Phriapatius, 'to ensure my loyalty. When King Orodes became high king the first thing he did was to send my sons back to me unharmed. That in itself was enough for me to pledge my loyalty to the new king of kings. I therefore hand over his miserable stepbrother to you, King Pacorus, to do with as you see fit.'

I could not contain my joy as I slapped Nergal on the arm and then pulled Gallia towards me to kiss her on the cheek. Phanes and Peroz grinned and Gallia politely shoved me away, smiling as she did so. I could not believe my luck. After all these years and after the spilling of so much blood I had him. I had killed his partner in treachery and now I saw Mithridates bound and helpless on a horse a few paces from me. It truly was a great day and I thanked the gods for their generosity.

I dismounted and picked up the sack that Phriapatius had yanked off Mithridates. I regained my saddle and replaced it over the tyrant's head.

'Much better,' I announced. 'There are no words that can convey my gratitude, lord king. I can only offer an invitation for you and your men to ride with me to Seleucia where justice will be administered.'

Phriapatius grinned and bowed his head as Mithridates thrashed around as much as his fetters allowed him to do so, and from under the sack we heard muffled sounds as he tried to shout something.

118

'We would be honoured,' replied Phriapatius.

I left Domitus to bring the legions back to the city as I rode at speed in the company of Carmania's, Dura's and Nergal's horsemen back to Seleucia. Once we had arrived Mithridates was confined in one of the palace's towers with Udall, the rapidly fading Nicetas and the Sarmatian commander. Guards were posted in and around the tower, on the walls and throughout the palace compound as a precaution against any rescue attempts, though as Domitus pointed out when he and his men reached the city six hours after we had arrived, who would want to rescue Mithridates?

After washing and changing into fresh clothes and when night had fallen I went with Domitus to see him and the others. They had all been given food, water and fresh apparel, though I had ordered that Nicetas be removed to a separate, more comfortable room as he was falling in and out of consciousness and Alcaeus informed me that he would probably not last another day.

'He has lost too much blood. The arrow that Gallia put in him shattered his shoulder joint and I could not stop the bleeding.'

'She knows how to shoot a bow,' I replied. 'Try to keep him alive until the morning.'

'So you can execute him,' said Alcaeus.

'Yes,' I replied coldly.

'Hardly seems worthwhile,' he mused.

'Justice has to be seen to be done,' I told him.

'He's the son of Narses,' said Domitus, 'if he lives he will try to kill Pacorus to avenge his father. I would rather have him dead than Pacorus.'

Alcaeus laid a hand on my arm. 'So would I.'

We were on the ground floor of the tower that held the prisoners and from the first floor we could hear the almost hysterical voice of Mithridates.

'I demand to see King Pacorus! How dare you hold me here like a common criminal. I am the king of kings!'

The six legionaries who guarded the entrance to the tower looked at each other and rolled their eyes. I had placed Thumelicus in charge of the prisoners and he now descended the stone steps next to the wall that led to the floor above.

'Do you want me to put his gag back on?' he asked.

'No,' I replied. 'I will see him, if only to shut him up.'

Domitus looked concerned. 'He might try to attack you. You know what a slippery bastard he is.'

'I'll take that risk,' I said. 'Let's get it over with.'

Domitus drew his sword. 'I'm coming with you.'

Thumelicus preceded us as we ascended the steps to arrive at the storeroom in which the captives were held. Two guards stood either side of the thick wooden door and two more sat at a table opposite, standing to attention when they saw us. Thumelicus ordered the door to be opened and then went inside, reappearing moments later with a firm hold on Mithridates' arm.

'Unhand me you brute,' he snapped as he struggled in vain to free himself of Thumelicus' iron grip. He froze when he saw me and for a second I thought I saw fear in his eyes, to be quickly replaced by contempt.

'I wish to see my brother,' he demanded.

I nodded at Thumelicus to let go of his arm. 'Your *stepbrother* is at Hatra dealing with the Armenian threat, but then you would know of that.'

His dark brown, almost black eyes looked away. 'I know nothing of the affairs of Armenia.'

Domitus guffawed, earning him a hateful stare from Mithridates.

'And I suppose you know nothing of the recent Roman threat to the empire, notwithstanding that you have been their guest these past few months?' I queried.

'I do not deny it,' he replied haughtily. 'The Romans were kind enough to offer me and my mother sanctuary after my brother and his deluded allies forced us to flee for our lives.'

'And provide you with an army to invade the Parthian Empire,' I replied.

A smirk creased his lips. 'As king of kings I have every right to use whatever means I deem fit to regain my throne from usurpers.'

'Such as bringing Thracian and Sarmatian mercenaries into the empire to slaughter its inhabitants,' I suggested.

'No worse than enlisting Agraci vermin into your service,' he shot back, then turned his reptile-like face towards Domitus. 'But then, what can one expect of a king who surrounds himself with freed slaves, criminals and the like?'

'You and the others are to be executed tomorrow morning,' I announced, prompting Domitus to raise his eyebrows.

Mithridates laughed. 'Even you would not dare to commit such an outrage. I have the right to be tried by a council of my peers.'

Anger began to stir within me. 'You have no rights! You are a murderer who is responsible for the deaths of countless thousands of people. You killed your father, sent assassins to kill me and plunged the empire into a ruinous civil war that has left it weak and vulnerable to outside aggressors. You have furthermore entered into treasonous negotiations with external powers aimed at destroying the empire and reducing it to a vassal state of Rome. One of these crimes alone would warrant a death sentence.'

'That is your opinion, King Pacorus,' he sneered, 'but it may not be the view of the other kings of the empire, kings who regard *you* as the reason the empire is in its present dire state.'

'I am not a murderer,' I snarled.

His eyes opened wide with surprise. 'Are you not? How many kings have you killed? Let my see. There was Porus and Narses. And how

120

many other kings have you got killed? Vardan, Farhad and your father. I hardly think you are qualified to lecture me about the spilling of blood. You should look at your own hands; there is enough of it on them. Have you considered that if it had not been for you and your army there would have been no civil war? All the other kings of the empire accepted my accession to the high throne, all except you. And because of your continued intransigence you provoked me into taking actions to safeguard the future of the empire.'

I was dumbfounded. 'You mean sending assassins to kill me?'

'The king of kings must take all necessary measures to safeguard the empire's security,' he replied seriously.

He actually believed his own words. I was rendered speechless.

'The death of one man,' he continued, 'in order to preserve the integrity of the empire is a small price to pay. But I failed and then you marched against me, and the conflict that followed sucked in the kingdoms of Babylon, Mesene, Hatra, Margiana, Hyrcania and all the eastern realms. Ask yourself this, King Pacorus: was it you or I who was responsible for this? I think the Council of Kings should decide.'

The Council of Kings met at Esfahan, a city nearly two hundred miles east of Susa, where all the rulers of the empire's kingdoms came together to settle disputes by diplomacy rather than by the sword. At least that was the theory. At such a gathering many years ago we had elected Phraates, the father of Orodes and Mithridates, to be king of kings and where King Narses of Persis had put himself forward to wear the high crown. Mithridates looked at me with a smug expression. Legally he was right: a council should be called to determine his fate. And I knew what the result of such a meeting would be – his serpent tongue would most likely extricate him from any blame regarding the empire's troubles. Even Orodes, who had suffered banishment and disgrace at his stepbrother's hands, would baulk at sanctioning his execution.

I looked at Domitus and then at Mithridates. 'This is your last night on earth. There is nothing left to say.'

I nodded to Thumelicus, turned and walked down the steps followed by Domitus. As we did so the voice of Mithridates echoed round the tower.

'You would not dare kill me. I am high king! I demand to see my brother!'

Then he was bundled back into the storeroom and the door was slammed shut.

Domitus replaced his sword in its scabbard as he walked beside me back to the palace.

'Is he right about that council?'

'In theory, yes,' I answered, 'but it could take months to organise, perhaps longer while we are preoccupied with the Armenians and Romans, and time tends to blur the collective memory. Mithridates knows this and thinks that he will be sent into exile once more. Sent back to Roman Syria to foment more plots. I cannot allow that.'

121

He stopped and grabbed my arm. 'If you kill him there are those who will frown upon your actions.'

I sighed. 'You mean Orodes.'

He nodded. 'Among others. It is no small thing to execute a king. All the other rulers that have fallen have done so in battle. When was the last time a Parthian king was executed by one of his own?'

'Mithridates murdered his father, Phraates,' I answered.

'There is no proof of that, Pacorus.'

'I believe it to be so, Domitus. That is all the proof I need.' I looked at him. 'Tell me, if you were in my position what would you do?'

He thought for a moment. 'Kill him.'

And so we did.

In front of the palace at Seleucia, between the gatehouse and the grand building itself, is a large paved area that was created during the time of the founding of the city by Seleucus I Nicator. I decided that it would be a suitable venue for the executions, being able to accommodate a large number of people who would bear witness to the event. I ordered Domitus to use the Durans to man what was left of the city walls and patrol the streets to enforce the curfew that was put in place until the condemned had been executed. Three cohorts of the Exiles would be drawn up on three side of the square, with more of their comrades lining the walls facing inwards to bear witness. On the north side of the square where the palace stood, I, together with Gallia, my senior officers, Nergal, Praxima, Phriapatius and his sons, would observe proceedings from the top of the palace steps.

So eager had I been to rid the world of Mithridates that I had given no thought to the manner in which he would be put to death. Domitus suggested crucifixion while Vagises favoured impalement. Though the thought of Mithridates wriggling on the end of a sharpened pole hammered into his rectum or nailed to a cross was appealing I decided against both methods. For one thing the victim could take days to expire and I wanted Mithridates dead as quickly as possible. In the end we settled on strangulation, but then had to organise the making of four crosses that would be set upright in the ground, against which the condemned would be secured. That night a dozen of the city's carpenters laboured to fashion the crosses, which when ready were transported to the palace and planted in the ground, but not before several of the flagstones had to be removed so holes could be dug in the earth underneath.

The dawn came soon enough and with it the procession of the condemned from their tower to the place of execution. Rank upon rank of Exiles stood motionless as three of the prisoners were escorted in a single file into the square, two legionaries carrying the unconscious Nicetas by the arms behind them.

I stood between Gallia on my right side and Nergal on my left as the men made their final journey on earth. I think Mithridates still did not believe he was going to die as he cast disdainful glances left and right before fixing me with a hateful stare. Gallia sneered at him but he ignored her as he scanned those gathered on the steps. He noticed Phriapatius and spat on the ground to show his disgust. Phriapatius grunted contemptuously in reply.

Four burly centurions had been given the task of being executioners, the one earmarked to throttle Mithridates being Thumelicus. As two legionaries manhandled the former king of kings against his cross the realisation that he was going to die finally gripped him. His eyes bulged wide as his arms were pinioned to the crossbeam and then he began shaking violently as his legs were bound tightly to the post.

Beside him Udall threw up and began pleading with the guards to let him go, saying he had been forced into Mithridates' service. When the leather straps were fastened around his legs he pissed himself in fear. In comparison the Thracian showed no emotion as he was secured against the cross, looking at me with an unwavering iron stare, while next to him the limp body of Nicetas was lashed to his cross.

Mithridates was whimpering by now, looking at us with tear-filled eyes, imploring us to save him, after which he began sobbing like a small child, entreating us to show pity. But there was no mercy within us that day. I took no pleasure in killing helpless individuals but the memory of my father, Godarz, Drenis and Kronos steeled my determination.

With the victims secured those standing behind them placed leather straps around their necks, the straps being twisted with sticks behind the posts to tighten them round the condemned necks. The executioners looked at me and I nodded, then they twisted the sticks further to choke the prisoners. Thumelicus, being the big angry brute he was, twisted the stick so quickly that he actually broke Mithridates' neck, the sharp crack being heard around the windless square. Within a minute it was all over and the victims' bodies hung limply on their crosses.

Domitus dismissed the cohorts as we returned to the palace. I thought I would be elated but actually I felt relieved; relieved that the spectre of Mithridates that had haunted the empire for so long was no more. But in many ways his death was an irrelevance to the strategic situation. The Armenians still controlled all of northern Hatra and parts of Gordyene, and soon Crassus would arrive at the head of his army to further add to the empire's troubles.

Domitus suggested that we hang the bodies of the executed from the city walls but I ordered them to be burned and their ashes scattered over the Tigris. Those Cilicians and Sarmatians that had been captured were sent under escort to Axsen at Babylon, there to serve her kingdom as slaves for the rest of their lives. They numbered less than five thousand but at least they could be distributed among the kingdom's villages to assist in the rebuilding work being undertaken in the aftermath of two invasions at the hands of Narses and Mithridates.

The captives left the next morning, a column of unshaven, barefoot, filthy men chained together and escorted by five hundred of Vagises' horse archers, who were under orders to kill any that showed any signs of rebelliousness. Sitting on Remus near what had been Seleucia's gatehouse

I watched them trudge out of the city west towards Babylon, their heads cast down, a sullen silence hanging over them. The only sounds were the tramp of their feet on the ground and the clinking of the chains around their ankles.

'You do not seem very pleased with your victory,' said Gallia on Epona beside me.

I pointed at the line of slaves. 'That was me once, in Cappadocia many years ago. Chained just like that and condemned to a life of slavery.'

'Then free them,' she said, 'it is within your power if you find their circumstances so disagreeable.'

'I cannot. They will only cause trouble and Babylonia needs all the manpower it can get to repair the devastation visited upon it.'

'You could always enlist them in the army,' she suggested.

I was appalled. 'Dura does not use mercenaries, men who would change sides for a few drachmas. They are untrustworthy, expensive and lack discipline.'

'Well, then, you are better off without them. At least Axsen will be able to make use of them.'

In front of us the end of the column walked disconsolately out of Seleucia and into the desert.

The next day Axsen herself arrived at the city escorted by a hundred purple-clad riders. This time we stood at the foot of the palace steps to greet the queen whose city this was. She slid off her horse as I bowed my head to her. She embraced me and then Gallia, Nergal and Praxima and I introduced her to Phriapatius and his sons. It was a potentially awkward moment as the king had formerly been an ally of Mithridates and Narses. But Axsen smiled warmly at him and Phriapatius for his part was most eager to endear himself to Babylon's queen and the king of king's wife.

'Carmania stands ready to assist your majesty in any way that you see fit,' he promised as he and his sons laid their right hands on their chests and bowed deeply to her.

Axsen was delighted by their pledge of allegiance. 'You are very kind and I thank you. Babylon is delighted to have Carmania as an ally.'

Axsen turned and ushered forward the commander of her escort. I recognised him as the officer I had first encountered at Babylon's Marduk Gate following Narses' second siege of the city.

'This is Demaratus. I have appointed him commander of Babylon's garrison. He is a man Lord Mardonius had great faith in.'

I thought I detected Axsen's voice falter when she mentioned the dead commander of Babylon's army, but she smiled when Demaratus bowed his head to us.

'It is good to see you again, Demaratus,' I told him.

'And you, majesty,' he replied.

I walked beside Axsen as we ascended the steps and entered the palace. Legionaries were standing at every stone pillar and at every doorway.

'I see that my palace is well guarded, Pacorus,' Axsen noted as we walked across the intricately laid mosaics that led to the columned courtyard.

'Babylon's security is always uppermost in my mind, majesty,' I replied.

Axsen giggled. 'Oh, Pacorus, always so formal. And thank you for the gift of the slaves. We passed them on the road. They will prove most useful.'

At the entrance to the royal suite we halted and bowed to her as she took her leave, asking for Gallia and Praxima to accompany her into her private chambers. In the palace square meanwhile, workmen were re-laying the stone slabs that had been removed to allow the wooden crosses to be planted in the ground.

Later Axsen gave a great feast in the banqueting hall in celebration of our victory at Seleucia. Thus far she had said nothing concerning the execution of Mithridates but did so now as I sat beside her at the high table before the assembly of all the senior officers of the armies of Dura, Mesene and Carmania and the queen's Babylonians.

'I am glad he is dead,' she told me, 'but I fear Orodes may not approve of your actions.

This came as no surprise to me. 'As his lord high general I acted according to what I believed would serve the empire best, majesty. At the very least Mithridates will no longer be a figure for malcontents to rally around. The empire cannot afford to be fighting a civil war at the same time as a conflict with the Romans and Armenians.'

'What will the Armenians do now that the Romans have decided to invade Egypt rather than Parthia?' she asked, a slave pouring wine into her gold *rhyton*.

I waved the girl away when she held the silver jug over my drinking vessel. 'Tigranes has conquered northern Hatra and his soldiers are camped only sixty miles or so from the city itself, but without siege engines he has little hope of seizing it, especially now Orodes is there to reinforce Gafarn.'

Axsen sipped at her wine. 'But Tigranes has agreed to a cessation of hostilities, has he not?'

I smiled. 'Only because it suits him to do so. His forces muster at Nisibus and his son campaigns to conquer Gordyene. With a hundred thousand men at least he can afford to pick his moment to attack us again, and let us not forget that Crassus will be arriving in Syria soon.'

She replaced her *rhyton* on the table. 'You do not paint a very rosy picture, Pacorus.'

'It would have been far worse had Aulus Gabinius struck east instead of south.'

'It was a miracle that he did so.'

I thought of Dobbai's night ritual. 'Yes, a miracle indeed.'

The assembled officers enjoyed the evening immensely and as the time passed and the wine flowed drunken oaths of loyalty were pledged between all and sundry. Thumelicus managed to find a Carmanian who was bigger than he and the two of them stood on a table and declared their undying friendship. The bearded Carmanian monster held Thumelicus' arm aloft and declared to the assembled that the German was the slayer of *maskim*, to which everyone cheered and drank more wine.

'Who is *maskim*?' asked Gallia as Thumelicus and his new companion fell off the table onto the floor to rapturous applause.

'Demons of the underworld,' answered Axsen.

'He was the one who strangled Mithridates,' I said, pointing at the very drunk Thumelicus whose nose was bleeding profusely from hitting it on the floor.

'Then his new title is most apt,' replied Axsen.

Notwithstanding the descent into mass drunkenness the evening went well and it was good to see Axsen smiling, though she must have been grieving for the dead Mardonius and missing Orodes terribly. I drank too much wine and had to be helped to bed by a very merry Gallia who wanted me to make love to her. I remember hurriedly stripping off as my wife disrobed. I lay down on the bed, and then inexplicably tried to unwind the bandage on my left arm before passing out.

I woke up to loud banging on the door to our room and opened my lead-like eyelids with difficulty, the banging and shouting from behind the door making my headache worse.

'Majesties,' I heard a man shout, 'your presence is required in the throne room.'

The thumping on the door continued and I saw Gallia rise from the bed.

'Enough!' I shouted, sending a spasm of pain through my skull. 'We hear you! Stop banging on the door or I will have you flogged.'

The banging ceased abruptly and I hauled myself to my feet. I had a mighty hangover, my head hurt, my stomach was delicate and my mouth felt parched.

'Queen Axsen is asking for you, majesties,' said the male voice.

I walked over to the door and was about to open it when Gallia called to me.

'Are you going to put some clothes on or are you intent on frightening the guards?'

I realised that I was naked and so picked up my shirt and then pulled on my leggings as Gallia wrapped a robe round herself.

'Tell the queen we will be with her shortly,' I called to the guard.

Ten minutes later, feeling the worse for wear, we walked into the throne room to find Nergal, Praxima and Phriapatius already in attendance.

'I am sorry for disturbing your sleep,' said a smiling Axsen, 'but I thought you would like to hear the latest news from the north.'

My heart sank. The Armenians must have taken advantage of our disappearance from Hatra to launch an attack against the city. I looked forlornly at Gallia. Surely the city had not fallen?

126

Axsen stood with a letter in her hand. 'The gods have sent another miracle. Tigranes is dead.'

Gallia smiled and then threw her arms round me. Nergal offered me his hand and I took it before Praxima kissed me on my unshaven cheek.

'Dead?' I asked. 'How?'

She sat back down on her throne and held up the letter.

'This arrived earlier from Hatra. Word reached the city two days ago that the Armenian king had died peacefully in his bed at Nisibus.'

I was most surprised. 'The last time I saw him he was fit and healthy, despite his great age.'

Axsen nodded. 'Orodes states that all the reports he has heard confirm that Tigranes was in rude health and after an evening meal retired to his bedchamber as normal. Rumour is that a wolf was heard howling very near to the palace in the city and that despite soldiers carrying out searches in and around the building no animal could be found, but its howling was heard by all and sundry throughout the night.

'In the morning servants went to rouse the king but found him dead in his bed. Most strange.'

I looked at Gallia who cast me a knowing glance – the magic of Dobbai continued to work it would appear.

'What does this mean?' asked Phriapatius.

'It means, lord,' I said, 'that Parthia is in a far better position that it was a week ago. Mithridates and his rebellion have been crushed and now Tigranes is dead. His son Artavasdes will become the King of Armenia, but he does not have the talents of his father.'

'The gods smile on the empire,' said Phriapatius with satisfaction.

'They might still piss on it,' pondered Nergal, looking at the surprised faces of Axsen, Gallia and Praxima, 'begging your pardon, ladies. But the Armenians still have an army of one hundred thousand men and Crassus is still on his way.'

'Nergal is right,' I agreed, 'but at least we have more time in which to plan our next course of action.'

After I had washed and eaten breakfast Axsen convened a council of war on the spacious veranda in the palace's north wing.

Against a backdrop of stunning views of the Tigris and the surrounding terrain the queen asked for my advice in my capacity of lord high general. It felt more like a gathering of friends for a picnic than a council of war. Apart from Phriapatius I had known the others present for years so the meeting had a very relaxed air about it. Nergal sat with his feet on a stool while Gallia and Praxima were seated either side of Axsen.

'I will take my army back to Dura,' I announced first. 'Despite Tigranes' death the Armenians remain the main threat before Crassus arrives.'

'We will be coming with you,' said Nergal, prompting Praxima to smile at me. 'If Hatra falls then there will be nothing to stop the Armenians and Romans marching south into Babylon and then Mesene.'

'I will stay with my army if you wish, Pacorus,' offered Phriapatius, prompting Axsen to smile at him.

It was a generous offer and thirty thousand troops would certainly strengthen a weakened Babylon. However, thirty thousand men and thirty thousand horses, to say nothing of the thousands of camels that attended the king's army, would place an enormous strain on the already overburdened resources of the kingdom. Such a large number of men and beasts would quickly empty the granaries of Seleucia and nearby Kish and Jem det Nasr.

'I was thinking rather, lord,' I said to him, 'that you would consider being deputy lord high general to keep the east of the empire secure, and to garrison the cities of Persepolis and Sigal on behalf of King Orodes.'

Persepolis was the capital of the Kingdom of Persis, formerly ruled by Narses, while Sigal was the capital of neighbouring Sakastan, formerly ruled by King Porus but subsequently absorbed by Narses. Now those two cities were garrisoned by troops taken from Babylonia and Susiana. It made sense for them to be replaced with loyal troops so that they could be sent back to their respective kingdoms, especially Babylon, which had recently lost its garrison at Seleucia.

Phriapatius was surprised. 'A most generous offer, King Pacorus,' he looked at Nergal, 'but there may be those who would object to such an appointment. It was not long ago that we were at war and now you wish me to keep watch over the lands east of the Tigris.'

'I know that you were an unwilling participant in the alliance of Narses and Mithridates,' I said, 'but I leave it to King Nergal to have the final say in the matter. It was, after all, his kingdom your army marched into during the recent civil war.'

Everyone shifted uncomfortably in his or her chairs but Nergal bore no grudges. The fact was that he had confined the Carmanian Army into a narrow corridor and had forced it to retreat back across the Tigris before it could do any major damage to his kingdom, and Phriapatius to his credit had kept his men under tight control and had not allowed them to rape or plunder.

'Mesene has lost sons and so has Carmania,' said Nergal. 'Parthia will not benefit from our continued enmity.'

'Well said,' commented Axsen.

'There is an old saying, lord,' I said to Phriapatius. 'Actions speak louder than words. Of all the eastern kings only you have offered aid; only you have marched your army hundreds of miles to stand by our side. Not only that, you handed over Mithridates and in so doing helped to finally put an end to the civil war that had bled the empire white. All these things you have done and asked no reward in return. The truth is that we are in your debt, lord king, and to bestow this position on you is the least I can do.'

Phriapatius seemed very pleased by my words and accepted my proposal while Axsen was most content that her soldiers would be returning to garrison Seleucia, the walls of which would have to be rebuilt.

'What is left of the royal treasury at Ctesiphon can pay for that,' said Axsen. 'If we have time to do so before the Romans and Armenians arrive.'

'It is my task to ensure that they do not, majesty,' I said.

After the meeting I was cornered by Phriapatius as the others were leaving.

'A word, Pacorus.'

'Problems, lord?'

'It is my youngest son, Peroz.'

'A fine young man,' I said, 'you must be very proud of him.'

'He wishes to serve under you.'

'I am flattered, lord, that he should think so highly of me.'

Phriapatius nodded. 'So you would not object if he accompanied you north to Hatra?'

I was surprised to say the least by his request. 'We go to fight, lord. That being the case I cannot guarantee the safety of your son. It would sit heavily with me if he was killed in my service.'

Phriapatius took my elbow. 'Walk with me.'

We followed the others from the north wing of the palace towards the large open courtyard.

'Peroz has talked incessantly of Pacorus of Dura ever since he heard about you defeating the elephants of King Porus. He is brave if a little headstrong and yearns to prove himself in battle. Phanes, my eldest son, is the heir to my throne and the star of Carmania, but Peroz grows restless in his shadow. Alas there is little love between them and I fear that soon their mutual animosity may erupt into open hostility. Peroz is popular among the people and there are many who would rally to his side if, after I have left this world, hostilities break out. It would suit me and my kingdom if they could be kept apart.'

'If he came with me he would be very far from home, lord.'

The king put his arm round my shoulder. 'But in excellent company. What do you say?'

'I repeat: I would not be able to guarantee his safety.'

He smiled. 'Tell you what, if I allocated five thousand of my soldiers to take care of him would you be more amenable to him joining you?'

Five thousand horsemen would indeed be a welcome addition to the army that would be marching north to face the Armenians.

'Very well, lord,' I answered. 'And you say Peroz is happy to join me?'

'He will be ecstatic,' beamed Phriapatius.

And so he was. The next day the army marched north back to Hatra along with Nergal's men and five thousand Carmanian horse archers. Phriapatius headed back to his homeland via Persepolis and Sigal where he would leave garrisons to ensure the continued loyalty of those kingdoms. I had to admit that I was most satisfied by the turn of events.

Not only did Musa and Khosrou safeguard the northeast corner of the empire but now the southeast of Parthia was also secure. These two bastions of loyalty would at the very least ensure that the eastern part of the empire remained at peace for the foreseeable future.

Like Nergal's troops the Carmanians also wore red tops, though long-sleeved shirts rather than woollen kaftans, but Peroz himself wore a blue silk shirt with gold stitched to the arms. Like his father he was of medium height though he was more handsome, with a square jaw, light brown eyes and a clean-shaven face. He did not seem concerned in the slightest that his father had left him behind. In fact he seemed positively relieved to be away from his brother.

'In my homeland he is called the "gilded peacock" because he spends all his time strutting around in his bronze and silver armour.'

'He will be king one day, Peroz,' I said.

'As he never fails to remind me,' replied the prince dryly.

'You should try to get on with your brother,' I told him, 'he is family after all.'

'A man can choose his friends, majesty,' he replied, 'but he has to put up with his family.'

Gallia and Praxima laughed and he smiled at them. He was an agreeable individual who was fascinated by Dura's army, particularly the Durans and Exiles and Marcus' machines, which were now disassembled and loaded back on their ox carts. These beasts limited our progress to between fifteen and twenty miles each day and so it took us fourteen days to reach Hatra. Each night we slept in a camp surrounded by a ditch and palisade despite being in friendly territory. Peroz thought this highly amusing.

'Parthians do not fight at night, majesty,' he informed us all on the first night as we dined in my tent.

'The Romans do,' replied Domitus curtly.

'But surely the Romans are many miles away in Syria?' he said.

A wicked grin spread across Domitus' face. 'Are you sure about that?'

'What my general is saying, Peroz, is that the army is more secure behind defences rather than having hundreds of tents, horses and wagons exposed in the open.'

Marcus complained about the extra food and fodder required to support the Carmanians and their horses but I told him that we would need all the troops we could muster when we fought the Armenians.

'You reckon we will be fighting them, then?' queried Domitus as he walked alongside our horses the next day, the usual dust cloud hanging over the army like a huge yellow desert phantom.

'Of course,' I replied. 'With Tigranes dead they have lost their most able commander and their morale will be low. It is the perfect time to fight them. We also need to deal with them before Crassus arrives.'

He nodded. 'Makes sense.'

'We also need to retake Nisibus,' I added. 'It is an affront to my father's memory that the second city in his kingdom is in the hands of the enemy.'

He raised his vine cane in acknowledgement and then headed towards the rear to inspect the Durans and Exiles in their marching order.

'Majesty,' Peroz said to Gallia, 'Domitus is the general of your army?'

Gallia nodded.

'Why then does he have no horse?'

'He prefers to walk,' she answered.

'What happens to him if your army is forced to make a hasty retreat?' he asked.

'Dura's army never makes a hasty retreat,' I said. 'Sometimes a slow and methodical tactical withdrawal but never a hasty retreat.'

'I will have my father send General Domitus one of his largest elephants,' said Peroz, 'and then he will be able to sit on a throne on its back so he can look down on his foot soldiers.'

Gallia, Nergal and Praxima burst out laughing and even Vagharsh riding behind us chuckled.

'I think Domitus is happier on his own two feet, Peroz,' I said.

'General Domitus does not like elephants?' enquired Peroz.

'He is a Roman, Peroz,' said Gallia, 'so he dislikes thrones. The Romans have no kings.'

Peroz looked horrified. 'No kings? Then who rules them?'

'They have what is called a republic,' I answered, 'in which the people elect their rulers.'

Peroz shook his head. 'Most odd.'

Gafarn and Orodes met us five miles from Hatra's eastern gates accompanied by the whole of Hatra's royal bodyguard, which I was delighted to discover was led by Vistaspa. Looking a little gaunt and somewhat awkward in the saddle he was still an imposing figure.

'It is good to see you on a horse again,' I told him.

'The leg has never healed properly,' he replied, 'but at least I can still ride.'

'We will need you when we fight the Armenians,' I said.

'Yes, majesty,' he replied flatly.

Gafarn seemed much happier than when I had left him and Orodes was his usual correct and charming self, making a great fuss of Peroz and enquiring after his father and brothers and making no mention of Carmania's former hostility.

When we reached Hatra there was no longer a pall of despondency hanging over it. The streets were bustling, the markets busy and there were caravans on the roads both entering and leaving the city. People cheered our party as it wound its way towards the palace where it was met by a beaming Diana dressed in a long white gown, a glittering golden crown on her head. My mother, similarly attired in white, sported a diadem. In addition to Assur, Addu and Kogan, a small army of priests, lords, their wives and palace officials were standing to one side.

As stable hands took our horses I walked forward to embrace Diana and then my mother, who had regained some of her former vim but still looked a little drawn. I was pleased to discover that neither of my sisters was present but slightly surprised that Atrax was also not in attendance. That night we were treated to a lavish feast at which I was introduced to an Armenian envoy! I initially thought it was one of Gafarn's jokes but Orodes informed me that the man had been given a house in the city to facilitate negotiations between Parthia and Armenia.

'We have agreed a fledgling peace treaty with Artavasdes,' he replied.

I was dumbfounded. 'Peace treaty?'

'Yes, Pacorus, we are no longer at war with Armenia.'

Chapter 6

'Peace treaty?'

The consumption of wine at the admittedly magnificent feast the night before had done nothing to deaden my sense of outrage concerning the accord that had been agreed behind my back while I had been dealing with Mithridates. I paced up and down in the spacious and well-appointed lounge in the palace's private wing as Gafarn and Orodes looked at each other. The latter had convened the meeting after I had made it clear the night before that I strongly disapproved of the treaty. He had also asked my wife, Diana, Nergal, Praxima and Vistaspa to attend in an attempt, I believe, to make me see sense. It did not work.

The women reclined on couches and the men in spacious, padded wicker chairs while I paced up and down like a caged lion.

'Mithridates is dead, the east of the empire is secure and Dura's army is here, supported by the troops of Mesene. The time is right to assault and recapture Nisibus.' I threw up my arms. 'And where is Atrax and his Medians?'

'As a sign of good faith,' replied Orodes calmly but firmly, 'it was agreed that King Atrax should withdraw from Hatra. In return the Armenians agreed to withdraw their forces from Mount Sinjar, which they have done.'

'Hatra is no longer threatened by enemy forces a mere sixty miles to the north, Pacorus,' added Gafarn. 'And for that we have to thank Orodes.'

Diana smiled at Orodes who acknowledged her sign of approval.

'The Armenians still hold Nisibus and northern Hatra,' I continued, 'and in a few months Crassus and his army will be in Syria, after which they will combine with the Armenians to renew hostilities.'

'The cessation of hostilities, albeit temporary,' replied Orodes, 'gives us time to prepare, Pacorus, to marshal the empire's resources to confront Crassus and convince him not to attack Parthia.'

I shook my head. 'Rome is intent on conquering Parthia, Orodes. We must destroy the Armenians before Crassus arrives.'

I walked over to stand directly before him. 'As your lord high general I strongly advise you to authorise an assault against Nisibus. With Tigranes dead they are vulnerable. The time to strike is now.'

Orodes stood to face me. 'I have given my pledge to Artavasdes, Pacorus, and cannot break it. That is my final word on the matter. I am responsible for the welfare of the whole empire and not just the affairs of Hatra and Dura.'

'When Crassus arrives the Armenians will join with him and attack the empire, Orodes,' I countered. 'Surely you know this?'

He sat back down. 'The Armenians approached us with an offer of peace, indicating to me that they do not believe that they could take any more Parthian territory. If we persuade Crassus that it would be foolish for him to attack the empire, then afterwards we may reclaim Nisibus and the rest of northern Hatra without a war.'

'The Armenians were most keen on peace, Pacorus,' confirmed Gafarn.

I stopped pacing and sat down in my chair. They had been duped and the Armenians, or at least Artavasdes' closest advisers, had been very clever. They must have known that he was no Tigranes and therefore sought to buy him time in which he could consolidate his father's conquests. The easiest way to do this was to seek peace with Parthia, offering to withdraw their forces north as a sweetener. They gave up a stretch of desert in return for a few months of peace, knowing that a large Roman army was on its way. Time was on their side rather than on ours.

'What about Armenian forces in Gordyene and Atropaiene?' I asked, taking a cup of fruit juice offered me by a beautiful slave girl with olive skin whose shapely body was covered by a long white gown.

'Artavasdes has given me his word that all his troops will be withdrawing from those kingdoms immediately,' replied Orodes.

'Surena has been mauling the Armenians in Gordyene, we hear,' added Vistaspa with satisfaction.

'At least someone has the right idea,' I mumbled.

Orodes was not amused. 'We cannot allow Surena to wreck the treaty with the Armenians. To this end I ask you, Pacorus, to go to Gordyene and ensure that Surena understands the current situation and abides by the agreement I have brokered with Artavasdes.'

I nodded curtly. Being an errand boy hardly appealed but out of respect for Orodes I would of course obey his wishes.

The meeting over, Orodes called me back as the others were leaving the room, asking me to shut the door to ensure we were alone.

'Pacorus, I thank you for defeating Mithridates and ensuring the safety of Axsen and her kingdom.'

'It was a pleasure, believe me.'

He looked slightly uncomfortable as he retook his seat, gesturing for me to do likewise.

'I cannot blame you for executing Mithridates, considering the insults and losses you have endured at his hands, but I have to act according to the office of king of kings.'

I knew where this was leading. 'Of course.'

He shifted uneasily in his chair and avoided my eyes. 'I have therefore no alternative but to issue a declaration to the other kings of the empire expressing deep regret concerning your actions at Seleucia. I am sorry, my friend, but at this time Parthia is in a fragile state and I do not wish to offend the sensibilities of the eastern kings of the empire. I need them to stay loyal to me if we are to prove victorious against the Armenians and Romans.'

'I understand, Orodes. I will resign as lord high general if it will help.'

He looked at me with gratitude in his eyes. 'That will not be necessary. I hope you are not offended.'

'No, but I believe that it is a mistake to adhere to a peace treaty with the Armenians.'

'It is done, Pacorus, and cannot be undone.'

That was debatable.

He frowned. 'But I worry about Surena.'

'You need not. He is a most excellent commander,' I said.

He nodded. 'That is what worries me. If he attacks Armenia from Gordyene the peace will be broken. You must impress upon him the necessity of curtailing his warlike tendencies.'

'And you?'

'I shall return to Babylon to be by the side of my wife. You did well winning over Phriapatius, by the way.'

'He will prove a valuable ally.'

Orodes looked thoughtful. 'I really must organise a Council of Kings to ratify my accession to the high throne. It would be a good opportunity to begin a new era for Parthia.'

More meaningless talking and arguing, more like.

He looked at me. 'What do you think?'

'An excellent idea, though perhaps it could be held after we have dealt with the Romans and Armenians.'

He nodded. 'Perhaps you are right. But I shall notify all the other kings of my intention to gather them at Esfahan soon.'

Not too soon, I prayed. 'Once again, an excellent idea, my friend.'

Later I visited my mother who was again tending to her flowers in the royal gardens. She seemed happy enough though totally unconcerned about the affairs of the empire. The trees, ponds, shrubberies and flowerbeds had become the limits of her world, beyond which nothing of significance occurred. She rarely attended official functions and shunned guests, seeing only family and old friends. Vistaspa was a frequent visitor, though, and sat for hours in her pagoda as she served him food and wine and they talked of the old days. I was glad that they had each other and that their conversations kept alive the memory of my father. Vistaspa walked with a pronounced limp now though he refused to use a walking stick. He was nearly seventy and a lot of his savagery had drained away, though he still cut an imposing figure. I got the impression that the Battle of Susa and the death of my father, a man he had devoted his life to, had taken a great toll on him and now he too yearned for peace in his dotage.

As Gallia chatted to my mother about her flowers and plants I asked Vistaspa how his leg was.

'It has never really healed properly and in the mornings it takes me a few minutes of stretching before I can put any weight on it, but otherwise it is fine.'

'Hatra's army still needs its commander,' I told him. 'Next year there will be a new war to fight.'

'You do not think the peace treaty will last?'

'No. If I had my way we would be marching against Nisibus by now, but I am not high king so it is not to be.'

135

He rested both hands on the arms of his chair, his black eyes fixed on me. 'You think Orodes underestimates the Romans?'

'The Romans want Parthia, that much is certain. I would prefer to have destroyed the Armenians before we have to face them. Orodes thinks that a united Parthia behind him will make the Romans think twice before they invade, but the Romans do not think the way he does. He desires to keep Parthia free and strong whereas the Romans wish to conquer the whole world.'

'When war comes, do you think we can win it?'

'I honestly do not know, Lord Vistaspa,' was the best answer I could summon, but in my heart of hearts I feared that we had let a golden opportunity slip through our hands and might pay a high price for doing so.

The next day Domitus took the army back to Dura. He too was most unhappy that we were not going to march north against the Armenians but I told him that Orodes' decision on the matter was final. The high king himself left Hatra with his men at the same time, with Nergal and Praxima accompanying him. I had to admit that it was a disappointing end to a campaign that had started so well.

I myself, as requested, rode to see Surena who had been asked to travel to Assur. I took with me Vagises and his three thousand horse archers plus Peroz and his five thousand Carmanians. I asked Gallia if she wanted to accompany me but she declined, saying that although she would love to see Viper again she had no interest in meeting Surena. Her view of him as a cocky, arrogant individual with too much to say for himself had never altered and she was glad that he was out of her sight in Gordyene.

Byrd and Malik and their scouts accompanied me, since the army would not need their services as it made its way west across Hatran territory back to Dura. We were not going to make war so I also left the camel train with Domitus though we did take five hundred mules loaded with food and fodder.

We struck east to Assur and found that Surena had already arrived and was lodged in the governor's mansion, along with Atrax whom I had also invited. Media bordered both Hatra and Gordyene and its fate was inextricably linked to those two kingdoms. Surena had brought with him a hundred horsemen but had left his now pregnant wife, Viper, and Silaces, his second-in-command, in Gordyene in case the Armenians launched an attack. Surena had matured into a serious, thoughtful king who had a thorough understanding of the principles of warfare and thought the same as I regarding the treaty with the Armenians.

We sat in the private quarters of the governor's palace with Lord Herneus and Peroz.

I brought Peroz along because it would have been bad manners to exclude him. After all he was a Parthian prince and he had brought five thousand horsemen with him. Besides I found his company agreeable enough, as I did Scarab's who stood behind me as I relaxed in the spacious and airy white-walled room that was Herneus' study. The

136

governor looked the same as the last time we had met, dressed as he was in a simple beige linen shirt, brown leggings and sandals. His inexpensive clothes and bald head contrasted sharply with the long black hair of Atrax, Surena and Peroz in their expensive silk shirts, leggings and leather boots. But Herneus did not need fancy attire to impress anyone: his record of holding the east of the Kingdom of Hatra against all threats for nearly thirty years had established his formidable reputation long ago.

Slaves served us fruit, pastries, sweet meats and fruit juice as Peroz sat nervously in the company of kings whom he had never met and who had previously been the enemies of his father.

'This is Prince Peroz,' I told the others. 'He has come all the way from Carmania to fight by our side.'

Atrax smiled at him. 'We welcome you, lord prince, and your men.'

'Welcome indeed,' added Surena. 'We will need all the troops we can muster next year when we are once again at war.'

'Orodes has bought us time,' I said, 'but that is all. When Crassus arrives the Armenians will undoubtedly break the peace treaty and join with their Roman allies.'

'Orodes believes that if we beat Crassus then the Armenians will not start a war with Parthia,' said Atrax.

'It would be better,' interrupted Surena, 'if we gave the Armenians a bloody nose now so that they will think twice before starting another war when their friends arrive.'

I looked at him. 'On behalf of Orodes I must ask you not to launch any attacks against the Armenians, Surena. We must bide our time.'

'Orodes is mistaken, lord,' he replied, causing Atrax and Herneus to raise their eyebrows. 'However, as he is now high king and I have no wish to undermine his authority I will do as you ask.'

'I too would have preferred to settle affairs with the Armenians before Crassus arrives,' I added, 'but Orodes has decided otherwise and so we must abide by his decision.'

'Who is Crassus?' asked Peroz, blushing slightly at his intervention.

'A very rich and powerful Roman,' I answered, 'who wishes to make himself even richer by conquering Parthia.'

'He is a tyrant,' spat Peroz disapprovingly.

'Actually,' I said, 'he is a pleasant enough individual but suffers from the affliction that possesses many Romans.'

'Affliction?' asked Herneus.

I sipped at my freshly squeezed apple juice. 'An unshakeable belief that it is Rome's destiny to rule the world.'

'Forgive me, lord,' said Peroz, 'but you have met this Crassus?'

'Indeed, I was a guest in his house in Rome once, a long time ago.'

'Perhaps he desires to be a guest in your house, Pacorus,' offered Atrax mischievously.

'He would be made welcome if he came in peace,' I replied. 'He is congenial enough.'

Peroz looked confused. 'You would have him under your roof, majesty?'

'Of course,' I replied, 'as long as he does not bring his army with him.'

'Crassus is your enemy, lord,' said Surena darkly.

'Even enemies can be civil to each other,' I replied.

I could tell that Surena was straining at the leash, eager to attack the Armenians in retaliation for their assault on Gordyene, though he had once again proved to be their superior when it came to strategy and tactics.

'Artavasdes once more struck for Vanadzor, so I let him advance to nearly the gates of the city before launching a series of attacks against his strung-out army. After three weeks of being attacked night and day he withdrew.' Surena shrugged. 'Simple enough.'

'You did well, Surena,' I told him.

He smiled. 'I had a good tutor.'

'What do you know of this Apollonius that holds the towns in northwest Hatra?' I asked Herneus.

He rubbed a hand over his bald crown. 'Capable enough, though overly ambitious and I think he has too few troops to hold the towns under his control.'

With the Armenians in control of Nisibus and much of northern Hatra the towns in the west of my brother's kingdom were exposed to attack from the Armenians to the north and the Romans just across the Euphrates.

'Militarily it would make sense to evacuate them,' suggested Surena.

'My brother would never agree to such a thing,' I said, 'because to do so would quite rightly be interpreted by the Romans as sign of weakness. And both he and I know that the Romans respect only strength, if they respect anything, and despise weakness. For that reason alone those towns must remain Parthian.'

We left for Dura the next day as Atrax headed for Irbil and Surena rode back to Gordyene. After six days of hard riding we crossed over the pontoon bridges below the Citadel and entered my kingdom. Vagises took the Duran and Carmanian horse archers to the legionary camp while Peroz and I trotted through the Palmyrene Gate. I drew my sword and saluted the stone griffin as I passed under it and then headed up the main street towards the palace. It was good to be back home and my wife and children were waiting to greet me as I rode into the Citadel's courtyard and jumped off Remus' back. I ran up the stone steps and threw my arms round my daughters and then embraced Gallia. Domitus nodded at me and Rsan and Aaron bowed their heads as stable hands came to take Remus and Peroz's horse to the stables.

Gallia looked at the young man standing at the foot of the steps.

'Prince Peroz,' she called to him, 'come and meet my daughters.'

He bowed his head and ascended the steps where he was introduced to Claudia, Isabella and Eszter, who reached for his hand and pulled him towards the palace.

'You had better go with her,' I said to him. 'She probably wants you to see a new toy.'

'And there is someone who wants to see you,' Gallia said to me.

'Oh, who?'

'A man from the east who arrived two days ago and who brings a great gift.'

I was intrigued. 'What gift?'

'I have no idea. He is on the palace terrace with Dobbai who sent for him.'

Domitus and the others trailed after Gallia and me as Peroz was being tormented by my two youngest daughters, who were tugging at his hands and waving their fingers at him as they pulled him towards the terrace. He smiled, teased them and listened intently as they told him about their horses and which of the palace servants were their favourites.

'This guest turned up with a hundred warriors and a hundred camels,' remarked Domitus. 'We housed them in Orodes' old quarters in the city. Apart from their commander they have not moved from there. Very strange.'

We walked through the porch and into the reception hall and then into the throne room, the squeals of my daughters resonating in the empty chamber. Gallia told them to keep their voices down as they led Peroz towards the door at the far end that led to our private wing giving access to the terrace.

'Dobbai organised their quartering and instructed Rsan to furnish them with whatever they wanted,' continued Domitus. 'You can imagine what he thought of that.'

I looked behind and nodded at my stern-faced governor who was walking beside Aaron. He tilted his head curtly in reply.

We reached the terrace to find Dobbai ensconced in her chair next to a figure in a yellow turban. He rose when he saw us arrive, helping Dobbai out of her chair after he had done so. He stood before me as Dobbai clapped her hands and scowled at Eszter and Isabella who were still tormenting Peroz. They let go of the prince and became statues beside him, not daring to look into Dobbai's eyes.

'So you have returned, son of Hatra,' she said, examining Peroz, 'and you bring help with you. Former enemies have become allies. Good.'

She held out a bony hand to the individual who stood beside her, a man of medium height, thin, with very dark skin and small brown eyes.

'This is Patanjali Simuka, a lord of the Satavahana Empire, a great power to the east of the River Indus.'

Patanjali bowed deeply, 'Hail, King Pacorus, Lord High General of the Parthian Empire.'

He certainly looked like a lord, dressed as he was in a red silk shirt, white cotton leggings embroidered with gold and leather boots. Around his waist was a wide leather belt from which hung a curved sword, and in the front of his turban was a large red ruby that must have been worth a small province.

'I am glad to make your acquaintance, Lord Simuka,' I replied.

'He brings a great treasure for you, son of Hatra,' said Dobbai.

He was obviously a man of some wealth and importance but a hundred warriors hardly constituted a great gift. Still, if he was offering his services I would not turn him away.

'You and your men are welcome to join us in our fight,' I told Lord Simuka, who looked perplexedly at Dobbai.

'He and his men are not the treasure,' said Dobbai irritably. 'Please show him, Lord Simuka.'

The dark-skinned lord from the east smiled and stepped away from her, then drew his sword.

'Guards!' screamed Domitus who drew his *gladius* and stood in front of me. Seconds later the six legionaries who had been in the throne room rushed on to the terrace, swords in their hands. An alarmed Lord Simuka slid his sword back into its scabbard and held up his hands.

'Idiots!' hissed Dobbai. 'Put away your sword, Roman, and tell your men to return to their posts. Lord Simuka has travelled a great distance from his homeland to be here and his reward is to be threatened with death?'

I laid a hand on Domitus' shoulder. 'We appear to have a misunderstanding.'

Domitus stood like a rock in front of me. 'It is death to draw a sword in the presence of the king, that is crystal clear.'

'I merely wished to show the king my sword,' protested Lord Simuka.

I ordered the guards to return to their posts and told Domitus to sheath his sword.

'Please give me your sword, Lord Simuka,' said Dobbai.

He did as he was asked and she handed me his weapon. It was a fine curved sword and had a most curious blade, having what appeared to be swirling patterns along its entire length.

'A fine sword,' I said.

'It is more than that, majesty,' he smiled. 'With your permission I would like to arrange a demonstration to show you its qualities.'

I really did not see where this was leading but to accommodate the wishes of our guest and placate a clearly irate Dobbai, who was glowering at Domitus, I suggested we all retire to the throne room while female servants took away our two youngest daughters. I allowed Claudia to stay as she was ten years old now and understood what was expected of a young princess. Compared to her sisters she had a serious nature and smiled little, a consequence of spending too much time in Dobbai's company no doubt.

Gallia and I sat down on our thrones as Dobbai stood next to her and Domitus beside me, a hand on the hilt of his *gladius*, while Lord Simuka stood near the dais and slashed the air with his sword. I gave the order to summon one of the officers of the company of cataphracts that was on garrison duty in the Citadel. Rsan and Aaron were clearly bored by it all, which resulted in my governor's face wearing an even darker expression, while Peroz seemed fascinated.

'You should let me fight him,' growled Domitus.

'He is not here to fight,' I corrected him.

In any case though Domitus handled a *gladius* with aplomb it would be unfair to match him against the longer blade wielded by Lord Simuka. Minutes later an officer from my heavy cavalry appeared in his white shirt, his *spatha* dangling from his sword belt. He was a broad-shouldered man in his thirties who stood at least six inches taller than our visitor from the east.

'This shouldn't take long,' muttered Domitus, grinning evilly.

I told the officer that he was to fight Lord Simuka but that it was a demonstration only and no blood was to be shed. They both bowed their heads and withdrew to the centre of the hall. All my horsemen practised swordsmanship on a daily basis, especially the cataphracts. The hours and hours spent training was evident as the officer directed a number of slashing strokes against Lord Simuka. As it was a demonstration only neither man attempted any thrusts to stab his opponent.

Every horseman in Dura's army carried a *spatha* based on the one that Spartacus had given me in Italy. Weighing around twelve pounds, their double-sided blade was over two feet in length with a walnut hilt whose grip had an eight-sided cross section with finger grooves to give the holder a firm purchase. The even distribution of the sword's weight made it easy to wield as was now apparent as the officer made a striking movement towards Lord Simuka's shoulders. Our guest whipped up his sword to meet the blow, the two blades crashed against each other in a blur, and the *spatha* was cut clean in half.

The steel clattered onto the tiles as I stood and looked at it in disbelief, as did the officer who now held a broken sword. Lord Simuka took two steps back, bowed at his opponent and sheathed his sword. The officer sheepishly stooped and retrieved the top half of his sword from the floor and stood to face me.

'Fetch another sword,' I told him.

He bowed and left the chamber hurriedly to equip himself with a fresh sword from the Citadel's armoury.

'Do you think your eyes have deceived you, son of Hatra?' asked a smug Dobbai.

I did not reply. Dura's armouries were famous throughout the empire for producing high-quality weapons and armour. Vast amounts of gold had been lavished on them over the years to procure the best armourers who worked with the finest materials to produce armaments that were the envy of other kings. One broken sword proved nothing.

The crestfallen officer returned with another *spatha* and again Lord Simuka bowed to his opponent and drew his curved sword, and then the two of them once more engaged in swordplay. The first attacks and parries were half-hearted until Domitus called to them 'to make a fist of it', after which my man pressed his attacks with more vigour. He was

141

stronger that his opponent but Lord Simuka was more agile and managed to evade most of his blows. The officer delivered a lightning-fast succession of strikes, slashing left and right as he forced Lord Simuka back towards the wall, before raising his *spatha* above his head and then slashing it down against his opponent. Lord Simuka's blade slammed into the officer's sword and again went straight through it, severing the blade a few inches above the hilt. Once again metal clattered on the stone tiles as we all looked on in stunned silence. How can this be?

Lord Simuka bowed to his shocked opponent, sheathed his sword and then calmly bent over and retrieved the broken blade.

Dobbai stepped from the dais and walked over to Lord Simuka and took the blade from him.

'Many years ago, when King Sinatruces ruled the empire, he received a number of gifts from a ruler named Satakarni from beyond the Indus in gratitude for him stopping raiders crossing the river and laying waste his lands. Among these gifts was a sword such as Lord Simuka now carries, a weapon with a black blade covered with strange swirling patterns. This sword could cut through the blades of other swords with ease and was among the high king's most treasured possessions.'

'What happened to it?' asked Gallia.

'No one knows,' replied Dobbai. 'He lost it or gave it away in his dotage, no doubt, or perhaps swapped it for a young slave girl. But I remembered and sent a message to the court of the Satavahana Empire that Dura wished to purchase this wondrous material to fashion its own weapons. My gift to you, son of Hatra.'

'It is as your adviser says,' remarked Lord Simuka. 'I have brought a thousand ingots of *ukku* with me.'

'A thousand swords to equip all your cataphracts,' added Dobbai.

'*Ukku*?' I asked.

'The name of the steel from which the swords are made,' answered Dobbai.

I pointed to one of the guards standing near the dais. 'Go to the armouries and bring Arsam here.'

He saluted and scurried from the hall. I looked at Lord Simuka.

'A most impressive demonstration. You have brought a thousand ingots of this metal, you say?'

Lord Simuka flashed a smile. 'Yes, majesty.'

'And what price do you ask?'

'A thousand ingots for a thousand bars of gold, majesty.'

There were loud gasps from both Rsan and Aaron and even Domitus, who usually never quibbled about the price of weaponry, looked surprised.

'Majesty,' said Rsan, 'that is an exorbitant price for a few swords, especially as your horsemen already have them.'

'I would have to agree with Lord Rsan,' added Aaron. 'The army already places a heavy demand upon the treasury.'

142

'What use is a full treasury if the Romans are battering down Dura's walls?' said Dobbai scornfully.

'I will leave the decision to my chief armourer,' I said at length, still finding it hard to believe that a brace of Dura's swords had been cut in two so easily. He arrived fifteen minutes later dressed in a leather apron and looking flustered. He was also in a foul mood. He didn't bother to bow as he stomped into the throne room and stood before me.

'Arsam,' I said, nodding at our guest, 'this is Lord Simuka from east of the Indus, whose sword has just cut two of your *spathas* in half.'

Arsam's eyes narrowed as he mulled over what I had told him. Then he smiled. 'Impossible.'

I nodded at the officer whose swords had been destroyed. He walked forward and showed him the broken blades. Arsam frowned, snatched one of the fragments and then another, turning them over in his hands.

'I am assuming that there is no fault in the blades,' I said.

Arsam looked furious. 'Impossible,' he said again, glancing at Dobbai, 'it must be some sort of devilment.'

'The metal that made the weapons that cut through your swords,' she snapped at him, 'was forged by the gods, that much is certain, but it is a gift not a curse.'

'Lord Simuka has brought a thousand ingots of the metal he calls *ukku* for you, Arsam,' I said, 'so Dura can benefit from this divine gift.'

Lord Simuka smiled at my grizzled, scarred chief armourer. For his part Arsam curled up a lip at him. 'I will need to see these ingots myself, and forge a blade from one of them to see if it is of the required standard.'

'I would not expect anything less,' smiled Lord Simuka.

Partially placated, Arsam agreed that he himself would create the blade and so the next morning we all gathered in his workshop in the city's armouries. Lord Simuka arrived in the company of an armourer he had brought with him, a wiry man with sinewy arms and thin legs dressed in baggy leggings and a leather apron. Arsam also wore a thick leather apron to protect him from red-hot splinters. In addition, he wore a pair of thick leather gloves on his hands and iron shields over his boots to protect his feet from being smashed if he dropped any metal he was working on.

Arsam's most experience armourers crowded round the fire to witness the creation of a blade from the magical metal from the east. Though all the workshops had roof shutters that were nearly always open it was still unbearably hot and sweat was already pouring down my face. Most of the armourers and their young assistants worked in loincloths only beneath their leather aprons, though I thought it unbecoming of their king to wear such attire so I stood and sweated.

Lord Simuka's man handed Arsam the ingot that was round and resembled a baked cake. He explained that once the ore had been extracted from the earth it was packed with charcoal, the bark of an evergreen shrub called cassia and the leaves of milkweed. It was then encased in clay and heated in a fire for up to seven days. The resulting

143

ingot was possessed of the remarkable strength and flexibility that we had all witnessed in the throne room.

Arsam's workers stood on benches and stools behind us to catch a glimpse of the process as the armourer from across the Indus instructed him in the proper procedure. Domitus and Vagises stood riveted as Arsam place the ingot in the red-hot fire with a pair of tongs and left it there until it was a dull red. Lord Simuka's man then ordered that it be taken out of the coals and left to cool naturally, during which time Arsam hammered it on an anvil to stretch and flatten it to make a sword blade. After it had cooled it was again placed in the fire until it once more looked a dull red, following which Arsam took it out of the heat and worked it on the anvil once more, his expert hands soon creating a straight blade. This process was repeated a third and final time before the wiry armourer informed Arsam that the blade was now ready to be tempered.

This involved returning it to the fire and heating it to red-hot before withdrawing it to allow it to cool naturally. He informed us that the blade must be left for six hours before it could be hardened, so we all left the workshop to walk back to the palace. Even though the process was not finished the metal already showed the unusual swirling patterns that characterised Lord Simuka's sword.

Rsan and Aaron did not attend the lesson on sword making and when I returned to the palace I found them both waiting for me in the throne room where Gallia was dealing with a complaint from the head of the city's guild of prostitutes concerning soldiers of the army demanding free services in return for keeping order in Dura's brothels.

The great number of trade caravans that passed through Dura on their way to Palmyra were staffed by thousands of young men who were guards, camel drivers and merchants, all with money in their pouches and lust in their loins. Every city along the Silk Road attracted whores, both male and female, to service the carnal needs of the men of the caravans, and Aaron had hit upon the idea of establishing licensed brothels within the city to service these needs. The amount of tax paid was related to the number of prostitutes employed in each brothel, and in return for their taxes the prostitutes were given protection from the city authorities. The number of brothels grew in proportion to the increase in Dura's prosperity and soon the establishments had formed themselves into a guild and elected a woman to represent them.

Samhat was at least fifty years old now and her once beautiful face showed signs of years of hard usage at the hands of drunken, lecherous men. But her hair was still immaculate and she wore rich robes and gold jewellery on her fingers and in her hair. The throne room was filled with the aroma of her intoxicating perfume.

Gallia did not approve of prostitutes, mainly because Praxima had been forced by the Romans to be one but also because she thought it demeaned women and made them the slaves of men. Anything that even hinted of slavery was bound to raise my wife's hackles. That said, Samhat was a strong and forceful woman who could hold her own in any argument and

144

after their first few meetings their relationship had stabilised into one of mutual respect, if not admiration. Gallia liked Samhat's honesty and plain speaking while the city's head whore liked the fact that my wife was forthright and a warrior.

Now Samhat stood before Gallia, her voice echoing around the chamber.

'All the city brothels pay their taxes on time, lady, I can show you their records if you so desire.' She pointed at Aaron. 'And the royal treasury benefits handsomely from my girls opening their legs.'

Rsan looked mortified and Aaron shifted uneasily on his feet.

'And in return,' continued Samhat, 'we expect the city authorities to maintain order and protect my girls.'

Gallia looked at the squirming Rsan and Aaron and then at Samhat.

'The soldiers who patrol the streets do not protect your girls?' she asked.

'Only if they lie on their backs and spread their legs in payment,' replied an indignant Samhat. 'They are therefore paying twice. It is outrageous, lady.'

I smiled to Gallia as we walked towards the door at the far end of the chamber.

'Domitus,' she called. 'May we have a moment of your time?'

Domitus, his tunic soaked with sweat, stopped and smiled politely at Gallia.

'Of course.'

I followed him as he stood near Samhat who regarded him coolly.

'This is Samhat,' said Gallia, 'head of the city's guild of prostitutes. It would appear some of your men have been abusing their position.'

Domitus looked at Samhat disapprovingly. 'I find that hard to believe. My soldiers are the most disciplined in the world.'

I nodded at Samhat who was not in the least intimidated by our sudden appearance in the throne room.

'Oh they are disciplined all right,' she continued, 'the way they extort my girls to lift their robes for them after they have thrown out the troublemakers from one of our establishments was obviously thoroughly pre-planned and expertly executed.'

Gallia smiled but Domitus was far from amused. Hot and irritable, the last thing he wanted was to be berated by an aged whore.

'Report the incident to the camp prefect in the headquarters building in the Citadel. He will have the offenders flogged.'

'Flogging is no good,' insisted Samhat.

Domitus' nostrils flared at her insolence. 'What would you suggest, that I have them executed?'

'They stuck their manhoods in my girls, a service that other men pay for, so they should also be charged,' replied Samhat. 'We all have to make a living.'

'That seems reasonable,' added Gallia.

145

Domitus smiled at Samhat through gritted teeth. 'Very well, report to the prefect and tell him that those responsible are to reimburse you from their wages.'

A delighted Samhat bowed to Gallia, then to me, ignored the others and sauntered from the chamber, her expensive jewellery jangling as she did so.

'It is her who should be flogged,' mumbled Domitus.

'Aaron and Rsan have been waiting for you, Pacorus,' said Gallia.

'It is about the purchase of these new swords, majesty,' said Rsan.

'A thousand gold bars is a very high price, majesty,' added Aaron.

'If they help to give the army victory then the price is worth paying,' I replied. 'Besides, nothing is decided as yet. The decision is Arsam's to make.'

Aaron began to protest once more. 'But, majesty…'

'Enough!' I shouted. 'I have told you of my decision. Raise the matter again at the weekly council meeting if you must, but I will hear no more on the issue now.'

They both meekly bowed their heads and retreated from the hall. As they departed Dobbai entered from the door at the far end and made her way to my throne.

'Marvellous,' I said to myself.

She sat herself down next to Gallia. 'The demonstration went well in the armoury, son of Hatra?'

'Arsam has some more work to do before the sword is finished, but yes, so far it appears to be going well.'

'It is a good job that our enemies are not armed with such weapons,' remarked Domitus.

'The metal is confined to only a few areas east of the Indus and is therefore rare and expensive, Roman,' she replied.

'As my governor and treasurer keep informing me,' I added.

'And as I told them, son of Hatra, what use is a treasury full of gold when the enemy are battering down the gates of your city. And as Orodes has decided not to fight the Armenians you have the time to equip your horsemen with the black swords before you fight them, for fight them you must.'

'You disapprove of Orodes being high king?' I asked.

'I did not say that. I was eager for him to sit on Ctesiphon's throne for I knew he would bring unity to the empire, which he is doing. He has others to think about butchering his enemies, chief among them being you, son of Hatra.'

'Pacorus thinks Orodes has made a mistake making peace with the Armenians,' said Gallia.

'Events decided that peace would break out,' insisted Dobbai, 'not Orodes or the Armenians. The death of Tigranes was responsible for the cessation of hostilities, and the gods decided that would happen, not men.'

'Were you responsible for his death?' Domitus asked her, wiping his sweaty brow with a cloth.

She looked at him as though he was deranged. 'How could I be responsible for his death? He was a great king who lived an immense distance from here and I am a frail old woman.'

But Domitus continued to press his point. 'I heard that a wolf was heard howling the night he died.'

Dobbai spread her arms. 'That is what wolves do, in addition to pissing over everything and scavenging. Next you will be telling me that I turned into a wolf with wings and flew to Tigranes' palace.'

Domitus feigned indifference. 'It is nothing to me.'

But like me he must have been thinking of that night when she had performed the ritual with the clay dogs that had disappeared by the morning. It was uncanny that just at the moment when the Romans had been poised to invade the empire and link up with a victorious Tigranes, with a prostrate Hatra at their mercy, they had marched south to Egypt and Tigranes had died suddenly.

In the armouries, meanwhile, the blade that Arsam had been working on was once more heated in the fire until it was red hot before being plunged into a vat of heated oil. Afterwards it was allowed to cool naturally to bring the tempering and hardening process to an end. The next day it was fitted with a walnut grip and Arsam himself brought it to the palace in the afternoon.

The throne room was packed when he strode across the stone tiles to present me with it. It had been encased in a red leather scabbard with brass fittings and Arsam looked very pleased with himself as he bowed before me and held out the sword. I rose from my throne, took it and then drew the sword from the scabbard. Like Lord Simuka's weapon it had a black blade that had strange swirling patterns along its length.

I looked at the dozens of faces staring at me, including Kronos' replacement, a serious native of Pontus named Chrestus who had travelled from his homeland with his former commander in the aftermath of his land's occupation by the Romans.

All the company commanders of the cataphracts were present along with Vagises and his senior officers from the horse archers, while opposite them stood the cohort commanders from the Durans and Exiles. I smiled to myself – how tribal men were. Despite Dura's army being composed of a myriad of different races once men joined a formation their immediate allegiance was to that unit and the men who were a part of it. They all owed loyalty to me but they died for their friends.

I stepped from the dais and nodded at Domitus who left his officers to face me. He raised his arms.

'This should not take long,' he shouted, prompting cheers and whistles from those around the walls. Gallia and the Amazons grouped around her laughed as Dobbai waved a hand dismissively at the racket and sat down on my throne, much to the consternation of Rsan and Aaron. Peroz glanced at the tall Scarab nervously but the latter was all reassuring smiles. I saw Arsam standing near the doors to the chamber, arms folded, in the company of Lord Simuka's armourer. The latter, surrounded by a dozen of his brightly dressed warriors, stood nodding and smiled at me.

I drew my new sword from its sheath and threw the scabbard at Chrestus.

'Remember,' I said to Domitus who stood like a ravenous wolf gripping his *gladius*, 'this is only to test my sword.'

He grinned evilly and then came at me with a series of blistering attacking strokes, hacking left and right in quick succession. I parried his blows as he forced me back towards the dais. The chamber was filled with whoops and screams as the spectators cheered us on. As I had a longer blade it should have been easy for me to keep him at bay, but he wielded his blade so deftly that I had difficulty and it took all my concentration to block it.

I jumped to the left and aimed two scything strokes at his shoulders that he met with his *gladius* before aiming a downward cut at my left leg. I blocked this and then raised my sword above my head and used it to deliver a vertical cut. In combat the intent would be to split an opponent's skull but as Domitus was one of my dearest friends I aimed the blow to miss his head and left shoulder. Nevertheless, he instinctively raised his *gladius* above his head, parallel to the ground, to block the blow. The two blades struck each other and the top half of the *gladius* was sheared off and fell to the ground.

I stepped back as the tumult died instantly and a wall of faces stared in disbelief at what they had just witnessed. Domitus stopped, picked up his broken blade and looked at me.

'That settles it, then.'

I examine the black-bladed *spatha* etched with its magical swirling patterns. 'Yes, it is settled.'

The cataphract officers nodded to each other and smiled because they knew that they and their men would now be receiving these marvellous swords. I walked over to Lord Simuka.

'You have your thousand gold bars.'

He bowed his head to me. 'Majesty.'

After everyone had left I instructed Aaron to pay Lord Simuka immediately. He generously offered to stay at Dura for a few more weeks to ensure that there was no problem with the rest of the ingots, which in the proceeding days were transported from the storerooms in Orodes' old mansion to the armouries. Arsam made the production of the new swords a priority, his task made easier by the fact that his armouries were already highly efficient centres of production. The small and costly army of smiths and their apprentices meant that the manufacturing process was both speedy and cost efficient, though if the cost of procuring the base metal was taken into account then Dura's new swords would be the most expensive weapons in history!

Though Arsam himself had made the first sword, which had been fitted with a temporary hilt, it went back to the workshops to be fitted with a proper grip and was also sharpened. At Dura sword production was carried out in stages and in different workshops. First a blade was forge by two strikers, after which it was sent to a separate workshop for grinding. From there it went to a third workshop for hilting and then to a fourth where it was fitted with a scabbard. On average it took ten days to turn a round ingot into a sword complete with scabbard.

Even working day and night and paying for extra shifts the maximum that the armouries could produce was a hundred of the new swords a month, which meant ten months of work devoted to them alone. In addition, Arsam was also tasked with producing the new arrows as well as manufacturing replacement items – mail armour, scale armour, tubular steel armour for arms and legs, helmets, swords, daggers, bows and arrows – for the army. Aaron's hair began to show flecks of grey as the weekly council meetings revealed the amount of gold that was being spent on the army.

A month later Lord Simuka and his men made ready to depart Dura with a thousand gold bars loaded on the backs of their camels. He had brought only a hundred men with him on his journey to the city but I gave him an escort of two thousand horse archers for his return trip. It became common knowledge that I had paid him a great sum for the precious metal he brought with him from east of the Indus and a paltry hundred men would be scant protection as Lord Simuka travelled back east. I was especially worried about his crossing of Susiana, Elymais and Persis, all of which were probably filled with roving bands of former soldiers of Narses now turned bandits. I therefore sent a courier to Nergal asking that he allocate more horsemen to Lord Simuka's party when it reached the borders of Mesene, and another to Carmania to request that King Phriapatius meet with him when he reached his own frontier.

Soon afterwards we had a welcome visit from Orodes in the company of Axsen who had never visited Dura. The day was hot and sunny when he rode through the Palmyrene Gate in the company of his wife and received an ecstatic reception from the population, who lined the main street and threw flowers at the royal couple and their bodyguard as they passed. Many of the latter had been quartered in the city when Orodes had lived in Dura and they tipped the points of their lances towards the crowds so they could be garlanded.

Typically, Orodes and Axsen dismounted to get closer to the crowds, which the legionaries who lined the route had difficulty in holding back. Orodes had always been a popular resident of the city, famed for his generous and warm nature and the people had taken to him as one of their own. Now he was king of kings and they were doubly pleased. It took a full hour for the royal party to reach the Citadel and I was worried that that it might be overwhelmed by a wave of adulation and so despatched Domitus with two hundred legionaries to ensure the royal couple reached the palace in one piece.

Eventually they walked through the Citadel's gates to polite applause from the city's most important citizens who had been invited to attend the

149

palace. Soldiers lined the walls and a hundred cataphracts on foot and in full dress stood to attention either side of the palace steps.

Gallia was dressed in a flowing white robe with gold earrings and a diamond-studded gold necklace. She held the hands of Eszter and Isabella as she stood beside me. Claudia was similarly attired, her hair gathered up on top of her head and held in place by a gold diadem. Domitus, Vagises and Chrestus were in their parade dress but I wore a simple white silk shirt and brown leggings.

Orodes and Axsen both wore purple silk shirts and white leggings, Orodes also sported his rich scale armour cuirass covered in shimmering silver scales, and his helmet inlaid with silver and gold. They walked over and embraced us and then Axsen was introduced to our daughters, kissing each one in turn and telling them how beautiful they looked. They remembered Orodes of course and made a great fuss of him. Isabella, now seven, asked if he had been on holiday and was he now coming to live back in Dura? It was a happy occasion and Axsen charmed all and sundry with her kind words and radiant nature.

That night a great feast was held in the banqueting hall to celebrate the arrival of our new guests. I apologised to Axsen that Orodes' mansion was not available to them and hoped that their quarters in the palace were adequate, as I knew that Babylon's royal residence was a hundred times grander than our smaller and somewhat spartan home. Slightly inebriated after drinking too much wine, she told me not to be silly and that she thought Dura a charming place.

Byrd and Malik had come from Palmyra bringing Rasha and several of Haytham's lords with them. Axsen stared at their tattooed faces as they sat a few paces from the high table. In their black robes they cut a fearsome appearance and she thought it most unusual and slightly disturbing that the traditional enemies of Parthia should be sitting a few paces from the empire's king of kings.

'They are not our enemies,' I said, trying to eat baked carp soaked in butter without the juices dripping on my shirt. 'The Romans and Armenians are.'

'We have peace with the Armenians at present, Pacorus,' said Orodes.

'Until the end of this year,' I reminded him.

'I am hopeful Artavasdes might be open to making the treaty permanent.'

I smiled at him but said nothing. Making the peace treaty permanent would de facto make the Armenian conquest of northern Hatra permanent, something that neither I nor Gafarn would ever agree to.

Orodes must have read my mind. 'I do not intend to sign away parts of the empire, Pacorus, but for the moment we must let Artavasdes think that he has permanently expanded his empire. Once the Romans have been dealt with he will be more amenable to renegotiating the treaty.'

Orodes was no fool but he was taking an enormous risk in thinking that we could defeat Crassus with ease before intimidating the Armenians into meekly withdrawing from northern Hatra. I still favoured attacking and hopefully annihilating the Armenians first but Orodes had decided otherwise.

'It was most fortuitous that Tigranes died,' remarked Axsen casually.

'Indeed,' agreed Orodes, 'a stroke of luck.'

'Or divine assistance,' I said.

They both looked at me questioningly but I merely smiled and raised my silver cup to them.

The next morning I took them both on an inspection of the legionary camp and showed Axsen the golden griffin of the Durans and the silver lion of the Exiles and the Staff of Victory. Orodes had seen them all many times but he explained to his wife their symbolism and significance and Domitus arranged a display of ten cohorts on the parade square in front of his command tent. Afterwards he joined us as we rode back to the Citadel and took refreshments on the palace terrace. In the distance the road to the city was filled with traffic and on the blue waters of the Euphrates below fishing boats were going about their business.

When we arrived we found Dobbai asleep in her chair, much to the disappointment of Axsen who had wanted to speak to her. She had failed to attend the feast the night before – Gallia explaining that she hardly ever graced such occasions – and now she added insult to injury by sleeping in the presence of the king of kings and his wife. Orodes merely smiled and shrugged – he had spent too long at Dura not to know that Dobbai did entirely as she pleased and came and went according to her own desires.

We spoke in hushed tones as we reclined on couches beneath the gazebo and servants served us cool fruit juices.

'Phriapatius is most pleased that you made him your deputy,' remarked Orodes.

'I thought it best that one of the eastern kings should be trusted with the high offices of the empire,' I replied, 'lest they think we do not trust them.

He grinned. 'And I thought I was the diplomat.'

'There is another reason why I selected Phriapatius,' I said. 'In the event that we cannot halt the Romans between the Tigris and Euphrates, it would be prudent to have another army east of the Tigris ready to give battle.'

Axsen looked surprised. 'You think we cannot defeat the Romans?'

'I think, lady, that the Armenians will throw in their lot with Crassus when he arrives, and then we will be fighting perhaps up to two hundred thousand enemy troops. Against such numbers we may not initially prevail.

'But while Dura, Hatra, Mesene and Gordyene slow the enemy Orodes can assume command of the army that Phriapatius has assembled and wait on the other side of the Tigris.'

Orodes looked mortified. 'I will not abandon Dura nor any other kingdom, Pacorus. It would be dishonourable to do so.'

'You would not be abandoning anything,' I reassured him. 'You would be merely trading space for time. If I can inflict serious damage on the

Romans and Armenians then you can attack their weakened forces and hopefully destroy them.'

'You forgot to add Babylon to those kingdoms who will stand in the first rank against the barbarian invaders,' said Axsen defiantly.

Gallia reached over and touched her friend's arm reassuringly and I smiled but the reality was that what was left of Babylon's army would be next to useless on the battlefield. The kingdom had lost many soldiers during the two invasions it had suffered at the hands of Narses and Mithridates, to say nothing of the thousands of men it had lost at the Battle of Susa. But the walls of Babylon were still high and strong and the kingdom's soldiers could still do the empire a great service in holding those walls against an invader until a relief force could be organised.

'The Romans will not cross the Tigris,' snarled Dobbai, 'and neither will the Armenians for that matter.'

Axsen grinned at Gallia like an excited child.

'You have seen this, lady?' enquired Axsen.

Dobbai began to rise unsteadily from her chair as Orodes left his seat to assist her. She smiled at him.

'The son of Hatra desires a noble, heroic death on the battlefield so his name shall be remembered for all eternity just like the slave general he adored. Is that not correct, son of Hatra?'

I frowned at her. 'Not at all.'

She sniggered at me. 'Oh I think so. But it shall not be.'

'You mean I will be defeated?' I asked.

Her wrinkled brow furrowed. 'I did not say that. Do not put words into my mouth. I merely remarked that you will not die in battle; it is not your destiny. Your destiny is to save the empire but you will get no thanks for doing so.'

'We value Pacorus highly,' insisted Axsen.

Dobbai nodded at her. 'Naturally. Someone who regularly kills your husband's enemies is most useful. Is that not so, Orodes?'

'Pacorus is first and foremost a friend,' Orodes corrected her.

She weighed up Orodes, dressed as he was in his silver scale cuirass, rich shirt and leggings and expensive boots, his hair immaculately groomed as usual.

'You are both forgiving and magnanimous, which are most desirous qualities in a king of kings. I chose well, I think. But then there wasn't much of a choice. It was between you and the son of Hatra.'

'You are too kind,' I remarked dryly.

'Let us not talk about the past,' said Orodes diplomatically, 'but rather plan the future.'

'That is simple enough,' remarked Dobbai. 'Defeat the Romans and Armenians and recover those parts of Hatra that are occupied by Artavasdes.'

'Is that all?' I said.

Dobbai walked forward to stand over me. 'With the help of the gods and using what wits you have it should be straightforward enough.'

152

Axsen was intrigued. 'Help of the gods?'

Dobbai examined her. 'The Romans unexpectedly turn around and decide to butcher the inhabitants of Egypt instead of Parthia and Tigranes dies suddenly. You think these things just happened by chance?'

Axsen's eyes were wide with excitement. 'You mean the gods made them happen?'

Dobbai said nothing but merely looked immensely smug.

'You asked them to help and they granted your request?' Axsen sat in awe of the frail old woman in her presence. She may have been the queen of one of the world's oldest cities, a city that had high priests and priestesses who carried out elaborate rituals and prostrated themselves before their gods, but here was a woman who had called upon the gods and they had answered. Not only that but had performed miracles that had saved the whole empire.

'You must tell me how you made the gods answer your appeal,' ordered Axsen excitedly.

Dobbai shook her head. 'It is forbidden.'

I thought of the evening of the ritual, the dank mist and the snarling hounds and shuddered. Dobbai had sent Gallia and the children out of the city to protect them. Including Dobbai there had been eight of us that night and now two – Kronos and Drenis – were dead. I knew that the gods did not grant their favours freely and, as Dobbai had warned, there was always a price to pay.

Dobbai suddenly turned and shuffled from the terrace, leaving a frustrated Axsen who looked indignantly at Orodes. But he merely smiled at his wife and said nothing. Dobbai stopped and looked back at us.

'You need to kill her.'

Gallia looked at me as though I knew whom she was speaking of but I shrugged.

Orodes looked slightly alarmed. 'Kill who?'

'Your stepmother, of course.'

'Queen Aruna?' I said.

'Of course, and do it quickly.'

Orodes was both shocked and appalled by the idea. 'My stepmother lives in exile in Antioch. She must be at least sixty years old now. I will not sanction any attempt on the life of an old woman who is no threat to us.'

Dobbai nodded to herself. 'Too forgiving.' She continued to walk from the terrace, calling out as she did so.

'Send the son of Hatra, then, or better still ask Haytham to send his assassins to slit her throat.'

'I will not be sending anyone to kill my stepmother,' said Orodes seriously, looking at me. 'And would ask that you also refrain from attempting to murder her.'

'I am delighted that Queen Aruna is far away in Antioch,' I replied, 'and hopes she dies there.'

153

'Your sorceress could weave a spell to kill her,' mused Axsen, much to the amusement of Gallia and the disapproval of Orodes.

'There is always a price to pay for such endeavours,' I found myself saying.

'What price?' asked Gallia.

I thought of Drenis and Kronos. 'A high price, sometimes too high.'

The next morning, following my ride and yet another lesson in swordplay from Domitus, whose reflexes appeared to quicken as he got older, I rode back to the Citadel, unsaddled Remus and afterwards stood by the gates looking at the granite memorial to the Companions. One hundred and twenty men and women had travelled back with me from Italy in the aftermath of Spartacus' death. That was sixteen years ago and in that time over half had died, some from natural causes but most in battle. Each one of their names was now carved on the stone before me, Drenis being the most recent one. I looked at the empty space that was yet to be filled. How long would it take until the memorial was filled with the names of all those who had fought with Spartacus, including my own and Gallia's?

'Pacorus?'

I turned to see Axsen dressed in leggings, purple silk shirt and red boots. Her face appeared flushed and her hair was in a long plait down her back.

'I have been on morning exercises with the Amazons. Most exhilarating.'

She looked at the memorial. 'What is this?'

'A monument to those who sailed back with me from Italy after Spartacus had died.'

She read aloud the word that was twice the size of the letters that spelled the names below it.

'Companions.'

'That is what we were, what we are,' I said, 'individuals who were thrown together in the enemy's heartland and who had to fight for their survival every day. A host of different races united by two things: a desire for freedom and devotion to one man.'

'You mean Spartacus? I have heard Orodes talk of him, though he did not know him.'

I smiled. 'I fear I bored Orodes to death talking about him. But yes, his name was Spartacus.'

'What was it like, being a slave, I mean?' she asked sheepishly.

'Terrifying, humiliating and unbearable in equal measure, and I was a slave but for a short time. After I was liberated I met others who had been slaves for many years. After fighting beside them I swore that I would never own another slave in my life.'

'We have slaves in Babylon,' she said almost apologetically.

'So does every kingdom in the empire, as do many mansions in this city. It is the way of things in the world.'

'Did your friend, Spartacus, seek to change the world?'

154

I thought for a moment. 'If he had been victorious and destroyed Rome then yes, he would have changed the world, or at least the Roman part of it, but I do not think he set out to do so. He was a very simple man, really, who wanted nothing more than to live in peace and freedom.'

'Just as we do in Parthia.'

I thought of her great palace in Babylon, the golden throne she sat on, the opulence she lived in and the small army of slaves who pandered to her every wish. Her notion of freedom was perhaps very different from that of Spartacus'.

I smiled at her. 'Yes, just as we do.'

'Do you think we can beat the Romans?' I detected a note of concern in her voice. Babylon, after all, was only a month's march from Roman Syria.

I smiled at her. There was no point in alarming her. 'Yes, we can beat the Romans.'

She looked past me to the gates. 'He looks like an angry young man.'

I turned to see a well-built individual, with black shoulder-length. He was wearing a white shirt edged in blue, an expensive sword at his hip and a bow in a hide case attached to his saddle. His quiver was slung over his shoulder and a helmet was fixed to one of the front horns of his saddle. He rode a well-groomed brown horse. Behind him were half a dozen other riders on white horses wearing scale armour cuirasses of alternating steel and bronze plates, helmets on their heads – members of Hatra's Royal Bodyguard.

The angry young man walked his horse into the courtyard and then noticed me standing by the memorial and half-smiled.

'Uncle,' he called, raising his hand to me.

I acknowledged his excuse for a salute and pointed at him. 'The angry man is Prince Spartacus, son of the man we were just speaking of and heir to Hatra's throne.'

And I could tell from his demeanour that something was wrong.

155

Chapter 7

I held the letter from Gafarn in my hand as the son of the man I had revered stood in front of me in the throne room. Gallia, having changed after her morning on the shooting ranges, had taken her seat beside me after learning that Hatra's prince had arrived at Dura. Orodes had taken Axsen to see Spandarat in his stronghold where they would spend the night, leaving me to deal with this unexpected problem. Gafarn had entrusted the officer of his escort with the letter, which I read and handed to Gallia. She shook her head after perusing its contents and handed it back to me.

The prince had not known of the letter's existence until now and though his curiosity was aroused when he saw it he feigned indifference, maintaining an air of brashness bordering on insolence as he folded his arms across his chest.

I held the letter up to him. 'It does not make for pleasant reading and is hardly the conduct becoming of a prince of Hatra. Your parents must be very disappointed in you. If you had committed these offences in Dura you would have been flogged.'

At that moment Zenobia entered the chamber and Gallia beckoned her over. My wife's second-in-command wore a tight-fitting white shirt that clung to her ample breasts while her leggings accentuated her shapely behind and womanly hips. She bowed her head to me and then spoke softly to Gallia, who smiled and nodded before Zenobia turned on her heels and left our presence. The eyes of the young prince were glued to her body as she walked past him.

'He might get flogged today for his disrespectful attitude,' remarked Gallia casually when she noted his leering.

'How old are you, Spartacus?' I asked.

'Sixteen,' he replied proudly.

'Sixteen. And in the last twelve months you have broken the nose of a fellow squire, beat another senseless, had numerous fights with Lord Kogan's guards, insulted the priests of the Great Temple, had too much to drink at a royal banquet and tried to ravish a nobleman's daughter. Finally, and perhaps most seriously, you attempted to seduce a novice of the Sisters of Shamash. More mischief than most men achieve in a lifetime.

'Have you anything to say?'

He held my stare. 'I was provoked.'

Gallia stifled a laugh.

'I see. And how does an innocent young female novice of a religious order provoke a young prince?'

He shrugged.

'Your father believes that a period away from the pampered surroundings of Hatra will do you good, and it just so happens that there is a position here that is suitable for you.'

'What happened to your master?' asked Gallia.

'He was killed fighting the Armenians,' Spartacus replied.

156

I could see that he bristled with anger and resentment. 'Well, you will be my squire until you have finished your training.'

'What happened to your master's other squire?' asked Gallia, for every cataphract had two squires to attend him and care for his weapons and armour.

'I broke his nose,' came the reply.

I ordered a guard to go to the stables and fetch Scarab who was already my squire. When he returned Spartacus looked in horror at the black-skinned man with his sweat-soaked shirt and dirt-smeared face. Scarab bowed his head to Gallia and me and smiled at Spartacus.

'Scarab,' I said, 'this is Spartacus who will assist you in your duties of being my squire. Take him to the barracks and find him a place to sleep. Inform the duty officer who he is.'

Spartacus looked at me in surprise. 'Barracks?'

He was expecting to be lodged in the palace, of course, and normally he would have been out of respect for his princely status. But it was obvious that he had been indulged and spoilt and needed to learn the virtues of humility. His education would begin immediately.

'That is correct,' I answered slowly and sternly. 'You will sleep in the barracks, though you may be comforted to know that your duties will require you to be away from your bed for long periods to spare you the indignity of enduring your meagre accommodation. You may go.'

He nodded curtly to Gallia and then me and then turned on his heels and marched from the hall, Scarab trailing after him.

'And Spartacus,' I called after him.

He halted and looked back at me.

'You will find that Dura is not Hatra.'

Three days after the arrival of my nephew Orodes and Axsen departed Dura.

Spartacus was given no special treatment, shown no favouritism and no allowances were made for him because he was a prince. He slept in a bed next to Scarab in the barracks inside the Citadel; rose before dawn; cleaned out his horse's stall; and groomed and fed his mount before he ate his own breakfast. After eating he rode out of the Citadel with the other squires and their cataphracts to the training fields outside the city. The cataphracts, equipped in full armour, would practice battle tactics and the squires would also take part. In this way they would become intimately familiar with the drills and procedures of the heavy cavalry for when they made the transition from squire to cataphract.

I always tried to take part in these training sessions as I enjoyed them immensely and believed that a king should always be in the company of his soldiers rather than sitting on his throne in his great hall listening to whingeing petitioners.

Scarab had previously been a slave and although he could ride a horse when he first came to Dura he was ignorant in the ways of mounted warfare, and neither could he shoot a bow. So having Spartacus present meant that not only could he explain to the Nubian the nuances of the tactics of armoured horsemen, he could also teach Scarab to shoot a bow. Spartacus thought it an outrage that he should demean himself by teaching a former slave to shoot, something that he had learnt to do from before he could walk. In reply to his protests I informed him that he would do as he was told.

He hardly spoke to me during the first two weeks he was at Dura. He was angry with me, angry with Scarab, angry with everyone. He thought it an insult that he was partnered with Scarab who was the oldest squire in the army. Squires began their training at the age of fourteen and finished it at eighteen, those that had lasted the course that is. Not every boy who began to train to be a cataphract was found to be suitable. So the angry young prince from Hatra spent his days in sullen silence, except when he was shouting at Scarab during archery practice.

'Let the bowstring slip out of your fingers, do not close your eyes when you shoot, gently exhale when you release the string. Think about what you are doing you stupid Nubian.'

He quickly became exasperated with Scarab and with his duties in general and a month after he had arrived I saw him storm out of the barracks building one afternoon and stride across the courtyard. I was standing at the top of the palace steps passing the time with the newly arrived Malik and Byrd, Peroz and Domitus and saw him approach, rage etched on his face. Domitus, dressed in a white tunic, black leather belt and sandals, stood facing me as Spartacus bounded up the steps and shoved him aside.

'Out of the way, old man.'

Malik looked in disbelief at what had just happened while Byrd shot an angry look at Spartacus.

'Uncle, I demand to be allowed to live in the palace. That black slave is an imbecile who is fit only for shovelling dung.'

I was not listening to him but rather looking at Domitus who tapped the youth on the shoulder with his cane.

'Your father would be disappointed in you.'

Spartacus could scarcely believe that his royal person could be violated so. He spun round to face Domitus.

'You will be flogged for daring to touch me.'

Around us men stopped what they were doing to watch the drama unfolding before their eyes. Surely this was a joke, or at the very least a mistake? Did this boy know whom he was talking to? I doubted whether my nephew recognised Domitus, for he had probably never seen him, and even if he had it would have been when he was dressed in full armour and headdress.

'Flogged will I?' said Domitus calmly. 'Well I might as well be flogged for a major offence rather than a minor one.'

He then lashed Spartacus across the face with his cane.

'How many lashes does that deserve?'

For a few seconds my nephew did nothing but clutch the side of his face. His body started to shake and I thought he was sobbing, but realised that his quivering was rage because he faced Domitus and drew his sword; his jaw tensed and pushed forward, his teeth bared.

The guards standing by the stone pillars of the porch moved towards the pair but I waved them back. This would be a useful lesson for young Spartacus. At that moment Gallia and the Amazons rode into the courtyard after an inspection some of the royal estates south of the city. The queen and her warriors halted to stare at the boy who stood with a drawn sword facing the general of the army.

'Arrest him, uncle,' shouted Spartacus, 'so he can be punished.'

More and more individuals began to gather around the edges of the courtyard to stare at the scene, and on the walls groups of sentries were talking to each other and pointing at the spectacle below.

As quick as a striking cobra Domitus swung his cane to strike the other side of my nephew's face, before calmly walking down the steps and heading towards the headquarters building. Spartacus screamed with rage, his face red as he ran after him and drew back his sword ready to cut Domitus in two. But Domitus spun round, saw the blow coming and deftly moved aside so my nephew sliced only air with his blade. His sword skills were finely honed, even at this early age, and he instantly repositioned himself to face Domitus and then thrust his sword forward, aiming at the older man's stomach. Perhaps he believed that the shorter, crop-haired middle-aged man who stood in front of him, armed only with a vine cane, would just stand still and allow himself to be run through. More likely he was not thinking at all, so possessed by wrath as he was. The strike was lightning fast but Domitus, who had spent his whole life fighting, saw it coming before it was launched and hopped to one side, transferred the cane to his left hand and again struck Spartacus across the face. This time, though, he did not allow his young opponent to wield his sword again: he grabbed his right wrist and kicked the back of the knee of my nephew's extended right leg, knocking him to the ground. In a flash Domitus kicked the sword out of his hand and placed his right foot on my nephew's neck, pressing down hard to pin him to the ground.

Domitus gestured to two guards standing outside the headquarters building who ran forward.

'Lock him in the armoury,' he ordered them.

They yanked my nephew to his feet and hauled him to the stout building with iron grills over its windows next to the headquarters building.

'My sword,' cried Spartacus, looking back at his blade lying on the flagstones.

Domitus walked over and picked it up.

'A fine weapon. You can have it back when you have learned to use it properly.'

He looked around and saw the crowd of spectators.

'Show's over!' he bellowed and then calmly walked back up the palace steps. He handed me the sword.

'Let him stew for a few hours and then let him out.'

'He is proving somewhat of a problem,' I said.

'You could always flog him,' suggested Domitus.

'That would only make him angrier and having been flogged myself I am reluctant to subject him to such humiliation. I apologise on his behalf, Domitus.'

'You were flogged, majesty?' said a shocked Peroz.

'It was a long time ago, prince,' I answered.

'On board a boat,' added Byrd, 'I remember it well.'

'As do I, Byrd. I still carry the scars.'

That night I had my nephew brought to me as I relaxed on the palace terrace in the company of Gallia. My daughters had been put to sleep and Dobbai had retired to her room so we sat sipping wine while small boats with lanterns at their bows cast their fishing nets on the marble-smooth waters of the Euphrates below us. The night was warm and still but not unpleasant. Gallia, her blonde hair loose around her shoulders, stretched out her arms as a dejected Spartacus was escorted into our presence. I dismissed the guards and gestured to an empty chair nearby. He saw his sword leaning against my chair but said nothing as he nodded to Gallia and slowly eased himself into the wicker chair.

A servant, a beautiful young girl with almond-shaped eyes and a lithe figure, walked over to him and offered him a cup from the tray she was holding, dazzling him with a smile, while another daughter of Ishtar filled it from a jug. He once again glanced at his sword.

'The man you attacked today was the commander of Dura's army,' I said. He looked surprised. 'Just because a man is not dressed in silver and bronze and does not have a plume in his helmet does not mean he is not important. As I told you, this is not Hatra.'

'You must learn to control your temper.'

I sipped at my wine and he did the same. 'Lucius Domitus, my commander, was perfectly within his rights to slay you today. Lucky for you that he was only carrying his cane.'

'He could still have you flogged,' added Gallia, flashing me a mischievous grin.

'You cannot fight the whole world, Spartacus,' I said. 'You must learn to be more tolerant, especially with regard to Scarab.'

'He torments me with infantile questions,' he replied.

'He wishes to learn, that is all,' Gallia rebuked him.

'He was a slave until recently and has not had your privileged upbringing,' I said. 'He is my squire and so are you, unless you would rather be an orderly for my general?'

A look of alarm spread across his bruised face. I smiled.

'I thought not.'

I stood up, picked up his sword and walked to the balustrade and peered at the boats on the river.

'Soon the empire will be at war with the Romans, Spartacus, and the Armenians as well, probably. In that war we will need all the soldiers we can mobilise. So you can appreciate the importance of teaching Scarab the use of the bow and other weapons.'

I held out the sword to him.

'You can help us win this war or you can wage your own private conflict against us all while Parthia is destroyed. It is up to you.'

He walked forward and took his sword from my hand.

'I did not mean to disrespect you, uncle.'

'We will say no more on the matter, Spartacus. But try to think before you assault anyone in future, especially crop-haired men shorter than you.'

He bowed his head to Gallia who smiled at him and then walked quietly from the terrace. I dismissed the servants and told them to leave the wine. I refilled Gallia's cup and then my own and retook my seat.

'It is hard to believe that it was sixteen years ago when we rode from the Silarus Valley with Diana cradling him in her arms,' she reflected.

I rubbed my eyes. 'They have passed in an instant, and once again we find ourselves about to fight Marcus Licinius Crassus.'

'This time he will be the one fighting far from home,' she said defiantly.

'I wish I shared your optimism. The reality is that he will have many legions plus horsemen and auxiliaries, and to the north we will face the Armenians who will add their great numbers to his own.'

She looked surprised. 'You think we cannot win?'

I emptied my cup. 'I think, my love, that when war comes it may last a long time. Parthia has been weakened after many years of civil strife and the last thing it needs is more war.'

'Perhaps Crassus will suddenly die as Tigranes did,' she said.

'Perhaps,' I replied. I hoped that the magic of Dobbai would indeed cause him to drop down dead, for without a miracle I had grave doubts as to whether we would be able to defeat him when he came.

At least the next few weeks passed without incident as far as young Spartacus was concerned. He was still prickly and prone to angry outbursts, especially towards Scarab. But his mornings were filled with onerous duties and his afternoons were spent teaching my Nubian squire archery and swordsmanship. So his time was filled and his apparently limitless reserves of energy were expended. The situation was helped greatly by Peroz taking them both under his wing and spending most afternoons with them to act as a mediator between the two, patiently teaching the Nubian how to use a bow and proving himself a better shot than Hatra's prince.

I had quartered the Carmanian horse archers in the ruins of Mari. Once, seventeen hundred years ago, it was a great city but had now become a collection of mud-brick ruins converted into stables for horses and barracks for their riders. Located south of Dura it had originally housed Silaces' eight thousand horse archers from Elymais when that kingdom had fallen to Narses and Mithridates. Now Silaces and his men were in Gordyene assisting Surena. Strabo, the quartermaster responsible

161

for the health and feeding of Dura's horses, camels and mules, organised weekly deliveries of fodder from the royal granaries and Marcus, the army's quartermaster general, supplied the Carmanians with food, clothing and horse furniture. Happily neither Aaron nor Rsan complained about their presence at the weekly council meetings because Phriapatius sent regular payments of gold to reimburse Dura's treasury for the upkeep of his son's soldiers.

I liked Peroz. He had an amiable, thoughtful nature and a mind with a thirst for knowledge. In fact he reminded me greatly of Orodes. By the autumn he had been accepted by the officers of the army as a valued ally and had seemingly managed to tame Spartacus and turn Scarab into a decent archer to boot.

During this time an eerie quiet descended over the empire as we waited for Crassus and his army. Byrd provided me with regular reports concerning the Roman governor of Syria who was still embroiled in Egypt's affairs and enriching himself greatly in the process, while in the north Artavasdes stuck to the terms of the peace treaty. Orodes wrote that this was because he did not feel confident of launching a war against Parthia without the towering presence of his father by his side. But when Byrd came to Dura he reported that Artavasdes was recruiting great numbers of mercenaries in preparation for the final war against the Parthian Empire.

In Gordyene, meanwhile, Surena strained at the leash to attack Armenia from his kingdom. So concerned was Orodes that my protégé would initiate a war against Armenia that he asked me to go to Gordyene to reason with Surena.

I took Scarab and Spartacus with me in addition to a hundred horse archers and a hundred mules loaded with fodder, food and spare clothing. Because the year was drawing to a close the latter included woollen mittens, thick woollen tunics and heavy cloaks complete with hoods for the mountains and valleys of Gordyene are cold in winter. The high peaks were already blanketed with snow and a cruel wind blew from the north.

We rode east to the city of Assur, across the Tigris and then struck north along the eastern bank of the river before heading northeast towards the Shahar Chay River that marked the border between Media to the south and Gordyene to the north. Ordinarily I would have visited Atrax in Irbil, the capital of Media, but I was in a hurry and had no wish to see my sister Aliyeh, whose infantile hostility towards me was beginning to test my patience. We made the three-hundred mile journey in twelve days and arrived at the river to find the far bank lined with five hundred horse archers commanded by Silaces.

There was a bitter northerly wind blowing that swelled the huge white banner of Elymais sporting a four-pointed star so it resembled a great sail. A frozen Vagharsh, hood over his head and a scarf shielding the lower half of his face, held my fluttering griffin banner as I edged Remus into the grey, wind-ruffled icy water and led my horsemen across. Opposite the horse archers raised their bows in salute and Silaces walked his horse forward towards me, bowing his head as Remus trotted from the water.

'Greetings, Silaces,' I said, 'I had forgotten how cold this kingdom could be.'

He looked into the leaden sky heaped with dark grey clouds.

'Indeed majesty, some of the high passes are already blocked by snow.'

'Well, at least that will stop Surena from waging war against the Armenians, then. How is he?'

He fell in beside me as we rode north to join the main road leading to Vanadzor, the kingdom's capital, the rider carrying his banner falling in behind us.

'He is a king with a mission, majesty,' he replied flatly.

'And what would that be?'

He smiled to himself. 'To emasculate the Armenians.'

'I am here to persuade him to delay his neutering,' I replied.

The first night, we camped by the side of a luxuriant forest of oak and roasted the meat of two huge stags that Silaces' men had shot that afternoon. On the second day we reached the town of Khoy, around which were several salt mines whose produce Silaces told me was traded with the kingdoms of Media, Atropaiene and Hyrcania for iron and bronze to make weapons and armour. In addition to salt Gordyene was abundant in cattle, sheep, horses and camels, which were also exported to nearby kingdoms.

'Surena means to make Gordyene another Dura, majesty,' said Silaces as we rode north towards Vanadzor, the wind having abated somewhat and a clear sky bathing the landscape in bright winter sunshine. Overhead a snowcock showed us its white flight feathers as it passed over our column.

'He has turned Vanadzor into a giant armoury to equip his army.'

I had to admit that I was filled with pride at his words. Surena had once been nothing more than a wild boy who lived in the great marshes south of the city of Uruk, an uneducated half-savage of the Ma'adan.

Our paths had crossed when I had been captured by soldiers of the treacherous King Chosroes, at the time the ruler of Mesene. Surena and his band of young mavericks had fortuitously ambushed the column in which I had been a captive and had freed me. I had subsequently fled with them into the marshlands and afterwards Surena had joined me on my journey back to Dura. He had become my squire, had again saved my life in the battle against Narses and Chosroes before the walls of Dura and had then entered the ranks of the army's cataphracts. He had been enrolled in the Sons of the Citadel scheme whereby the most promising individuals were groomed for command and had graduated to become an officer in the heavy cavalry.

Surena's meteoric career had continued when I had given him command of half of my cataphracts at the battle near the Tigris against Mithridates and then command of a dragon of horse archers – a thousand

163

men – in the subsequent retreat from the army of Narses. Surena never knew it but he was given command of an expeditionary force into Gordyene because Claudia, the dead wife of Spartacus, had talked of him in oblique terms when she spoke to me in the Temple of Ishtar at Babylon. I had expected him to be an irritant to the Armenians, who at the time were occupying Gordyene, but nothing more. But his leadership and courage had resulted in him liberating the kingdom and returning it to the Parthian Empire. A grateful Orodes had rewarded him with Gordyene's crown and I felt very satisfied with myself for finding him.

Peroz was most intrigued by this grey, cold land filled with high, snow-clad mountains, rivers bloated with raging waters and seemingly endless forests of beech and oak and wind-swept mountain steppes. He rode on my right side with Silaces on my left; the banners of Dura, Carmania and Elymais fluttering behind us as we entered the wide, long valley before Vanadzor and saw a most wondrous sight.

Before us was arrayed the army of Gordyene: rank upon rank of foot soldiers in front of companies of horsemen, and before them all, mounted on a grey horse and surrounded by his senior officers, framed against a huge banner sporting a silver lion on a blood-red background, was Surena, Lord of all Gordyene.

'Where is Viper?' I asked Silaces.

Viper was a former member of the Amazons whom Surena had married and was now Queen of Gordyene.

'Because she is pregnant, majesty, he has ordered her not to ride until the baby is born. He dotes on her greatly and loves her, too much perhaps.'

Surena urged his horse forward and cantered across the ground to bring it to a halt in front of me, flashing a smile.

'Greetings, lord. Gordyene's army stands ready for the inspection of the Lord High General of the Parthian Empire.'

I held out my arm to him and he clasped my forearm. 'Greetings, Surena, I am here to convey the gratitude of King of Kings Orodes in making Gordyene once again the northern shield of the empire.'

Now nearly thirty, his youthful enthusiasm and arrogance had been replaced by determination combined with common sense and great tactical and strategic awareness. He also looked older and more careworn, but then the responsibility of administering a kingdom bore down heavily on all of us.

His officers, all of them young and very serious, were dressed in conical iron helmets, scale armour cuirasses, red long-sleeved tunics, baggy black leggings and boots. And as I rode slowly up and down the ranks of the assembled army I was struck by the age of the troops. This was a young army. The only middle-aged men I saw were among Silaces' men from Elymais.

Looking at the army I could see the influence his time at Dura had made upon Surena because he had modelled his forces on my own, tempered by financial practicalities. Gordyene was not as wealthy as

Dura. There were no cataphracts present but Surena had raised two dragons of medium horsemen, men in scale armour comprising rows of overlapping iron scales riveted onto thick hide and reinforced with scale armour shoulder guards. They also wore pteruges – strips of leather that hung from the waist and protected their thighs and upper legs.

These horsemen carried spears as their main weapons instead of the longer *kontus,* axes instead a swords, with daggers in sheaths on their right sides. Their round wooden shields were faced with hide painted red, each embossed with white lion's head.

Surena's horse archers wore no armour and had soft pointed hats on their heads, but each one was equipped with two quivers and a short sword for close-quarter fighting. There were eight thousand of them drawn up in their dragons and companies, the standard bearer in each of the latter carrying a lion windsock. The last dragon of horse archers seemed to be composed of particularly fresh-faced youths, as I remarked to Silaces.

'Take a closer look, majesty,' he said.

I peered at the front rank. 'They are women!'

'The queen's dragon,' stated Surena proudly. 'My wife was in the Amazons and so to make her feel more at home I raised a thousand female horse archers in honour of her and the Amazons. They are called the Lionesses.'

'They can shoot as well as any man,' remarked Silaces.

Gordyene's foot soldiers resembled the legionaries of Dura with their helmets, large oval shields and short swords, though these men also wore greaves on their lower legs and wore leather armour instead of mail. There were five thousand of them and they made for a very impressive sight.

Finally we came to Silace's horse archers – the exiles from Elymais – who had numbered eight thousand when Surena had led them into Gordyene. Since then a thousand had fallen fighting the Armenians but they were still an impressive body of horsemen and represented the most experienced element of Surena's forces.

'It is a fine army,' I said to Surena.

He beamed with delight and pointed towards his city. 'Viper is waiting to receive us with warm wine and hot food, lord.'

There were small flecks of snow in the wind and our faces were pinched with cold so I was glad to ride through the thick oak gates and into Vanadzor. The city had never been an attractive or gracious place filled with wide streets, rich buildings and beautiful statues, but rather a dour, bleak stronghold designed to withstand external foes. Its ugliness was due in no small part to the local hard black limestone used in the construction of its walls and buildings. Many of its stone structures were squat and unsightly but their walls were thick and its citizens hardy and strong. Curiously local quarries also produced marble but it was hardly ever used in Gordyene; instead, it was exported to neighbouring kingdoms for profit.

165

The Romans had carried off many into slavery when they had conquered the kingdom but others had escaped to the mountains to eke out an existence and to await deliverance. Surena had proved their deliverer after the Romans had given Gordyene to the Armenians, who had believed that all the flames of resistance had been extinguished. After Surena had taken the city the people had returned from their hovels in the mountains.

When they did they found a very different Vanadzor. As we were riding through the muddy streets of the city Surena proudly informed me that he had increased the number of stables and barracks within its walls to accommodate his new army. While in the hills and mountains detachments of lightly armed scouts, many former members of King Balas' army, watched for enemy incursions into the kingdom and launched raids against hostile forces entering Gordyene.

'As well as raiding across the frontier,' muttered Silaces.

Surena heard him. 'Our enemies must learn to respect our borders, Lord Silaces. Besides, it is best to have neighbours who fear us rather than regard us as lambs to be slaughtered.'

The palace was surrounded by a high square stonewall with round towers in each corner and an impressive three-storey gatehouse on its south side. Wooden shutters on each storey indicated shooting platforms for archers and spearmen. The gates opening to allow us to enter were, like at the entrance to the city, made from thick oak and reinforced with iron strips and spikes.

Bleak, functional and strong were the qualities that the palace imparted; its stone-paved square surrounded by barracks, stables, armouries and ironworks. The chimneys of the latter were spewing black smoke and the air was heavy with the aroma of burning charcoal and hot metal. As we dismounted from our horses and stable hands took our shivering beasts to warm and cosy stalls I was struck by the high level of activity around me. It was as though we had wandered into a giant colony of ants.

Surena escorted us up the black stone steps, through the porch and into the main hall of the palace, which was well lit and had white marble tiles on the floor to brighten what would otherwise have been a chamber that resembled a cave in the underworld with its black walls, stone pillars and dark ceiling. In front of the wall at the far end stood a stone dais holding the king and queen's thrones and behind, hanging on the wall, was a massive red banner embossed with a silver lion. The shields of the guards who stood at every pillar also carried lion motifs. The scene projected strength and power and any visitor would be left in no doubt that this was a kingdom organised for war.

We walked across the tiles with helmets in the crooks of our arms to where Viper stood in front of the dais. She still looked like a teenage girl, though because she was pregnant her breasts had swelled and her extended belly made her look a little plumper. She smiled girlishly at me and melted my heart as I stepped forward and embraced her tenderly. I had always been fond of her and though she had been a member of the Amazons and knew how to use a bow and a sword, in this bleak stronghold she looked vulnerable and a little fragile. I could see why Surena was so protective towards her.

'Welcome, lord,' she said as I kissed her on the cheek and released her from my arms.

'Gallia sends you her love and wants to know when you will be visiting Dura.'

Surena also kissed her, took her hand and gently led her to her throne, seating her before taking his seat. Silaces stood on his right side to face us.

'After the baby is born,' she grinned, 'all three of us will pay you a visit.'

'Orodes and Axsen also send you their love,' I said, 'as do the rest of the Amazons.'

Slaves brought cups of heated wine to warm our insides and Surena ordered hot braziers to be fetched to warm the hall, though in truth now we were out of the cold feeling began to return to my hands and feet.

Peroz stood as straight as a spear shaft beside me, much to the amusement of Viper.

'This is Prince Peroz, the son of King Phriapatius of Carmania,' I said to her, 'who has brought troops to fight alongside my own.'

Surena smiled at him. 'Welcome to Gordyene, lord prince. It is good to see you again.'

Peroz bowed his head to him and Viper in a most punctilious manner, causing Viper to giggle.

I stepped aside and held out a hand to my squires standing behind us. 'And these two are my squires. Scarab is a Nubian who joined us recently and Prince Spartacus is from Hatra.'

They both bowed to the king and queen.

'Spartacus?' said Surena. 'Is that not the name of the general you fought under in Italy, lord?'

'It is indeed,' I answered, 'and this is his son.'

Surena admired the strapping youth for a few seconds and then pointed at a stout, middle-aged man with a ruddy complexion standing by the wall.

'Show our guests to their quarters,' he ordered.

That evening Surena gave a great feast in our honour, his officers placed at tables before us. I informed him of the latest developments in the empire. I told him that Phriapatius had been made my deputy and was responsible for raising a second combined army in the east to act as a reserve in case the army I commanded was destroyed.

'You think that is likely, lord?' he asked, ripping at a piece of roasted leg of chamois with his teeth. The chamois was a cross between a goat and an antelope whose meat was extremely tasty.

'Hopefully not,' I replied, shoving a strip of piping hot gazelle meat into my mouth.

'It all depends on when we engage the enemy,' I told him. 'Timing is of the utmost importance. That being the case, I would emphasise to you the importance of not launching any unprovoked aggression against the Armenians. Orodes thinks the peace will hold and does not want Parthia to break it.'

He continued chewing, not looking at me but admiring his pregnant wife. He did indeed love her greatly. She smiled at him and he smiled back and I decided that now was the time to broach the subject of taking Silaces and his men back with me. They had been an integral part of the campaign that had freed Gordyene and now they provided a seasoned corps of veterans that stiffened Surena's army. In theory, as I was lord high general of the empire, I could order Silaces to accompany me south when I left Vanadzor, but I had no wish to treat a man who had been of such service to the empire disrespectfully. In addition, I both liked and admired Surena and so had to tread carefully.

'I have a favour to ask you, Surena.'

He smiled again at Viper. 'Name it, lord, and it will be done.'

'You will know that the army of Hatra has suffered a number of reverses in recent months.'

He nodded gravely. 'Your father's death was a great blow to the empire, lord.'

'When Crassus arrives he will cross the Euphrates at Zeugma and then march south along the river, straight through Hatran territory,' I continued. 'At the same time the Armenians will advance from Nisibus to strike at the city of Hatra itself.'

He was nodding as I said these words, chewing on more meat as he did so.

'This being the case, I need all the soldiers I can get my hands on to meet and defeat these threats.'

He wiped his hands on a cloth. 'The army of Gordyene will be ready to answer your call, lord.'

'You may be occupied with your own Armenian invasion when fighting recommences,' I said. 'Therefore I have to request that Silaces and his men return with me when I leave your city.'

'You do not need to request such a thing, lord. They are yours to command.'

He did not appear shocked or surprised by my request. Was I so predictable?

'Nevertheless, Surena, I would have your agreement in this matter, for to lose seven thousand veteran horsemen is no small thing.'

'Today you saw but part of my army, lord,' he said. He then spread his arms out wide. 'These men are the senior commanders who serve Gordyene, including the men from Elymais. As well as the twenty-two thousand soldiers on parade today Gordyene can raise an addition five thousand horse archers and I have allies to supplement my army.'

'Allies?'

He suddenly stood up and men began to rap tabletops with their knuckles in salute when they saw him. He raised his hands to still the hubbub and then pointed to where a group of men with wild beards and moustaches sat.

'Lord Diophantes, how many of the brave Aorsi do you bring to fight by our side?'

A tall man with a big round face, long unkempt hair and small eyes stood up. He was wearing a rich red leather jacket with a sheepskin trim fastened at the front by two large silver brooches. He grinned devilishly at Surena.

'Eight thousand warriors ready to slaughter your enemies, great king,' he answered in a booming voice.

There were whoops and cheers and more rapping on tables as the big man slapped his companions on their backs and Surena sat down.

'So you see, lord, I have taken measures to ensure the security of Gordyene for my son when he is born.'

'Who are the Aorsi?' I asked.

'A tribe of the Sarmatians who live north of the great Caucasus Mountains.'

I was horrified. 'Sarmatians? I had to kill a host of them at Seleucia. They were in the pay of Mithridates.'

He was unconcerned. 'They are hardy warriors who will fight anyone as long as they are rewarded for doing so. Some of Balas' old warriors, the wild men who act as guardians of the northern frontier, told me about the famed Sarmatian horsemen from beyond the mountains, so I sent envoys to the tribal chiefs of the Aorsi asking for soldiers to fight for gold and horses. They sent Diophantes and eight thousand men in reply.'

'They might not be as easy to get rid of,' I warned him.

He looked and me and smiled. 'I do not wish them to leave. I have asked them to stay and have promised them rich lands that they can call their home.'

'In Gordyene?'

He shook his head. 'In Armenia.'

I was about to remind him that we were currently at peace with Armenia when Viper rose and declared she was tired and would have to retire. Surena immediately took her arm and said he would take her to their bedroom. I rose and embraced her and Peroz bowed, took her hand and kissed it, much to her delight. As Surena led her to their private quarters located to the rear of the banqueting hall everyone rose and began to chant 'Dasna, Dasna' as the couple exited the chamber.

I looked at Silaces in puzzlement.

'It means "short dagger",' he replied. 'The nickname they have given the queen. It is not only the king who adores her in these parts, lord.'

While they were gone slaves brought great platters heaped with the meat of roasted mouflons – sheep that were much larger and bigger than the ordinary variety – plus cooked sturgeon and salmon caught in local rivers. They also served prodigious quantities of *dolma*, a local dish that

169

consisted of minced lamb mixed with rice and flavoured with mint, fennel and cinnamon.

I watched Spartacus and Scarab at the table in front of me devouring everything put in front of them, even the boiled sheep's head soup that had been served before the main meal. In these parts it was believed that soups consumed before a feast began had healing powers. They were both tall, sturdy framed individuals and would make fine warriors, if they did not kill each other first. Silaces pointed the mutton and spice kebab he was holding at them.

'A curious pair, majesty.'

'The black one was a slave at Emesa and Spartacus is with me because he needs taming.'

'Can the son of the slave general be tamed?'

'I hope so,' I replied.

Silaces nodded. 'It is appropriate that he should be by your side when he fights the people who killed his father.'

Before Surena returned I told him that he and his men would be leaving Gordyene with me.

'Initially you will be quartered at the city of Assur,' I told him. 'You will be close to the city of Hatra and can reinforce King Gafarn if he is threatened, but will also be able to return to Gordyene if necessary should Surena get into difficulties with the Armenians.'

'I do not think you have to worry about Surena, majesty. He is more than capable of holding this kingdom.'

What I did not tell him was that by taking him and his men I hoped it would make Surena more cautious when it came to provoking the Armenians.

The next morning, as snowflakes whirled around the icy courtyard, we said our farewells in the entrance of the palace to Surena and Viper, who was wrapped in a great fur-lined cloak and felt hat, her girlish face barely visible. I shook the hand of Surena and embraced his wife fondly and then took to my saddle. All of my party were wrapped in their thick cloaks, hoods and mittens, especially Scarab who seemed to feel the cold more than most.

I nudged Remus forward and leaned forward to speak to Surena.

'Remember, do not provoke the Armenians. We want to fight the coming war on our terms, not theirs.'

'Yes, lord.'

'And take care of yourself and Viper. I look forward to seeing you both after the baby arrives.'

I raised a hand to Viper, wheeled Remus around and trotted from the courtyard, followed by my horse archers. Outside the city Silaces and his men were waiting for us, all of them with their quiver flaps closed, their bows in their cases. Grey clouds were hanging low and the northern wind stung our faces as we rode from Vanadzor south back to the border.

I sent riders ahead to Irbil to inform Atrax that I was bringing back Silaces and seven thousand horsemen who would be traversing his

170

territory on their way to Assur. Though as lord high general I could go where I wanted within the empire, with or without a small army as an escort, it would have been discourteous not to acquaint him with my movements. I also did not want to give Aliyeh another excuse to criticise me if word reached Irbil that I had marched through her husband's kingdom without permission.

Happily Atrax himself rode from his capital to meet us at the Shahar Chay River with a thousand of Media's horse archers in their blue tunics and grey leggings, grey cloaks around their shoulders. Fortunately the wind had abated and sun shone through the breaks in the clouds to bring a degree of light and warmth to the stark winter landscape as we rode our horses through the icy waters.

Despite being married to my sister Atrax had a warm, magnanimous character that everyone warmed to. Quick to laugh and praise and slow to criticise, he was a brave and loyal friend and a good king to his people. I never understood what he saw in my aloof, serious sister but they say that love is blind and he certainly adored her. And, to be fair (loathe though I was to be so), she had borne him two fine sons to secure his dynasty.

That night we camped ten miles inland from the river and warmed ourselves around great fires made from chopped wood Atrax had brought with him from Irbil. As we stood looking into the yellow and red flames I told him that that Crassus would soon be arriving.

'What is he really like, this Crassus?' asked Atrax, tossing the thighbone of the roasted chicken he had been gnawing into the fire. 'You said you met him once.'

'Many years ago. He invited me to his house in Rome to try to persuade me to leave the army of Spartacus and return to Parthia. He offered me and Gallia safe passage if I would abandon the slave army.' I smiled to myself. 'I said no of course.

'As to what he is really like; he is formal and polite, generous I suppose, very rich and very powerful. He also has that Roman certainty that everything he does will be to his advantage and every decision he takes will be the right one.'

'He is arrogant?' suggested Atrax.

I laughed. 'We are all arrogant to a degree, my friend. We all believe that our abilities are superior to the majority of other men, and that we take the right decisions to ensure the safety of our kingdoms and the empire. But with Roman commanders such as Crassus it is different. They believe that they have a divine right to make the world Roman; that it is not just their duty but the will of their gods that they should conquer the world.'

'Let us hope, then, that our gods have more power than theirs,' he replied.

I thought of the ritual that Dobbai had performed; the diversion of Aulus Gabinius to Egypt and the unexpected death of Tigranes. The rational part of me dismissed these things as mere coincidences; after all, if the gods had been summoned then surely they would strike Crassus dead and open the earth to swallow his army. But then I remembered that she also once told me that the gods loved chaos and bloodshed. Perhaps they only helped a little, just enough to ensure Parthia was not destroyed, but not enough to grant us outright victory. Perhaps they wished for war between Parthia and Rome to go on and on for all eternity until every inch of ground between the Himalayas and the Euphrates was soaked in blood. The fire hissed and spat and above us the gods toyed with us mere mortals.

Chapter 8

Dura had always been a frontier city. Originally founded by a general named Nicanor, one of Seleucus I's commanders, it had subsequently passed to Parthian control and became a bulwark against the Agraci on the western bank of the Euphrates. The lords who settled on the strip of land north and south of the city lived in great strongholds and existed in a state of perpetual war with the Agraci tribesmen who inhabited the vast desert to the west. The Agraci raided their lands and they in turn launched reprisals and the desert ran red with blood. And then a great and terrible king called Haytham became the ruler of the Agraci tribes and all the lands between Emesa in the west, Dura in the east and the vast expanse of desert to the south. He inspired fear and loathing and his cruelty sent a shiver down the spine of the hardiest warrior. Dressed entirely in black and riding a black stallion that legend told had been sent from the underworld to bear this scourge of civilisation, Haytham led a host of black-clad devils that plundered and killed without mercy. And nowhere had Haytham been more feared and despised than in Dura.

Eszter giggled, tugged on Haytham's sleeve and then ran away. Now five years old, she had inherited a mischievous streak from somewhere and wore a permanent smile on her round face.

Haytham jumped out of his chair and growled at her, causing her to scream with delight and race round the terrace. Gallia told her to be quiet and sit back in her chair. Isabella giggled and Claudia frowned and looked away. Dear Claudia. Now eleven, she was old and serious beyond her tender years as a consequence of spending so much time in Dobbai's company, not that the old woman had corrupted her in any way. Rather, she had taught our daughter about the gods, the signs they gave mankind, the plants that could heal and harm and how to ask for divine assistance. She largely ignored our other two daughters and apart from periods spent with her tutors she devoted the rest of her time to the company of Dobbai. Now she sat beside her on the palace terrace as we entertained Haytham and Rasha.

'Cannot a man get any peace in this world?' opined Haytham, screwing up his face at Eszter who giggled and stuck out her tongue at him. Gallia told her not to be so rude.

'Malik would have come,' said Haytham, retaking his seat, 'but Jamal insisted he stayed at Palmyra. Ever since the death of her father she is worried that the Romans will assault Palmyra again. She nags him incessantly.'

Jamal was Malik's wife and a beautiful woman who would one day be queen of the Agraci.

'Aaron's religion,' I said, 'states that his god created the world in seven days and rested, and then he created man and rested. But what it does not teach is that after he created woman no one has rested.'

The eyes of my wife, Claudia, Rasha and Dobbai bored into me to indicate that my attempt at levity had failed miserably.

Haytham laughed. 'You are a brave man, Pacorus, to make such a statement in front of so many women.'

'Foolish is a word that would be more suitable,' growled Gallia.

I had asked Spartacus and Scarab to be present so they could both meet Haytham, which for the young prince was at first difficult. He had been brought up in Hatra where the Agraci were looked upon as little more than pests to be exterminated. It was well known that I had forged an alliance and friendship with the Agraci ruler but this had resulted in Hatran opinion of me being lowered. To most Parthians the Euphrates marked the boundary where civilisation ended and barbarity began. Spartacus had been surprised when I had informed him that Haytham was visiting the palace and astounded when I told him that Rasha had her own room there.

Rasha was now a stunning young woman with hair as black as the night, flawless skin and the most beautiful brown eyes. When she had arrived, those eyes lingered upon the handsome face of the young prince who was introduced to her. He in turn had bowed most graciously to her and had insisted on escorting her into the palace. I had been worried that he might be aloof with Haytham and Rasha but her striking looks were enough to make him forget her race easily enough.

'How is Byrd?' enquired Gallia.

'Rich and growing richer,' replied Haytham. 'Perhaps one day he will be able to purchase a new robe. He has gone to Antioch to inspect his offices there.'

'I hope he will be safe,' I said with alarm.

Haytham laughed. 'They will think that he is desert lord, nothing more. No one will know that he is the chief scout and close friend of King Pacorus, lord high general of Parthia. He will outlive us all, of that I am sure.'

'Hopefully he will learn more about the arrival of Crassus,' I said.

'I remember that name,' reflected Haytham. 'He once tried to bribe me to permit a Roman army to march through my territory to attack Dura. And now he comes himself.'

'It is the will of the gods,' announced Dobbai, 'that the son of Hatra and Crassus should battle each other to determine the fate of the empire. The forthcoming clash between these two great warlords will be watched by the divine ones and the victor will be granted his wish.'

'Surely the victor will have already been granted his wish,' I said, 'for he will have vanquished his foes.'

She threw back her head and cackled. 'And after the slaughter; what then? It is your destiny, your fate to fight Crassus, son of Hatra, but what do you wish for in the next life?'

I was confused. 'The next life?'

She beckoned Claudia to help her get out of her chair. 'When all of us are ashes and dust, when we are not even someone's memories, where would you be then, wandering alone for all eternity or with your friends and loved ones?'

174

'With my friends and loved ones, of course.'

She took Claudia's arm and then shuffled from the terrace. 'Exactly. So fight well, son of Hatra, and the gods will reward you.'

Haytham looked contemplative and Gallia confused, while Spartacus and Rasha glanced at each other furtively and thought of nothing but their attraction to each other.

'You must kill this Crassus when he arrives,' declared Haytham after a long silence.

'I would rather destroy his army, lord,' I replied. 'Besides, I have to say that I quite like him.'

Haytham was shocked. 'A great warlord shows his enemies no mercy.'

I smiled at him. 'I remember a time when a small group rode into the desert and returned a daughter to the King of Agraci. He did not kill them.'

He winked at Gallia. 'That is because the beauty of your wife intoxicated me and made me forget that we were enemies.'

Gallia blushed and looked away and Isabella and Eszter pointed at her and laughed.

'And yet we are friends now, lord, and the ancient enmity between Parthian and Agraci is no more,' I said.

He shook his head at me. '*We* are friends, Pacorus, but you delude yourself in thinking that our two peoples can ever live in friendship. Hatreds can be difficult to forget.'

'Not for the saviour of Dura,' said Gallia, her face no longer flushed. 'How is the fat King of Emesa?'

Following the defeat of the army sent from Emesa to capture Palmyra, Haytham had come to be regarded by the citizens of Dura as a hero who had turned back a foreign army intent on seizing their city and reducing them to slavery. The gossip carried by the caravans on the road had reported great Agraci casualties, which had perversely been interpreted as a sign that Haytham and his people had fought desperately to save Dura – no thought had been given to the idea that the Agraci might have actually been fighting for their own land and people. As a consequence, when Haytham and Rasha had arrived in the city a grateful populace had mobbed them.

Scarab looked at Haytham with interest. 'Sampsiceramus does not want war. He desires only to live in opulence surrounded by an army of slaves satisfying his every need. Is that not so, Nubian?'

Scarab bowed his head at Haytham. 'It is as you say, great king.'

'He is not the problem,' continued Haytham. 'If only the same could be said of his Roman overlords.'

The next day we went hunting south of the city. Along the riverbank the land was irrigated and filled with fields and villages, plus the royal tanneries that were situated far enough away so their stench would not disturb the city's residents, including those who lived in the palace. Away from the irrigated strip, however, the land was desert and largely uninhabited. It was also mostly flat aside from a few wadis that cut deep

175

into the earth. The old year was failing fast as I rode with Haytham, Gallia, Rasha and a score of Haytham's warriors and my own squires into the arid land of shrubs, grasses and desert lichens. It may have appeared empty but this land was teeming with snakes, lizards, hares and rabbits. Today, though, we were hunting gazelle.

The women were bare headed with their hair free as the day was mild but not hot and was unlikely to get so with a sky filled with white clouds. Spartacus and Scarab fell in behind us as we headed in a southwesterly direction.

'When this Crassus arrives the Romans may attempt to assault Palmyra once more,' said Haytham to me. 'If Dura's army is in the north fighting him I may not be able to hold off another Roman army, Pacorus. We can melt into the desert but your city cannot do the same.'

'I appreciate your warning, lord king, but Dura's walls are strong and will resist any assault until I return with the army.'

He frowned. 'It might be wise to leave some of your army behind to safeguard your city.'

He obviously did not realise how weakened Parthia was at this present juncture.

'Alas, the empire will need every man to face the Armenians and Romans.'

He looked more serious. 'We hear that the Romans have settled affairs in Egypt to their advantage and Prince Alexander, the man you furnished with weapons, has suffered more defeats in Judea. He and his men still fight but they have been reduced to holding a few isolated strongholds.'

I had hoped that Alexander Maccabeus, a Jewish prince who had paid me in gold for a great many weapons produced in Dura's armouries, would keep the Romans occupied in Judea and may even eject them from the country altogether. But his army had been defeated and my hopes had been dashed.

'Soon they will once again turn their attention to the east, towards Palmyra and Dura,' he continued.

'Dura will not forget its friendship with the Agraci people,' I declared grandly, not knowing how I would be able to help him if the Romans decided to once more strike from Emesa.

'And the Agraci will not abandon you, my friend.'

'I see a group ahead,' said Rasha suddenly.

I had not been paying attention to the terrain in front of us but I did so now and peered directly ahead to where Rasha was pointing. I saw shapes in the distance but they were not moving.

'Your eyes are keen,' said Gallia.

We halted to take stock of the situation. We had been moving slowly so as not to kick up any dust that would betray our presence and as the wind was blowing from the west we were downwind of our quarry. But gazelles are intelligent, nervous beasts and require patience and excellent horsemanship to bring down.

Rasha wrapped her reins around her left wrist and pulled the bow that had been a gift from Gallia from its case; young Spartacus did the same.

'Come Gallia,' said Haytham, 'let us show these youngsters how it should be done.'

She grinned and followed him as he walked his horse left.

'You are with me, young prince,' Rasha said to Spartacus, urging *Asad* to the right. He moved his horse forward to be adjacent to me and stopped, his face pleading with me for permission to join the desert princess.

'Off you go, then,' I told him, 'and make sure she does not come to any harm.'

He flashed a smile and followed Rasha. I turned to Scarab.

'That leaves just you and me.'

Our escort waited in their saddles as we walked our horses forward to form a wide circle around our prey. In such a hunt there are never more than two riders together so as not to alarm the gazelles.

Gallia and Haytham and Rasha and Spartacus walked their horses to each flank and then began to slowly decrease the circle as Scarab rode parallel to me as we moved forward.

I could see the gazelles clearly now – four of them – and they had spotted us. As one they bolted a short distance, stopped, changed direction, darted forward again and eventually broke into a canter.

'Keep by me, Scarab,' I said as Haytham and Gallia urged their horses into a fast walk.

As we closed in on the gazelles we resisted the urge of our horses to break into a canter until our prey decided on the direction of their escape route. I pulled my bow from its case and strung an arrow in the bowstring as the other two groups continued to close in on the gazelles. The latter then broke into a fast run and raced right, towards Rasha and Spartacus who screamed at their horses and dug their knees into their flanks to intercept the prey. Their horses bolted and both riders leaned forward in the saddles with their bowstrings drawn back. As the gazelles ran across the front of them they released their arrows.

Two of the gazelles immediately collapsed in a cloud of dust as the missiles found their mark. Rasha then whipped another arrow from her quiver, nocked it and released it, the missile hitting the hindquarters of a third beast and sending it crashing to the ground. The fourth gazelle raced away as Spartacus put more arrows into the wounded prey to kill them. Haytham looked pained as he and Gallia came alongside me and shoved his bow back in its case, while the youngsters whooped with joy and grinned at each other like idiots.

That night I gave a feast in honour of Haytham and his daughter at which the gazelles were roasted and served to the guests. The king returned to Palmyra the next morning but his daughter remained at Dura for another week. During this time she spent the mornings training with the Amazons and the afternoons in the company of Spartacus, Scarab and Peroz. Because Dura was her second home Haytham did not feel compelled to leave a bodyguard behind, as he knew she would be safe and I would give her an escort back to Palmyra, though usually Gallia and the Amazons took her back.

On the third day of her stay, in the early afternoon after I had spent a tedious two hours in the weekly council meeting, I saw Rasha and Spartacus leading their horses from the stables, Scarab and Peroz following behind. They were holding hands and looked like two young doves, gazing into each other's eyes. Domitus and Gallia were chatting behind me when I stopped and bellowed across the courtyard.

'Spartacus! Come here at once.'

Stable hands, servants and guards all turned to look at me as Spartacus stared in bewilderment, then at Rasha.

'Now!' I ordered.

Domitus and Gallia came to my side as Spartacus ran over while Rasha held the reins of his horse and her own. Peroz followed him. Spartacus halted in front of me.

'Uncle?'

'What are you doing?'

'Going to the archery ranges to train with Scarab and Peroz,' he replied, smiling at Gallia, who smiled back and shook her head.

'Not that,' I snapped. 'You must not touch Rasha.'

'We were only holding hands, uncle.'

'She is a princess of the Agraci,' I told him, 'not some servant girl to be seduced and tossed aside. You are not to see her anymore.'

My nephew looked most upset at this command and just stared at me.

'A little harsh, Pacorus,' said Gallia.

'Is it?' I hissed. 'Every time Rasha comes to Dura Haytham entrusts her wellbeing and safety to us. Imagine what he would think if he learned that his daughter had been pawed by a squire.'

'He would not like it at all,' gloated Domitus, smirking at Spartacus.

My nephew bristled at Domitus' words but did not respond. He may have been at least six inches taller than my general and almost as broad, but he had learned the hard way that Lucius Domitus was not a man to be tangled with lightly.

'I am a prince,' he corrected me.

'Well, *prince*,' I said slowly, 'I am a king and I order you to report to the commander of the guard in the headquarters building. I am sure he can find you some floors to clean.'

Spartacus was going to protest but gave me a surly bow of the head, turned around and with sunken shoulders walked back to Rasha. He spoke a few words to her, kissed her on the cheek, took the reins of his horse and trudged back to the stables.

'It is entirely my fault, majesty,' apologised Peroz.

'It is not your fault at all,' I assured him.

'It is no one's fault,' said Gallia, looking at me. 'Spartacus is a handsome young man and Rasha is a beautiful young woman. It is obvious that they would find each other attractive. Sometimes Pacorus you are such a fool.'

'I do not want to be standing before Haytham in his tent explaining why his daughter is carrying the child of a Parthian,' I replied.

'I do not think anything untoward has happened, majesty,' said Peroz gravely.

I looked at him. 'What? No, of course not. But we must take precautions to see that nothing does happen, lord prince.'

'Agraci war party approaching,' said Domitus, nodding at Rasha striding across the flagstones. Behind her Scarab was now holding the reins of three horses and finding it difficult to control them. 'Do you want me to form a *testudo* you can hide in?'

'Back me up on this matter,' I pleaded with Gallia.

'You are on your own,' she replied flatly.

Domitus was chuckling. 'It is so hurtful when allies desert you on the eve of battle.'

Rasha halted before me, her brown eyes narrowed and her nostrils flared.

'Why have you forbidden Spartacus to see me?'

I sometimes forgot that she was Agraci, a people noted for their bluntness as well as their savagery. I placed my hands on her arms and smiled.

'When you are at Dura you are my responsibility, Rasha. I am sure that your father would not approve of such familiarity with a Parthian.'

She fixed me with her eyes. 'You have forbidden him to see me but am I allowed to go where I wish within these walls?'

I smiled again. 'Of course, this is your home.'

Out of the corner of her eye she saw my nephew walking towards the headquarters building. She smiled back at me disarmingly, and then turned to Peroz.

'I would like to stay here in the Citadel, lord prince.'

Peroz stepped back and bowed to her. 'As you wish, princess.'

He really was getting more like Orodes every day.

Rasha kissed me on the cheek. 'Thank you, Pacorus.'

I let go of her arms and looked smugly at Gallia.

'Would you ask Scarab to take *Asad* back to the stables, lord prince?' she said to Peroz, who bowed his head once more to her and us and then returned to where Scarab was struggling to retain control of the horses. Rasha walked past us towards the headquarters building.

'Where are you going?' I called after her.

She turned and smiled. 'You did not say that I was forbidden to see him.'

Domitus slapped me on the arm. 'Ha! Out-foxed by a girl.'

Gallia shook her head at me and walked back to the palace with Domitus in tow as Rasha disappeared into the headquarters building.

Later in the throne room the duty officer reported to me after I had been bored rigid for an hour by Rsan, who as the city governor was responsible for the smooth day-to-day running of Dura's affairs. He took his duties extremely seriously to the point of obsession. Today's topic was the programme for the paving of all the major streets in the city, which had been temporarily suspended on account of Aaron not issuing funds for the purchase of paving stones.

'Why not?' I asked.

'Because of the yearly tribute.'

'Yearly tribute?'

Rsan nodded. 'When Mithridates, that is King Mithridates, sat on the high throne Dura did not pay any tribute, as you are aware, majesty.'

I smiled to myself. In theory every Parthian king paid a yearly tribute to Ctesiphon according to how many soldiers he could put into the field. Usually paid in gold, I had always refused to pay any tribute to Mithridates at the start of a new year, sending a letter to him instead saying that if he wanted tribute he should come to Dura and take it by force. He never did, of course, but it was an opportunity to insult him and show Dura's defiance. But now Orodes was high king I paid the yearly tribute, as did all the other kings of the empire.

'We have to pay the annual tribute, Rsan,' I told him.

'Indeed, majesty, but Aaron has informed me that because of the purchase of the Indus metal to make swords for your horsemen there is not enough money for the road-paving programme.

'The roads will just have to wait,' I said.

He pursed his lips. 'We could always raise taxes, majesty.'

'No, Rsan, we are not raising taxes. The people and the caravans are taxed enough. If they are raised the caravans might decide to travel to Syria via Hatra instead of Dura, then the treasury will be in a parlous state.'

After he had departed mumbling to himself the Citadel's duty officer updated me concerning the activities of my nephew and Rasha.

'They are both cleaning up in the granary, majesty.'

'The princess should not be given any duties.'

'She insisted, majesty,' he said. 'She is very tenacious.'

'Indeed. Well, just make sure they are accompanied at all times. On no account are they to be left alone for long periods.'

'Majesty?'

'Just keep an eye on them.'

I was glad when Rasha returned to Palmyra but I did allow her and Spartacus to say goodbye to each other in the courtyard before she rode back to her father with Gallia and two score Amazons for company. My wife wanted to see Byrd and Noora and would escort them both back to Dura for the annual gathering of the Companions, which would take place at the start of the new year.

Rasha threw her arms around my nephew and kissed him on the cheek before vaulting onto *Asad*'s back. She waved at me and then Peroz and Scarab and looked longingly at Spartacus as she rode from the Citadel. For his part my nephew looked a little forlorn and I realised that Rasha was no longer a bright little girl but a young woman and I felt sad. It seemed only yesterday when we had taken her back to her father. Where do the years go?

My spirits were further dampened at the gathering of the Companions, not because it was not good to see them all; it was. But now half of them were dead and existed only as names carved on a memorial. But at least it was good to see Diana, Gafarn and their young son Pacorus, who was now a teenager. He had inherited his parent's cheerful disposition and Diana's charm, which made him very popular among the Companions. Spartacus welcomed his parents warmly and was perhaps appreciating what a privileged life he had been living at Hatra. After my annual humiliation at the hands of Thumelicus in arm wrestling I sat with the rulers of Hatra and discussed their eldest son while the Companions made a fuss of him. All of them had ridden from the Silarus Valley all those years ago when he had been a new-born child. Now they regaled him with tales of themselves and the man he was named after.

'He looks happy,' said a smiling Diana. 'We thank you.'

'Yes,' agreed Gafarn. 'Dura obviously suits him.'

'His temper has improved,' I said, 'but it can still flare up when provoked.'

'Just like his father,' smiled Nergal.

'He looks just like him,' added Praxima.

'He is in love,' said Gallia.

Diana and Gafarn looked at her in amazement.

'It is true,' she insisted. 'A young woman has stolen his heart.'

'That is welcome news,' said a happy Diana. 'He needs someone to temper his anger.'

'It is not a straightforward matter,' I said. 'The young woman who Gallia alludes to is the daughter of King Haytham.'

'She is Agraci?' said Gafarn with concern. I nodded.

'What does that matter?' remarked Diana.

I smiled at her. 'To you, my friend, nothing at all. But to Hatra's lords and ladies and the kingdom's people a great deal. However, you will be relieved to know that I have put a stop to it.'

'Pacorus believes that he can control affairs of the heart by barking a few commands,' sniffed Gallia derisively. 'He has as much chance of that as ordering the sun not to rise each morning.'

Nergal and Praxima burst into laughter and Diana grinned at them. As always they had made the trip from Uruk to be with the Companions, and as the years passed it had become obvious that they would not have children themselves. They were now both in their forties and Praxima's child-bearing years were behind her, though Dobbai had foretold long ago that Praxima would never give birth due to the abuse her body had suffered at the hands of the Romans. And I reflected that Axsen, who was the same age as me, would also probably never have children and that saddened me – she and Orodes would have made excellent parents.

'How is mother?' I asked.

Diana looked at me with sympathy. 'Still a lost soul, I am afraid to say. She seems happy enough in her garden and Vistaspa is a great source of comfort to her, but I often catch her crying at night before she sleeps. She misses your father terribly.'

'We all do,' said Gafarn.

'All Parthia misses him,' remarked Nergal glumly.

Spartacus stayed with me at Dura when his parents returned to Hatra with their bodyguard a week later. Gafarn had told me that all was quiet with regard to the Armenians though they still occupied Nisibus and the north of his kingdom. That obviously pained him but I said there was nothing to be done about it at the present. Everything hinged upon us defeating the Romans, after which we could turn the full might of the empire against the Armenians. Though 'might' was an inappropriate word to use.

In the month after the turn of the new year I became a scribe rather than a general, sending letters to and receiving them from all four corners of the empire. Parthia may not have had paved roads such as the Romans enjoyed but it was fortunate in possessing an excellent postal system. Post stations established every thirty miles or so along major roads, at which couriers could pick up fresh horses, ensured that messages traversed the empire speedily enough.

I received word from Phriapatius at Persepolis that his eldest son had returned to Carmania to rule in his place while he organised an eastern army. He told me that progress was slow on account of the other eastern kings having few troops to spare due to their great losses in the recent civil war. He tactfully did not mention that I had been responsible for a great number of those losses but assured me that the army would be assembled in time. He asked about his son and I wrote back that Peroz was a fine young man who was well liked at Dura, and that his horsemen were a valuable addition to the army. I broached the subject of Peroz being sent back to him but his father replied that as long as I was satisfied with his son's conduct then he saw no reason for him to leave Dura.

Less welcome news came from King Khosrou of Margiana and King Musa of Hyrcania. These two rulers held the northeast frontier of the empire and could field great numbers of troops; soldiers that I had hoped could be brought west to fight the Romans and Armenians. But Khosrou informed me that the nomads who lived in the land between the Caspian and Aral seas were still raiding his northern frontier. These tribes had originally been bribed with gold by Mithridates to raid Margiana and Hyrcania so Khosrou and Musa would be fully occupied and thus not able to assist Orodes and me, but now they wished to invade Parthia and settle there. These peoples, the Saka and Huns, were wild, fierce warriors that were causing Khosrou and Musa great difficulties. As a consequence they would be able to contribute few if any troops to the army that Phriapatius was assembling.

At the end of the month I rode to Ctesiphon to see Orodes. I took Spartacus and Scarab with me as well as Peroz, who provided an escort of a hundred of his Carmanians. The whole of the empire's western border from Dura north to Hatra and Gordyene was very quiet, though I had received letters from Byrd at Palmyra telling me that his sources reported that the Armenians were still being reinforced with mercenaries from Galatia, Cilicia, Cappadocia and Pontus. And Sarmatia, no doubt. Like us the Armenians were awaiting the arrival of Crassus before opening hostilities.

Orodes and Axsen had made the massive, ramshackle palace complex their official home now that he was king of kings and the empire's treasury was once again located there.

A vast, sprawling edifice filled with several palaces, Ctesiphon's walls were covered with wooden scaffolding when we rode through the main gates. Banners showing the horned bull of Babylon and the symbol of Susiana – an eagle clutching a snake in its talons – hung from the gatehouse and from flagpoles along the central avenue leading to a second gatehouse that gave access to the walled grounds of the complex's main royal enclosure. In between these walls and the outer perimeter were barracks, stable blocks, granaries, storerooms, temples to Shamash, Ishtar and half a dozen other deities, and spacious ornamental gardens.

We left our escort to be shown to their barracks and made our way through the second gatehouse and into Ctesiphon's inner sanctum of palaces, gardens, ornamental pools and stucco statues. We trotted along the paved road that led to the courtyard fronting a huge open-ended vaulted reception hall. Before this Demaratus and four of his Babylonian officers were standing. Dressed in scale armour cuirasses of overlapping silver scales, they wore purple long-sleeved shirts and baggy purple leggings. As I slid off Remus' back and a stable hand took his reins, Demaratus walked over and bowed his head.

'Greetings, majesty, welcome to Ctesiphon.'

I had been here before, once when Sinatruces had lured me here in an effort to steal Gallia from me, other times when Phraates had been high king, and none of those visits was particularly rewarding. I found it a nest of vipers and intrigue that dripped with treachery. Hopefully it would change now Orodes was high king.

'I see the defences are being strengthened,' I said.

'The walls have been much neglected, majesty. It will take at least a year to finish the restoration work.'

I hoped we had that long before Roman sandals were tramping across the Mesopotamian desert. I held out a palm to Peroz.

'This is Prince Peroz from Carmania who has brought horsemen to fight by my side.'

Peroz smiled at Demaratus who stood to attention and bowed his head.

'Highness.'

I unstrapped my helmet and took it off as Demaratus escorted us into the reception hall towards the great red doors that led to the main throne room. Babylonian guards armed with short spears and shields stood either side of these doors and others stood along the walls.

'The walls of Seleucia are also being repaired, majesty,' remarked Demaratus, 'though it will take years to restore them to their former strength.'

Spartacus and Scarab followed behind in silence and behind them walked Demaratus' officers. The guards opened the doors to allow us to enter as we walked towards the dais at the far end of the hall where Orodes and Axsen awaited us. White marble tiles and white-painted walls and ceiling made the chamber look cavernous and the sound of our boots on the tiles echoed around the room.

I halted before my friends and bowed my head while Peroz, Spartacus and Scarab went down on one knee before Parthia's king of kings and his wife. Near the walls stood nobles and their wives dressed in rich robes, the ladies adorned with fine jewellery. Around the dais itself were stewards and scribes, and dressed in red robes bearded priests from the Temple of Marduk in Babylon. Axsen had obviously brought her nobles and spiritual advisors from her city to Ctesiphon. Demaratus bowed to them both and then took his place beside the dais on Orodes' right side.

'Welcome, King Pacorus,' said Orodes formally, 'Lord High General of Parthia and victor of many battles.'

There was polite applause at his declaration.

'Welcome Prince Peroz, son of King Phriapatius and our valuable ally, please rise.'

Peroz rose to his feet, leaving Spartacus and Scarab kneeling with heads bowed.

'Rise all of you,' commanded Orodes.

'We are glad to see you, Pacorus,' said Axsen who was wearing a rich purple robe with gold edging, a jewel-encrusted crown on her head and a gold necklace at her throat.

'And I you, highness,' I replied, causing her to smile.

The formalities out of the way, Orodes dismissed everyone in the throne room and asked to see me in his study in the palace's private quarters to the rear of this chamber. Axsen asked Peroz, Spartacus and Scarab to escort her on a tour of the palace while I walked with Orodes along a corridor with walls decorated with paintings of animal hunts.

'Axsen does not like it here,' he complained. 'She would rather be at Babylon.'

I could understand that. Babylon was where she grew up and its palace was just as splendid as Ctesiphon's, perhaps more so.

'Do you have to live here?'

He frowned. 'The high king of the empire should live in its capital, inconvenient though it may be. Besides I am having it renovated, at considerable cost I may add.'

'I noticed,' I replied.

We arrived at his study, a slightly austere room with pigeonholes along one wall filled with old documents. I had visited it many years ago just prior to the Battle of Surkh when I had helped to defeat Narses, and afterwards had been rewarded with a great quantity of gold by a grateful

Phraates. The large desk was in exactly the same position in front of wood panelling that was decorated with a beautifully painted map of the Parthian Empire. Orodes sank into the ornate chair behind the desk and pointed at another in front of it, in which I sat.

Orodes looked deflated as slaves offered us wine, pastries, wafers, fruit and yogurt. He took a *rhyton* of wine but waved away the offer of food. I helped myself to both wine and food as he ran a finger around the rim of his *rhyton* and then dismissed the slaves and ordered the two guards in the corridor to close the door.

'The Armenians have refused my overtures to extend the peace treaty,' he muttered.

'Hardly a surprise,' I replied, taking a mouthful of what was excellent wine. 'Crassus and his army will be arriving soon. Artavasdes no doubt sees little merit in peace with the prospect of conquest dangling before his eyes. But he will not make any hostile moves before Crassus arrives.'

He looked up at me. 'Perhaps we might think of striking at the Armenians before he does so.'

I rose from the chair and walked over to the map of the empire on the wall behind him.

'Unfortunately, geography does not favour such a move.' I pointed at Nisibus, which was occupied by the Armenians. 'If we muster our forces at Hatra for a strike against Nisibus it will take around a month before the troops of Dura, Babylon, Media, Hatra, Mesene and Atropaiene are gathered together. Before that happens the Armenians will themselves muster over one hundred thousand troops and march them south to seize the city of Assur and the crossing point over the Tigris. If they hold that place then they can prevent troops from Media and Atropaiene to the east from reinforcing us.'

He too rose and stood next to me, tracing a finger from Nisibus down to Assur. 'There is nothing to prevent them doing so now, Pacorus.'

I smiled. 'I have reinforced Assur's garrison with Silaces and seven thousand horse archers. The Armenians have no siege engines and so it is too hard a nut for them to crack.'

'How many soldiers can be raised to fight the Armenians and Crassus?' he asked.

'Just over one hundred thousand in total, not including Surena's forces in Gordyene.'

He raised an eyebrow at this.

'To call upon Surena will leave Gordyene exposed to another Armenian invasion,' I said.

'A pity, Pacorus, he is an excellent commander.'

'He is,' I agreed, 'but at the start of the war we need him in the north to stop Gordyene falling and then, after we have hopefully dealt with Crassus, reinforcing our efforts against the Armenians.

'We are fortunate that Artavasdes is the Armenian king and not his father. He would not have waited until Crassus arrived before striking south.'

185

'It was a greater stroke of luck the Romans diverting their attention to Egypt when they did,' added Orodes, who retook his seat and gestured for me to do the same.

'I have to tell you, my friend,' I said, 'that even if we manage to defeat Crassus there is no guarantee that we can also stop the Armenians. I have heard reports that they are recruiting great numbers of mercenaries to swell their army. You may wish to consider relocating your court to Esfahan or another eastern city.'

He looked aghast at my suggestion. 'To do so would in an instant destroy any authority I might have. The king of kings of the empire does not flee from his enemies, Pacorus.'

'At least consider moving to Babylon, then,' I suggested. 'Its walls are at least strong and sit behind a moat. The defences here are derisory.'

'I have every confidence in you, Pacorus,' he smiled, 'to prevent the enemy reaching these parts.'

Unfortunately I did not share his confidence though I did not tell him so. The army of Hatra had formerly been the western shield of the empire, a highly trained force of professionals who were the envy of other kings. But now that army had suffered great losses at the Battle of Susa and subsequently at Nisibus and north of Hatra. It had lost its commander, my father, and its morale was low. Of the armies of the other kingdoms that would be called upon to fight Crassus, Media and Babylon had lost many sons at Susa and the soldiers of Atropaiene were average at best. That left only Nergal's horse archers from Mesene and my own army as a match for the Romans but they would be heavily outnumbered. How I wished my father was still alive.

I looked round the room and saw the empty chairs and thought of another time when I was in this study.

'Is something troubling you, Pacorus?'

'I was just thinking of when I was in this study with your father, just before the Battle of Surkh where we defeated Narses. He was sitting where you are now. Across the table were my father, Gotarzes, Vardan and that snake Chosroes, and myself of course. Of all of them I am the only one left alive. It seems an age ago.'

He looked at me with sympathetic eyes.

'You know,' I continued, 'when I escaped from Italy I thought that life would be so simple. I would marry Gallia, inherit my father's throne and live out the rest of my life as the King of Hatra.'

Orodes nodded thoughtfully. 'The gods had other plans for you. They decided that you should be a great Parthian warlord.'

'The next few months may make you re-evaluate that assessment,' I replied.

The next day we rode back to Dura.

With Byrd's network of informers in Syria and Cilicia I would know the moment Crassus arrived at Antioch, which would give me time to gather together the armies of Dura, Hatra, Babylon, Media, Atropaiene and Mesene. Garrisons would be left at Hatra and Assur, reinforced by sizeable numbers of horse archers to attack the Armenians should they advance south from Nisibus. Artavasdes would attack Hatra, of course, and I hoped he would because I knew that he would be unable to breach the city's walls and would be compelled to besiege it. But there were no water supplies near the city and so he would be forced to send detachments to the Tigris sixty miles to the west. There Silaces and his horse archers riding from Assur would assault them. While the Armenians rotted in front of Hatra I would fight an outnumbered Crassus and at least stop him in his tracks. And afterwards I would march east and engage the Armenians before the walls of Hatra and destroy them – a fitting tribute to the memory of my father.

As we rode across the pontoon bridge over the Euphrates towards Dura's Palmyrene Gate I began to whistle to myself. With luck and the help of the gods we would be able to resist the Roman invasion and throw the Armenians out of my brother's kingdom. But as I trotted up the city's main road to the Citadel I was unaware that the death of a young woman would throw my carefully prepared plans into chaos.

The first intimation of the event that was to plunge the empire into turmoil was when I rode through the Citadel's gates into the courtyard and saw Gallia surrounded by the Amazons at the foot of the palace steps. Many were in tears and others were comforting each other and I felt my stomach tighten. I dismounted, gave Remus' reins to a stable hand and walked to my wife's side. She looked pale and shaken and I saw she was clutching a letter in her hand. A disconcerting silence filled the courtyard and I saw that Gallia's eyes were misting with tears.

'What is it?' I asked.

She did not answer but held out the letter to me. She had been holding it so tightly that the words were difficult to read but I straightened it out as the eyes of the Amazons bore down on me. It was from Silaces at Assur, who had been informed by Surena that Viper had died giving birth to his son, who had been delivered stillborn. I closed my eyes and prayed to Shamash that He would welcome them both into heaven. I opened them to find the eyes of my wife's bodyguard still looking at me. What could I say to assuage their grief? Nothing. I remembered the woman who had looked like a girl, my young squire who had fallen in love with her and who had made her his queen and felt immensely sad.

'I am sorry,' was all I could say.

I was also sorry for Surena for now he was alone in his cold, grey palace with nothing to do but brood over his loss. I decided that I would write to Atrax to ask him to visit Surena. They were close friends and the King of Media's cheerful disposition would hopefully stop Surena sinking into the pit of despair.

'How little you know him, son of Hatra,' remarked Dobbai as I sat alone with her that evening on the palace terrace after our daughters had been taken to their bedrooms. Gallia and the Amazons had locked themselves in the banqueting hall where they were holding a farewell meal for Viper and her child. It was a strictly all-female affair and so I was left to reflect on her death alone.

'I have known him as a boy from the great southern marshes, as a squire, as an officer in my army and as a king,' I snapped at her. 'I think I know him very well.'

'You know part of him. He was a wild creature that you took out of its environment and you sought to tame him like a horse. But a beast that has been taught to perform and dressed in fine clothes is still wild underneath.'

I held my head in my hands in despair. 'Surena is not a beast; he is a man who has just lost his wife and child.'

She waved a hand at me dismissively. 'Have it your own way. But I tell you that he will lash out like an enraged demon because of this, disregarding the consequences. You should prepare.'

'Prepare for what?'

'The unexpected.'

Knowing that Dobbai's warnings were not to be dismissed lightly during the next few days there was a permanent knot in my stomach as I expected bad news to arrive at Dura. Perhaps Crassus had speeded up his journey, or maybe Artavasdes had decided to start the war without waiting for the Romans to arrive. But after a week nothing had happened and so I began to relax. The army was up to full strength and ready to march. The cataphracts had received their new swords and production of the new arrows for the horse archers was almost completed. All was quiet along the border with Roman Syria and Haytham's kingdom was not being troubled.

I visited the Agraci king a week after my return to Dura and took Spartacus and Scarab along with me. As usual the road to Palmyra was thronged with traffic going east and west and the desert oasis itself was filled with caravans. Haytham gave a great feast the night we arrived and I kept a close eye on my nephew and Rasha, but though they exchanged pleasantries and spent some time in each other's company there was no show of affection between the two, for which I heaved a sigh of relief. Her father had almost certainly earmarked a potential husband for his daughter and it would not be a Parthian, even if he was a prince.

Between the courses of roasted lamb stuffed with rice, nuts and raisins, and dates; platters heaped high with succulent mutton; and great quantities of unleavened bread, Byrd informed me that thus far there was no sign of Crassus but his arrival was eagerly awaited in Antioch.

'He has boasted that he will conquer all Parthia and reduce its kings to servants of Rome.'

'Servants?' I said, scooping up a slice of lamb covered with cooked onion. 'I think "slaves" is more appropriate. What do you hear of Alexander Maccabeus in Judea?'

Byrd screwed up his face. 'He still fight but is more the hunted than the hunter. Romani tighten their grip on Judea and Egypt.'

I thought of the thousands of weapons that I had supplied to the Jewish rebels and the high hopes of their leader. 'Still, at least he is still resisting. Are the Armenians still recruiting mercenaries?'

He nodded. 'Artavasdes has sworn to make Hatra an Armenian city just like Nisibus. Rumour tell of a great map he has commissioned that shows Kingdoms of Hatra, Gordyene, Media and Atropaiene as provinces of Armenian Empire.'

I nearly choked on my piece of lamb. 'What?'

'He thinks he is the new Tigranes,' said Byrd.

I took a gulp of water. 'We will have to disabuse him of that notion.'

The next day I spoke with Haytham and told him that everything was in place with regards to dealing with Crassus and the Armenians.

'What part would you like me to play in this plan?' he asked me.

'You may do as you like, lord king.'

We sat alone cross-legged on carpets and among cushions in his great tent. Outside the bustle and noise of Palmyra filled the air. They were the sounds of much activity and indicative of great prosperity, but Haytham seemed concerned.

'I must wash the swords of my warriors in the blood of my enemies, Pacorus, to avenge the death of Vehrka, else I will appear weak to my people.'

'When the Romans arrive, lord,' I said, 'there will be more than enough enemy blood to go round.'

'The Romans will again try to take Palmyra. Though we are a nomadic people and can relinquish this place easily enough, I must defend it. To abandon it would be shameful.'

'The Romans will invade Parthia first, lord,' I told him.

He looked surprised. 'It would make more sense to march from Emesa east to Palmyra and then Dura.'

'The Romans will wish to join with their Armenian allies to the north, lord. They will cross the Euphrates at Zeugma to gain access to the land between that river and the Tigris.'

'Your squire, the tall one with broad shoulders and black hair,' he said suddenly. 'He pays too much attention to Rasha. I saw them exchanging glances last night. Tell him that she is not for his eyes.'

The threatening tone in his voice told me that it had been a mistake to bring Spartacus to Palmyra. I assured Haytham that in future I would leave my squires at Dura.

'The Nubian you can still bring. He at least knows his place.'

Despite his incurring the animosity of Haytham, which would normally have resulted in his swift execution, Spartacus was in high spirits as we made our way back to Dura. As usual the road was heaving with traffic – mules and camels loaded with goods, carts being pulled by mangy donkeys, travellers on foot, mystics, guards on horseback escorting their masters' caravans – the air was filled with dust and the aroma of animals and their dung. These sights and smells gladdened my heart for they were a sign of commerce and Dura's prosperity.

'These people and their animals stink,' complained Spartacus behind me.

We were riding by the side of the road, the smell and dust of hundreds of animals and men filling the hot, still air.

'What you are seeing is the lifeblood of the empire,' I told him. 'Without the Silk Road and the caravans that travel along it Parthia would be impoverished. Hatra would be nothing but an outpost in the desert without the Silk Road.'

'They still stink,' he mumbled.

'What do you think of the princess, Scarab?' I heard him say to my Nubian squire.

'A jewel of the desert,' replied Scarab.

'I like her,' proclaimed Spartacus.

'You cannot have her,' I said to him. 'Haytham was most displeased by your behaviour at the feast.'

'I did not touch her,' he protested.

'Haytham is no fool. He sees and hears everything. Do you think he did not notice a great strapping oaf leering at his daughter, or catching her eye and eliciting a smile from her? You delude yourself and you would be wise not to get on the wrong side of him.'

'He does not frighten me,' he remarked casually.

I halted Remus and wheeled him around. The fifty horse archers of my escort behind also halted.

I jabbed a finger at my cocky nephew. 'You should fear him. He would slit your throat without a thought if he thought you had dishonoured his daughter.'

He was outraged. 'I would never dishonour Rasha.'

I let my hand drop. 'I know that. But you must understand that she is Agraci and will marry an Agraci lord.'

'I am a prince and higher than a lord,' he declared proudly.

Scarab grinned at me from under his floppy hat.

'He does not care if you are a prince. You are Parthian and Rasha is Agraci and the two do not mix.'

'You are his friend, uncle. In Hatra people say that the Agraci and Parthians are mortal enemies, and yet you and he visit each other and regard yourselves as brothers.'

I shook my head. 'It is not the same. I am not lusting after his daughter, which by the way is conduct unbecoming of a Parthian prince.'

'I am only half Parthian,' he said. 'I was raised a Parthian but I was born a Thracian.'

I smiled. Gafarn and Diana had promised that he would know of his blood parents and they had kept their word.

'What is a Thracian?' asked Scarab as we resumed our journey back to Dura.

'A native of Thrace,' I said.

'And where is Thrace, majesty?' he enquired further.

'A land far to the west of here,' I replied.

190

'You were born in this land?' he asked Spartacus.

'I did not say that. I said I was born a Thracian,' he snapped.

Scarab, clearly intrigued, continued to press my nephew for answers. 'Then where were you born?'

'Italy if you must know. I was born in Italy and my father and mother were both slaves. Are you satisfied?'

Spartacus' smile and cheerfulness disappeared as he sat sullenly in his saddle.

Scarab broke the silence. 'I too was born to slaves. We have no say over the circumstances of our birth, only the life we live afterwards.'

'Well said,' I told him. 'What Spartacus forgot to tell you, Scarab, was that when they died his parents were both free. More than that, his father was also a great warlord, one of the greatest the world has ever known.'

I looked back at them both and saw Scarab slap my nephew on the arm. 'I had no idea. I thought you were just a rich, pampered prince.'

'He is that too,' I said.

Chapter 9

Two days after we had returned to Dura another letter arrived from Silaces, this time addressed to me. It was delivered during the weekly council meeting in the headquarters building where a sweating Arsam, fresh from his workshop, was informing everyone that the last deliveries of the new arrows had been issued to Vagises' horse archers: the final batch of half a million steel-tipped missiles that could go through our own shields with ease and could also pierce mail armour. The expenditure, as Aaron informed us after Arsam had been dismissed, had been extremely high, not only in steel but also in additional labour costs.

'The armouries are already filled with bronze arrowheads,' he stated, reading from the detailed itinerary handed to him by one of his clerks, 'and now they are to be packed with additional arrows. I have to tell you, majesty, that the army is draining your treasury.'

'You sound just like Rsan when he was treasurer,' said Domitus, causing my governor to frown.

'We must be prepared for when hostilities break out, Aaron,' I said.

'My men are eager to test their new arrows on the Romans,' said Vagises.

'I remain to be convinced,' sniffed Domitus. 'No Roman army has ever been defeated by arrows alone. It will take more than a few archers to stop Crassus.'

'We will have more than just a few archers,' I told him.

'Perhaps Prince Peroz might like to issue his men with the new arrows,' suggested Aaron, 'then we could charge his father and thus alleviate the burden on Dura's treasury.'

Domitus shook his head and smiled while Rsan nodded in agreement and Dobbai snoozed in a chair by the window. She opened her eyes and tugged on Gallia's sleeve as she gazed into the courtyard at a courier pacing towards the headquarters building.

'Ill tidings.'

Moments later one of the guards knocked on the door and entered, saluting stiffly.

'Letter from Assur, majesty.' He handed me the folded parchment, bowed his head and then left, closing the door as he did so.

I broke the seal and read the contents. I threw the letter on the table.

'Surena has attacked Armenia.'

Domitus took the letter and read it himself, running a hand over his cropped skull as he did so.

'Looks like the peace with the Armenians is over, then.'

I placed my elbows on the table and held my head in my hands. Silaces had reported that Surena had written to him that he had unleashed his Sarmatian mercenaries, supported by five thousand horse archers, against the Armenians. Silaces did not know why he had done so other than to provoke Artavasdes into retaliating and launching another invasion of Gordyene, which Surena could once again defeat.

'I told you, son of Hatra,' said Dobbai, 'when a wild creature is in pain it will lash out in fury, and so it is.'

'You should write to Surena ordering him to desist his activities,' said Gallia.

'It is too late for that, child,' said Dobbai. 'The marsh boy has tossed a burning torch onto a pile of hay. It will cause an inferno that will sweep over the land.'

'Even if Surena obeyed you,' said Domitus, 'the Armenians will want revenge for what he has done.'

'They will want his head on a spear and Gordyene returned to Armenian rule,' said Dobbai. 'Are you prepared to grant them those things, son of Hatra?'

I looked at her. 'No.'

At a stroke my carefully laid plans for the forthcoming campaign had been wrecked by Surena's foolishness. In his black despair the notion of burning and looting Armenian towns and villages may have been appealing but his actions had placed Hatra in great danger. At the end of the meeting I gave the order to prepare the army to march north and afterwards sent riders to Ctesiphon and Uruk to alert Orodes and Nergal respectively of developments and to ask them to bring their armies north. I wrote other letters to Atrax and Aschek alerting them of events in Gordyene and requesting that they march their forces west to Hatra. We would now have to fight and destroy the Armenians before Crassus arrived.

Dura's army was up to strength and fully equipped but I worried about the forces of the other kingdoms. Babylon had been ravaged in the recent civil war and had lost many fine soldiers at the Battle of Susa, as had Media, and while I did not doubt the courage and leadership of Orodes and Atrax I was concerned about the quality of the soldiers they led.

Nergal's horse archers I had no worries about: they were well-equipped and professional soldiers. My only regret was that there were only five thousand of them, the other five thousand he had previously brought with him being the retainers of his lords and thus part-time warriors. And then there was the problem of Hatra's army, formally one of the most formidable in the empire but now shaken by losses and defeats. Only Dura's army remained as strong and formidable as it had always been.

As the cataphracts and horse archers were gathered at Dura and squeezed into the legionary camp that held the Durans and Exiles, I summoned the lords to the city to explain to them my plan of action and their part in it. As usual the one-eyed Spandarat was their leader of choice. His hair was almost entirely grey now and was thinning alarmingly, though he was still possessed of that irreverence that he had displayed when I had first come to Dura.

I sat beside Gallia in the throne room and explained to the score of grizzled old warriors that once more they would be responsible for the safety of my kingdom and would provide garrisons for the two large forts at the northern border, the other one on the southern border as well as the additional smaller forts in between. Apart from a small retinue of full-time soldiers that were in effect their bodyguards, the only soldiers that Dura's lords could call upon were the farmers that worked their lands and the servants that lived in their strongholds.

'We would prefer to fight,' said Spandarat to murmurs of agreement from his hoary companions.

'Believe me,' I said, 'there will be plenty of fighting to do in the coming months, but for the moment I need you here watching my back while I deal with the Armenians.'

Gallia smiled at him. 'Spandarat, we would like you to move into the palace and take care of our daughters.'

Once it had become clear that I would have to march north to fight the Armenians, Gallia had declared that she and the Amazons would be joining me to avenge Viper's death. I could not see how the Armenians were responsible for Viper's demise but made no protest – in this war we would need every bow and sword.

He winked at her and smiled. 'Would be an honour, princess.'

'Excellent,' I said, 'that is settled.'

They grumbled between themselves for a while but Gallia mingled among them and won them over. It was not difficult to do. They had always admired her for her fighting prowess and forthright nature and she in turn always told them how dear they were to her. Initially they had lusted after the blonde-haired, blue-eyed Queen of Dura but now they were older they regarded her as an adopted daughter and doted on her.

It was just as well that they were so compliant as the next day I received a despatch from Gafarn stating that Armenian troops were mustering at Nisibus. A great many of them! His missive dripped with fear and uncertainty and it was clear that his nerves needed steadying.

'Hatra is a mighty fortress,' said Domitus dismissively as I sat in his tent while he read the letter. 'The Armenians have no siege engines and even if they did it would take them many weeks to drain the city's moat and breach the walls.'

'Gafarn is not a soldier like you. All he sees is the Armenians massing to the north and Crassus about to arrive to the west. Hatra badly needs a victory.'

He tossed the letter on the table. 'Hatra badly needs a king who can fight.'

'You are being unkind, Domitus. Gafarn is capable enough and he has Vistaspa to command his army.'

Domitus stood and started to pace up and down, tapping his right thigh with his vine cane as he did so – always a bad sign.

'Vistaspa is old and had the stuffing knocked out of him at Susa. Does he even command Hatra's army now? Vata should have been leading it but he managed to get himself killed. There is only one logical course of action.'

He stopped pacing and fixed me with his stare.

'Would you care to enlighten me, Domitus?'

'You must go to Hatra and take command of its army.'

In theory it might have been a laudable idea but if I did as he was suggesting it would fatally undermine the authority of Gafarn and make it impossible for him to remain king. There was already a growing number of dissenting voices within the city that were questioning the legitimacy of his reign. They said that it was not right that a former slave of the royal household should have succeeded my father, especially as the rightful heir was alive and ruling Dura. They wanted the two kingdoms to be united under one ruler and it was not Gafarn.

'I cannot do that, Domitus, for to do so would emasculate my brother's authority and that I am not prepared to do.'

He walked back to his chair and retook his seat. 'You've been spending too much time in the company of Orodes. You are beginning to sound like him. In any case you are lord high general so in theory you can take control of Hatra's army as part of your duties.'

'No. Gafarn needs actions that reinforce his authority, not undermine it. We shall muster the armies of the kings at Hatra and then engage the Armenians, and afterwards march north to retake Nisibus.'

'And what about Crassus?'

I managed a weak smile. 'Hopefully we will have defeated the Armenians before he appears. But if he arrives sooner then I will have to deploy the reserve to delay him until we can march back south to engage him.'

He looked baffled. 'Reserve?'

I tapped my nose. 'Bringing back Silaces from Gordyene was not only designed to muzzle Surena's aggression.'

'Just as well,' he said ironically.

'It was also for the purpose of creating a reserve. Lord Herneus, the governor, can muster ten thousand horse archers from the lords under his control. Added to the seven thousand under Silaces that makes a sizeable number of horsemen who can be deployed rapidly north or west.'

Domitus was not convinced. 'Seventeen thousand horse archers cannot defeat the Roman legions plus auxiliaries and Roman cavalry.'

'You are right, my friend, but they can slow them down and give us time. Time, Domitus that is the key. I also intend to transfer the horse archers under the command of Apollonius in western Hatra to Herneus. That will give him an additional five thousand men.'

'And in doing so,' said Domitus, 'you will sacrifice those towns in western Hatra.'

I held out my palms. 'What can I do? I cannot be in two places at once. Thanks to Surena the Armenians are preparing to launch an attack against Hatra. Ideally we would have been waiting for Crassus at the border but now have to battle the Armenians instead.'

It took only a week before Nergal and Praxima arrived with their five thousand Mesenian horse archers and the thousand camels loaded with food, fodder, tents, spare weapons and arrows. They had crossed the

195

Euphrates near Uruk and then travelled up the western bank of the river through Agraci territory before reaching Dura's southern border. They camped two miles south of the city while their king and queen were lodged in the Citadel. I was disappointed that Nergal did not bring ten thousand men but he told me that he could not empty his kingdom of soldiers in the face of the impending Armenian and Roman threat.

From Palmyra came Byrd and Malik with their fifty bearded, dishevelled scouts on their wild horses, some of them approaching middle age now but having lost none of that semi-feral nature and appearance that set them apart from the rest of Dura's army. They really were a law unto themselves; paid by Byrd from an allowance that was sent to him each month by Aaron and taking orders from no one save their paymaster and Malik. Most of them were Agraci but even Malik said that his own people viewed them as rough loners. Domitus believed Dobbai had created them by casting a spell but the truth was that they had become the lucky mascots of the army. Soldiers are very superstitious and when setting out on campaign every man always looked for the wiry men dressed in ragged robes that galloped out of camp before dawn and were not seen again until dusk.

It took a further week for the Babylonians to arrive: five hundred cataphracts of Orodes' bodyguard, a further five hundred horsemen of Axsen's Royal Guard, seven thousand horse archers and five thousand spearmen on foot. There were in addition a further three thousand foot soldiers from the Kingdom of Susiana, Orodes' homeland that had been the location of the battle where we had finally defeated and killed Narses. Unfortunately for Susiana its troops had been on the losing side that day and had suffered accordingly. Still, it was fitting that a small number had marched with their king to represent him and their kingdom. I was delighted to discover that he had also brought Demaratus with him as his second-in-command.

The Babylonians made camp across the Euphrates opposite the Citadel, a sprawling collection of different sized and coloured tents pitched in ever widening circles around the purple marquee of Orodes, which though rectangular and larger than the rest was not as grand as the great pavilion used by his predecessor, King Vardan, while on campaign.

'And there are no half-naked slave girls to serve you wine,' he informed me as I settled into a plush chair in the central area of his marquee.

'That is a shame. I always looked forward to seeing their oiled bodies when I visited Vardan on campaign.'

In order to leave us alone he dismissed the four officers from the Royal Guard in their gleaming dragon skin armour. He slumped into a chair opposite. He looked as though the weight of the world was on his shoulders.

'Axsen has gone back to Babylon,' he said. 'She would not stay at Ctesiphon alone and when I am away she likes to have Nabu and Afrand close by her.'

Nabu was the high priest at the Temple of Marduk in Babylon, a dour, imposing individual who exerted great control over the city's population. Afrand was high priestess at the Temple of Ishtar, a beautiful seductress who wore few clothes to cover her voluptuous body.

He sighed. 'So we march again, my friend. It appears to be our destiny to spend our lives living in tents and tramping to war.'

'The gods have willed it so.'

'I sometimes wonder if they are any gods,' he said bitterly, 'or if there are why we waste our lives worshipping them and building great temples in their honour.'

'You sound just like Surena.'

His brow furrowed. 'What are we to do with him? I made him King of Gordyene as a reward for liberating the province but it seems I have created a monster that is out of control.'

'He is still a good commander,' I said, 'but the deaths of his wife and child have unhinged him.'

He looked at me sympathetically. 'As a man I cannot blame him for his anguish but as high king I must rebuke him for his recklessness when I next see him. Unless the Armenians kill him and defeat his army, that is.'

I thought of the training that Surena had received at Dura and that day when I had inspected his army.

'I do not think you need worry about his battlefield prowess, Orodes.'

My friend's mood was lifted later when I gave a great feast in the palace and invited all my senior officers and those of Mesene, Babylon and those with Peroz, the banners of these kingdoms hanging on the wall. The chamber was filled with laughter and chatter as the wine and beer flowed and men reaffirmed friendships and forged new ones. Thumelicus insisted on arm wrestling a great hairy brute from the Zagros Mountains who served in the ranks of the Susianans and we were stunned when he failed to beat him with ease. The bout ended in a draw and with the two of them, both very drunk, embracing each other and weeping like small children. It was a most curious spectacle.

Orodes was seated on the top table in the place of honour flanked by Nergal and me, with our wives beside us. Next to Gallia sat Domitus with Miriam beside him. She was uncomfortable with the rowdiness going on a few feet in front of her. She picked at her food and engaged in polite conversation but appeared horrified at the behaviour of some of her husband's officers.

'It is good that they can indulge themselves,' he told her, 'some of them won't be coming back.'

Matter-of-fact as usual, his words did nothing to brighten her mood.

Gallia, once again in the company of her former second-in-command Praxima, displayed no such concern. She and the Amazons were eager to get to grips with the Armenians and the Romans, particularly the Romans. Much about Rome I admired, especially their military methods and just as Spartacus had copied them in Italy so had I adopted them for Dura's army, but Gallia hated the Romans. She hated them all for enslaving her, for invading Dura when we had returned to Parthia and, strangely, for reducing the Gauls to a subject people, despite the fact that she derided her own race for their passivity.

I was still worried about Peroz's welfare and was debating whether to leave him and his men behind at Dura. But the affront to his honour would have been great and in any case I needed all the soldiers I could muster, especially with Nergal's shortfall, and so he would be coming with us. In any case he and his men had been doing a lot of work on the training fields working with Vagises and his horse archers, so to leave him behind would be most unprofessional on my part.

Regarding the Babylonians, their foot had fought beside the legions at Susa and their horsemen had likewise battled the army of Narses and Mithridates. The purple-clad foot soldiers had suffered heavy casualties and had crumpled during the battle but at least they were professional soldiers, unlike those from Susiana who had been recruited from farmers and hill men judging by their threadbare appearance. I would have preferred it if Orodes had left them in his homeland but for political reasons he had felt compelled to bring them.

Dura's army, marching twenty miles a day, could reach Hatra in under ten days, but Babylon's foot soldiers were not as physically fit as Domitus' men and so the rate of march our combined forces achieved was fifteen miles a day. Fifteen miles tramping across hard-packed dirt under a hot sun with the air thick with dust kicked up by thousands of feet and tens of thousands of animals. The assembled army numbered fifteen hundred cataphracts plus their squires and camels, five hundred men of Babylon's Royal Guard, twenty thousand horse archers, eighteen thousand foot soldiers and their hundreds of wagons and mules, and the camel trains of Dura and Mesene – two thousand beasts in all.

And because there were no water holes between the Euphrates and Hatra water was strictly rationed. So we marched with parched throats, sweating bodies and dust-covered clothes. The luckiest ones were the scouts: companies of horse archers who provided an immediate screen around the army and, further out, Byrd and Malik's ghost riders riding far and wide to ensure we not surprised by bands of Armenian raiders. If the enemy was mustering at Nisibus it was highly likely that they would send parties of horse south to gather intelligence as to our movements.

'There is no point in them sending out scouting parties,' said Domitus sweating in his helmet under a spring sun. 'All they need to do is talk with the drivers and guards of the caravans to learn what is going on.'

'One of the disadvantages of so many caravans traversing the empire,' I said. 'The Silk Road carries gossip as well as goods.'

Apart from the scouts on patrol all the other horsemen were on foot leading their horses. There was no point in sitting in the saddle tiring our horses while we marched at the rate of a legionary on foot carrying his *furca* – a four-foot long pole with a crossbar at the top, to which was strapped a rolled-up leather bag holding his stash of personal equipment, which could weigh up to sixty pounds. Then there were of course the oxen pulling wagons loaded with Marcus' siege engines. So Gallia, Peroz, Nergal, Praxima, Orodes and myself led our horses as Domitus left his position in front of the colour party of the Durans carrying their golden griffin standard to join us.

He looked at Orodes. 'Shouldn't you be on your horse, being king of kings and all that? I bet your brother never walked while on campaign.'

'First of all,' said Orodes, 'he was my stepbrother. Secondly, I do not intend to change my habits just because I am high king.'

Domitus turned to Peroz. 'What about you, young prince? Do you think King of Kings Orodes should be on his horse?'

Peroz, clearly awed by being in Orodes' presence, was reticent to say anything, smiling awkwardly and then bowing his head when Orodes looked at him.

'Leave him alone, Domitus,' said Gallia. 'Orodes has always been down to earth and will not change despite being high king.'

Orodes smiled at her. 'Exactly.'

'What is more remarkable?' I asked. 'That Orodes is king of kings, that Nergal and Praxima are regarded as gods in Mesene, or that Domitus managed to find a woman who would agree to be his wife.'

Everyone laughed and Nergal slapped Domitus on the back. It was just like the old times when we had all been together and Orodes had been a mere exiled prince. How things had changed since then.

For five days we made steady progress in a northeasterly direction towards Hatra. Each night we erected a large camp with an earth rampart, ditch and palisade toped by stakes that contained all the men and animals. It was a giant square in the middle of the barren landscape, each side measuring twelve hundred yards with four gates at each point of the compass. The men of Dura and Mesene slept in oiled leather tents; the officers of Babylon in round, voluminous tents and the foot soldiers of Babylon and Susiana in the open with only a blanket for warmth. I thought it most unprofessional but Demaratus informed me that the royal treasury did not have the money to purchase tents for its foot soldiers.

'But it has enough money to provide the men of the Royal Guard with great canvas lodgings when on campaign,' I remarked one night as I walked round the camp with him and saw the sorry sight of his foot soldiers sleeping on the ground, huddled together in their threadbare blankets.

'They are lords and the sons of lords, majesty. Men of quality who live in fine houses and enjoy rich living.'

'They are soldiers, Demaratus, just like these men lying on the ground.'

He looked in puzzlement at me and then at his foot soldiers. 'These men are not nobles, majesty, they are merely poor villagers or homeless city dwellers who joined the army because it gives then regular pay and food.'

'But you expect each one of them to lay down his life if called upon.'

'Of course, it is their duty.'

'And what of your duty?' I asked him.

'My duty is to serve my king and queen, majesty.'

'Of course, but what of your duty to your men?'

He looked at me as though I was trying to trick him. 'I do not understand, majesty.'

'Every man in my army is clothed, fed, housed and treated the same regardless of whether he is the highest-ranking cataphract or the lowliest legionary. Each soldier in Dura's army knows that his weapons and armour are the best that money can buy, and he also knows that his commanders, right up to the king, will never waste his life needlessly.'

'But everyone knows that Dura's army is...' he stopped himself from saying any more.

'Speak freely.' I ordered him.

'Forgive me, majesty, but it is common knowledge that Dura's king is beloved of the gods and that its army is protected by the spells of his, that is your, sorceress. That is why it is invincible.'

I laughed aloud. 'If it is invincible then it is because it is well trained and well armed and every one of its soldiers is proud to be a part of it. It is the small things, Demaratus, that make the most difference.' I put an arm round his shoulder. 'For example, if you provide your foot soldiers with tents they will fight better for you.'

He looked at me and then at the thousands of men sleeping on the ground in front of us in bewilderment.

'Truly,' I said.

He obviously found it hard to believe me but it was hardly surprising. Parthian nobles were born into privilege and viewed those beneath them with contempt, especially lowly foot soldiers who could not even afford a horse. It was convenient for them to believe that Dura's army was so effective not because of its lowly foot soldiers but rather because it had the favour of the gods and its very own sorceress.

On the sixth day, roughly halfway between Dura and Hatra, Byrd and Malik came galloping back to the army with a score of Hatran horse archers. It was two hours before midday and their horses were sweating and breathing heavily as they were brought to where the kings were once again walking with their own horses. As Byrd and Malik raised their hands to us their commander slid off the back of his horse and went down on one knee in front of me.

'Urgent message from the King of Hatra, majesty.'

He reached into a small leather bag slung over his shoulder, pulled out a folded parchment and handed it up to me.

I held out a hand to Orodes. 'Get up. This is King of Kings Orodes. His eyes should read it first.'

The officer, mortified, looked wide eyed at Orodes and went down on his knee again.

'Forgive me, highness.'

Orodes took the letter, broke the wax seal and read the contents. He shook his head, sighed and handed it to me. Peroz, Nergal, Gallia and Praxima looked with interest at the document I was reading. I finished and pointed at the officer.

'You and your men report to the quartermaster and get those horses watered. They look as though they are about to drop, and get up.'

He rose to his feet. 'I am ordered to return with an answer as quickly as possible.'

Behind us the great column of men, wagons and animals continued to march northwest towards Hatra as Orodes took off his floppy hat and wiped his brow with a cloth. He looked at the others.

'It was from Gafarn. A great Armenian army is approaching Hatra and he urgently requests our presence in the city.'

'It will take us another seven days to reach Gafarn,' I said as the Hatrans followed Byrd to find Strabo. Malik dismounted from his horse and joined our little group.

'The horsemen could be there in three days,' suggested Orodes.

I heard footsteps and turned to see Domitus and Chrestus running towards us.

'Problems?' asked a concerned Domitus.

'A large Armenian army is approaching Hatra,' I said. 'Our presence there is urgently requested.'

Domitus shrugged. 'So they close the gates and let the Armenians waste themselves in a useless siege. They will retreat in a few days anyway when they learn of our approach.'

'Gafarn has sent an urgent appeal,' said Orodes gravely, 'we must answer his request. It would be best for the horsemen to ride to Hatra as quickly as possible.'

Domitus looked at me in alarm. 'I would strongly advise against dividing the army.'

Orodes looked most concerned. 'Ordinarily, Domitus, I would agree with you. But these are not ordinary circumstances. Hatra is one of the largest cities in the empire. If it falls it would do irreparable harm to our cause and would embolden the Armenians further, to say nothing of the Romans.'

Domitus took off his helmet and ran a cloth over his sweaty crown. 'Why would Hatra fall? Have Armenian siege engines suddenly sprung from the earth?'

Orodes frowned at his levity. 'I intend to ride forthwith to Hatra with my horsemen. I will not command you to do the same Pacorus and Nergal, but as friends I ask you to do this for me.'

What could we say? Domitus was correct in what he said but Orodes only saw Hatra in danger and believed that he had the means to save it. Above all he believed that the office of high king demanded that he put the interests of the empire foremost in all things. Gafarn, shaken by his earlier defeats, had obviously panicked but Orodes could not refuse an appeal for assistance from another king in need.

'My horsemen are at your disposal,' I said.

'As are mine,' added Nergal.

'And mine,' said Peroz loudly before blushing.

Domitus stood with his hands on his hips shaking his head as Orodes laid a hand on Peroz's shoulder.

'I have heard that there was courage in Carmania and now I have seen it with my own eyes.'

Peroz puffed out his chest with pride as Domitus replaced his helmet on his head.

'You and Byrd and your scouts will remain with us,' he told Malik, 'otherwise we will be blind.'

'I will stay with the foot,' I announced. 'It would be wrong for all the kings to desert them.'

Orodes and Nergal nodded. Nergal used to be my second-in-command and was used to leading horse archers in battle while Orodes had formally commanded Dura's cataphracts, so I had every confidence that they would reach Hatra safely.

An hour later fifteen hundred cataphracts and their squires, five hundred Babylonian Royal Guards and twenty thousand horse archers were riding into the distance and kicking up a great cloud of dust in the process. Gallia had decided that she and her Amazons would also remain with the army to assist Byrd and Malik's scouts.

'Has anyone thought that another Armenian army might be heading south towards us?' she asked as she stretched out her lithesome legs in my command tent that evening.

'Have seen no enemy,' remarked Byrd as he chewed on a hard biscuit and sipped at a cup of warm water.

'Gafarn needs to get a grip on his imagination,' said Domitus, pointing at me. 'If you were king of Hatra, which you should be, you would relish the prospect of luring the Armenians into a siege knowing that a relief army was only a few days away.'

I held up a hand to him. 'Don't start all that again.'

Later, as Spartacus and Scarab were cleaning my own and their swords, my nephew casually mentioned that he had spoken to a woman earlier.

'Woman?'

He slid my sword back in its scabbard and picked up his own.

'Yes, she was standing by my horse while I was grooming him.'

I looked at Gallia in confusion. 'There are no women in Dura's army aside from the Amazons.'

Spartacus shrugged. 'She was not one of the Amazons. Perhaps she was attached to the Babylonians.'

'I doubt it,' I replied. 'Are you sure you haven't been suffering from sunstroke?'

Scarab laughed but Spartacus froze him with a stare. 'She was real enough. Said that the city of Assur was in danger.'

Alarm coursed through me like a raging torrent. 'What did you say?'

Spartacus stopped cleaning his blade. 'She said that Assur was in great danger.'

'What did she look like, this mystery woman?' queried Gallia.

Spartacus thought for a moment. 'Tall, thin, long black hair. It was a most curious thing. Even though I had never met her before she felt familiar. Her eyesight must have been poor, though.'

Gallia leaned closer to him. 'Why?'

Spartacus grinned. 'She called me "little one".'

The next morning he and Scarab were mounted on their horses in front of the Amazons as I stood before an increasingly irate Domitus. Zenobia held the reins of Epona as Gallia, her hair tied in a plait behind her back, put on her helmet.

'You are riding to where?' asked my general.

'Assur, Domitus, it is in danger.'

He looked behind him at Byrd and Malik who had been alerted that we were riding to Assur.

'Have your scouts been riding near to Assur.'

Byrd shook his head, as did Malik.

'Assur too far east,' said Byrd.

Domitus turned back to face me. 'Why would you want to go to Assur?'

'It is in danger, Domitus.'

'We have received no word from Herneus appealing for aid,' he said, still disbelieving that I was riding with my wife, two squires and the Amazons to Assur.

'We received word last night, Domitus,' I replied.

Domitus would not let the matter go. 'No one entered the camp last night or I would have heard of it.'

I walked over to him so that Spartacus would not hear me. 'It was Claudia, Domitus, she was the one who delivered the message.'

He did not realise who I was alluding to. 'Claudia?'

'The wife of Spartacus.'

He went to laugh but then saw that I was deadly serious. 'She is dead. I saw her body burn to ashes.'

'Listen my friend. You will have to trust me in this. Get the army to Hatra and await me there. But I cannot ignore this warning.'

He looked at me and then Gallia and scratched his head. He then looked at Byrd and Malik. 'These two and their scouts are staying with me otherwise this army is blind and one of us has to keep his wits about him.'

I smiled and slapped him on the arm. 'I will see you at Hatra.'

It took us two days of hard riding to reach Assur.

A rider galloped ahead of us to announce our arrival as our tired beasts plodded their way along the dirt track, their heads bowed from exhaustion. A squad of foot guards from the gatehouse dressed in white leggings and shirts barged people out of the way with their spear shafts and shields to allow us to enter Assur. The city was its usual bustle of disordered activity on our right side, the southern part of the city where the general population lived and worked: a sprawling collection of one- and two-storey homes and businesses squeezed together alongside stables, brothels, market squares and animals pens. Overcrowded and noisy it also stank of animals, rotting food and sweating people.

'I need a bath,' said Gallia, stating aloud what I was thinking, and turning her nose up at the pungent aroma that was being brought to our nostrils by a southerly wind.

Our escort left us at the gatehouse of the governor's palace, a large, three-storey building with shuttered shooting ports on every level. The palace was surrounded by a high stone wall with round towers positioned in each corner and along its length, though I saw few guards either on the walls or standing guard by the open twin gates. The palace itself was a single-story rectangular building arranged around two courtyards and as I dismounted in front of its steps the governor, Lord Herneus, escorted by three of his senior officers, descended them and bowed his head to me.

'Greetings, majesty.'

Gallia also dismounted and handed the reins of Epona to a stable hand. The Amazons behind us did likewise.

I stretched out my arms as Remus and the other fatigued horses were led away to the stables.

'Get their saddles off quickly and rub them down,' I commanded, 'they have had a hard ride.'

I turned to Herneus. 'As have I. Are you well, Herneus?'

He nodded his bald head. 'Well, majesty. This is a most unexpected visit, and it is good to see the Queen of Dura grace this city.'

Gallia had taken off her helmet and smiled wanly at him. She looked pale and tired, we all did.

'We need to bathe to wash the grime from our bodies,' I said, 'but while we are taking advantage of the palace's comforts you need to send couriers to your lords to order them to muster their men and bring them here, and fetch Lord Silaces also.'

He looked confused. 'Lord Silaces is not here, majesty. He and his men left for Hatra a week ago, along with my lords and their horsemen.'

My legs suddenly felt weak. 'Hatra?'

'Yes, majesty. The king summoned all the horse archers in and around Assur to his side to meet the Armenian threat, foot soldiers too.'

I hardly dared to ask the next question. 'How many men of the garrison remain?'

'Five hundred.'

I looked at Gallia and then back at Herneus while the Amazons stood in tired groups.

'Is there a problem, majesty?' he asked.

'Has there been any reports or sightings of Armenians in this area?' I replied.

He looked at his men.

'None, lord,' said one dressed in a bronze and iron scale armour cuirass and a sword in a rich red leather scabbard at his hip.

I looked at Gallia and the Amazons, then at Spartacus and Scarab, all of them wearing tired expressions.

'We will refresh ourselves, Herneus. Please arrange it.'

The guest quarters in Assur's palace were even more luxurious than the ones at Babylon, though not as expansive. The walls were painted white and decorated with murals of Parthian victories over the eastern nomads, while the rooms were both airy and spacious. As we changed out of our dirty clothes slaves filled with water a great round bath sunken into the floor in a white-tiled room next to our bedroom. Throughout the palace grooves in the paved floor brought fresh water to the kitchens, latrines and private chambers, and other tiled channels beneath the floors carried wastewater to the city's sewer and then to the nearby Tigris.

Slaves laid out fresh robes on our bed and took away our old ones to be cleaned as I eased myself into the clear, cool water as Gallia did the same opposite me. She had untied her plait and she slid under the water and then re-emerged and began to refresh her supple body with soap made from water, mineral salts and cassia oil. Despite giving birth to three children her belly was still flat and her skin did not bear any stretch marks or scars, unlike mine. By comparison I had scars on my back, one on my face, another on my leg and a new one on my left arm courtesy of Nicetas at Seleucia.

After we had bathed sweet-smelling slave girls wearing short white gowns massaged the aches and pains from our bodies with oil, their long fingers working the balm into my flesh and lulling me into a sense of utter calm.

We were awakened from our deep slumber by frantic banging on the door.

'Majesties, the governor urgently requests your presence in the hall.'

We rose bleary eyed and dressed in our new robes; I in a white silk shirt and baggy red leggings and Gallia in a flowing white robe.

'You look ridiculous,' she told me as I pulled on my boots and buckled my sword belt.

'And you look very feminine,' I smiled.

She went to the door, opened it, told the guard to be silent and ordered him to fetch her a pair of leggings and a top. He returned breathless with brown leggings and a beige shirt. The slaves had taken away our silk vests so to hide her modesty she put on her mail shirt and then we went to see the governor.

The sight of guards and officials running round and the ringing of alarm bells outside told me that something was wrong before I set eyes on Herneus' grim expression. He was a man of only medium height but his iron-like visage and deep, commanding voice gave him an air of authority. Now in his fifties, he had held the east of the Kingdom of Hatra for over twenty years.

205

I strode into the main chamber and Herneus rose from his chair on the dais to let me sit in it. He had also arranged for another to be placed beside it for Gallia.

'I take it the Armenians have arrived,' I said indifferently.

Herneus raised an eyebrow. 'You knew they were on the way, majesty?'

'I suspected. Where are they?'

Herneus pointed at a dust-covered soldier. 'Tell the king.'

The man went down on one knee and bowed his head. 'Ten miles north of here, majesty.'

'Get up,' I told him. 'How many?'

He glanced nervously at Herneus before answering. 'Thousands, majesty, mostly foot soldiers. I also saw rafts on the river being pulled by ropes from the bank.'

I dismissed him and turned to Herneus. 'You have closed the gates?'

'Yes, majesty.'

'Get the people into the temple district.' Herneus nodded to one of his officers who scurried away to organise the evacuation of the people from their homes and businesses to the temples in the northeast area of the city. These buildings were large and could accommodate the city's residents, and hopefully their priests would provide them with solace. The main temples in the city were dedicated to Marduk, the supreme god of Babylon, the Sky God Anu and the Sun God Shamash. But there were also places of worship dedicated to the Storm God Adad and Assur, the chief deity of the city since Assyrian times.

'Our defences will be stretched thin, majesty,' said Herneus. 'There are not enough men to man the entire length of the walls.'

I nodded. 'That was the intention all along. We will reconvene in an hour.'

With Gallia I went back to our quarters where our cleaned clothes were laid out on the bed. I changed into my leggings, vest and white shirt and Gallia did the same. Spartacus and Scarab brought my leather cuirass and helmet, the latter having a fresh goose feather crest. Zenobia reported to Gallia and after eating a quick meal of fruit and cakes the five of us walked to the main hall. Herneus and his officers were waiting for us in their scale armour cuirasses, helmets in the crooks of their arms.

'Let us take a look at the enemy,' I said, striding past them towards the entrance hall.

As we walked from the palace across the courtyard and through the gatehouse groups of soldiers ran past us heading towards the walls. I thanked Shamash that both my father and his father, King Sames, had devoted much time and resources on strengthening Assur's defences. In addition to the river that protected two sides of the city and a moat that covered the other two sides, a double wall, the space in between filled with buildings to house troops of the garrison, surrounded the city on the landside. On top of the outer wall was a parapet protected by battlements, the latter containing narrow slits from where archers could shoot on attackers below.

I gestured for Herneus to walk beside me.

'I had hoped that when Tigranes died Armenian military expertise would die with him, but it appears that I was wrong. By massing a great army north of Hatra they have drawn all the forces of the western empire there, including my own army, but it appears that it was a ruse to divert our attention from their real target – this city.'

'If Assur falls,' he said grimly, 'then the enemy will control the kingdom's main city in the east and a major crossing point over the Tigris.'

'And will deny our allies in the east the means to get forces over the Tigris,' I added. 'They have played their hand well.'

I could tell that Herneus was infuriated with himself that he had allowed his lords, Silaces' horse archers and half his garrison to be taken away from him, and perhaps a part of him was also annoyed with his king, but his sense of loyalty would never allow him to say so.

We walked through the gate in the inner wall and then ascended the steps that led to the parapet on the outer wall beside the Tabira Gate, in the northwest of the outer wall. All three of the city's gates had been closed by now and troops of the garrison, armed with bows, stood ready behind the battlements, but they were spread very thinly. The length of the outer wall facing the landside was over a mile in extent, with the rest of the perimeter fronting the river to the north and east.

The Armenians were making no attempt to approach the walls; rather, they were deploying their forces to the west and south of the city in preparation for an assault against the three gates. Their troops were dressed in bright uniforms of blue, red and orange; huge banners bearing the Armenian six-pointed star fluttering in the southerly breeze. I thanked Shamash that a deep, wide moat encompassed all the landward side of the city else the enemy would swarm over the walls and into the city with ease.

It was now three hours past midday and despite the breeze it was very warm notwithstanding that the sun was beginning to descend in the west, right into our eyes. The battlements were high on the outer wall to protect everyone on the parapet so we stood on large steps to see over the walls.

'They mean to attack immediately,' I said. 'They wish to take advantage of their superiority in numbers and will have the sun behind them when they assault us.'

I turned to Herneus. 'Send pigeons to Hatra and Irbil to request aid.'

He turned to one of his officers and gave him the order, the man running down the stone steps to a waiting horse that would take him back to the palace. Hatra was only sixty miles to the west; Irbil ninety miles in the opposite direction. A pigeon could reach Hatra in just over an hour and Irbil thirty minutes more. If we could hold out for two days then Assur might yet be saved.

'They are going to try to smash through the gates,' said Herneus, pointing ahead at what appeared to be a great tree trunk mounted on a large four-wheeled carriage. I now understood why the Armenians had been using rafts on the Tigris: it was to transport their battering rams. One ram was drawn up directly in front of the Tabira Gate and I could see another opposite the Western Gate. A messenger confirmed that a third was being readied to smash through the South Gate.

'When they get near the gates they will be cut down easily enough,' said Gallia confidently.

But I could see frantic activity around the battering ram as its large crew assembled a protective roof of planks topped with iron sheets over the tree trunk and its carriage. And behind the ram I could also see foot archers in bright blue tunics and leggings. They would provide covering missile volleys when the ram approached the gates.

'We must concentrate our forces at the three gates,' I said. 'Herneus, give the order to abandon the defences on the riverside. The Amazons and a hundred of your men will defend the Tabira Gate, the rest of your garrison will be divided between the other two gates.'

He nodded and then beckoned over another of his officers to convey my order.

'One more thing,' I said. 'Send soldiers to the temples asking that anyone who can shoot a bow is to report to the walls immediately.'

Each of the gatehouses on the outer wall had two storeys, each one having shooting slits for ten archers, and now they began to fill with troops as the garrison was concentrated at the three entry points to the city. Slaves from the palace ferried quivers of arrows from the armouries as the Armenians completed their preparations and made ready to assault Assur.

After an hour the enemy began its advance. In the van were the battering rams – sharpened tree trunks mounted on sturdy carriages with four thick wheels fashioned from the same thick trees that had been used to make the rams, each of them protected by crude iron and wood roofs.

Men wearing no armour or helmets clustered all around the ram's carriage underneath its roof. They strained to heave the heavy ram towards the Tabira Gate. The trunk was secured to the carriage by ropes so the Armenians would have to literally ram it against the gates, relying on its weight and momentum to smash through the thick wood.

Behind the ram were the foot archers and behind them blocks of spearmen who would force their way into the city once the gates had been smashed in. They looked very colourful in their red tunics and yellow leggings, though as far as I could see they wore no armour on their bodies or heads. Armed with short stabbing spears and oval wicker shields, they would be useless in a battle but very effective for butchering civilians if they got into Assur. The archers and spearmen were grouped in blocks that numbered around a thousand men: two thousand archers and five thousand spearmen in total. Seven thousand Armenians were about to assault the Tabira Gate.

Herneus received reports from the other two gates that approximately the same number of Armenians was deployed against them – over twenty thousand troops against six hundred.

'Long odds, majesty,' he said without emotion.

'Hopefully we can thin their numbers before they reach the gates,' I replied. The Amazons were now lining the walls either side of the Tabira Gate and were inside the gatehouse itself, ready to shoot at the oncoming enemy. Full quivers lay on the parapet behind each Amazon, though I was concerned that there appeared to be too few for our requirements.

'My lords and Lord Silaces took many quivers with them when they rode to Hatra,' reported Herneus.

'We will need runners, then,' I replied.

Gallia looked at me. 'Runners?'

'Boys, children, majesty,' replied Herneus, 'who run around picking up the arrows that the enemy shoots into a city under siege.'

'They run the risk of being hit by other arrows while they do so, surely?' she said.

I shrugged. 'If the enemy captures the city they will be either killed or enslaved anyway. See to it Herneus.'

He bowed his head and left us at the same time as those who had answered my summons from the civilian population began to ascend the steps to the parapet. My heart sank when I saw them. Most of them were either very old or crippled and deformed in some way: humpbacked, bandy legged, crook-backed or one-eyed.

'This lot would be better off dead,' I mumbled.

Gallia jabbed me in the ribs. 'As they have volunteered to stand against the enemy the least you can do is show some courtesy.'

I smiled at her. 'If it will amuse you, my sweet, then of course.'

An elderly man, tall with sinewy arms turned dark brown by years in the sun, was brought before us by one of the garrison's officers. He must have been over seventy at least and had a bow slung over his shoulder.

He went down unsteadily on one knee before us. 'I am Asher, majesty, and have been instructed to report to you.'

Gallia walked forward and helped him to his feet. 'Rise, Asher. We are glad you and your men are here, are we not Pacorus?'

'Ecstatic,' I replied without conviction, earning me a Gallic glare.

'I served under your grandfather, King Sames, majesty,' Asher declared with pride.

I nodded. 'I am sorry that the Armenians have dragged you out of retirement, Asher.'

'I can shoot a bow as well as any man, majesty,' he said defiantly.

'I have no doubt,' I replied, doubting whether his aged eyes would be able to even see the Armenians let alone shoot at them. 'You and your men will take up positions either side of my wife's warriors.'

'The famed Amazons,' he beamed.

'Indeed,' I said.

209

'They're coming,' shouted Spartacus behind me as suddenly the air was filled with the din of drums and horns.

I turned and walked to the steps next to the shooting position he was standing behind and stood on them so I could see over the battlements. Already arrows were hissing through the air and striking the walls as the archers behind the ram began shooting at us.

I jumped down. 'To your positions!' I shouted.

Asher and his hundred misshapen wretches were directed to their positions as Gallia kissed me on the lips. 'The gods be with you.'

'And you,' I replied.

She stood next to Zenobia as I pointed at Scarab and Spartacus. 'You two are with me.'

I ran into the gatehouse and then ascended the steps to the roof clutching my bow with two quivers slung over my shoulder. Each quiver held thirty arrows and on average a skilled archer could loose up to three aimed shots every seven seconds, but such a rate of arrow expenditure would soon exhaust our ammunition supplies and also our archers, particularly the Amazons. Like all Parthian archers they used recurve bows made from sinew, horn and wood, but because they were women their bows were slightly smaller and thus had a reduced draw weight so they would tire less quickly. It did not mean their arrows were any less deadly than those used by any of my other soldiers, though. A bow is, after all, no more than a spring whose power comes from its user and the springs of the Amazons were deadly.

I watched the ram edge closer to the walls and above the tumult of the horns and drums I could hear the curses of the officers who were in charge of it as they shouted at their men to redouble their efforts. Behind the machine the blue-uniformed archers maintained a steady barrage of missiles at the gatehouse and walls, and then the Amazons began shooting.

The ram was around six hundred paces from the walls when their arrows were shot from the battlements. Gallia had given orders that half the Amazons were to shoot at the men pushing the ram, the other half loosing missiles at the archers behind them. Above all they were to shoot accurately.

Loosing arrows at a steady rate of five every minute, soon unprotected enemy archers were being felled as bronze tips landed among their densely packed ranks: two hundred and fifty arrows being shot at them every minute. The other half of the Amazons, including all those in the gatehouse, shot at the approaching lumbering ram. I released an arrow then nocked another, my nephew beside me relishing the chance to show off his archery skills to Scarab beside him. He shot an arrow, nocked another, shot that and then strung another in the space of a few seconds.

'Don't waste arrows,' I told him. 'Choose your targets.'

He flashed a grin. 'Even Scarab could not miss that ram, it is so large.'

Arrows clattered against the walls and hissed overhead as the Armenian archers tried to silence our shooting. But Assur's defences had been well designed and it was all but impossible to shoot an arrow through the slits in its battlements from several hundred paces away.

Many of the ram's crew were hit and disabled and killed, but replacements were sent from the ranks of the spearmen who were following the archers. Individuals ran forward holding their shields above their heads as they tried to reach the ram. Most did but some were hit and collapsed to the ground with arrows in them as more of their comrades were despatched to take their places. And all the time the ram got closer to the gates.

I left my position and ran to the right side of the gatehouse to check on Gallia. There she was, calmly selecting a target and loosing an arrow. I kept my head down for the volume of enemy arrows being shot at us was prodigious. I saw Asher pull back his bowstring and release it, and then watched the man beside him jump onto a step to look over the wall and being struck in the face by an Armenian arrow.

I returned to my shooting position and used another five arrows then reached again into my quiver. Empty!

'Arrows!' I shouted but there were none left and one by one those either side of me stopped shooting once they had exhausted their ammunition. After a while only empty quivers remained.

I looked ahead and could see the amount of missiles being directed at the enemy was dropping alarmingly as we ran out of arrows. I ran down the steps to the next level and out onto the parapet. Gallia and some of her Amazons were still shooting but the others were similarly out of arrows.

I ran to Gallia's side. 'Deserting your post, Pacorus?'

'We have no arrows left. As soon as you are out withdraw to the inner wall.'

Above our heads hissed dozens of arrows being loosed by the Armenians, many more hitting the walls in front of us.

'We are going to die here,' she said, looking above at the hundreds of arrows in the air.

Suddenly slaves from the palace came up the steps to the battlements clutching large bundles of arrows and began dumping them on the parapet. Others carried bundles into the gatehouse. A man in a short-sleeved white tunic and sandals placed at least a hundred arrows behind Gallia and bowed his head.

'These are arrows shot into the city?' I asked.

'Yes, highness.'

'Have many boys died collecting them?' asked Gallia.

'Dozens, highness, both boys and girls.'

I touched Gallia's elbow. 'This is no time to die,' and then I ran back into the gatehouse as other slaves brought more bundles of arrows to the outer wall. Our shooting re-commenced and felled dozens of enemy archers but now the ram was close to the gatehouse – no more than three hundred paces away – and though resembling a pincushion was slowly but inexorably rumbling towards the gates. I cursed the fact that the bridges across the moat were made of stone otherwise we could have fired them, but as it was even if we poured burning oil onto the ram its roof would have protected it.

Armenians archers were collapsing in heaps as Gallia's women and the army of cripples shot them down but still the ram came on. Now it was less than two hundred paces from the gates and I could hear the men groaning as they hauled its bulk forward.

'They will reach the gates soon,' said a concerned Spartacus.

'Then we will greet them with our swords,' shouted Scarab, releasing his bowstring.

The roof at the front of the ram was angled down to prevent us shooting arrows into its interior as it got nearer and so our arrows became less effective as it closed to within fifty paces and stopped.

'They are about to ram the gates!' I shouted.

Though wagons and braces had been piled up behind the gates there had been no time to reinforce them with rubble to build a bank of earth. We heard a great collective groan and then the ram rumbled forward across the bridge and into the gates. There must have been forty or more men under its roof and they managed to give the ram enough momentum to splinter the gates and force them apart. The spearmen out of range of our own archers began cheering and hoisting their spears aloft as the ram was hauled back in preparation for another charge. By now my right arm and shoulder ached from shooting arrows and the inside of my fingers were red-raw from clutching the bowstring.

The Armenian archers were taking a fearful battering as every arrow loosed by the Amazons found its target, but to give them credit they held their ground and carried on shooting, though I noticed that the density of arrows being directed at us had dropped markedly since the start of the assault. They too must have been suffering ammunition shortages.

There was a great blast of horns and those archers still left standing about-faced and ran back towards the spearmen, while the latter lifted up their shields in front of them and began to march forward, just as the ram was once more hurled against the gates. This time there was a cracking sound and then a grinding noise as the ram prised the gates apart and forced the supports behind them back. The outer wall had been breached.

'Back to the inner wall!' I screamed as the spearmen approached the stone bridge.

I was nearly out of arrows again so I grabbed the three remaining behind me and gestured frantically to the others to get down the steps in the gatehouse and to the inner wall.

And then I heard a new sound.

Chapter 10

At first I thought my mind was playing tricks on me. But I stopped and cocked my ear to where the attackers were positioned and heard it again: a clear, pure sound that cut through the tumult of the Armenian drums and horns and the shouts and cries of their soldiers. I heard it again and this time it was louder and nearer and I knew that it was not in my imagination. I walked to the shooting slit and stepped onto the stone steps beside it to peer over the battlements. The shrill sound of dozens of trumpet blasts echoed across the plain once more and I saw the horizon filled by a wall of white shields and helmets as five thousand Durans and five thousand Exiles marched to our relief.

I ran to the right side of the gatehouse and shouted at those below.

'Domitus is here! Relief has arrived!'

Gallia and Zenobia looked up at me in confusion and then both peered through their shooting slits and then hoisted themselves onto the battlements and raised their bows in the air and began shouting 'Dura, Dura'. Soon all the Amazons were chanting the same followed by Asher and his ragged recruits.

Below us the Armenian spearmen, on the verge of forcing their way into Assur, halted their advance as their officers received word that a hostile army had suddenly appeared in their rear. The Armenian archers were already reforming to shoot at the oncoming mail-clad soldiers, but they were short of ammunition, tired and their numbers had been drastically thinned and they were no match for Domitus' men. They loosed one volley, which thumped harmlessly into the wall and roof of locked shields, and then melted away as the legionaries abandoned their *testudo* formation and increased their rate of advance.

Beneath the gatehouse there was silence as the ram's crew abandoned their monster and hurried back to what they perceived to be the safety of their spearmen, but not before a few were felled by eagle-eyed Amazons who had some arrows left. There were still five thousand Armenian spearmen remaining and as they shuffled into position to form one great block to face Domitus' men, half of the latter suddenly veered to their right to swing round the left flank of the enemy spearmen who had been facing the Tabira Gate.

I saw the light catching a golden emblem and knew that it was the Durans who were going to attack the spearmen below us. The latter were now moving slowly towards the legionaries, their densely packed formation resembling a great rectangle. Moving closer towards their destruction.

I stood from my vantage point and thanked the gods that they had given me an opportunity to witness Parthia's finest soldiers in action. The Durans were drawn up in two lines, each one made up of five cohorts, but it was only the first line that was sent in against the Armenians: two and a half thousand men against twice their number. I felt sorry for the Armenians.

Each cohort was made up of six centuries – three in the first rank and another three behind – each century made up of eight ranks, each rank containing ten men. But on this occasion the Duran front line was reorganised to extend each cohort so that all six centuries were in the first line. Ordinarily this would take some time but Dura's army was so well trained and drilled that it took only a few minutes before there was a frontage of thirty centuries advancing against the Armenians.

The Duran line was now only eight ranks deep and was mighty thin but it made no difference. A blast of trumpets signalled the attack and the legionaries increased their pace. The first two ranks hurled their javelins at the advancing Armenians at a range of around thirty paces – six hundred long, thin iron shanks attached to a heavy wooden shaft arching into the air before smashing into enemy shields, flesh and bone. These ranks then drew their swords and sprinted at the enemy as the legionaries in the third and fourth ranks behind them, as they had done many times before, launched their javelins over the heads of their comrades in front before also drawing their short swords. Train hard, fight easy.

The first two ranks of the Durans used their shields as battering rams against the ill-equipped and poorly trained Armenians, smashing steel bosses into faces or toppling over hapless spearmen before stabbing at them with frenzy. The Armenians, their front ranks almost annihilated by Duran javelins, began to give ground immediately as *gladius* blades cut through wicker shields with ease and pierced torsos, sliced open bellies, put out eyes and mutilated groins. Then the spearmen ran.

It was as though a collective madness had seized the Armenians for as one those still living dumped their spears and shields and fled in all directions. The Durans maintained their formation as they continued to advance at a steady rate, stepping over pierced and mangled bodies as they did so.

So engrossed had I been in the spectacle that I had not noticed that Gallia had joined me on top of the gatehouse. She smiled as I turned to see her and in my elation was suddenly gripped by a desire to rip off her clothes and make love to her, here, on the top of the tower while death was being meted out to the enemy below. I grabbed her and kissed her long and hard on the lips as below us the Armenians were being slaughtered. I pressed her tightly to my body, clutching her buttocks and forcing her groin into my loins. Surprised, she pulled back.

'What are you doing?' she giggled.

'I want you,' I said, pulling her back against me.

'It is a miracle, uncle,' I heard a voice behind me declare.

'If Haytham does not kill him I might,' I whispered in her ear as I reluctantly released her.

Spartacus and Scarab came to my side, both grinning like fools.

'It is a miracle sent by the gods,' declared Scarab.

The Durans were close now, the front ranks walking towards groups of Armenians who had halted a few paces from the moat below and were falling to their knees and holding up their arms in a plea for mercy. In the distance I could see the other half of the Durans marching to support the Exiles who were engaging enemy forces at the Western and Southern gates.

In the general excitement I had not noticed that fresh bundles of enemy arrows that had been collected by runners had been deposited on the parapet behind the Amazons and Asher's men. I heard fresh screams below and saw that Gallia's warriors were shooting at the hapless Armenians grouped on the other side of the moat. Asher's men soon enthusiastically joined them and a general slaughter ensued. I did not order a stop to it and neither did Gallia. The Armenians had been on the verge of entering the city and if they had succeeded would have put everyone to the sword, such is the fate of cities that fall to an assault. Every one of the Amazons would also have been raped before being killed so they had little inclination to show mercy.

The Durans halted while the Armenians were cut down, resting their shields on the ground and admiring the archery skills of the Amazons. In five minutes around two thousand men had been either killed or wounded, the survivors being saved only by the fact that once more there were no arrows left.

I saw Domitus, white crest atop his helmet and greaves around his shins, walking up and down the line congratulating individuals and sharing jokes with others. He then walked forward to within shouting distance of the gatehouse.

He cupped a hand to his mouth. 'Have you finished your archery training?'

I raised a hand to him. 'All done, my friend. It is good to see you.'

He pointed his cane at those Armenians still standing, who were rooted to the spot in terror.

'Do you want them killed?' he asked.

'They should join their comrades in the underworld,' hissed Gallia.

'Kill them, uncle,' agreed Spartacus, who drew his sword. 'I will lend a hand.'

'No,' I called to Domitus. 'Disarm them and bind them. Lord Herneus can sell them as slaves.'

He raised his cane in acknowledgement and then arranged details to secure the prisoners.

'You show mercy in victory, majesty,' said Scarab admiringly.

Gallia shook her head but said nothing while Spartacus slid his sword back in its scabbard.

'Go to the Western Gate,' I told him, 'find out what is happening and report back to me when you have found out. Take Scarab with you.'

They raced away and Gallia and I went to ground level to welcome our saviours into the city. When we reached the smashed gates I heard the thunderous voice of Thumelicus hurling abuse at a hundred men manhandling the ram back across the bridge.

'Put your backs into it, you lazy bastards, its just a sapling tied to a cart. Heave!'

Actually the ram was far larger and more imposing than it had appeared from the top of the gatehouse, and it took a good ten minutes before it had been shifted back over the bridge. It must have weighed tons with its iron-plated roof and great trunk that had forced the gates apart.

'Even you look small beside it,' I shouted to Thumelicus as his men sat on the ground panting after their exertions. He smiled and raised his arm in salute.

'Looks like we got here just in time,' said Domitus, striding towards us and tapping his cane against his thigh. He looked as though he had just completed a short walk.

Gallia embraced him, eliciting cheers and whistles from those of his soldiers nearby. I extended my hand and he clasped my forearm.

'You are a most welcome sight, my friend,' I told him. 'Where are Demaratus and his Babylonians and the soldiers of Susiana?'

He smiled. 'Guarding the wagons and mules. About five miles away. Nice and safe and far enough away not to do any damage.'

I put an arm around his shoulders as we turned and walked back into the city.

'I thought I ordered you to take the foot to Hatra? Not that I am ungrateful that you disobeyed my orders.'

'I would never disobey your orders, Pacorus,' he said with a straight face. 'Truth is we were on our way to Hatra via Assur when we came across this city being attacked and decided to lend a hand.'

Gallia laughed. 'Very droll,' I replied.

He winked at Gallia. 'You gallop off into the desert with a hundred riders heading for Assur, mumbling some nonsense. So I think: "Something's wrong." Remember I have known you a long time. So I gave the order to march after you. In any case there are enough troops in Hatra to beat off a dozen armies.'

'More than you think,' I replied. 'Gafarn ordered Assur's lords and Silaces to present themselves at Hatra, in addition to half the city garrison.'

Within the hour we had all gathered at the palace where Herneus gave a report on the day's events. It was dark now and the legions, men from Susiana and the Babylonians had made camp a mile west of the city; the Armenian prisoners having been placed under armed guard in the area between the inner and outer walls north of the Tabira Gate. A preliminary head count had put their numbers at eleven thousand.

'Yours to do with as you see fit,' I told Herneus.

Of the rest of the Armenians, many had been killed at the Western Gate when they were assaulted by the Exiles and rather less at the Southern Gate, some having given themselves up and the rest having fled over the stone bridge across the Tigris into Media.

'King Atrax's forces will deal with them,' said Herneus.

'We will wait here for Atrax to arrive with his men,' I announced, 'before continuing our march to Hatra.'

216

The next day I stood on top of the gatehouse at the Tabira Gate and watched the Armenian prisoners collect the bodies of their comrades who had been killed the day before. Under armed guard they had first created funeral pyres from their own wicker shields, the rafts they had used to bring the battering rams down the Tigris and wood from the rams themselves. The bodies were dumped on top and the wood lit. The nauseating stench of roasting flesh soon filled our nostrils as black smoke rose into the sky from the dozen pyres that ringed the city.

'I never get used to that smell,' I said to the others.

'Better Armenian flesh burning than Parthian,' said Herneus grimly.

'Clever attempting to take this city, though,' mused Domitus. 'If it had fallen then Hatra would have faced being threatened from three directions – Nisibus, Assur and Zeugma.'

I stared at the heaps of black, charred cadavers being licked by flames. 'Wars are not won by standing on the defensive. It is time to march against the Armenians and defeat them once and for all.'

The next day there was a service of thanksgiving in the city's temple dedicated to Shamash, at which all those who had volunteered to stand beside the garrison and the Amazons on the city walls were honoured. Almost five hundred had fought on the battlements shooting arrows at the Armenians and a further six hundred had been formed into a reserve at the palace, ready to be committed against any enemy incursions. The Armenians would have made short work of the collection of cripples, old men, young boys and men missing limbs who now stood near the altar being blessed by the high priest for their courage. They were each given five drachmas for their loyalty, paid out of Herneus' own pocket. He was a rich and powerful man and could afford to do so but I thought it was a nice touch.

The most poignant scenes were the cremations of the runners, the young boys and girls who had been killed while scouring the ground behind the inner wall for enemy arrows. They had thought it great fun and were encouraged by officers of the garrison to collect as many arrows as they could for a reward of sweets and fruit. But many had been hit and killed while doing so and I hated the Armenians for forcing us to resort to such measures.

A touching scene was when an emotional Asher was presented with a silver arrow for his service during the assault. I learned that he had been instrumental in raising volunteers from among the general population that had taken refuge in the temples, and I thanked Shamash that we still had men of iron like him left in the empire.

Afterwards, when everyone had filed out of the temple to return to their daily lives, I sat near the altar next to Gallia as sunlight streamed in through the high windows. She was wearing her white shirt and tan leggings and boots, her hair loose around her shoulders. I held her hand.

'I am tired, Gallia.'

'Of course, you have had hardly any sleep these past three days.'

217

I smiled at her. 'I did not mean that. I am tired of war, tired of battles and bloodshed. I have been fighting for over twenty years, and for what?'

'So we can stay free,' she said, surprised at my despondency.

I sighed. 'Freedom. We were free when we escaped from Italy, but instead of living in Hatra and being content to wait for my inheritance, in my impatience I took the throne of Dura. I have often wondered if I had not done so whether the empire would have been plunged into civil war, whether Phraates would have been murdered and whether my father would have been killed.'

I looked into her blue eyes. 'Am I responsible for all those things?'

Her look hardened. 'No, you are not. Had you been responsible for Mithridates and Narses being vomited into the world then I would have said yes, but you cannot blame yourself for what has happened since we returned from Italy. It has been your destiny.'

I chuckled darkly. 'My destiny? My doom, more like.'

She stood up. 'Come on. No more despairing. We have a war to win.'

I stood up and pulled her close, her full lips inches from mine. 'Perhaps you should be lord high general.'

She kissed me tenderly. 'I would like that. What will you do now?'

'We wait for Atrax and then march to Hatra to fight the Armenians.'

The King of Media arrived the next day with five hundred cataphracts, their squires, four thousand horse archers and five thousand foot soldiers. Media's soldiers wore blue tunics and grey leggings but it was the first time I had seen Atrax's professional foot soldiers.

'I have spent the last three years equipping and training them,' he said with pride as I rode with him, Demaratus and Herneus as we inspected his troops on the Plain of Makhmur, the great flatland across the Tigris opposite Assur, which could accommodate an army with ease. Following Domitus' relief of the city I had sent a second despatch to Atrax telling him that he need not rush to our aid. This had allowed him to bring his foot soldiers with his horsemen. At the same time I had also sent a courier to Hatra to assure Gafarn that Assur was safe and asked him not to engage the Armenians until I arrived.

Each of Media's foot soldiers was ensconced in a helmet with a large neck protector and cheekguards, a short-sleeved scale armour tunic, similar to that worn by his heavy horsemen, thick leather greaves over leather boots and a large oval shield faced with hide painted black and sporting the white dragon of Media. But the most remarkable thing about these soldiers was that their main weapon was a mace, a short length of wood topped with a spiked iron head. They also carried swords and daggers but these troops were obviously equipped and armed to literally batter their way through an enemy formation.

'The Armenians have heavy foot soldiers,' said Atrax, 'so these men have been created to fight and destroy them.'

'They do Media credit, majesty,' remarked Demaratus.

'They certainly do,' I agreed.

The next day we left Assur for Hatra. I hoisted myself onto Remus in the palace courtyard while outside the city twenty-three thousand foot soldiers and four and a half thousand horsemen marched west into the desert. Beside me Gallia was on Epona with the Amazons drawn up behind us. Herneus and his officers stood at the foot of the palace steps, flanked by the high priests from the temples and the city officials. The city governor stepped forward and bowed his head.

'You have saved this city, majesty,' he said to me, then looked at Gallia and bowed once more, 'and this city will talk of your warriors with reverence and awe for generations, highness.'

'It was an honour to have fought beside the men of Assur,' she replied, breaking into a smile.

I leaned forward. 'I will have your lords and their men returned to you as soon as I get to Hatra, Herneus. And Silaces and his men too.'

He nodded. 'Thank you, majesty.'

'One more thing, Herneus. King Aschek and the army of Atropaiene will be arriving here soon on their way to Hatra. Aschek has a tendency to dally when he should make haste, therefore please do not encourage him to stay here and enjoy what will be I'm sure your excellent hospitality.'

He smiled wryly as I raised my hand to those assembled before me. 'Shamash be with you all,' then I tugged on Remus' reins and rode from the courtyard with Gallia and the Amazons following. The city had given thanks to the gods for its deliverance, cremated the dead and had now returned to the greater battle that was the daily struggle for survival.

The march to Hatra was uneventful.

Byrd and Malik scouted with their men and Atrax sent parties of horse archers far and wide in case there were any more Armenian forces in the area but they reported seeing nothing, and when we arrived at the city three days later I learned that the Armenian host that had been advancing from Nisibus had suddenly retreated in haste back to the city. There were thus tens of thousands of horsemen and foot soldiers camped around Hatra with nothing to do but eat up their rations and cover the ground with animal dung.

Marcus established the Duran camp to the north of the city near the city's northern gates. These gave direct access to Hatra's vast royal quarter housing the mansions of the kingdom's richest and most important nobles, the Great Temple dedicated to Shamash, the treasury, the palace and its accompanying gardens, and the royal barracks, armouries and stables. A high, thick wall reinforced by one hundred and fifty towers along its length surrounded the entire city, while a separate wall encompassed the royal quarter. It really was a formidable fortress and one that even an enemy with siege engines would find difficult to reduce.

While Domitus settled the legions and Demaratus' men into camp I rode with Gallia, Spartacus and Atrax to the palace. As ever it was a place of calm, order and authority; Kogan's guards in their smart uniforms standing at every pillar and doorway. Clerks and city officials went about

219

their business without any fuss and priests spoke in hushed tones in the corridors.

We walked into the throne room where Kogan himself stood by the dais, along with Vistaspa and a very frail Assur, his hair and beard now totally white. Courtiers standing around the sides of the hall bowed their heads as we made our way to the dais. A rather gaunt Gafarn rose and stepped onto the floor to greet me, and then Gallia and Atrax, while a smiling Diana greeted her son and then embraced Gallia. Orodes, who surprisingly had been standing beside Kogan, came forward and shook my hand, as did Nergal who followed him, while Praxima kissed my cheek. I nodded to Peroz who was standing on the other side of the dais and I also noticed Silaces in the assembly. Worryingly, the sour-faced Apollonius was also present. I hoped Gafarn had not denuded the garrisons of the towns of western Hatra, which were closest to Roman Syria.

The welcomes over, Gafarn returned to stand on the dais.

'King Pacorus, hero of Assur,' he said in a loud voice, 'Hatra salutes you.'

His words were followed by warm applause and I felt myself starting to blush, though as I raised an arm in acknowledgement and turned left and right I noticed that my sister, Adeleh, was not clapping. She had obviously been taking lessons from Aliyeh on how to bear a grudge.

Gafarn stilled the applause. 'Tonight we will give a feast in honour of King Pacorus and his valiant wife, Queen Gallia, whose warriors stood like a rock to turn back the Armenian tide at Assur.'

Fresh applause broke out and Gafarn and Diana both rose and beckoned us to accompany them as they walked from the throne room to their private quarters. I walked beside Diana as Orodes took the arm of Gallia behind me, followed by Nergal, Praxima, Peroz and Spartacus, who had an arm around the shoulders of his brother, Prince Pacorus.

'Spartacus fought well at Assur,' I said to Diana. 'He is turning into a fine young man and good soldier.'

'Dura agrees with him,' she said, linking her arm in mine. 'He is happy?'

'It was difficult at first but he has calmed down and applied himself to his duties. Prince Peroz has helped him enormously, for which I am grateful.'

'What about the Agraci girl?' asked Gafarn.

'I wouldn't worry about that,' I replied, 'it was a just a passing fancy. He's too busy to worry about women.'

The feast that night was truly spectacular. The banqueting hall was crammed with tables at which sat the city's nobility, Hatra's senior officers, Assur's head priests, as well as the commanders of the assembled armies. Dozens of slaves served food heaped on great silver platters while others poured beer and wine into jewel-encrusted gold and silver drinking vessels. My mother made a rare appearance, dressed in a pure white long dress, her hair oiled, curled and fastened in place with gold hairclips, with additional gold at her neck, on her fingers and round her wrists. She sat between me and Gafarn in the place of honour at the top table, laughed and talked, and was once more the Queen of Hatra. I was truly happy that, if only for one night, she was once more the forceful, gracious and witty woman who was the mother I remembered. Everyone was happy it seemed, even Adeleh, though she said nothing to me. But it was a most agreeable occasion and contrasted sharply to the gathering that was held the next day in the office adjacent to the throne room.

Kogan started by giving a very long and detailed account of the numbers of troops in and around Hatra, which, not including the city garrison, numbered two thousand, seven hundred cataphracts, sixty-six thousand horse archers and twenty-three thousand foot soldiers. And these figures did not include the troops that Aschek would be bringing from Atropaiene, which would undoubtedly swell the number to a combined total of over one hundred thousand soldiers.

'What news do you have of Surena?' I asked Gafarn.

He leaned back in his chair. 'My sources inform me that he continues to strike at the Armenians from Gordyene.'

'And what of the Armenians?' I probed further.

'Their forces have dispersed from Nisibus, apparently,' he replied. 'They retain a large garrison there but their army has dissipated, it would seem.'

'Surena holds their attention,' I said.

'He fights his own private war,' stated Orodes disapprovingly. 'He has answered none of my summons to present himself to me here. It is as if Gordyene has once more been lost to the empire.'

'We must recapture Nisibus,' stated Gafarn.

I was not so sure. The Armenians had tricked us once and nearly taken Assur. They had now seemingly dissolved their army they had mustered there, leaving only a garrison behind. Perhaps they hung the prize of Nisibus before us like a fisherman dangles a piece of bait on his rod.

'No,' I said.

They all looked at me in surprise.

Gafarn was stunned. 'No? Have not we mustered this army here, at Hatra, with the sole purpose of curbing the Armenians, brother?'

'It is as Gafarn says,' added Orodes.

I shook my head. 'The fact that the Armenians have retreated from Hatra indicates that they do not wish to engage us in battle. They tried to capture Assur and nearly succeeded, but if they were intent on forcing a battle they would have kept their army together and marched it against Hatra.'

'Then what do they want?' asked a confused Atrax.

'To let Crassus fight their war for them, after which they can pick over the bones of Parthia like a vulture,' I replied. 'Artavasdes is not his father, who would have sought victory without any aid.'

Gafarn was unconvinced and began stroking his beard with his hand.

'Crassus is, and always has been, the biggest threat,' I said. 'Defeat him and the Armenians can be dealt with at leisure.

'Gafarn, you must return the horse archers that Apollonius has brought here back to your western towns, and send Silaces and Herneus' lords back to Assur.'

'You would weaken the army by doing so, Pacorus,' said Atrax.

'The Armenians may attempt another attack against Assur to give them a strategic crossing point over the Tigris,' I replied. 'From Assur they could strike into Media and southern Gordyene, as well as west at Hatra. And the towns of Ichnae, Nicephorium, Carrhae and Zenodotium need reinforcing as they will be in the path of Crassus and his army.'

'Crassus has not even arrived in Syria,' said Gafarn irritably.

'He soon will be,' I said.

'And that is why we need all the troops we can muster here, at Hatra,' he said resolutely.

'One hundred thousand soldiers,' I said slowly so everyone could understand, 'cannot remain at Hatra indefinitely. For one thing they and their animals will quickly exhaust the city's granaries and will have to disperse anyway. Send Apollonius and his men back to the west and Silaces and the lords of Assur back east. When Crassus arrives in Syria we will march west and meet him at the border.'

'And the Armenians?' queried Orodes.

'The Armenians, my lord,' I replied, 'will sit and wait for the outcome.'

Gafarn was shaking his head. 'They will attack Hatra while our attention is diverted towards Crassus.'

'It does not matter,' I said. 'They will not be able to storm the city but will rather have to mount a siege against it. And how will they water their men and animals? The nearest source is the Tigris, some sixty miles away.'

I could tell that he was still unconvinced but the truth was that we were wasting our time sitting on our backsides at Hatra. If the Armenians were serious about assaulting it they would have already done so. I was therefore relieved when a guard knocked and entered the room to interrupt the uncomfortable silence. He bowed to Gafarn and then whispered something in his ear.

'Well give it to him, then,' he said, exasperatedly.

The guard walked to my side, bowed his head once more and held out a papyrus scroll. I took it and unrolled it. It was from Spandarat at Dura and informed me that he had heard from Haytham that an Egyptian army was mustering at Emesa in preparation for an attack against Palmyra.

'Problems, Pacorus?' enquired Orodes.

I threw the missive on the table. 'It would appear that we have been duped again, my friends. That letter was from Dura. An Egyptian army is assembling at Emesa and intends to march west to capture Palmyra, and in my absence Dura no doubt.'

'Why would the Egyptians attack Dura?' asked Gafarn.

'Why? Because Egypt is under the Roman heel and dances to Rome's tune. Just as we watch the Romans so do they observe us. Crassus has always coveted Dura and now he sees a cheap and easy way to take it: with an Egyptian army that he has no doubt hired.'

'What will you do?' asked Atrax.

'I must return to Dura with my horsemen,' I replied. 'Haytham will fight, of that I have no doubt, but he cannot defeat an army of horse and foot on his own. He will need my support.'

Orodes, who had lived at Dura and knew Haytham well, was nodding in agreement but Gafarn was ashen faced. 'You will take your army back to Dura?'

'Only the horse archers, Gafarn. The rest will stay here.' I stood up. 'And now, if you will excuse me, I have to consult with my officers.'

As I rode back to camp I was in a strange way relieved that this crisis had suddenly appeared as it gave me an excuse to leave Hatra and concentrate on defeating the enemy. Had I been Hatra's king I would have dispersed its horse archers to the south and east and leave the city as bait for the Armenians and Romans. Once they took it their supply lines would be mercilessly harried by thirty-five thousand horse archers, to say nothing of the forces that Dura, Babylon, Media and Atropaiene could assemble. Even the Romans with their siege engines would find their effectiveness quickly diminished by a Mesopotamian summer sun and a parched desert devoid of any pasture or oases. But I was not Hatra's king. Perhaps I should have been after all. Useless thoughts; concentrate on the here and now.

'It's a bad plan, Pacorus.'

Domitus was pacing up and down in my tent, tapping his cane against his thigh, always a bad sign. I sat with Chrestus, Gallia, Marcus and Peroz while my general mumbled to himself and had a face like thunder. He stopped and pointed the cane at me.

'The moment you leave your brother will realise that he has an additional ten thousand well-trained foot soldiers and a thousand cataphracts to play with and we will be marching north to recapture Nisibus to avenge your friend's death. What was he called?'

'Vata,' I answered.

'And he will also realise that you have brought your siege engines. The temptation will be too great for him.'

I held up a hand to him. 'You are the general of Dura's army, Domitus, and it is not to go anywhere without your permission, and your authority supersedes even that of Orodes as king of kings.'

He eyed me warily. 'And you will tell him that?'

'I will.'

'And your brother?' he pressed me. 'I will also be able to ignore his commands if I think it is prudent to do so?'

'Yes.'

He grunted and retook his seat. 'How many riders will you take?'

223

'All the horse archers,' I told him, smiling at Peroz, 'as well as the Carmanians. The cataphracts can stay here. Eight thousand horsemen should be enough.'

'Eight thousand plus the Amazons,' added Gallia. 'I'm coming with you.'

Immediately after I had convinced Domitus of the wisdom of my plan I wrote a note to Spandarat ordering him and his fellow lords to stay at Dura until I arrived, which would be in six days. I emphasised to him that on no account was he to ride out and fight the Egyptians on his own. The courier left my tent as Malik and Byrd halted their horses outside before entering. They and their scouts had been riding to the north of the city searching for Armenians.

'Find anything?' I asked.

Malik filled two cups with water from a jug on the table and handed one to a dust-covered Byrd. 'Nothing.'

'Sit down,' I told them. 'I have some news that will be of interest to you.'

I informed them about the army assembling at Emesa, its plan to attack Palmyra and my riding to assist Haytham.

'You will be coming with me I assume?'

They both nodded.

'Good. You have another chance to avenge Vehrka, Malik.'

Malik drained his cup and refilled it. 'Egypt is many miles from Emesa. Why is its ruler interested in Palmyra?'

'Rome is the ruler of Egypt now,' I replied. 'Aulus Gabinius must have restored Egypt's king to his throne and now we see the consequence of him being Rome's puppet.' I smiled at Byrd. 'Your network of spies in Emesa has served us well.'

'I will lop off that fat king's head with my own sword,' swore Malik.

Whether or not Sampsiceramus himself led the army did not concern me. I was more alarmed by the prospect that Mark Antony, the young commander we had captured, might now have a senior position in the Egyptian force or perhaps might be leading it in person.

'I said you should have killed him,' was Gallia's only remark when I revealed my fear to her.

I told Spartacus and Scarab that they would also be accompanying me. There was nothing for them to do at Dura and I was eager for my nephew not to slip back into his old, undisciplined ways while at Hatra. I therefore instructed him to visit the palace with me to say his farewells to his parents while Gallia and I took our leave of them and said goodbye to my mother. As usual she was on her knees in her beloved garden, trowel in hand planting fresh flowers. The deranged Rubi sat in a chair nearby as slaves fussed around them both. Gallia sat with Rubi and talked softly to her as the mad woman rocked to and fro in her own little world, baring her teeth and hissing when I approached. I sometimes thought that the insane were the only truly happy people in this world.

We left the next morning at dawn, just over eight thousand riders carrying waterskins, sacks of fodder, saddlebags filled with food and four quivers each slung over our shoulders. We left the camel train at Hatra and would be able to pick up additional ammunition at the armouries in Dura, but I had a feeling that we would need a great quantity of arrows in the days ahead. We would not take any of the new steel-tipped arrows with us – they were reserved for Crassus' legions.

Our rate of advance was a steady thirty-five miles a day across the sun-blasted landscape, riding hard but always walking the horses during the hottest hours of each day. We trotted across the pontoon bridges at Dura on the sixth morning and rode straight to the Citadel where Rsan and Aaron were waiting for us at the bottom of the palace steps. Peroz and Vagises took their men to the now deserted legionary camp where they would water their horses in the animal troughs fed by the Euphrates. Malik and Byrd, following a short break, would continue on to Palmyra.

I slid off Remus' back as stable hands came forward to take him, Epona and the horses of the Amazons and my squires to the stables. Vagharsh stood on the paving stones, leaned on his flagpole and arched his back.

'I'm getting too old for careering around the empire,' he said.

'Me too,' I agreed.

The griffin banner was safely enclosed in its wax sleeve but after returning to Dura it was always placed on the wall behind the dais in the throne room and that is where he now took it, ignoring my governor and treasurer as he walked slowly up the steps.

'Where are our children?' asked a concerned Gallia.

Rsan bowed. 'Awaiting you in the throne room, along with Lord Spandarat and Dobbai.'

They both trailed after us as we walked through the reception hall into the throne room, to be greeted by the sight of Spandarat and Dobbai side by side on our thrones and our three children in a line in front of them. Vagharsh was unrolling my banner to place it back on the hooks on the wall, ignoring the two occupants of the thrones and our children. Isabella and Eszter ran to us when they saw us though Claudia remained where she was, curtseying to us when we stood before the dais. She had now seen eleven summers and was growing tall like her mother, though unlike Gallia her long hair was now dark like my own.

'I hope your majesties are well,' I said sarcastically.

Spandarat winked at Gallia and stood up. 'Sit yourself down, princess.'

Gallia took her seat and Eszter climbed onto her knee while Isabella stood next to her.

'To my knowledge Lord Spandarat did not request your presence here, son of Hatra,' said Dobbai irreverently.

I did not rise to her bait. 'With an Egyptian army approaching my place is defending my kingdom.'

She looked amused. 'Defending your kingdom from what? A bunch of ill-armed scrapings from the Nile who could be blown away by a desert wind?'

'I'm glad you think so little of our adversaries,' I retorted, 'but then it is not you who will have to face them in battle.'

Servants brought large cups filled with cool fruit juice for us to drink.

'And neither do you,' she snapped back. 'Haytham is quite capable of dealing with the Egyptians. You should have remained at Hatra.'

'It is true, majesty,' agreed Spandarat, 'me and the other lords could have reinforced Haytham if he found himself in difficulties.'

'Nothing is happening at Hatra,' I said, getting rather annoyed at having to explain myself, 'whereas a great army is heading for Dura.'

'*Great army*,' said Dobbai incredulously, 'your wits are becoming addled. The gods have sent omens indicating that danger lies to the north not in the west. Tell him, Claudia.'

'It is true, father, for I have seen them with my own eyes – a dog urinating against a wall and then lying down and wagging its tail.'

'An omen of impending disaster,' said Dobbai.

Claudia continued. 'And afterwards I saw a man leading a bull by its nose ring in a northerly direction, and a rat snake was following them.'

'As clear as the scar on your face,' commented Dobbai.

'Thank you children, you may return to your rooms,' I said.

Claudia was going to protest. 'Now!' I shouted, causing Eszter and Isabella to jump. Gallia nodded at them and they scuttled away. Vagharsh walked past me in the opposite direction.

'A dog taking a piss. Imagine that,' he remarked.

'Be gone,' Dobbai snapped at him, 'what are you but a dog carrying a pole that follows his master around?'

Vagharsh curled his lip at her and then slapped me on the arm as he took his leave.

'You will ride to fight by the side of Haytham?' Dobbai asked.

'I will,' I said defiantly, pointing at Spandarat. 'And you and your lords will be coming with me.'

Spandarat slapped his hands together. 'Lovely!'

Dobbai rose unsteadily from my throne, Gallia jumping up and taking her arm. The old woman smiled at her, tenderly cupped her cheek with her hand and then they both walked towards the door that led to the private wing of the palace.

'You may go and slaughter the Egyptians, son of Hatra, but the real danger lies to the north,' she called to me. 'Heed my words.'

But I ignored her ramblings and, three days after arriving back at Dura, the lords and their men having assembled in the legionary camp, I rode at the head of twenty-eight thousand horse archers to Palmyra. I had asked both Byrd and Malik to try to persuade Haytham not to offer battle to the Egyptians until I arrived. He had many warriors but few archers and I feared, just as before, that bowmen and slingers would slaughter them when they attempted to get close to the enemy. Gallia stayed behind with the Amazons to guard Dura.

We arrived at Palmyra five days later to find a great assembly of Agraci warriors filling the ground around the green oasis – thousands of black-clad horsemen equipped with spears and round shields, curved swords in black scabbards at their hips and daggers tucked into their belts. All Haytham's lords were present, including Yasser, the man who ruled southern Arabia in his name. It was he who had greeted us with a hundred of his men half a mile east of Palmyra.

He extended a hand to me. 'Good to see you again, King of Dura.' He raised a hand to Spandarat. 'Come to watch how the Agraci slay their foes, old man?'

Spandarat spat on the ground and laughed. 'Come to save your arse, more like.'

Yasser greeted Vagises warmly and was introduced to Peroz before falling in beside me to continue our journey.

'The king wants blood,' said Yasser, 'he is like an angry snake, ready to strike. It took all of Malik's persuasion to convince him to wait until you got here. He's talking about burning Emesa to the ground.'

'Has the enemy left the city?' I asked.

'Yesterday. We have scouts outside the city and along the road here who use smoke signals to keep us abreast of developments.'

My horse archers camped immediately east of Palmyra as there was no room in the settlement itself. I noted that the traffic on the road had all but disappeared and in Palmyra itself there were few caravans. The traders who plied the Silk Road had a sixth sense when it came to impending war and made plans accordingly. Most either delayed their journey or took an alternative route. When I rode into Dura I noticed that the caravan park to the immediate north of the city was unusually full. The merchants were waiting for the slaughter to end before continuing their journeys.

I rode with Yasser to the great tent of Haytham in the centre of Palmyra where he and his lords were waiting. It was a great honour to be allowed to sit on the king's council as he made plans for war but I was proud to be his friend and fight by his side. What did Dobbai know of pride and loyalty?

Haytham embraced me warmly and then asked me to join him and Malik as they sat with their lords on the carpets and cushions in his tent. I recognised them all and they made room for me as they sat cross-legged in a circle while servants brought refreshments. Byrd, sitting on Haytham's left, nodded as I took my place next to Yasser. In addition to him there were another eleven lords, all of them menacing, cruel warriors who had achieved their high positions with their swords.

'Now my brother Pacorus has arrived with his warriors,' started Haytham, 'we can ride west and kill the invading army. We will leave in the morning. How many riders have you brought with you, Pacorus?'

'Twenty-eight thousand, lord,' I answered.

Yasser slapped me on the shoulder and the others nodded approvingly.

Haytham smiled evilly. 'When you all see the enemy remember Lord Vehrka and avenge him, and remember that nothing is forgotten or forgiven.'

After the meeting Rasha was waiting for me outside her father's tent, accompanied by a dozen guards.

'Are you under arrest?' I teased her.

She rolled her eyes. 'My father thinks that my virtue needs guarding at all times.'

'He is worried about you,' I assured her.

She spoke softly so her guardians would not hear. 'Is Spartacus with you?'

'He is, but he has a battle to prepare for and is confined to camp.'

She pressed a letter into my hand. 'Would you give him this?'

I should have refused and given it back to her but she looked at me with such imploring brown eyes that my heart melted. So much for being the chief warlord of Parthia!

'Of course,' I replied.

She threw her arms round me, kissed me on the cheek, ordered me to keep safe and then hurried away with a spring in her step. What it is to be young and in love.

The Agraci did not fight as my army fights. Like my own nobles each of Haytham's lords brought his own followers and they fought and died for him, fighting alongside him in battle and sharing in his victories and defeats. Agraci tactics, such as they were, consisted of getting to grips with the enemy as quickly as possible and slaughtering them in a close-quarter mêlée. Against well-disciplined, trained and equipped soldiers it was a recipe for disaster. Courage and bloodlust alone were not enough to overcome a professional army, that is why I wanted to be here, not for glory or a chance to kill Egyptians, though I was not averse to sending any race to the afterlife if they made an enemy of me, but to save Haytham. I would never have told him that, of course, but with my horse archers he and his men stood a better chance of defeating the enemy.

Three days out from Palmyra, marching along the road to Emesa, our scouts came across the enemy. It was not hard to find them: the vast dust cloud kicked up by their soldiers matched that of our own and could be seen miles away. The flat, hard-packed dirt across which we rode was littered with small stones and sparse grass and scrub vegetation. Occasionally a patch of greenery would appear as if by magic where water seeped to the surface to create a small oasis, but mostly the terrain was unending arid earth, made bleaker by a sun scorching our backs from a cloudless sky.

At midday, as the sun's rays were warming the ground to turn the horizon into a shimmering haze, Haytham ordered a halt and called his lords together. As he did so waterskins were brought forward from the hundreds of camels that had accompanied us from Palmyra, on which were also stored food, tents and fodder.

'The enemy are ten miles distant,' said Haytham, 'they will be here in three hours.'

'How many?' asked one his lords.

'Nearly forty thousand foot, six or seven thousand horse.'

Forty-five thousand soldiers was below our own strength of thirty thousand Agraci plus my own horsemen from Dura – a good omen.

'Are there are any Romans present?' I asked.

'My scouts reported seeing no Romans,' answered Haytham.

The day was getting better and better.

'I would like to take a closer look at our opponents, lord,' I said to Haytham, pointing at Vagises and Peroz to accompany me.

I jabbed at finger at Spartacus and Scarab. 'You two stay here.'

We cantered forward over the dusty ground with Vagharsh and a dozen horse archers behind us. The mood of the army was relaxed and confident, sentiments I shared as there were no Romans present.

'How do these Egyptians fight, majesty?' asked Peroz.

'Like Greeks,' I answered.

He was confused. 'Greeks?'

'Alexander of Macedon conquered Egypt around two hundred and eighty years ago, and ever since then the kingdom's rulers, named Ptolemy after the first king, have been Greeks and the descendents of Greeks. Many men from Greece settled in Egypt in the intervening years and have brought their ways with them, including the Greek way of war.

'Like the Romans they believe in the power of their foot soldiers. Their horsemen are equipped only to scout, raid and support the foot.'

Within fifteen minutes we had halted and were observing the mighty host advancing across the desert at a steady pace, creating a huge dust cloud that must have been choking the men in the rear of the formation. I pointed at an unbroken black mass in the centre of the Egyptian battle line.

'That is their phalanx, made up of battalions of two hundred and fifty-six men, called *syntagma*, arrayed in ranks of sixteen men sixteen deep. They carry long spears called *sarissas* that are around fifteen feet in length. The first five ranks advance with their spears levelled to form an impenetrable hedge in front of the first rank, while the raised spears of the rear ranks help defeat enemy missiles. And there are sixty-four battalions of them – over sixteen thousand men.

'Each phalangist wears a helmet, linen armour called *linothorax*, a shield slung over the shoulder covering his left side so he can hold his spear with both hands.'

I could see other foot soldiers either side of the phalanx and horsemen on the extreme ends of each wing. I estimated the frontage of the Egyptian army to be a mile and a half.

Half an hour later I was in my saddle at the head of Vagises' men on the right wing of the army. It had been decided that Peroz and his men would take up position on the left wing. In such a way Haytham's warriors would have missile support once the battle began. The enemy also had archers, which were deployed in two great blocks either side of the phalanx.

We were now around a mile from the enemy, walking forward at a slow pace with arrows nocked in our bowstrings. Vagharsh had removed my banner from its sleeve but it hung limply on the flagpole, as there was no wind. Already my silk vest was soaked in sweat and perspiration covered my face and neck. Each dragon of horse archers was arrayed in ten companies in a line, each company arranged in ten ranks of ten men. As each man had only three quivers of arrows I had given orders not to waste any missiles. With this in mind I had placed Spandarat and his lords behind Vagises – twenty thousand men. Haytham was most surprised but I knew that as soon as my lords were committed they were effectively beyond control so their one and only charge would have to be well timed. Needless to say Spandarat and his fellow nobles were most unhappy.

The eerie quiet that had descended over the battlefield was ended when both wings of the enemy army suddenly galloped forward. These were light horsemen wearing tunics and leggings only and riding wiry horses bred for speed. They carried wicker shields and each rider was armed with up to half a dozen javelins and they raced across the ground towards us, ready to launch their short spears.

Answering the command of horns, the front rank in each company waited until the widely spaced Egyptian horsemen were within four hundred paces before drawing back their bowstrings and loosing an arrow volley at them. The missiles arched into the air and fell among the enemy horsemen, hitting several horses and their riders. The Egyptians immediately halted and retreated back to their own lines as fast as they could. Trained for hit-and-run tactics, they had failed in their objective of goading us into action. But then with horror I looked to my left and saw masses of Agraci warriors galloping after them.

Haytham, seeing the enemy horsemen easily beaten off, had unleashed a general assault against the Egyptians.

'What do we do?' asked Vagises.

'Nothing,' I replied.

'You are not going to support our allies, uncle?' queried Spartacus.

'Not until they return after having many of their saddles emptied,' I replied.

And so it was. As soon as the Agraci got close to the enemy centre they were peppered with lead shots from slingers that hugged the flanks of the phalanx and the foot archers either side of them. In the space of a few minutes Haytham lost dozens of men and horses for nothing, the Agraci falling back as rapidly as they had advanced to get out of range of enemy missiles.

Wild cheering erupted from the Egyptian ranks and the phalanx began to march forward once more. I raised my bow to signal the advance and behind me three thousand horse archers urged their horses forward.

They cantered past me as Spartacus moved his horse ahead.

'Not you,' I told him. 'You will stay here until I tell you otherwise.'

He slammed his bow back into its case in frustration as Vagharsh's face wore a broad grin.

The horse archers rode to the right before arching inwards to assault the light horsemen on the Egyptian left flank. As they broke into a trot large amounts of dust were kicked into the air and hung there like a yellowish cloud. I glanced to my left and could still see the huge phalanx advancing but beyond that was a wall of dust. The thousands of horses' hooves were beginning to reduce visibility drastically.

In front of us I could hear the whoosh and hiss of thousands of arrows being loosed as Vagises' companies neared the Egyptian army and wheeled inwards to strike the flank of the enemy line, files of ten horse archers riding at the enemy, shooting their bows and then wheeling right to take them back to the rear of the file. In this way a continuous, withering storm of arrows would be directed at the opposition.

Using this tactic each horseman usually got off at least three arrows. As he reached the front of the file he released his bowstring, nocked another arrow and shot it as he wheeled his horse right and loosed a third arrow over the back of his horse as he returned to the rear of the file. In this way each of Vagises' dragons shot around six hundred arrows a minute at the enemy.

After ten minutes a dust-covered Vagises rode back to where I watched.

'The Egyptian horsemen have fled, Pacorus. We are shooting down black men carrying hide shields and spears. Hundreds are dead.'

'Nubians,' remarked Scarab with sadness.

'What of the enemy's archers and slingers?' I asked.

'Most have been cut down with the Nubians, their bows do not have the range of ours,' he answered. 'Though their slingers have the measure of them.'

'Spandarat,' I called. 'Time for your and your lords to assault what is left of the enemy's left flank.'

He whooped with joy and rode back to his fellow nobles.

'Pull back your men, Vagises,' I ordered. 'Let them save their arrows and let us hope that Peroz has enjoyed similar success against their other wing.'

I coughed as dust entered my mouth.

'This ground is very sandy,' remarked Vagises, who dug his knees into his horse's sides and sped off followed by a score of men.

A few minutes later there was a great rumbling sound behind us and then the earth began to tremble as Spandarat and my other lords led their horse archers forward. It was not a disciplined approach to the target followed by an ordered attack to maintain a steady rate of missile expenditure; rather, a wild charge of men possessed of a feral rage and desirous to kill as many of the enemy as possible.

Too late, and to my horror, I realised that I had made a grave error in throwing Spandarat against the Egyptians for soon the visibility was further drastically reduced by the thick dust cloud created by twenty thousand galloping horses. We started coughing as the fine particles got in our eyes and entered our throats. I could hear shouts and screams to the front and the cries of wounded and dying horses but I was effectively a useless bystander to the battle, unable to dictate its course.

I heard horns in the distance and then trumpet blasts coming from ahead and to the left. The phalanx! It must have halted. I smiled to myself. Perhaps Peroz or Haytham had shattered the enemy. Perhaps they themselves had been shattered! I could see no more than a hundred paces in any direction so thick was the dust enveloping the battlefield. For all I knew the Egyptians could have been behind me.

The earth shook once more and somewhere in front of me a sizeable number of horsemen were galloping from the right to left. I peered into the yellow haze but saw nothing and then they were gone. Most strange.

'I saw breastplates and helmets, uncle,' said Spartacus, whose eyes were obviously keener than mine.

'Are you certain?'

He nodded.

I turned to the commander of the company of horse archers that was with us.

'Follow me,' then tugged on Remus' reins to turn him left. One thing was certain, neither Haytham nor I had horsemen wearing armour, which meant they could only be enemy riders.

We trotted forward keeping close order with arrows nocked in our bowstrings. The sounds of battle were initially on our right as we moved towards the centre of our battle line but then I heard shouts and cries and the sounds of blades striking each other ahead.

'Ready!' I shouted as we broke into a fast canter and rode straight into a huge mêlée.

Agraci warriors were fighting a multitude of other horsemen wearing bronze helmets and breastplates and greaves around their shins, armed with the *xyston* – a long spear – and the *machaira*, a vicious short sword with a curved cutting edge. Four of my men were speared immediately as we rode among the turmoil.

'All-round defence,' I shouted.

I raised my bow and shot an Egyptian in the chest as he spurred towards me with his spear levelled. The company closed around me and began loosing arrows in all directions, scything down enemy horsemen like a farmer cuts crops. I was not worried about my men hitting Agraci, only that they would run out of arrows.

Then, directly ahead, I saw Haytham and Malik fighting among a dwindling band of their men, black shapes lying on the ground all around where Agraci had been killed by the enemy.

'Forward!' I shouted. We had to get to Haytham's side or he would be cut down. There seemed to be an endless supply of enemy horsemen. Where were the rest of the Agraci?

Suddenly Spartacus broke ranks and galloped forward, shooting an Egyptian who was closing in on Haytham from the right.

'Come back you idiot,' I called to no effect.

'Maintain formation,' I shouted, just as Scarab also bolted forward on his horse to join my other squire.

They both made it to Haytham's side just as half a dozen Egyptians with spears levelled closed in on the Agraci king. Spartacus shot two of them in quick succession and then killed the horse from under a third who was about to ram his spear into Haytham's unguarded right side. Spartacus and Scarab rode to the king's side and loosed arrow after arrow at the enemy, killing two more before the sixth beat a hasty retreat.

If anything the dust was getting thicker as I drew level with Haytham and the soldiers of my company formed a cordon around what was left of his bodyguard. He let his blood-covered blade fall to his side.

'You are a most welcome sight,' he said.

Malik on his other side raised his sword to me.

'Are you hurt, lord?' I asked.

Ahead of us Spartacus loosed an arrow that went into the eye socket of an Egyptian. Haytham pointed his sword at him.

'That young puppy saved my life.'

'My nephew has his uses,' I replied. 'Where did these Egyptians come from?'

'Emerged from behind that great group of spearmen in the centre. Speared hundreds of my men and forced us back. I sent Yasser and most of my other lords to support your archers on the left after they had smashed the enemy in front of them.' He shook his head. 'That appears to have been a mistake.'

He had had a narrow escape but as my men sat in their saddles with arrows nocked in their bowstrings the sounds of battle in front of us began to recede.

'Keep watch,' I shouted, 'the enemy might return.'

Sure enough there came the sound of hooves pounding the earth to our left and so I redeployed my men to face the new threat, with Haytham and his Agraci formed up behind. The riders drew closer and out of the dust came hundreds of black riders – Agraci!

'Stand down,' I ordered as Yasser halted his horse in front of his king and hundreds of Agraci warriors fell in behind Haytham. He looked at the dead bodies spread across the ground.

'The enemy have been broken, lord. Those who have horses are fleeing west; the others are being killed at our leisure. What happened here?'

'We had our own private battle,' was all that Haytham said.

I rode with him, Malik and Yasser forward to where small groups of the enemy were desperately trying to defend themselves against Agraci attacks, supported by Peroz's horse archers on the left and Spandarat and his men on the right. The phalanx had collapsed and great piles of enemy dead lay where they had been killed, most by the spears and swords of the Agraci after they had attempted to run and had been cut down.

As we continued to ride forward the dust began to clear and I saw Peroz and his senior officers in front of their horse archers. A company would ride forward and unleash arrows against a group of Egyptians, after which the waiting Agraci would ride in and hack the survivors to pieces like a pack of ravenous wolves.

I peered across to the left where Agraci and Parthians were intermingled in a great chaotic mêlée against isolated groups of enemy foot soldiers. And from the right came Vagises accompanied by a company of horse archers. He raised his hand to me and then Haytham.

I pointed at the confusion on the right. 'Spandarat and my lords are enjoying themselves, it seems.'

'Do you wish me to stop it?' he asked.

'No, let them have their fun.'

Haytham slapped me on the shoulder. 'We will make an Agraci out of you yet, Pacorus.'

I ordered Vagises to organise a pursuit of the enemy horsemen with a thousand of his men after the rest had surrendered their arrows to him. They were to pursue and kill as many of the enemy as possible, not engage in any battles. If more enemy horsemen appeared they were to withdraw.

The slaughter petered out with the onset of nightfall. I have no doubt that some among the enemy survived, either feigning death and waiting for night before making their escape west, or slipping through the roving bands of Agraci, Duran and Carmanian horsemen in the haze. Nevertheless the bulk of the Egyptian army lay dead on the bloodstained earth and with it any chance it may have had of capturing Palmyra.

Haytham was ecstatic: I had never seen him laugh and grin so much. Though his good humour did not extend to the few enemy soldiers who had been captured. The next morning he had them stripped naked, flogged severely, buried in the ground up to their necks, had their eyelids cut off and left them to die in the sun. Our own losses had not been light, particularly among the Agraci who had lost over two thousand men, but with ten times that number of enemy dead covering the earth Haytham did not care. He had won a great victory, Vehrka had been avenged and his reputation as a mighty warlord had been enhanced.

Duran losses amounted to less than a hundred horse archers, though Spandarat and his lords had suffered nearly nine hundred dead and wounded – the consequence of launching ill-disciplined attacks against the enemy.

'They died fighting,' was all that he said, 'what else can a man hope for?'

'To live into old age?' I suggested.

He spat on the ground. 'Old age is like a living death, mark my words.'

Peroz, who had kept his men under tight control throughout the battle, had likewise suffered only light casualties: two hundred and twenty killed and a hundred wounded. Vagises returned to us two days later to report that he had added around five hundred or more of the enemy to the butcher's bill but had called off the pursuit when he had neared Emesa.

'What was left of them would no doubt inform that fat king that King Haytham and his army would soon be besieging his city.'

When we returned to Palmyra Haytham gave a great feast to celebrate his victory. He seemed to have invited the whole army as every inch of ground inside and outside his tent seemed to be occupied by his lords, their warriors and Dura's soldiers. Byrd brought Noora and the radiant Rasha stuck by Malik's side and dazzled us with her smile. As the evening wore on Haytham gathered his lords around him in front of a huge raging fire and called on me to come forward. When I did so he put an arm around my shoulder and called for quiet.

'Years ago a man rode from the city of Dura into my kingdom with his wife, a scout and a young girl. He was a Parthian, a member of the race that is the sworn enemy of the Agraci. And yet, disdaining certain death, he brought my daughter back to me.'

There was loud acclaim. Haytham raised his hands to still the noise. He continued.

'That man stands before you, a man I am proud to call brother, and the scout who rode with him that day,' he pointed at Byrd, 'is now one of my most trusted advisers.'

Malik slapped Byrd on the arm and Noora hugged him close.

'And now my brother Pacorus,' continued Haytham, 'has brought his warriors to fight by my side and together we have destroyed a great army that was sent to enslave us. I therefore declare that Pacorus, King of Dura, is now officially my brother and may make decisions concerning the Agraci in my absence, so much do I value his judgement.'

I was taken aback. This was indeed a great honour and I was about to thank him when he yanked his dagger from its sheath, grabbed my right hand and drew the sharp blade across my palm. I winced in pain as he likewise cut his own palm, pressed it onto my bloody hand and then held it aloft. The crowd erupted into wild cheering.

Haytham waved forward two women who brought dressings to bind our wounds.

'You do me a great honour, lord,' I said to him, wondering how long it would be before I could shoot a bow or wield a sword again.

'You are to call me brother from now on,' he told me.

Once the women had finished applying the dressings Haytham raised his hands again and the commotion faded way, the only noise the spitting of burning logs behind us. Haytham searched out Spartacus standing next to Scarab and beckoned him forward. My nephew, who had probably drunk too much already, stepped forward, smiling at Rasha as he did so. Haytham's daughter was beautiful tonight, dressed as she was in a flowing blue silk robe with jewel-embroidered wide sleeves. Her headscarf was also blue silk and from the centre parting of her hair was tied a silver *teeka* that rested on her forehead. She wore silver bracelets and anklets and around her neck hung a simple silver necklace holding an exquisite and priceless pear-shaped blue diamond. It had been brought

235

from the lands east of the Indus and was called the 'idol's eye' and must have cost Haytham a small fortune.

The Romans believed that diamonds were tears of the gods, others like Dobbai thought them useful talismans to ward off evil, while some wore them to attract others. Rasha held my nephew's eyes with her own as he paced forward to her father and I could only think that she wore this rare precious stone to entrap his feelings.

Haytham raised the right arm of Spartacus.

'This boy saved my life in battle and now I repay the debt I owe to him. Ask what you will of me, boy, and I will grant it.'

The crowd chanted his name and the hairs on the back on my neck stood up. I never thought that I would hear the name 'Spartacus' be acclaimed again but that night the air rang with the name of my dead friend and lord once more and I looked at Vagises and Vagharsh among the assembly and they smiled at me. Like me they had been transported back in time to another place when we had stood with Gauls, Dacians, Germans, Greeks, Thracians and Parthians and chanted the same name.

Haytham stilled the tumult. 'Speak boy.'

I knew what he was going to say and closed my eyes as the brave young fool looked at his beloved.

'I wish the hand of your daughter in marriage.'

His declaration was met by a deafening silence as Haytham's lieutenants looked at each other in disbelief and then back at Spartacus who stood with a self-satisfied smile on his face. Rasha wore a smile of victory and stepped forward.

'I accept.'

Haytham spun round and glared at her.

'Stay where you are,' he bellowed, causing her to jump.

He whipped his sword from its scabbard and held the point at Spartacus' neck.

'The debt is paid,' he said menacingly.

My nephew looked at the blade and then at Haytham in confusion. 'I do not understand, majesty.'

Malik was shaking his head and Byrd was frowning with disapproval as Haytham pressed the point of his sword into my nephew's neck.

Haytham smiled savagely. 'You saved my life and now I have saved yours by not cutting off your head for your insolence.'

Agraci laughter greeted this pronouncement though neither Spartacus nor Rasha were smiling.

'We love each other,' proclaimed Rasha forlornly.

'It is not becoming for the daughter of a king to have feelings for a lowly squire.'

'I am a prince,' said Spartacus with difficulty, the point of Haytham's sword still pressing into his neck.

'It is true, lord, er, brother,' I said, 'he is a prince of Hatra.'

Haytham looked at me and slowly lowered his sword. 'It makes no difference. I will never permit my daughter to marry a Parthian. You may be my brother, Pacorus, but there is too much hatred between our two peoples to allow the blood of each to be mixed. A child of such a match would be an outcast from both races.'

Rasha's head dropped and she visibly wilted at her father's refusal to countenance their union. I sometimes forgot that most Parthians hated the Agraci and vice versa. Poor Rasha.

'But I am not Parthian,' declared Spartacus.

Haytham regarded him warily. 'What trickery is this?'

'No trickery, majesty,' he replied, his cockiness quickly returning and declaring. 'I am a Thracian.'

Haytham's face was blank. He looked at me as his men shrugged their shoulders in indifference.

'It is true, brother,' I said. 'He was born in Italy to Thracian parents. I was one of those who brought him to Parthia to be raised as a prince of Hatra. But he is the son of the general I fought under against the Romans.'

Rasha, given fresh hope, now looked at her father imploringly. Haytham slid his sword back into its scabbard and looked thoughtfully at Spartacus and Rasha, then smiled slyly.

'It is not enough.'

Rasha's eyes misted with tears and Spartacus' shoulders sank, but to his credit he did not give up on his love.

'Name the conditions which will win me the hand of your daughter, majesty, and I will fulfil them.'

Haytham, momentarily taken aback by his fresh impertinence, glared at him and I was about to step between them to prevent him lopping off my nephew's head, when Haytham smiled cruelly.

'You're brave, boy, I will give you that, and so, in light of your valour in battle and your strange pursuit of lost causes, I make you this offer.

'Years ago, word reached me of a battle between the Romans and Parthians and the tale of how a young prince from the city of Hatra had taken a silver eagle standard from the enemy single-handedly. I have heard that these silver eagles are sacred to Roman soldiers and that they would lay down their lives to protect them.'

Haytham pointed at me. 'My brother was the man who stole that eagle from under the noses of thousands of Roman soldiers and it now sits in the temple of his forefathers in Hatra.'

He looked at Spartacus. 'You have seen this thing?'

'I have, majesty.'

'And now the Romans once again threaten our borders and King Pacorus once again marches against the eagles.'

He stood before his assembled lords and warriors and raised his arms.

'I, Haytham, King of the Agraci, hereby make this offer to the boy who saved my life in battle. If he wants my daughter then he will bring me one of these Roman eagles that he has taken in battle to lay it on the ground before me. This offer stands for one full year, after which I will give my daughter to the son of one of my lords.'

237

He spun round and pointed at Spartacus. 'You have one year, boy. One year in which to do this thing. But know that when you leave Palmyra after this night and return to Dura you are prohibited from entering my kingdom, on pain of death, unless you bring a silver eagle with you for company.'

The Agraci cheered and laughed at Haytham's words and Rasha looked most concerned, with good reason. To capture a Roman eagle was all but impossible, notwithstanding that I had done so in my youth, and then only due to a combination of sheer luck and youthful folly. Spartacus had enough of the latter but the gods alone would decide if he would have any of the former.

Haytham was both clever and cruel. He dangled the prospect of a union between Rasha and Spartacus knowing full well that Spartacus would probably die attempting to win the one thing that would give him Rasha. Haytham laughed along with his warriors as my nephew considered what he had agreed to.

The next day, as we rode back to Dura, he was unusually quiet.

'It was brave of you to declare your love for Rasha in front of Haytham and his lords,' I told him. 'I was most impressed.'

'It did me little good,' he mumbled.

'There are many fine young women among the nobility of Hatra,' I said, 'when you return there it might be best to look to them for your future happiness.'

'Why should I?' he snapped.

'Because if you venture into Agraci territory,' said Vagharsh behind him, 'your head will be on a pole outside Haytham's tent.'

'Unless I win an eagle,' he replied defiantly.

'You have more chance of sprouting a pair of wings,' scoffed Vagharsh.

When we reached Dura Spartacus' spirits had sunk lower with the realisation that he could no longer enter Agraci territory unless he had a Roman eagle with him. A year was a long time and if he failed to get his trophy he would probably never see Rasha again, at least as an unmarried woman. My own humour was troubled when I saw the legionary camp was full of soldiers, wagons and horses – the rest of the army had returned to Dura.

I left Vagises and Peroz to organise the quartering of their men in the camp and rode immediately with my squires and Vagharsh to the Citadel, the guards at the western gates of the camp having informed me that Domitus and Chrestus were waiting for me at the palace. As I galloped past the camp and through the Palmyrene Gate into the city the knot in my stomach tightened. Something was very wrong.

The guards at the gates of the Citadel had seen us riding up the main street and so, as we trotted into the courtyard, Gallia, Domitus and Chrestus were waiting for me. I slid off Remus' back and told Spartacus and Scarab to take him and their own horses to the stables. I embraced Gallia and then looked at my two commanders.

'I assume there is a good reason why the army is back at Dura.'

'We were sent back,' replied Domitus.

'Sent back by whom?'

'By your brother,' he answered.

'Gafarn?'

'Just tell him, Domitus,' sighed Gallia.

Domitus looked at her and then me. 'Crassus and his army arrived in Syria, crossed the Euphrates at Zeugma and attacked the towns in western Hatra before Orodes had chance to organise a response. Crassus then garrisoned the towns and withdrew back into Syria. It would appear that the Egyptian army sent against Palmyra was a decoy to mask the main enemy attack.'

Chapter 11

An hour later, after I had washed and changed, I sat in the headquarters building as Domitus told the sorry tale of what had happened after I had left Hatra. Byrd's spies had alerted Gafarn that Crassus had arrived in Syria and was preparing to strike across the Euphrates, but then news reached Hatra that once more a large Armenian force had left Nisibus and was heading straight for the city. Orodes, in consultation with the kings, decided to march north and engage the Armenians prior to advancing to the border to meet Crassus.

'We spent two weeks chasing the Armenians in the desert before realising that we had been deceived,' he reported. 'Our scouts caught up with one group of Armenian horsemen who had tied branches to the tails of their horses.'

'Why?' asked Gallia.

'So they kicked up a lot of dust to give the impression that there was a multitude of horsemen on the horizon,' he replied.

Dobbai burst into laughter. 'They well and truly duped you, didn't they Roman? And all the while Crassus was sneaking across the border.'

Domitus did not rise to the bait but continued to recall how, upon realising that there was no Armenian army north of Hatra, and receiving messages that Crassus had crossed the Euphrates, Orodes despatched Silaces and his seven thousand horsemen to reinforce Apollonius.

I raised my hand. 'Silaces? I thought I had ordered that he and his men should be sent back to Assur.'

Domitus looked apologetic. 'They never left Hatra. Your brother is obsessed by the notion that the Armenians will capture Hatra and refuses to release any troops from under his control.'

'Then Assur is defenceless,' I said with alarm.

Domitus shook his head. 'Fortunately King Aschek was tardy in his advance to Hatra.'

'No change there,' sniggered Dobbai, 'he was ever reluctant to draw his sword.'

'He is at Assur with just over fifteen thousand men,' continued Domitus.

'You still have not explained how you came to be back at Dura,' I said to him.

'After we had wasted our time chasing a non-existent enemy in the desert we heard that Crassus had captured the towns of Ichnae, Nicephorium, Carrhae and Zenodotium,' he stated. 'At the last place Apollonius lured a Roman delegation into the town and had them killed in the marketplace.'

'The idiot,' I said.

'It cost him his life when the Romans stormed the place,' Domitus continued, 'and we learned that they sold the population into slavery as a lesson to other towns that are thinking of resisting them.

240

'Silaces arrived too late to save Zenodotium but managed to get himself wounded and lost a sizeable number of men to enemy arrows from the walls.'

'Was he badly injured?' I enquired.

Domitus shook his head. 'Just a flesh wound in his arm, or so I heard.'

'Talking of which,' said Gallia, nodding at my bandaged hand, 'what happened to your hand?'

'Another battle wound?' suggested Chrestus.

'No,' I replied. 'After his victory Haytham insisted that we become blood brother so he cut his palm and mine and then we clasped hands to mix our blood.'

'A great honour,' said Chrestus.

'A great honour?' scoffed Dobbai. 'You should fetch that Greek doctor of yours and get him to cut off your hand before the Agraci poison infects the other parts of your body.'

'I agree with Chrestus,' I said defiantly. 'It is a great honour to be called "brother" by the king of the Agraci.'

She waved a hand at me. 'Desert thieves and murderers, that is what the Agraci are, though I admit you have been clever to enlist them as your allies.'

'They are valued friends,' I replied.

'To you, perhaps,' she said. 'But Parthians and Agraci will never live in peace with one another; there is too much bad blood between them. You must have a care, son of Hatra, that you are not seen as being more Agraci than Parthian.'

'You like Malik and Rasha, do you not?' Gallia asked her.

'Of course, child,' she smiled, 'but you must understand that Parthians do not regard the Agraci as you do, as you all do, here in Dura.'

'We won't be seeing Rasha in Dura for a while,' I said sadly.

Gallia was most concerned. 'Why? Is she ill, or hurt?'

'Worse,' I said, 'she is in love.'

My wife looked at me quizzically. 'Haytham has found her a husband?'

'Not quite,' I replied. 'Young Spartacus saved Haytham's life in the battle and afterwards Haytham asked Spartacus what he would like as a reward. He requested Rasha's hand in marriage.'

Domitus rolled his eyes and Dobbai laughed again.

'What did Haytham say?' asked Gallia.

'He was not pleased but managed to stop himself from cutting off Spartacus' head there and then. He told him that if he brought a captured Roman eagle to him at Palmyra then he could marry Rasha, but that until he did so he was banished from Agraci territory on pain of death. He has a year to fulfil this condition, after which Haytham will give Rasha to an Agraci lord.'

'There are many daughters of nobles in Hatra who can be a wife to the little prince,' sneered Domitus, 'because he has more chance of taking an eagle than that stone griffin at the gates has of flying away.'

241

'Poor Rasha,' was all Gallia could say. 'I will visit her.'

'You underestimate the son of the slave general,' said Dobbai. 'The gods have chosen a path for him, just as they have for you, son of Hatra. He will wear a crown one day.'

'Of course he will,' I said irritably. 'He is the heir to Hatra's throne.'

Dobbai looked smug. 'I did not say that he would wear Hatra's crown for that is reserved for the one who was born in the city and who carries your name.'

'Pacorus?'

'Indeed.'

'Then what crown will Spartacus wear?' asked Domitus.

Dobbai glowered at him. 'Do I ask you about your daily duties, Roman, about how many men you have flogged or hanged each month, or give advice to you regarding how to fight your battles? No! Then kindly do not pester me with your infantile questions. But seeing as you are here, why were you banished from the Kingdom of Hatra?'

She smiled at him while he shifted uncomfortably in his seat.

'Banished?' I said, shocked.

'I was not banished,' he snapped. 'After we had returned to Hatra your brother wished to march west to retake the towns that had been captured by the Romans, using our siege engines. But Byrd's spies in Syria continued to send us messages that informed us that Crassus had garrisoned each town and had placed his army near the border, on the western side of the Euphrates. I therefore said that we should wait for your return until anything further was decided. He grew angry at this and demanded that I obey his orders. I declined to do so whereupon he ordered me to depart his city. So here we are.'

Poor Gafarn. The plight of his kingdom was obviously affecting his judgement. In his eagerness to achieve any sort of victory he was making rash decisions.

'What did Orodes say on the matter?' I asked.

'Privately he supported me,' said Domitus, 'but publicly he could not be seen contradicting the decision of another king lest it fatally undermine Gafarn.'

'A wise decision,' I said. 'Fear and panic can spread like a plague through a kingdom. What is Crassus doing now?'

Domitus shrugged. 'Nothing as far as we know.'

'Autumn approaches,' said Chrestus. 'It is doubtful he will make any further moves until next spring.'

I nodded. Why should he? He had arrived in Syria and had achieved a series of easy victories while using the Armenians and an Egyptian army to divert our attention.

'And what of our Armenian friends?' I asked.

'Artavasdes does nothing but sit on his arse,' said Domitus. 'Surena is still raiding his territories, though.'

'High King Orodes demanded his presence at Hatra,' said Chrestus.

'He ignored the summons,' added Domitus.

242

I sighed. 'I may ride to Gordyene to see Surena, to convince him that he must act in unison with us all for the good of Parthia.'

'He does not care about Parthia,' remarked Dobbai. 'He is lost to you, son of Hatra. You made him a king and now he turns his back on you. And yet he may still have a part to play, for good or ill.'

'I always knew he would turn out to be no good,' said Gallia. 'He was always too sure of himself, too full of his own importance. He will not be missed.'

She had always disliked Surena, notwithstanding that he had married Viper, but now her Amazon was dead she felt no need to hide her animosity towards the King of Gordyene. For myself I had always liked Surena and still felt responsible for him. In my eyes he remained that wild boy of the Ma'adan who had rescued me from a cruel death at the hands of King Chosroes all those years ago.

'Surena is a valuable ally in our war against the Armenians,' I insisted. 'His anger will burn itself out.'

'You are wrong, son of Hatra,' said Dobbai, 'it will grow in intensity until it consumes him.'

'He fights his own private war,' remarked Domitus disapprovingly. 'If he had coordinated his efforts with ours then we might have beaten the Armenians, leaving us free to face Crassus.'

'Well,' I said, 'nothing more will happen until the spring most likely, which gives us time to prepare at least.'

But in truth we had achieved nothing. Crassus had made easy gains, Artavasdes hovered over Hatra like a thundercloud and Gafarn's nerve was visibly crumbling. The Romans and Armenians had witnessed his propensity for rashness and were almost inviting him to attack them, knowing that if he did they would easily defeat him.

'We should invade Syria,' remarked Domitus casually, 'take the fight to the enemy.'

'You would like that, wouldn't you,' I said.

Domitus stood and began pacing in front of the map of the empire, then stopped and pointed at Antioch with his cane.

'With Peroz's men we have nearly twenty thousand troops. We can march north, cross the border and be in Antioch in a week.'

'To what aim?' I asked. 'Crassus' army is mustered in the north, near Zeugma.'

'To burn Antioch,' replied Domitus.

I shook my head. 'No, Domitus. Burning Antioch would avail us nothing and would only provoke Crassus into action. If he severed our line of retreat we would have to fight him, outnumbered most likely, in hostile territory. The risk is too great.'

'Then enlist Nergal and Atrax to your cause,' he suggested, 'that will even the odds.'

'Syria,' I told him, 'is not the problem, Crassus is. And I would prefer to fight him on a ground of my own choosing.'

243

Domitus muttered to himself and sat back down, which brought the meeting to a close. As my right hand was still sore afterwards I borrowed one of Aaron's treasury clerks and dictated a number of letters, one to Gafarn accepting responsibility for Domitus' insolence and promising that I would deploy troops on my northern border to give the impression that I was preparing an invasion of Syria. I sent a letter to Phriapatius saying that Peroz had turned into an excellent commander and had distinguished himself in the recent battle with the Egyptians. Finally I sent a despatch to Surena requesting that he travel to Assur where we could discuss recent events.

The next few weeks were remarkable only for their inactivity. The troops of Mesene, Media, Babylon and Susiana returned to their homelands as an uneasy peace descended on the empire. Byrd rode from Palmyra and brought news that Crassus was awaiting the arrival of horsemen from Gaul who were commanded by his son. It was an indication of his lack of trust in Syrian cavalry that he was wished to receive reinforcements from hundreds of miles away rather than recruit mounted troops locally. Gafarn sent a terse note complaining about Domitus' attitude but thanking me for deploying more troops on the Syrian border. Phriapatius, on the other hand, sent a very long and appreciative letter thanking me for nurturing the talents of his son and informing me that his eastern army was assembling slowly but steadily. Accompanying the letter was a consignment of gold to pay for the wages of Peroz's soldiers and fodder for their horses. Aaron was most pleased when I informed him.

I stood with him in the courtyard as the bars of gold were unloaded from the camels and itemised on papyrus. Two thousand Carmanian horse archers had escorted them, and in gratitude I sent back with them two-dozen warhorses bred on Dura's stud farms for their king.

When Godarz had been city governor it had been agreed that Dura should breed its own horses for the army, though it had proved a long, difficult and costly business. Even my father had refused to sanction the purchase of stallions from Hatra's studs to Dura. My father's pure whites that provided the mounts for his royal bodyguard were the envy of the empire and were fiercely protected. Horse theft was a capital offence and the sentence was also visited upon the family of the perpetrator. I had dreamed of my own cataphracts riding pure white horses but Strabo, whose knowledge about horses and how to breed them was exemplary, told me that I was wasting my time.

The finest Parthian horses were a breed called Nisean that were found in Hatra, Media, Atropaiene and Hyrcania. Descended from ancient Scythian stock they were very strong, tough and resilient. Noted for their speed and endurance on long marches they were ideal for Parthian warfare. My friendship with Atrax and Aschek resulted in Strabo being able to purchase a number of pure blood mares and stallions from both of them that formed the foundation of Dura's breeding programme. My father also relented and authorised the sale of a number of horses from his own farms, though no whites.

I had wanted Remus to sire a line but Strabo was at first against it.

'We don't know his ancestry,' he told me. 'He might pass on a deformity or weakness to a foal.'

'Remus is a fine warhorse,' I said to him.

'None finer,' he agreed, 'but within him he may have an ailment that he is immune to but one that he could still pass on to his offspring.'

'We will just have to take a chance on that,' I replied.

And so we did, mating him with a cremello mare brought from the lush green plains of Media. Despite Remus being the king's horse and the veterans of many battles the mare must have had the dominant blood for the foal that she produced was golden in colour like many Nisean horses, with a coat that shimmered in the sun. We named him *Tegha*, meaning 'blade'. Like all Niseans he had long ears, almond-shaped eyes and a sparse mane and tail, with a lightly muscled long back, flat croup, deep chest and long neck. My dream of having a herd of whites may have come to nothing but as the years passed Dura produced a good number of homebred bays, blacks, palominos, chestnuts and greys.

Though the cost may have been high the revenues from the trade caravans, the taxes paid to the treasury from the lords' estates and duties imposed on the businesses inside the city meant the treasury was always full, and that meant Aaron was mostly happy. Rsan had trained him well, though, and he kept watch over the kingdom's wealth like a hawk. To the continual annoyance of Domitus every item of expenditure had to be discussed at the weekly council meetings and itemised once it had been agreed upon.

Two weeks after the horses had been sent to Phriapatius I went to see Aaron in his treasury, as usual surrounded by diligent and serious clerks making notes. The treasury was positioned directly opposite the palace and was a two-storey building above ground with a basement beneath that had been hewn out of the rock upon which the Citadel stood. This was where the bars of gold and chests of gold coins and drachmas were stored. The ground floor comprised two rooms that held records and another two where Aaron's clerks worked. The first floor was where Aaron had his own office, with three other rooms that housed more records and his chief clerk.

Two guards always stood outside the treasury's main entrance when the door was open during the day, with another two standing at the top of the stone steps that led down to the underground basement where the gold and money was stored. At the top of the steps was a metal grill that barred access to the gold and money, and only Rsan and Aaron carried keys to the lock that secured it. The basement itself had been converted into a number of rooms where the kingdom's wealth was stored behind iron bars. Only a select few individuals were allowed in the treasury: including myself, the queen, Domitus, Rsan, Aaron and his trusted clerks.

I walked up the steps and into Aaron's spacious and bright office, the pair of shutters at the windows open to give a view of the Citadel's courtyard below. He stood up and bowed his head but I gestured for him to sit. I sat down in the chair in front of his large desk as he finished his writing and put down his pen.

'How can I help you, majesty?'

'Have you heard from Alexander lately?'

Alexander Maccabeus was a Jewish rebel who had been fighting the Romans for years. With gold he had purchased a great numbers of weapons from Dura with which he hoped to liberate Judea, his homeland, from Roman rule. But Aulus Gabinius had defeated him and though he still carried on his war against the Romans, he was now little more than a bandit hiding out in the hills of eastern Judea.

'Still battling the Romans, majesty, I believe, though I have not heard from him in several months.'

'I have had an idea to assist our ally and your friend,' I told him.

Aaron looked down at his desk. 'He has no more gold to purchase weapons, majesty.'

'It will not require any gold, at least not from him. I intend to send him soldiers so he may carry on the fight against Rome.'

He looked concerned. 'You intend to march your army into Judea, majesty?'

'No, Aaron. Dura's army is needed in Parthia. But there are other soldiers who would be more than willing to go to Judea. For the right price. I thought we might use the gold that Phriapatius sent to hire some mercenaries to send to Alexander.'

Aaron's concern increased. 'But that gold is for the upkeep of Prince Peroz and his soldiers, majesty.'

I smiled. 'Dura has enough food and fodder to support Peroz's men and their animals, and the meticulous records that you present each week at the council meeting have shown me that the kingdom's finances are in excellent shape, therefore I see no problem with diverting a portion towards assisting Alexander.'

'To what end, majesty?'

'To divert the Romans' attention away from Parthia, Aaron. To give us time to prepare our defences so that when they turn their gaze once more towards us we will be in a stronger position.'

He fell silent, deep in thought. I noticed that he was wearing a necklace of a silver hand with an eye painted in its centre. I nodded at it.

'What is that strange symbol you wear at your throat?'

'A gift from Rachel. It is called a *Hamsa* and symbolises the Hand of God. It is supposed to bring its wearer health, happiness and good fortune. The eye is to ward off evil influences.'

'Well, perhaps with the help of your god,' I said, 'we might be able to cause trouble for the Romans in Judea.'

He shook his head. 'God will not help us.'

'Why not?'

'We are paying for our own sins and the sins of our fathers. God punishes us for not following His laws.'

'He has abandoned you?' I asked.

'We are His chosen people, majesty, He will never abandon us.'

I was confused. 'But he allows the Romans to conquer your homeland and to enslave your fellow Jews. It seems to me that he has chosen you for nothing more than misery.'

He smiled knowingly. 'The Jews were chosen to hear His truth and relay God's message to the world.'

I found the religion of the Jews most strange. They worshipped a god who had no name and did not help them when they most needed assistance. It was a testament to their faith that they did not stop their worship of him.

When I raised the issue at the next council meeting Domitus was most unimpressed.

'Mercenaries? And where are you going to get them from?'

'The Zagros Mountains, of course. Surely you have not forgotten our great victory at the Battle of Susa? You remember when we were assaulted by the hill men on the second day of the battle.'

'I remember,' he sniffed. 'Half-naked savages armed with clubs and other makeshift weapons. I would not call them soldiers.'

'We can furnish them with weapons easily enough,' I replied, 'and then Alexander can come to Dura and take them back to Judea.'

'We slaughtered thousands of them at Susa,' remarked Domitus. 'Are you sure there are any left.'

'Oh believe me, Domitus, if there is one thing I can say with certainty: there is an endless supply of hill men.'

The Zagros Mountains occupied a large area of central Parthia. Made up of numerous parallel ridges of limestone and shale whose highest peaks were permanently covered with snow, the Zagros were also filled with fertile plains, fast-flowing rivers, ravines and villages filled with wild people called hill men. The people of the Zagros lived in tightly knit clans whose leaders spent most of their lives in blood feuds with neighbouring clans, though they were more than willing to temporarily put aside their differences to fight on behalf of others as long as the price was right. Mithridates had used gold to hire tens of thousands of hill men in an attempt to destroy us at Susa and now I was determined to go down the same route.

I rode with Domitus, my two squires and a hundred horse archers to the city of Susa, the capital of Susiana and Orodes' homeland, to recruit my detachment of hill men. Before we departed Dura I wrote to Orodes requesting that he meet us at Susa to both facilitate the raising of my mercenary band and to discuss the strategy for next year. He and his men had returned to Babylon by this time and Atrax and Aschek had also travelled back to their homelands. As promised I had moved troops – a thousand horse archers – to the frontier with Syria where they rode into the desert each day and arrayed themselves on the border in a provocative

247

manner. On the other side of the border Roman legionaries did the same in what became a daily ritual.

I took Spartacus with me to take his mind off Rasha, or at least place several hundred miles between him and her, as I did not trust him from trying to sneak into Agraci territory to see her. I knew they wrote to each other on a regular basis but also knew that Haytham would kill him without a thought should he set foot into his domain. I took Scarab because I wanted to show him as much of the empire as possible.

It took us eighteen days to reach Susa – a distance of five hundred miles – following a similar route that our army had taken in the civil war against Narses and Mithridates. Seleucia was still being rebuilt and Ctesiphon refurbished and when we reached the latter we were informed that Orodes and Axsen had travelled together to Susa with the soldiers of Susiana who had marched all the way from Hatra.

After crossing the Tigris and riding along the eastern side of the river for four days we left the waterway and travelled across the desert for two days before reaching the verdant foothills of the Zagros Mountains. It was still hot but the humidity rose markedly as we entered the Valley of Susa and then headed south to the city itself.

'A bit different from the last time we were here,' said Domitus.

'Indeed,' I agreed. 'Then we had to fight our way to Susa.'

'I remember being in Hatra when the heralds announced your great victory, uncle,' said Spartacus. 'It was a day of great joy and even greater sadness when we learned that King Varaz had been killed. I wish I could have been by your side at that battle.'

'We lost a lot of good men that day,' commented Domitus sadly. 'We could have done with them by our side when we face the Romans and Armenians.'

'I fear we will lose many more good men next year,' I said.

'It is the enemy who will be losing men, uncle,' boasted Spartacus, 'if they are anything like the Egyptians.'

I looked at Domitus who shook his head. My nephew had had a taste of battle and had found it agreeable and now he thirsted for more. Whereas I saw death and the promise of ruin he saw nothing but glory, reinforced by the youthful conviction that he was invincible. He was now nearing the end of his time as a squire and would soon be joining the ranks of Hatra's cataphracts, which he might one day command. If he stayed alive; if we all stayed alive.

'Actually it was not my victory at Susa,' I told him, 'Surena was the architect of triumph.'

'We could certainly do with him by our side next year,' remarked Domitus.

'You have changed your tune,' I said. 'I remember the first time I rode into camp with him next to me. You were most disparaging about him then.'

'That was a few years ago now,' he replied. 'You made him into a fine soldier and commander. You tamed him.'

'I fear I only tamed him for a while, Domitus. I think he has turned wild again.'

'All over the death of a woman,' mused Domitus. 'Pity he cannot find another to warm his bed.'

I looked at him. 'Viper was his true love and now the flame that burned inside of him for her has been extinguished, to be replaced by the cold of his wrath and suffering. Finding another to soothe his rage against the world will not be easy.'

'Rasha is my true love,' Spartacus declared.

'You might do well to forget her,' urged Domitus, 'if you know what's good for you.'

'One day she will be my queen,' Spartacus continued, ignoring Domitus' words. 'I will take a Roman eagle to Haytham. I have seen the one that you captured in the Great Temple at Hatra, uncle. You have shown it can be done.'

'The gods were with Pacorus that day,' said Domitus. 'They might not be so accommodating with you, young pup.'

'Why do the Romans take the eagle to be their symbol?' asked a curious Scarab.

'Because, my Nubian friend,' said Domitus, 'the eagle is the bird of Jupiter, the king of the gods.'

'The king of the Roman gods,' I added.

'Don't start all that again,' said Domitus. 'The eagle is therefore the symbol of strength, courage and immortality, all virtues that a Roman legion seeks to possess. The eagle is additionally the king of the birds, able to ascend above a storm, and is also the messenger of the gods. Eagles carry souls into the presence of the gods. That is why they are revered so.

'The legionary eagle is a sacred object and will be defended as such by each legion's soldiers. That is why it is almost impossible to take one in battle, unless of course you slaughter every single legionary beforehand.'

'Then that is what I shall have to do,' boasted Spartacus.

Susa was built on high ground between the Karkheh and Dez rivers in the fertile Valley of Susa, at the foot of the Zagros Mountains. The city had once been at one end of the Persian Royal Road that went all the way to the Aegean Sea in the west, and was now part of the Silk Road that went south to Persepolis and then east to the Indus and beyond. Susa itself was a formidable fortress, being surrounded by a high, thick mud-brick wall and a dry moat that was eighty feet wide. People had inhabited the site of the city for over four thousand years, gradually improving and expanding it over the centuries.

Like Dura Susa had a citadel, located in the north and surrounded by its own wall. We entered the city via the eastern gate where a huge three-story gatehouse sat above two pairs of great oak gates. Above the gatehouse flew the banners of Susiana and Babylon to indicate that both Orodes and Axsen were in residence. The paved road from the gatehouse wound its way through the crowded city and was lined on either side by one- and two-storey mud-brick houses. The commander at the gatehouse had been given orders to facilitate our movement on the congested road and so a company of his spearmen moved aside pedestrians, two- and four-wheeled carts and ill-tempered mules overloaded with goods. As usual the air was thick with the pungent aroma of thousands of unwashed bodies, animals and their dung and refuse.

It was only half a mile from the east gate to the royal quarter but it took us nearly thirty minutes to traverse the route, Domitus swatting away a plague of beggars with his vine cane and Scarab frightening them off with his black face and the frequent growls he directed at them. Ahead of us the black-uniformed Susianan spearmen grew angrier and began barging aside all and sundry with their shields in an effort to speed our journey. Looking at them I wondered how many had fought against me at the Battle of Susa, or who had been part of the garrison that had defied Orodes after the battle.

Eventually we reached the calm and majesty of the royal quarter, which if nothing else smelt fresher than the rest of the city. A guard of honour snapped to attention on the paved square as I halted Remus in front of the grandiose palace. A teenage stable hand in white leggings and shirt took his reins as I dismounted and a portly, middle-aged man with a neatly trimmed light brown beard and thinning hair approached and bowed to me.

'Greetings, majesty,' he said in a slightly tremulous voice, his eyes cast down. 'I am Timius, chief steward. King of Kings Orodes and his queen, Axsen of Babylon, await you in the audience hall if you would care to follow me.'

'My men require food and stabling for their horses,' I said.

He turned and looked at a younger, slimmer man with small hands who waved forward a host of waiting stable hands.

'They will stable your men's horses, majesty,' squeaked Timius, 'after which they will be shown to the barracks.'

Domitus came to my side and Spartacus and Scarab fell in behind as Timius led us into the palace, a building that had originally been built by the Persians over five hundred years ago. It had been constructed around three courtyards, titled "courts", around which were offices, temples, guardrooms, kitchens, quarters for slaves and the private apartments of the king and queen. The audience hall, the *Apadana*, formed the northern annex of the residence and was like a palace in its own right. It had been erected on a raised stone terrace and was reached by a columned portico.

The audience hall itself contained thirty-six white-painted stone columns that supported wooden ceiling beams. The edges of the roof were covered with gold leaf so that travellers would see its magnificence from afar when the sun's rays caught them. The walls were decorated with friezes of enamelled bricks that portrayed lions, archers and hunts. It was certainly a palace fit for a high king.

Timius left us when we reached Orodes and Axsen, who rose from their golden thrones and embraced Domitus and me. They were both attired in long purple robes with gold crowns on their heads, and Axsen wore gold jewellery around her neck, wrists and fingers.

'We are glad to see you,' she giggled as Spartacus and Scarab went down on their knees before them.

Orodes ordered them to get up. 'Welcome Spartacus, Prince of Hatra, and Scarab, squire to King Pacorus.'

My nephew, used to grandeur and opulence, nodded and smiled while Scarab stood open-mouthed at the high king of the empire who retook his seat alongside his wife.

'I have had my officers send word to the hill men that we are looking for recruits to fight in a land far away from here,' said Orodes.

Domitus nodded at me. 'I told him that we had killed most of them at Susa but he would not have it.'

Orodes stroked his chin. 'Unfortunately, Domitus, the gods have sent the people of the Zagros to inflict misery upon the empire and so they are numberless.'

'They have been giving you trouble?' I asked.

'No more than usual, but it grieves me that I have to commit soldiers to defend against their raids who could be better employed fighting the Armenians and Romans.'

'How many of these barbarians do you wish to recruit?' asked Axsen.

'Two thousand should suffice,' I answered.

'They will fight in your army?' she enquired.

'They will not be fighting anywhere near Dura's army,' Domitus answered for me.

Axsen was most perplexed. 'Then what?'

'Judea,' I answered. 'They will be sent to Judea to fight the Romans.'

We stayed at Susa for two weeks, during which time a message arrived at the palace from one of the chiefs of the Zagros clans that he would meet with me concerning supplying mercenaries. He sent one of his men to the city to act as a guide, a swarthy individual named Gourlay with a thick black beard and wild hair who rode a scrawny horse with only a blanket on its bowed back for a saddle. He stood barefoot before Orodes in the audience hall in his dirty, torn leggings and threadbare shirt with his arms folded. His long knife had been taken from him as a precaution before he entered but still the garrison commander had doubled the number of guards around the king and queen.

'Why does your leader refuse to come to the city?' demanded Orodes.

The man shrugged. 'He does not wish to see his head stuck on your walls,' he answered insolently. He spoke a bastardised version of our language which, combined with his strong accent, made his words difficult to understand.

'My chief's village is two days' ride from here,' he continued, 'you come to him.'

'Out of the question,' replied Orodes impatiently.

'I will go,' I said.

251

The messenger looked at me. 'You bring no soldiers. I will be your guide.'

'I will bring three others with me,' I told him, 'that is all.'

He agreed to meet me at the city's eastern gate the next morning and after he had been dismissed Orodes urged me not to go, fearing that it would be a trap and that I might be killed.

'What purpose would killing me serve?'

'No purpose at all,' he said, 'but that does not mean they will not do it. The hill men do not live by our rules. The hill men do not live by any rules.'

I shrugged. 'Mithridates managed to recruit a good number so they are not averse to offers of gold.'

'That is the point, Pacorus. My stepbrother reneged on his agreement with the hill men and paid them nothing for their services. He duped them and they lost thousands in the battle against us for nothing. That is one of the reasons they have been so troublesome of late: they seek revenge for his treachery.'

I laughed. Even though he was dead, Mithridates was still causing us problems.

'If I don't meet with this man, Orodes, then I will have come all this way for nothing. I would ask a favour of you, though.'

'Name it.'

'Get your treasury to release some gold coins for me so I may take them to this chief, as a sign of good faith.'

He looked horrified. 'That will be the quickest way to get your throat cut.'

'I will have to take that risk. There is little point in turning up with only words. If I can convince this man that there is more gold to be had he may agree to supply me with men.'

'Is it worth it, Pacorus?'

I thought for a moment. 'I do not wish to send any Parthians into Judea to certain death. If I try to recruit mercenaries from lands near to Armenia the Romans will get to know of it. Enlisting a few hill men seems the cheapest and easiest thing to do.'

He placed a hand on my shoulder. 'This world will be an emptier place without your friendship to fill it.'

'I will return, I always do.'

We left the next day, Gourlay leading the way on his mangy horse. Domitus was most unimpressed by this venture and spent the whole of the first morning complaining, much to the amusement of Scarab who was amazed that someone could address a king so.

'King? I knew him when he was a slave, boy, just like you.'

Scarab looked embarrassed by his words.

'It is true,' I told him. 'It is no secret that I was captured by the Romans and forced into bondage. I have never sought to hide my past. But what my general did not tell you was that I was the one who rescued him.'

Domitus smiled sarcastically. 'I thought it was Spartacus who led the raid on the silver mine.'

'It was my archers that tipped the scales in that battle,' I said. 'Without them you would still be hacking at rock deep under the earth.'

'Majesty,' interrupted Scarab, 'I have heard about this man called Spartacus. Men talk of him in hushed tones and with reverence as if he was a god.'

I was riding next to Domitus with my two squires behind me and now I turned and looked at Scarab and at Spartacus, who was staring ahead in silence though no doubt listening to every word.

'He was not a god,' I replied, 'though the Romans liked to think of him as a devil sent from the underworld, but he was a great general and a fine man I was proud to call friend.'

Scarab turned to my nephew. 'You must be proud to bear his name.'

Spartacus did not respond for a few seconds but finally he spoke. 'For many years I did not think so. But since my time at Dura I have begun to change my mind. My parents were wise to send me to you, uncle.'

'You are the one who has learned wisdom,' I said.

'Not when it comes to women,' said Domitus.

Spartacus bristled with anger. 'Rasha is beautiful.'

Domitus laughed. 'I have known her since she was a young girl and she has turned into a fine young woman, but I know enough about Parthians to understand that she could never be a queen of Hatra, even if you do manage to capture an eagle, which you won't.'

'I do not wish to be King of Hatra. My brother, Pacorus, who was born in the city, will be king, not I,' he insisted. 'They do not like me in Hatra and I do not like them.'

'Who?' I asked.

'The nobles,' he spat. 'They sneer at me and plot behind my parents' back.'

Domitus looked at me but said nothing and we rode on in silence for a while. In front Gourlay led us through ravines and across steppe filled with long grass and wildflowers, before coming into a valley whose steep sides were covered in oak. The air was pure and cool as the valley narrowed and we threaded our way through the trees, not only oak but also pistachio, hawthorn, almond, nettle and pear. This was a rich country for the Zagros was a haven for bears, eagles, wolves, wild goats, foxes, jackals, deer, mongoose and marten.

'We make camp here,' Gourlay announced suddenly while we were riding through thick woods following the course of a fast-flowing stream. It was late afternoon and these were the first words he had spoken for several hours.

Spartacus caught sight of a group of Persian fallow deer around four hundred paces away, their tawny coats and white spots blending into the sun-dappled surroundings and making them difficult to spot. We halted and slid off our horses and stretched our limbs as he pulled his bow from its case and strung an arrow.

'You think you can hit one from here?' I asked. The deer stood around three foot at the shoulder with flattened antlers like those of a miniature moose and presented a small target.

He drew back his bowstring and then released it, the arrow lancing through the air before striking the neck of one of the deer, which collapsed to the ground as the others bolted.

'No problem,' he beamed triumphantly.

'Then you can go and collect it.'

As we unsaddled the horses Gourlay threw his mount's saddlecloth on the ground and tethered the beast to a nearby tree. Scarab prepared a fire and Domitus skinned and gutted the deer that Spartacus had killed and roasted its flesh over the fire. We sat in a circle around the flames and feasted on the warm meat, our guide saying little before he wrapped himself in his saddlecloth and fell asleep.

Later I took the first watch as Scarab and Spartacus slept and Domitus sat sharpening his sword. I crouched by him.

'What did you make of my nephew's remarks about Hatra's lords plotting behind Gafarn's back?' I whispered.

He continued to run the stone along his sword's edge. 'A boy who feels he is an outsider will imagine people are against him when they are not.'

'Perhaps,' I replied.

The next day, after we had washed in the stream, attended to the horses and eaten a sparse meal of cured meat, we continued on with our journey, travelling east into the Zagros. I made several attempts to engage our guide in conversation but his surly one-word answers to my questions indicated that he had no interest in what any of us had to say and so we rode on in silence. The light was fading when Gourlay held up an arm to signal us to halt and then called out into the gloom of the forest. We looked at each other in confusion but then several figures emerged from the undergrowth – men dressed in poor quality tunics and leggings carrying axes and spears.

'I had forgotten how ragged these hill men are,' Domitus said to me softly. 'If they manage to survive the journey to Dura the Romans will make offal of them in no time.'

'You must try to look beyond the raw material, Domitus, to what may be.'

He grinned. 'What may be? A lot of dead hill men littering the earth in Judea.'

Our guide rode over to me while his newly arrived companions stood and eyed us warily.

'These men are watchers from my lord's village. It is in the next valley, an hour's ride away.'

We continued our journey among the trees, the foliage growing denser as we followed a single track through the forest. After a while we began to climb and the sun lanced through openings in the forest canopy as we ascended to reach a wide expanse of lush mountain steppe and felt the

254

wind on our faces once more. We crossed the steppe and then rode down a slope into thick forest once more. After half an hour we encountered a wide stream at the bottom of the valley and followed its course until we reached a clearing where a village stood.

From what I knew of the tribes that inhabited the Zagros they grew no crops but lived on what they caught in the rivers and forests and the animals they kept, as well as raiding the settlements of other tribes and Parthian farms and villages. The long Zagros winters combined with the rugged terrain meant that growing crops was impossible, so the herdsmen spent half their time living in goat-hair tents on the high pasture lands grazing their sheep and goats, and the rest of the time in these lowland villages. The chieftains and their subordinates had a marginally better time in that they stayed all-year round in the villages.

Gourlay dismounted as a group of burly men approached him led by one I assumed was the village chief. They were all dressed in loose-fitting green woollen tunics that extended down to their knees, with baggy brown leggings and crude boots. They carried a mixture of spears and axes, though only the chief had a sword that hung in a scabbard from his brown leather belt. He had long light brown hair, a thick beard and, most unusually, blue eyes that now fixed on me as he looked up at me.

'It is considered polite for a guest to dismount when meeting his host.' His voice was calm and polite.

I smiled and slid off Remus' back to stand before him. He was taller and broader than me, though I noticed that his hands were not like the paws of a bear but were slender with long fingers.

I bowed my head to him. 'I thank you for agreeing to see me and hope that my visit will be of benefit to us both.'

'That remains to be seen,' he replied. 'I am Zand, leader of the Sagartian people and I welcome you to my village, King Pacorus.'

I could tell from the expression on Spartacus' face that we were a long way from the well-appointed palace at Susa and its luxurious royal stables. He dismounted and stood with a look of disgust on his face as half-naked infants ran around him as we were shown to our quarters.

'Look happy,' I said to him, 'your face is showing contempt.'

'These people stink,' he remarked with disdain.

He was right: the place reeked of animal and human dung and sweat. 'Think of Rasha to take your mind off it.'

The village was made up of round and rectangular wooden-framed huts with thatched roofs of varying size, and animal pens for sheep and goats alongside them. Our 'quarters' consisted of a round hut that had a crude stable beside it, in truth nothing more than a pen with a thatched roof. A fire had been lit inside the hut to warm it that also had the unfortunate effect of filling it with smoke, which was supposed to exit via the hole in the centre of the roof. The floor was covered in animal skins and the entrance was also covered with skins.

'This is cosy,' remarked Domitus after we had unsaddled our horses and carried the saddles inside the hut.

255

Like the other dwellings in the village the walls were made up of wattles – interwoven branches made weather resistant with daub, a mixture of mud, straw and animal dung.

'It is like a stable,' said Spartacus, dumping his saddle on the ground.

'I would readily exchange it for a stall in Dura's stables.' I said, 'but needs must. At least we don't have to sleep with meat hanging from the ceiling rafters.'

Spartacus looked at me with surprise. 'Meat?'

'Just as we cure meat, so these people hang meat from the rafters so the smoke from the fire cures it. All very practical.'

'All very uncivilised,' he replied.

'What about you, Scarab?' I asked, 'what do you think of our lodgings?'

'They will suffice, majesty.'

Spartacus rolled his eyes as he bent down and lifted one of the animal skins to discover how many insects he would be sharing his bed with.

We may have been guests but Zand posted two guards outside the hut's entrance and another two to watch our horses, though this may have been to deter any thieves, or at least that is what I liked to think. After we had placed the food and fodder in the hut we went back outside to groom the horses and check their shoes and hooves. Looking around I could see a large rectangular hut that I took to be the chief's home, in addition to food stores and warehouses. There was also an open-fronted smithy where two squat bearded men were hammering iron on an anvil. I wondered how many such villages Zand controlled and how many people his tribe numbered, many thousands if the numbers that were arrayed against us at the Battle of Susa was anything to go by. I clutched the leather bag that contained the gold that was slung over my shoulder. Hopefully its contents would be proof of my good faith. Then again, it might get all our throats slit. I was about to find out just how civilised or not the hill men of the Zagros Mountains were.

In honour of our arrival at the village a feast was held in Zand's long hut where we were seated on benches arranged around the walls. Women served us roasted mutton and chicken. They filled cups with milk, wine that tasted of vinegar and an equally foul-tasting alcoholic beverage made from fermented mare's milk. I sat next to Zand on one bench, flanked by his warriors, while Domitus and my two squires were accommodated at another bench. The hut was filled with smoke that made my eyes smart. It came from the great fire that burned in the centre on the earth floor, over which fresh meat was roasting on spits. I noticed Zand drank very little while his warriors got roaring drunk and tried to grope the female servants, who seemed to like being mauled by the stinking oafs.

The Sagartians largely ignored Domitus and my squires but the women brought them wooden platters heaped with meat and ensured their cups were always full. Domitus kept looking at the entrance where his sword and dagger lay on the floor, along with everyone else's weapons. Only Zand, the chief, was permitted to carry weapons in his hut, which was probably a sensible precaution as a group of ill-disciplined, drunken warriors armed to the teeth was a certain recipe for bloodshed.

Zand tore at a piece of meat with his teeth, the juices dripping onto his hand.

'You wish to buy some of my warriors, King Pacorus of Dura?'

I nodded. 'I will pay you gold for them.'

He glanced at me with narrowed eyes. 'The last Parthian king who wanted the Sagartians to fight for him promised the same but paid me nothing,' he said bitterly. 'Why should I believe or trust you?'

'For one thing, I have come to your village in person to signal that I trust you and wish to deal with you face to face.'

I reached into the bag that was slung over my shoulder and pulled out a small ingot of gold. I placed it on the bench before him.

'Secondly, I bring gold as an act of good faith.'

He put down the meat on his platter, wiped his hand on his tunic and picked up the ingot, belched and examined it. He passed it to Gourlay who sat on his left and who turned it over in his hand.

'How many of my warriors do you wish to take back with you to your kingdom?' he asked.

'Two thousand.'

He sat back in his chair and stared at the raging fire before him. 'Why does a great Parthian warlord wish to hire Sagartian warriors, and so few? We have heard of your name in these parts, of the Parthian king who rides a white horse and leads a terrible army that has never been beaten. Tell me, King Pacorus of Dura, how many of my people did you slaughter in the Valley of Susa?'

Gourlay passed the ingot back to his lord as the din in the hut subsided and Zand's warriors nudged each other and turned to look at me. I suddenly felt decidedly uneasy. I glanced at Domitus who was frowning severely and also looking at his sword and dagger, no doubt wondering if he could reach them before any of Zand's warriors stopped him.

I sipped at my cup of warm milk. 'As many who wished to kill me.'

Zand stood and walked round the bench to stand in front of me with his back to the fire.

'I cannot decide if you are very brave or very stupid for coming here, King Pacorus of Dura. You are a man who has many enemies in this place,' he declared in a loud voice.

There were murmurs of assent and several hateful stares were directed at me.

I remained calm, sensing that he was testing as opposed to threatening me. 'All warlords have enemies, King Zand. How many fathers and sons have you killed during your reign with the sword that hangs from your belt? You decided to send warriors to aid Mithridates, my enemy, at Susa. Most of them died. On another day perhaps they would have lived and I would have died. Men die in battle. It is the way of things.'

I stood and spread my arms. 'You can slay me now if you wish to avenge the deaths of your men. It makes no difference to me.'

I took off the bag that hung from my shoulder and emptied its contents onto the bench.

'You can kill all of us with ease and take this gold, our horses and our weapons. Your people and mine have always waged war against each other and no doubt always will while there are men in the world.'

He folded his arms. 'Why should I, Zand, king of the Sagartians, extend mercy to you, King Pacorus of Dura?'

'Perhaps because I will give you gold for your men and with it you may purchase weapons to arm your people against their enemies,' I answered.

He said nothing for what seemed like minutes but then nodded his head and roared at his warriors to stop staring at me and to continue feasting. They were soon emptying their cups and demanding the female slaves bring more wine as Zand returned to his seat.

'And horses,' he said before belching loudly once more.

'Horses?'

'You want two thousand warriors. Then you will have to pay gold and supply me with two thousand horses as well. The coming winter may be harsh and our enemies, the Lors and Kashkai, press on my borders.'

'You wish to raid their lands?' I asked.

He grinned savagely. 'I wish to empty their warehouses. They will starve if they have no food for the winter.'

There were a number of tribes who inhabited the Zagros Mountains but in the western region the Sagartians held sway against the incursions of the Lors and Kashkai. It would appear that after their losses at the Battle of Susa Zand's people had lost territory at the hands of the other two tribes.

'Very well,' I agreed. 'Two thousand horses. When can you supply the warriors?'

He smiled. 'You can have them as soon as you bring me the gold and horses. What will you do with them?'

'They will be sent to a place called Judea, to fight the Romans.'

The blank look on his face told me that he had never heard of Judea or the Romans. How lucky he was.

He looked surprised. 'You do not have enough warriors to fight these Romans?'

'My warriors will be needed elsewhere.'

What I did not tell him was that his warriors were ideally suited to the type of warfare that Alexander waged in Judea. Having been defeated in battle he had been forced to live the life of a bandit leader, launching hit-and-run raids from the hills of eastern Judea. The hill men of the Zagros Mountains had been carrying out such raids since time immemorial. It was in their blood.

At the end of the evening the benches were cleared from the hut and Zand his warriors slept on the floor while we were escorted back to our lodgings. Spartacus and Scarab were both drunk and Domitus and I had to help them stagger back to our quarters, after which they both collapsed on

258

the floor in a deep sleep. The men who had escorted us from Zand's hut stood guard outside our own as I sat on the floor propped up against my saddle while Domitus secured the animals skins over the entrance. He came and sat by my side, talking in hushed tones.

'I thought that chief was going to kill you.'

'He needs gold and horses more than my head,' I said. 'The losses he suffered at Susa have dented his power. The other tribes are increasing their strength as his diminishes.'

'Why does he need horses?'

'To raid his enemies' villages before winter to destroy their stores so the inhabitants will starve. In this way he will re-establish the Sagartians as the region's strongest tribe.'

'Have you thought that he might also use them to mount raids against Orodes' lands?'

'It is easier for Zand to raid the lands of the other Zagros tribes,' I replied.

'Let us hope you are right,' Domitus commented dryly.

The next morning a subdued Spartacus and Scarab doused their bodies in the cool waters of the stream as I stood bare-chested nearby and used my dagger to shave the stubble from my chin. Another two guards stood nearby as villagers went about their daily affairs. I saw no one coming from Zand's hut and assumed that he and his warriors were still deep in slumber. Looking round at the different-sized huts and animal pens I realised how poor these people were, especially as this was the home of the tribe's chieftain. I also realised that two thousand horses to mount raiding parties would greatly increase their power.

'What is that, uncle?'

I turned to see a wet Spartacus wading to the bank who was looking at the lock of hair around my neck.

I clutched the chain. 'A lock of Gallia's hair. I wear it always.'

He came out of the water and sat on the earth. 'I will ask Rasha to send me a lock of her hair and then I too can wear it close to my heart.'

I slid my dagger back in its sheath. 'Just make sure you do not wander into Agraci territory.'

He smiled and pointed at Scarab ducking his head in the water. 'Perhaps Scarab can ride to Palmyra and bring it back.'

I shook my head. 'Are you determined to get him killed as well as yourself?'

He peered up at me. 'My parents told me that you killed Gallia's father.'

I put on my shirt and sat next to him. 'Not quite right. It was in fact your father, the king, who killed him, with a shot that I have never seen bettered in all the years since. That was a good day.'

Scarab walked from the stream and stood with the early morning sun warming his muscular torso.

'What did Gallia, I mean Queen Gallia, say about it?' asked Spartacus.

'She has never said a word about it to me then or since, but I like to think that she approved.'

Spartacus looked surprised. 'Of killing her father?'

'King Ambiorix, Gallia's father, was a cunning, ruthless bastard who sold his own daughter into slavery, something that Haytham would never do whatever you think of him. Besides, Ambiorix sided with the Romans against us and deserved his fate.'

I looked at Spartacus. 'You should concentrate on staying alive rather than filling your head with dreams.'

'If I take an eagle my dreams will become reality,' he said with conviction.

'I think,' I said, 'that the key word in all of this is "if".'

'The gods must have placed Spartacus in a position where he could save King Haytham for a reason,' remarked Scarab, to the delight of my nephew who grinned at him.

'Really, Scarab?' I said. 'And what reason would that be?'

'I am not in the confidence of the gods, majesty,' he replied, 'but all things on earth happen for a reason.'

I looked at him. 'Do you believe that you were sent to me for a purpose?'

He flashed his white teeth. 'Yes, majesty.'

'And what is it.'

'I do not know, majesty.'

I stood up and buckled my sword belt. 'Listen to me, both of you. The gods meddle in the affairs of men but do not believe that they do so for the benefit of mortals. They do so for their own amusement, of that I am certain.'

'It is said that you are beloved of the gods, majesty,' said Scarab, 'that you are immune from enemy weapons and that your army is invincible.'

I thought of the many scars that covered my body as a result of wounds received at the hands of enemies. I slapped Scarab on the arm.

'Don't believe everything you are told, Scarab.'

Chapter 12

The hung-over warriors eventually staggered from Zand's hut and threw themselves in the stream to restore some sense to their dulled brains. A few threw up outside the hut first to provide a breakfast for the mangy dogs that stalked the village. They really were a disgusting people, and yet they were also hardy and had resisted foreign powers for thousands of years. As his warriors splashed in the water and engaged in boorish horseplay Zand himself appeared from out of the forest carrying the body of a wild goat and a bloodied spear, Gourlay beside him. He nodded at me and shouted at his men to get out of the stream and attend to their duties as Domitus sidled up to me fully dressed in his mail shirt, helmet in the crook of his arm.

'I have attended so many feasts that they now bore me,' said Zand, handing the dead goat and spear to Gourlay who walked back to the hut with them.

'Too much drinking eventually deadens the mind so I prefer to stay sober these days,' he continued. 'I trust you and your men slept well, King Pacorus of Dura.'

'Yes, thank you,' I replied. 'You like to hunt in the early hours?'

'It is the best time to take life,' he said. 'The senses of both men and beasts are befuddled at such times so a hunter can get close. Their blood can be watering the earth before the first of the sun's rays brings light to the world.'

I wondered how many people would die as a result of the horses that I would be supplying him with, how many pre-dawn raids he would lead in the coming months? It was not my concern. My concern was the safety of the empire, though I had to admit that it irked me that I was assisting such people. But then, I too was almost certainly sending the warriors I would be hiring to their deaths.

'Gourlay will escort you back to Susa,' he continued. 'When can I expect delivery of the gold and horses?'

'When will you send the warriors?' I asked.

'Gourlay will lead them to Susa as soon as I have received your payment,' he replied.

'What is to stop you from taking the gold and horses and not fulfilling your part of the agreement?' asked a sceptical Domitus.

Zand's pitiless blue eyes narrowed. 'Nothing, you will just have to trust me.'

'I have never put much stock in trust,' growled Domitus.

Zand studied the short, crop-haired individual in front of him dressed in armour and armed with a short sword and dagger, so different from the wild, long-haired warriors of his own tribe.

'You are not Parthian, are you?'

'I am a Roman,' said Domitus.

Zand glanced at me. 'The same people that King Pacorus of Dura wishes to send my warriors to fight against.'

261

'They won't be your warriors once he has paid for them,' said Domitus, 'they will be his.'

'The gold and horses will be accompanied by soldiers to ensure that the exchange goes smoothly,' I said.

Zand did not take his eyes off Domitus. 'And what is to stop those soldiers from shooting down my men with your Parthian bows, King Pacorus of Dura.'

I smiled. 'Nothing. You will just have to trust me.'

Zand burst into laughter. 'I think we can do much business, you and I. Come, let us eat breakfast before your journey.'

We retired to his hut that still stank of human odour and smoke but which was soon filled with the more pleasant aroma of fresh bread as the female slaves prepared food for us to eat. Fresh logs had been thrown on the fire and then domed metal plates were placed on top of the flames and left to get hot. The benches had been replaced around the fire and we took our seats and watched the women toss dough balls made from flour, salt and water on the hot plates and then flick them over and over, sprinkling water over the bread to prevent it from getting too dry. The bread was served with kebabs made from the wild goat that Zand had killed earlier, honey from the tribe's hives and eggs that had been collected that morning. It was an altogether delicious meal.

Two hours later Zand himself was escorting us back to Susa, following the same route that we had used to reach his village. This time we had an escort of a dozen of his warriors on horseback, each one armed with a spear, round wooden shield and a long knife. Compared to Dura's horsemen they were a sorry sight but I knew they were masters at moving unseen through hills and forests and would make much trouble for the Romans in Judea.

We bid farewell to Zand in the foothills of the Zagros east of the River Dez and continued on to Susa alone. The chief said that he would send Gourlay to the city in two weeks' time to see if the gold and horses were ready, and if not at two week intervals after that. He emphasised the importance of receiving the horses and gold before the autumn ended so he could raid the lands of his enemies to kill and steal their winter foodstuffs.

'You pay a high price for his assistance,' said Orodes as we relaxed in a small lounge in the private apartments of his royal palace at Susa.

'Dura will reimburse your treasury for the gold and the horses,' I told him.

'You trust this man, this Zand?' asked Axsen as she reclined on a couch opposite my own.

'I trust his ambition and ruthlessness,' I answered. 'He wishes to attack the villages of his enemies and with his warriors mounted he can raid far and wide.'

'Including Susa's farms and villages,' said Orodes with concern.

'That's just what I said,' remarked Domitus casually.

'It is a risk,' I admitted, 'but the other tribes are pressing on Zand's borders, especially after his losses at Susa. He will be concentrating on expanding his power at the expense of the other tribes rather than attacking Susiana's territories.'

'These tribes need to be subdued,' said Axsen.

'Alas, lady,' I replied, 'thus far no one has succeeded, not even the great Alexander of Macedon. The Zagros Mountains are too expansive and the tribes too dispersed to make their subjugation possible. Far better to encourage them to kill each other.'

'What is he like, this Zand?' asked Orodes.

I thought for a moment. 'Intelligent.'

'For a savage,' added Domitus.

'We are all savages to someone, Domitus,' I retorted, 'but Zand is someone whom a high king might be able to deal with, if only to play off his enemies against each other.'

'We will honour your agreement with him,' said Orodes, 'I will see to it that he receives his gold and horses. Having fought the Romans and the hill men, I do not think that the latter are capable of defeating the former.'

'That is putting it mildly,' said Domitus.

'Then why are you purchasing hill men as mercenaries?' asked a concerned Axsen.

I drained my cup of wine and held it out for a slave to refill it. 'My desire is not for the hill men to defeat the Romans but to keep them and Crassus occupied in Judea. He will not invade Parthia until Judea is subdued and by the time he does we will be ready for him.'

'And the Armenians?' asked Orodes.

'I still believe that if we defeat the Romans then the Armenians will be relatively easy to deal with,' I replied.

Orodes stared at his cup. 'Surena is still waging his private war against the Armenians, which at least distracts them. Have you had any word from him, Pacorus?'

I shook my head. 'None. He may be dead for all I know, though I suspect that he still lives. He is a most resourceful individual.'

'It was very sad that his wife died,' said Axsen wistfully, 'I liked her. It is very romantic that her death has spurred him on to battle the Armenians.'

Domitus looked askance at her and rolled his eyes.

'You should bring him to heel,' Domitus said to Orodes.

'Alas, my friend,' he replied, 'the only way I could do so would be to march an army into Gordyene and conquer the kingdom, which I have neither the resources nor desire to do. Parthia is not Rome. The empire is made up of separate kingdoms whose rulers swear allegiance to the king of kings whom they have elected. In my grandfather's time any disloyalty was severely punished but then Parthia was strong and was not threatened by powerful external enemies.'

'Surena's war serves our interests for the moment,' I said, 'in that it keeps the Armenians from marching south against Hatra. My main

263

concern is that his depredations may enrage Artavasdes and goad him into launching an offensive at the same time as Crassus invades the empire.'

'You could attack the Armenians first,' suggested Domitus.

'But then Crassus would surely cross the Euphrates while we were preoccupied in the north, swinging north to trap our army between him and the Armenians. I cannot risk that.'

'The scales are finely balanced,' said Axsen.

'Indeed,' I replied, 'which is why we need to buy as much time as possible.'

'And what of the eastern kings,' probed Axsen, 'will they assist you?'

'Phriapatius is loyal,' I replied, 'but if the western kingdoms fall I doubt those in the east of the empire will mobilise their forces to fight a war west of the Tigris. They will prefer to wait for the Romans to come to them, thinking they will be stronger on home ground, which will be their undoing.'

'But you have fought and defeated the Romans before, Pacorus,' said Axsen, 'and you have your sorceress on your side.'

I smiled at her. 'Perhaps I should send her to fight Crassus.'

'It will take more than sorcery to defeat the Romans,' said Orodes glumly.

I looked at Domitus who caught my eye but remained stony faced. He had been at Dobbai's ceremony and had witnessed the strange mist, the ghostly howling and seen the empty places where the clay hounds had been. Did he believe? Did I believe? I wanted to and was thankful when Tigranes had died and Aulus Gabinius had turned back from invading Parthia, but were these events miracles or just coincidences? I wanted to see more miracles to convince me that the gods were truly on our side, but would thinking these things anger them and stop them from assisting us further? I tortured myself with such thoughts as I rode back to Dura from Susa with my horse archers, Domitus and two squires. The latter were in high spirits, Spartacus because he was going back to Dura and so would be nearer to Rasha, Scarab because I had told him that he would be my permanent squire when Spartacus became a cataphract. Scarab would never make it into the ranks of the heavy horsemen. He could shoot a bow with a reasonable degree of accuracy but his sword skills were almost non-existent and his horsemanship left a lot to be desired. Spartacus, like most Parthian males, had been in the saddle almost before he could walk and had learned to shoot a bow and wield a sword and lance from the saddle at an early age. These skills he took for granted because they had been part of his upbringing, but years of experience and learning could not be condensed into months. Some had been surprised that Surena, being from the southern marshlands, had adapted so well to Dura's horse archers and cataphracts, but he too had been fighting and riding from an early age, albeit horses stolen from the enemy.

So Scarab would remain my squire and servant, but as a free man.

'There are no slaves in Dura's palace,' I told him as we rode along the eastern bank of the Euphrates on the way back to Dura, 'you know this.'

'That means you can leave Dura at any time,' Domitus told him, 'if you get tired of washing Pacorus' shirts.'

'The king saved me,' said Scarab, 'therefore I am forever in his debt and will only leave him if he dismisses me.'

He really did not understand the concept of freedom.

'Being free means taking your own decisions, Scarab,' I said, 'not being told what to do. To forge your own destiny and live your life in freedom and not in chains.'

'My destiny is to serve you, majesty. That is what the gods have decreed and it is unwise to ignore their wishes. Therefore I pledge my life to your service.'

'Sounds like slavery to me,' grinned Domitus, who then eyed Spartacus, 'a bit like marriage.'

'What about your family, Scarab?' I asked, 'would you not like to search for them. Being free means that you can travel back to Egypt and find them.

He shook his head. 'I was sold into slavery when I was an infant and do not know the location of the market where I was sold. I have no knowledge of my family.'

'I am sorry,' I said.

'It is the will of the gods,' he replied casually. 'You have known your family, majesty, and Spartacus his, a great blessing. And you, lord general,' he asked Domitus, 'do you have knowledge of your parents?'

I smiled knowingly. Scarab might as well ask a stone by the side of the road to explain its ancestry for Lucius Domitus never spoke of his past.

'My mother was a kitchen slave, a cook, in the villa of a Roman patrician in Capena, near Rome. The man was very rich and had been a commander of a legion, a legate, and had been richly rewarded for his services by a grateful Senate. My mother was the daughter and granddaughter of slaves so she told me and had been purchased in the slave market by her master, a white-haired man named Quintus Sergius.

'You are probably thinking that I was born to slave parents but you would be wrong. My father, if you can call him that, was the son of Quintus Sergius, a tribune who took a fancy to the good-looking slave girl in the kitchens and raped her, though others might say he seduced her. I believed my mother in the matter. He returned to Spain where he was killed soon afterwards but his father knew the truth and when she gave birth to me he treated her kindly, giving her light duties in his household and ensuring that her son prospered. She was still a slave of course and he would never admit that the slave baby she bore was his grandchild, but the guilt he felt over his son's actions compelled him to attempt to atone for the great affront done to my mother, and I think that in me he saw a memory of his son. He was quite old when I was born and his wife was older and so they would never have any more children.

'I grew up a kitchen slave but one who was taught to read and write. Quintus Sergius also told me stories of Rome's wars and life in the legions and was delighted when I said that I wanted to join the army. And

265

so, on my seventeenth birthday, he gave me a formal *manumission*, which meant I was free and became a Roman citizen. As a citizen I could join the army and with my former master's letter of recommendation my acceptance was assured. My mother did not wish me to leave, of course, but he had filled my head with notions of glory and adventure and I could not wait to wield a sword and kill Rome's enemies.

'I can still see her, standing near the villa's entrance in her apron with the other slaves as I rode with Quintus Sergius to the nearby legionary barracks. It was a bright spring day and the air was full of the aroma of pine and I thought myself very special riding next to a war hero to follow in his footsteps.

'I never saw my mother again though she wrote to me often. Two years later Quintus Sergius himself wrote to me saying that she had died of a fever. So you see, Nubian, like you I have no family except those I call family who live in Dura.'

I nearly fell off my horse. In all the time that I had known Domitus I had never heard him divulge this information.

'I am glad that Quintus Sergius died before I was condemned to the silver mine,' Domitus continued. 'It would have upset him greatly and I did not desire that. He was always good to my mother and me and I owed him a great deal. If he is watching me now I hope that he is pleased with the army I have helped to create.'

'He will be,' I assured him, 'for you have created the finest army that Parthia has ever known and its reputation and history will be lauded by generations of Parthians to come.'

Domitus looked at Scarab and then nodded towards me. 'The king is such a dreamer.'

It took a month for the hill men to reach Dura – two thousand scruffy, poorly dressed and equipped men, many of whom had no footwear. They were led by Gourlay and escorted by five hundred of Orodes' horse archers to ensure they did not indulge in rape and pillage on their journey. Most of them were armed with a variety of axes, spears and long knives and only Gourlay rode a horse, the same pitiful beast that he had ridden when he had escorted me to Zand's village. It looked as though it was about to collapse and expire but it must have been hardier that I thought because it had survived the journey to Dura.

It stood next to Remus with Gourlay on its back as I inspected his ragged band the day after they had arrived at Dura. Domitus had insisted that the hill men be quartered in a tented compound erected ten miles south of the city. He did not want them in the city or the legionary camp but in their own enclosure where they could be more easily confined. He was mounted on my other side and wore an expression akin to a father who has just found out that his youngest daughter was pregnant by a travelling salesman. Nevertheless, Gourlay informed me that they were all single men in their late teens or early twenties who were eager to fight and kill so they could return to their tribe as great warriors. I kept silent regarding the fact that most of them would probably meet their deaths at the hands of Roman soldiers.

'Miserable bunch,' mumbled Domitus contemptuously, fortunately out of earshot of Gourlay.

'You have done well, Gourlay,' I said. 'They are a fine group of young men.'

Domitus suppressed a laugh.

'Thank you, majesty,' said Gourlay. 'All of them are eager to slit a few throats to show their keenness.'

'I can believe that,' muttered Domitus.

Marcus supplied their tents and cooking utensils and sent daily food deliveries to the new camp to bulk up the hill men, many of whom looked as though they had not eaten in weeks. And to prevent boredom setting in while I waited for Alexander to arrive from Judea, each morning they were taken out into the desert on a long route march. This caused an immense amount of grumbling among them at first, but their resentment was assuaged by what awaited them on their return. Domitus complained that I was indulging them but I believed that if they at least looked like soldiers then they might act like them and not a bunch of bandits. So they first received new tunics to replace the flea-infested rags they wore – which was another reason Domitus did not want them mixing with the rest of the army. Next they were issued with two thousand pairs of sandals, which they would need when they were in the barren, rocky hills of Judea.

Dura was fortunate in that its armouries not only produced weapons and armour but also contained equipment that had been captured from the enemy during the army's campaigns. Thus I was able to issue the hill men with an assortment of helmets, spears and swords that gave them a more martial appearance. In addition, Gourlay selected a hundred of them who had experience of archery to be issued with bows and full quivers. An archery field was built near their camp and each day the bowmen practised shooting arrows at straw targets. A month after the hill men had arrived Alexander came to Dura.

Before I had left for Susa I had asked Aaron to write to Alexander to invite him to Dura where he would receive reinforcements. I gambled that as a Jewish patriot he would be eager to acquire reinforcements for the fight to free his homeland. I did not tell him that I was sending fighters to Judea purely for my own interests, but then Alexander would probably have guessed the motive behind my offer. But he came anyway.

Aaron rode with a party of horse archers to Palmyra to bring him back to Dura and when the party returned I had the army drawn up in front of the city in salute. Alexander Maccabeus may have been a fugitive living in the hills but he was still a prince of Judea and an enemy of Rome and that made him my friend and ally. The cataphracts wore their scale armour with pennants fluttering from every *kontus*; the colour parties of the Durans and Exiles stood to attention grouped round their sacred emblems; the legionaries had white plumes in their helmets and the

267

mounted horse archers of Vagises and Peroz clutched their bows. Gallia was beside me with the Amazons behind in their full war gear as Aaron and Alexander rode up to us in front of the Palmyrene Gate.

The prince was riding a well-groomed brown mare and was wearing a rich white tunic edged with blue, blue leggings and leather boots. But as he halted his horse a few paces before me I was shocked by how he had aged. His shoulder-length hair was thinning and streaked with grey and there was grey in his beard. His cheeks were sunken and his brown eyes had a world-weary, haunted look about them – clearly the years of fighting the Romans and living in the hills had taken a great toll. When I had first met him I estimated his age to be similar to my own but now he looked like an old man.

'Greetings, King Pacorus,' he said. 'Your army is a most impressive sight.'

'Welcome to Dura, Prince Alexander,' I replied, holding out a hand to Gallia. 'This is my wife, Queen Gallia.'

He bowed his head to her solemnly and she returned the compliment.

'You must be tired after your journey,' I said to him, 'but before we retire to the city I have something to show you.'

I raised my right arm and Gourlay and his hill men, who had been positioned behind the Exiles, marched forward towards the city gates. Alexander turned in his saddle as the fully armed hill men, organised into hundred-man companies, advanced and then halted two hundred paces from us. I had to admit that they looked very different from the threadbare wretches who had marched from the Zagros Mountains. Each warrior now wore a new tunic, a helmet on his head and sandals on his feet. A regular supply of wholesome food had bulked them up so they presented a threatening appearance. Alexander looked at them in confusion.

'A gift from the Kingdom of Dura to the Jewish people,' I said. 'Soldiers for you to take back to Judea to continue the fight against the Roman occupiers.'

A broad grin spread over his face as he admired his new army.

'You are most generous, majesty,' he said.

'Judea's enemies are our enemies, Alexander, and Dura will never abandon its allies. These men will reinforce your own troops to allow you to take the fight to the enemy.'

He turned back to face me. 'They will be most welcome for I have few soldiers of my own left.'

His careworn demeanour returned.

'I hope Ananus and Levi are well,' I said. They were two of Alexander's lieutenants whom I had encountered in Judea.

'They are both long dead,' he said glumly.

We rode in silence through the city to the Citadel where Alexander was shown to his quarters in the palace. I had toyed with the idea of letting him stay with Aaron and Rachel but that may have been construed as a slight. I wanted to promote the perception that Alexander was a powerful ally rather than demean him, even if the truth was that he was currently no better than a hill man.

Alexander's mood had improved by the time he attended the feast I gave in his honour at the palace that evening. He sat next to me on the top table along with Gallia, Miriam and Domitus and Aaron and Rachel. I had also invited a Jewish priest, a rabbi, who said prayers before we ate, and who stayed to partake of the lentil stew – a traditional Jewish dish – which the kitchens had prepared, along with roasted beef, goat and mutton. Two days later Alexander left Dura with Gourlay and his hill men, along with two hundred mules loaded with food, spare weapons, clothing and cloaks. After they had left I rode to the Palmyrene Gate, and standing next to the stone griffin I watched the column of men and animals disappear into the west. I prayed to Shamash that He would let the hill men taste victory before they died.

Affairs at Dura continued as normal: the armouries produced weapons and armour, the caravans travelled east and west and the army drilled and prepared for the coming war. I was in frequent contact with both Orodes and Phriapatius, though none of my letters to Surena in Gordyene were answered. Orodes wrote that he had also received no answer to his request that Surena visit him at Seleucia. I did hear from traders who were travelling through Dura that their fellow merchants who had been in Gordyene had informed them that Surena was rarely in Vanadzor, preferring the company of the wild men of his northern borders, who were constantly raiding Armenian territories. I had toyed with the idea of asking Gafarn to send Silaces to Gordyene to speak to Surena, but when I mentioned it in a letter to Gafarn I received a message back that Silaces and his men could not be spared.

There was better news from Phriapatius who reported that he had assembled forty thousand men at Persepolis as part of his Eastern Army, ready to reinforce us when the Romans invaded. However, he stated that most of the men in this force were his own Carmanians, the other eastern kings having been reluctant to send him any troops because they did not wish to weaken their own armies. And from Khosrou and Musa came news of unending war with the nomads of the northern steppes, the vast land between the Caspian and Aral seas.

'Mithridates started a fire that cannot be extinguished,' remarked Dobbai as I finished my summary of events in the empire to Dura's council.

'That is a pity,' said Domitus, looking at the map of the empire hanging on the wall of his headquarters, 'we could have done with some of their soldiers.'

Dobbai scoffed at him. 'The kingdoms of Margiana and Hyrcania are a thousand miles distant whereas the Romans and Armenians are but a stone's throw away. Even if they could provide assistance it would arrive too late to be of any use.'

'What of Gordyene?' asked Domitus.

'I have received no word from Surena though I have heard that he still raids Armenia.'

'He will never stop killing until he himself gets what he desires,' said Dobbai.

Domitus exhaled loudly and looked out of the window while everyone else looked at her in confusion.

'And what is that?' I asked.

'To be with his wife and child of course,' she replied, 'I would have thought that much was obvious.'

'He has a kingdom to rule,' I said, 'he will find another wife in time.'

'You are wrong, son of Hatra. He cares for nothing, not his life, much less his kingdom. You trained him well but made a mistake by unfastening his collar. He has become a wild dog that even you might find difficult to control. Still, at least he keeps the Armenians from seizing more of your brother's kingdom. And sending men to aid the Jews will divert the Romans' attention away from Parthia for a while. That was a clever ploy, son of Hatra.'

'I am glad you approve,' I said through gritted teeth.

'Of course they will all be killed,' she continued, 'that much is certain. But what are the lives of few savages from the Zagros?' She sneered at Aaron. 'Or a few Jews for that matter.'

'How dare you!' snapped Aaron, his nostrils flaring. 'Prince Alexander is an ally and friend of Dura, the king has said so himself.'

'Prince?' said Dobbai mischievously, 'the last time I heard he was living like a hunted animal in the hills. He will never regain his position and is condemned to the life of a bandit, and the Jews will return to their position.'

'What position?' I enquired.

'Slaves,' she said. 'They were slaves of the Egyptian pharaoh many years ago until he grew tired of their incessant nagging and threw them out of Egypt and now they will be slaves of the Romans.'

Aaron jumped up from his chair. 'I really must protest, majesty.'

I held up a hand to him. 'Please be seated, Aaron. I'm sure Dobbai meant no offence.'

'I am merely stating the truth,' she said innocently, 'if some are displeased by this there is little I can do.'

'You can be silent,' seethed Aaron.

'Enough!' I said. 'If the Romans and Armenians triumph we shall all be slaves.'

'Just like the Jews,' said Dobbai, grinning maliciously at Aaron. 'Of course if you sent assassins to kill Crassus there would be no Roman invasion of Parthia.'

'Not a bad idea,' suggested Domitus.

'If Crassus is murdered and it is discovered that Dura is responsible it will enrage the Romans further,' I said. 'And may I remind you that there would still be Roman legions in Syria waiting to invade the empire. No. Crassus and his legions have to be defeated to send a clear message to

270

Rome that if they attempt to invade Parthia their armies will be destroyed. That is the whole point of what we are trying to achieve: to not only defeat Crassus but also destroy the Roman desire to conquer Parthia.'

Byrd and Malik had made the trip from Palmyra and I asked them both to give an account of what was happening in Syria and on Haytham's western border.

'My spies in Antioch report that Crassus recruits Syrians to his army,' said Byrd. 'He has eight legions in Syria. Seven he brought from Italy plus one that garrisons the province. Other legion is in Judea and Egypt.'

'There has been no aggression from Emesa,' stated Malik. 'The rumour is that the fat king is living in fear of an assault upon his city by my father.'

'Good,' I said. 'Fear will hopefully prevent him participating in any more assaults against Palmyra.'

'One thing that I have also heard,' said Byrd. 'Queen Aruna has found a new lover. A Roman called Marcus Roscius.'

Gallia, who had been bored by the meeting thus far and had spent most of it either daydreaming or looking out of the window, now looked interested. 'He was the Roman tribune who came to Dura wanting to take Aaron back to Syria.'

'I remember,' I said.

'Tribune now deputy governor of Syria,' reported Byrd.

'Poor tribune,' I quipped.

Dobbai was far from amused. 'You should take care, son of Hatra, Aruna is full of malice and desires you dead.'

'Well,' I replied, 'with me here and her in Syria I think I am safe enough.'

That night Gallia and I dined with Rachel and Aaron in their house near the Citadel. Rachel was pregnant with their first child and both of them were very excited about their impending parenthood. We were joined by Miriam and Domitus and soon forgot about the Armenians, Romans and war as we talked about children, getting old and our time in Italy. It was a relaxed and enjoyable evening. I liked Aaron and his wife and Miriam, whom I thanked Shamash for sending to Domitus. He was very relaxed in her company and for a while I forgot that he was a ruthless killer, consummate soldier and commander.

We had a most excellent meal and were relaxing on couches in the dining room when there was a commotion outside and a centurion from the Durans entered the room, the headman of the house protesting loudly at his interruption. Aaron rose from the couch and stilled the man as the centurion saluted me and then Domitus.

'This had better be good,' I said to him.

'Begging your pardon, majesty, but there is trouble in the city.'

Domitus raised an eyebrow. 'What sort of trouble?'

'At one of the brothels general.' He suddenly realised there were women present. 'Begging your pardon, majesty, ladies.'

271

I stood up and jabbed a finger at him. 'You interrupt my evening just to bring me news of trouble in a whorehouse?'

The centurion looked alarmed. 'Not just any trouble, majesty, it involves Prince Peroz.'

I folded my arms and stood in front of him.

'Go on.'

'The prince has barricaded himself in one of the rooms and a few men from one of the caravans are threatening to break down the door and kill him. As it is him I thought you should take charge of the situation, majesty, seeing that he is a royal guest at Dura.'

I sighed. 'I suppose so.'

'And your nephew is with him, majesty.'

'What?'

'Prince Spartacus is with Prince Peroz, plus your black servant.'

'Scarab?'

'Sounds interesting,' mused Domitus.

'Spartacus should not be frequenting brothels, Pacorus,' said an unimpressed Gallia. 'Diana would be most upset if she knew.'

'You have obviously been a bad influence on the boy, Pacorus,' grinned Domitus.

'You are not helping,' I told him.

'You had better go and sort it out,' Gallia told me.

'I will come with you,' said Domitus, 'you don't mind do you, Miriam?'

Miriam was not amused by talk of brothels. 'Apparently not.'

After conveying my apologies to my hosts and Miriam I left Gallia in their company and walked with Domitus, the centurion and four of his legionaries to the scene of the trouble: the house of Samhat just off the main square in the centre of the city. The evening was warm and so we wore just our shirts, our swords at our hips with Domitus carrying his trusty cane.

When we arrived at the brothel – an imposing two-storey building with twin oak doors that fronted the street – there was a sizeable crowd of curious onlookers outside.

'Make way for the king,' the centurion shouted, his men barging aside the spectators with their shields. Two soldiers were standing guard outside the brothel to ensure no one entered, and they snapped to attention as Domitus and I entered the house of sin.

'Clear these people from the street,' Domitus ordered the centurion. 'Crack a few heads if you have to but get it done quickly.'

The centurion saluted and went back outside as an irate Samhat saw us and confronted me.

'We are a respectable establishment catering for a wide variety of important clients who pay a great deal of money for discretion. This is not a back-street fighting pen.'

'Please calm yourself,' I told her, admiring the expensive mosaics on the floor, the copper flower stands in the entrance hall and the silver oil lamps mounted on the red-painted walls.

Beyond the entrance was a large hall around which were doors leading to what I assumed were bedrooms, with a fresco of an erotic act painted above every one.

To one side, guarded by half a dozen legionaries with drawn swords, were a group of rough-looking individuals in loose robes and leggings who were staring at us in an aggressive manner. I nodded at them.

'Are they some of your high-ranking clients?'

'They arrived in the city two days ago as part of a caravan,' she replied. 'They may look like beggars but one has paid well for the services of one of my girls and returned tonight to spend more of his money.'

'So what is the problem and where is Prince Peroz?' asked a bemused Domitus eyeing the scantily clad young women who had started to gather outside their rooms.

'The problem,' said Samhat slowly and loudly so everyone could hear, 'is that one of them,' she pointed at the caravan crew under guard, 'paid for a night with Roxanne but Prince Peroz arrived unexpectedly and threw him out of her room when she was discovered with him. So he returned with some of his friends looking for trouble and the prince has barricaded himself in her room, along with others.'

'I have paid a lot of money to be with her,' shouted one of those under guard, a sour-faced man with broad shoulders and large knuckles. 'I demand to lie with her, either that or my money back.'

'Why don't you give him his money back?' suggested Domitus.

Samhat looked at him angrily. 'Because I run a business, not a meeting place for young lovers. I called the city guard because I want the love-struck prince upstairs to be taken away so Roxanne can earn her keep, that's why.

She smiled at me. 'I did not realise that you would come, though, majesty.'

The hall was slowly filling with prostitutes, musicians and eunuchs as we stood conversing.

'What about my refund?' shouted the brute with large knuckles.

'Hold your tongue,' shouted Domitus.

'If you could sort this matter out, majesty,' said Samhat with concern, 'I would be eternally grateful.'

I indicated to Domitus that he should follow me as I walked up the wide staircase that had an intricately carved wooden banister with inlaid ivory. The staircase itself was covered with a rich red carpet that felt soft underfoot.

'I never knew there was so much money in prostitution,' remarked Domitus.

'It is not only the oldest profession, my friend, but also one of the most lucrative.'

273

There were ten rooms on the brothel's first floor and like on the ground floor there were erotic frescos above the entrance to each one. Two guards stood outside one of the doors on the right and they came to attention when they saw us. Domitus told them to go downstairs as I knocked on the door.

'You cannot enter,' shouted Peroz from inside.

'It is Pacorus,' I said, 'open the door.'

I heard muffled voices and then heard what sounded like a heavy object being moved from the other side of the door before it was unbolted and Peroz stood in the doorway with a sword in his hand.

'You can put that away,' I said sternly, and then saw Spartacus and Scarab similarly armed standing behind him. 'And you two can sheath those weapons as well.'

Peroz bowed his head and slid his sword back into its scabbard as I walked into the spacious, lavishly furnished room that had a large bed against one wall facing wooden shutters leading to a balcony. The floor was covered in a plush light red carpet and oil lamps hanging from wall brackets provided light. The alluring aroma of perfume and incense entered my nostrils and my eyes settled on a young woman sitting on the bed. Her oval face was most beautiful, with flawless olive skin, high cheekbones, a narrow, delicate nose and luscious lips. Dressed in a white gown with delicate gold chains around her ankles and more gold hanging from her ears, she looked nervous as her brown eyes darted between Peroz and me. The prince stood next to her protectively as her hand reached for his.

'It is a good job those soldiers came when they did, uncle, otherwise we would have killed those fools downstairs,' boasted Spartacus, which earned him a congratulatory slap on the back from Scarab.

I looked up at the ceiling in despair, to discover to my surprise that it was painted with depictions of fornicating couples, both male and female. I blushed and looked at Domitus.

'Would you escort my squires downstairs and ensure that they do not get into a fight?'

I smiled at Peroz. 'Perhaps we may have a few words together, prince?'

Domitus ushered Spartacus and Scarab out of the room and closed the door behind him as I pulled up two chairs so that Peroz could sit down and I could do the same. I smiled at the nervous young beauty sitting on the bed.

'You must be Roxanne,' I said. 'I am delighted to meet you.'

Those brown eyes met mine and then she looked down at the floor. 'Thank you, majesty,' she replied softly.

I sat and listened to his story, about how he had been visiting Roxanne for a number of weeks at a regular time and how he had decided, on a whim, to take Spartacus and Scarab to see her. The three of them had spent much time together during the preceding months and Peroz had wanted to show them the woman he had obviously fallen in love with.

274

And so they had sauntered down to the brothel not realising that this was not the usual time that Peroz visited, and had arrived to discover that Roxanne had been sold to the oafish brute downstairs for the evening. Enraged at what he perceived to be the abuse of his beloved he had thrown the man out of her room and barricaded himself in, along with my two squires. As he talked I began to realise that Peroz did not think of Roxanne as a prostitute but as a sort of princess from a fable, always waiting for him each week when they would spend hours in each other's arms. So besotted was he with her that the thought that she would lie with other men had not even entered his mind, either that or he purposely shut it out of his thoughts.

My heart sank when, still clutching her hand, he stood up and announced. 'Roxanne will be a princess of Carmania, lord, for after the war I will be taking her back to my homeland.'

I smiled politely as my mind was filled with images of his enraged father and mocking brother when he presented a whore at court. And it would hardly reflect well on Dura or its king that Peroz had been allowed to consort with prostitutes. But then, the Kingdom of Dura was held in low esteem by many in the empire and what did I care about what others thought? I did care about the thousands of Carmanian horse archers that were a valuable addition to my army and I liked the young prince who commanded them. Two things were obvious: that Peroz would never agree to leave this establishment without his beloved by his side, and the owner of the brothel would never allow her to leave without compensation.

'I think it would be best for everyone, Peroz,' I said to him in a calm manner, 'for you to escort Roxanne back to the palace. I will wait at the foot of the stairs so Roxanne may gather together her clothes and possessions to take with her.'

'I have no possessions, majesty,' she said softly.

I look around at the rich furnishings and her expensive dress. She saw my surprise.

'Everything I wear and all the things in this room are owned by Samhat, majesty.'

When they came downstairs Samhat, who was not amused that I was removing one of the most profitable girls from her establishment, pointed this out to me.

'You can't take her,' she hissed.

Domitus drew his *gladius* and placed the point at her throat.

'The king can do what he likes, including having you and your girls crucified if he has a mind to.'

To her credit Samhat stood her ground though her concubines and girls looked decidedly nervous and some were clutching each other for comfort. 'Big knuckles', still penned into the corner with his friends by the legionaries, was outraged.

'I've paid good money for the whore.'

Spartacus jeered at the man and beckoned him forward, goading him that he was nothing more than a lowborn animal. Before violence flared Domitus removed his sword from Samhat's throat and grabbed my nephew by the scruff of his neck and bundled him outside as 'big knuckles' and his friends, held back by the shields of the legionaries, hurled abuse and threats at him.

'Give him back his money,' I instructed Samhat. 'You will receive compensation from the treasury, and for the girl. She will not be returning to you.'

Samhat was infuriated. 'I have invested a lot of money in her and now you are kidnapping her just because a pampered prince has been love-struck.'

My patience was fast running out. 'First of all, madam, if you had not encouraged him to frequent your premises he would never have met the young girl in question. Secondly, as I have just informed you the treasury will recompense you for your losses, within reason. However, if you continue to insult your king then I will have no option but to close your establishment and have you and your whores flogged from the city.'

My threat had the desired affect and she said no more but I could tell that she was fuming and in truth I was not unsympathetic. But when it came to choosing between Peroz and her there was no contest. Afterwards I strolled back to the palace in the company of Peroz, the woman he wanted to make a princess, Domitus and my squires.

'You should have that old whore flogged for her disrespect,' grumbled Domitus. 'I'll do it.'

'A most generous offer, Domitus,' I replied, 'but in this instance that "old whore" as you call her was correct.'

I nodded at Peroz and Roxanne walking ahead of us. 'He sees her as his future princess whereas Samhat views her as a valuable commodity. I fear the compensation I will have to pay will be prohibitive.'

'You are not actually going to pay her anything?' asked a disbelieving Domitus.

'Samhat pays her taxes and runs a profitable and legal business. If word spreads that the King of Dura arbitrarily ruins businesses then it might affect trade, and less trade means less taxes, which means less money to spend on the army. So you see, my friend, I have little choice.'

'Aaron will be most unhappy,' he said.

I laughed. 'Yes, I suppose he will. But with a war coming I would rather have an unhappy treasurer than an unhappy Prince Peroz.'

'Very sensible, uncle,' said Spartacus behind us.

'Unlike your behaviour tonight,' I scolded him. 'Have you noticed how trouble follows you around like a loyal dog?'

'If trouble comes looking for me I will not shy away from it,' he replied defiantly. 'I was brought up to stand shoulder to shoulder with my friends. Peroz and I have been discussing a double wedding, uncle.'

Domitus rolled his eyes.

'A double wedding? You are both to be congratulated.'

'What are the most extreme odds, do you think?' posed Domitus. 'Your nephew taking a Roman eagle or Peroz's father accepting a whore as his daughter-in-law?'

I wondered the same thing but was strangely comforted by the prospect of the coming war, which might settle things one way or another. Spartacus and Peroz might both be killed, or they might cover themselves in glory and return home as heroes. If so would Haytham let my nephew marry his daughter and would Phriapatius allow his son to marry a whore? Perhaps I would be killed, thus saving me the trouble of having to worry about it all.

Roxanne was given a room in the palace well away from Peroz's though he assured me that nothing untoward would happen while they were under my roof. Gallia thought Peroz most gallant and complimented him on his actions. Early the next day, after Peroz had taken Roxanne south to review his men, she quizzed me if I would inform his father that he desired to marry a whore. I could give her no answer. Although Gallia did not approve of prostitution she had no problem with prostitutes themselves. Her closest friend, Praxima, had been forced to work in a Roman brothel as a whore and Gallia took the view that all prostitutes were forced into their trade, a not wholly accurate view. Some positively relished their profession!

Later that morning the representative of Samhat came to the palace to discuss compensation for Roxanne. I received him in the throne room with Gallia sitting beside me and had summoned Aaron from the treasury. Our visitor strode into the throne room flanked by two guards, having first been searched for concealed weapons. He was a portly man of medium height dressed in a fine orange robe with a purple silk sash around his ample waist and red leather sandals on his feet. He was completely bald and had dark makeup around his eyes. After bowing his head at me and then Gallia we saw he held a bundle of papyrus sheets in his manicured hands.

'Hail, King Pacorus of Dura, son of Varaz and grandson of Sames, Kings of Hatra, and lord high general of the empire and noble defender of all the kingdoms of Parthia. Husband to Queen Gallia, daughter of King Ambiorix...'

I held up a hand. 'You are very well informed but to save time perhaps we might move straight to the business in hand.'

He cleared his throat and smiled. 'Of course, majesty. My name is Chigaru, secretary to Samhat and I have been asked to present to you the details concerning compensation for Roxanne, lately employed at my mistress' establishment.'

I pointed at Aaron. 'This is Lord Aaron, the kingdom's treasurer, who will advise me on the veracity of your claim.'

Chigaru bristled at the implication that his mistress' demands might be fraudulent but quickly composed himself and smiled weakly at Aaron.

'You are a eunuch, are you not?' asked Gallia.

'I am, majesty,' he replied without emotion.

'What are your tasks?' she was clearly fascinated by him.

'I keep a record of all the clients who visit the brothel, fix the price for a night of each girl's favours, receive the money for said favours and provide clothing and other essentials for each of my mistress' women and men.'

'Why are eunuchs employed in brothels?' she quizzed him further.

'Sexually impotent men make the best guardians for young women, majesty' he replied proudly. 'They can be trusted not to spoil the goods and do not covet power. My mistress trusts me completely.'

She leaned forward. 'How long have you been a eunuch?'

'Fourteen years, majesty.'

'Well, this is all most interesting,' I said, 'but...'

Gallia ignored me and continued to stare at Chigaru. 'Did it hurt?'

Chigaru looked at her quizzically. 'Majesty?'

'The ritual by which you became who you are now,' she explained.

He smiled obsequiously. 'Ah, I understand. Your majesty is most inquisitive and people do not normally enquire about how I came to be a eunuch. But I have heard that you are not only a great warrior but also possessed of a keen mind. I was fifteen years of age when they came for me, three huge slaves in the service of my master who had decided that I should be a eunuch.

'I was taken to the kitchens where a physician smeared my groin in pepper broth while one man held my wrists and the other two my legs. The physician then took a small curved knife that resembled a sickle and sliced off my genitals. The pain was excruciating.

'He then with great care inserted lead needles and wooden nails into the gaping wound to staunch the flow of blood and then covered the wound with papyrus that had been soaked in water and used a bandage to keep it in place. Two of the slaves then walked me around my master's house for two hours, after which I was allowed to lie down. I was forbidden to drink any water for three days to allow the wound to partly heal. On the fourth day the physician removed the needles and nails and I passed water like a spurting fountain. I fell to my knees and cried with joy for I knew that the operation had been a success. Those who are castrated and cannot pass water afterwards die a most painful death you see.

'That, majesty, is how I became a eunuch.'

Gallia, far from being revolted, was impressed. 'I congratulate you on your courage, Chigaru.'

He bowed his head solemnly. 'From one whose courage is known throughout the world that is a compliment indeed, majesty.'

'And now, Chigaru,' I said, slightly disgusted by what had been done to him, 'perhaps you will enlighten us as to the amount of compensation your mistress deems reasonable for the girl Roxanne.'

He smiled at me and bowed his head, then glanced at one of his parchments. 'Considering her age, beauty and the expenses that have already been lavished on the young lady in question, the amount of compensation comes to half a talent of gold.'

'Half a talent!' Aaron said loudly. 'That is thirty pounds of gold. For a whore?'

Chigaru remained calm. 'A very accomplished whore.'

Aaron was not amused. 'This is outrageous, majesty. In any case she belongs to Prince Peroz so it is he who should pay Samhat compensation and not Dura's treasury.'

'Roxanne does not belong to the prince,' Gallia said to Aaron, 'she is with him of her own free will. She is not a slave to be bartered in the marketplace.'

'Of course, majesty,' said Aaron in a muted tone, 'but the fact remains that Prince Peroz should pay the indemnity for this young woman.'

Aaron had made a good point but if I asked Peroz to pay the brothel he would no doubt write to his father requesting that he send him the gold. Phriapatius would find out eventually that his youngest son had fallen in love with a whore but he did not need to know yet. Then again, so besotted was Peroz with Roxanne that he might announce his impending marriage to her to the whole world anyway.

'The fee is agreed,' I told Chigaru, 'my treasurer will see that the amount is sent to your mistress forthwith.'

Chigaru looked at Aaron in triumph and then bowed deeply to me and then Gallia. Aaron was fuming but my decision had been made. I had more urgent things to think about than the price of a whore, beautiful though she was.

The guards escorted Chigaru from the throne room and closed the doors behind them.

'It would be wise to request that Carmania's treasury reimburse our own for this amount, majesty,' suggested Aaron.

'Dura's treasury will bear the cost. King Phriapatius has other things to occupy his mind.'

'I do not understand,' said Aaron.

'Though it is none of your business, Aaron, because I am in a good mood I will tell you why we will not be asking Peroz's father for the gold. The King of Carmania will take a very dim view of his son falling in love with a prostitute, and an even dimmer view of his son's hosts for allowing such a thing to happen. He may demand that Prince Peroz and his men leave Dura and return home, in which case I will lose five thousand horse archers that I would rather have by my side when we fight the Romans and Armenians.'

Aaron looked contrite and said nothing further on the matter.

'The eunuch was most efficient,' I had not noticed that Dobbai had entered the chamber but now she shuffled from behind me to stand just in front of the dais. 'Perhaps you should castrate all the members of your council, son of Hatra, to ensure their loyalty and curb their tongues.'

Aaron glared at her as she said the words.

'I have no reason to doubt the loyalty of those who serve me,' I said to her.

'You are fortunate, son of Hatra, that your palace is not infused with malice and treachery but a great warlord has the luxury of knowing that his subordinates fear him.'

'I thought they loved me,' I teased her.

'Love is the most poisonous emotion of all for it blinds men to the obvious and wraps them in a madness from which they do not wish to escape. If Peroz had had his manhood removed then he would not be chasing whores.'

'We are not going to discuss Peroz's manhood,' I told her.

She continued to goad Aaron. 'Jewish priests cut off part of the manhoods of their male infants, is that not correct Jew?'

'I did not realise you knew so much about our customs,' he replied with embarrassment.

'They should lop them off totally,' she said wickedly, 'to make all Jewish males eunuchs, then they would be far less troublesome.'

'Enough, Dobbai,' I snapped, 'you give me a headache. The Jews have proved valuable allies of Dura and the longer they continue to fight the Romans in Judea the more time we have to make our own preparations. Please leave us.'

She sneered at Aaron, smiled at Gallia and ignored me as she ambled back to the private apartments in the palace. I regretted that I had spoken to her so brusquely because that afternoon Dobbai fell ill. At first it was a troublesome cough that had afflicted her while sitting in her chair on the palace balcony. Servants brought her fruit juice and water but she could not shake it off and as the afternoon wore on a concerned Gallia sent for Alcaeus, who prescribed grape juice mixed with honey. However, despite the application of this well-known remedy Dobbai continued to cough, her frail body pitching forward as she did so. Gallia sat holding her hand and an increasingly alarmed Claudia rushed to the kitchens to prepare a concoction of crushed turmeric root. But this and all the other medicines had no effect and Dobbai continued to cough so I assisted Alcaeus in taking her to her bedroom.

After she had been made comfortable her coughing seemed to subside and I breathed a sigh of relief, but as I was about to leave her she grabbed my arm.

'I told you there would be a price to pay, son of Hatra,' her grip was frail and she suddenly looked very old.

'I don't know what you mean,' I said unconvincingly.

She looked at me mockingly. 'Do not insult me. You know full well what I mean. The gods always demand payment, son of Hatra, remember that.'

Gallia stayed with her and Alcaeus returned to his quarters but was later urgently recalled when Dobbai developed a fever. One minute the sweat poured off her and she could not bear a blanket to be over her, the next she was shivering and desperate for warmth. This continued into the late afternoon and early evening. She could only ingest small amounts of water and then with great difficulty, her throat closing as she was wracked by violent spasms. Gallia held her hand, ashen faced, while Claudia became distraught and had to be taken from the room.

Alcaeus was at a loss what to do. He ordered her bedding to be changed and the straw in the mattress to be taken and burnt, and then sent orders to the kitchens to soak two small pieces of cloth in egg whites and bring them to him. When they arrived he wrapped them around the soles of Dobbai's feet. We all looked at him as though he had gone mad.

'An old Greek trick. The egg whites draw the high temperature down from the brain to the feet.'

It worked as Dobbai's temperature began to fall and she became lucid once more.

'Thank you, doctor,' she said weakly, 'but your skills, great as they are, will not work here.'

Alcaeus stayed for another hour, in which Dobbai slept and he suggested that we leave her to get some rest. I sat with him on the palace terrace as Claudia burned dragon's blood resin, which was resin from a palm tree, in Dobbai's room to both purify it and protect her from evil influences

'She is a remarkable young girl,' said Alcaeus, 'her knowledge of herbs and medicines is amazing.'

'I did not know you had been teaching Claudia your craft,' I said.

'I have not. She visits me often and questions me about the workings of the human body but when it comes to treatments she needs little tutoring.'

'She has been close to Dobbai since she was an infant,' I said, 'perhaps too close. How ill is Dobbai?'

He shrugged. 'She is old, Pacorus, and like all elderly people is more susceptible to ailments. She has caught some sort of fever that I have not seen before but the next twenty-four hours should determine whether she survives or not.'

'It is not a fever.'

As we sat in the dark with oil lamps illuminating our faces I told him about the ceremony that Dobbai had carried out and my participation in it, along with the others, about the celestial mist and the howling hounds. He was naturally sceptical and told me that all these things had a rational explanation.

'Drenis and Kronos both took part in the ritual and they are both dead,' I told him.

'They were both soldiers killed on the battlefield; it happens.'

He smiled at me. 'When Dobbai recovers, all these thoughts you are having will disappear. I advise you to get some rest.'

But Dobbai did not recover: over the next two days she got worse. The fever returned and with it violent convulsions that wracked her old body and made her progressively weaker. She drifted in and out of consciousness and visibly diminished before our eyes. The servants were frightened by her sunken cheeks and eye sockets and refused to enter her room. An angry Gallia told them to leave food, water and fresh bedding outside in the corridor and performed all their duties herself. With the help of Claudia she washed Dobbai, changed her soiled bedding and recited prayers that her daughter suggested. It was all to no avail. On the third day Dobbai's hair began to fall out and her breathing became extremely shallow.

That afternoon I stood beside Alcaeus at the foot of the bed staring at the shell of what had been a fierce, determined woman and felt a chill sweep over me. Gallia sat beside her dabbing her forehead with a damp cloth and Claudia sat on the other side of the bed holding Dobbai's hand, her young face pale and her eyes bloodshot from tears and lack of sleep.

'It won't be long now,' he whispered to me.

Dobbai opened her eyes and looked at Claudia, speaking words to her that I was unable to hear. My daughter leaned forward and Dobbai spoke into her ear as tears ran down Claudia's cheeks. She next spoke to Gallia who held the old woman's skeletal-like head in her hands and gently kissed her on the forehead. My wife was also deeply upset and shaking with anguish, trying to suppress the heartache that was threatening to erupt like an angry volcano. Dobbai whispered something to Gallia and my wife nodded. She rose from her chair and walked over to me.

'She wants to speak with you.'

Alcaeus smiled at Gallia and gently placed his arm around her shoulder, reassuring her that she was doing everything she could. My drained and distraught wife looked far from the fearless warrior the world knew.

I sat in the chair and leaned forward as Dobbai once again opened her eyes to look at me.

The fire had gone out of them and they were now dark pools of world-weariness. She moved her hand towards me and I reached out and took it, the fingers cold and bony.

'My time has come, son of Hatra. My ancestors are waiting for me on the great eternal steppe.' Her voice was very faint. 'It will be good to see them again after so many years. Burn my body on a northern wind to quicken my journey.'

Her grip tightened slightly. 'You must stay strong and determined to save the empire. Have faith in the gods, son of Hatra, for they have not forsaken you and will give you what you most desire when all has been settled. That will be your reward for your service to the empire.'

Her voice became even fainter and I had to place an ear next to her mouth to hear her words.

'Thank you, Pacorus, for allowing me to share your home and your family, I have known peace here and for that you have my gratitude. Everything I have done has been for your and their welfare. The gods keep you safe.'

I continued to hold her hand as she close her eyes for the last time and Dobbai, a woman of the Scythian people and sorceress of King of Kings Sinatruces, departed this world. Claudia buried her head in her hands and sobbed as a distressed Gallia comforted her.

282

We burned the body the next day after Gallia and Claudia had washed it and dressed it in a white silk gown. Thousands gathered on the other side of the Euphrates, opposite the Citadel, where the great funeral pyre was sited. Dobbai had spent countless hours sitting on the palace terrace gazing across the river and so it seemed fitting that she should be cremated on this spot. I held the torch as an ocean of faces stared at me – civilians, merchants, servants, legionaries, cataphracts, squires and horse archers. Though none of them had known her they had all known of her and her reputation. They knew that she had commissioned the stone griffin statue that stood sentry at the Palmyrene Gate and had heard of her prophecy that no army would take the city while it remained there. And every legionary in the Durans knew that his beloved golden griffin standard had been Dobbai's brainchild, as I knew that it was she who had given me the griffin as an emblem when she had sent me my battle flag even before I had seen Dura. The Durans and Exiles sported griffin wings on their shields and the *kontus* of every cataphract flew a griffin pennant. So they all came to pay their respects and say farewell to her.

I stood with an ashen-faced Gallia and our children, along with Alcaeus, Domitus, Chrestus, Vagharsh, Vagises, Marcus, Aaron, Peroz and Rsan. The light was fading by the time everyone had gathered around the pyre. It had been a warm, windless day but as I held up the lighted torch I saw the flame flicker and felt a slight breeze on my face. A wind from the north increased as I thrust the torch into the great pile of logs soaked in oil. I stood back as flames erupted around the pyre and the wind picked up to carry her soul back to the resting place of her ancestors.

'Farewell, safe journey.'

I watched the flames consume her body and stayed until nothing was left but a great pile of ashes as the crowd dispersed. Gallia took our children back to the palace and the soldiers went back to their duties.

'She was very old, you know,' the words of Alcaeus came from behind me.

'I know.'

'What I mean is,' he continued, 'old people die and when they do so it does not mean that the gods have taken her as payment for their favours.'

'I know,' I replied without conviction for I knew that the gods had taken Dobbai just as they had seized Drenis and Kronos. I was suddenly fearful for Domitus, Vagises, Thumelicus and Vagharsh who had also taken part in the ceremony. I prayed to Shamash that He would take me before them should the gods demand more souls. Alcaeus placed a reassuring hand on my shoulder and then departed to leave me standing alone in front of a pile of ashes. I bowed my head to the ash, turned and walked with head bowed back to the city. There was a sudden gust of wind that buffeted my cloak. I looked back and saw that there were no longer any embers where the funeral pyre had stood, just a patch of black earth.

As I wandered back over the pontoon bridge and then along the edge of the deep wadi that stood in front of the city's northern wall, I decided that Peroz and Roxanne could make their home in Dura should his father disown his son. Orodes had been a landless prince once and had made his home here so why not Peroz? I walked through the Palmyrene Gate and looked up at the stone griffin above mounting his unceasing guard over all of us.

That night a pall of gloom hung over the palace as I sat with Gallia and we ate in silence. She picked at her food and snapped at servants who went about their duties with heads bowed. Claudia had locked herself in her room as soon as she had returned to the palace and Isabella and Eszter had also been taken to their rooms.

Gallia shoved aside her plate of meat and rice and leaned back in her chair.

'Life here will never be the same.'

I nodded. 'Her departure leaves a void that cannot be filled, I agree.'

'Do you think that her magic died with her?'

'I do not know,' I replied.

'The ritual, I mean, when she sent the girls and me away. Do you think that now she is dead the gods will not honour her spells?'

I thought of Crassus' legions in Syria and the Armenian hordes in the north. 'I hope not, I sincerely hope not.'

Soon after Dobbai's death the old year also died and Byrd rode to Dura with news that Crassus had taken some of his legions south to crush a rebellion that had suddenly flared up in Judea. I asked Aaron to be present as we sat with Domitus and Gallia in the headquarters building and Byrd recounted what he had heard from his sources in Antioch and Damascus, of how Alexander's rebels had terrorised the local population and had been forced back into the hills by Crassus, who had gone on to sack Jerusalem and its temple. I avoided Aaron's eyes as Byrd related how Crassus had plundered the temple and taken away gold to the value of eight thousand talents. It was an incredible sum and a gross insult to the Jewish people and I knew that it had been my fault because I had sent mercenaries to Judea so that Alexander could continue his war against the Romans. I also knew that I did not care and was glad that Judea was being laid waste and not Parthia.

A visibly shaken Aaron left the meeting after Byrd had relayed his tale of woe and we relaxed and talked about Haytham, Malik and Emesa.

'Fat king very subservient to Haytham,' said Byrd, 'send him gifts and offer of one of his daughters, one very young and a virgin.'

'How disgusting,' spat Gallia.

'Haytham said no,' said Byrd, 'he say she probably fat like her father.'

'So the border is quiet?' I asked.

Byrd shrugged. 'It is common knowledge that Crassus will cross Euphrates into Parthia as soon as Judea is quiet. He says he will conquer Palmyra after he has subdued Parthia.'

'How many men has he recruited in Syria?' I asked.

'Three thousand horsemen and four thousand foot. He also awaits his son who will bring a thousand more horsemen.'

'His son?' complained Gallia. 'Is not one Crassus enough?'

Byrd cracked a smile. 'His name is Publius Crassus. My office in Antioch inform me that he has been fighting with another Romani named Caesar in Gaul.' He looked at Gallia. 'Your people are still killing Romans.'

'They are not my people, Byrd,' she replied, 'the citizens of Dura are my people.'

Byrd reached into his tunic and pulled out a piece of folded calfskin.

'This is for your squire, Spartacus' son.'

'What is it?' I enquired.

He twisted his mouth. 'Not know.'

I called for a guard and told him to go and fetch my squires who would be in the stables after their morning training sessions. They arrived a few minutes later, with dirty faces and smelling of horse dung. I pointed at Byrd.

'Byrd has something for you, Spartacus.'

He wiped his face on his sleeve and took the piece of folded calfskin.

'From Rasha,' said Byrd.

Grinning like a halfwit, Spartacus carefully unfolded it to reveal it contained a lock of hair. He smiled at Gallia and then held it up to Scarab.

'It is a lock of Rasha's hair. She said she would send it to me. Now I can wear it around my neck just as the king wear's a lock of the queen's hair.'

Gallia smiled back at him and Byrd looked totally disinterested.

'You still banned from Haytham's lands.'

But Spartacus was elated and stated that he would take the lock of hair into the city this very day where a silversmith would place it on a chain, and afterwards he would wear it around his neck where it would remain until the day he died. This touched Gallia and Scarab embraced him but I reminded him that he might have a piece of Rasha's hair but he still had much to do if he was to take possession of the rest of her. But his high spirits could not be dimmed and he went back to his dung shovelling a happy young man.

'You think he will capture a Romani eagle?' asked Byrd.

I thought for a moment. 'You know, Byrd, the young fool just might.'

His chances of doing so improved slightly at the end of the following week when he was formally inducted into the ranks of the cataphracts. He had served his apprenticeship and now my nephew, the adopted son of King Gafarn and Queen Diana of Hatra, became one of Parthia's élite horsemen. I asked him if he wished to return to Hatra to be inducted into its Royal Bodyguard but he was insistent that he wished to take the oath of allegiance at Dura. I pointed out to him that when he returned to Hatra he would have to take a new oath of allegiance to Gafarn and the city but he replied that he would always be loyal to his father and the city he had been raised in, but that he believed that if he took the oath at Dura it would increase his chances of marrying Rasha because it was nearer to her. I agreed but immediately wrote to Gafarn and Diana informing them of his decision and also begging their forgiveness. Strictly speaking I should have sent him back to Hatra but I had grown fond of him and in truth wished to keep hold of him a little longer.

I need not have worried because Gafarn and Diana answered my despatch with their arrival at Dura. They left young Pacorus in the care of my mother and their city in the capable hands of Vistaspa and Kogan. I stood with my friends on the palace steps as twenty former squires stood on the flagstones of the Citadel's courtyard and became cataphracts. The gates were closed and the guards on the walls faced inwards to bear witness to the sacred ceremony.

A priest from the city's Temple of Shamash conducted the oath taking. His building was a far cry from the grand structure of the Great Temple in Hatra but his authority was no less diminished for it. He stood in front of the row of young men and waited until the sun was at its zenith to honour Shamash, then ordered them all to kneel and bow their heads. In front of each squire was laid his suit of scale armour, complete with leg and arm protection, his helmet and his weapons: *kontus*, sword, dagger, mace and axe. I remembered when I had taken the oath all those years ago at Hatra when I had knelt beside my friend Vata and where my father and his general, Lord Bozan, had stood on the palace steps looking on with pride. How long ago that seemed.

The priest, a barrel-chested man with a huge thick beard and booming voice, commanded the squires to repeat the words he now spoke:

'I will never disgrace my sacred arms,
Nor desert my comrades, wherever I am stationed.
Nor will I take a step backwards in battle.
I will fight for things sacred,
And against things profane.
And both alone and with all to help me.
I will defend my homeland, its people, its crops and its sacred waters.
I will obey the king, who rules reasonably,
And I will observe the established laws,
And whatever laws in the future,
May be reasonably established.
If any person seeks to overturn the laws,
Both alone and with help I will oppose him.
I shall protect the king in country and in town, fall and die for him.
I shall speak with him in the truth of my heart,
Give him sound advice loyally, and smooth his way in every respect.
I will also honour the religion of my fathers.
I call on the great Sun God Shamash to witness this my oath of allegiance.
May I be struck down by Your mighty power if I fail You.'

Thus did Spartacus, son of the slave general of the same name and Prince of Hatra, become a cataphract and thus passed into manhood.

Afterwards all of them were entertained in the banqueting hall for this was one of the most important days in their lives.

'He looks happy,' remarked Diana after her son had embraced her and returned to his table to sit next to Scarab.

'He is very happy,' I replied, 'though that has more to do with Dura's proximity to a certain Agraci princess than his becoming a cataphract.'

Gafarn sipped at his wine. 'He is still besotted with her, then?'

'Totally,' I said.

'Then perhaps it is as well that he stays here for the moment. I have enough grumbling among my lords without adding to their grievances with my heir marrying an Agraci woman.'

'Your lords are restless?' I was surprised because Hatra's nobles were previously reckoned among the most loyal in the empire.

'Nothing that cannot be handled,' he replied unconvincingly.

But of course Spartacus could not stay at Dura indefinitely and I told him that as he sat with his parents, Gallia and our children on the palace balcony the day after the ceremony. I felt myself glancing at Dobbai's chair often and still felt a pang in my heart when I thought of her. I did

287

not know why: she had always adopted a condescending attitude towards me and had openly mocked me on many occasions. And yet she had watched over my wife and children like a hawk and for that I was grateful. Claudia was very morose at this time and took to wearing black robes just as her tutor had done. She also covered her head with a black shawl that hid her hair and part of her beauty. Gallia was also withdrawn though she tried to put on a brave face.

'We were sorry to hear about your sorceress,' said Diana.

'Her loss is keenly felt by the whole kingdom,' my wife replied.

'She watches over us still,' announced Claudia, who then went and sat in Dobbai's chair and stared east across the blue waters of the Euphrates.

Spartacus sat next to Diana fingering the lock of Rasha's hair that hung around his neck from an expensive gold chain. Gafarn noticed it.

'A lucky pendant, Spartacus?'

'Yes, father,' he beamed, 'a lock of my beloved's hair. It will keep me safe from the weapons of the enemy and means we will always be close to each other. I have sent her some of my own hair.'

Diana smiled and laid a hand on his arm. 'Most romantic.'

'I have heard that you are banished from the Agraci's lands on pain of death,' said Gafarn smugly.

'It is a test, father, nothing more, to ensure that I am worthy of marrying Rasha. Once I have fulfilled my quest then her father will allow me to marry his daughter.'

Gafarn shook his head. 'Quest?'

'Yes, father,' replied Spartacus, 'to capture a Roman eagle and plant it in the soil in front of King Haytham.'

Gafarn's brow furrowed. 'It is no small thing to capture a Roman eagle. In the whole history of the Parthian Empire only one man has done it and he sits next to you.'

'I know that, father,' Spartacus replied, 'I have seen the eagle in the Great Temple at Hatra and have heard the tale of its taking since I was a small boy.'

Gafarn pointed at him. 'There was only one legion that day. I remember because I was there but it took all the guile and skill of Hatra's army to defeat it and now there are many legions preparing to invade Parthia. What use will it serve to throw away your life on a futile adventure?'

I agreed but said nothing.

Spartacus thought for a moment before replying. 'Have you ever considered, father, that it may have been fate that I came to Dura, that I fell in love with Rasha and then saved Haytham's life? It is as if the gods have planned out my life for me and I believe that it is to be beside Rasha.'

Gafarn looked up at the sky. 'You saved Haytham's life? There will be many Parthians who will be shocked that a prince of Hatra did so.'

'What do I care about what others think?' my nephew replied.

'You should,' said Gafarn, 'there are many in Hatra who disapprove that their king is a former Bedouin slave and their queen a former Roman slave. Their displeasure will be compounded when they learn that the heir to the throne is a friend of the Agraci king.'

'My uncle is a friend of Haytham,' said Spartacus defiantly.

Gafarn nodded. 'Indeed, but he is a feared warlord who has won many victories and, above all, he is a Parthian whose father and grandfather were great servants of the empire. You must learn to see yourself as others perceive you, Spartacus. That is a lesson I have learned the hard way.'

I looked at Gallia but said nothing though it was obvious from the bitterness in Gafarn's voice that he did not have the unconditional support of the kingdom's lords, which was very worrying. But I did not pay much heed to Gafarn's grumblings – defeats at the hands of the Armenians would not have improved the humour of his nobles but a victory would easily dispel any doubts they may have had about their king.

The next day Spartacus prepared to leave Dura and return to Hatra with his parents, but his and their plans were disrupted when a courier arrived from Ctesiphon telling of a great disaster in the east.

I called together all the members of the council, together with Gafarn and Diana, in the headquarters building and relayed the news that I had received from Orodes.

'The northern nomads have defeated the combined army of Kings Khosrou and Musa near the city of Nisa in Margiana. They have subsequently flooded south and west to devastate large areas of Margiana and Hyrcania and now threaten the Kingdom of Atropaiene.

'The nomads, the Saka and Dahae peoples, have united under a leader called Attai, which means "father" apparently, and now stand on the verge of conquering much of northeast Parthia.'

'What of the other eastern kingdoms?' asked Gafarn.

'Unfortunately,' I said, 'they are also under attack, or at least some of them are. Orodes has further informed me that the Yuezhis, a people who inhabit the lands to the north of the Kingdom of Yueh-Chih, have begun raiding this kingdom and also as far south as Aria, the kingdom immediately south of Yueh-Chih.'

'Sounds more than a coincidence,' snarled Domitus.

'I agree,' I replied. 'This Attai obviously has a strategy that appears to aim at carving a great slice off the east of the empire. Orodes has requested my presence at the city of Assur to determine a course of action.'

Gafarn was surprised. 'Why Assur?'

'Because Aschek and Atrax will not wish to be far from their kingdoms with a horde of nomads threatening their borders and Orodes has also asked Surena to present himself.'

'You think he will answer the summons?' asked a dubious Gallia.

In truth I had no idea. 'I hope so for the sake of the empire.'

'He is not a Parthian,' muttered Gafarn, 'what is the empire to him?'

289

His dark mood had obviously not brightened since yesterday. After the meeting he and Diana hastened back to Hatra with their bodyguard but without Spartacus, who requested that he be allowed to stay at Dura until after the gathering at Assur. Gafarn, no doubt concerned that in addition to the Armenians in the north and the Romans in the west, he may have nomads raiding his eastern border, offered no protest. We said our farewells to our friends and then I made ready to ride to Assur. After they had left Domitus came to see me as I was inspecting Remus' saddlery next to his stall.

'This business in the east could not have come at a worse time.'

'I know,' I concurred, 'Aschek will never commit his army in the west with the threat of a nomad invasion of his kingdom from the east.'

He kicked at some straw on the floor. 'And Atrax?'

I placed the bridle back on its hook. 'Aschek will want him to deploy his troops on his eastern border so they may readily reinforce his own army if necessary.'

He leaned against the wall. 'Our forces diminish by the minute. We will need all the troops we can muster to meet the Romans and Armenians in the next few months. Losing Atrax's army would be a grievous loss. And then there is the matter of Surena.'

'Surena has become a law unto himself, though I am grateful that he is still waging war against the Armenians,' I said.

'Do you think he will show his face at Assur?'

I sat down on the bench opposite Remus' stall. 'I have no idea. But even he must realise that if we fall then Gordyene will be an island surrounded by a sea of enemies and will surely be overwhelmed itself.'

Domitus shrugged. 'Perhaps that is what he wants: to die in a blaze of glory and join his wife and child in the afterlife.'

He slapped me on the shoulder. 'Safe journey,' and then sauntered away.

Remus poked his head over the half-door that gave access to his stall.

'Another journey for you, old friend.'

I stood up and walked over to him to stroke his cheek.

'I bet you did not think when I took you from the stables of that rich Roman in Nola all those years ago that you would spend your life traversing the Parthian Empire.'

He flicked his ears and pushed his muzzle into my chest.

'Perhaps one day you will be able to retire and live out the rest of your days in peace.'

'And that should be soon.'

The unkempt figure of Strabo shuffled into the stable and walked over to me. He stroked Remus' neck.

'You are riding to Assur, majesty.'

'I'm glad palace gossip is as efficient as ever, Strabo.'

He ignored the sarcastic remark. 'Another campaign beckons, then?'

'Yes, I will be riding him into battle once more.'

He stopped stroking my horse and looked at me. 'This should be his last campaign.'

'His last campaign? Why? Is he ill?'

'Not ill, majesty, no. But he is not getting any younger and his heart and legs are not as strong as they were.' Strabo smiled at Remus. 'You may think he is immortal and he certainly does, but the truth is that all the battles and campaigns he has taken part in have taken their toll. After the coming campaign you should ride *Tegha*.'

'There is nothing wrong with Remus,' I said angrily, 'he looks the same as he did twenty years ago.'

Strabo sighed. 'You are the king and can of course do as you wish. You may ride your horse until he collapses and dies under you if you so choose, but I know that you would not do such a thing for you are not such a king. I would be failing in my duty if I did not give you my opinion. I know you love this horse and do not wish to be parted from him, but not even kings can halt time and the toll it exacts upon all living things.'

From being angry I became alarmed. 'Are you saying that another campaign may kill him?'

'Another campaign may kill you first,' he replied disrespectfully. 'Wearing armour and charging around a battlefield places a great strain on a horse's heart. The mounts of the horse archers do not have to carry such a burden, though they risk being cut and pierced by arrows. Then there is the stress of battle. It's not only men who piss themselves with fear in combat.'

'Most eloquently put, Strabo.'

He tickled Remus under the chin. 'I know you will make the right decision.' He nodded slightly then turned and ambled away.

I sat back down on the bench, placed my elbows on my legs and rested my chin in my hands. I had never given the health of Remus a second thought. He had always been a strong and sturdy horse who had ridden in many battles to emerge unscathed. When other horses had died due to heart failure at the dreadful Battle of Susa he had survived, obviously making me think that he could go on forever. But nothing lasts forever, it seems, as Dobbai's death should have taught me. *Tegha* was a good horse and I resolved to ride him after the coming campaign, but retiring Remus would be akin to losing my right arm. But then he deserved to rest on his laurels in his autumn years. I wondered if I would be allowed the same privilege: would I even see my autumn years? No matter how many enemies I vanquished there always seemed to be an unending supply of new ones to fight.

The next day I left for Assur.

It took us five days to reach the city. At Dura patrols were increased along the borders in case Crassus decided to launch any surprise raids into the kingdom, though Byrd assured me that his network of spies and informants in Syria and Judea would give him prior warning of any such attack. The northeast of the empire may have been burning but that was nearly a thousand miles away and in the west of Parthia there existed a surreal peace. The roads were filled with traffic and farmers worked in their fields. West of Dura the road to Palmyra was never busier and the city was ringed not by Romans but by trade caravans, whose crews and guards flooded into the city each day to spend their money on food, hospitality and whores. I had to admit that it had been a masterstroke by Aaron to place a tax on the brothels whose dues went directly to the upkeep of the army. The city's markets were blossoming and peace guaranteed that the farmers who worked on the lords' estates prospered and paid their rents. And when the lords prospered so did the city treasury when they paid their annual tributes.

Aaron was always pestering me to raise taxes and the tribute but I resisted his pleas. The treasury was almost always full and so there was enough money to maintain the army and thus ensure a peaceful kingdom. And where there was peace there was trade and where there was trade there was a constant flow of money into the treasury.

Occasionally a slave trader would present himself at the palace and petition me to allow him to establish a slave market in the city, promising to share equally the profits with the crown if he was allowed to do so. I always refused. I could not besmirch the memory of Spartacus by permitting such a thing. There were no slaves in the palace and there would be no slave markets in the city, at least not while I was king. Aaron was most distraught when he heard that I had turned my back on a lucrative venture but I informed him that I was king and not a businessman, but that he was welcome to take up the matter of slave trading with the queen if he so wished. He bowed politely and I heard no more about it.

I took Spartacus, Scarab and a hundred horse archers with me to Assur, the city looking none the worse for the Armenian assault it had suffered recently. The gates had been repaired, the moat had been cleared of debris and bodies and Hatra's banner of the white horse's head flew from every gatehouse. A captain of the garrison and half a dozen of his white-uniformed riders met me a mile from the city and asked that I camp my horse archers on the Plain of Makhmur located opposite the city, on the eastern side of the Tigris. The return of Silaces' horse archers and the rest of the garrison had resulted in there being no spare quarters for the escorts of the other kings who had arrived. I asked the officer who was present.

'High King Orodes, majesty, in addition to King Gafarn, King Atrax and King Nergal. All their men are camped on the plain.'

'King Surena has not arrived?' I asked him.

'No, majesty.'

My escort rode with the captain and his men to the Plain of Makhmur while I entered the city with Spartacus and Scarab, leaving our horses outside the governor's palace where Lord Herneus received us. He looked meaner and more unforgiving than ever, his head devoid of any hair and his features looking as if they had been carved from rock. He walked beside me as we made our way through the palace to my quarters.

'I hear that Surena is not here.'

'Arrogant little bastard,' spat Herneus, who had been appointed by my father for his iron-hard determination and loyalty and not for his etiquette. 'He was willing enough to receive support from me and Atrax when he was fighting the Armenians in Gordyene, but now he does not need us any more he treats us like lepers.'

'His war with the Armenians must be absorbing much of his time.'

He was seething. 'Rumour is that he has unleashed his Sarmatian mercenaries on Armenia where they can amuse themselves butchering women and children while Surena broods in his palace, plotting his next move, and his army camps outside its walls.'

'We will need that army in the coming months, Herneus.'

I was shown into the reception hall where Orodes, Gafarn, Atrax and Nergal were waiting. It was good to see them all again and all thoughts of eastern nomads, Armenians and Romans were temporarily forgotten as we greeted each other and reminisced about old times. Orodes told me that the rebuilding of Seleucia's walls was proceeding apace and that Axsen had finally agreed to move permanently to Ctesiphon, which was also being renovated. Nergal informed me that Praxima was well and was looking forward to slaughtering Romans when they invaded and hoped to kill Crassus himself, while Atrax reported that his boys were growing up fast and would soon be riding into battle beside him. I asked after my sister's health and he said that Aliyeh was fine but said no more about her. Gafarn embraced Spartacus warmly and announced to everyone that he was now a cataphract and would soon be taking his place among Hatra's Royal Bodyguard. My nephew blushed as everyone congratulated him and patted him on the back.

As I was tired after my journey I retired to my quarters and bathed to wash the desert from my body and then enjoyed the company of a nubile young slave girl who massaged my back, arms and legs with oil. In a semi-daze I felt her slim fingers trace the lines of the numerous scars that decorated my back.

'You have many scars, high-born,' she purred.

'A memento of my time in a foreign land.'

'It must have been terrible for you to suffer such injuries.'

'It was not something that I would have chosen,' I agreed.

'The foreigners must have been savages to treat a great king in such a way.'

'I was not a king at the time,' I corrected her, 'I was a slave like you.'

Shocked, she momentarily stopped weaving her magic with her fingers. 'A slave? I do not understand.'

'A long time ago I was captured by a people called the Romans who put me in chains and took me back to their homeland to live as a slave until I died. One Roman whipped me and gave me the scars you see with your own eyes.'

She resumed her massaging. 'What happened to these Romans, great one?'

293

'They now stand on the borders of the empire and wish to conquer Parthia.'

'But you will fight them?'

'Oh yes,' I replied, 'that is my destiny – to fight Romans forever.'

The next day I sat around a table with the other kings plus Herneus in the governor's private quarters to determine our course of action. Orodes, as ever a stickler for procedure, had requested that clerks record the conversation for posterity. I often wondered why we bothered with all these records. Who would ever read the stacks of parchments that gathered dust in the archives of every city and town in the empire?

'So, my friends,' began the king of kings after slaves had served us all wine, 'we are here to decide the course of action in this, a year of grave danger for the empire. In the east the steppe nomads have united under one leader and threaten to sweep into the empire like a great flood, while to the north and west the Armenians and Romans muster their forces to invade Parthia.'

'Do we have any recent news from Musa and Khosrou?' I asked.

Orodes looked at Atrax who now spoke. 'Aschek has mustered his forces on his eastern border to meet the nomads should they sweep west, but at the moment they are content to plunder Hyrcania and Margiana.'

'Where are the armies of Khosrou and Musa?' asked Nergal.

'Khosrou licks his wounds in his capital, Merv,' replied Atrax, 'while Musa rallies his men at his capital, Hecatompylos.'

'And there is more bad news from the Kingdom of Yueh-Chih,' interrupted Orodes, 'where King Monaeses contains the Yuezhis with difficulty. They have all appealed for my help and I must send it.'

I looked at him with alarm. 'Send who?'

I glanced nervously at Atrax. 'If you despatch Atrax and Aschek then it will seriously weaken the size of the army that will face the Romans and Armenians in the west.'

Orodes took a gulp of wine. 'I know that, Pacorus, but as high king I cannot stand by and do nothing while the empire is being overrun. Aschek has stated that he will go to Musa's aid as his kingdom borders Hyrcania.'

That came as no surprise to me though I doubted whether Aschek was the man to lead a relief expedition, but I held my tongue on that subject. But if Orodes suggested that Atrax supported Aschek then that was another matter. The King of Media was a fine commander and had an excellent army whose loss in the west would be keenly felt.

'What about the other eastern kings?' I suggested. 'Cannot they send men to the north?'

'They are like rabbits hypnotised by a cobra,' replied Orodes. 'Aria is already being raided by the Yuezhis and so Anauon and Drangiana to the south of that kingdom look to their own defences. There is only one man who can shore up our eastern frontier and that is Phriapatius.'

'He leads our reserve army should we need it against Crassus and the Armenians,' I said.

Orodes was not to be moved. 'I cannot help that, Pacorus. Phriapatius has thousands of men at Persepolis and they are needed in the north. He can link up with Aschek's army and together they can aid Musa and Khosrou.'

Orodes smiled at Atrax. 'Such a course of action will also safeguard Media's eastern frontier to allow Atrax to support us in the west.'

Atrax nodded in agreement and I had to admit that the plan made sense. The nomads had to be cleared from the northeast and the Yuezhis also had to be taught a lesson they would not forget and Phriapatius did command a large army, which could be mobilised to achieve these things. But it also meant stripping troops from the west.

'Surena's absence is keenly felt,' fumed Gafarn.

Orodes tactfully ignored the mention of the man who had snubbed him by not being here and instead nodded to one of the guards standing by the door, who opened it and went outside into the corridor. Orodes stood.

'Amid all the gloom that has engulfed us I have decided to fill the vacant throne of Elymais.'

King Gotarzes, a friend and ally of my father who had been killed by Narses and Mithridates during the civil war, had formerly ruled Elymais. Mithridates had subsequently taken over the kingdom but since his overthrow Orodes had ruled it. I heard footsteps and saw Silaces enter the room.

'Welcome Silaces,' said Orodes, 'please take a seat.'

He pointed at an empty chair beside me that Silaces walked to after bowing his head to Orodes.

'The office of king of kings is an onerous one,' said Orodes, who remained standing, 'though one of the more agreeable privileges that comes with it is the ability to reward loyalty and courage. Silaces, you have never faltered in your loyalty to your dead king or your homeland. During the terrible years of civil strife when you and your men were exiles from Elymais you continued to serve the allies of your kingdom, first with Pacorus and then assisting Surena in liberating Gordyene.'

Everyone began rapping their knuckles in the table in agreement, much to the embarrassment of Silaces. Orodes raised his hands to request silence.

He continued. 'And so as a reward for your unfaltering loyalty I have decided to appoint you King of Elymais. May your reign be long and prosperous.'

Silaces' mouth opened and closed but no words came out so shocked was he. I slapped him on the shoulder and once again the other kings rapped their knuckles on the table.

Orodes sat down. 'But I am afraid you and your men are still needed here for the time being so you will not yet be able to sit on your throne. And well done.'

I rose and offered my hand to Silaces who also stood. The others likewise offered him their congratulations and such was the commotion that no one noticed the figure of Surena framed in the doorway.

295

Dressed in an iron scale armour cuirass, black shirt, black leggings and black boots, he looked like an avenging demon. Gone was the carefree, impious youth I had brought back with me from the great marshlands many years ago. His long black hair was unkempt and his eyes were cold and menacing. In truth I scarcely recognised him.

'The wanderer returns,' said Orodes with a trace of mockery. He pointed at an empty chair. 'We have left a place for you but thought you would not be attending, such is the paucity of communications with Gordyene of late.'

Surena sauntered over to the chair and flopped down in it. 'I have had important matters to attend to.'

He nodded at Silaces and managed a half-smile in my direction.

'Is not the summons of the high king important?' asked an exasperated Gafarn.

Surena snapped his fingers at a slave to indicate he wished to be served wine.

'Not more important that defending my kingdom, no,' Surena replied insolently. The company of Sarmatians had clearly not improved his manners.

It was fortunate that Orodes was a master at diplomacy as he let the insult pass and everyone retook their seats. The high king acquainted Surena with what had happened in his absence who was genuinely pleased that Silaces, whom he had fought beside in the liberation of Gordyene, was now the king of Elymais, and thought the plan to send Phriapatius north a sensible one.

'And so the only matter that is left to be resolved is Crassus and the Armenians,' announced Orodes. 'We cannot fight one war in the east and another in the west at the same time; the risks are too great. As we are already at war in the east I see no option but to try to postpone conflict in the west until matters in the east have been resolved to our advantage. This being the case I have decided to request a one-year truce with the Romans.'

Atrax, Nergal and Silaces said nothing though Gafarn looked disappointed, which was noticed by Orodes.

'I realise that the Armenians still have control of the north of your kingdom and Roman troops occupy your western towns, Gafarn, but when the nomads and Yuezhis have been dealt with the full might of the empire can be turned west to eject the Armenians and Romans from Parthian lands.'

Orodes smiled at me. 'I would like Pacorus to go to Syria to treat with Crassus, a man whom he has had previous dealings with, and persuade him that peace is preferable to war.'

'How will I do that?' I enquired.

'Simple, my friend. Your fame as a great warlord, combined with your position as Parthia's lord high general and the offer of gold, will be difficult for the Romans to resist.'

I was confused. 'Gold?'

Orodes leaned back in his chair. 'This Crassus is a greedy man, that much I know. He covets wealth above all and so I will offer him riches. Ten thousand talents of gold to be precise, if he agrees to twelve months of peace.'

Ten thousand talents was a colossal amount of gold. 'I did not realise that the treasury at Ctesiphon was so full,' I said.

Orodes placed his hands behind his head. 'It isn't. I will have to request donations from every kingdom in the empire to amass such an amount, but the point is that you dangle it in front of Crassus so he will take the bait.'

'It will not deter him from wanting to conquer Parthia,' I said. 'It will more likely make him more desirous to take possession of a land that has seemingly limitless riches.'

'But it will buy us time, Pacorus,' replied Orodes, 'and at the moment that is a more precious commodity than gold.'

'You are wrong.'

Surena had contented himself with drinking his wine and seemed not to be taking much notice of proceedings, until now.

'You have something to say, Surena?' asked Orodes.

Surena drained his cup and pointed at a slave holding a jug of wine and then at his empty vessel. 'You waste your time talking to the Romans. I agree that Pacorus, that is King Pacorus, should go to Syria, but he should have an army at his back with which to destroy the legions there and burn Antioch to the ground. That is the only language the Romans understand.'

For a moment everyone thought he was joking but we quickly realised that he was deadly serious.

'Have you forgotten about the Armenians?' asked a somewhat discomforted Orodes.

'The armies of Hatra, Gordyene and Media can take care of the Armenians,' Surena replied confidently, 'while Dura's army, supported by Babylon and Mesene, can lay waste to Syria.'

'My sources have informed me that Crassus has nine legions in total,' I said to him, 'in addition to troops he has raised locally. He can put fifty thousand men into the field.'

'And you can match those numbers, lord. With your army and your lords you can march with over thirty thousand men, plus the armies of King Nergal and King Orodes, another fifteen thousand men. And there are Haytham's warriors.'

Gafarn was appalled. 'Haytham?'

Surena cast him a disparaging glance. 'It is well known that Dura and Haytham are allies and have assisted each other in their wars. Haytham would gladly provide warriors to plunder Syria.'

'Just as your men have plundered Armenia?' said Orodes.

Surena smiled. 'Of course. Gordyene is no longer troubled by Armenian incursions now that my soldiers have taken the fight to the lands of Artavasdes. The soldiers of this Crassus already sit in some Parthian towns. It is an insult to the empire.'

'Perhaps we should make you lord high general, Surena,' said Orodes mockingly.

'Perhaps you should,' Surena replied.

'Careful boy,' snarled Herneus, 'just because you've butchered a few Armenians does not give you the right to speak to the high king disrespectfully.'

Surena sneered at him. 'Take care, old man, you might talk your head off its shoulders.'

Herneus jumped up and grasped the hilt of his sword. Surena laughed.

'Sit down, Herneus!' commanded Gafarn.

Surena grinned triumphantly at him as the governor of Assur, his cheeks flushed with anger, slowly retook his seat. Nergal looked at me and shook his head.

'You should have a care who you insult, Surena,' I said, 'one day you might need those whom you now mock.'

'Your behaviour is unacceptable, Surena,' said Orodes sternly.

Surena held up his hands. 'I apologise for my enthusiasm. I prefer fighting to talking and only war will remove the enemy from the empire's lands. The fact is that every day the Romans and Armenians piss on Parthian land the more we appear weak and helpless. Only by striking at the enemy's lands can we reassert our greatness.'

'We will take back all our lands,' promised Orodes, 'but to wage two wars at once is folly.'

'No,' said Surena firmly, 'your plan is folly.'

There were murmurs from the others that he had spoken to the high king so but Surena was unconcerned.

'Crassus will reject your offer of gold for a truce,' he continued. 'It will serve only to make him more determined to launch his war sooner so that he may take possession of all the empire's riches. He sits in Syria and prepares his army and we do nothing. It is better to kill an enemy than to talk with him, that much I have learned.'

I stared at him and saw a man eaten away by bitterness and anger: bitter that the woman he adored had been cruelly snatched from him and angry against the whole world because of it.

'Perhaps,' said Orodes calmly, 'another high king might agree with you, Surena. But I do not and while I am high king we will follow my plan. If Crassus rejects my offer then you will have your war but we will attempt to buy time first, which will ultimately serve our purpose more.

'In addition, I have no desire to add Syria to the empire. If we invade Syria; what then?'

'Then it becomes a wasteland and a buffer between the empire and Roman territory,' replied Surena casually.

'We are not Romans, Surena,' I told him. 'We do not create a desert and call it peace. What about the thousands of people who live in Syria? Will you kill them or sell them into slavery? I have spent all my life opposing such things and I tell you that I will have no part of a war with such objectives.'

'It is as Pacorus says,' added Orodes.

'You will not be attacking the Armenians and Romans?' he asked.

'Not yet,' answered Orodes.

Surena looked resigned. 'I see that my words have fallen on stony ground, which is a shame.' He suddenly stood up. 'I see little merit in remaining here if all we are to do is talk about appeasing our enemies.'

'Yet again you show disrespect to your high king,' remarked Gafarn disapprovingly.

'You should concern yourself more with defending your kingdom, Gafarn,' said Surena dismissively, 'before more of it is eaten up by our enemies.'

'Is your memory so short, Surena,' growled Gafarn, 'that you have forgotten who created you a king? It was Orodes. Or the man who raised you up from living among marsh dwellers and gave you an education in the military arts? It was Pacorus. Do you not think that you are in their debt?'

Surena pointed at Gafarn. 'I brought Gordyene back into the empire and have been drawing Armenian soldiers to the north to defend their borders when they could have been marching south to Hatra. Given support I could defeat Artavasdes and retake Nisibus, something that you appear incapable of. So in answer to your question I think I have more than repaid any debts I may have accrued.'

He bowed his head ever so slightly to Orodes and then walked from the room, throwing his empty cup at a slave standing near the door.

'Surena,' I said before he disappeared into the corridor, causing him to halt and face me. 'I hope I can rely on your support when the fighting begins.'

'The fighting has already begun,' he replied sullenly.

'If we all go our separate ways,' I told him, 'in the end we will all go the same way.'

He turned on his heels and walked briskly from the room, the guards outside closing the door as he left.

'Arrogant little bastard,' seethed Herneus, looking at Orodes. 'You should let me take some men and I'll bring him back from Vanadzor in chains so he can be punished.'

Herneus was a man of iron and an excellent governor of Assur but he grossly underestimated Surena, a man who had liberated an enemy occupied Gordyene single-handedly.

'We cannot spare you, Lord Herneus,' said Gafarn, 'much as I concur with your proposed course of action.'

'Surena is intemperate, I agree,' said Orodes, 'but his rashness is a result of his immaturity and eagerness to wage war against the enemy. His behaviour was unacceptable and men have lost their heads for less, but right now I cannot afford to lose him or his army.'

'When the war begins he will bring his army to fight by our side,' I said, 'of that I am certain.'

Orodes nodded. 'Notwithstanding Surena's opposition to the idea, I would still like you to go to Syria, Pacorus, to offer Crassus my proposal.'

'You have been to his house before,' Gafarn said to me, 'so he should be amenable to hearing what you have to say at least.'

'That was a long time ago,' I replied.

'What is he like, this Crassus?' asked Herneus.

I thought for a moment. 'Generous, polite and hospitable are words that could be applied to him.'

'And merciless. Don't forget he had six thousand of our comrades crucified in Italy,' said Nergal bitterly.

'He is ruthless, certainly,' I agreed, 'like most Roman leaders, but Crassus is also greedy. He not only covets land for Rome but also wealth for himself. Twenty years ago he was perhaps Rome's richest man and the passing of time has not reduced his appetite for gold, his looting of the temple at Jerusalem is testimony to that. It is as if he has to accumulate wealth in the same way that a man needs air to breathe and that may be his undoing.'

'How so?' asked Atrax.

'Because,' I replied, 'his perception that Parthia is overflowing with gold may lead him to make rash decisions that will play into our hands.'

'It is agreed, then,' said Orodes. 'Pacorus will go to Antioch and play the role of peacemaker.'

I left Assur the next day, Orodes having sent a courier to Phriapatius at Persepolis requesting him to march north at speed to the Caspian Gates and thence to relieve King Musa who was in his capital of Hecatompylos. Thus did I lose forty thousand well-trained and led soldiers, who would be campaigning in the northeast corner of the empire for at least six months, perhaps longer. It would take Phriapatius three weeks alone to reach the Gates, a strategically important pass that runs east and west through a spur of the Alborz Mountains that lay below the southern shore of the Caspian Sea. If Aschek was a competent commander then he could have led the relief expedition but as it was he would be supporting Phriapatius. I cursed the memory of Mithridates and hoped that he was enduring torments in the underworld because he had been responsible for inciting the northern nomads to strike at the empire.

Khosrou and Musa had always had volatile frontiers but any violence was usually restricted to minor raids and looting. When I had first met Khosrou at the Council of Kings at Esfahan all those years ago he had told me that he had encouraged the nomads to try trade instead of raids and had had some success, and had even enticed some of them into the ranks of his army. But Mithridates had bribed the nomads' chiefs with gold to attack Margiana and Hyrcania during the civil war and their appetite for plunder had returned with a vengeance. Worse, new tribes came from the steppes in the far north, enticed by tales of easy plunder and untold riches. And now they had been united under this Attai. The last thing the empire needed was hordes of barbarians pressing on its northern borders as the Romans prepared to renew hostilities in the west.

'It is a mistake, Pacorus.'

Domitus reclined in his chair after I had briefed him on what had been decided at Assur. We were sitting in his tent in the legionary camp as the late afternoon was giving way to early evening. I had arrived back at Dura that morning and went to see him after he returned from the exercise that he had been taking part in. It had involved the two legions plus all the cataphracts and two thousand horse archers and had ended with a mock battle five miles south in the desert, in which the legions had drawn up in a hollow square formation and had been assaulted all day and into the night by the horsemen. I picked up the sheet of papyrus from the table and looked at the 'casualty' figures for the exercise.

'Five killed, fifty wounded and twenty-three horses dead. Was it a real battle?'

'No, but as near to one as we could get. Keeps everyone on their toes and their skills sharp. They will need them to be when we fight Crassus.'

'You do not think he will accept Orodes' offer?'

Domitus laughed. 'Orodes is a good man and a brave fighter, but until all men think as he does we should keep our swords sharp. Crassus will interpret his offer as a sign of weakness, which it is.'

He picked up a blank sheet of papyrus and laid it before him and then took a pen and began scribbling on it.

'You say Aschek and the Carmanians that were located at Persepolis have been ordered east.'

I nodded as he scribbled some more.

'And Surena will not fight?'

'Oh he will fight,' I replied, 'just not on Orodes' terms.'

He frowned and shook his head as he added up a column of numbers. 'Then you have lost around seventy thousand troops before the fighting has even begun. Like I said, a grave mistake.'

I told him about Surena's disagreement with Herneus and Orodes concerning strategy and that he wanted me to invade Syria and reduce its towns and cities to rubble.

'At least he has not forgotten everything he was taught here,' said Domitus approvingly.

'I know you have always wanted to invade Syria, Domitus, but as I told you and as I told Surena it would be a mistake. We may prevail initially but in the end Rome would send more armies to take it back and I do not want an endless war on my frontier.'

'You have a war on your frontier whether you like it or not,' he replied, 'all I was and am suggesting is that it is always better to strike the first blow.'

'How are Peroz's horsemen?' I asked, changing the subject.

'Fully trained in Duran strategy and tactics,' he answered proudly. 'I like him and he's like an eagle who has discovered a field of lambs now that he has taken up with that whore.'

'Roxanne.'

Domitus nodded. 'Pretty thing, I have to admit. I hear she cost you a tidy sum to release her from her contractual duties. Aaron is forever bending my ear about it. It is amazing how similar to Rsan he is in his parsimony.'

'He would. Still, it was worth it to keep Peroz and his five thousand horse archers at Dura.'

Domitus raised an eyebrow. 'Peroz proudly informed me while you were away that he intends to marry his whore soon.'

I held my head in my hands.

'I assume by your demeanour that his father does not know he has fallen in love with a whore.'

I sighed and looked at him. 'She is no longer a whore.'

He grinned maliciously. 'You think his father will see it like that? I think he will think that you have led his boy astray and will be most displeased.'

'When did you become such an expert on Parthian kings?' I said.

Domitus was clearly in a mischievous mood. 'And what with young Spartacus wanting to marry an Agraci you are fast earning yourself a reputation as a man who creates undesirable marriages.'

I wagged a finger at him. 'Spartacus will be going back to Hatra soon and will hopefully lose interest in Rasha.'

'You really believe that?' he said. 'And why has he not returned to Hatra to his father?'

'I thought I would take him to Antioch with me to show him what the enemy looks like, Scarab too.'

I saw his dagger in his hand, which he started to fiddle with. 'You know that bitch Aruna is in Antioch.'

'So I believe. Do you wish me to relay your compliments to her?'

'Just watch your back, that is all,' he said with deadly seriousness. 'I remember Dobbai telling me that she was as evil as her son. It is a curious thing; I never thought I would miss the old woman but I do.'

'As do I,' I agreed.

'If she was still alive you could have taken one of her talismans as protection.'

'I will be under a flag of truce, Domitus.'

'Perhaps,' he sniffed.

While I waited for an official reply to the message that I had sent Crassus requesting a meeting with him at Antioch I had Scarab clean and burnish my leather cuirass, replace the crest in my helmet with fresh white goose feathers and polish the helmet itself. I knew Crassus would be dressed in rich attire and did not want to appear a pauper by comparison. I dallied with the idea of taking a company of cataphracts with me but decided against it. If they were not going to fight there was little point in having an escort of a hundred men sweating in scale armour and full-face helmets and their horses similarly attired, impressive spectacle though they would have made. In addition, I wanted to keep their new swords a secret so I left them at Dura. Instead I took Vagises and a hundred horse archers, each man being issued with a long sleeved white silk shirt, red leggings and helmet. I also gave the order that they were to wear mail shirts to make them look more impressive, even though only the Amazons among Dura's horse archers normally wore armour.

'You should take them instead,' remarked Gallia on the evening before I left, a rider having arrived at the palace earlier from Syria with confirmation of my safe passage to Antioch.

'They are your bodyguard so should stay here with you,' I replied.

'As should you: there is no point in talking to Crassus. You should have told Orodes that.'

'Orodes is high king,' I reminded her, 'and so he does the telling.'

She grabbed my arms and looked into my eyes. 'Do not go; you will face danger in Syria.'

I looked at her rather bemused.

She let go of my arms. 'You think I am a fool? Well, while you were away I was talking to Claudia about you and she suddenly got a tickling sensation on the sole of her right foot. She told me that it meant that you would soon be going on another journey, but later that same day when she was at the gates of the Citadel a dog stood in front of her and began barking at her. She said it was a bad omen.'

I could scarcely believe my ears. 'A ticklish foot and a barking dog? Claudia is twelve years old, Gallia. I hardly think she is qualified to interpret omens from the gods, if they are indeed that.'

She regarded me coolly. 'I believed her and so should you. Have you forgotten who raised her? Have you also forgotten that it was Claudia who warned you about Crassus taking the towns in western Hatra, a warning that you chose to ignore.'

I had no time for this. 'I do not go to Syria to make war but rather to put a proposal to Crassus. Whatever he is he is not a common criminal. He would gain nothing by killing me.'

'Except to remove the one general who can defeat him, the one person who stands between him conquering the Parthian Empire,' she replied caustically.

'I think you exaggerate. I will be away for no longer than three weeks and I do not go alone.'

She was not convinced but knew that it was useless to argue with me further. The next day I embraced her and my children at the top of the palace steps while Vagises and his overdressed horse archers stood waiting in the courtyard with twenty fully laden camels behind them. Spartacus sat on his horse holding Remus' reins with Scarab beside him. I shook the hands of Domitus and Vagharsh, who was most aggrieved that he was not accompanying me. Opposite stood Aaron, Rsan and Peroz, who looked resplendent in his silver scale armour cuirass.

I walked down the steps and vaulted into the saddle. I raised my hand to signal the company to move out when Claudia ran down the steps and raced over to me. She held out an outstretched hand in which was a silver amulet.

'Take this, father, it will protect you from harm.'

I leaned down and took the amulet from her.

I smiled at her. 'Thank you.'

I looked at the talisman in my hand. It was a beautiful silver *Simurgh*, an ancient mythological beast that had the head and foreparts of a dog, the wings and tail of a peacock and a body covered with scales.

Claudia did not smile back but looked deadly serious. 'It is a protective guardian for your journey. Beware the mother of snakes.'

I nodded to her in acknowledgement and then wheeled Remus around and trotted from the courtyard as my daughter ascended the steps. Vagises fell in beside me and Spartacus and Scarab took up position behind as we rode down Dura's main street towards the Palmyrene Gate. The last time I had ridden to see Crassus was in Italy twenty years ago. Then I had been accompanied by his personal slave and had been the commander of all the horsemen in Spartacus' slave army. Now I was the lord high general of the Parthian Empire and commanded my own army, but more than anything else I was intrigued by the prospect of seeing Crassus again. The last time I had ridden to Rome itself, the heart of the enemy's empire, and had emerged unscathed. I had no reason to believe that this time would be any different.

Chapter 14

The commander of my horse archers was most unhappy that we were going to Syria and even more melancholic that we would be meeting Crassus. Vagises was an excellent officer and a valued Companion but one who saw no purpose in talking to the Romans. He had been with me since that fateful expedition into Cappadocia all those years ago when we had been young and foolish and had gotten ourselves captured and shipped to Italy as slaves. I am sure that he thought the whole thing was a Roman ruse to recapture us.

'How can it be a trap?' I asked him. 'It was Orodes who suggested that I meet with Crassus.'

Vagises did not reply but stared ahead as our horses trotted across the border where a detachment of Roman horsemen waited to escort us to Antioch some eighty miles to the west. As we crossed the frontier between the Kingdom of Dura and Roman Syria I caught sight of a *gladius* set in a stone base next to a *kontus*. It was at this spot where I had met the Roman general Pompey and where our two armies had faced each other, ready to do battle. Instead we had agreed a truce and he had thrust a sword into the earth to delineate where Roman Syria ended. I had plunged a *kontus* into the ground beside it to mark the northern extent of my own border and thus had part of the frontier between the empires of Rome and Parthia been fixed, at least until now. Afterwards the two weapons had been mounted on a four-sided stone base, the side facing east being inscribed 'Kingdom of Dura', the one facing west bearing the words 'Romana Syria'. Vagises saw me looking at the monument.

'I remember that day, when you faced down Pompey and his legions. That is the only language the Romans understand.' He spat on the ground as we passed into Syria.

'Bastard Romans.'

'I trust I can depend on your discretion when we arrive at Antioch,' I said.

'I will conduct myself according to my rank, Pacorus. I will not give the Romans the satisfaction of thinking that Parthians are uncouth, much as I would like to.'

He looked behind him at Spartacus and Scarab.

'It was a mistake bringing Spartacus,' he said softly, 'if Crassus gets wind that the son of the slave leader is with us he will have him thrown into a cell.'

He really was in a foul mood.

'If Crassus was like that,' I reasoned, 'then he would have arrested me when I travelled to his house in Rome twenty years ago. The Romans may be many things but they are sticklers for the rule of law and they will not violate the safe passage that we have been granted.'

He mumbled something that I could not hear and then lapsed into a surly silence as our escort rode up and its commander, a man in his early thirties with olive skin and a thick black beard, bowed his head to me. He was obviously Syrian and commanded a detachment of horsemen who were serving the Romans as auxiliaries. His name was Bayas.

'I am here to escort you to Antioch, majesty,' he said in Greek.

Like most of the population of Syria he was probably descended from either the Greek or Macedonian settlers who had arrived in the province in the aftermath of its conquest by Alexander of Macedon. Before then Syria had been ruled by the Persians and before them it had been home to the Egyptians, Sumerians, Assyrians, Babylonians and Hittites. And now it was ruled by Rome.

Bayas led fifty horsemen, all dressed in long-sleeved brown tunics, protected by leather cuirasses painted white, and baggy white leggings. On their heads they wore so-called Phrygian caps. Hanging from the horns of their saddles were small round shields, which were made from laminated strips of wood glued together, with bronze around the circumference to prevent them from splitting in a fight. Covered in white-painted hide, they were designed to stop a sword blow or arrow strike. Each horseman was armed with short javelins that he carried in a case dangling from his saddle and a longer thrusting spear designed for the mêlée. I wondered how many other similar horsemen Crassus had raised thus far?

Bayas was agreeable enough and I did not bother to pester him with questions concerning where he was based or the size of the unit he was attached to. Byrd's spies in Syria would be able to provide that information when the time came.

We moved west at a steady pace of twenty miles each day, riding on paved roads and watering our horses at wells that had been sunk beside them. Syria had been a Roman province for over ten years now and the evidence of its new masters was all around. The roads were not only efficient transportation systems; they were also statements of power. It was not only traders and their goods that travelled over their smooth slabs but also the hobnailed sandals of Roman legions marching to conquer foreign lands. It always amused me that Roman horsemen had to ride on the verges either side of the road whereas my horsemen could ride on the smooth flagstones because our mounts wore iron shoes. How I would have liked to see such roads criss-crossing my kingdom and indeed the empire but the cost was colossal. Underneath the slabs was a layer of gravel and sand with lime cement, and beneath that a layer of rubble and smaller stones set in lime mortar. The base layer comprised flat stones also set in lime mortar, and beside the roads were drainage channels so that rainwater could run off.

Syria had always been a rich region, with intensive irrigation systems to water the fields, and the Romans had been fortunate in that its population had always been subject to taxation. It had thus been relatively easy for them to exact taxes from their new province as a network of officials was already in place. All they had to do was employ them to collect taxes on behalf of Rome. And as time went on Roman weights, measures and coinage replaced their Greek equivalents and Latin became the legal language of the province.

The journey to Antioch was uneventful, though Vagises' humour did not improve and he insisted on extra guards around the camp each night. Mostly we pitched our tents near a village and Bayas negotiated with the headman so that Vagises and I could use the village bathhouse for relaxation after a day's riding. As we travelled nearer to Antioch the villages became larger and were surrounded by drained marshes and dams. We also saw legionaries working in details organising the construction of *qanats* – underground irrigational canals – that brought water to the surface to irrigate the land. Syria was certainly thriving that much was certain. Bayas told me that the Romans provided the engineering skills of the legions to towns and villages for free, which somewhat surprised me.

'The Romans' tax system is based on the harvest of farmlands, majesty,' he explained, 'so the more crops that are harvested the more taxes they collect. Very clever.'

The plain that we travelled through before we reached Antioch had red soil and was filled with olive orchards. The slopes of the high hills that surrounded it were also covered in olive trees and oaks. The land was green and fertile and as we continued and came to the Orontes River I saw an abundance of vineyards, fig trees, myrtle, ilex, arbutus, dwarf oak and sycamore. The Orontes had deep and swift waters with which to irrigate the land and it wound its way round the bases of high and precipitous cliffs before entering the Mediterranean Sea that was some thirty miles away.

We rounded a bend in the road and were confronted by dozens of Roman horsemen around three hundred paces away. I instinctively raised my hand to signal a halt and then reached behind me to pull my bow from its case hanging from one of the rear horns of my saddle. Vagises did the same and shouted 'ready!' as ahead the Romans made no attempt to move.

From smiling and looking relaxed Bayas' face registered alarm.

'No danger, majesty,' he stuttered, 'it is a guard of honour to welcome you to Antioch.'

I already had an arrow knocked in my bowstring and when I glanced behind I saw that every one of my horsemen had done likewise.

'Stand down,' I shouted, placing the arrow in my quiver before sliding the bow back into its case. Vagises sneered at the stationary Romans and did the same as Bayas galloped forward to greet the new arrivals.

'I don't like this,' growled Vagises, who had finally begun to relax and accept that he was probably not going to be murdered in his sleep. I noticed the new Roman horsemen had no spears, continuing to sit motionless in their saddles, hands holding their reins as they gazed at us. Bayas halted in front of a man I assumed was the officer in charge. Some of the Roman horses were grazing.

'I do not think they are about to charge us, Vagises,' I said, nudging Remus forward, 'so it would be bad manners to shoot at them, do you not think?'

He grumbled a reply and then joined me as behind us our Syrian hosts and my horse archers rode ahead to meet the Romans. We had moved forward around fifty paces when Bayas wheeled his horse around and began trotting back to us accompanied by a Roman officer. I raised my hand to signal a halt and waited for them to arrive.

The Roman commander, whose face was hidden behind his large closed cheekguards, sported a magnificent red crest atop his burnished helmet, and as he closed on us and brought his horse to a halt I saw that like me he was also wearing a muscled leather cuirass, but it made mine look a poor article indeed. It was white and sported silver griffins on the chest with a candelabra between the mythical beasts and surmounted by a gold gorgon. Below the candelabra was a golden she-wolf suckling Romulus and Remus, the founders of the city of Rome. He wore *pteruges* at the shoulders and waist whose ends were decorated with gorgon motifs. Whoever this Roman was he was certainly wealthy.

He removed his helmet and handed it to Bayas, then clasped his clenched right fist to his chest. Broad shouldered with a handsome face, square jaw and a full head of brown hair, I estimated his age to be around thirty. He fixed me with his piercing brown eyes.

'Greetings, King Pacorus, I am Publius Licinius Crassus, *Praefectus Alae* in Syria.'

So this was Crassus' son and the men he led were presumably some of the horsemen he had brought with him from Gaul. I too removed my helmet and handed it to Vagises, whose hand was resting on the pommel of his sword. I frowned at him to show my disapproval of his gesture and so he let his hands rest on the front of his saddle.

'Greetings Publius Licinius Crassus,' I replied, 'I am pleased to meet you. You have the same title as another commander of horse named Mark Antony that I had the honour of meeting.'

'He has returned to Italy, sir.'

That was something at least. I held out a hand towards Vagises.

'This is Vagises, the commander of my horse archers.'

Publius stared at the white uniformed horsemen behind us.

'They are a fine body of soldiers.'

'We have a lot more of them in Parthia,' said Vagises with barely concealed contempt.

'Would you care to inspect my men, sir?' Publius asked me.

I nodded and rode forward with him as trumpets sounded and his soldiers sat erect in their saddles. Each man was dressed in a red short-sleeved tunic, light brown breeches that ended just below the knees and open sandals on his feet. Mail shirt, sword, helmet and oval shield completed his appearance. I had to admit that they were a fine body of men.

Afterwards he rode beside me as a detachment of his men trotted ahead of us and the rest fell in behind my horse archers. Bayas and his men were unceremoniously relegated to the rear of the column. Publius was in a talkative mood and so we discussed his journey from Gaul, my encounter with Mark Antony and the recent civil war in Parthia.

'I remember seeing you when I was a boy, sir,' he said.

I was most surprised. 'Really?'

'Yes, when you visited my father's house in Rome during the slave revolt. A man from the east riding a white horse.'

He looked at Remus.

'Is he the same horse, sir?'

I patted Remus on the neck. 'Yes. Remus and I are old friends.'

'It is most strange that a Parthian should ride a horse named after one of the founders of Rome.'

'That was his name when I found him,' I replied, 'and it would have been unfair to give him another one.'

He looked sheepishly at me. 'In Rome parents invoke your name to put fear into their children when they misbehave. They say that the Parthian on his white horse will come and kidnap them if they are not virtuous.'

I laughed. 'I did not realise I had made such an impression.'

'The slave revolt made a lasting impression on all Italy, sir. I have heard rumours that Spartacus escaped with you and now lives in Parthia.'

'Spartacus died in the Silarus Valley,' I told him. 'I watched his body being cremated the day after the battle.'

I did not say that Spartacus' son was riding a few paces behind us out of earshot and diplomatically avoided bringing up the subject of his father having crucified six thousand slaves along the Appian Way.

I rode beside Publius on the verge while my men trotted over the road's stone slabs. There was no other traffic on the road, which led me to believe that it had been cleared for our benefit, an opinion that was confirmed when we rounded a bend and the city of Antioch came into view. And in front of it, arranged each side of the road for a distance of at least a half a mile from the walls, were Roman legionaries standing to attention. It was an impressive display of military might. Each man was attired in bronze helmet, mail shirt, red tunic and sandals and armed with a *pilum*, *gladius*, dagger and *scutum*.

Behind the Roman soldiers were the green slopes of Mount Silpius on our left and Mount Staurin on our right that both rose up to an impressive height to dwarf us. We carried on towards the eastern entrance to Antioch, which Publius informed me was called the Iron Gate. As we got nearer I saw the walls either side of the gates were also lined with soldiers, the sun glinting off the whetted points of their javelins. A few minutes later, escorted by the son of Crassus and surrounded by hundreds of Roman soldiers, I rode into the city of Antioch.

I had heard that Antioch was called the Athens of the East and whereas I had never been to Athens and therefore could not comment on the claim, I had been to Rome and seen its size and wealth and although Antioch

309

could not compare with it in terms of size it was certainly a place of great opulence. The gatehouse we passed through was large and impressive, holding two sets of massive twin gates strengthened by iron strips on both sides. The city had been founded two hundred and fifty years ago by one of Alexander of Macedon's generals named Antigonus Monophthalmus but had been captured by his rival, Seleucis I Nicator, who had gone on to found the Seleucid Empire. And the heart of that empire was the so-called *Tetrapolis* – 'land of four cities' – the ports of Seleucia and Apamea, like Antioch situated on the banks of the River Orontes, and the port of Laodicea.

As I exited the Iron Gate I glanced back at the slopes of Mount Silpius where many houses had been built to accommodate the city's eastern sprawl and where the walls snaked across the craggy slope higher up. Those walls had been designed by an architect named Xenaeus and were both high and thick and on the eastern side virtually impregnable. I should have asked Surena to accompany me on this journey so he could see for himself the strength of the Syrian cities he wanted to plunder.

As a major trading centre at the western end of the Silk Road Antioch received an unending supply of silk, furs, porcelain, spices and gems from China for shipment across the Mediterranean to Rome, and from the west came cargoes of gold, silver, ivory, carpets, perfumes and cosmetics to be sold in China. It was rumoured that Antioch was so wealthy that every house had its own fountain and though I could not verify this I did see magnificent two-storey buildings fronted by marble columns and public baths. We rode along a wide street that ran from the Iron Gate west bordered by marble colonnades. Other, lesser streets crossed it at right angles. Legionaries stood guard along this route as behind them a sea of curious faces gazed at me. They did not cheer or jeer but watched in silence as I rode with the son of Crassus to meet his father. Like all cities Antioch stank of human sweat and filth and animal dung mixed with exotic spices, but at least the temperature was bearable with a pleasant northerly breeze blowing.

Eventually we reached Antioch's royal palace located in the northwest of the city on an island in the middle of the Orontes and connected to the metropolis by five stone bridges. Surrounded by a high stonewall, it had a large portico entrance of marble columns topped by huge wooden beams that supported a roof of thick marble tiles.

We rode through the entrance, into the spacious courtyard and towards the palace steps opposite. In front of these was a large crowd of Roman officers, local priests and senators. A senate composed of wealthy property owners administered every Syrian town and city; in Antioch they numbered two hundred balding, middle-aged men. A slave walked forward, bowed at me and held Remus' reins as I halted in front of the assembled dignitaries and slid from the saddle. Trumpets blasted and a guard of honour at the top of the steps stood rigidly to attention. Remus, alarmed by the sudden, loud noise, shifted nervously so I stroked his neck to calm him.

'Greetings, King Pacorus, welcome to Antioch.'

I turned and saw a face I thought I would never see again in this lifetime. Now around sixty, the last time I had clapped eyes on him he had a full head of neatly cut brown hair, but now Marcus Licinius Crassus was balding which made his large ears look even bigger. That said he looked remarkably good for his age and his broad forehead was largely free of worry lines. He still had a rather serious face with thin lips but now they parted in a smile as he walked forward and raised his right hand in salute.

Like most Romans Crassus was shorter than me and had a slighter frame but his appearance projected wealth and prestige. He wore a pristine white tunic that had broad purple stripes and had a purple cloak draped over his left shoulder that was fixed in place by a large gold brooch. Mt eyes were also drawn to his rich blue boots.

I reciprocated his salute. 'Greetings Marcus Licinius Crassus, Governor of Syria. It has been a long time.'

He walked forward and took my elbow as the slave led Remus away to the stables. Crassus nodded to one of his officers. He walked over to Vagises who had also dismounted.

'Your men will be shown to their quarters,' said Crassus. 'You must be tired after your journey.'

Spartacus and Scarab had handed their horses to slaves and strode over to follow me up the steps as Vagises oversaw the movement of his men and their animals to the barracks that had been allocated them.

Two Roman centurions, angry red crests atop their helmets, went to intercept them and stop them entering the palace.

'They are with me,' I snapped as Spartacus' hand went to the hilt of his sword.

Crassus stopped and waved the centurions back and then gestured to my two young companions to follow us. I saw my nephew's hand on his sword.

'Behave yourself, Spartacus,' I ordered.

Crassus heard the name and raised an eyebrow but said nothing as we passed the priests, sweating senators and Roman officers to enter the palace, but he must have known that it could not have been a coincidence that the strapping young man behind him with long black hair had the same name as the man he had defeated in Italy twenty years ago. Did he know that the son of the slave leader was walking behind him or did he think that perhaps one of my followers had named him thus?

Publius walked beside Spartacus and engaged him in polite conversation as his father escorted us into the palace, a large, sprawling structure containing many halls and rooms. If it was not as grand and expansive as Axsen's royal palace at Babylon then it came a close second. Its long and richly decorated corridors led to private apartments, reception rooms, dining halls, offices and temples, and it seemed an age before Crassus stopped and nodded to a slave standing at the entrance to yet another corridor who stepped forward and bowed his head to me.

'King Pacorus, if you would please follow me I will show you to your quarters.'

I recognised him. 'Ajax! It is good to see you.'

He looked older and perhaps a little thinner but like his master was remarkably well preserved. I was taken back twenty years to Spartacus' tent in Italy where he had been escorted in by a guard with an invitation for me from Crassus to visit his house in Rome.

'It has been a long time, majesty. Time has been a good friend to you, I think.'

I smiled at him. 'You are still the accomplished diplomat, Ajax.' He must have seen the scar on my cheek and the weariness in my eyes and to him I probably looked ten years older than I was but I was grateful for his compliment. I turned to Scarab.

'This is Scarab, my squire, who will require a room,' Ajax smiled at the Nubian.

'And this,' I continued, looking at Spartacus, 'is my nephew, Prince Spartacus of Hatra, who will likewise require accommodation.'

Ajax's eyes widened slightly at the mention of the name of the man who had terrorised Italy but he instantly regained his composure and smiled at them both.

'There are rooms for all, majesty.'

Publius had allowed his mouth to open in surprise and was staring at my nephew while his father maintained his expression of civility. The silence, though, was deafening. It was Publius who spoke first, smiling at my nephew.

'Your name is not a Parthian one, prince.'

Spartacus knew the history of his father and his revolt against Rome. He flashed a smile at Publius. 'It is Thracian because my father was a Thracian and was known to your father, I think.'

The cobra was out of the sack as Ajax shifted uncomfortably on his feet but Crassus was too skilled in politics to allow the unexpected to disconcert him. He looked thoughtfully at Spartacus.

'You must have travelled back to Parthia with King Pacorus all those years ago. And now you are a prince in that land. My congratulations.'

'Well,' I said. 'It has been a long day and I for one would welcome a bath and a change of clothes.'

Crassus smiled at me and nodded to Ajax who bid us follow him down the corridor to our accommodation as the governor of Syria and his son took their leave of us.

My room was spacious and airy and led to a balcony that gave an excellent view of the River Orontes below. Its twin doors were made from Syrian cedar with handles of red copper. Like the corridor outside the walls were painted with mythical scenes of hunting and war with a ceiling of cypress wood. The bedroom floor was white marble and in addition to the large bed my quarters contained a writing desk, four plush couches and three chairs with wooden arms and backs inlaid with ivory.

The rooms of Scarab and Spartacus either side of mine were similarly well appointed.

Ajax knocked at my door a few minutes after showing me to my room and offered to show us to the bathhouse, a great structure in the northwest corner of the palace complex that was a marvel of engineering. With Scarab and Spartacus we left our clothes at its reception and walked into the warm room, the *tepidarium*, and then into the hot room, the *caldarium*. These rooms were heated by means of a system called a *hypocaust* where the floor was raised off the ground by pillars and spaces were left inside the walls so that hot air from a furnace could circulate beneath our feet and in the wall cavities.

I sat on a bench and sweated and watched my two young companions immerse themselves in the warm water. I had to admit that the Romans were great builders but nevertheless had to remind myself that they were also great destroyers and that their empire was built on the misery of subjugated peoples. And even in this place of calm and relaxation I was reminded of this when our bodies, after we had sweated in steam rooms, were scraped clean by slaves holding a curved metal tool called a *strigil* that removed oil, sweat and dirt from the skin. It was most relaxing though I noticed that Scarab, being a former slave, was slightly uncomfortable and took every opportunity to thank the man scraping his body. For his part Spartacus, having never felt the lash on his back or known what it is like to be treated like an animal, basked in the attention he was receiving.

Vagises came to the baths to report that his men had settled into their barracks and the horses were receiving excellent attention in the stables. He also took the opportunity to wash the journey from his body and although he too had the dirt scraped from his flesh, he demurred when it came to being massaged with oils.

'Our hosts are bending over backwards to make us feel welcome,' I said.

'That is what bothers me,' he replied. 'I feel as though we are being fattened up for a feast. Make sure you keep your bedroom door bolted tonight.'

'We are perfectly safe.' I told him. 'The Romans frown upon murdering their enemies in the dark; they prefer to slaughter them in the open, on the battlefield, where the whole world can bear witness to their victory.'

'We are wasting our time here,' he said. 'I have known the Romans too long not to know that they will interpret Orodes' offer as a sign of weakness.'

'I know,' I agreed.

He looked at me with surprise. 'If you knew why did you not persuade him to abandon the plan?'

'Because he is high king and it would have been unseemly for his lord high general to disregard his orders. Besides, I have to confess that I wanted to see Crassus again, to see if he had changed or mellowed.'

313

'And has he?'

'No.'

But that night it was Crassus the impeccable host who was on display as he feasted my men in the palace's large banqueting hall. The Romans normally liked to recline on couches during their banquets but on this occasion long tables had been arranged at right angles to the top table where I sat between Crassus and his son. Vagises sat on the other side of Publius and my nephew and Scarab sat opposite each other at the end of one of the tables directly in front of me. All the city senators were present, along with Crassus' senior officers and a collection of differently dressed priests from the many temples in the city. I knew that the temples dedicated to the Greek gods Athena and Ares were over two hundred years old but also that the Romans had brought their own religion and had shrines in the city dedicated to Mars, Apollo and Jupiter. I scoured the faces of the Roman officers dressed in their rich tunics but could not see Marcus Roscius.

'Tell me, governor,' I said to Crassus, 'is Tribune Marcus Roscius still in Syria?'

He seemed rather surprised that I knew that name. 'He is a legate now and commands his own legion. He is unwell and could not attend the feast. You know him?'

I feigned disinterest. 'He came to my city one time concerning a legal matter, that is all.'

He must have known that Queen Aruna was resident in Antioch and that Roscius was her lover but he kept his council and said no more about his legate. Perhaps he truly was ill but I doubted it; more likely he was ordered to stay away by his viper of a mistress. Instead he introduced me to a pale, thin man dressed in a purple-bordered tunic who sat next to him named Gaius Cassius Longinus. About thirty years of age, he had a square face, thick curly hair and large brown eyes. He seemed affable enough and was obviously one of Crassus' senior officers according to where he was seated. I was surprised to learn that he was actually a *quaestor*, a sort of glorified treasurer, though bearing in mind Crassus' obsession with money I suppose his elevation had a certain logic to it.

Crassus may not have been interested in discussing his absent officer but he was most eager to find out more about my nephew. As a slave filled his silver cup adorned with images of Dionysus, the Greek god of wine, he pointed at Spartacus.

'He is the son of the leader of the slave rebellion?'

'He is,' I answered.

'He must have been an infant when he, and you, escaped from Italy in the aftermath of my victory,' he said. 'His mother resides in Parthia?'

The first course of our meal had comprised bread rolls sprinkled with poppy seeds and honey, delicious spiced sausages, lettuce and olives. But now the slaves were carrying sliver trays heaped with the second course, which included roasted livers of capon steeped in milk and dressed in pepper, roasted peacock, eels, prawns, pork, boar, mushrooms and truffles.

'His mother died giving birth to him, the night before we gave battle in the Silarus Valley,' I replied.

'He knows of his father, that he was a slave and a renegade?' probed Crassus.

'Of course, he knows that his father was a great commander who at one time had the whole of Italy at his mercy.'

Crassus stiffened but then drained his cup and held it out to be refilled. 'History is interpretation, King Pacorus, and is being constantly rewritten to reflect the opinion of the victor. And in the end that is all that matters: who is the victor.

'I trust your wife, Queen Gallia, is well.'

I nodded. 'She is, thank you.'

He again looked at my nephew. 'And he is the heir to the throne of Hatra?'

'He is, though I hope that he does not accede to it for many years.'

Crassus put down his cup and leaned back in his chair. Around us the hall was filled with the noise of men becoming louder as the consumption of wine increased.

'How would the people of the Kingdom of Hatra feel about a slave becoming their king?'

'He is not a slave,' I corrected him. 'And their feelings are irrelevant. They are subjects and they obey their rulers.'

'I see your time with Spartacus in Italy did not blind you to the realities of life. Let me ask you another question: what would be the opinion of Hatra's lords to the son of a slave being their king?'

I could not discern the logic of this conversation. 'They too are subjects and they too would obey their king. Kings rule, subjects obey. That is the natural order of things. And you seem to forget that I too was once a slave and yet I have the unquestioning loyalty of my people.'

He wagged his finger at me. 'Not quite the same. Your fame as a fearsome warlord is known throughout the world. Who would dare to raise his sword against the man who rode beside Spartacus, killed Narses and Mithridates and placed King Orodes on his throne?'

'You are well informed,' I said brusquely.

'Information is power, King Pacorus, perhaps even more than military might.'

The third course, desserts, was a lavish affair of cakes, fruits, pastries stuffed with raisins and nuts, snails, oysters and scallops. While the senators gorged themselves, the priests frowned and shook their heads, and my men and the Roman officers found much in common with each other, Crassus ate little and drank sparsely. He kept his emotions in check and I felt as though I was being subtly probed and tested throughout the whole evening, though not in an aggressive way. Publius was very courteous and though Cassius was dour and boring Crassus was charm itself. He was a most interesting and complex character.

315

The next day Publius took Spartacus and Scarab hunting while I sat with his father, Vagises and Cassius to relay to the Romans Orodes' offer. To be truthful I would rather have been chasing animals with my two younger companions. The terrain around Antioch was teeming with bears, wild boars, antelopes and gazelles and I was sure that they would have more success than me.

The gathering was held in a spacious circular meeting room that had marble columns around the sides decorated with floral motifs. Greek armour and shields hung from the walls themselves – relics of a bygone era – while the ceiling was adorned with large gold images of eagles – emblems of Antioch's current rulers. I sat beside Vagises on one side of a large rectangular oak table with a perfect, polished surface. Crassus sat directly opposite me and Vagises stared at Cassius. Ajax sat on the other side of Crassus and smiled at me as slaves served us wine diluted with cool water and offered us cakes and yoghurt. The atmosphere was both convivial and tense.

Crassus spoke first. 'Well, King Pacorus, perhaps you would be kind enough to elaborate more on the reason for your visit here, agreeable though your company is, and the nature of King Orodes' offer.'

Cassius already looked bored and yawned without covering his mouth, earning him a frown of disapproval from his commander.

I smiled at Crassus. 'First of all I would like to convey my gratitude for the courtesy you have shown myself and my men, especially in this time of difficult relations between Parthia and Rome.

'It is with those relations in mind that King Orodes is most concerned. He does not desire war between our two great empires but rather wishes to pursue the path of peace. He believes that war between Rome and Parthia would serve neither side but would rather lead to great and unnecessary bloodshed that would be detrimental to both. He realises that you have incurred considerable expenses in transporting your army to Syria and is therefore prepared to offer a sum of ten thousand talents of gold in return for your pledge that you will suspend hostilities for a period of one year.'

Cassius' eyes lit up at the mention of such a huge sum but Crassus, who had been studying me carefully, sat impassively. I began to think that he had not heard my words but then he folded his hands across his chest.

'That is a most generous offer and one that would normally deserve careful consideration.' He drew himself up. 'However, these are not normal circumstances, King Pacorus, far from it. No less than the honour of Rome itself is at stake and that cannot be bought.'

That was debatable because I knew that to Crassus everything had a price, but I was eager to know more about his reason for dismissing Orodes' offer so quickly.

'I was not aware that Parthia had insulted Rome's honour,' I said.

He looked at me sternly. 'Were you not? Then let me elucidate. It is common knowledge that the region known as Gordyene was Roman territory that had been granted to the Armenians, our valued allies. It was subsequently invaded by a Parthian army that committed many outrages and forced the Armenians, who were greatly outnumbered, to withdraw.'

This was not how I remembered events.

'Aggression against one of Rome's allies,' Crassus continued, 'is an act of violence against Rome itself and cannot go unpunished.'

'The Kingdom of Gordyene is Parthian,' I said firmly, 'not Armenian or Roman and it was not invaded but rather liberated from foreign rule.'

Crassus smiled thinly. 'And then there is the matter of Judea.'

'Judea?' I replied. 'That does not concern King of Kings Orodes or Parthia.'

Crassus leaned forward and placed his elbows on the table. 'No indeed, but you have taken a keen interest in its affairs, have you not?'

'I take an interest in all things that happen near the borders of my kingdom,' I said casually.

'Such as arming the Jewish rebel Alexander Maccabeus with weapons that were produced in your armouries at Dura,' suggested Crassus. 'An act that is nothing short of a declaration of war against Rome. And imagine my surprise when I myself campaigned recently in Judea, only to discover that this rebel, whom my predecessor had crushed, had received reinforcements from the Parthian hinterland.'

'Life is full of surprises,' I replied.

Cassius was staring at me with hateful eyes, which I found not in the least intimidating while Vagises looked bored.

Crassus grew more serious. 'The fact is, King Pacorus, that I am charged with avenging the many wrongs that have been committed against Rome by yourself and Parthia and have no choice but to wage war until these wrongs have been righted. My hands are tied in the matter.'

'So your intention is to wage war against Parthia?' I asked, already knowing the answer.

He nodded gravely. 'It is.'

'And what is the purpose of that war?' I probed.

He seemed thrown by this query and cleared his throat. I surmised that he coveted Parthia because he wanted control of the Silk Road and all the riches that would bring him, though he would never admit that it was simple greed that motivated him. He thus sought to disguise his real motive by portraying his presence in Syria as being the guardian of Rome's honour. If Rome had any honour!

'I will state my reasons for waging war on the Parthian Empire when I stand in the royal palace at Ctesiphon,' he replied grandly.

Vagises laughed and showed the palm of his left hand to Crassus, pointing at it.

'Hair will grow here before you see Ctesiphon.'

Cassius smirked and Crassus was confused but my fears had been confirmed. Having plundered Jerusalem's temple Crassus was in no mood to let further riches slip out of his hands, and the fact that I had mentioned that Orodes was willing to pay him ten thousand talents of gold had only increased his avarice. His mind must have been racing with thoughts of the treasury at Ctesiphon, which he no doubt believed to be stuffed with gold though the truth was very different. And Ctesiphon was only a month's march from Syria. How tempting a target it must have appeared to him.

'Wars are easy to start,' I said, 'but harder to end.'

'Rome's wars end when the enemy has been vanquished,' said Cassius smugly. 'As the Carthaginians, Armenians, Syrians, Jews and the people of Pontus have learned, to defy Rome is folly.'

Crassus was nodding in agreement and then rested his hands on the table.

'Let us for a moment be logical. We know that Parthia is weak as a result of years of internal strife and that it is beset by external foes. The Armenians occupy the northern half of the Kingdom of Hatra while my own forces occupy towns that were once part of that kingdom, a kingdom that I believe was esteemed the strongest in the Parthian Empire.'

He spread his hands. 'Now it lays prostrate and helpless before its enemies. The truth is, King Pacorus, that Parthia's star is waning. Your high king would be well advised to consider that.'

Vagises beside me stirred with anger but I laid a hand on his arm.

'It is true that the empire has been plagued by civil war,' I said. 'But that war has now ended and its instigator Mithridates is dead. The empire is united under King of Kings Orodes. You speak of the Armenians but you should know that it was not a great army that evicted them from Gordyene but a mere boy in command of a few thousand soldiers that I gave him. And now that same boy has grown into a man who torments Artavasdes as a lion harries a wounded prey.

'I regret that you have rejected my high king's offer because the easy victories you experienced last year have lulled you into a false sense of superiority. If you cross the Euphrates this year you will find that easy victories are hard to come by and you may experience the bitter taste of defeat instead.'

Cassius grew angry at my words. 'You dare to insult us.'

I remained calm. 'I do not threaten like an angry child, Cassius, I merely point out that Parthia will not lie down and let itself become one of Rome's slaves.'

'I am sure that other peoples who now call Rome "master" thought the same,' he shot back.

'They were not Parthian,' I answered.

'Your loyalty does you credit, King Pacorus,' said Crassus, maintaining his calm demeanour, 'but not even you can reverse the tide of history. You came to this city with an offer from your high king but now I make you an offer. If you submit to the authority of Rome then the Kingdom of Dura will be untouched by my army when it crosses the Euphrates. What is more, when the conquest of Parthia is complete you will be appointed king over all the territories from the Euphrates to the Indus to rule in Rome's name, though I will naturally retain control over all trade routes. But you and your heirs will be the guardians of a new Roman eastern empire that will dwarf that of all previous kingdoms.'

I felt a sudden urge to laugh in his face though I controlled my emotions. Did he really think that I would sacrifice my friends, my family, my kingdom, my empire and my race to become a Roman puppet? In his mind he probably thought it a reasonable offer and perhaps regarded me with a degree of affection, like a man views his favourite dog. I picked up my silver cup filled with wine and took a sip.

'Many years ago a man once told me that it is better to die on your feet than live on your knees,' I said. 'You think you offer riches and prosperity but in reality you offer nothing more than slavery; slavery for me and my heirs, for my kingdom and the people of my empire.'

'I can take by force what I now offer, it makes no difference to me,' he said dismissively.

Now I leaned forward and placed my elbows on the table. 'Then do so, for by all that I hold dear I swear that I will never bow down to Rome or its servants.'

Cassius began to say something but Crassus silenced him. 'That is your final word on the topic?'

I nodded. 'It is.'

He pursed his lips. 'That is regrettable. Twenty years ago you came to my house in Rome and I made you an offer.'

'I remember,' I said.

'You refused it just as you refuse my offer now,' he continued. 'Then I promised that I would pursue Spartacus and the slave army until it was destroyed and I was true to my word. I also told you that when I took the field I would show no mercy to the enemies of Rome. I make the same promise to you now – there will be no quarter shown to you, your high king or any others who stand in my way.

'Twenty years ago you managed to escape Italy and return to Parthia but now there is nowhere left to run to. Rome stands on the frontier of your empire. In your heart you must know that resistance is futile. Look around you, King Pacorus, at the magnificent palace we sit in. Where once the kings of the mighty Seleucid Empire walked now Roman soldiers patrol. Go north to Cappadocia and Pontus and you will see Roman banners flying from the walls of every town and city; travel south and you will see Roman legionaries keeping the peace in Judea and Egypt. Rome is destined to rule the world. No kingdom can stand against it, no empire can stand against it, much less one man.'

There was nothing left to say. The meeting ended with strained smiles and icy politeness but I knew that I had to get back to Dura as quickly as possible. The only comfort I could take from my visit to Antioch was that Crassus was supremely confident and that might make him casual in thinking that his march into Parthia would be nothing more than a victory parade. But perhaps he would act with speed and skill and be over the Euphrates with his legions before my army had left Dura. My heart sank with the thought that Marcus Licinius Crassus might indeed reach Ctesiphon before the month was out.

As I strolled from the meeting room with Vagises accompanying me I looked at the commander of my horse archers.

'Please let me know the instant hairs begin to sprout on your palm.'

The next day we left Antioch, which appropriately was cold and wet with the peaks of mounts Silpius and Staurin wreathed in mist. Crassus maintained the role of perfect host, allocating his son to be our escort and bidding me farewell at the foot of the palace steps. Spartacus was delighted that Publius would be riding with us to the border and rode next to his new friend, both of them laughing and joking with each other.

'It is a great shame that soon they will be trying to kill each other,' I remarked as I observed them.

Crassus held out his hand. 'It does not have to be so, there is still time for you to consider my offer.'

I took his hand. 'I prefer freedom to slavery.'

He smiled. 'Farewell, King Pacorus.'

I vaulted onto Remus' back and led my men from Antioch's palace. My soldiers wore their white cloaks around their shoulders and those of Publius scarlet mantles. The city streets were busy but not crowded as we rode along the main street and exited the city via the Iron Gate. This time there were no legionaries lining the road and so we had to thread our way past camels and mules loaded with wares and people on foot carrying great bundles of goods on their backs. After we had travelled past the two mountains it was easier to ride on the grass verge beside the road, and more convenient for the unshod horses of our hosts.

I rode at the head of the column beside Vagises but did not engage him in conversation. My mind was filled with thoughts of the coming clash with Crassus and the Armenians. From yesterday's meeting it was clear that Rome wished to see Gordyene returned to Armenian control and that Crassus had the conquest of all the land between the Euphrates and Tigris as his initial aim. And after that? No doubt the rest of what was left of the Parthian Empire.

'What's this?' Vagises' voice brought me back to the present. Ahead a column of riders was approaching, perhaps a hundred or more, horsemen armed with spears and carrying shields on their left sides, though none were wearing helmets. At first I thought it was Bayas and his band of Syrian warriors who had returned to escort us to the frontier but as they got closer I saw that the man leading them was dressed in Roman war gear. I raised my hand to halt the column and Publius walked his horse forward to be beside me.

'It appears that your father does not trust us to return to Parthia, Publius, and has sent additional soldiers to ensure we leave Syria as quickly as possible.'

'I was not informed of an additional escort, sir,' he replied.

It was not Bayas who led these Syrian riders but an individual I had hoped to avoid during my visit to Syria. He halted his horse before me, a haughty expression on the face that was enclosed by a shiny helmet with a ridiculously large red crest, while his torso was protected by a bronze muscled cuirass inlaid with silver and on his feet he wore ornate boots decorated with flaps in the shape of lions' heads. His white tunic with a narrow purple stripe and large red cloak completed his appearance. Tall and imposing, Marcus Roscius regarded me coolly.

'Greetings Marcus Roscius,' I said. 'I hope you have recovered from your illness.'

'Legate Marcus Roscius,' he replied stiffly. 'I am here to ensure you leave Syria promptly.'

He saluted Publius. 'Hail Publius Licinius Crassus. I will save you the trouble of having to ride all the way to the frontier.'

Publius was perplexed. 'I was not informed that you would be joining me.'

Roscius smiled. 'You have a campaign to prepare for, sir, now that Parthia has declared its hostility to your father. I have learned that King Artavasdes will be arriving at Antioch sooner than expected and I assume your father will require you to escort the retinue of a valued ally into the city.'

Publius glanced nervously at me. 'I see. Well, it would seem that I must take my leave of you here, sir.'

I smiled at him. 'You and your father have been excellent hosts, Publius. I thank you for your courtesy.'

He clasped his clenched fist to his chest. 'Hail and farewell, King Pacorus. It has been an honour.'

He wheeled his horse about, clasped forearms with Spartacus and then signalled for his men to follow him. They rode back to the city leaving me with Roscius and his soldiers, who now took up position on the flanks of my own soldiers.

'Nice lad, that Publius,' remarked Vagises loudly. 'Not like most Roman officers who are arrogant bastards.'

Roscius looked angrily at him but kept his mouth in check.

'We must be one our way,' he said curtly, yanking the reins of his horse to turn it around before trotting forward.

I gave the signal to follow and we recommenced our journey east. The weather was finally improving and the sun's rays began to filter through the grey clouds above us to warm the earth. There was still coolness in the air, though, and so we kept our cloaks wrapped around us. Roscius rode ahead of Vagises and myself which was not only bad manners but also highly irritating. After a mile I had had enough.

'Legate,' I called to him, 'is our company so disagreeable that you deem the only things worth showing to us are your horse's arse and your back?'

Vagises laughed and Spartacus behind us guffawed. Roscius instantly halted his horse and sat still. I looked at Vagises in bewilderment and then heard a scraping noise. And then the killing began. The scraping sound had been Roscius drawing his sword that he now raised in the air as he wheeled his horse around and screamed at his men to charge. Fortunately the animal reared up on its hind legs, giving me a chance to react as behind me the air was filled with screams and shouts.

Instinctively I threw off my cloak and reached behind me to grab my bow in its case as I turned in the saddle to see my men being speared and killed by Roscius' men. They thrust their spears into mail shirts, thighs and arms before my men had a chance to react and within no time the ground was littered with dead and dying horse archers. Vagises' reflexes were quicker than mine and he had already nocked an arrow in his bowstring, which he released to send the missile into the back of a spearman who was thrusting his lance into the chest of a horse archer lying on the ground. The Syrian gave a yelp and then toppled from his saddle. Vagises shot another spearman, then another and another as he strung arrows in his bow and released them in a blur.

I shot Roscius' horse in the chest as it began its charge, causing it to collapse and spill its rider who sprawled on the ground. I heard a scream behind me and saw Scarab gallop past and then leap from his saddle to fall on top of Roscius. They tussled on the ground in a life-and-death struggle but I had no time to intercede as the Syrian horsemen, having butchered my men, were now regrouping to finish the only Parthians left alive – myself, Spartacus and Vagises. But they had grossly underestimated our skill with a bow and shooting from a stationary position we loosed arrow after arrow at the horsemen who were less then a hundred paces away.

We each carried three full quivers and released arrows at a rate of seven missiles a minute. We killed the first group of riders – a dozen men – with ease and then shot at the group behind, our arrows piercing eyes and noses as we aimed at our opponents' faces. A hundred of my men were dead but the number of enemy bodies lying beside them was rapidly increasing as I emptied my second quiver and plucked an arrow from my one remaining full one. Spartacus was shooting with deadly accuracy as he urged his horse forward to get closer to the enemy, who had decided that they had had enough and promptly turned tail and ran. They galloped back down the road in the direction of Antioch but he raised his bow and let loose a final arrow that hissed through the air and slammed into the back of the rearmost rider, who threw out his arms before falling to the ground.

'Nice shot,' I said to him.

'Pacorus,' I heard Vagises say behind me. I turned Remus around to see Marcus Roscius standing around fifty paces away holding a wounded Scarab as a shield in front of him. My squire was bleeding heavily from a wound to the belly and he also had a red stain on his mail shirt at his left shoulder where he had been stabbed by a blade, no doubt the bloodied *spatha* that Roscius was holding in his right hand. His own horse was lying a short distance away, groaning in pain form the arrow I had put into it, but there was another horse further away that was standing still observing our little scene. Roscius had seen it and was heading for it.

I nocked an arrow in my bowstring and jumped down from the saddle and walked towards the Roman who was dragging the injured Scarab with him.

'Let him go,' I ordered, shortening the distance between Roscius and me.

The Roman, his left forearm at Scarab's neck, stopped and pulled my squire closer, only half his face showing behind him. The Nubian was wilting, his mail shirt now soaked in blood, his breathing very shallow.

'Those riders will return with reinforcements, Parthian, and when they do you will join the rest of your men,' he gloated.

'Let him go,' I said calmly, 'and you will live.'

He continued to inch towards the horse. 'You are finished, Parthian, you and the rest of the horse thieves in your motley empire. Even as we speak the Armenians are marching on Hatra, the city of your birth, and will take it easily. You think you are so clever but you know nothing. We have friends in Hatra, members of your own people who have sword allegiance to Rome. You and Parthia are finished.'

I raised my bow and pulled back the bowstring.

'Slave,' he sneered as the string slipped from my fingers.

The arrow went into his right eye socket and the point exited the rear of his helmet. He stood, dead, the arrow sticking out of his eye and blood spurting onto Scarab's face.

'He's dead Scarab,' I said as I ran over to my squire.

I kicked the body of Roscius away and grabbed Scarab whose knees buckled under him.

'Get that horse!' I shouted at Vagises as Spartacus slid his bow back into its case, vaulted from the saddle and ran over to me. I rested Scarab on the ground and supported his head with my hand.

'Is he dead, majesty?'

I smiled at him. 'Yes. Do not talk. We will get you out of here.'

Spartacus knelt beside Scarab and looked with alarm at his wounds as Vagises arrived with the spare horse.

'Spartacus,' he said, 'get your bow.'

He nodded back down the road and I turned to see a rider galloping towards us, a man dressed in a turban and black robes who was holding his arms aloft.

'Do not shoot,' he was shouting, 'I am a friend.'

Vagises raised his bow but I told him to lower it as the mystery rider slowed his horse and halted around twenty paces away.

'State your business,' Vagises ordered.

Another two riders appeared, also dressed in black robes, and halted a hundred paces away. They appeared to be carrying no weapons.

'My name is Andromachus,' the first man said, 'and I am the brother of Noora, Byrd's wife.'

Vagises looked at me and lowered his bow.

'Byrd sent you?' I asked.

Andromachus shook his head. 'No, lord. I have offices in Antioch and a network of informers. I heard a tale that your life was in danger and came as quickly as I could.' He looked at the dozens of dead bodies on the ground. 'You must come with me, quickly. The Romans will be sending out patrols to hunt for you when they learn of what has happened.'

'We have done nothing wrong,' insisted Vagises.

Andromachus pointed at the corpse of Marcus Roscius. 'Killing a legate is a grave offence in Roman eyes. You must all come with me!'

His two companions were looking down the road towards Antioch, from where any patrols would come from, and so I told Spartacus to assist me in getting Scarab onto the back of the horse Vagises was holding. We used a rope to secure him in place and then I regained my saddle.

'Follow me,' said Andromachus.

We doubled back down the road past wild-eyed and frightened travellers who huddled by their animals as we thundered by them. After a few hundred paces Andromachus led us into the trees and onto a track that rose up into the hills. We were heading south, climbing slowly as we threaded our way through walnut, myrtle, fig and mulberry trees. Andromachus led the way and his two companions brought up the rear as we moved at speed through the trees, Spartacus riding by the side of the wounded Scarab to ensure he did not topple from his saddle or was struck by a low branch.

Andromachus called a halt after we had been in the trees for ten minutes or so and cocked his head to discern if we were being followed. His two companions also looked back and strained their ears but shook their heads and so we continued our journey. We rode beneath hanging rocks, across shallow streams of gushing waters and saw waterfalls foaming and roaring from the cliff face above. This was certainly a place of life and beauty though we had no time to enjoy the scenery as our horses traversed the dozens of fast-flowing rivulets that sprang from the rocks above.

After a while we descended into an area of lush grooves of laurel, cypresses and bay trees and gently rippling streams, before coming unexpectedly upon a great walled villa among the trees. Andromachus led us to the entrance – two closed wooden gates – in front of which stood a pair of black-robed guards armed with spears and swords. One of them banged on the gates and after a few seconds they opened to allow us to enter the villa. The main building in front of us consisted of two wings that were connected by a columned frontage accessed by stone steps.

'This is your home?' I said to Andromachus, marvelling at its size.

'Do not be too surprised, lord,' he said, sliding from his saddle. 'Byrd and Noora choose to live in a tent; I do not.'

I assisted Spartacus and Vagises in getting Scarab down from his saddle and then we carried him into the villa. The chief steward, an old man with black tattoos on his face, led us to a small sleeping room off the large central courtyard, where Scarab was laid on a bed. Two women wearing black headdresses began stripping him of his mail shirt and clothes so we left him in the care of the steward who Andromachus informed me had some knowledge of medicine. We retired to the large study that looked out onto the courtyard.

I flopped down into a chair as Spartacus, his tunic smeared with Scarab's blood, perched on a couch and Vagises did the same.

'I hope your slaves are trustworthy,' I said to Andromachus who had seated himself behind a large desk with intricately carved wooden legs.

'They are not slaves they are Agraci,' he replied, 'and they are totally trustworthy. They will not betray your presence here.'

'And where are we?' asked Vagises as a woman served us cool fruit juice from a silver platter.

'Six miles south of Antioch,' said Andromachus. 'This area is named Daphne and is home to the city's wealthiest and most influential citizens. There are many villas here among the groves and fountains. The Greeks built a temple here dedicated to their gods Apollo and Diana and many believe that the waters have healing properties.'

'Let us hope they help my squire,' I said.

Andromachus raised an eyebrow. 'It is only a belief, lord.'

'I have to get back to Dura,' I said. 'The Armenians are marching on Hatra.'

'There will be Roman patrols out looking for you, lord,' said Andromachus, 'so your escape from Syria must be carefully planned. But in the interim I have the means by which you may get a message to your city.'

Andromachus took me to the aviary that formed part of the villa's outbuildings and which contained at least a score of pigeons. He told me that I could send a message to Byrd at Palmyra that could be couriered to Dura, which would be safer and faster than a rider on horseback running the gauntlet of Roman patrols.

Our horses were quartered in the stables and Spartacus and Vagises were given rooms adjacent to where Scarab lay, though I was give a large bedroom away from theirs. Everything about the villa was large, from the shingle-covered roof to the library, dining room and Andromachus' study. The sprawling building also contained storerooms, kitchen, servants' quarters, cellar and a bathhouse. The exterior walls were covered with white plaster and the interior with colourful paintings depicting mythical creatures and floral scenes.

After I had ensured that Remus was settled into his stall I sat down in my room and penned a note to Gallia on a small piece of papyrus:

'The Romans have rejected peace. Armenians are marching south. Get the army to Hatra with all speed. I will join you there. Inform Orodes that Crassus will cross the Euphrates soon. He must rally all available forces at Hatra. Shamash protect you.

Pacorus.'

325

The message was tied to the leg of Andromachus' swiftest pigeon and then the bird was sent on its way. He informed me that his pigeons made regular trips to and from Palmyra and was confident that Byrd would be reading the message well before nightfall. That provided some comfort but my spirits sank when the villa's steward knocked on my door with news that Scarab's condition was hopeless.

'The wound is too severe and he has lost too much blood, majesty. There is nothing to be done.'

I went at once to where Scarab lay on a bed surrounded by Vagises and Spartacus. His head was resting on a cushion and he smiled weakly at me when I entered the room. Vagises looked thoughtful – he had seen death too many times to let his emotions get the better of him – but Spartacus was distraught. From initially disliking the big Nubian Spartacus had grown to like his fellow squire and now he was angry that he was slipping away. I rested a hand on my nephew's shoulder and then sat on the stool beside Scarab's bed. His wound had been bandaged but blood was still seeping through the material. The room was so quiet that I could hear Scarab's laboured breathing.

'Is there anything I can do for you, Scarab?' I asked softly.

His eyes turned to me. 'No, majesty, thank you.'

He looked at Spartacus. 'Farewell, my friend, I will speak with the great god Amun and ask that he grant you your wish to be with Rasha.'

Spartacus smiled and nodded, desperately fighting back tears.

He once again looked at me. 'Thank you, majesty.'

'For what?'

He smiled weakly. 'I have lived a life as a slave, a low-born no better than an animal, but because of you I die a free man.'

'Not only that,' I said, 'but a friend and loyal soldier of Dura.'

He looked at the ceiling and smiled one last time and then Scarab passed from this life and joined his ancestors in the afterlife. I closed his eyes and then stood and bowed my head as Spartacus angrily wiped away a solitary tear that ran down his cheek.

We cremated Scarab that evening in the presence of Andromachus and all his workers and servants. I stood in silence watching the flames devour the Nubian's cadaver and then heard Spartacus talking angrily with our host a few paces away. I walked over to them as my nephew began jabbing a finger in Andromachus' face.

'What is going on?' I enquired.

Spartacus, his face a mask of frustration, turned to me. 'Scarab's killer is but two miles away.'

I looked at Andromachus. 'The lad mistook my words. What I actually said was that the person who probably organised the attack on your men lives in a nearby villa.'

'Who?' I asked.

'Queen Aruna,' answered Andromachus, 'the mother of Mithridates.'

I clenched a fist. 'Yes, I know who she is.'

'All I said was that as she and that Roman legate were lovers, and I have heard that she is a mistress of intrigue, it seems highly unlikely that she knows nothing about the attack against you.'

Before I could answer Spartacus stomped away towards the stables. Andromachus shrugged and Vagises rolled his eyes as I followed. The stables, lit by oil lamps dangling from the walls, smelt reassuringly of horses, wax and leather. I caught sight of Spartacus taking his saddle off a wall hook.

'What are you doing?' I asked him.

'Going to avenge Scarab,' he snarled.

I laid a hand on his arm. 'It is dark, you have no knowledge of this area and the queen's villa will undoubtedly be heavily guarded.'

'One of Andromachus' men can guide me,' he replied defiantly.

'And what will you do if you manage to find your way there and get past the guards?'

'Kill the bitch,' he replied.

'Well, she is a bitch and she does deserve to die, but not tonight and not by your hand. So put the saddle back on the wall and come back to the villa.'

He stood, rock-like, before me.

'That was an order,' I told him, 'not a request.'

'She deserves to die.'

'That is probably what she is saying right at this moment to whatever Roman officer she has decided will replace Marcus Roscius. My first duty is to get back to Parthia to meet the Armenian and Roman threat, or do you think that the life of one squire outweighs that of every citizen of the empire?'

He appeared confused. 'You will not seek to avenge Scarab's death?'

'Grow up, Spartacus. This is not some childhood game. We were lucky to escape with our lives today and still have to get out of Syria alive. My first duty is to the empire. So put the saddle back on the wall and get some food and rest.'

He slammed his saddle back on the peg and walked away without saying anything. I followed him as the embers of Scarab's funeral pyre crackled in the warm night air.

The next morning we gathered in Andromachus' office once more to ascertain how we would escape Syria. Vagises suggested journeying south towards Emesa and then striking for Palmyra. I rejected the idea.

'There is no point in going to Palmyra,' I said, 'because by the time we get there Dura's army will hopefully be on its way to Hatra, which is where we must reach as quickly as possible. Therefore I need to get across the border at the same spot where we entered Syria.'

'That will be heavily guarded, lord, I would advise against it,' said Andromachus. 'You will also have to be disguised.'

Unfortunately we spent the rest of that day in enforced idleness while Andromachus sent his servants on a trawl of the area surrounding the villa to collect walnut husks. When they returned the husks were chopped into small pieces and tipped into a large metal cauldron containing water that was heated over a fire until it boiled. It was left to simmer for an hour. The resultant dark brown liquid was allowed to cool and then Andromachus asked me to bring Remus from the stables.

I was confused. 'Why?'

'Because, lord, it is known throughout the world that King Pacorus of Dura rides a white horse, and even the most unintelligent Roman soldier will know to be on the lookout for anyone riding a white horse. Since we cannot hide your horse we must disguise him.'

Remus stood mortified as his gleaming white coat was turned a dark brown by the dye.

'Don't forget the tail,' Andromachus shouted at the two women who were applying the liquid.

'Don't worry, lord,' he said to me, 'it won't harm him and will brush out.'

'When?' I asked.

He rubbed his chin. 'Not sure, but no longer than a month.'

Afterwards a bay coloured Remus was returned to the stables to let the dye dry and we prepared to make our escape from Syria the next morning.

Chapter 15

The quickest way to Hatra was to ride directly east towards the border of my own Kingdom of Dura and then cross the Euphrates before striking northeast across the desert to Gafarn's city, but Andromachus suggested a different route. He advised travelling northeast to the city of Zeugma, crossing the river there and then riding east along the Euphrates before striking for Hatra.

'Zeugma will be crawling with Romans,' said an unimpressed Vagises.

'And so will the Syrian border,' replied Andromachus. 'The difference being that the Romans in Syria are looking for you whereas those at Zeugma are not.'

I was convinced, and so the next morning we loaded food and fodder on two spare horses that Andromachus gave us, on which we also hid our helmets, armour, bows and quivers so as not to draw attention to ourselves. We wore black Agraci robes over our tunics and leggings and donned black headdresses to hides our faces.

'Be sure to cover your face, lord,' he told me, 'it is well known that the face of the King of Dura carries a battle scar.'

We wore our swords under our robes, as it was unwise for even the most poor-looking traveller not to have a weapon to hand – despite the best efforts of Romans, Parthians and Agraci there were still bandits in the hills and among the woods of Syria, Arabia and Parthia. I thanked Andromachus warmly for his help and hospitality but was concerned about his safety.

Servants brought our horses into the courtyard of his villa and we vaulted into our saddles. 'If the Romans find out that you have assisted me they will crucify you,' I said to him.

He looked up at me and smiled. 'They probably won't find out, but if they do I shall say that you took me hostage and forced me to assist you. I have too many of Antioch's senators in my pay to believe that I will receive anything more serious than a rebuke.'

I looked at the large villa in its luxuriant surroundings. 'Do the authorities know that Byrd is my chief scout?'

He looked surprised. 'Of course. They also know that he is your friend and the friend of King Haytham and High King Orodes and that makes them want to be his friend. Better that than him being a powerful enemy. And every rich merchant in Cilicia, Cappadocia, Syria and Judea knows that his goods are safe when they are transported on one of Byrd's caravans.'

'One day I think he will rule over all of us,' I said, offering my hand to him. 'Farewell Andromachus, Shamash keep you safe.'

'Farewell, lord. Safe journey.' He pulled something from his robe. 'And take this.'

'What is it?'

'A pouch full of drachmas. You may need it on your journey, especially as you are impersonating poor travellers.'

He was right. Journeying via Zeugma meant that our route covered four hundred and fifty miles and at the end of every day, during which we covered at least forty miles, we stopped at one of the many halting places that had been established on the numerous lanes and tracks that made up the Silk Road. Called *caravanserai*, they were usually roadside inns that had a rectangular walled enclosure abutting them that gave protection from attack as well as from the elements. Accessed by a single gate that was wide and high enough to allow fully laden camels to enter, inside there were washing facilities, cooked food and fodder for animals. Most caravans, especially the larger ones, had their own guards as well as fearsome caravan dogs that were used to drive off predatory wildlife and also warn of approaching bandits. But both Parthia and the Romans realised that trade was the lifeblood of their empires and so they devoted significant resources to protecting the Silk Road. In Parthia small mud-brick forts, such as existed in my own kingdom, were built along major roads to maintain security, while the Romans also built strongpoints from where road patrols were launched to keep road traffic safe.

The *caravanserai* were always vibrant places, filled with many different races carrying goods from the east and west. And as well as merchants and their guards and servants, caravans would also attract religious teachers, entertainers moving between cities, mystics and even escaped slaves. There was safety in numbers and the larger the caravan the more chance it would have of reaching its destination unmolested. That was the theory at least. And of course large caravans meant substantial customs duties for the kingdoms they passed through. I often wondered how the merchants made a profit from their commerce, what with being charged tolls when they entered every kingdom, but then I remembered that they were carrying silk from China, a material that was literally worth its weight in gold.

On the night we stopped at a *caravanserai* on the outskirts of Zeugma, Spartacus wandered off after we had eaten a meal of roasted mutton kebabs, rice and raisins. We had seen many Romans on the road in addition to civilian travellers: men on horseback and columns of legionaries making their way to the camps they had established around the city. This was where Crassus would be crossing the Euphrates to commence his campaign in Parthia and thus his forces were mustering here.

I leaned against my saddle and saw a horse taking a piss in its stall. Our horses were in the adjacent stalls and I had elected to camp on the ground in front of them. There were small rooms that we could have hired but I wanted to give the impression that we had little money and were therefore of no consequence.

'How long before Crassus crosses the river?' asked Vagises, picking a piece of meat from between his teeth.

'Two weeks, perhaps longer. Andromachus confirmed that Artavasdes was visiting Antioch so he will be preoccupied with him for a few days at least.'

'No doubt they will discuss dividing the spoils of their forthcoming campaign.'

'No doubt,' I said. 'If what Marcus Roscius said was true, that the Armenians are already on the march, then Crassus must have promised Artavasdes the Kingdom of Hatra. If the Armenians take the city then Crassus will be free to march south along the Euphrates and strike at Babylon, Seleucia and Uruk.'

'And Dura,' added Vagises glumly.

'If the Armenians manage to capture the city of Hatra then the empire is finished,' I said to compound Vagises' melancholy.

He was horrified. 'It is that serious?'

I saw no reason to disguise the truth. 'If Hatra falls then the Armenians will be free to strike west at Assur and then across the Tigris into Media and Atropaiene, while Crassus and his legions will easily crush any resistance in Babylon and Mesene. Then he will be able to cross the Tigris at Seleucia and invade the eastern half of the empire. And there will no army to stop him, not with Phriapatius already on his way north to aid Musa and Khosrou. It all hinges on us stopping the Armenians and Romans at Hatra.'

'You have forgotten something,' he said.

'Oh?'

'Surena and his army.'

I looked up at the myriad of stars in the clear night sky. 'Surena goes his own way now, that much is certain from the meeting at Assur.'

'Surely he will assist us?'

I spread my hands. 'I have no idea. It appears that by unleashing Surena into Gordyene I created a monster that is uncontrollable.'

'Surena may abandon the empire but he will not abandon you,' Vagises stated with conviction.

Our conversation was interrupted by the return of Spartacus who was carrying something in his arms. As he got closer I saw a pair of small black eyes peering at me.

'What is that?' asked Vagises.

Spartacus carefully sat on the ground next to his saddle and showed us a puppy as black as night.

'One of the merchants' bitches had a litter a few weeks back and this was one of her puppies,' he held out the dog, a bundle of black fluff. 'I saw him and thought it an auspicious omen.'

I rolled my eyes. 'How so?'

'The other puppies were brown or white and brown but this one was pure black. I immediately thought of Scarab and knew I had to have him. The price was very reasonable.'

'What are you going to call it?' asked Vagises.

'He will be called "Scarab" in honour of my dead friend,' replied Spartacus who began petting the animal.

The next day the three of us plus the mongrel rode into Zeugma, crossed the Euphrates and headed east. Normally the river marked the western frontier of the Kingdom of Hatra but Crassus' invasion of the previous year had resulted in the loss of Gafarn's western towns and their occupation by Roman soldiers. On the road we saw more legionaries going to and from the towns of Nicephorium, Ichnae, Carrhae and Zenodotium. The latter place was where Gafarn's governor of the west, Apollonius, had enticed a Roman delegation into the town and murdered them, resulting in Crassus storming the place and selling its citizens into slavery as a punishment for their treachery. Alas for Apollonius, he had no doubt been either killed in the assault or crucified in front of the city afterwards.

After twelve days of hard riding we at last came to Hatra and rode through the western gates of the city. Kogan's guards stood sentry on the bridge over the moat, above the gates and in the towers that flanked them. The road was filled with traffic, the streets were heaving with citizens going about their daily business and everything appeared surreally normal. We entered the city and made our way to the walled royal quarter located in the north of Hatra where the palace and the houses of the kingdom's richest lords were sited.

Our Agraci robes were filthy and stank, our faces were unshaven, black rings surrounded our eyes and we must have looked like a trio of bandits as our tired horses approached the imposing gates in the southern wall of the royal compound. Beyond them was the quiet, ordered wealth and power of Hatra's rulers, a world usually forbidden to the city's ordinary citizens. The gates were open to allow access to the paved road that went through the marbled mansions to end at the Great Square, to the north of which stood the palace.

Without thinking I let Remus continue walking up to the gates when he was brought to a halt by two guards armed with spears and carrying bronze-faced shields, an officer standing behind them.

'Halt!' barked their commander, a brawny, bearded man whose face was hidden by his bronze helmet. He wore greaves, had a white plume in his helmet and his hand rested on the hilt of his sword.

'And where do you think you are going?' he barked aggressively.

'To see the king,' I snapped, 'now out of my way.'

One of his subordinates grabbed Remus' reins and the other pointed his spear at my belly as Vagises and Spartacus drew level with me.

'The king is busy today so piss off before I arrest you.'

'I am King Pacorus, his brother, now for the last time get out of my way.'

With hindsight, considering my dishevelled appearance, it was the wrong thing to say as the guard commander burst into laughter.

'Of course you are. I should have realised from your kingly attire.' He bowed mockingly. 'Would your majesty like me to bring you some refreshments?'

His two men grinned at each other but I was failing to see the funny side of the situation.

'I will tell you one last time. Get out of the way.'

'He is the king and you are only making trouble for yourself,' announced Spartacus, whose dog peeked from his robes and began yapping at the gate commander.

'Guards!' shouted the officer, who pointed at me, 'you are under arrest. Get off your horse.'

A dozen other soldiers exited the gatehouse, ringed us and levelled their spears. I dismounted and took off my headdress.

'I tell you again, I am King Pacorus of Dura.'

The commander stepped forward until our faces were only inches apart.

'Even the lowliest beggar knows that King Pacorus rides a white horse and not a mangy, flea-bitten nag like yours.'

Then two of his men behind began to manhandle me towards the gatehouse.

'Get your hands off me!' I shouted, which drew the attention of a rider who was down the road some fifty paces. The commander drew his sword and forced its point into my stomach.

'Right, I can spill your guts here and now, it makes no difference to me, so I suggest you behave yourself before I add chopping off one of your hands to the flogging you are going to get.'

Spartacus and Vagises went to protest but were silenced as spear points were pressed into their bellies and they were ordered to dismount.

Lord Vistaspa, who was not concerned with the arrest of three troublemakers, rode stiffly by, the guard commander bowing his head to him as he did so.

'Lord Vistaspa,' I called, causing him to bring his horse to a halt. He turned in the saddle and his eyes opened wide as he recognised me.

'Release him at once you imbecile,' he ordered the commander, 'you dare threaten and lay your hands on the King of Dura.'

He slid from his saddle and walked over with a slight limp, his permanent souvenir from the Battle of Susa. The guards, now shamefaced and alarmed, withdrew their spears and retreated from us. Vistaspa bowed his head to me.

'My most sincere apologies, majesty.' He looked in confusion at my appearance and horse. 'The last I heard you were in Syria.'

I laid a hand on his arm and smiled. 'I was and now I am in Hatra on urgent business. I must see my brother.'

He nodded. 'Of course. Follow me.'

Spartacus and Vagises regained their saddles and I went over to the guard commander, who knelt before me.

'Get up,' I told him. 'Your diligence does you credit. Remember, though, that sometimes things are not as they appear.'

Two hours later, after having bathed, shaved and changed my clothes, I sat in the company of Gafarn and Diana in Hatra's palace. Spartacus and his new pet were also present, the young pup scampering around the marble floor to the delight of Diana. My brother looked relaxed and his wife happy; it appeared that the foreboding that had previously hung over the city had disappeared. I told them how my mission to Syria had ended and why I and the other two had arrived at the city in disguise.

'Very clever dying Remus' coat,' mused Gafarn, 'it certainly fooled the guards at the gates. Do you want them flogged for their insolence, by the way?'

I shook my head. 'That will not be necessary. In any case we will need every soldier we can get our hands on to fight the Armenians.'

Gafarn looked surprised. 'The Armenians?'

'Yes, brother. As we sit here Artavasdes and his army are marching south against this city.'

Gafarn looked at Diana and then at me. 'We would have received intelligence from Lord Apollonius if this were true.'

I heard the name but did not understand. 'Lord Apollonius?'

Gafarn smiled. 'Yes, after his heroic exploits in the west I appointed him Commander of the North. He has taken an army of horse archers north to beyond Mount Sinjar to demonstrate our strength to the Armenians. If they were marching south I would have received word of it.'

I felt sick, my mouth was dry and my heart began racing. The mocking words of Marcus Roscius filled my mind and it all suddenly made sense. I tried not to look concerned.

'How many men did Apollonius take north with him?' I asked Gafarn.

'Twenty thousand horse archers.'

I closed my eyes and cursed my luck. 'How many men are left in the city?'

'The Royal Bodyguard – five hundred men – a thousand other cataphracts, five thousand horse archers plus the two thousand men of Kogan's garrison.'

'What is the matter, Pacorus?' asked Diana, seeing the colour drain from my face.

Half an hour later I told her as she and her husband sat around the table in the office that abutted the throne room and which had been used many times by my father. Vistaspa and Kogan had been ordered to attend, and Chief Priest Assur's presence had been requested. I also invited Vagises and Spartacus to the meeting, the latter having given his pet to a steward to look after. When the doors had been closed I told them of my journey to Syria, the ambush sprung by Marcus Roscius and how before his death he had boasted that the Armenians were marching against Hatra, which had been betrayed.

'Gafarn has informed me that Apollonius has taken twenty thousand men out of the city, which confirms to me that he is the traitor in the pay of the Romans.'

Kogan and Vistaspa looked at me in disbelief while Assur raised his bushy white eyebrows. Gafarn laughed nervously.

'You are mistaken, brother. Lord Apollonius fought the Romans in the west last year and has been most vocal in his determination to recapture the towns that were lost.'

334

'The fact that he escaped with his life condemns him,' I said. 'The Romans always make an example of any town or city that defies them, as they did with the inhabitants of Zenodotium last year. Apollonius must have brokered a deal with the Romans; that is the only reason he was allowed to live.

'In addition, Artavasdes visited Crassus after I spoke with the governor of Syria, which confirms to me that the two of them have been working in conjunction to coordinate their attack on the empire and specifically the Kingdom of Hatra.'

'Lord Apollonius will be recalled,' said Vistaspa sternly, 'so he can speak for himself on these matters.'

'These are serious charges, Pacorus,' remarked Gafarn, 'and yet though I want to believe you I have seen no evidence of Lord Apollonius' treachery.'

'Alas, brother,' I replied, 'the evidence of his treason is his absence from this city in its hour of need.'

Gafarn was beginning to get angry. 'But we have received no reports that there are Armenian troops to the north of Hatra.'

I held out my hands. 'Of course not, not with Apollonius himself responsible for the security of the north of the kingdom.'

Vistaspa rose from the table and went outside to dictate a letter to Apollonius ordering him to present himself at the palace immediately, though I was certain that the courier would be killed when he arrived at Apollonius' camp. He was not my immediate concern – I needed to know where the Armenians were. To this end I asked Vistaspa to send out scouts to the north and east to discover their whereabouts, plus the despatch of another courier, to the city of Assur, to bring Silaces and his horse archers to Hatra.

'I heard Marcus Roscius boasting,' said Spartacus, looking very much like a prince in his white silk shirt, tan leggings and black boots. 'He killed Scarab and I am going to kill that bitch.'

Diana frowned. 'Language, Spartacus, please.'

'We should have killed her before we left Syria,' he hissed.

'Who?' asked Gafarn.

'Queen Aruna.'

'The mother of Mithridates?' Gafarn seemed surprised.

'Yes indeed,' I said. 'She has made her home in Syria and Marcus Roscius was her lover. I have no doubt that she instigated the attack on our column.'

'Her temperament has not mellowed, then,' commented Gafarn dryly.

'Having failed to kill me she is irrelevant to the current situation,' I said.

'She still deserves to die,' seethed Spartacus.

'There are many people worthy of a death sentence,' I remarked, 'but right now we must concentrate on an Armenian army intent on putting us all to the sword.'

'And if Apollonius returns to the city with his men?' queried Assur in his deep tone.

'Then, sir,' I replied, 'I will apologise for the gross disservice I have done him.'

But it was too much of a coincidence that he was out of the city, the more so having taken most of the city's soldiers with him. That night I stood on Hatra's walls and looked north but saw no glow on the horizon to indicate an army's campfires. Later, in my old room, I wrote a letter to Orodes informing him of the danger that threatened Hatra and that Crassus had rejected his offer and would be launching his campaign soon.

The next morning I rose early and joined a war council convened by Gafarn. Hatra's king still did not believe that Apollonius had betrayed him but agreed with his being recalled to clear up any uncertainty. I suggested that it might be prudent to impose a curfew as Apollonius could have friends inside the city who might try to seize any of the four gates to allow the Armenians to enter.

'I think you are letting your imagination run wild,' commented a slightly annoyed Gafarn.

'I will double the guards at the gates, majesty,' stated Kogan. 'I can vouch for the loyalty of all my men.'

Vistaspa said nothing but nodded approvingly at my suggestion. I did not wish to undermine my brother's authority but I kept thinking of Spartacus' words regarding murmurs of discontent among Hatra's lords concerning their low-born king. It was but a short journey from discontent to outright treachery, especially in times of uncertainty and strife.

'Still,' I said, trying to be optimistic, 'at least my army and Silaces' men will be arriving soon, and after them Orodes, Nergal and Atrax.'

'As lord high general,' said Vistaspa, 'what will be your plan, majesty?'

'I would have liked to have engaged Crassus first before the Armenians,' I replied, 'but now we have no option but to give battle to the Armenians before the Romans.'

'The Armenians are more numerous,' said Vistaspa, remembering the hordes that Tigranes had brought to Nisibus when my father had requested a meeting with them.

'That they do,' I concurred, 'but the Romans have always presented the greatest threat and that has not changed. The Armenians are mere puppets of Rome. If we had stopped Crassus then Artavasdes would have yielded to our demands, of that I have no doubt.'

There were voices outside and then the doors of the meeting opened and a guard entered. He bowed to Gafarn and then spoke into Kogan's ear.

'Let them in,' he commanded.

The guard exited and seconds later a dust-covered Byrd and Malik entered and nodded to Gafarn. A wave of relief swept through me as I rose and embraced them both.

'Your army half a day's march away,' said Byrd.

I closed my eyes and thanked Shamash for safeguarding a small pigeon that flew from Andromachus' villa to Palmyra.

'Gallia leads the army,' reported Malik.

I slapped Byrd on the arm. 'Your brother-in-law has saved the day for without him I would be either dead or in a Roman prison.'

'He was under orders to keep an eye on you,' replied Byrd nonchalantly.

'Who guards Dura?' I asked.

'Spandarat,' replied Malik, 'much to his frustration, especially as Claudia told him that she was perfectly capable of organising the city's defence. However, she has appointed him her official military adviser to keep him happy.'

'At least I do not need to worry about my city,' I said. I turned to Gafarn. 'And, my brother, Hatra now stands a fighting chance.'

I made my apologies and left the meeting to summon Vagises before going to the stables to saddle Remus. Byrd and Malik acquired fresh horses and the four of us rode south into the desert to go and find my wife.

Two hours later on a small hillock we saw a party of Byrd's scouts sitting on their horses. They observed us warily before recognising their commander as we drew closer to them. They trotted down the hillock and their leader, a lean man with a straggly beard, reported that the army was five miles to the south. We left them to continue their scouting duties and continued on, fifteen minutes later encountering a company of Vagises' horse archers who formed part of the army's forward screen. Finally we saw a vast cloud of dust in front of us and then a great column of horsemen and foot soldiers that seemingly had no end. A group of riders left the column and galloped towards us – figures wearing helmets, mail shirts and white tunics. I slowed Remus and waited as Gallia pulled up Epona beside me and removed her helmet.

'I thought you might miss the war,' she grinned.

I leaned over, pulled her to me and kissed her on the lips. 'Never has a sight been more welcome.'

She glanced at Remus. 'Where is Remus?'

'This is Remus,' I replied.

She was confused. 'Why is he brown?'

'I will tell you later.'

I returned with her and the Amazons to the front of the column where we were joined by Domitus and Chrestus, both of whom were on foot. He immediately noticed the colour of my horse.

'Where's Remus?'

I sighed. 'This is Remus.'

'Why have you painted him brown?'

'I will tell you later.'

It took four more hours to reach Hatra, the army pitching its camp on the hard-packed dirt half a mile from the city's southern gates. I sat down

337

with Gallia and the others in the command tent and told them what had happened in Syria, and specifically Crassus turning down Orodes' offer.

'I could have told you that and saved you a journey, plus the lives of a hundred horse archers,' remarked Domitus, chewing on a piece of cured meat. 'All your trip will have achieved will have been to make Crassus more eager to seize the great riches he believes are at Ctesiphon.'

'He is as arrogant as ever,' said Vagises bitterly, who looked at me. 'Tell them what he offered you.'

'He wanted to make me king of kings of a Parthia that was a client state of Rome.'

'You mean he wanted to enslave you,' hissed Gallia.

I smiled at her. 'That is what I told him.'

'And that bitch Aruna tried to have you killed,' said Domitus, smiling. 'You made a lifelong enemy there. You should have heeded Dobbai's words and killed her long ago. You still might have to.'

'I have bigger things to worry about than an embittered mother,' I told him. 'The Armenians for one thing.'

I informed them of my concerns about Apollonius, his departure from Hatra with a large number of soldiers and how I believed that an Armenian army was on its way to Hatra.

'I thought you said Byrd's brother-in-law told you that Artavasdes was at Antioch,' said Domitus.

I nodded.

'Seems highly unlikely that his army would be making its way south without him,' he continued, finishing off his strip of meat. 'And you base your theory on what Marcus Roscius spouted at you before you killed him.'

I nodded again.

'That's a lot of assumptions.'

'You may be right,' I agreed, 'but I just cannot reconcile how Apollonius escaped with his life last year without making some sort of agreement with the Romans.'

Domitus stuck out his lower lip. 'That is strange, I agree.'

'What does it matter?' said Gallia. 'We are going to have to fight the Armenians and Romans anyway.'

Domitus and Malik laughed and Chrestus smiled.

'Succinct as ever, my love,' I said.

'Have the Armenians any siege engines?' asked a perplexed Marcus.

'Not as far as I know,' I replied. 'Why?'

He ran a hand over his nearly bald crown. 'Well, even if the Armenians are advancing on Hatra, how will they capture it without siege engines?'

'They do not have to,' I answered him. 'All they have to do is sit in front of the walls while Crassus is free to run amok between the Euphrates and Tigris. And don't forget that the Romans do have siege equipment. You are an engineer, Marcus, how long can a city of one hundred thousand people hold out for without hope of relief?'

'Orodes and Nergal have been alerted and will bring their armies here, as will Atrax,' said Gallia determinedly.

'Let us pray they arrive in time,' I added.

'Orodes will be here in two days,' said Domitus, 'and Nergal will hopefully be with him.'

'Atrax might take longer to get here,' I said, 'especially if he has taken his army to Media's eastern border to support Aschek.'

Domitus frowned. 'I thought Peroz's father was marching to aid Aschek.'

'He is,' I agreed, 'but Aschek is apt to panic and so it is wise to support him in his hour of need.'

'I don't know how he became king,' sneered Domitus.

'The same way my father and Atrax did,' I replied. 'Their fathers died and they inherited the throne.'

Domitus pulled out his dagger and began toying with it. 'The Romans did away with their kings over four hundred years ago. Their republic is much more efficient.'

Peroz was shocked. 'Rome killed its kings?'

Domitus smiled maliciously at him. 'That's right, and since then Rome has gone from strength to strength.'

'Even though Domitus has lived in Parthia for twenty years there is still a part of him that is forever Roman,' remarked Gallia, 'is that not correct, Domitus?'

'Old habits die hard,' he replied wistfully.

'You can take the man out of Rome but you cannot take Rome out of the man,' I added mischievously.

Domitus bared his teeth and pointed his dagger at me. 'What will you do if the Armenians do not turn up and this Apollonius turns out not to be a traitor?'

'In those happy circumstances,' I replied, 'then we will meet Crassus and after we have defeated him we will march north, retake Nisibus and then invade Armenia to teach Artavasdes a lesson in manners.'

Peroz thumped the table in triumph and Malik smiled at him.

'He reminds me of Surena,' said the Agraci prince.

Domitus placed the point of his dagger on the table and began turning it. 'Talking of him, can we expect your former squire to make an appearance in our hour of need?'

I held out my hands. 'I have no answer to that.'

'Impudent boy,' snapped Gallia, 'you should order him to attend you here.'

'I could do that,' I smiled at her, 'and he would probably ignore me. He stormed out of a meeting with the high king so I hardly think he is going to obey a command from his lord high general.'

Gallia shook her head. 'You say this Apollonius is a traitor but Surena's actions are just as criminal. His troops could be the difference between defeat and victory.'

Domitus stopped turning his dagger. 'She has a point, Pacorus.'

'Surena, for all his faults, liberated Gordyene, raised an army and now spends his time killing Armenians. For all his insolence I cannot find it in myself to condemn him for his actions.'

'That is because you found him, raised him up from the swamp he was living in, made him a warlord in your own image and unleashed him into the world,' said Domitus. 'I admire you for your loyalty, Pacorus, but he has reverted back into a wild savage, only this time he has an army and a kingdom to back him up.'

'Surena is loyal,' I insisted.

'To you, yes,' said Gallia, 'but not to Parthia.'

Her hostility towards Surena had not abated since the first time she had met him and he had inadvertently touched her hair, so fascinated had he been by her blonde locks. Their relationship had deteriorated further when he had pursued Viper, one of her cherished Amazons. That he had gone on to marry the girl had infuriated my wife further but I knew Surena to be both brave and capable and I had viewed his achievements with a mixture of pride and admiration. If that was construed as weakness on my part by some then so be it.

The rest of the meeting was more agreeable, with Marcus reporting that his siege engines were all in working order and the camel train was loaded with not only replacement bronze-tipped arrows but also quivers full of Arsam's new steel-tipped missiles. I gave orders that the latter were to be issued only when we faced Crassus, when we would put the theories of my chief armourer to the test. The arrival of Dura's army meant that there were twenty-five thousand troops at Hatra, not including Kogan's garrison of two thousand. To the west were Herneus' ten thousand horse archers and another seven thousand under Silaces, which would swell our numbers to just over forty thousand men, enough to at least hold the Armenians until Orodes, Nergal and Atrax arrived.

At the end of the day, as I lay beside a sleeping Gallia in the palace, much of the anxiety that had gripped me since my journey from Syria had disappeared. The arrival of my troops and old friends had done much to dissipate it and the fact that no enemy army had been detected made me think that perhaps I had indeed let my imagination run away with me. I had, after all, based all my assumptions on the words of Marcus Roscius, the lover of Queen Aruna who had no doubt tutored him in the arts of deceit. What were the words of a Roman to me? Outside the warm night air was scented with the nectareous fragrance of the palace gardens where peacocks strutted, white doves roosted and fountains gushed sweet water from the eternal springs that gave the city life. This was Hatra, the impregnable fortress in the middle of the desert whose walls had never been breached by an enemy. As my wife's chest rose slowly and subsided as she slept beside me I drifted into a sleep of contentment.

The next day the Armenians arrived.

I was standing in the palace's large throne room in the presence of Hatra's king and queen seated on their thrones with my mother looking very regal on the other side of Gafarn. She was wearing a long white gown with a crown on her head. Her black hair was loose and hung around her shoulders and she was had a gold belt around her waist and gold jewellery on her fingers. To the right of the dais upon which all three of them were seated was the severe Assur and his white-robed priests, and to the left Vistaspa and the commanders of the Royal Bodyguard and horse archers, plus Kogan and his senior officers. Diana's son, Prince Pacorus, now thirteen years old, stood nervously next to Spartacus. Tall like his father, he had brown shoulder-length hair and a kindly face like his mother. When he caught my eye I smiled at him.

I stood beside Gallia in front of the dais and bowed my head at my brother and his wife, Diana rising to embrace her friend and Zenobia standing next to her. Diana also kissed Byrd and Domitus, much to the discomfiture of the latter, who stood as straight as a spear shaft beside me in his full armour, helmet in the crook of his arm. The hushed room was filled with the aroma of incense that had a calming effect. Spartacus smiled at Peroz who faced him.

'Welcome Prince Peroz,' said Gafarn, 'brave son of King Phriapatius, our ally who holds the east of the empire.'

Peroz bowed his head. 'Thank you, majesty.'

'And welcome Pacorus, King of Dura,' continued Gafarn, 'whose martial fame is known throughout the world and who brings the great and undefeated army of Dura to stand by our own.'

'It is an honour to be here, brother,' I replied.

The exchanges were all highly formalised but Hatra was a very traditional city where Assur and his priests held great sway, believing that adherence to time-honoured rituals would win the favour of Shamash and benefit the city and its rulers. My father had been a stickler for rules and regulations just as his father before him and I realised that Gafarn had followed in their footsteps. Some of the city's nobles may grumble but while Gafarn had the support of Assur, whose priests controlled the masses, there would never be an outright challenge to his rule. Most of the city's great nobles were standing near him now, in the uniform of the Royal Bodyguard, while their sons rode in the ranks. But I did not see any sign of Apollonius among them, the man responsible for losing the west of my brother's kingdom. Despite the despatch of couriers no word had reached the city of the errant lord's whereabouts, or the twenty thousand horse archers he had led out of the city, but at least news had reached us that Silaces was on his way from the city of Assur.

The high priest who had been named after the city where Herneus was governor had just finished reciting a prayer when the doors of the throne room opened behind me, and all eyes focused on the guard who marched stiffly towards Kogan. Even before the contents of the sheet of folded papyrus that he carried in his hand were read I knew that something was awry. Where before there was calm and reassurance there was suddenly apprehension. With every step that the guard took towards Kogan the tension palpably rose until it became almost unbearable as he handed the note to his commander. Kogan did not read it but instead walked in front of the dais, bowed and then held it out for Gafarn to take. My brother did so and read its contents, then handed it to Diana to peruse.

He stood. 'Scouts have detected a large Armenian force advancing towards the city from the northeast.'

Men looked at each other and some may have been alarmed but no one spoke. The officers of the Royal Bodyguard were too professional to allow their emotions to show. Assur was impassive – all the demons from the underworld could be converging on the city and he would be unconcerned, believing that Shamash would protect Hatra as long as the people remained pious.

'How many Armenians?' I asked.

'We have not been able to discover that as yet,' replied Gafarn.

'May I suggest we convene a council of war to determine our next move,' I said.

My mother suggested the gazebo in her secret garden and insisted on attending. It was now mid-morning and the temperature was already rising, though it was pleasant enough in the shade of the arbour. Immaculately dressed slave girls with painted fingernails and oiled hair brought us fruit juice, yoghurt, wafers, fruit and pastries as we reclined on couches and determined how best to slaughter the enemy. As we did Gafarn received more updates on the composition of the Armenian army and its distance from the city. As I devoured a delicious honey cake topped with seeds he revealed that around one hundred thousand Armenians were four hours away.

'Outnumbered four to one,' remarked Domitus casually. 'Sounds decent odds.'

Vagises laughed while Vistaspa frowned but Gafarn said nothing.

'Do Romans always give battle no matter what the odds?' my mother asked Domitus politely.

He wiped away crumbs from around his mouth with the back of his hand. 'Yes, lady, always. They believe that if you attack first it gives you an advantage and also pleases the gods.'

'And what gods are those?' she enquired further.

'Chiefly Mars, god of war,' replied Domitus proudly, 'and the god of death.'

My mother was intrigued. 'And does he have a name, this god of death?'

Domitus nodded. 'He does, lady, but I prefer not to say it in case he notices me and takes me away into the next life for doing so.'

My mother smiled. 'How quaint. And do you believe that we should fight the Armenians, Roman?'

Domitus grinned broadly. 'Yes, lady.'

She looked at Gafarn and then me. 'And what do my two sons think?'

I waited for Gafarn to speak first even though technically I outranked him as lord high general.

'I await the decision of the empire's lord high general,' he replied.

I finished another honey cake. They really were most palatable.

'By the time the Armenians get here we will still have five hours of daylight left, more than enough to fight a battle. The enemy will be tired after marching all day in the heat whilst our men will be fresh, but if we allow them to make camp then tomorrow we will have to fight an invigorated opponent. I therefore propose to fight the Armenians outside the city, today.'

'Even though we are outnumbered?' asked Vistaspa.

'It is not the size of the man in the fight, Lord Vistaspa,' said Domitus, 'but the size of the fight in the man.'

My mother laughed and clapped her hands. 'You really are a most intriguing individual, Roman.'

'Even though we are outnumbered,' I replied. 'I have no stomach to be cooped up inside this city like lambs in a pen awaiting slaughter. Silaces is on his way from Assur and Orodes and Nergal are advancing from the south. If we allow the Armenians to lay siege to Hatra they will be able to engage our friends separately while we are trapped inside the city. This I cannot allow.'

I looked at Gafarn who smiled at me. 'I agree. Kogan, bring all the caravans that are camped outside the city within the walls and quarter them in the squares.'

'I will need to bring my mules, wagons and siege engines into the city as well,' I told Gafarn.

'Put them in the Great Square,' he replied.

Assur raised his bushy eyebrows. 'Adjacent to the Great Temple?'

'I'm sure Shamash will understand,' said Gafarn. 'We are, after all, defending His sanctuary from the heathens.'

'We will all defend your temple, Lord Assur,' said my mother, 'I will fetch my bow and stand on the battlements beside Lord Kogan's men.'

Domitus looked at her in surprise.

'You think I am a frail old woman, Roman,' she asked, 'fit only to be raped and murdered if the enemy breaches the walls? I can shoot a bow as well as any man.'

'I don't doubt it, lady,' he replied admiringly.

Diana, who had once been an Amazon, also declared her intention to stand on the walls beside her mother-in-law, but when I suggested that Gallia might like to join them I was met by an icy glare.

'I will be fighting alongside you with the Amazons, my dear,' she insisted.

So I kissed my mother farewell and ordered Domitus to pass the word on to Marcus that the Duran camp was to be dismantled and the wagons and animals brought into the Great Square. He was to use the city's northern gates, which gave direct access to the royal quarter. In addition to Kogan's guards, the three thousand squires of Hatra's cataphracts and Royal Bodyguard, plus a further two thousand from Dura, would reinforce the garrison. This gave Kogan a total of seven thousand men and boys, plus my mother and Diana.

343

The Armenians had hugged the Tigris on their way here before heading southwest into the desert to advance on Hatra. They had also probably diverted a number of troops to the city of Assur to keep Herneus occupied and prevent him from reinforcing Hatra. I was not worried about him: he had ten thousand horse archers plus his garrison to defend the city. But I was concerned that any assault against Assur would prevent Silaces from reaching us.

I walked with Domitus from the gardens, through the palace and into the Great Square, which would soon be filled with mules and wagons.

'We will place Marcus' smaller ballista among the first line cohorts,' I said, thinking aloud. 'Because we are greatly outnumbered we will deploy the Durans and Exiles in two lines to extend their frontage, with the horse archers on the wings and the cataphracts held back as a reserve. The Armenians will be confident of victory and we will use that against them by drawing them onto our javelins and swords.'

'You have been doing a lot of thinking,' he said.

I stopped and looked at him. 'This is the city where I grew up, Domitus, a place of great strength and certainty in an uncertain world. When I was in Italy the thought of Hatra was a comfort to me: its many towers, its high walls and great moat. Whatever calamities befell the empire, the one constant was the strength of Hatra, the capital of the greatest kingdom in the empire.

'But now much of that kingdom lies in enemy hands and this city itself is in peril. I will not stand idly by and watch it fall to the Armenians, not while there is breath left in my body.'

He smiled and laid a hand on my shoulder. 'Do not fear. You have created an army that would follow you into the underworld if you asked it to.'

'Just a few miles outside the city will suffice.'

I looked at the entrance of the Great Temple. 'I think I will take a few minutes in the temple Domitus.'

'Not thinking of becoming a priest are you?'

'Not yet. Deploy the army immediately north of the city. I will meet you there. By the way, what is the name of the Roman god of death?'

He looked pensive before shrugging. 'Mors.'

We clasped arms and then he marched off to organise the movement of thousands of men and animals. It would take about three hours for the camp to be dismantled and the tents and palisade stakes to be loaded onto wagons and mules and brought into the city. The squires would be earmarked for the menial tasks while the legions, horse archers and cataphracts marched by the city's eastern wall to take up position beyond the northern gates. Hatra's horsemen, meanwhile, would exit the city via the northern gates and join their Duran and Carmanian allies to await the Armenians.

I walked across the square to the steps that led to the entrance of the impressive colonnaded temple, its great bronze-faced doors positioned facing east to welcome the Sun God each day as He made another journey

344

through the heavens. I walked through the doors and into the spacious, airy interior that was flooded with sunlight coming through the many high windows cut in the walls. White-robed priests moved across the white marble tiles in soft slippers in order to make as little noise as possible so as not to disturb the Sun God.

The temple was filled with the aroma of frankincense, which was burned every morning to purify its interior of any malign influences. In the middle of the day myrrh was burned to unite heaven and earth and in the evening the priests always burned kapet, a mixture of cedar bark, juniper berries, cinnamon, wine, honey, raisins, galangal, myrrh and benzoin, to purify the temple. I walked up the central aisle to where the high altar basked in bright sunlight. I took a seat and stared at the silver eagle that was laid before it, the eagle that I had taken all those years ago. As far as I knew it had not been touched since Assur had placed it there as an offering to Shamash, though I suspected that it had been dusted if not cleaned during the past twenty years, since it looked immaculate.

Though one or two priests moved silently around inside the cavernous structure it seemed as though I was alone before Shamash. I closed my eyes and prayed to Him – that He would grant our forces victory over the Armenians and deliver up this, His city, that He would look over and protect my mother and my family, and finally that He would safeguard the empire against its many enemies in its hour of need. I opened my eyes and saw a young girl standing in front of the altar. She wore a simple brown dress; her feet and her arms were bare. She had long black hair that cascaded down her back. She knelt down in front of the altar and extended her arm to touch the eagle.

'Do not touch that,' I ordered.

She withdrew her arm and got to her feet, then turned to face me. She had a pretty face with big brown eyes and a mischievous grin. She sauntered over and sat down beside me. She looked at the eagle.

'Is it yours?'

'No,' I replied, 'it belongs to the Sun God.'

'Where is he?'

'He is god; he is all around us.'

'Why were you sitting with your eyes closed?'

'I was praying in quiet contemplation,' I replied. 'You should try it.'

She looked at me with a quizzical expression. 'What were you asking for?'

She was an irksome child. 'Where are your parents?'

She looked at her bare feet. 'Dead.'

'I am sorry.'

She giggled. 'Why? You did not know them. You have not answered my question.'

I sighed and looked around for someone to take the urchin away but could see no one. We were totally alone.

'If you must know I was asking the Sun God to grant me victory.'

She began swinging her lower legs that dangled from her seat. 'Victory over who?'

I smiled at her innocence. 'The Armenians who are approaching the city.'

She suddenly jumped off her seat and ran over to the eagle and stood by it. 'Where are the other eagles?'

'Other eagles?'

'Yes, the other eagles who look like this one.'

I was mildly surprised by this question to say the least but decided to indulge her infantile mind. Someone had obviously told her about the Romans. 'They are gathering in the west.'

'You will have to beat them as well and then you can place all seven eagles beside this one.'

I stood up as she once more knelt beside the Roman eagle. 'How do you know this?'

She giggled. 'Everyone knows that the Romans are invading Parthia just as they know that you will save the empire.'

At that moment the rays of the sun shone on the eagle and reflected into my eyes, temporarily blinding me. The girl giggled again.

'You should have faith, son of Hatra.'

I moved aside and looked at the altar but there was no one there. I glanced left and right and then behind me but saw no one and heard only my own footsteps on the tiles as I searched the temple in vain for the girl. She was nowhere to be seen. I saw a priest and was about to question him regarding seeing the child but thought better of it. Perhaps the incense had befuddled my senses and I had dreamt the whole episode. And yet...

I left the temple and walked to the stables to collect Remus who had been brushed and was beginning to return to his original colour. Around me hundreds of squires were assisting their masters into their scale armour while others were encasing horses in thick hide covered with iron scales. Farriers were replacing horseshoes, veterinaries were examining horses and cataphracts were checking their weapons.

I mounted Remus and rode him from the royal quarter and out of the city via the eastern gates. I had to thread my way through a great press of camels that were being brought into Hatra as the caravan parks around it were emptied on Kogan's orders. The Duran camp was likewise a hive of activity as legionaries gathered in their centuries and cohorts and horsemen in their companies and dragons. Already a long line of wagons was making its way to the city and mules were being loaded with equipment. It was very hot and already my silk vest under my tunic was drenched in sweat. For the cataphracts and their horses in their heavy armour it was far worse but at least they did not have the prospect of a long march ahead of them.

Most of the tents had been stashed on the wagons but Domitus' command tent still stood and inside he and the others awaited me, the Amazons sitting on the ground around it waiting for their mistress. I

346

dismounted, handed Remus' reins to Zenobia, took off my helmet and went inside.

'Ah, the priest returns,' quipped Domitus. 'We were beginning to think that you might sit out the battle in meditation.'

'Very droll,' I replied.

I looked at Malik and Byrd. 'Get your scouts out to ensure the Armenians do not detach forces to sweep around our rear.'

They nodded and both left. I turned to Marcus.

'Are your ballista ready?'

He smiled. 'The crews are fully briefed.'

I turned to Vagises and Peroz. 'Vagises, your horse archers will initially be deployed dismounted behind the first line cohorts. The Armenians will endeavour to smash our centre with their overwhelming numbers of foot. Three thousand archers shooting at them will hopefully diminish the force of their initial assault.'

'What of my men, majesty?' requested Peroz.

'You, lord prince, will be positioned on the army's left wing. King Gafarn will take up position on the right with his horse archers.'

An hour later I was mounted on Remus reiterating my battle plan with Vistaspa and Gafarn to the rear of the army that was waiting for the Armenian host. I suggested that Vistaspa take command of all the cataphracts that were grouped in two large blocks to the rear of our position, every man having planted the butt spike of his *kontus* in the hard earth and the Durans having shoved their full-face helmets up onto their heads. Vistaspa was most pleased by my suggestion but it made sense: of all of us he had the most experience and was respected by both Hatra's élite horsemen and my own heavy cavalry.

'That's decided, then,' I said happily.

The ground we would fight the battle on was ideal for horsemen, comprising largely flat terrain with the occasional depression or mound. In the spring rains there is a brief covering of young green grass but this quickly disappears to leave an environment as it appeared now: sun-roasted hard earth with a sprinkling of the only plants that can live in this harsh land – southernwood, wormwood and dragonwort. Domitus had positioned his legions so they faced northeast, which meant that the sun was behind his men's backs as it began its slow descent in the west. We were around half of a mile from Hatra's northern gates, allowing the army room for manoeuvre and also being close enough to provide an escape route back to the city should disaster befall us. The legions covered a frontage of a mile and either side of them each wing of horse archers presented a frontage of half a mile. Our battle line looked impressive but we were as thin as papyrus and everyone knew it.

We did not see the Armenians first but rather heard them – a low, rumbling sound to the northeast that slowly got louder as the enemy approached.

'Kettledrums,' I mumbled to myself.

347

If there was one thing that I had come to loathe it was kettledrums, which always reminded me of the armies of Narses and Mithridates, though they were both dead. As soon as I heard that awful drumming sound my mind conjured up images of the pair, sitting on their horses mocking me. The Durans and Exiles had been sitting or lying on the ground and when they heard the annoying racket some stood up and peered into the distance. Most, though, continued their rest or conversation with their comrades. They had heard it too many times to let it bother them and had become expert at using it to judge how far away the enemy was.

Minutes later a group of horsemen galloped through the gap between the legions and Gafarn's horse archers on the right flank, most of whom were also sitting on the ground beside their mounts.

Byrd and Malik brought their horses to a halt in front of me and raised their hands in salute. I saw that their horses were both sweating from a long gallop. Their arrival was a signal for others to gather around us as the figures of Domitus, Vagises and Chrestus strode from the ranks of legionaries ahead and Gafarn left his horse archers with a company of bodyguards following him. And from the Carmanians rode Peroz and fifty other horsemen with Vistaspa also riding from his cataphracts. He joined Gafarn and the prince of Carmania as they drew level beside Malik, their escorts remaining fifty paces away.

Byrd uncorked his water bottle and took a sip. 'Armenians half an hour away.'

'Numbers?' I asked, though I already knew that they greatly outnumbered us. Domitus, bareheaded, nodded at Malik as he stood in front of Remus next to the sweating Chrestus.

'A hundred thousand foot and fifty thousand horse,' replied Byrd without emotion.

Domitus pointed his cane at me. 'I thought you said we would be outnumbered four to one? I make it six to one. You sure you didn't count some of the enemy twice, Byrd?'

Byrd patted his horse on the neck. 'You take my horse and count them for yourself if you no believe me.'

'We've seen enough armies to be able to estimate their strength, Domitus,' said Malik.

Domitus raised his cane to salute his old friend and then looked at me. 'You still want to fight them?'

I looked at Gafarn in his cuirass of steel scales and helmet adorned with Hatra's crown. 'It is your city and your crown, brother.'

Gafarn may have found the demands of kingship taxing but today his face was a mask of determination. It was as if he could finally dictate events rather than them ruling him. 'We fight. They will arrive soon and it would be a grave discourtesy not to be here to greet them.'

'Good,' I said, 'the Armenians have treated Parthia with contempt for too long.'

I looked at Domitus and Chrestus. 'I am afraid that your men will be acting as the seawall against which the Armenian waves will crash. You will have Vagises' archers for support but it is imperative that you hold their attack.'

'You are certain they will attack, majesty?' asked Vistaspa.

I smiled. 'If I had one hundred and fifty thousand men under my command I would wish to sweep the enemy from the field. They will attack, especially when they see how few we are.'

I looked at Gafarn and then Peroz. 'You must use your horse archers to goad the enemy so they will launch their horsemen against you. Once they do withdraw to allow Lord Vistaspa to commit his cataphracts. The heavy horsemen of Hatra and Dura are the empire's finest and nothing the Armenians possess can match them. When Lord Vistaspa charges with his cataphracts the enemy's horsemen will be shattered, then Peroz and Gafarn will commit their horse archers.'

Vistaspa nodded approvingly and Peroz looked thoughtful.

'Remember, lord prince, goad the enemy, entice him to attack. Use the tactics you have learned at Dura.'

'Yes, lord,' Peroz beamed.

I next addressed Vagises. 'As soon as the legions are engaged in a mêlée get your men mounted and pull them back to my position here. They will act as a reserve just in case events take an unexpected turn.'

'You mean if we get our arses kicked,' said Domitus.

'In which case,' I added, 'the horsemen will act as a shield to allow the legions to retire to the city.'

Domitus slapped Vagises hard on the back. 'Don't worry about us; we'll be dead most likely so you and your horse boys don't need to concern yourselves with our safety.'

Peroz was horrified. 'My men and I will never abandon you, Lord Domitus. We will never dishonour our homeland by fleeing.'

Domitus squinted at Peroz. 'You remind me of Orodes and Pacorus with all that nonsense about honour.'

'You honour me, general,' smiled Peroz.

Domitus looked at him and shook his head. 'See what I mean.'

The kettledrums were getting louder and the horizon was now filling with small black shapes as the Armenians approached.

'To your positions,' I said, 'and may Shamash be with you all.'

Peroz and Gafarn raised their hands in acknowledgement and then galloped back to their men as their escorts grouped round them. Vagises and Chrestus were deep in conversation as they made their way back to the legions deployed in the centre, while Domitus took off his helmet and brushed its white crest.

'You take care of yourself, Pacorus,' he said.

'I will take care of him, Domitus,' replied Gallia.

Satisfied that the crest looked presentable, he replaced his helmet on his head and raised his cane at us before ambling back to take command of his men.

'He looks as though he is taking an afternoon stroll,' remarked Vistaspa, though not in a mocking way.

'He is the finest soldier I have ever met,' I said. 'One day mothers in Parthia will tell stories to their children of Lucius Domitus, the Roman centurion who forged the army of Dura into an invincible weapon that put all of its enemies to the sword.'

I heard the shrill blast of trumpets and saw ten thousand legionaries hoist up their shields and javelins and form ranks as the Armenians flooded the ground to the front of the army like ants swarming from a huge nest. The infernal din of kettledrums filled our ears as the enemy manoeuvred into position. Spearmen clutched their weapons, archers tested bowstrings, slingers pulled lead shots from their pouches and horses scraped impatiently at the earth as tension and foreboding gripped tens of thousands of men who were about to fight the Battle of Hatra.

Chapter 16

I knew that we were greatly outnumbered but also knew that every one of the soldiers who faced the Armenians was a professional: a man who spent every day training with his weapons and learning drills until they became second nature. My old tutor Bozan, now long dead, had always stressed the importance of training.

'Train and train until you carry out drills unthinkingly,' he used to say, 'so fighting becomes instinctive and your weapons become extensions of your arms. Train hard, fight easy, boy, that's the secret.'

Even Peroz's horse archers had been schooled in Dura's ways and were now every bit as good as Vagises' mounted archers. Except that today the latter were not mounted. The Durans were drawn up in the centre, five cohorts in the first line and five in the second. On their left stood the Exiles, also arrayed in two lines of five cohorts, and between the first and second lines in each legion stood Vagises' archers, ready to spring a nasty surprise on the enemy when they attacked. Their horses were positioned to the rear of the legions, behind the line of wagons that were loaded with spare javelins, swords and shields, water bottles and medical supplies for Alcaeus' orderlies who stood ready with their bandages and instruments to patch up lacerated bodies and shattered bones.

Every tenth Duran horse archer was detailed to stay with the horses to keep them calm when the fighting began and the air would be filled with the cries of the dying and the stench of urine and dung.

The vanguard of the army were Marcus' fifty small ballista, each one positioned behind two large wicker screens faced with thick hide and over six feet high, behind which the crews could work in safety. The screens were closed up so there was only a small gap between them, through which the ballistae could fire their iron-tipped bolts. These machines were ideal for softening up the enemy or goading them into action.

I looked down at my right hand, which was shaking.

'Are you all right, Pacorus?' asked a concerned Gallia beside me.

'Mm? Yes, of course. The shakes, that is all. Strange, I have not had them in years. I cannot remember the last time I experienced them.'

'A sign of getting old, perhaps,' quipped Vagharsh behind me, holding the griffin standard.

I reached over and laid a hand on Gallia's arm. 'If things go awry I want you to get back to the city. You will be safe there.'

She took my hand and kissed it. 'My place is by your side. I flee from no enemy.'

Vagharsh laughed. 'That told you. You didn't really think Gallia would turn tail and run, did you? It's not in the Gauls' nature. You must remember Crixus and his feral followers. Gallia may be Queen of Dura but she is still a wild Gaul at heart.'

My wife turned and smiled at him and behind us the mail-clad Amazons grinned at each other. The vexatious kettledrums were still

351

sounding as both armies stared at each other across the five hundred paces of no-man's land.

Then there was a mighty blast of horns and the Armenians opened the battle.

'No parley, then,' remarked Vagharsh, 'they must fancy their chances.'

'Their commander is probably thinking that he will be dining in Hatra tonight,' I said.

'Then we will have to disabuse him of that notion,' said Gallia defiantly.

Whoever the Armenian commander was he knew what he was doing because first he sent in his slingers with archers following behind. A long line of slingers recruited from the wild regions of the Caucasus walked forward to pepper the legions and ballista crews with their shots. Many people scoff at slingers, believing them to be threadbare shepherds who are worthless on the battlefield. But what many commanders do not realise is that a lead pellet or stone propelled by a sling at a straight angle has greater force than an arrow. So now hundreds of men wearing no armour or helmets and carrying no other weapon but a long knife calmly walked forward, reached into the leather pouches slung across their shoulders to extract lead missiles, and released them from their slings using an underhand motion.

As soon as movement had been discerned in the Armenian ranks in front of them and their officers had spotted the slingers and archers, trumpets had blasted among the Durans and Exiles and seconds later twenty cohorts formed *testudo*. The legionaries knelt, the first ranks forming a shield wall and the succeeding ranks lifting their shields above their heads to form a roof of leather and wood. The lead shots slammed into the shield wall as the slingers continued to walk forward, and then the ballistae began shooting.

The Armenians had no doubt noticed the pairs of what appeared to be wooden panels deployed in front of the army but had probably dismissed them. But now from between these panels came iron-tipped bolts that went straight through bodies to impale those behind. The crews worked feverishly to shoot four bolts a minute – two hundred deadly projectiles smashing bones and piercing flesh at a range of four hundred paces. Instinctively the slingers stopped, unsure what to do, as their own missiles made no impression on the locked shields of the Durans and Exiles. And as more and more of them were cut down by ballista bolts, their commanders decided to withdraw them out of range. Horns sounded and the surviving slingers ran back to beyond the range of the ballistae, which stopped shooting. I smiled. First blood to us.

The Durans and Exiles remained in their *testudo* formation as the Armenians next sent forward their archers to saturate our ranks with arrows. Vagises' horse archers were huddled behind the first line of the Durans and Exiles and Alcaeus and his orderlies had taken shelter under the wagons in the rear of the legions as the first Armenian arrows began to land among them.

352

Armenian bows were not like our recurve type, being straight limbed and longer. As such their range was shorter and so the archers were forced to close to within two hundred paces of our front ranks to achieve maximum effect. Once more the ballistae began shooting as the thousands of densely packed men wearing green tunics and cloth caps rushed forward and then stopped to release their arrows. The front ranks released arrows directly at the shield wall in a vain attempt to literally shoot the shields to pieces, while those behind loosed their arrows in a high trajectory so they would fall on the rear ranks.

From where I was sitting it looked impressive as a blizzard of arrows arched into the sky and then fell on the legions, but the men had been subjected to such volleys before and had made sure there were no gaps in the roof that protected them. The bronze-tipped arrows did not have the force to pierce our shields and after about five minutes the arrow storm abated and then stopped altogether as the Armenians exhausted their ammunition. The ballistae had also stopped shooting, their crews having taken shelter behind their wooden screens, and thus another lull descended over the battlefield as the Armenian archers pulled back to their own lines. Again the *testudo* remained in place as Domitus and Chrestus awaited the next enemy assault.

Riders came from Gafarn and Peroz to inform me that, though they both faced Armenian horse archers at least equal to the number of their own horsemen, the enemy had made no aggressive moves, both sides merely observing each other nervously.

'Why don't you order an assault?' said an impatient Gallia.

'Because, my sweet, the enemy is only testing our strength, probing our lines. He wants us to attack so he can bring his greater numbers to bear but I will not give him that satisfaction.'

'Once a Gaul, always a Gaul,' commented Vagharsh.

There was a great cacophony of drums from the enemy ranks and then a huge mass of Armenians began advancing against the legions: rank upon rank of foot soldiers armed with spears and carrying round wicker shields. The drummers within their massed ranks banged their instruments wildly so that it sounded as if a huge herd of animals was bearing down on the Durans and Exiles. The latter responded with trumpet blasts and the men abandoned their *testudo* to meet this fresh onslaught.

The Armenian spearmen were dressed in brown tunics and red leggings but wore no armour and only linen caps on their heads. But there was a great many of them, upwards of forty thousand or more. And at the same time the horse archers on the Armenian flanks entered the fray, companies riding forward to loose arrows at their opponents before withdrawing to their original positions. These movements were designed purely to keep our horse archers occupied and prevent them shooting missiles at the densely packed ranks of the unarmoured levy spearmen that were marching against the legions. Gafarn and Peroz duly obliged and became willing partners in this desultory duel, sending parties of their own horsemen forward to loose a few arrows and then pulling them back. Dura's camel train was located to the rear of Peroz's dragons and the amply furnished train of Hatra was positioned behind Gafarn's horse archers, so neither of our wings would run out of ammunition any time soon.

The Armenian commander, having got the attention of my two wings, probably believed that his spearmen would at least be able to push back my centre due to sheer weight of numbers alone. But I had a surprise in store. As the spearmen increased their pace and began shouting and cheering to fortify their courage, Vagises' archers standing behind the first-line cohorts drew back their bowstrings and released their arrows. Two thousand, seven hundred arrows arched into the sky and then fell among the densely packed spearmen, followed six seconds later by a further volley. The Armenians ran into this arrow storm of thirteen and half thousand missiles every minute at around three hundred paces from the legions, the missiles scything down hundreds of men as they pierced shoulders, necks, chests and legs. Cheers were replaced by high-pitched screams and yelps as the front ranks of the spearmen were turned into heaps of groaning, twitching wounded.

Vagises' men kept shooting their arrows as they emptied the spare quivers they had been issued with, mounds of dead Armenians being created in front of the legions as the missiles easily found unprotected flesh. But as quickly as spearmen were killed or wounded others behind them ran forward to get to grips with Domitus' men.

Vagises' archers could only fire over the heads of the centuries in front of them, which meant that their killing ground stopped two hundred paces out from the front rank of legionaries. Those spearmen who had emerged unhurt from the strip of ground that was saturated by arrows now formed up in front of the legions. They had been badly unnerved by seeing hundreds of their comrades being killed by Parthian arrows, but now their officers cajoled and threatened them to reform their ranks and charge the white shields sporting red griffin wings that stood in front of them. And their courage was fortified as the arrow volleys lessened and stopped as Vagises' men ran out of ammunition and more and more additional spearmen came forward to swell their numbers. As they formed their ranks to charge many raised their weapons and shook them at the silent legionaries, spitting curses and threatening to send them to the next life on the end of their spears. Then as one they issued a blood-curdling scream and hurled themselves forward at the legions, and to fresh horror.

When they were fifty paces from my men there was a blast of trumpets and then the whole first line charged forward, the first five ranks in each century hurling their javelins against the Armenians. Once more hundreds of the latter were cut down by this fresh missile storm and then the legionaries were among them. The ranks that had thrown their javelins drew their short swords and sprang at the stunned spearmen, smashing their shield bosses into faces or bodies to push opponents over, stabbing *gladius* points into groins, necks and eye sockets as they hacked their way into the enemy.

Now it was the turn of the legionaries to cheer and shout as the Armenian ranks buckled under this terrifying onslaught. They had already been shaken by the arrow storm but had managed to salvage some of their discipline and courage, but now these part-time soldiers collapsed under the unrelenting assault of the Durans and Exiles. Within minutes thousands of spearmen had been cut down, those still living being trampled and stamped on by the advancing legionaries. Hobnailed sandals were smashed down onto windpipes, arms and groins and the air was rent with high-pitched screams. Some Armenians lying face-up had their heads severed as legionaries slammed their metal-rimmed shields down hard on their necks.

Whistles and trumpets sounded and the front-line cohorts halted and reformed as the Armenian spearmen fled in headlong retreat. I nodded with satisfaction. Our centre still held and that attack had cost the Armenians thousands of casualties. The ballistae had been abandoned during the assault of the spearmen but now their crews, who had sought sanctuary behind the first-line cohorts, ran forward to retrieve their machines before the next attack.

I looked over to the right wing to see Gafarn's horse archers still in their companies adjacent to the right flank of the Durans, but on the left it was a different story. Though Peroz's men were still extant in their companies there was a large gap between them and the left flank of the Exiles. The Armenian horse archers facing him had obviously enticed him further away from our centre and now there was a yawning gap that could be exploited by the enemy.

I turned and pointed at Zenobia. 'Ride forward immediately and find Vagises. Tell him to mount his men and bring them here.'

She saluted and shouted at her horse to move, the beast jerking forward as it sped across the ground.

I pointed at the gap. 'The enemy had lured Peroz further over to the left, you see?' Gallia nodded.

Vistaspa had also noticed the gap and was manoeuvring his heavy horsemen to meet whatever threat came through it. But as yet nothing appeared and while I was absorbed with what was happening on the left the Armenians launched a fresh assault against our centre.

Perhaps up to ten thousand levy spearmen had been killed or wounded by Vagises' archers and Domitus' legionaries but to the Armenian commander they were expendable: farmers and townsfolk who had a minimum of training and deficient weaponry. They were chaff and Armenia would not weep for their lost souls. A far tougher proposition was now approaching the legions: heavy swordsmen.

As Vagises drew up his horse in front of me his men flooded the ground to the rear of the Amazons and then companies peeled away to make the trip to the camel train to replenish their stocks of arrows.

'They are just toying with us,' he said, nodding to Gallia beside me. 'But I have a feeling that the real battle is just beginning.'

'Your men did well, Vagises,' I said.

He moved his horse to take up position on my left side and pointed at the widening space between our centre and left flank.

'I don't like the look of that.'

'No,' I agreed, 'take two dragons of your men and seal the gap. The rest will stay here with me as a reserve. I have a feeling we may need them.'

He peeled away to consult his officers as there was a great tumult in the centre and the Armenian heavy swordsmen attacked. Just as I had modelled my foot on Rome's legions so had the Armenians based their heavy swordsmen on the Roman model. Protected by conical helmets with cheekguards, mail shirts and oval-shaped wooden shields faced with bronze or iron, these men carried two short throwing spears that they now hurled at my frontline cohorts before drawing their swords and charging. These men were professional soldiers who were recruited from the Armenian heartlands. They were well paid, well equipped and highly motivated and they numbered at least twenty thousand men.

Just as Dura's legions were trained to hurl their javelins and then charge at an enemy with their swords drawn, so the Armenians threw their missiles and launched themselves at the legions. Three things prevented them breaking our line. Firstly, they faced soldiers who were even better trained and motivated than they were, which meant that that the first-line cohorts were able to withstand the hail of spears that were thrown at them. Though dozens of legionaries were killed or wounded the line did not break. Secondly, the first-line cohorts that received the Armenian charge were actually the cohorts that had begun the battle as the second line. In the aftermath of the defeat of the levy spearmen Domitus had brought up his fresh second line to take the place of those cohorts that had battled the spearmen. Thirdly, and perhaps decisively, the ground in front of the legions was literally carpeted with dead spearmen, which broke up the momentum of the heavy swordsmen's charge as enemy units negotiated their way through and over piles of dead men.

The awful din of a huge mêlée erupted as the swordsmen finally got to grips with the Durans and Exiles, the front ranks of both sides stabbing and hacking at opponents with their swords. The frenzy of sword strikes produced fewer casualties than expected, though, as men kept their shields tight to their torsos and tucked their chins into their chests to protect their necks. The reality was that a small number of men in the front ranks of both sides duelled with each other as the ranks behind them waited for the breakthrough that never came.

The centre was a scene of deadlock but on the left a disaster was unfolding.

Vagises was leading two thousand of his horse archers towards the gap between Peroz's rapidly fading horsemen on the left wing and the left flank of the Exiles when groups of enemy horsemen suddenly began pouring through said gap: a seething wedge of horseflesh made up of mounted spearmen in green tunics, scale armour cuirasses and helmets. They were moving fast towards the cataphracts that stood motionless in front of them.

There were dozens of dragon windsocks fluttering among the Armenian horsemen, each one being the standard of a company of around a hundred men. From my position I could not determine how many enemy horsemen there were but a guess would put the figure at fifteen thousand or more.

Horse archers are not able to engage in a close-quarter battle with enemy horsemen who are armoured and equipped with lances and shields. Their most effective tactic is to shoot at an enemy from a safe distance, like a swarm of hornets, arrows being their deadly sting. But now Vagises led his men directly towards the Armenian swarm, his companies deploying into a long line of wedge formations, each one four ranks deep. His horse archers were galloping towards the right flank of the Armenian mass and began loosing arrows at a range of seven or eight hundred paces from them.

Shooting around four arrows a minute, two thousand missiles landed among the Armenians every fifteen seconds. They struck horses and their riders, sending animals careering to the ground where they thrashed around in agony. Dozens of injured beasts, wild-eyed with terror and pain shooting through their bodies, collided with other horses and knocked them off-balance. Riders were thrown from saddles and trampled under hooves as Vagises' men inflicted carnage on the Armenian flank.

When they were around two hundred paces from the enemy the companies of Dura's horsemen wheeled their horses to the right and then right again as they about-faced and retreated, twisting in the saddle and shooting arrows over the hind quarters of their animals as they did so.

Now Vistaspa led his cataphracts forward and the ground began to shake as two and half thousand armoured horses and their riders broke into a canter and then a gallop, hundreds of *kontus* shafts lowered as they were held two handedly on the right flank of the animals. It took my breath away as I beheld the steel-encased horseflesh of Dura and Hatra race across the ground and then smashed into the Armenians. I punched the air as I heard the sickening scraping noise that told me that *kontus* points were going through shields and armour.

'Pacorus!' Gallia shouted.

'I know, it is a magnificent sight. Hail victory!'

'No, Pacorus, Look!'

I turned away from admiring the unstoppable charge of the cataphracts to see with horror Gafarn's horse archers fleeing from a great number of Armenian heavy horsemen who were now dividing into two parts: one that continued to pursue Hatra's horsemen, and another that was riding towards our position. The Armenian commander had timed the charge of his horsemen with perfection – on one wing unleashing them into an inviting gap; on the other committing his mailed fist to smash through the horse archers on our right flank. I stared open-mouthed as at least three thousand heavy horsemen, followed by Armenian horse archers, galloped after Gafarn's men who were shooting arrows over their horses' hind quarters as they retreated back to Hatra. The army's right wing had evaporated.

The Armenian horsemen who had peeled away and who were now bearing down on us wore steel arm armour, scale armour cuirasses and green plumes on their helmets. Each man carried a long lance and no doubt was also armed with a sword and perhaps also a mace or axe. One thing was certain: the thousand horse archers with me plus the Amazons would not be able to withstand them.

The Armenians had now halted and were dressing their lines preparatory to a charge to destroy us. Frantic and frequent trumpet blasts to my front indicated that the legions' commanders had also witnessed the collapse of Gafarn's wing.

'The legions are forming square,' I said to no one in particular.

'What are we going to do?' asked Gallia.

I peered at the Armenians horsemen and saw that though their horses wore scale armour, the suits covered the animals' bodies only, not their heads or necks. I called forward the company commanders.

I pointed at the Armenian horsemen beginning to walk their animals towards us.

'The horses' heads and necks are vulnerable. We are therefore going to charge them and drop as many of the beasts as we can before taking refuge in the square being formed by the legions. Go!'

They saluted and rode back to their commands, horns sounded and then the Duran dragon and Amazons slowly swung right to face the Armenians. The latter had now broken into a canter as they closed the gap between them and us, their lances lowered to skewer Parthian flesh. I raised my hand and signalled the advance and we too broke into a trot and then a canter. Gallia leaned forward in her saddle and without thinking pulled an arrow from her quiver and nocked it in her bowstring. Horns blew and we broke into a gallop, Remus straining his muscles to outrun Epona beside him. I strung an arrow and released it, then nocked another and another and another as missiles flew at the Armenians and scythed down their front ranks. Horses pulled up and collapsed as arrows hit them, catapulting their riders onto the ground.

Then, just as we had done a hundred times before on the training fields, fresh horn blasts signalled a wheel to the right and then right again as we about-faced and retreated from the Armenians. I twisted in the saddle and shot an arrow at the oncoming enemy, and then a second before turning away and shouting at Remus to move faster to escape our pursuers.

Then I diverted him right and the others followed as we headed towards one side of the square that had now been formed by the Durans and Exiles.

I pulled up Remus as the cohorts opened to allow my riders to enter the square as Gallia pulled up beside me, the Amazons grouped around us while Vagises' dragon flooded into the square. The Armenian heavy horsemen had not pursued us and were content to form up into a long line around five hundred paces away.

'Why don't they charge?' asked Gallia.

'There is no need,' I answered. 'They have succeeded in swatting away one of our wings and have got into our rear. We are now surrounded, my sweet, like sheep in a pen.'

I pulled on Remus' reins and walked him into the square with my wife and her warriors as the cohorts closed ranks and faced their shields towards the Armenians. Gafarn was gone, Vistaspa and Vagises had been separated from the main body of the army and I had no idea where Peroz was. As the sun descended in the west I was facing certain defeat in front of the city of my birth.

I thanked Shamash that Lucius Domitus commanded the army for as soon as he had discerned that both our wings had disappeared and that there was fighting in the rear he had disengaged his front cohorts from the Armenians swordsmen and formed square. He had also fortuitously ensured that the wagons carrying spare weapons and shields were within that square. An additional bonus was that most of the animals from Dura's camel train had also sought sanctuary within the square so at least we had replacement arrows to shoot at the enemy.

The Armenian swordsmen did not follow the legionaries as they withdrew, having lost a not inconsiderable numbers of men to *gladius* strikes. The Durans held the top and right-hand sides of the square, the Exiles its left-hand side and rear, as all round it enemy troops deployed into position.

I slid off Remus' back as I saw the white-crested helmet of Domitus coming towards me. Gallia ordered Zenobia to dismount the Amazons as the rest of Dura's horse archers also jumped down from their horses. A curious quiet engulfed the square as the officers of both sides worked feverishly to rearrange their men and ignored their opponents. Quartermasters issued fresh javelins, shields and swords to battered and bruised legionaries who formed orderly lines at the wagons while Alcaeus and his physicians ran around patching wounds and carrying the seriously wounded into the centre of the square.

Domitus had taken off his helmet and was wiping his sweaty forehead when he reached me. 'Bit careless of you to lose both of your wings.'

I too took off my helmet and wiped my brow on my sleeve. 'There are too many of them, I realise that now.'

'What do you want to do?'

Chrestus ran over as Gallia began counting the arrows left in her quiver.

'We are only half a mile from Hatra,' I said. 'Gafarn has most likely withdrawn to the city and Vistaspa is too good a soldier to allow his

359

heavy horsemen to be trapped and destroyed, so I must deduct that he too has sought refuge in Hatra. We should do the same.'

Gallia was unimpressed. 'You will give victory to the enemy?'

'Either that or stay here and be slaughtered,' said Domitus flatly.

'We take the wounded with us,' I said. 'Those who are seriously injured can be loaded on the wagons, the others can walk back to the city.'

I smiled at Gallia. 'Take command of the horse archers. Divide them between the four sides of the square and tell them to kill any slingers or archers they see. The enemy will try to soften us up with missiles before they launch a fresh assault.'

She nodded curtly and then went off with Zenobia to organise our archers.

'It is best that the queen has something to occupy herself,' I said to Domitus and Chrestus.

Domitus winked at Chrestus. 'To stop her bending your ear, more like. Reminds me of that time when we were surrounded by Narses and Mithridates. The horsemen buggered off then as well.'

'I sent them away,' I corrected him. 'Besides, it is not quite the same: at least we are within walking distance of safety.'

'If we can break out of the position we are in,' Chrestus reminded us both.

A roll call revealed that the legions had lost a hundred and fifty dead and nearly four hundred wounded, most of the casualties being inflicted in the mêlée with the Armenian swordsmen. The latter now stood facing the Durans in front of the top of the square, retreating fifty paces when the archers Gallia posted among the legionaries began shooting at them with great accuracy. The Durans on the right side of the square faced thousands of levy spearmen, our archers having great sport against these men who had already been badly mauled by the legions, shooting arrows that pierced thin wicker shields and struck unarmoured torsos, necks and faces. They were quickly withdrawn out of range. The Armenian slingers and archers took up position in front of the spearmen and attempted to counteract our missile fire, but our recurve bows had greater range than the Armenian ones and after a short while their archers also withdrew, leaving only the slingers to duel with our bowmen before they too were pulled back.

It was the same on the other side of the square where the Armenian commander also placed a great number of levy spearmen, who were very effectively culled by Dura's expert archers before being pulled back. But it was a different story at the foot of the square where we would have to make our breakout attempt. Here the enemy placed his professional spearmen: soldiers wearing leather cuirasses and helmets and carrying large, rectangular wicker shields of almost shoulder height that were faced with leather. Our arrows were unable to penetrate them and so the archers were reduced to trying to hit the Armenian horsemen who were arrayed behind the spearmen, to no avail. I received a report from

Chrestus whose Exiles faced these heavy spearmen that they numbered at least twenty thousand men. The Armenian general knew that this was the direction any breakout attempt would come from and had deployed his men accordingly. Smashing through such a barrier would be an epic struggle indeed.

The ordered calm was suddenly shattered by the sound of hundreds of kettledrums, trumpets and horns as the Armenian ring around us sprang into life and thousands of spearmen and swordsmen charged our square. The charges against the right and left sides of the square were disordered and half-hearted as hundreds of levy spearmen, their morale already fragile, were cut down by dozens of archers standing among the ranks of the legionaries. But at the top and bottom of the square it was a different story. The Armenian swordsmen, now without their javelins, locked shields and ran at the Durans with swords drawn. The latter, having been resupplied with javelins, hurled two volleys to cut down the first ranks of the Armenians and temporarily disrupt their momentum. But there were still many thousands of Armenians left and the two lines smashed into each other to recommence their grim close-quarters battle. At the bottom of the square the locked shields of the Armenian heavy spearmen advanced steadily and methodically but were stopped as the first five ranks of the Exiles hurled fifteen hundreds javelins at them. The thin, soft iron points embedded themselves in shields and bodies, chopping down hundreds of men in the front ranks and halting those behind. Then the Exiles charged, clambering over dead and injured spearmen to get to grips with those behind. The Armenians began to fall back slowly as *gladius* points stabbed groins, necks and faces. But the truth was that the enemy was keeping us fixed where we were and he had greater numbers to grind us down with relentless attacks against all sides of the square, trading lives for time.

And then I heard a new sound to the northeast and heard the telltale low rumble created by thousands of hooves pounding the earth and knew that we were finished, for a new army had arrived on the battlefield.

It was then that I saw in the distance the Armenian commander; a figure wearing a tall white conical hat with a cuirass of shimmering steel plates, riding a huge black horse up and down behind his swordsmen, no doubt urging them on.

All thoughts of a breakout disappeared as I ran to where the Durans were having difficulty holding back the masses of swordsmen who were hacking at their front ranks. Behind the tiring cohorts dismounted horse archers and Amazons were still loosing arrows over the heads of the Durans and were undoubtedly finding targets, but their missiles were cutting down only a few of the tens of thousands of Armenians who were attacking the legionaries.

Gallia and Zenobia stood beside their female companions as others rushed off to bring fresh quivers from the camel train. Inside the square it was chaos as drivers struggled to retain control of camels and mules and horse archers tried to calm horses frightened by the screams, shrieks and war cries of tens of thousands of men.

I ran past Gallia to the rear of the line of cohorts where a steady stream of wounded men were either hobbling from the ranks or being dragged by medical orderlies and then unceremoniously dumped on the ground before being worked on. I saw one legionary, his mail shirt torn and bloody, stagger from the rear of a century. I ran over to him, put his arm over my shoulder and assisted him to where Alcaeus was binding the wounded arm of another soldier.

'Another one for you,' I said to him, gently easing the wounded man on to the ground.

Alcaeus said nothing, glanced at the man I had assisted and then called to one of his men to attend to him.

'Pacorus.'

I turned to see Domitus sprinting towards me.

'We are having trouble holding them,' he said, his mail shirt torn and his helmet dented.

I pointed to the northeast. 'Armenian reinforcements have arrived.'

I then heard a great whooshing noise as the new arrivals unleashed a volley of arrows. The legionaries instinctively hoisted their shields above their heads but I saw the line of Amazons and archers standing behind the battling cohorts and knew they would be scythed down in seconds.

'Take cover!' I screamed at Gallia.

But it was too late. She did not hear me above the din of battle and I watched, helpless and horrified, as my wife stood in the open to be engulfed by thousands of arrows. I held a clenched fist to my mouth in terror as I was given a front-row seat to my beloved's death.

But nothing happened.

No arrows fell in the square, not one. I heard another mighty whooshing sound and looked into the sky. Nothing. Domitus likewise gazed upwards and then around and looked at me in bewilderment.

'Perhaps we are already dead and this is the afterlife,' he said.

The sounds of battle seemed to grow louder beyond the right side of the square as Gallia, in blissful ignorance, continued to shoot at the enemy. In between arrows she looked at me and spread her arms to suggest I should not be standing around conversing with Domitus while a battle was raging.

'What's he doing?' I heard Domitus say.

I looked to where he was staring and saw the hulking figure of Thumelicus bounding towards us. He arrived panting and hardly able to speak.

'Compose yourself, you great German oaf,' said Domitus affectionately.

Thumelicus drew himself up and grinned at me.

'You remember that filthy, half-starved wild boy you brought back with you from the marshlands all those years ago?'

I had no time for this. 'Have you been hit on the head?'

'Surena, your former squire,' said Thumelicus, still grinning like an idiot.

'What about him?' asked Domitus.

'Well, he and his army are beyond those groups of Armenian spearmen. Looks like he did not forget the debt he owed you, Pacorus.'

I too began grinning like a madman and jumped up and down as I hugged Thumelicus and then tried to embrace Domitus, who was having none of it. But he too looked relieved.

Within minutes word spread around the square that salvation had arrived as the Armenian army began to collapse. The enemy had methodically scattered our wings and surrounded our foot but now their troops were spread too thinly to even withstand an assault by fresh troops, let alone defeat it.

I gave orders that the horse archers were to mount up in preparation to ride out of the square as Gallia desisted her shooting and ran over to me.

'What is happening?'

I grabbed her hands and kissed them. 'Surena has arrived with his army, my love.'

In fact it was not only Surena who had arrived but also Silaces and his seven thousand horse archers. Reports reached me that as well as the lion banner of Gordyene, the four-pointed star flag of Elymais was also flying proudly beside it.

Surena's first assault, in conjunction with Silaces, was against the levy spearmen who were assaulting the right side of our square. Fifteen thousand horse archers unleashed a series of devastating volleys – the whooshing noise I had heard – against their rear ranks, felling thousands and prompting those still living to flee in panic.

Having been on the verge of triumph the Armenian commander attempted to snatch victory from the jaws of defeat by ordering his heavy cavalry, which were deployed behind his heavy spearmen to the rear of our square, to attack the relief force. But his horsemen were then suddenly assaulted from behind – Gafarn's horse archers had returned to the fray.

My brother told me afterwards that he and his men had lured the Armenian horsemen on their left wing away from the battlefield, falling back in successive waves and shooting arrows as they did so. The Armenians continued their pursuit as Hatra's horsemen whittled down their numbers with accurate archery. The Armenian bows did not have the range of those of their adversaries and so soon the enemy's numbers had been considerably reduced. Gafarn led three thousand men back to the battlefield as the rest continued to toy with the Armenians and, more importantly, keep them occupied.

Gafarn's reappearance panicked the Armenian horsemen backing up their spearmen, their alarm compounded when Surena's two thousand medium horsemen struck their right flank. Assaulted from the rear by accurate archery and in the flank by hundreds of mounted spearmen, the

Armenians retreated rapidly in the only direction that was open to them – west into the desert – straight into the ranks of Vistaspa's cataphracts.

The Armenian mounted spearmen had been routed and scattered by the cataphracts easily enough in a battle that had spread across an area of several miles. Vistaspa's horsemen charged and reformed several times as they cut the enemy to pieces, literally in some cases where Dura's armoured horsemen used their new swords to sever arms, cut through sword blades and armour and split helmets with ease. Many Armenians fled north to escape the butchery and Vistaspa let them go, recognising that there was still a battle to be won. And now his companies of cataphracts smashed into the fleeing Armenian heavy horsemen, whose cohesion disintegrated in the face of this fresh onslaught.

The levy spearmen that had been massed to the left-hand side of our square were charged by ten cohorts of Exiles, led by Chrestus in person. Using the last of their javelins, the Exiles reaped a rich harvest in enemy dead when they hurled their missiles before charging the ill-armed enemy and driving deep into their ranks. In reality the spearmen were beaten before the Exiles had even launched their charge so low was their morale, and it became a test of who could run the fastest – helmetless spearmen wearing no armour or mail-clad legionaries – as the Exiles gave chase to a fleeing enemy. The legionaries were speedily recalled by whistles and trumpet calls and reformed in their ranks – the horsemen could round up the spearmen later.

And what of Peroz and his horse archers? Like Gafarn his soldiers utilised the greater range of their bows to shoot down their opponents. The Armenian commander had deliberately sacrificed the horse archers on his right wing to enable his mounted spearmen to charge into our rear. What were a few thousand horse archers compared to victory? Except that there was no Armenian victory, and as Peroz and his men reappeared on the battlefield the fate of the enemy was sealed.

As Surena's horse archers amused themselves butchering hapless enemy spearmen the King of Gordyene rode up to me as Domitus was organising the Durans and Exiles for an assault on the last remaining body of enemy troops that had not been routed: the swordsmen. Surena jumped from his horse, his standard bearer grabbing the reins as his senior officers halted their horses. He walked up to me and smiled, and then we embraced each other.

'It is good to see you, Surena.'

'You too, lord. Men will speak of this day and your name with awe and respect.'

I slapped him on the back. 'They will tell the truth: that the King of Gordyene saved my arse.'

He grinned. 'With the King of Elymais, lord.'

'Where is Silaces?'

'With my Sarmatians, lord, ensuring that the enemy do not escape our wrath,' he replied.

So he had brought his Sarmatian jackals with him, mercenaries who delighted in killing and devastation. Still, nothing could diminish the extent of the Parthian victory that was unfolding or Surena's part in it.

Sunset was creeping upon the world now, the sky filled with red and orange hues as Armenian swordsmen formed an all-round defence directly in front of the legions, once more formed into two lines with the Durans on the right and the Exiles on the left. Surena's medium horsemen and horse archers, working in conjunction, were busy trawling the battlefield for pockets of Armenians, spearing any injured they came across and surrounding and then destroying any groups of enemy soldiers who tried to resist them. The Sarmatians, meanwhile, had taken up position behind the enemy swordsmen, while Silaces' men were arrayed on the Armenian left flank and the returning Peroz lined up his men against the enemy right flank. Thus were the Armenians and their commander now completely surrounded.

The number of dead men and animals was not as great as the butcher's bill of the dreadful battlefield of Susa but there were still tens of thousands of slain scattered across the ground, along with the corpses of hundreds of horses and camels.

An eerie quiet descended over this field of carrion as men thanked their gods for still being alive and drank greedily from water bottles, while the Armenians contemplated their fate. It was regarding the latter that I sent riders to the various contingents to gather the kings and commanders together to decide our next course of action.

I stood behind the second line of Durans with Gallia as the Amazons sat on the ground next to their tired horses. Domitus ambled over to us tapping his vine cane against his thigh, his sword back in its scabbard. Behind us Vagises, having returned with Vistaspa's men, was organising his companies to take up position behind the legions, ready to move into the space between the first and second lines once more should we need to shoot at the Armenians, not that we had many arrows left.

Domitus, now relaxed and very happy, slapped me on the arm. 'You are one lucky bastard. I never thought we would beat them.'

I winked at Gallia. 'Now he tells me.'

Domitus took off his helmet and examined the dent near the crest holder.

'You remember that ritual we took part in all those months ago?' he said to me. 'I thought it was all nonsense but, looking around today, I think that old witch knew what she was talking about.'

He smiled at me and amidst the carnage was genuinely happy, basking in the victory that the army that he had created had made possible. And died as the lead pellet struck the side of his head. He dropped like a stone as the slinger who stood no more than two hundred paces away reached into his pouch for another missile. Perhaps he meant to kill me, or Gallia, but he had no opportunity to loose another pellet before Gallia killed him with an arrow that struck him in the chest. Where he had come from I did not know. Perhaps he had been knocked unconscious and lay on the ground as fighting raged around him, or maybe he was very brave and wanted to kill a senior enemy commander before he himself was killed, or perhaps he was sent by the gods to exact payment for our victory. But whatever the explanation he had slain my friend and the man who had been my right arm.

I knelt beside the body of Lucius Domitus and felt his neck for a pulse. There was none. I heard hooves and saw Surena on his horse. He looked down at the body of my friend and then wheeled his horse away. Within minutes the slaughter had begun.

I had no interest in the aftermath of the battle as I organised a party of Durans to take Domitus to one of the wagons for transfer to Hatra, but Surena thought otherwise. Word quickly spread through the ranks of the Durans and Exiles that their commander was dead, and then among Dura's horse archers and the soldiers of Hatra, Gordyene and Elymais. Soon the remnants of the Armenian Army were surrounded by soldiers who had vengeance on their minds, a sentiment encouraged by Surena who rode up and down the lines exhorting them to slay the enemy.

Then the horse archers began shooting, not rapid volleys but rather aimed shots that found their mark. Thousands of arrows were loosed at the Armenians from all four sides and soon there were heaps of dead on the ground in the half-light. No quarter was asked for or given as archers methodically moved their horses nearer the rapidly shrinking square of Armenians. Finally the archers ran out of arrows and the dreadful hissing that had enveloped the square died down as the shooting ceased, to be replaced by groans, whimpers and cries of wounded and dying men. And then the legions attacked.

Gripped by a cold fury over the loss of their commander, the officers and centurions had had difficulty in holding their men back. But now, as the horsemen who had been deployed in front of them retreated, the Durans and Exiles marched forward. They did not forget their training and retained their ranks as they stepped on and over dead and dying men on the ground in front of them to get at those still living.

There were perhaps six or seven thousand Armenian soldiers still standing, though many of those were wounded and a few had no weapons. As the Durans and Exiles advanced against the pitiful remains of the enemy square, the cataphracts lined up on one side, Surena's medium horsemen opposite them and the Sarmatians sealing the square. The Armenians were caught in a giant trap as the legionaries threw their few remaining javelins and then charged with swords drawn uttering blood-curdling screams.

There was no battle as such, just a methodical slaughter as the legionaries stabbed and hacked men to pieces. Some Armenians threw down their shields and weapons and ran, only to be cut down by horsemen with spears, axes, maces and swords. Some fell on their knees and begged for mercy but they found none, only death meted out by Parthian weapons, or at the hands of Surena's Sarmatians. It was dark by the time the killing stopped, the foul stench of blood and gore filling the

366

air and our nostrils and infusing our clothes. It was perhaps the greatest victory that the Parthian Empire had ever enjoyed over its enemies but I would have gladly swapped it for the life of my dead friend.

As the last remaining Armenians had their throats slit I stood with Gallia by the wagon that held the body of Domitus. We were joined by Gafarn, Vistaspa, Peroz and Silaces. Guards held torches to cast our faces in a red glow as Gafarn lifted the cloak that had been placed over the body and laid a hand on Domitus' shoulder.

'Farewell, my friend. He was the best of us.'

I had nothing to say to any of them and they stood in an awkward silence until I saw the figure of Alcaeus approaching leading four legionaries carrying a stretcher. My chief medical officer looked downcast and dragged his feet as he ordered the men to load the body they were carrying on the wagon.

'Wait,' I ordered.

'It is the body of Thumelicus,' said Alcaeus, 'he would want to make this final journey with his friend.'

Gallia walked over to the stretcher and kissed Thumelicus on the forehead, then ordered the men to place the body next to Domitus.

'I heard he charged headlong into the enemy ranks,' said Alcaeus, 'wanted to avenge the death of Domitus all on his own. By the time his men reached him he had been cut down, though they say he killed many before he fell. I will miss him.'

'I too. How many others have we lost, Alcaeus?'

He stretched his back. 'Not as many as I thought we would. Just over four hundred dead at the last count and six hundred wounded among the legions; I do not know what losses the horsemen have suffered.'

The lights of Hatra on the horizon were our guide as we made our way back to the city – a bedraggled column of exhausted men leading tired horses with their heads down, mules pulling wagons and camel drivers urging on their beasts. The Durans and Exiles marched in stoic silence, the golden griffin and silver lion both covered as a mark of respect for the loss of their general. Behind us we left a patch of ground covered with tens of thousands of dead men. I walked with Gallia, Gafarn, Vistaspa, Silaces and Peroz but not Surena, who decided to camp near the battlefield rather than just outside the city.

'He will send his Sarmatians to scour the land for Armenian stragglers,' said Silaces. 'They like to take scalps.'

'Scalps?' said Gallia.

'Yes, majesty,' he replied, forgetting that he too was now a king. 'Sarmatian warriors like to take the scalps of men they have killed so they can hang them from their saddles.'

'Surena should not have brought these savages into Hatra,' complained Gafarn.

'Surena saved us, brother,' I said, 'we owe him a debt of gratitude for he has turned you into the vanquisher of Armenia. You will find that

Artavasdes will be more eager to enter into negotiations now you have destroyed his army.'

'And killed his brother,' added Silaces.

'His brother?' queried Gafarn.

'Artashes,' continued Silaces. 'It was he who commanded the Armenian Army. That is why Surena was eager to get here. He and Artashes have been conducting their own private war for many months. Surena left his foot at Assur to await the arrival of Atrax's army when he learned that Artashes was nearing Hatra. Surena will be making sure he does not escape.'

Dura's army returned to its camp outside the city while Hatra's soldiers trudged back to their barracks inside the royal quarter. I stayed with Gallia in the command tent with the body of my friend and did not sleep as I sat in silence at the table with my wife sipping at wine. How many times had I sat with my friend at this very same table and joked and planned the future? And now he was gone; gone like Thumelicus, Drenis and Kronos.

'There are only three of us left,' I said.

'What are you talking about?' asked Gallia.

'The night of Dobbai's ritual. Of those who took part there are only three left: myself, Vagises and Vagharsh. The others are dead, as is she. She said there would be a price to pay.'

I heard horse hooves outside and then one of the entrance flaps was swept aside by a sentry.

'Prince Spartacus, majesty.'

'Let him in.'

Dressed in a simple white tunic and brown leggings, Spartacus appeared remarkably fresh-faced as he walked over to Gallia and embraced her, then nodded to me.

'I am glad to see you unharmed,' I told him, indicating that he should sit with us. I walked over to another table holding wine, poured a cup and handed it to him.

He held it up to me. 'To you, uncle, and the glory of the empire.'

Gallia rolled her eyes but I smiled at him. He was young, a prince of this city and had just taken part in a battle that had crushed Armenia's might. He had every reason to feel proud.

He suddenly looked melancholic. 'I heard about Lucius Domitus. I grieve with you. He was a great soldier.'

'And a greater friend,' added Gallia with a cheerless voice.

'You go now to fight the Romans, uncle?' he asked.

'After we have recovered our strength and been reinforced by our allies, yes. I had wanted to deal with Crassus first but the gods dictated otherwise.'

'I would ask a favour of you,' he said.

'What favour can I grant the triumphant Prince of Hatra?' I teased him.
'A boy no longer but a valiant member of your city's Royal Bodyguard.'

'I wish to come with you when you march against the Romans,' he said.

I drank some wine. 'That will be for your father to decide, Spartacus. You are no longer my squire.'

Gallia laid a hand on his arm. 'Pacorus will ensure that you are beside him when he faces Crassus, Spartacus, have no fear.'

He leaned over and kissed her on the cheek. 'You have always been and will ever remain my favourite aunt.'

He gulped down his wine, bowed his head to me and then asked if he could take his leave. I stood and shook his hand and he embraced Gallia and then sauntered from our presence.

'What did you say that for?' I asked.

She shook her head. 'You think he has forgotten about the quest that Haytham set him? You think he has forgotten about the woman whose strand of hair hangs around his neck?'

I sighed deeply. 'That nonsense again. I had forgotten.'

'Just make sure you take him with you.'

I laughed. 'The chances of him taking a Roman eagle are infinitesimal, they really are.'

'You took one,' she shot back.

'That was different.'

'How?'

'It just was.'

She pointed a finger at me. 'You promised Claudia that you would take care of her son.'

Sometimes the female mind baffled me. 'What?'

'If you deprive him of the chance of marrying Rasha he will be deeply unhappy. You do not want that, do you?'

I gave up. 'Apparently not. Very well, I will ask Gafarn if his son can accompany me.'

Once more the sentry disturbed us to announce that my senior officers were outside. I ordered him to let them in and also to fetch more wine as they entered and slumped into the chairs around the table. They all looked dead on their feet, their faces showing stubble and their clothes dirty and torn. I emptied the wine jug and then half of the fresh one brought in by a sentry to provide them with refreshment as they made their reports.

'The legions lost four hundred and fifty dead and seven hundred wounded,' said Chrestus without emotion.

'Of the wounded around a quarter will not last through the night,' added Alcaeus.

Vagises looked up. 'The horse archers lost one hundred and twenty killed and two hundred wounded, with a similar number of horses lost. Losses among the cataphracts are considerably less. Ten killed and fifty wounded.'

'Three hundred of my men were also slain today,' reported Peroz, 'with a further five hundred wounded.'

369

'It was a hard fight,' I agreed, 'though the Armenians suffered far more so let us thank the gods for that.'

'And now?' asked Vagises.

'And now, my friend,' I answered, 'we cremate our dead, await our allies and prepare to fight Marcus Licinius Crassus.'

'I have lost all my smaller ballista,' said a distraught Marcus. 'They were destroyed by the Armenians.'

'They can be replaced,' I told him, 'but at least the larger ones are safe in Hatra. They will be needed against the walls of Nisibus.'

Before they lay down on the carpets and wrapped themselves in their cloaks to sleep I told Chrestus that he now commanded the legions. He had served a long apprenticeship under Kronos and I knew that Domitus rated him highly, which was all the recommendation I needed.

The next day Orodes and Nergal arrived from the south with the armies of Babylon and Mesene – eight thousand foot, twelve thousand horse archers, five hundred cataphracts and Orodes' Royal Guard – while from the west came Atrax leading the army of Media and Gordyene's foot soldiers, an additional ten thousand foot, four thousand horse archers and five hundred cataphracts. And with Atrax rode the King of Gordyene with his horsemen, which included the Sarmatians, many of whom had bloody scalps dangling from their saddles.

There was a service of thanksgiving in the Great Temple, which was so full that the congregation spilled out of its main entrance, down the steps and onto the Great Square. The mood of the city, previously apprehensive, became happy and carefree, pretty young women kissing any soldier they could find and citizens acclaiming King Gafarn the greatest ruler that had ever sat upon Hatra's throne. It was amazing how victory was a panacea for all ills. In the aftermath of the battle blind people apparently regained their sight and the crippled discarded their crutches and walked again so beloved of the gods was Hatra, or so I heard.

Amid the delirium of triumph I ordered Kogan to keep the Sarmatians out of the city, suggesting to Gafarn that he send ample quantities of wine and beer to their camp to keep them in a state of stupefaction rather than raping the female population of his capital.

After the service of thanksgiving kings, queens and nobles gathered in the throne room where those who had showed exceptional bravery in the battle were rewarded with gold, expensive swords and even grants of land. I was not only pleased for Gafarn and Diana, whose rule had finally been vindicated, but also for my mother who sat on the dais beside them. The past few years had been hard for her. Not only had she lost her husband, my father, but had also seen parts of his kingdom seized by enemies and the authority of her adopted son challenged. But one of those enemies had been dealt a heavy blow and today she smiled and radiated majesty.

Surena, who had deliberately missed the service in the temple, believing that there were no gods, now came into the chamber with his senior officers. They walked to the dais and bowed their heads at Gafarn and then Surena stood before Adeleh and bowed his head. Behind him two of his officers unfurled a great purple flag bearing an eight-pointed flower flanked by two eagles and placed it on the floor before her. We all looked on intrigued as Surena went down on one knee before my sister.

'Behold, lady, the banner of Artashes, the Armenian upstart whose army was yesterday destroyed outside this city. He is now but one of the many thousands of Armenian dead who litter the ground. I present you with his banner, princess, with the promise that his death and the liberation of Nisibus, your late husband's city, will avenge Prince Vata's death. This I swear in front of you and all those assembled in this great hall.'

There was warm applause at these words and Adeleh, her eyes moist with tears, walked forward and bid Surena to rise. She held out her hand and he kissed it before stepping back and bowing his head to her. It was a nice gesture, I thought.

Hatra felt like the city of old, with a king basking in victory and strengthened by allies. Gallia and Praxima chatted with a radiant Diana and Spartacus teased the young Prince Pacorus. Assur stood next to a pillar surrounded by his stern priests while Vistaspa was deep in conversation with Orodes, no doubt discussing the next phase of the campaign. And it was to Vistaspa that a guard handed a note that caused my brother's general to frown and pass it on to Orodes.

The high king read it and then turned and saw me, beckoning me over. A knot tightening in my stomach told me that it was bad news before I reached him.

'Crassus is preparing to cross the Euphrates at Zeugma,' said Orodes. He handed me the note. 'He is bringing fifty thousand men with him.'

Vistaspa was in a bullish mood. 'Having just defeated over one hundred thousand Armenians we do not have anything to fear from half that number of Romans, majesty.'

Orodes smiled at him but I knew as he did that the Romans were a far tougher proposition than the Armenians.

Chapter 17

The next day I sat with the other kings on couches in the private wing of my brother's palace. Outside peacocks roamed freely in the royal gardens and the scent of cedar and jasmine filled the ground-floor room, the doors leading to the veranda outside open to allow the air and sunlight to enter. Gafarn looked like a man reborn, his eyes afire with vigour and the haunted looked he had worn exorcised by the great victory we had won. Orodes, dressed in a rich purple silk shirt, baggy white leggings and red boots, also looked relaxed, despite knowing that the Romans were at long last on the march. Only Surena looked like a man who had just returned from the battlefield, attired in his black shirt and leggings, scale armour cuirass and helmet, which he had placed on the tiled floor in front of his couch.

After slaves had served us wine in solid gold *rhytons*, Orodes held up his drinking vessel to Gafarn.

'A toast to the Kingdom of Hatra, whose forces have vanquished a great threat to the Parthian Empire.'

We raised our *rhytons* and drank the wine that was perhaps the finest I had ever tasted.

'And to the Kingdom of Dura and the lord high general of the empire,' added Orodes, raising his goblet a second time, this time to me.

We emptied our drinking vessels and the slaves refilled them as the king of kings leaned back on his couch.

'And so, my friends, in the afterglow of victory we must turn our attention to dealing with another threat to the empire. Yesterday we received news that Crassus is about to cross the River Euphrates and begin the campaign that he believes will lead to the conquest of Parthia.'

Gafarn looked thoughtful but not particularly troubled while Silaces and Atrax looked at each other, Surena said nothing and Nergal sneered contemptuously.

'What advice would my lord high general give?' asked Orodes.

I drained my goblet and held it out to be refilled, but before I could say anything Surena spoke.

'The Armenians must be pursued and Nisibus retaken before Armenia itself is invaded. The more time we spend here acting like debauched Persians the more opportunity Artavasdes has to raise another army.'

Atrax and Nergal looked wide-eyed at him while Silaces, who had spent many years campaigning with the King of Gordyene, merely shook his head resignedly. Gafarn frowned at Surena and Orodes looked aghast at his impertinence. Manners and etiquette were everything to Orodes. Even when he had been a landless, exiled prince at Hatra he had retained his strict sense of protocol and graciousness at all times.

'I was not aware that you were now Parthia's lord high general,' he rebuked Surena, who looked at Orodes' grave demeanour and blushed. I decided to save him from further embarrassment.

'What Surena says is correct. We must send an army north to retake Nisibus and prevent the Armenians from raising fresh forces that can threaten Hatra. And if that means invading Armenia then so be it.' Surena smiled to himself, no doubt thinking of how he and his Sarmatians would ravage Armenian lands.

'And the Romans, Pacorus?' asked Nergal. 'What of them? If we march north then Crassus will surely be at the gates of this city when we return.'

'You are right, my friend,' I agreed, 'we cannot allow Crassus a free hand in Parthia. Therefore I propose sending a force west to slow down his advance while the bulk of our armies deal with the Armenians, what is left of them.'

I smiled at Surena. 'Dura's legions, together with their siege engines and accompanied by the foot soldiers of Gordyene, Media and Babylon, can go north to lay siege to Nisibus. This will total twenty-eight thousand men. With them will go the heavy horsemen of Babylon, Media and Hatra – two and a half thousand men – plus the horse archers of Prince Peroz, Babylon, Media, Hatra, Mesene and some drawn from the ranks of Surena's mounted bowmen, plus Gordyene's medium horsemen. This gives a total of around thirty thousand horsemen, including Babylon's Royal Guard. It is only fitting that King of Kings Orodes should lead this army.'

'Some of my horse archers, lord?' queried Surena.

I smiled at him. 'Indeed so, my young lion, for you and I will be riding west with Dura's cataphracts, horse archers and a portion of your own horse archers to engage Crassus.'

Orodes looked alarmed. 'If I take sixty thousand men north, Pacorus, how many men will be left to accompany you and Surena to face Crassus?'

'Ten thousand,' I answered.

The others shook their heads in disbelief. 'Ten thousand horsemen cannot defeat a Roman army of fifty thousand men, Pacorus,' said Nergal in alarm.

'You go to certain defeat,' remarked an even more alarmed Atrax.

I held up a hand. 'My friends, please understand that the last thing I desire is a noble death at the hands of the Romans. I do not go to engage them in battle but rather to harry them, to both slow them down and wear them down. It is three hundred miles from Hatra to Zeugma. Crassus will cross the Euphrates in a few days' time and I will leave this city tomorrow. He will march twenty miles a day whereas I can cover over thirty each day. Once I reach him my horsemen can launch hit-and-run attacks and stay out of range of his best units, his legions.'

'He will march down the Euphrates,' said Gafarn, 'towards Babylon and Seleucia.'

'That is correct,' I said.

'And towards Dura,' added Nergal whose frown was increasing by the minute.

'He will never get that far,' I said. 'How far can an army march each day while being under constant volleys of arrows and being raided by horsemen? The Romans will form a square with their shields locked, which will slow them down. Some days they might not even venture from camp.'

'They will send their horsemen against us,' said Surena.

I nodded. 'True, but that is why I will take my cataphracts. They are more than capable of scattering any Roman horsemen.'

'It is a risky strategy, Pacorus,' said Orodes.

'Less risky than allowing Crassus to reach Seleucia,' I replied.

'Would it not be better to send a larger force to engage Crassus and a smaller one to deal with the Armenians?' suggested Atrax.

'If Artavasdes had been killed outside Hatra, then yes,' I replied. 'But the Armenian king still holds Nisibus and can still send another army south into Hatra. Therefore a large force is required to both lay siege to Nisibus and deal with a second Armenian army that he will undoubtedly lead to relieve that city once it is besieged.'

Atrax remained sceptical but thankfully Orodes accepted my advice and agreed that he should march north with the bulk of our forces. I was convinced that at the very least I could slow Crassus' advance to a crawl, giving us time to capture Nisibus, defeat any forces that Artavasdes gathered and then muster an army at Hatra to engage Crassus.

Our strategy agreed I walked with the others through the palace to return to camp. Surena walked beside me, his helmet in the crook of his arm.

'I should go north with my army, lord,' he said.

'Most of it will be going north, Surena, but I would like you to come with me.'

'Why me?' he asked.

'Because your army is the most experienced among the empire's kingdoms: it has been fighting the Armenians for years and you yourself are among the most successful of Parthia's generals.'

'No more successful than you, lord,' he shot back. 'And both Nergal and Silaces have far more experience than me.'

What he said was true but what I did not tell him was that I did not want him and his men rampaging through Armenia butchering all and sundry. Artavasdes would hardly be agreeable to peace if his kingdom was invaded and his people slaughtered. However, I hoped the threat that this might happen if he did not acquiesce to our demands would be sufficient to his agreeing to peace, especially after we had taken Nisibus back and Orodes stood on Hatra's northern border ready to invade Armenia.

I put an arm round Surena's shoulder. 'I would esteem it a great honour and special favour if you would accompany me.'

'Very well, lord,' he said. 'Would you like me to bring my Sarmatians?'

The thought horrified me. 'I think they should accompany Orodes. They will be useful for raiding enemy territory.'

Orodes chatted to the others as we walked from the palace's private chambers, into the throne room and then along the corridor that led to the building's entrance. It was a beautiful late spring day, the sun in a cloudless blue sky highlighting the power and majesty of the Grand Temple and the vastness of the adjacent Great Square that was now empty of Dura's wagons and mules.

I was walking down the stone steps to go to the stables to collect Remus when I saw a group of riders approach. They drew closer and then halted before dismounting and leading their horses towards the palace steps. I saw that the swarthy figure leading them was Apollonius, fresh from his journey to the north. He handed the reins to one of his companions and strode over to stand before Gafarn.

'Lord Apollonius,' he said without enthusiasm.

Apollonius bowed deeply before his king. 'Hail, great king, slayer of the Armenian barbarians. I hurried back as quickly as I could when I heard that Hatra was in danger.'

I looked at his immaculate scale armour cuirass of overlapping steel plates, his spotless white shirt and brown boots that did not have a mark on them. His horse looked as though it had just been groomed and the attire of his fellow lords was similarly spotless and unruffled. Wherever they had been they had not been hurrying anywhere.

'Where are the horse archers you led from the city?' asked Gafarn.

'Safely returned to barracks in the city, majesty' Apollonius replied.

I looked past him to where his companions were shifting uneasily on their feet, glancing at each other furtively. They stank of treachery.

I walked down the final two steps and held out my right hand to Apollonius.

'All will be settled soon.'

He bowed his head to me and took my hand, a look of relief on his face. I kept hold of it as his expression changed from one of gratitude to being perplexed and then slightly nervous. His eyes momentarily recorded terror when I rammed the point of my dagger through his neck with my left hand. The blood gushed from the wound in great spurts, covering the blade, my hand and sleeve as I continued to grip Apollonius' hand and watch the life ebb from his body. The others gasped in disbelief as I let go of his hand and his lifeless body collapsed on the flagstones, blood still pumping from the wound.

'Arrest them!' I shouted to the guards on the steps as Apollonius' stunned companions gaped at the corpse at my feet.

'What are you doing?' shouted an enraged Gafarn.

'Vermin control,' I replied as Surena and Nergal both drew their swords and assisted the guards in surrounding the captives, who were bundled away, protesting, towards the guardroom.

Gafarn grabbed my blood-soaked arm. 'Explain yourself!'

I removed his hand. 'It is quite simple, brother; Lord Apollonius was a traitor who had brokered a deal with the Romans to betray you. Unfortunately for him, though fortunately for you, our recent victory put paid to his plans. If you search his mansion I am sure you will find evidence of his treason, either that or interrogate his accomplices in crime to reveal the truth.'

A subsequent thorough search of Apollonius' home revealed letters from Crassus promising him the crown of Hatra in return for his assistance. Following a brief trial his companions were found guilty and subsequently hanged from the city walls for their perfidy, their bodies left to rot in the sun as a warning to others who might be considering treason.

We burned the bodies of Lucius Domitus and Thumelicus on two pyres in the centre of the Great Square, the only time that individuals who had not been members of Hatra's royal family were cremated in that location. Gafarn had every man of his bodyguard on parade as a mark of respect for two Companions, friends and one who had been the commander of his brother's army. I stood with him, Gallia, Diana, Nergal, Praxima, Spartacus and young Pacorus at the top of the palace steps as Vagises and Vagharsh both carried torches to the oil-soaked pyres and lit them.

As I had done a hundred times before I watched as the flames spread round the bottom of the piles of wood and then engulfed the bodies in a great roar and explosion of fire. The Durans and Exiles filled two sides of the square, my cataphracts and horse archers another and the ranks of Hatra's heavy horsemen the fourth. The colour parties of the Durans and Exiles stood next to the raging pyres holding the golden griffin and silver lion in salute, as tears ran down Diana's cheeks and Gallia stood ashen-faced beside her friend.

How many more times would I stand and watch the bodies of my friends and comrades being consumed by flames? Would those who stood by me now be watching my own body being cremated in the coming months? I found myself scanning the ranks of the legionaries, trying to search out that tell-tale white crest atop a helmet worn by a man of iron gently tapping a vine cane against his right thigh, but then brutal reality hit me like a spiked mace as I realised that I would never see Domitus again, never hear his reassuring voice on the eve of battle or shake his hand after the army he had created had added another silver disc to the Staff of Victory that was now held by Chrestus between the griffin and lion emblems. Without Lucius Domitus there would have been no staff, no victories and probably no army of Dura.

The fires roared again and the bodies of our friends disappeared from view as ravenous flames greedily devoured them. I had given the order that when the fires had died down the ashes were to be placed in copper urns and taken back to Dura where I would build a great mausoleum to house them. It was the least they deserved. We had lost another ten Companions during the battle and with their deaths a few more links with my time in Italy had been severed. I wondered how many of us would live to enjoy old age.

Gafarn had little time to grieve for our losses as Kogan brought a most pressing matter to his attention: the burial of the Armenian dead. Our own dead had been speedily cremated with due military honours but there remained tens of thousands of corpses lying half a mile to the northeast of the city. Ordinarily men from the army could be used to carry out the grisly task of stripping the dead and throwing them on pyres. However, the various armies would soon be marching north and east and could spare neither the time nor the men for burial duties. Gafarn therefore ordered a proclamation read in the city calling for volunteers to assist in disposing of the Armenian dead. To encourage willing participants he promised a few drachmas daily to those who came forward. Treasurer Addu protested at this but was overruled. It was now almost summer and very hot and soon the stench of rotting bodies would be carried on the wind to the city. But far worse would be the plague of flies that would envelop Hatra. Lacerated bodies lying in the sun became breeding grounds for maggots and flies by the million. And with the flies would come the threat of disease that might ravage the city.

So a long line of wagons and people trudged to the battlefield under the supervision of city engineers and companies of the garrison to deal with the army of corpses that we had created. The people who took part were the poorer sort who hoped to find valuables on the bodies of the dead, such as a pouch of money or a gold or silver necklace that they could sell. And after the corpses had had been searched they were loaded on wagons so they could be transported further away from the city where they could be thrown into burial pits. The city's chief engineer was worried that to bury so many bodies near the city might risk polluting the underground springs that gave Hatra life, and so the dead had to be transported five miles further north.

Bodies that had been cut to pieces, together with severed limbs and the corpses of animals, were cremated where the battle had taken place, the shields of the vanquished providing wood for the mass pyres. Soon great columns of black smoke were snaking into the cloudless sky as the cadavers were burned.

I stood with Surena on the city's northern battlements and watched the columns of smoke rise like giant cobras rearing up, about to strike.

'Why don't the city authorities burn all the Armenian dead?'

'They do not have the wood,' I answered. 'There are simply too many.'

'There are never enough Armenian dead,' he sneered.

'Ordinarily, of course,' I continued, 'we would use enemy prisoners or burial details but your Sarmatians appear to have killed all the stragglers and those who wished to give themselves up.'

'Prisoners need feeding,' he said dismissively. 'We do not take prisoners in Gordyene.'

'You cannot kill everyone, Surena.'

He looked at me with eyes that were devoid of emotion. 'I learned long ago that in this world you have to kill to prevent yourself being killed.'

'Is that the king or the marsh boy speaking?'

He suddenly looked very sad. 'My grandparents died.'

'I had no idea. I am sorry, truly. I liked them.'

He looked into the sky. 'I used to receive regular reports about them from Nergal at Uruk, who was notified by couriers sent by my people. They died peacefully, my grandfather first, then my grandmother a month later. They say she died of a broken heart. They had many years together and one could not live without the other. It is an emotion I know only too well.'

He attempted a half-smile and then left me as the black cobras of death filled the horizon.

Later, after a meeting with my senior officers in my command tent, I sat with Gallia at the table and discussed with her the imminent expedition into the west. She had declared that she and the Amazons would be accompanying me, seeing little merit in remaining at Hatra.

'You could always return to Dura,' I suggested.

She shook her head. 'I do not intend to remain idle while a Roman army invades my homeland. Besides, I want to test out these new arrows that Arsam has produced.'

'Remember we go not to give battle to Crassus but to slow his advance,' I reminded her.

'If I put an arrow in his guts that will slow him down for good,' she growled.

Our conversation was interrupted by the appearance of Spartacus, who was in a most agitated state.

'You ride west tomorrow, uncle?'

'Yes,' I answered.

'You will not forget your promise to take me with you.'

I had forgotten. 'Your place, as a prince of this city,' I said, 'is beside your father. Lord Vistaspa for one will be expecting you to accompany Hatra's army north to Nisibus.'

He began pacing up and down and fidgeting with the hilt of his sword.

'I would ask you to speak to my father, uncle.'

'Of course Pacorus will speak to him,' said Gallia reassuringly.

'I will?'

She frowned at me. 'Yes.'

So half an hour later we sat with Gafarn, Diana and my mother in a small dining room near to the royal bedrooms. Slaves served us pastries and fruit juice as two others cooled my mother with great fans made from ostrich feathers.

'I was sorry to hear about your Roman,' she said. 'I liked him.'

'He will be sadly missed,' I said.

'And now you both go once more to fight our enemies,' she said. 'I pray that you both return. We seem to have nothing but war now, not like in the reign of Sinatruces when the empire had peace.'

'His death heralded many testing times for Parthia, I agree,' I said, 'but now we have a chance of forging a new era for the empire.'

'Pacorus has a favour to ask you,' Gallia said to Gafarn.

My brother opened his hands. 'Consider it done. Nothing should be refused the hero of the hour.'

378

'I would like Spartacus to accompany me tomorrow.'

Gafarn looked perplexed. 'If you are deficient in cataphracts I will get Vistaspa to give you some of Hatra's companies.'

'This concerns the Agraci girl, does it not?' smiled Diana.

Gafarn held his head in his hands. 'Not this again.'

My mother was most curious. 'What Agraci girl?'

'Spartacus has fallen in love with the daughter of King Haytham, who has insisted that he can only marry the girl if he captures a Roman eagle.'

My mother's eyes lit up. 'Like the one in the Great Temple.'

'That is correct, mother,' I said.

'I think it would be better,' insisted Gafarn, 'if I took Spartacus with me to Nisibus so he can forget these nonsensical ideas about marrying an Agraci woman. He is the heir to the throne of this city and should start acting like it.'

'Princes should not marry beneath them, I agree,' said Diana, 'after all, we do not want a member of a low-born race sitting on Hatra's throne, such as an Agraci woman.'

Gafarn nodded triumphantly. 'Precisely, my dear, I could not have put it better myself.'

'Or a Roman kitchen slave,' continued Diana.

Gafarn stopped nodding. 'What?'

'Or a Bedouin slave, even,' Diana carried on.

Gafarn looked uncomfortable. 'I think we are straying from the point, my dear.'

Diana looked at him reproachfully. 'No we are not. Have you forgotten your roots, Gafarn, or mine? If Spartacus wishes to pursue his dream then who are we to stand in his way?'

'The people of this city will not tolerate an Agraci queen, that much I know,' insisted Gafarn.

'Then he must give up the throne,' replied Diana, 'for that is the price he must pay if he truly wants this girl.'

'Most eloquently put,' said my mother, which did nothing to improve Gafarn's humour. 'After all, you have another son who was born in this city. He will make an excellent king, I think.'

Gafarn looked hurt. 'You do not think Spartacus will make a good king?'

My mother thought for a few seconds. 'Spartacus has a restless spirit that bridles against convention. He needs to make his own way in the world, that much I know. You may think you can chain him to this city but you would be wrong. He was born to rule but not this kingdom. I believe he is destined to win a crown by his own efforts.'

'Is he outside?' Gafarn asked me.

I nodded.

'Guard!' he shouted.

The doors opened and one of Kogan's soldiers walked in.

'Is Prince Spartacus in the corridor?' snapped Gafarn.

'Yes, majesty.'

'I request his presence.'

Moments later my nephew stood to attention before his father.

'You wish to ride with Pacorus tomorrow?'

'Yes, father.'

'To take a Roman eagle?'

'If Shamash wills it,' he replied.

Gafarn looked at Diana. 'So you can take it to Haytham and claim his daughter.'

'Yes, father,' said Spartacus with pride.

'You cannot be King of Hatra and have an Agraci wife,' said Gafarn slowly so my nephew would understand the significance of his words. 'This city is ranked among the finest and most Parthian in all the empire, and its kings have always fought the Agraci. Haytham is more feared and hated than the Romans and Armenians combined. That being the case, his daughter can never sit on Hatra's throne.'

'What your father is trying to say, Spartacus,' interrupted Diana.

'What I am telling you,' said Gafarn, 'is that if you marry this Agraci princess you will never wear Hatra's crown. Your brother will inherit the throne. So what do you want more – Hatra or this Agraci girl?'

'Her name is Rasha,' said Spartacus.

'I know,' replied Gafarn.

'I am glad, father, for you will know how to address her at our wedding.'

Gallia laughed and Diana smiled as Gafarn's cheeks became flushed with anger.

'Very well,' my brother said, 'so be it. You may ride west with Pacorus tomorrow and may the gods keep you safe.'

Spartacus grinned at me boyishly before kissing his mother and grandmother and bowing to his father prior to his exit.

'I will keep an eye on him, have no fear,' I said.

'As will I,' added Gallia.

'All your fears may come to nought, Gafarn,' said my mother. 'There is no guarantee that he will take one of these eagles and then he will not marry Haytham's daughter.'

A glum-faced Gafarn nodded at my mother and the rest of us sat in silence, as above us the gods roared their approval at the reckless daring of a young prince.

The next day we left Hatra to face Crassus.

Surena had given orders that his Sarmatians, rather than accompany Orodes, were to return to Gordyene to provide additional security for his kingdom, though I doubted whether his realm would be troubled by any Armenian incursions bearing in mind that its army had just been destroyed. In addition, Vanadzor and all his major towns had their own garrisons in addition to the standing army he had raised. Nevertheless he was not to be dissuaded and so they promptly left Hatra at the same time as their king rode west. He did not bother informing Orodes, which could have been interpreted as an insult, and I had the feeling that Surena was glad to be away from the company of kings, priests and nobles so he could continue fighting his own private war.

He liked few men and trusted even less. He viewed Atrax as a friend who had supported him in his successful efforts to liberate Gordyene and also trusted Silaces, though was apt to see him more as a subordinate rather than a fellow king. I think he also respected me for giving him the chance to become a soldier and then commander in Dura's army and trusting him to lead an expedition into Gordyene, which had wildly surpassed my own expectations. But I realised that he viewed Orodes with disdain bordering on contempt and thought Gafarn and Aschek weak rulers. For the forthcoming campaign he had entrusted the command of his medium horsemen and foot soldiers to Silaces, who had once led them in Gordyene.

Now Surena led six thousand of his own horse archers west in the company of a thousand Duran cataphracts, two thousand squires, a thousand camels carrying spare arrows, three thousand of my own horse archers commanded by Vagises and Gallia's Amazons. The four thousand camels controlled by the squires were loaded with waterskins as well as food as we would be travelling across the barren desert to get to Crassus as quickly as possible.

As usual Byrd, Malik and their scouts formed the vanguard of our force, disappearing before dawn and reappearing at the end of the day to report that they had seen no signs of the Romans. We did not know if Crassus had crossed the Euphrates but I felt sure that he had done so and would be either at the Hatran towns he had captured last year or perhaps had even begun his march along the river. After five days we reached the Khabur River, a tributary of the Euphrates, and let our animals drink from its cool waters as the squires refilled our waterskins. Because it was now summer the water level was low so we were able to ford the river with ease. We halted for a day at the river to allow Byrd and Malik to scout west and also southwest towards the Euphrates in search of our prey, but they reported seeing nothing except a few nomads wandering across the barren landscape. I was pleased: the further west we travelled without encountering Romans meant the less Parthian territory that Crassus occupied.

That night I invited Surena to dine with us, which actually meant nothing more than sitting round a campfire since we had brought with us the eight-man tents used by the legionaries rather than my command tent. And because we had no tools or stakes we dug no ditch or rampart to surround our camp, though every third man was always on guard duty to prevent us being surprised during the night. Parthians did not fight at night but Romans did.

'I have always found that strange,' remarked Surena as the fire in front of him crackled and spat. 'Parthians prefer to fight during the day because it honours the Sun God, but if they kill the god's enemies, regardless of whether it is at night or during the day, then surely he will not be offended. If he exists, that is.'

Vagises looked at him with horror. 'You do not believe Shamash exists?'

'I do not believe any gods exist, and if my words are blasphemy then let the gods strike me down.' He looked up at the night sky and nothing happened.

'You see,' he continued, 'nothing.'

Vagises looked at me and smiled. He had been a part of Dobbai's ritual and had seen the strange events with his own eyes, plus the timely death of Tigranes afterwards and the unexpected withdrawal of Roman forces from Syria, and finally the great victory we had won before the walls of Hatra.

'Perhaps the gods helped you defeat the Armenians in Gordyene and made you King of Gordyene,' I suggested. 'Have you thought of that?'

'Why would they do that?' he sniffed.

'Perhaps because you are resourceful, brave and a great general,' I replied.

He looked at the flames in the fire. 'When men are desperate and at their wits end, when they are afraid and alone, then they will ask for the help of the gods. But only because they have no one else to turn to. They will beg and promise the gods anything to received an answer to their prayers. I know, I was such a person once.'

He was talking of the death of Viper, no doubt.

The corner of his mouth twisted into a sneer. 'But the gods do not answer and in the cold light of day when the one thing you wanted to live has been snatched away, you realise that the skies and mountains are not filled with benevolent immortals but only clouds, mist, ice and snow.'

He looked at each of us in turn. 'There are no gods.'

'We all miss Viper,' said Gallia, and Surena momentarily appeared as a lost boy, enraged with the world but alone and helpless, before his mask of steel returned.

He nodded at Gallia. 'She loved you, lady, you and all the Amazons. I thank you for your kindness.'

It was a touching moment, the more so because Gallia had never liked Surena. But she loved her Amazons and that was one thing that, at least momentarily, had bridged their divide.

'I believe in the gods,' announced Spartacus, to everyone's surprise. 'I have asked them to help me capture an eagle.'

Surena looked at him. 'An eagle?'

'A Roman eagle,' replied Spartacus.

'That is the gift that our young prince here must take to Haytham to win the hand of his daughter,' I said.

'Princess Rasha,' stated Spartacus with pride. Gallia smiled at him while Vagharsh shook his head.

'I remember her,' said Surena, 'from my time at Dura. She used to visit the palace often. Viper was very fond of her.'

He looked at Spartacus. 'And now she is a woman and you are to marry her. My congratulations.'

'If he can take an eagle,' I said.

'The sacred symbol of every Roman legion,' added Vagises, 'and protected by five thousand heavily armed legionaries.'

Surena looked at Malik. 'Your father does not mind his daughter marrying one who is not of her own kind, Prince Malik?'

Malik looked at Spartacus. 'My sister will not lead our people so he indulges her dreams, believing that they will be unfulfilled.'

'The son of Spartacus may surprise you yet,' muttered Byrd.

The next day he and Malik were in the saddle before dawn as we journeyed west once more across a landscape of shallow valleys, rocky outcrops and hillocks. The midday heat was unbearable and so during the hottest hours we dismounted and walked beside our animals to conserve their reserves of strength. I remembered Strabo's words about Remus not getting any younger and continually checked his body and head for signs of exhaustion, but he appeared to be as hearty and strong as ever. The Amazons took off their helmets and mail shirts and wore their floppy hats. Where we could we rested in the shade of rocks until the heat had abated before continuing our journey.

After journeying west from the Khabur River for three days, at the end of the third day, as the western horizon was filled with a giant yellow sun that turned the sky blood red, Byrd and Malik galloped into camp and slid off their sweat-lathered horses in front of me.

'We see Roman scouts,' reported Byrd, greedily drinking from a waterskin offered him by Gallia.

I handed another to Malik. 'Where?'

'Thirty miles to the west, near river,' said Byrd.

'Did they see you?' I asked.

Malik nodded as Gallia took the waterskin from Byrd and held it to his horse's mouth so it could slake its thirst.

'Romani give chase but we outrun them,' said Byrd.

During the next hour the rest of their scouts rode into camp and told their stories. Piecing together their reports it appeared that the Roman army was camped in the Plain of Carrhae, directly west of our position, on the western side of the Balikh River. The latter ran from north to south, almost parallel to the Khabur that we had crossed a few days before, and also emptied into the Euphrates.

The night was surprisingly cool as I sat with the senior officers of Dura and Gordyene to make our plans for the next day. We lit no fires so as not to betray our presence and sat on stools with our cloaks wrapped around us. The sky twinkled with stars and a full moon flooded the land with a ghostly pale light as I stood and addressed those assembled, the grunts and snorts of the animals in the camel park the only noises to disturb the quietness.

I had mentioned to Surena beforehand about speaking to his and my officers and he was quite happy for me to address them rather than him.

'You are lord high general, lord, after all. Besides, when the King of Dura talks I listen.'

And so I emphasised to them all that we were not here to engage Crassus in battle.

'That is what he will want: to draw us into an engagement. But we will remain beyond the range of his legionaries' javelins and their ballista. We ambush their patrols, raid their column when we have chance and generally retard their progress. Above all we must not get embroiled in a battle. We are too few and they are too many.

'If we force Crassus to form battle lines each day then we will drastically reduce his rate of march, which will give Orodes time to impose a peace favourable to Parthia on Armenia and then march back south to meet Crassus. We are here to buy Orodes time, nothing more.'

They all nodded in agreement, even Surena, giving me confidence that he and his men would adhere to the plan. The soldiers of Gordyene were all professionals and knew that ten thousand horsemen could not defeat an army of fifty thousand Romans, and so did their king.

'When we begin our campaign of harassment against the enemy, lord,' said Surena, 'I assume that we will be making night attacks against their camp.'

I nodded. 'That is correct. As soon as we lock horns with the enemy we cannot let go, and that means fighting at night, but that will entail nothing more than men on foot shooting at camp sentries from a distance in an effort to sow uncertainty and fear. I do not want Parthians impaled on Roman stakes or lying dead at the bottom of ditches.

'Now get some food and sleep. You will need it.'

After the meeting I pulled Vagises to one side.

'Your men have been issued with the new arrows?'

He nodded. 'We will finally see if Arsam's new weapons fulfil their promise.'

'I have every faith in my chief armourer,' I said.

'It has been a while since we faced Romans in battle and twenty years since the last time we fought Crassus. I remember that day in the Silarus Valley.'

He looked at me. 'Seems like yesterday all of a sudden. And now we ride into battle against Crassus once again, this time with the son of Spartacus by our side. Let us hope that it is a good omen and hope that his father is watching and grants us good fortune.'

I laid a hand on his arm. 'I am sure he is, his mother too for that matter.'

'What do you think he would have made of Surena?'

I laughed. 'He would have liked him, I think, but would have kept him on a tight leash.'

'His soldiers are well trained,' he said, 'but there is something wild about him. Dangerous. If his men get into difficulties tomorrow they are on their own. I will not sacrifice one of my horse archers to his rashness.'

'I think we can trust Surena, Vagises. Remember he was trained at Dura.'

He nodded unconvincingly and walked off into the night. But I had every confidence that Surena's men would be more than equal to the test set before them. Their king had been schooled at Dura, had been enrolled in the Sons of the Citadel and had risen through the ranks of Dura's army. It was no coincidence that his army was organised and trained along Duran lines, right down to the type of horn and trumpet blasts used by his horsemen and foot soldiers. This would make cooperation on the battlefield between our two forces easy and seamless.

The new day dawned cold and misty. As usual I slept little before facing an enemy and Gallia slept among her women on the eve of battle, so I woke in the pre-dawn darkness cold and alone and exited my tent wrapped in my cloak. Squires were already feeding and watering their masters' horses and sentries were returning from duty to grab a couple of hours' sleep before their day in the saddle. I felt the stubble on my chin and desired to wash and shave but would have to forego that pleasure as water was scarce, the nearest supply being the Balikh River where the Roman army was camped.

'You look like a beggar,' joked Malik as he walked towards me leading his horse, Byrd beside him and their scouts behind them already mounted on their mangy beasts.

I embraced him and then Byrd. 'You two take care of yourselves and don't try any heroics.'

'I too old for that,' said Byrd.

'I'm not,' grinned Malik, who looked around. 'This mist will soon clear. It is going to be a hot day.'

Byrd hoisted himself into his saddle. 'For some their last. We will return, Pacorus.'

He raised a hand and then wheeled his horse away, followed by Malik and the other scouts, all of them disappearing into the grey mist as they rode west.

The camp became a hive of activity, squires serving their masters meals as they too took the opportunity to fill their bellies with cured meat, biscuits and dried dates, all washed down with tepid water. Each cataphract had two squires and after their meals one youth would saddle his master's horse and fit it with the scale armour that covered its body, neck and head while the other would assist his master in putting on his scale armour and fixing his mace and axe on the front horns of his saddle. As well as these weapons each of my heavy horseman was armed with a sword made from the Indus steel, a dagger and the mighty *kontus*.

An hour after dawn, mist still clinging obstinately to the landscape, the companies of cataphracts and horse archers filed out of camp at a leisurely pace. Behind them came the beasts of the camel train loaded down with spare weapons and arrows and behind them the squires on their horses leading camels packed with tents, cooking utensils, tools, spare clothing and armour.

As it was still cool every horse archer and cataphract wore his white cloak, while the cloaks of the soldiers of Gordyene were grey. It was eerily quiet, which together with the mist made everyone nervous. Vagises threw out two companies of horse archers as an advance guard and two companies on each flank as we peered into the greyness. After half an hour of slow progress I called a halt to wait for the sun to burn away the vapour. Better that than horses and men falling into a wadi or other unseen natural feature.

Finally the sun, a pale yellow ball, burnt away the mist and we commenced our march, everyone still wearing their cloaks as it was still unusually cool, compounded by an easterly breeze that blew in our faces. The terrain around us was mostly flat save for a few isolated hillocks, giving excellent all-round views. The mood became more relaxed as we trotted west, secure in the knowledge that the enemy would not surprise us in this open ground. Everyone still had their cloaks wrapped round them as Vagises sent out half-companies ahead to search for our scouts who were beyond the horizon.

I rode between Gallia and Surena, Vagharsh and Surena's standard bearer riding directly behind us, their flags encased in wax sleeves, and behind them the Amazons leading the cataphracts. Dura's horse archers formed the head of the column and those of Gordyene behind them, with the camel train grouped in the rear, along with Dura's squires. As the morning wore on the wind increased to kick up dust that enveloped the column. The temperature was rising but in an effort to keep out the dust the cataphracts put on their full-face helmets and everyone else wrapped scarves around their faces. No one discarded his or her cloaks.

Then, suddenly, the wind ceased and the dust abated as the sun beat down on us from a clear sky. We halted and shook the dirt from our cloaks and took the opportunity to drink from our water bottles. It was mid-morning now and I could at last feel the sun warming my body. I patted Remus on the neck. I had decided to wear my leather cuirass and not my scale armour today – there would be no mass charges against the Romans. The cataphracts were in their armour to protect the other horsemen from any attacks from Roman cavalry, nothing more.

We continued the march but had not advanced two miles when a dozen horse archers came galloping towards us with Byrd and Malik in tow. They careered to a stop in front of us as I gave the order for another halt.

Byrd raised his hand. 'Romani horsemen approaching, five miles to west.'

'How many?' I asked.

'About a hundred,' replied Malik, 'but there are other groups of Roman horsemen scouting to the north and south.'

'We will continue our advance,' I said.

Byrd and Malik fell in beside Gallia as I saw a dust cloud ahead and knew it presaged enemy horsemen. I gave the order for the cataphracts to deploy into line and called forward Vagises.

'Bring in all your outriders,' I told him, 'we do not want to frighten off the Romans.'

As he rode away to send couriers forward to bring back his scouting parties more of Byrd's men rejoined us. I sent word to the cataphract company commanders for their men to continue wearing their cloaks, which would hide their scale armour.

'I do not understand,' said Surena.

'In this sun the light will reflect off the steel on scale armour,' I replied, 'thereby alerting our Roman friends that we have heavy horsemen. That might deter them from assaulting us, which we do not want. With any luck Crassus might be tempted to send his horsemen against us, which we can then destroy.'

But as Vagises' men returned to the ranks and we continued to trot west the dust cloud in front of us disappeared as the Roman horsemen returned to their commander. After an hour Byrd and Malik once again took their men ahead to discern the Romans' movements.

'It looks like there will be no fighting today,' I announced. 'The Romans will withdraw back to camp and Crassus will ponder his next move. But at least we know where he is and can shadow him from now on.'

It was getting very warm and so I gave the order that the heavy horsemen could take off their cloaks and also reform into column. They did so and also removed their helmets but they still sweated in their scale armour. The pace was no quicker than a slow walk to save the horses and I was considering ordering a halt when Byrd and Malik returned, their horses sweating and breathing heavily.

'Crassus approaches,' said Byrd, his face partly covered by a headscarf.

'He has crossed the Balikh River,' continued Malik.

'Crassus is leading his horsemen?' I asked with disbelief. Perhaps they were referring to his son, Publius.

Byrd shook his head. 'Whole Romani army come, spread across plain in a long line.'

'Horsemen on the wings and the foot in the centre,' said Malik.

'The Romans will not fight today, Byrd,' said Gallia, 'Pacorus has assured us all they will not, thus kindly go and ask them to return to camp.'

Surena burst out laughing and Vagises smiled.

'Very humorous,' I said.

'What do you want to do?' asked Vagises.

It was now midday and the sun was at its height roasting everything below. But the men were fully armed and in the saddle and the enemy were only a few miles distant.

'We might entice their horsemen away from the main body yet,' I said, 'where they can be whittled down by our horse archers. We advance.'

But first we halted as officers once again deployed the cataphracts in a long line of two ranks and the horse archers took up position behind them. Surena rode off to take command of his men while Vagises rode at the head of his troops, the drivers of the camel train marshalling their beasts to stay close to their designated companies of horse archers. In total there were ninety one-hundred-man companies of these, each one served by twelve camels loaded with full quivers of arrows. We had an abundance of the latter but I gave orders that the archers were not to be wasteful in their shooting – we might be battling Crassus for many days and would therefore require every missile.

'And that goes for the Amazons,' I told Gallia who was securing the straps of her helmet's cheekguards under her chin.

'You are becoming very bossy in your old age,' she said. 'In any case my women always hit what they aim at.'

'That may be, but you and they will remain with me today.'

She turned to Zenobia. 'He's frightened that all those hairy arsed Roman soldiers will rape him.'

Vagharsh laughed aloud.

'Is there any hope that you might one day respect your king and lord high general of the empire?' I remarked sarcastically.

'Not much,' he replied.

With the squires trailing well to the rear our outnumbered forces trotted towards the enemy who now filled the horizon: a great line of black shapes slowly getting larger as the range between the two sides decreased. As Gallia and I rode forward the cataphracts put on their helmets to present an inhuman visage of steel to the enemy and then brought down their lances to grip them with both hands lest the Roman horsemen suddenly charged us.

For a third time Byrd and Malik left us to gallop ahead as Vagharsh unfurled my banner and the red griffin spread its wings. I felt a sense of elation sweep through me as I turned to look left and right to see a thousand of the empire's finest horsemen break into a canter as we closed to within half a mile of the Romans.

I drew my *spatha* and peered ahead and saw that the Roman line was shortening. What trickery was this?

'They are forming square,' shouted Gallia, reading my thoughts.

I could discern trumpet blasts now and see Roman soldiers running back towards their centre as the horsemen on the flanks disappeared. I was tempted to order a halt and then a withdrawal as we would not be able to break the Roman square and at this very moment the enemy might be setting up their ballista to shoot at our horsemen. But then Surena appeared by my side. He too could see that the Romans had formed a square.

'Let my archers attack them, lord,' he begged, his eyes aflame with excitement.

'They may have ballista,' I cautioned.

'If they do then we will withdraw, but they are stationary and we are mobile and should take advantage of the enemy's mistake.'

He was right, of course. 'Very well, Surena, may Shamash go with you.'

He smiled and peeled away as we continued to canter towards what was now a huge hollow square of locked Roman shields. As we neared the enemy I noticed a hillock on the right and gave the order for the cataphracts to make for it. I heard a succession of horn blasts behind me and the heavy horsemen slowed and then changed direction to head for the hillock, while six thousand of Surena's men spread into line and prepared to engulf the Roman square.

We rode to the hillock where the horsemen thrust the butt spikes of their lances into the earth, shoved back their helmets on the top of their heads and watched the spectacle unfolding before them. Vagises arrayed his dragons of archers into three groups to the north, east and south of the square, well out of the range of any ballista bolts. He then rode with a company to join me on the hillock as Surena's horsemen swarmed round the square like angry hornets. The air was filled with a constant hissing noise as if a giant snake was above us as Gordyene's men shot at the enemy.

'I don't see many saddles being emptied,' he remarked.

'Perhaps they have no ballista or have left them in camp,' I said.

The companies of horsemen from Gordyene continue to rake the sides of the Roman square with arrows, loosing some at the locked shields but most over the heads of the legionaries, hoping to hit unprotected heads and torsos of Syrian auxiliaries taking cover behind them. Judging by the size of our own squares that we had formed in training and on the battlefield I estimated that each side the square in front of me was made up of twelve cohorts – around six thousand men – which meant that inside the square were a further twenty-eight thousand men, including horsemen.

A group of horsemen galloped towards us, the silver lion banner of Gordyene fluttering behind its king. Surena brought his horse to a halt and raised his hand in salute.

'No ballista, lord,' he grinned. 'The Romans are standing there like dumb animals.'

Vagises pointed past him. 'Not all of them.'

Surena turned in the saddle as the cohorts on the north side of the Roman square parted and hundreds of horsemen and foot soldiers flooded onto the plain.

'Syrian auxiliaries,' I said.

Crassus was no fool and knew that his legionaries could not get to grips with our light horsemen, but his similarly armed and equipped Syrian horse archers were ideal for dispersing the hundreds of enemy horsemen who were loosing missiles at his square. And so the legionaries moved aside to allow his Syrians to attack Surena's men. The horse archers thundered out of the square shooting their bows and immediately emptied dozens of saddles as their arrows hit both men and horses, the latter rearing up in pain before collapsing on the ground and writhing around in agony. And behind the Syrian horsemen came foot archers in light brown tunics, red leggings and wearing helmets, who sprinted in all directions, shooting more arrows at Surena's horsemen. Accompanying them were spearmen on foot who wore white tunics, white leggings and carried large, round wooden shields along with their short stabbing spears. Groups of spearmen followed the foot archers as the Syrians on horseback chased after Surena's men.

But the soldiers of Gordyene were well trained to deal with enemy attacks and they instinctively retreated out of the way of the Syrians, galloping away from the square and shooting arrows over the hind quarters of their horses at their adversaries as they did so. The Syrians, having seen how their charge had easily scattered the Parthians, gave chase in expectation of hunting down and slaying their prey. But they knew little of Parthian tactics.

The Syrian archers galloped directly north straight into a hail of arrows shot by the dragon of Duran horse archers that was positioned in front of them. Discovering this large body of horsemen the Syrians came to a halt, to be attacked on both flanks and in the rear by Surena's returning soldiers. Having a short time before been pursuing a seemingly defeated enemy, the Syrians now found themselves under a deluge of arrows as Surena's soldiers shot the densely packed Syrian block of horsemen to pieces. Having far outpaced their supporting foot soldiers, the Syrians had no answer to the rapid, accurate shooting that Surena's men subjected them to and soon individuals were fleeing for their lives, attempting to escape from the trap they had unwittingly galloped into. The majority failed to do so.

The Syrian soldiers on foot, having been deserted by their horsemen, attempted to run back to the safety of the square. But their initial charge had carried them at least five hundred paces from the locked Roman shields and now there were companies of horse archers galloping to head them off as they turned tail and ran. All semblance of order and discipline disappeared as individuals moved as fast as their legs could carry them towards the long line of Roman shields. Discarding their weapons and shields to lighten their load, many Syrians tripped and stumbled, twisting ankles and breaking legs. Horse archers rode parallel to groups of fleeing soldiers, loosing arrows at them as they did so, some drawing their swords to cut men down, while others galloped after them, shooting arrows into their backs as they closed to within touching distance of their foes. Perhaps a quarter of the Syrian foot made it back to the square alive but most of the horse archers were killed and none made it back to their Roman allies. At a stroke Crassus had lost most of his Syrian auxiliaries.

'Your men did well,' I said to Surena.

'They and I had a good teacher,' he beamed.

Gallia smiled at Surena in acknowledgement of his compliment. Perhaps she was warming to him at last.

A temporary lull descended over the battlefield as the horse archers of Gordyene were withdrawn in companies to replenish their ammunition and take a well-earned rest. As they did so Vagises moved his dragons closer to the edges of the square, though well out of arrow and javelin range. He also deployed five hundred men to cover the western side of the square to fully surround the Roman Army.

'What now, lord?' asked Surena.

It was a good question.

We had mauled the enemy's Syrian auxiliaries and had subjected the Roman square to a prolonged period of arrow volleys, but the Romans remained in their ranks and though they had undoubtedly suffered some casualties they retained a great superiority in numbers. It was now late afternoon; the enemy had only to remain in their ranks and we would have to retire from the field, to resume our tactic of harassment tomorrow. But I comforted myself with the knowledge that Crassus would not be able to march far with us hanging on his flanks.

With my permission Surena sent word for the camel train to be brought forward so the horse archers could replenish their quivers more quickly.

'We have time to subject them to more volleys before dusk falls, lord,' he said.

'You are right,' I agreed, 'the enemy will not make any further movements today so the more Romans we kill now the less we will have to face tomorrow. Vagises, it is time to discover whether all that money lavished on Arsam's new arrows has been well spent.'

'You think the Romans are just going to stand there and let you shoot them down?' asked a sceptical Gallia.

I laid a hand on her arm to reassure her. 'Believe me, I know the Romans better than myself. They will remain rooted to the spot until darkness falls. They will gladly trade a few casualties for time.'

A noise sounding like a dull scraping interrupted our conversation and from our vantage point on the hillock I saw movement among the Roman cohorts deployed on the northern side of the square, and then suddenly hundreds of horsemen poured from the enemy formation.

'It would appear that the Romans know you better than you know them,' remarked Gallia caustically, for behind the horsemen came rank upon rank of legionaries, accompanied by what appeared to be Syrian foot archers.

'Are they attempting a breakout?' said Vagises.

The Roman horsemen momentarily halted to dress their lines and then I heard trumpet blasts coming from their ranks, followed by fresh movement as what appeared to be well over a thousand enemy horsemen, plus at least four times as many legionaries in addition to a few hundred archers, veered right and began to head in our direction.

'They mean to kill the Parthian commanders,' remarked Gallia, who turned to Zenobia and ordered her to form the Amazons into line.

I looked at Surena and realised that just as we had been observing the Romans, so had Crassus been watching us. The banners of Dura and Gordyene had revealed our position to him and now he had sent a force to kill us.

'Form line!' I shouted to the officers of the cataphracts behind me. Seconds later horns were sounding and men were plucking their lances from the ground and pulling helmets down over their faces as the Romans trotted towards us. My eye was drawn to the centre of the line, to where a figure in what appeared to be white armour was riding ahead of the first line – Publius Crassus!

'We will meet the Romans head on,' I announced. 'Gallia, throw your Amazons in front as a screen and shoot arrows at the Romans to impede their advance. Vagises, return to your dragon positioned to the north of the square and divert them to assault the legionaries and archers accompanying the Roman horsemen.'

'What do you require of me, lord?' asked Surena as Gallia trotted away with Zenobia to organise the Amazons' attack.

'Bring one of your dragons to support Vagises. Once we have dealt with their horsemen we cannot let the Roman legionaries return to their square. The chance of destroying all their horse and a good portion of their foot is too good to let slip.'

He nodded and then galloped away with his bodyguard company with him. Vagises loitered for a few moments as the cataphracts began forming into a long line on the hillock and either side of it.

'Are you certain you do not wish my horse archers to soften them up first, Pacorus?' he asked.

'The finest heavy Parthian horsemen against the best Rome has to offer,' I replied. 'Let us see which side the gods favour.'

He smiled. 'May they be with you, my friend.'

He raised his hand and then wheeled his horse away to gallop behind the forming cataphracts to reach his companies of horse archers. The widely spaced Amazons were by now cantering across the half mile of ground that separated the two sets of horsemen. They would close to within four hundred paces of the Romans to loose half a dozen arrows, before retreating in a leisurely fashion, shooting missiles as they did so. Their arrows would not empty many saddles but might goad the Romans into charging prematurely.

The Roman horsemen occupied a frontage of around seven hundred and thirty paces. The thousand riders were organised into what was called an *ala*, which was made up of thirty-two units called *turmae*, each one comprised of just over thirty troopers. And now the *turmae* trotted towards us in one long line, each one three ranks deep. I also saw a few Syrian horsemen on the flanks that overlapped our own – the remnants of the auxiliary horsemen we had defeated earlier.

Gallia and the Amazons had no success in provoking the Romans even though they emptied a few saddles, and so fell back through the three ranks of the cataphracts to replenish their arrows from the camel train. I drew my *spatha* and pointed it forward to signal the charge as horns relayed my order along the line. The horses broke into a slow gallop as every *kontus* was lowered and grasped with both hands as the gap between the two sides rapidly diminished. From within full-face helmets came muffled war cries as horses broke into a fast gallop and the two sides collided with an ear-splitting bang that reverberated across the battlefield.

The Romans carried spears and held large oval shields on their left sides but in a head-on clash they were at a gross disadvantage. Their lances were nearly half the length of a *kontus* and the shields provided an excellent target for my cataphracts, who literally skewered most of the *ala*'s front rank, knocking riders from saddles as *kontus* points went straight through shields, mail shirts, torsos underneath and out through the backs of enemy horsemen. Around five hundred Romans died or were hideously wounded in that initial clash.

I had steered Remus straight at the rider in the white cuirass in an effort to kill Publius Crassus, demoralise his men and shatter the enemy's mounted arm. He had seen me too and I now became oblivious to the hundreds of armoured riders either side of me and to the Romans to my front as I raised my sword to crush the enemy commander's helmet as Remus strained every one of his mighty muscles to outrun the horses of the other cataphracts. I screamed as I was suddenly directly in front of Publius Crassus and brought my blade down, and completely missed as he ducked to the side and carried out a perfect back slash with his sword as I passed that cut deep into the rear of my cuirass.

I pulled Remus up but his momentum had carried me straight into the Roman second rank, and now the enemy's discipline and professionalism came to the fore as the battle changed from one of a headlong charge into a grim mêlée. The cataphracts in the second and third ranks instinctively slowed before moving into the developing maelstrom of swinging sword blades, spear thrusts and terrified bolting and limping horses that had been caused by the initial impact.

I had no time to look for Crassus the younger as a Roman lunged at me with his spear that I only avoided by grabbing one of my saddle horns with my left hand and collapsing down Remus' right side, before hauling myself up once the rider had passed me by. Other cataphracts closed around me, hacking at Romans with their swords, maces and axes to great effect. I saw one of my horsemen clash swords with an opponent and sever his blade before thrusting his sword point into the man's face.

The second and third ranks entered the fray, Romans lunging at armoured horses and riders with their spears and cataphracts thrusting their long lances into exposed horseflesh. Horses writhed in agony as *kontus* points were thrust into their guts, fell to the ground and threw their riders. One man, face-down on the ground, had the butt spike of a *kontus* thrust into his back that shattered his spine before he could rise. Dismounted Romans tried to get near our horses to stab them under their scale armour, their riders keeping them away with lance thrusts. I saw a Roman with a *kontus* embedded in his belly, gripping the lance with one hand as he thrust his spear into the scale armour of his opponent. Incredible bravery!

I heard hisses and a whooshing noise and knew that Vagises' horse archers were now assaulting the legionaries who had accompanied the horsemen. The ranks of the latter were gradually being whittled down as Dura's new swords were cutting through steel and iron with ease. Half a company was now grouped around me and I felt totally useless, being unable to fight anyone. Some cataphracts had discarded their lances and armed themselves with a sword in one hand and an axe in the other, using the pointed end of the later to embed them in Roman shields and then yanking the owner towards them before splitting his helmet with a downward sword strike.

The initial charge had destroyed the Romans' first rank, the mêlée had inflicted further losses on the enemy and our numbers were beginning to tell. I did not see any Syrian horsemen and suspected most had fled after the first clash, and the archers were also nowhere to be seen. A horseman came to my side, his sword and mace smeared with blood. He pushed his helmet back on his head to uncover his face.

'We are scattering them, uncle,' said Spartacus, his breathing heavy from the exertion of battle.

Suddenly arrows began falling from the sky, hitting horses and men but fortunately not piercing our scale armour.

'Put your helmet back on,' I commanded him, before giving the order to sound recall.

I saw Romans still in their saddles jerk in pain as arrows hit their backs, legs and pierced their horses as we disengaged and hurriedly pulled back. In the confusion of the mêlée our whole line had rotated so that we actually rode to the north. As the companies reformed around their commanders I saw that Vagises' archers were snapping at the heels of the leavings of the Roman horsemen and the locked shields of the legionaries, herding them towards the hillock that we had originally occupied.

'Pacorus.'

I turned to see Vagharsh wilt in the saddle, two arrows stuck in him, and then fall to the ground. I jumped down as he tried to rise, clutching the banner and using it as a prop. He fell back down as I knelt beside him and Spartacus leaned down and grabbed the banner to hoist it aloft once more.

I cradled Vagharsh's head as blood oozed from the wounds to his chest and belly. He looked up and smiled.

'I never would have thought that I would die at the hands of Parthian arrows.'

His face blurred as my eyes filled with tears. 'Hold on, my friend, hold on.'

He smiled once again as teardrops fell on his face. 'We will meet again, my friend, but for the moment I must depart from your side. It has been an honour.'

Gallia jumped down from Epona and knelt down, her face full of despair, as Vagharsh looked at her, smiled ever so faintly, sighed and then closed his eyes. I closed my eyes and growled through gritted teeth as another Companion left this life.

I ordered a company to guard his body as I mounted Remus and assessed the current situation. I ordered all the company commanders to report to me after a roll call had been taken as Vagises' horse archers lapped round the Romans who had now taken possession of the hillock. Crassus' square remained in the same position, for the moment undisturbed by our horse archers, but now the son of Crassus and several thousand of his soldiers had been separated from the main body and were isolated on the hillock. A decisive moment in the battle had been reached.

Vagises and Surena, his lion banner fluttering behind him, rode to where Spartacus held aloft my standard as cataphract commanders reported their losses, which were remarkably light: twenty men killed and fifty-three others wounded, none seriously. I saw a look of horror on Vagises' face as he halted his horse and stared at the body of Vagharsh on the ground, four dismounted cataphracts standing guard over it.

'Bastard Romans,' he hissed, not realising that it was arrows shot by his own men who had killed him. I saw no reason to reveal the truth.

'We have a battle to win before we can grieve,' I told him. 'It is time to unleash a hailstorm against the Roman square lest Crassus is tempted to rescue his son.

I turned to Surena. 'I would be eternally grateful if you would destroy those Romans occupying my hillock.'

A devilish smile crept over his face and he slammed his knees into his horse's sides, causing the beast to rear up on its hind legs, and then he bolted forward back to his waiting companies. Vagises followed him and then veered away to his waiting dragons of horse archers. Within minutes horn blasts echoed across the gloomy battlefield and horse archers once more began loosing arrows at all four sides of the square. To my left the Romans on the hillock faced the full wrath of two thousand horse archers as Surena's men shot what was left of the command of Publius Crassus to pieces.

Having destroyed the Romans' Syrian archers – those few still alive being confined to the hillock – our horse archers could now ride closer to the front ranks of the enemy square on the plain, riding parallel to the locked shields, each rider loosing around five arrows a minute before peeling away to reform in his company. The horsemen stayed out of javelin range but shooting at a distance of around fifty paces they ensured that every arrow struck its target. And the pace of their horses was a quick canter – there was no need to gallop – further aiding accuracy. Seven thousand horse archers were assaulting Crassus' square, shooting an average of twenty-eight thousand arrows every minute at his men.

I heard the sound of cheers resounding across the plain and realised that Surena had destroyed the Romans on the hillock. Groups of horse archers began redeploying to take part in the assault against the main Roman Army as others began herding a long line of Roman prisoners away from the battlefield. And all the time Crassus and his men were easy targets for our archers.

'Here comes the conquering hero,' remarked Gallia as Surena came galloping towards us, holding what appeared to be a spear in his hand.

As he and his bodyguard got closer I realised that there was a severed head on the end of the shaft he was holding, blood covering the wood and his hand.

'Behold, lord, I give you Publius Crassus,' he shouted at the top of his voice so my officers grouped behind me could hear, 'son of Marcus Licinius Crassus, who unwisely brought an invading army into Parthia.'

I stared at the lifeless eyes of the man I had liked. 'You should have accepted his surrender, Surena.'

'Unfortunately, lord, he took his own life but some five hundred of his men did give themselves up. Do you want me to kill them?'

'We will decide what to do with them after the battle is over.'

'Take it away,' Gallia said to Surena, 'it's disgusting.'

Surena grinned. 'Your wish is my command, lady. I shall go and show Crassus what has happened to his son.'

He gave a whoop of victory and then turned his horse around and galloped away with his men following.

As dusk was fast approaching Vagises began withdrawing his men plus those of Gordyene. The Roman Army still existed but it had been severely battered and had there been but two more hours of light left we might have shot it to pieces, just as we had done with the troops of Publius Crassus. As it was we withdrew from the field, taking as many of our dead as we could, leaving behind only those who were within javelin range of the enemy.

Byrd and Malik and their scouts stayed on the field until well after darkness had enveloped the land to ensure that the Romans did not send out any parties of horsemen to raid us, but they returned after we had made camp three miles to the east with news that the enemy remained immobile in their square. The last of our number to leave the battlefield was Surena and his bodyguard, the King of Gordyene riding up and down in front of the Romans, taunting them with the head of Publius Crassus and shouting insults at them, demanding that they send a champion from their ranks to fight him in single combat. He shouted for Crassus himself to come forward to avenge his son's death but the Romans remained stationary and silent in their ranks and eventually Surena tired of their lack of response and left them to endure a night without shelter, food and water. It had been a day that had exceeded all expectations and I was forced to rethink my strategy.

'Crassus is finished,' said Surena, sitting on a stool after having planted the spear on which the head of Crassus' son was impaled next to his tent before joining us round a fire.

'I am apt to agree with Surena,' said Vagises, chewing on a piece of cured meat.

The squires, who had taken no part in the battle, now stood sentry over the camp as the horse archers of Dura and Gordyene and my cataphracts rested their weary bodies under the stars.

'You have won a great victory, lord,' continued Surena.

'I have won nothing,' I contradicted him. 'The Roman Army still exists and tomorrow will attempt to reach the safety of the walls of Carrhae, ten miles to the north. Only after we have prevented it from doing so can we claim victory.'

Surena would have none of it. 'You did not see the damage inflicted on the Romans by our arrows. Men were being shot down where they stood and pulled back into the square, and on all four sides bodies were being pierced with ease.'

'I have to agree,' added Vagises. 'Arsam's arrows proved their worth today.'

'And do not forget the Romans that were killed on the hillock, lord, and at the hands of your own cataphracts,' continued Surena.

'We must have killed upwards of six or seven thousand,' suggested Vagises, 'plus the ones killed or wounded in the square.'

'That still leaves over forty thousand men to our less than ten,' I reminded them. 'We will wait until the morning before becoming too triumphant.'

I spent most of the night walking around the camp, talking to those who also could not sleep and congratulating them on their conduct during the battle. The morale of the men was high, especially among the cataphracts who had defeated their Roman opponents, and everyone was talking about the new swords and how their blades had sliced through Roman steel with ease. I also took the opportunity to view the five hundred Roman prisoners who had been corralled in a small gully near the camp. They had been given dates to eat but no water since we could spare none. They would have to wait for the dawn when they would be escorted to the Balikh to slake their thirsts. They looked tired, demoralised and frightened by their predicament, and many carried battle wounds. Two companies of bowmen guarded them but I doubted any would attempt to escape, unlike their comrades to the west on the Plain of Carrhae.

The only person who was not happy, and appeared close to despair, was Spartacus. When I returned to my tent I found him pacing up and down and muttering to himself.

'They say that talking to oneself is either a sign of madness or proof that one who does so has the ear of the gods,' I said.

He stopped pacing and muttering and looked at me, his unhappy face cast in a red glow by the fire nearby.

'I certainly do not have the ear of the gods,' he fumed.

I pointed to a stool and sat on another.

'Sit down, you will wear out your boots with all that pacing.'

He sat beside me, mumbling under his breath.

'What's the matter?'

He suddenly looked totally forlorn. 'I will never be with Rasha now.'

'Ah, I see. You think that your chance of taking an eagle has eluded you?'

'Yes.'

'The battle is not over, Spartacus, far from it. Tomorrow is another day. You must have faith.'

I was beginning to sound like Dobbai, much to my consternation.

'Surena says that that Romans are finished and will flee back to Carrhae.'

'He is right that they will make for Carrhae,' I said, 'but they are far from finished. They are only ten miles from safety. This battle is not over.'

Chapter 18

The new day dawned bright and sunny and the army was in the saddle early, three companies of Surena's horse archers having been left behind to guard the prisoners who would be transported west to the Balikh River after we had determined where Crassus and his army were. That was solved when we rode back on to the battlefield to discover it had gone, leaving behind hundreds of wounded men occupying the area where a day earlier the great square of legionaries had stood. Byrd and Malik had ridden out of camp before dawn and now they returned with news that the main force of Romans was strung out on the road to Carrhae.

'We ride very close but they make no moves against us,' reported Byrd.

'How far away?' I asked.

'Three miles,' answered Malik.

I waved forward Vagises.

'Take your horse archers and kill as many as you can but do not get too close to Carrhae. There are no doubt horsemen among the garrison.'

He saluted and gestured to his waiting officers to attend him.

'And Vagises,' I said, 'take care of yourself. No heroics.'

He smiled and then went to brief his commanders, and within minutes nearly three thousand horse archers were cantering north to harry the Roman retreat.

Most of the casualties we had suffered the day before had been among Surena's men – six hundred killed and another three hundred wounded – and so four hundred of his men remained in camp to care for the injured, in addition to those who were guarding the prisoners. But he still retained just under four and half thousand men and now those horsemen deployed around the groups of standing, lying or sitting Roman wounded. What a pitiful sight they were: cut and bleeding men with broken bones, listless faces and torn tunics, waiting in dumb silence as we decided their fate.

'What do you wish to do with them, lord?' asked Surena, who had thankfully left his gruesome trophy in camp.

Gallia looked at me in expectation that I would give the order to kill them. We did not have enough medicines to treat their wounds and no wagons to transport them to the nearest town, which in any case was occupied by the Romans. In truth I was reluctant to order their murder because they were unarmed and helpless and I liked to think of myself as a soldier not a butcher. As I heard the laughter of Dobbai in my mind I saw one of Surena's men dismount and offer a waterskin to a Roman whose left arm was in a sling. The Roman reached out to take the leather container when he saw a horse archer nearby pulling back the string on his bow to test the tension. Thinking an arrow was nocked in it the Roman drew his dagger and stabbed the Parthian in front of him, who collapsed to the ground clutching his stomach. Surena saw it too.

'Kill them all!' he screamed.

Gallia nodded approvingly as his men either shot down the Romans, hacked them to death with their swords or rode over those who lay

399

prostrate on the ground. I ordered the cataphracts to accompany me north and turned my back on the scene of slaughter as my ears were assailed by the wails and screams of dying men.

As we travelled towards Carrhae we came across whole centuries of disarmed Romans, marching in step and in their ranks, being escorted south by half-companies of Duran horse archers. The Romans were surrendering in droves, though a few still had some fight left in them. Halfway to Carrhae Vagises returned to report that his men had trapped around two thousand Roman legionaries on a hillock nearby. Spartacus behind me let out a groan when he saw that the commander of my horse archers was holding a pole topped by a silver Roman eagle. He noted Spartacus staring longingly at it and held it out to the young prince.

'You want it?'

'Certainly not,' he snapped. 'It is worthless if another has taken it.'

Vagises shrugged. 'I didn't take it; I found in lying on the ground. Still, it's a nice trophy. There's another one on that small rise ahead, though you might have to fight them for it.'

I turned to look at Spartacus and saw his eyes were wide with excitement. 'Very well,' I said, 'it looks as though you have the ear of the gods after all, Spartacus.'

He handed my standard to Zenobia mounted beside Gallia and drew his sword as I nudged Remus forward. I looked at the eagle being carried so casually by Vagises on my left side.

'My men have taken two more of these,' he said. 'The Roman Army is on the verge of collapse.'

I could hardly contain my excitement. To have not only turned back the Roman invasion but also shattered their army was nothing short of a miracle, one that I had Dobbai to thank for. How else could this marvel be explained? The sounds of thousands of horses' hooves snapped me out of my daydreams as Surena's men flooded the road in font of us to gallop on towards Carrhae, skirting groups of Roman soldiers trudging in the opposite direction.

'We killed them all, lord,' he announced proudly as Vagises moved his horse aside to allow him to join me. He saw the eagle that Vagises held.

'You should give that to young Spartacus so he can marry Rasha.'

'I will take my own or none at all,' insisted Spartacus.

'There is one but a short distance away,' I said to Surena, 'guarded by nearly half a legion. That is where we are heading.'

'Is Crassus there?' inquired Surena.

'No horsemen,' replied Vagises, 'most likely he is in Carrhae by now.'

'If he gets back to Syria he will raise another army to invade Parthia next year,' said Surena.

That much was true. Losing an army might be an inconvenience and a stain on his honour, but for a man of Crassus' wealth it would be only a temporary setback. If he raised another army and mounted a second invasion of Parthia then he could still achieve ultimate victory as well as avenge the death of his son.

But for the moment our thoughts were occupied by the two thousand Roman legionaries who had taken possession of a small rise of ground about five miles south of the town. Why they had stopped rather than press on to the sanctuary of Carrhae no one knew. Perhaps many wounded among their ranks had slowed their march or, more probably, they had become lost in the dark and strayed from the road that led north. Whatever the reason they were now being surrounded by horse archers as Vagises' men circled them like angry wolves.

The commander of my horse archers rode to where I sat with Gallia and Surena observing the Romans, who had formed a shield wall on all four sides of their ragged square and had also locked shields over their heads in anticipation of volleys of arrows.

Vagises halted his horse and raised his hand. 'Pacorus, the commander of the camel train informed me earlier that he has few quivers left. We used a prodigious quantity of arrows yesterday that has nearly exhausted our supplies.'

'How many do we have left?' asked Surena.

'Whatever your men and mine carry at this moment plus an additional two quivers,' answered Vagises.

'That few,' I said. 'Perhaps we should demand the surrender of these Romans rather than waste more arrows. We still have to deal with those Romans who have reached Carrhae, after all.'

I heard a groan of frustration behind me and Gallia laid a hand on my arm.

'I think you should fight these Romans, Pacorus.'

'Why? What is so special about them?'

She glanced at Spartacus behind us.

'Some have to fulfil their destinies, my husband, just as you have fulfilled yours.'

I looked at Spartacus, who because he wore the uniform of a Hatran cataphract had an open-faced helmet. I saw his eyes full of pleading.

'Very well,' I said. 'Vagises, your men will soften them up first, but controlled shooting. Tell your commanders to be frugal with their arrows. We may need them in the days ahead.'

Gallia, her face largely hidden behind the closed cheekguards of her helmet, nodded at me.

'Rasha will love you even more.'

'Not if Spartacus gets himself killed she won't.'

But Spartacus was not thinking about death or mortality, only glory and his beautiful young princess. After I had given the order for half the cataphracts – five companies – to deploy into battle formation he rode to join the front rank as the horse archers began to attack the Roman square. To break such a formation is not easy and even though Dura's horsemen were among the best trained in the empire I worried that the cataphracts would come to grief when they made their charge. The customary tactic was for the horse archers to shoot against all four sides of the square, with the heaviest concentration of missiles being directed against one of those sides, which would be the predetermined target for the heavy horsemen. The attacks against the other three sides were diversions only.

His company commanders under strict orders not to waste arrows, riders charged at the Roman shields with empty bowstrings and then swung right to ride along the wall of shields to discover if the enemy had retained their javelins during their retreat. The lack of missiles thrown from the square seemed to suggest that they had not.

The five companies of cataphracts earmarked for the attack were arrayed in a line facing the south side of the square, but I passed the word that their actual assault should be against its eastern side. The Roman commander would have seen the heavy horsemen lining up and would have deduced that they were going to assault his men once the archers had finished their work. Most likely he would have stripped legionaries from the other sides of the square to reinforce the one that faced south, but Vagises' horse archers were subjecting the eastern side to the heaviest volleys of arrows. His men were now riding parallel to the shield wall, loosing their arrows at a range of below thirty paces, the slim steel heads going through *scutums* with ease, though whether they were piercing flesh was impossible to tell.

I raised my hand to the commander of the half-dragon of heavy horsemen that was waiting patiently in three ranks, the butt spike of every *kontus* driven into the earth beside each rider and helmets pushed up on every head. It was already very warm and they were roasting in their heavy scale armour; to sit in the sun wearing a full-face helmet would only increase their discomfort.

But now the signal was given to move and so lances were plucked from the earth and helmets pulled down as five hundred men rode forward a few paces and then as one wheeled right into column formation, riding parallel to the south side of the square. The commander galloped to the head of the column as it turned again, this time left, to take it parallel to the eastern side of the square, all the time the horse archers continuing their shooting and doing their best to mask the movement of the cataphracts.

I drew my sword and turned to Gallia. 'It is not right that my horsemen should risk their lives while their king sits idly on his horse.'

'You and Remus wear no scale armour,' said Gallia.

'I will be in the third rank, have no fear.'

'I am with you, lord,' said Surena, who also pulled his sword from its scabbard.

'You and the Amazons are our reserve,' I said to Gallia, 'Shamash keep you safe.'

I dug my knees into Remus and he shot forward as Surena followed, both of us galloping after the column of cataphracts that was now deploying into line to face the eastern side of the Roman square. Upon seeing the movement of the cataphracts and their redeployment, Vagises issued orders for his men in front of the heavy horsemen to withdraw as five hundred lances were lowered and the heavy horsemen broke into a trot and then a canter.

No horse will charge into a shield wall and so the cataphracts rode forward at a slow, controlled gallop, the front rank grasping the shaft of each *kontus* not in the middle but nearer to the butt spike, thereby extending it forward beyond the shoulders of their horses. In this way they could slow their mounts just before impact so the beasts would not panic and either swerve sideways or rear up on their hind legs. The second and third ranks rode forward at a slower pace so as not to collide into the front rank when the impact came – a loud scraping noise that heralded over a hundred *kontus* points being driven through *scutums* and into their owners' bodies.

The riders in all three ranks of the heavy horsemen were widely spaced to allow the second rank to fill the gaps after the initial collision, the next wave of cataphracts moving forward into the openings to drive their lances into Roman shields and bodies. Horrible high-pitched screams pierced the air as men were literally skewered by lances that went through their bodies and into the earth behind, leaving legionaries pinioned to the ground.

Then the cataphracts drew their swords and hacked left and right at helmets, the dark metal splitting them with ease and the skulls underneath. Some Romans avoided the lances and swords and stabbed at horses with their short swords, the blows being deflected by steel scales and thick hide of scale armour. A few stabbed underneath the armour to slice open a horse's belly, felling the animal and its rider, the pair collapsing onto other legionaries.

The fight was brief and bloody, the cataphracts cutting into the four threadbare ranks that made up this side of the Roman square, prompting some men to flee before the horsemen. Others rallied around the commanders of their centuries, instinctively seeking the security of their comrades, but in so doing they created gaps through which my horsemen flooded. They ignored the groups of Romans who adopted an all-round defence in their centuries and rode into the centre of the square where the senior commanders stood ready to defend the legion's precious eagle.

One side of the square having been breached and fractured, Vagises sent in companies of horse archers to support the cataphracts, the bowmen shooting down fleeing Romans at short range. Some Romans, fatigued and demoralised, were now throwing down their weapons and attempting to surrender, a risky manoeuvre in the face of enemy horsemen who were not inclined to take prisoners while the battle was still waging. Some were lucky; others were not as more and more horsemen poured into the broken square.

With Surena beside me I accompanied the third rank as it entered the square killing any Roman who crossed its path. I swung my sword at the head of a Roman as he ran past me but failed to hit him. In front of me a lone rider in scale armour charged headlong at the group defending the legion's eagle.

'The idiot!' shouted Surena as Spartacus directed his horse at the score or more men – senior officers and centurions – who guarded the legionary eagle, the sacred symbol of the Senate of Rome and honour of the legion.

I screamed at Remus to move and he bolted forward as I saw with horror Spartacus' horse smash into the enemy soldiers and collapse to the ground, throwing its rider and rolling over those in its path. I pulled Remus up sharply and jumped from the saddle, sword in hand, as a centurion stood over Spartacus with his *gladius* drawn back, ready to plunge it into my nephew. I screamed at the top of my voice and ran at the Roman, plunging the point of my blade into his mail shirt. I tripped over Spartacus and tumbled to the ground as the dead centurion fell on top of me and then looked up, helplessly, to see an officer, a tribune in a muscled cuirass, pull the dead centurion off me so he could ram his sword through my chest. I stared, transfixed, as he stood over me, drew up his sword with both hands and then died as a *kontus* was driven through his body. He pitched forward with the point of the lance protruding from his chest as the cataphract releasing the shaft rode on past me, the point narrowly missing my throat as it stuck in the earth a few inches from my face. Once again a dead Roman had pinned me to the ground.

Surena hauled the body off me and helped me to my feet as Spartacus, oblivious to anything else, ran at the hulking figure draped in a lion skin holding the eagle. The Romans called them *Aquilifers*, these veterans who were the most senior standard bearers in every legion, and they were selected because they were seasoned soldiers who knew how to take care of the legion's most precious object.

The *Aquilifer* rammed the butt spike of the shaft that held the eagle into the ground and drew his *gladius* as Spartacus swung his sword at the man's head. The Roman ducked and thrust his own sword into the left arm of Spartacus, which was fortunately protected by tubular steel armour, causing the point to glance off it. My nephew attacked the Roman with a series of lightening-fast sword strikes, his blade moving so rapidly that it appeared that he was holding a weapon of the immortals as it flashed in the sunlight. But the *Aquilifer* parried every stroke and then smashed his small circular shield into Spartacus, knocking him to the ground.

The Roman raced to stand over him but Spartacus already had his dagger in his left hand and brought it down hard to go through the man's foot. The *Aquilifer* screamed in pain and hobbled backwards as Spartacus then swung his sword and cut deep into the side of the Roman's right calf. He screamed again and this time collapsed to the ground, blood gushing from his foot and lower leg. I ran to Spartacus and lifted him to his feet as Surena fought another Roman officer who had rushed to aid the *Aquilifer*. The latter had managed to haul himself to his feet but was knocked to the ground again as Spartacus swung his sword at the side of his helmet, severing the cheekguard and knocking the Roman senseless. He collapsed again as Spartacus jumped on him and launched a frenzied attack on him

404

with his dagger, stabbing at his face and neck again and again, showering his face, hands and armour with the *Aquilifer*'s blood.

I hauled Spartacus up once more as Surena killed his opponent with a downward strike of his sword splitting helmet and skull. Cataphracts were now forming around us as more and more horse archers darted around, killing Romans who had thrown down their weapons and raised their hands in a sign of submission.

Spartacus was oblivious to the scenes of carnage around him as he stepped forward and touched the silver eagle with up-raised wings surrounded by a laurel wreath. He grasped the shaft and yanked it from the ground, holding it aloft for all to see while Surena and I flanked him to ensure that the enemy did not ruin his moment of triumph.

Cataphracts swirled around us and cut down Romans with their swords and maces, supported by the bows of Vagises' men who were now shooting at point-blank range. Romans who had surrendered had been slaughtered, those who had attempted to run had been cut down and now the last vestiges of what had been half a legion were being methodically destroyed. I slapped Spartacus on the shoulder and left him in the capable hands of Surena as Gallia and the Amazons rode to where I was standing, my wife leading Remus by the reins.

'You should take more care of your horse,' she chided me.

I hauled myself into his saddle and pointed at Spartacus.

'I had my hands full keeping him alive.'

'So he will marry Rasha. All is well.'

I looked around at the hundreds of dead Roman bodies. 'Yes, all is well.'

The battle was now over, the ground littered with discarded *scutums*, swords, helmets and legionary standards, in addition to the hundreds of dead bodies with arrows or lances stuck in them. A few Romans, their heads horribly gashed by sword or mace strikes, were still clinging on to life as their lifeblood poured from their wounds, others sat upright on the ground staring in disbelief at their bellies that had been sliced open by Parthian blades. A few poor wretches were endeavouring to push their guts back inside them, not realising that the hand of death was already upon them.

After the frenzy of bloodlust had receded horse archers and cataphracts looked on with pity at their defeated foes, though there remained a small group of Romans still fighting. The calls of horns alerted me to their presence a short distance away from where Spartacus had taken the eagle. There were a score of them, most wounded, some helmetless and all grouped around a figure with a badly gashed head who was holding a century standard, made up of a number of silver disks called *philarae*, mounted above which was a metal plate bearing the century's title and from which hung two red leather strips. The standard was topped by an image of a human hand in silver. I had seen many of these emblems in Italy and Spartacus had amassed a great collection of them following his many victories.

The Romans stood in silent defiance, swords in hands as Vagises surrounded them with four companies of horse archers, who calmly strung arrows in their bowstrings and waited for the order to shoot.

'Wait!' I shouted, then nudged Remus forward to join Vagises.

'This won't take long,' he said.

'Don't waste your arrows, order your men to stand down.'

He looked at me in confusion. 'Why?'

'Young Spartacus has his eagle,' I replied. 'We could have accepted the surrender of the Romans but Gallia persuaded me to fight them so a boy could marry an Agraci princess. A lot of men have died to facilitate that union. I see no reason to add to the butcher's bill.'

He called forward one of his officers and relayed my order. Fresh horn calls led to the ring of horse archers placing their arrows back in their quivers and then wheeling about, leaving twenty Romans relieved and confused in equal measure.

'You are getting soft in your old age, Pacorus,' Vagises ribbed me. 'They would not show the same mercy if the positions were reversed.'

'That is why we are better than them, my friend.'

I nudged Remus forward and halted him around twenty paces from the Romans, who raised their swords at my approach.

'Soldiers of Rome, you have done all that valour and honour requires and are now free to go back to Syria. When you reach Roman territory once more you can tell all those who will listen that only defeat and death awaits those who invade Parthia. Tell Rome that I, Pacorus of Dura, will crush every army that it sends against the Parthian Empire, just as I have destroyed your army.'

I wheeled Remus about and rode him north as my wife and the Amazons fell in behind me and then company after company of horse archers and cataphracts formed column to follow me. Spartacus rode behind myself, Vagises and Gallia, grinning like a simple-minded fool to all and sundry as he held the trophy in his hand. But the decision to fight for the legionary eagle had been bought at a high price when Byrd and Malik returned to us with news that Crassus had reached the safety of Carrhae's walls.

Surena had chased him all the way to the town gates but a volley of arrows from the walls had forced his withdrawal. He had approached the gates under a flag of truce and requested a meeting with Crassus concerning the agreement of a peace treaty between Rome and Parthia, which was highly presumptuous on the King of Gordyene's part but did at least confirm that the Roman commander was in the town. An officer replied that Crassus would reply to Surena's demand the next day.

We made camp three miles south of the town, near the rippling waters of the Balikh River. At last we could immerse ourselves in its cool waters and wash the filth and blood from our bodies. We unsaddled our horses and brought them cool water to drink and then sat down to work out our next course of action. The prisoners were also allowed to drink from the river and wash their wounds, and their fate was our immediate concern.

'How many do we have?' I asked as we sat on stools in a circle round a fire as darkness enveloped the earth, the dim glow of torches on the walls of Carrhae visible in the distance.

'Just under seven thousand,' answered Vagises. 'If we take any more they will outnumber us.'

'The sensible thing would be to kill them,' said Surena without emotion.

'I am not in favour of killing prisoners,' I said, 'especially as we now have the means to feed them.'

Before night had fallen Vagises had diverted five hundred of his men across the river to take possession of the Roman camp a short distance away, from where Crassus had marched to engage us. They found it stuffed full of supplies and mules, which would all be conveyed back to Dura. A company was left to guard it while the rest brought back a horde of biscuits, wine, bread, cured pork and grain in wagons.

'Once they have been taken back to Dura,' I continued, 'Orodes can decide their fate. Vagises, how many of the enemy do you think lie dead on this plain?'

He shrugged. 'Difficult to say, but a guess would put the figure at around twenty thousand, give or take.'

'That still leaves over twenty thousand Roman soldiers in Carrhae, lord,' said Surena, 'plus their commander.'

'We must prevent him from getting back to Syria and raising another army,' added Vagises.

'We have no engines to lay siege to Carrhae,' said Surena.

That was true but Carrhae was a small town and although it had walls it would not have the provisions to sustain twenty thousand soldiers in addition to its garrison and the population.

'Crassus will have to either escape from the town or enter into a peace treaty,' I told them all. 'There is no other army in Syria to come to his aid and his Armenian allies have been defeated and are being pursued by Orodes. Tomorrow we surround Carrhae and wait for Crassus to come to us.'

Later, after the others had retired to their tents, I could not sleep and sat with Gallia, tossing logs onto the fire. We wrapped our cloaks around us for there was a cool wind blowing from the foothills of the Taurus Mountains to the north of Carrhae. It had been a remarkable two days that had seen Parthia defeat a numerically superior Roman army and take possession of no less than seven legionary eagles. As far as I knew this feat was unique in the annals of warfare. All that remained was to agree a peace treaty with Crassus.

'Can you make a treaty without Orodes?' she inquired.

'Orodes is not here and the time to treat with Crassus is now, when his army lies in tatters and Syria is open to invasion.'

'You think Crassus will agree to a treaty?'

I smiled at her. 'He has no choice. He cannot leave Carrhae without my permission and the price of his freedom is a binding treaty.'

She giggled. 'Crassus the slave, at the mercy of Pacorus, his master. I like that. And what are the terms of your treaty?'

'Quite simple. The Euphrates shall define the boundary between the empires of Rome and Parthia in perpetuity, and Armenia will no longer be a client state of Rome but will be independent, free to make its own destiny.'

She sighed. 'Even after all these years you still know so little of the Romans.'

'I do not understand.'

She tilted her head and looked at me lovingly. 'To you preservation is everything – preserving Hatra, preserving the empire and the ways of your father and grandfather.'

'What is wrong with that?'

'Nothing, absolutely nothing, but to the Romans it is anathema. Rome desires to rule the whole world and subjugate all the peoples who live in it to its rule, and it will not rest until it has done so. Twenty years ago we escaped Italy and came to Parthia, and now we sit round a fire after having fought another Roman army, just as we did when we were with Spartacus all those years ago.'

'Are you suggesting I should march against Rome?' I asked half-seriously.

She sighed. 'I am saying that it a waste of time talking to Crassus. He will say anything to secure his escape, and once he is back in Syria will raise a new army to satisfy his thirst for conquest.'

I leaned across and put my arm around her. 'I think you will find that he will be more than willing to talk to me tomorrow, my sweet.'

But Gallia was right and Crassus stole a march on me, leaving Carrhae as I sat on a stool talking to my wife by a fire.

It was two hours after dawn the following day when I learned from Malik that Crassus had left the town, along with what remained of his army. Byrd and their men had been scouting the area north and west of Carrhae when they witnessed three columns of legionaries leave the town and head towards the foothills of the mountains. My heart sank as I realised that Crassus was on the verge of making good his escape.

I hurriedly saddled Remus and collected together five hundred horse archers, the Amazons and a further thousand of Surena's men and rode with him and them north. We skirted Carrhae and headed north towards the foothills of the mountains. We left Vagises behind with orders to allocate guards to watch the prisoners, distribute the camel train's remaining spare arrows among the horse archers and then bring them and the cataphracts north to scour the area.

I cursed my luck as Remus galloped among the scrub and I searched for Crassus. In front of us were the hills of Sinnaca, an area of thick woods, steep slopes and rocky paths, country that was ideal for travel on foot and for eluding horsemen. If Crassus had managed to reach the hills the game was up and he would be back in Syria in two days. A mile north of Carrhae we encountered Byrd and a dozen of his scouts, one of whom was riding a donkey.

'This is Abgarus, a cousin of Andromachus,' reported Byrd. 'He inform me of whereabouts of Crassus.'

I closed my eyes and thanked Shamash for this miracle. The man on a donkey was an unprepossessing sight, with straggly long hair and a lazy left eye. Nevertheless, if accurate his information was invaluable.

The man smiled as Vagises arrived at the head of two companies of horsemen to swell our force.

'You saw Crassus?' I asked.

He shook his head. 'No, lord.'

I gripped my reins tightly in frustration. 'Then how do you know where he is?'

He smiled submissively again. 'I saw three groups leave Carrhae last night, lord, but only one contained lictors.'

Surena was confused. 'Lictors?'

'Special Roman administrators in plain white togas,' I told him. 'On their left shoulders they carry bundles of vine rods bound together by red bands from which an axe head protrudes. These rods are emblems of Roman unity and power but, more importantly, they escort Rome's consuls and governors on their journeys, the bearers acting as bodyguards.'

'These lictors half a mile away,' said Byrd, 'in a marsh.'

I smiled at Abgarus. 'My thanks to you. How can I reward you?'

'I have lived in Carrhae all my life, lord, and made a good living until the Romans came and brought with them their taxes. Now I live in penury.'

From his appearance I knew he was telling the truth.

'Their expulsion from Carrhae will be reward enough.'

Byrd thanked him and tossed him a bulging leather pouch. Abgarus' eyes lit up when he looked at the contents and began whistling as he tapped the donkey on the flank and rode back down the road to Carrhae. I had a feeling that he was poor no longer.

Byrd led the way as we left the road and headed in a southeasterly direction, riding over slightly undulating ground towards the hills of Sinnaca. The scrub was getting thicker now with small groups of oak and almond trees dotting the landscape. Byrd slowed his horse as a great expanse of marshland loomed into view, a lush green area of reeds, grasses and low-growing shrubs. The Romans were in the process of extricating themselves from this wetland, to head for the steep slopes of the hills that rose up on our left.

'Why would they enter such terrain?' asked Gallia.

'Get lost in dark,' replied Byrd, 'no moon last night.'

Our attention was diverted from the Romans in front of us by the sound of trumpets and I saw a second Roman force appear from those hills and began descending the slope. I estimated their strength to be four cohorts as they marched slowly down the hill to place themselves between Crassus and us.

Surena drew his sword and pointed it forward to signal the advance to his officers behind. We had perhaps two thousand horse archers to throw against two thousand Romans rapidly descending the hill to face us, plus perhaps another three thousand under Crassus. The ground was covered in bushes and we were on the edge of a marsh, which meant we would not be able to outflank the enemy, with the wetlands on one wing and the hills on the other. We would have to charge straight at the Romans, who even though were tired, hungry and deficient in weaponry would still be able to lock shields and halt our advance. We might be able to stand off and shoot down their front ranks but Crassus could still escape into the hills.

'Surena,' I said, 'we cannot destroy them.'

He held up his hand to stay his officers and then turned in the saddle to look at me.

'We have them, lord. One more charge and we will rid the world of Crassus.'

I smiled though I could have wept. 'We cannot outflank them and our horse archers are already low on ammunition. After they have used up all their arrows they will not be able to cut their way through ten ranks or more of legionaries.'

'My other horse archers and your cataphracts will be here soon,' he insisted, 'we can hold the enemy's attention until they arrive.'

I admired his tenacity but the thickening ranks of Romans in front told me our efforts would be futile. Whoever commanded the group of legionaries that had been on the hillside had not only saved Crassus but also his campaign. Now he would escape into the hills, return to Syria and raise another army. I suddenly felt tired and old as the fruits of our great victory withered before my eyes.

'What now?' asked Vagises as Surena slammed his sword back in its scabbard in frustration.

'We watch the Romans withdraw up the hillside,' I said.

The enemy force that had descended the slope to face us was now fully deployed and presented a shield wall to deter our arrows, with the ranks behind holding their shields above their heads to defeat our missiles. Remus scraped at the ground as more and more of Surena's horse archers swelled our ranks. It made no difference: we could have fifty thousand men and would still not be able to break the enemy before Crassus escaped. Then I saw a handful of white-robed individuals scrambling up the steep grassy slope and knew they were the lictors, which told me that the governor was with them, though I could not identify him.

I pointed at the small white figures ascending the hill. 'You see those men wearing white, they are the lictors and Crassus is with them.'

'How far are they away?' asked Gallia.

'Seven hundred paces, perhaps more,' said Vagises.

410

She pulled her bow from its case and nocked an arrow in the bowstring. 'Amazons! Aim shots at those whites figures on the hillside.'

'You are wasting your arrows,' I told her as she released her arrow at a high angle, the missile arching into the sky and disappearing from view. Seconds later dozens of arrows were flying towards the Romans scrambling up the hill as the Amazons vented their frustration.

'Excellent idea,' said Surena, who likewise began taking shots at the soldiers ascending the hill. Soon the front ranks of his companies arrayed in a line behind us were also loosing arrows, which as far as I could tell were having a negligible effect. I nudged Remus forward and then wheeled him about before raising both my arms.

'Stop shooting!'

Surena gave the order to desist shooting as one by one the Amazons lowered their bows and finally Gallia also halted her efforts. I returned to her side and looked at her half-empty quiver.

'You might need the rest of them.'

'At least Crassus would have had to duck his head,' she sniffed.

Those Romans who had been wading through the marsh had now all ascended the hill, after which those with locked shields in front of us began to inch to their right to follow them, all the time retaining their *testudo* formation. We sat on our horses and watched them go. There was no point in wasting any more arrows. We might kill a few and injure more but our prize had alluded us and with it the chance of outright victory.

It took at least half an hour for the huge *testudo* to traverse the slope and join the Romans who had been under Crassus' command. While they did so I discussed our next move with Surena.

'We should demand the surrender of Carrhae,' I said, 'and after that the other towns occupied by the Romans in this region – Nicephorium, Ichnae and Zenodotium. When the Romans return next year they will find that their defences and garrisons will have been greatly strengthened.'

'And Syria?'

I looked at him. 'What of Syria?'

'We are close to the border, lord, and could raid the Roman province with ease.'

I thought of the strong and high walls of Antioch. 'We will not be able to storm Antioch or any other town or city. That being the case, the most we could achieve would be to ravage the countryside.'

'At least that would give the Romans a taste of what they have inflicted on others,' said Gallia.

I doubted whether we would kill any Romans using such tactics. More likely the only people that would be affected would be poor Syrians trying to make a living.

'I will consider it,' I replied.

'Why aren't they moving?' asked Vagises, looking up at the enemy on the hillside.

411

I looked at the Romans who had formed into a long line of centuries arrayed several ranks deep facing our left flank in the plain below. But Vagises was right: they were standing immobile on the hillside around six hundred paces from us.

'Perhaps they intend to attack,' suggested Surena.

In the next few minutes we hurriedly redeployed and swung our line through ninety degrees to face the Roman line, our horse archers manoeuvring their companies into line order to match the extent of the enemy's frontage. There certainly seemed to be a high level of activity among the Roman ranks, with officers and centurions running around between the centuries and then towards the rear where the white-attired lictors stood out against the green background.

'I'll warrant you wished you hadn't wasted those arrows now,' I grinned at Gallia, who scowled back at me.

We stood ready to face the Roman onslaught but as the minutes passed the more I realised that such a manoeuvre would at best be ill advised and at worst suicidal. To launch an attack down a steep hill would result in units becoming disorganised and they would have to redress their lines at the bottom, prior to a charge. And even if they launched a charge we would simply withdraw before them. And what then? They would not wish to get back into Carrhae having crept out from there under cover of darkness; rather, they would have to retreat back up the hill. It made no sense.

'They are not going to attack,' I said, 'pass the word to stand at ease.'

'What are they doing, then?' asked Gallia.

I patted Remus on the neck. 'I have absolutely no idea.'

'I will ride up there and demand their surrender,' announced Surena with a wide grin across his face.

We all laughed at his proposition, but as sun beat down on us and the Romans continued to stand on the hillside his plan sparked an idea in my mind. I turned to the King of Gordyene.

'Surena, perhaps we might yet secure an advantage from this curious situation. I would ask you to go to the Romans under a flag of truce and request a meeting with Crassus regarding a peace treaty.'

Gallia, who had taken off her helmet, rolled her eyes. 'Why don't you send a squire instead, Pacorus, someone far more appropriate for dealing with the Romans than a king?'

'I don't mind, lady,' said Surena, 'anything rather than sitting here being bored to distraction. What terms do you demand, lord?'

'The immediate evacuation of all Parthian territories and a cessation of hostilities between Rome and Parthia for five years.'

Gallia burst out laughing. 'And ask Crassus to come down and clean Pacorus' armour at the same time, for you have more chance of achieving that than the aforementioned demands.'

I frowned at her to indicate my displeasure but she waved away my annoyance. Vagises grinned at Surena as he pulled his bow from its case and unfastened the bowstring, before riding forward holding the disabled weapon aloft so the Romans could see that he came in peace. He rode up the grassy slope with some difficulty, his horse losing its footing a couple of times. A group of men left the enemy ranks and came down the slope to meet him, centurions judging by the transverse crests on their helmets. I saw Surena pointing back to where we were sitting and then gesturing with his arms, then one of the Romans left them and went back up the slope to pass through the long line of centuries and stop at a group that included the lictors.

Gallia was clearly bored by it all. 'We should ride back to camp and then return to Hatra. Hopefully Orodes has had better luck than us.'

'We have still mauled the enemy and prevented them from invading the empire,' I reminded her, 'you are too harsh in your judgement.'

'You have won a victory but not the war,' was her unrelenting comment.

I gave the order for the horse archers behind us to dismount as midday approached and the sun roasted our backs, swarms of small flies from the marsh adding to our general discomfort as they plagued both horses and men. Eventually Surena returned with news that Crassus would consider my offer and give his answer presently.

'He and his men will be gone within the hour,' said an increasingly irritable Gallia.

I was apt to agree with her but then there appeared to be a great commotion on the hillside as we saw figures running around again and apparently arguing with legionaries in their ranks. I had no idea what was happening and neither did anyone else, but then a small group began to slowly descend the slope and head towards us. There were eight of them, seven attired in bronze muscled cuirasses, red-crested helmets, white pteruges around their thighs and shoulders and red cloaks pinned on their right shoulders. They formed a guard around a bald-headed man of medium height wearing a white tunic with purple stripes and a purple cloak – Marcus Licinius Crassus.

I rode forward with seven companions to match the number of Romans: Gallia, now with her helmet back on her head, Zenobia who carried my banner, Surena, Vagises, Malik, Byrd and Surena's second-in-command, a sour-faced man with a long scar on the side of his neck called Exathres. As we approached the Romans I saw that every one of their officers had their swords sheathed, a good omen.

We walked our horses forward in a line as the Romans adopted a similar formation, Crassus directly opposite me. At a distance of twenty paces from each other the two groups halted as if by mutual consent and stared at each other. Epona flicked her tail, Remus chomped on his bit while Surena swatted away a fly that was pestering him.

I raised my right hand. 'Greetings Marcus Licinius Crassus, Governor of Syria and consul of Rome.'

Crassus showed me a faint smile, though he looked very tired and slightly nervous. He raised his right hand in return.

'Greetings King Pacorus, son of Varaz of Hatra, Lord High General of the Parthian Empire.'

'It is with regret that we meet under such circumstances,' I said, 'but I hope that we may yet depart as friends.'

'Friends do not make war on each other,' retorted Crassus.

'Or invade each other's territories,' snapped Gallia.

The high-ranking Roman officers looked angrily at the helmeted figure wearing a mail shirt beside me but Crassus nodded knowingly.

'I do not think that we have been introduced,' he said to Gallia. 'You know my identity and I suspect I know yours, but perhaps we may be formally acquainted.'

Gallia snorted in contempt but fortunately her cheekguards masked her disdain, but then she slowly removed her helmet to reveal her face.

'I am Gallia, Queen of Dura,' she announced, fixing Crassus with steely blue eyes.

Crassus pointed up at me. 'Twenty years ago your husband came to my house in Rome and during our conversations he talked of your beauty, and even though it was two decades ago I can see why he was so eager to talk of your splendour.'

Gallia was unmoved by his flattery. 'Ten years ago your dog, Lucius Furius, came to my city and tried to take it. Just like you his army was defeated and he himself was killed.'

The other Romans with Crassus bristled at her words but Crassus raised his hand to quieten them. I frowned at Gallia but she was unapologetic and continued to taunt Crassus.

'Have you come to beg for your life, governor?'

Crassus did not rise to the bait but I could see that his officers were livid at the effrontery being shown to their commander.

'I have come here because your husband requested a parley. But perhaps you would rather shoot me down with your bow, warrior queen of Dura?'

Gallia reached behind and pulled her bow from its case, prompting the Roman officers to draw their swords and close around Crassus.

'You think I would not, Roman?' hissed Gallia.

Crassus gently pushed his officers away and clasped his hands in front of him. 'Your reputation as a slayer is know throughout the whole world, lady.' He spread his arms wide. 'If you wish to kill me then here I am. A famed archer such as yourself will have no difficulty hitting me from such a close range.'

'There will be no violence!' I said firmly. 'We are not here to fight but to determine once and for all the border between the empires of Parthia and Rome.'

Gallia sneered at Crassus and replaced her bow in its case. Out of the corner of my eye I saw Zenobia pass my standard to Byrd who sat next to her but thought nothing of it.

'Do you hold the authority to determine such a thing?' asked Crassus mischievously.

'I am lord high general of the Parthian Empire,' I replied, 'entrusted by King of Kings Orodes to negotiate with the enemies of the empire.'

Crassus looked around. 'And where is King Orodes?'

'Chasing what remains of the Armenian Army back north,' remarked Surena, his subordinate stifling a laugh.

'And you are?' snapped Crassus, cracks appearing in his composure.

'Surena, King of Gordyene,' announced Exathres, 'the scourge of Armenia.'

Crassus' eyes narrowed as he studied Surena.

'Artavasdes is not his father,' I said, 'his brother was defeated and killed before the walls of Hatra and now High King Orodes campaigns in Armenian territory. Your ally has been emasculated, governor.'

Whether he had heard of the crushing Armenian defeat I did not know, but even if he had not and did not believe me he knew that his own army had been destroyed and also that Artavasdes was unable to offer him any immediate aid.

'Your slave state has been crushed,' gloated Gallia.

'And now you seek to make me a slave, is that it?' said Crassus with irritation. 'Is that why you insist I stand on my feet while you all sit on horses?'

He was right: it was an insult for us to be in our saddles and speak down to him. He was, notwithstanding his defeat, still the governor of Syria.

'Vagises,' I said, 'please let the governor sit on your horse.'

An unhappy Vagises slowly dismounted and then led his horse towards Crassus. His path was blocked by one of the governor's subordinates, who pushed him aside roughly and tried to grab his horse's reins. Vagises, his right hand tangled in the leather straps, pushed the man away with his other arm as his horse began to panic and back away. But the Roman, like the other officers, was still holding his sword and without thinking lunged forward and drove the blade through Vagises' back. Or perhaps he was thinking and had had enough of being taunted by enemies on horseback, one of whom was a woman.

I cried out in anguish as blood came from Vagises' mouth, he fell to his knees and then pitched forward to lie face-down on the ground. I heard a hiss by my right ear and saw Gallia's arrow go through the bronze cuirass of Vagises' killer and then saw Zenobia kill another Roman. Crassus turned-tail and began running back up the slope as Malik's horse bolted forward and he sliced open a Roman helmet with his sword. Zenobia dropped another Roman with an arrow in his thigh, the man yelping in pain before he was silenced forever by Surena's sword. Byrd's horse reared up on its hind legs and threw him to the ground with a loud crack.

Zenobia put an arrow in another Roman as a second ran at me and tried to ram the point of his *gladius* under my cuirass and into my belly, but I drew my *spatha* and whipped it down hard onto his forearm, the blow shattering the bone and reducing the limb to a useless bloody pulp. He uttered a high-pitched scream and then rolled around on the ground in pain before Malik jumped down from his horse and silenced him. The last Roman officer was killed by Surena and Exathres, who manoeuvred their horses either side of him and then rained down blows on his head and shoulders, inflicting terrible wounds on his neck and face, notwithstanding that he was wearing a helmet. They laughed as they toyed with him, alternating sword blows to stab and slash him. His *gladius* was knocked from his hand when a downward strike by Exathres sliced open his knuckles, then Surena used all his strength to deliver a sideways sword strike against the side of the Roman's helmet, which knocked him to the ground. Half unconscious, he tried to crawl away but Exathres jumped from his saddle, kicked the man hard in his side and then stamped on his back. The Roman made no movement as Exathres stood over him, grasped his sword with both hands and held the point against the rear of his neck, before thrusting the blade down.

I heard another twang and saw the figure of Crassus stagger a few feet as Gallia's arrow hit him in the back. He had managed to run around a hundred paces before he was hit but he got no further. On the hillside above the Roman soldiers stood impassively in their ranks and made no attempt to save their general. How low their morale must have been.

'Go, bring me the head and right hand.'

I turned to see Exathres regain his saddle and then gallop forward to where Crassus was crawling forward on the ground. Surena's lieutenant jumped from his saddle, pulled out his dagger and slit Crassus' throat, then proceeded to hack off his head with his sword, and all the while the legionaries above stood as witnesses to the violation of their commander's body. I had no stomach for this. I turned and waved a group of Dura's horse archers forward.

'Retrieve the body of Lord Vagises,' I ordered their commander.

I rode past a smirking Gallia. 'Satisfied?'

'Immeasurably,' she purred.

Malik was helping Byrd back into his saddle. 'Ankle broken,' winced Byrd.

'Get him back to camp,' I instructed Malik. 'Everyone, fall back,' I ordered.

I left Surena and rode with the others back to our waiting soldiers and then withdrew through the ranks of the horse archers of Gordyene. I turned to see their king actually riding forward up the slope to be nearer the Romans but for what reason I knew not. I found out later when he and his horsemen returned to camp with two thousand Roman prisoners. Now we had around ten thousand captives to take back to Dura, from where they would be sent to Seleucia.

'Orodes can deal with them,' I said to Gallia as we stood watching flames consume the body of Vagises. 'He can have the Roman eagles and all the other standards we have taken. I have fulfilled my duty and now I am going home.'

I felt her hand in mine. '*We* are going home.'

I glanced at Surena on the other side of me. 'Was there any need for that?'

'What, lord?'

'Cutting off Crassus' head,' I answered.

'I will send it to Orodes so he can show it to the Armenians. His right hand too.'

'His hand?'

He smiled triumphantly. 'I had his right hand cut off as well, the common punishment for thieves.'

The next day we began the march back to Dura. I sent couriers to Hatra with the news that Crassus was dead and his army defeated and that troops should be sent west to secure those towns in the west of the kingdom that I knew would now be abandoned by their Roman garrisons. Surena despatched Exathres north with a company of horsemen to take his grisly gifts to Orodes so I gave him a note for the high king informing him of our victory and hoping that he had met with similar success. Surena was eager for more battle and declared his intention of joining Orodes prior to returning to Gordyene. So I gave him all the captured eagles, except the one that never left the side of Spartacus, the booty from the Roman camp and all the enemy prisoners and bade him farewell at the Khabur River, before the King of Gordyene journeyed on east. We went south to join the Euphrates to follow the river back to Dura.

We retained one of the captured Roman wagons to transport Byrd back to the city as his leg wound was worse than we first thought and it was impossible for him to ride in the saddle. I continued to let Zenobia carry my banner now that Vagharsh was dead, which led to great excitement among the Amazons. Gallia was in high spirits at the prospect of seeing our daughters again. We rode along the northern bank of the Euphrates past well-tended fields, peaceful and prosperous villages before crossing over the stone bridge north of Dura.

Fishermen manoeuvred boats on the river and cast their nets in the water. Near the bank naked children splashed in its cool waters and waved to the cataphracts in their white tunics and floppy hats as they passed. War and death seemed a million miles away as the aroma of camels wafted into our nostrils when we rode by the park that accommodated the animals of the trade caravans. The road leading to the pontoon bridges over the Euphrates and west to Palmyra was filled with traffic as the commercial life of the city continued undimmed and untroubled by Romans or Armenians.

The imposing sight of Dura's strong yellow walls and the squat edifice of the Citadel always filled me with reassurance and pride. My spirits began to rise as the cataphracts, their squires, Byrd's scouts and the horse archers peeled away to pitch their tents in the legionary camp west of the Palmyrene Gate. I rode with Gallia, Spartacus still clutching his eagle, Byrd in the wagon, Malik and the Amazons through the city to the Citadel. I bowed my head to the stone griffin above the gates as a guard of honour from the replacement cohort hastily formed up by the gatehouse. Our progress from the Palmyrene Gate to the Citadel was slow as word spread that the king and queen had returned to the city and the main street began to fill with cheering crowds. Spartacus held his eagle proudly aloft, the queen touched outstretched hands and young women begged Malik for kisses. And on a barren hillside north of Carrhae, crows picked at the headless body of Marcus Licinius Crassus.

Chapter 19

In the days following our arrival back at Dura couriers brought happy news from Orodes. His march north had turned into a victory procession as the Armenians abandoned Nisibus and Gafarn took possession of the city and all the surrounding villages that had been previously under enemy occupation. Then Orodes had crossed the border into Armenia and advanced to the gates of the Armenian capital, Armavir, deploying his army around the walls and showing Marcus' great siege engines to the garrison. Rather than seeing his city reduced to rubble and the population butchered, and more importantly to save his own skin, Artavasdes sent a delegation to Orodes offering a peace treaty. The high king agreed, though the conditions to guarantee Parthian friendship were harsh and Armenia became a client state of the empire and was forced to pay huge reparations to Hatra for the previous occupation of its territory.

'So Armenia becomes the slave of Parthia rather than Rome,' observed Gallia as she read Orodes' voluminous correspondence on the palace terrace.

I had little sympathy for the Armenians. 'I have no pity for Artavasdes. He is lucky to escape with his head. If I had been before the walls of Armavir he would not have been so lucky.'

She gave me back the letter. 'So the legions suffered no further casualties?'

I looked at the empty chair of Dobbai near the balustrade. 'It would appear so, though the casualties of this campaign have been grievous indeed. I wonder when my turn will come?'

Gallia looked at me and then at the chair. 'What do you mean?'

'I am the last survivor of those who took part in Dobbai's ritual. She, along with Domitus, Kronos, Vagises, Thumelicus, Vagharsh and Drenis, are all dead. I alone live. For the moment.'

'Perhaps the gods have spared you,' she said, more in hope than certainty.

I smiled faintly. 'Perhaps.'

'Did you notice in Orodes' letter that Gafarn had agreed to his youngest son marrying the daughter of Artavasdes?' she said, changing the subject.

'Yes. Young Pacorus is to be a future ruler of Armenia, it would seem.'

She screwed up her face. 'I do not approve of such things and am surprised that Gafarn would be a willing accomplice to condemning his son so.'

I laughed. 'Condemning? If you mean he has condemned Pacorus to a life of privilege, of being fed on the finest foods and sleeping in silk sheets and being waited on hand and foot by an army of courtiers, slaves and having a whole kingdom fawn at his feet, then I suppose you are right.'

'Don't be clever, it does not suit you.'

419

I saw Claudia come from the palace onto the terrace. 'Talking of which, we should start thinking of a husband for our eldest daughter.'

Claudia heard my remark. 'I will not be marrying anyone, father. It is not my destiny.'

'I will decide your destiny,' I teased her.

Her brown eyes flashed annoyance. 'Is that what you really believe?' She had inherited her mother's cheekbones and shapely figure and was turning into a great beauty, but her custom of wearing black robes and maintaining an aloof air made her severe and unapproachable. Too many years spent in the company of Dobbai had robbed her of her childhood and now the old woman's influence was threatening to deprive her of her womanhood.

'How is Byrd?' asked Gallia.

He had been placed in one of the palace's bedrooms so his broken leg could be attended to, which Claudia informed me would not heal properly.

'I have placed adder's tongue wrapped in cloth on the area of the break but the bone is too baldy shattered to heal properly.'

'You put a snake's tongue on Byrd's leg?' I said with disgust, 'no wonder it will not heal.'

She may have just turned thirteen years of age but Claudia was wise beyond her years. 'Adder's tongue is a healing herb, father, as most people know.'

'I have also placed a charm in his room to ward off evil and have asked for the assistance of Gula, goddess of healing, to look favourably on him,' she continued.

'What charm?' I asked.

She walked over to Dobbai's chair and sat in it. 'Elderberries, rosemary and tarragon all mixed together and wrapped in a white cloth tied together with red twine. Tarragon is a favourite herb of the goddess and will prevent the leg becoming rotten.'

'So it will heal?' I said.

She looked at me and sighed. 'The leg has been saved and Byrd will be able to walk on it after a fashion, but it will be painful for him to do so. He will probably need a crutch.'

'For how long?' I asked with alarm.

'For the rest of his life, father.'

The pall of gloom that had hung over me after the Battle of Carrhae suddenly returned as I realised that if my daughter's words were true then I had lost my chief scout. Gallia saw my head sink.

'Perhaps his leg will heal properly.'

'No, mother, it will not.'

The appearance of Spandarat lightened the mood somewhat. He had finished making his final rounds in his capacity of military governor of the city and now pulled up a chair, leaned back in it and belched, much to the consternation of Claudia.

'So, I suppose you want your city back?' he said to me.

'I would be most grateful.'

His eyes sparkled mischievously. 'Now that you have beaten the Romans you will be leading an expedition into Syria, no doubt.'

I shook my head at him. 'Not this year, Spandarat, but I promise that if there is an attack against Syria you and the other lords will be accompanying me.'

He rubbed his hands with glee. 'I have heard that Syria is dripping with riches.'

Claudia rolled her eyes and Gallia smiled. He may have been the foremost lord of the Kingdom of Dura but he was just an old horse thief at heart.

'Syria also has cities with high walls,' I said.

He winked at Gallia. 'But no garrisons now you have killed them all. I heard you killed Crassus and chopped off his head.'

'I neither killed him nor severed his head,' I answered.

'Surena killed him after I had shot him,' said Gallia coldly.

Spandarat nodded approvingly. 'He had it coming. I just wish I had been there to see it. There's no one left to fight now the Armenians and Romans have been defeated.'

'There is always someone left to fight, Spandarat,' I said.

But it appeared that my roguish lord was correct in his assessment, at least initially. With an oppressive peace forced upon the Armenians and Crassus dead and his army destroyed it seemed that all Syria lay at Parthia's mercy. But for one young man such matters paled into significance before the prospect of seeing his beloved again.

Spartacus had wanted to ride straight to Palmyra the day after he had taken his eagle but I reminded him that he was a soldier in Hatra's army seconded to Dura and was therefore obliged to obey my commands. So he had ridden back to my city and in the days following had continually pestered me regarding when he would be allowed to go to Palmyra. So irksome did his tormenting become that I threatened to have the eagle melted down before his eyes unless he silenced his tongue. So he paced the palace muttering to himself until, a week after we had arrived back at the city, in which time Byrd's leg had healed sufficiently to allow him to ride in a wagon back to his wife, we set off for Palmyra.

Initially our column was small – the Amazons, Malik, Byrd sitting on a wagon, Spartacus, Gallia and myself – but the day after we had left Dura we were joined by Spandarat and half a dozen other lords, who wanted to see Haytham hand over his daughter to this upstart prince who had made good his vow. Spartacus himself rode at the tip of the column holding the eagle in his right hand, the sun glinting off its silver wings. He was so happy that he could have left his horse at Dura and ran the route to Palmyra.

As we neared Haytham's capital more and more of the curious, the religious and those who wanted to see a piece of history attached themselves to our column that now trailed behind us for several miles. On the third day a hundred Agraci warriors met us on the road to ensure that

421

Spartacus did indeed have an eagle, otherwise their commander was under orders to kill him on the spot – Haytham never forgot his threats. Malik smiled as the commander of the Agraci force insisted on touching the eagle to ensure it was really silver and not a piece of painted wood!

Malik slapped my nephew on the back and then left us to ride on with the warriors so he could be at the side of his father when the king honoured his promise. On the last night of our journey before we reached Palmyra there must have been over a thousand hangers-on attached to our party. Their commotion filled the night air as we sat on stools round a fire and Spartacus cradled the eagle in his arms.

'Where will you live?' asked Byrd, his splinted legged stretched out in front of him.

'I have given no thought to that,' answered my nephew. 'Hatra I suppose.'

I thought of Gafarn's hostility to the notion of his marriage and raised an eyebrow but said nothing.

'You will live in the palace at Dura, of course,' insisted Gallia. 'Rasha should spend the first months of her new life in familiar surroundings before you take her away from her people.'

Spartacus beamed with delight. 'Thank you, aunt, that would be most agreeable.'

Indeed it would, for he found the relaxed atmosphere at Dura far more convivial than the strict social mores that existed at Hatra.

'Nevertheless,' I added, 'as the heir to Hatra's throne you will be expected to make your home in the city, notwithstanding that by marrying Rasha you will relinquish its throne.'

'Parthians no like Agraci,' said Byrd, 'you will not find peace at Hatra. Will have to find your own kingdom.'

'I will find my own kingdom,' boasted Spartacus, his delirium of happiness having warped his senses, 'and I shall make Rasha its queen.'

'You know he just might,' Gallia whispered to me as Spartacus took the gleaming eagle over to Byrd to show it off to him.

Later, as she lay beside me in our tent, I kept thinking about Byrd's words.

'He is right.'

Gallia was drifting off to sleep. 'Mmm?'

'Byrd. He was right about Spartacus and Rasha not being able to live in Hatra. The people would not look kindly on an Agraci princess in their presence.'

'You worry too much. Go to sleep.'

Dura was fast becoming a refuge for exiles, what with Gallia's offer that Spartacus and Rasha could live with us in the palace, plus Roxanne already living there and eagerly awaiting the return of Peroz. If they too got married I feared that the King of Carmania would not accept his son's union and might even banish him. All would be settled either way soon.

Roxanne was finding life as a prospective princess far more agreeable than that of a whore, albeit a highly paid one. Following her arrival at the palace she had been regularly entertained by Aaron and Rachel, Miriam and even Rsan, who felt it incumbent upon himself to offer her his hospitality as the future bride of Carmania's prince. Even the city's wealthiest residents had invited her to gatherings, no doubt hoping that by doing so they would ingratiate themselves with Prince Peroz, whose reputation had soared following his battlefield triumphs.

After my return to the city I had visited Miriam to convey to her my deep sorrow at the death of Domitus, a loss I think I felt more keenly than she did. They had only enjoyed a brief time together and now she was a widow for a second time. I was filled with remorse concerning his death but she was very kind as we sat in the mansion that they had made their home, assuring me that her god was kind and that she and Domitus would be reunited in the afterlife. I thought of my dead friend's worship of Mars, the Roman god of war, and wondered if that angry deity would release the soul of such a great warrior as Lucius Domitus to be with his wife. Shortly afterwards Miriam left the mansion to live in the residence of Aaron and Rachel, who were now parents to two young sons, preferring the laughter and unruliness of children to a life of lonely solitude. Thus once more did the mansion that had formally belonged to Godarz become empty.

The next day dawned resplendent and sunny with a slight easterly breeze that brought welcome relief from the heat that was already stifling by mid-morning. Long before that Spartacus had risen to prepare himself for the entry into Palmyra, ensuring his appearance matched his position as a Parthian prince. On his feet he wore black leather with silver studs and a silver horse's head at the top of the front and rear of each boot. His red leggings were striped with gold and he wore a long-sleeved white silk shirt over his silk vest. Over the shirt he donned an armour cuirass made up of overlapping silver scales that shimmered in the sunlight and resembled the skin of a mythical serpent. And his open-faced steel helmet had a large white horsehair plume that extended down his neck.

He had been grooming his horse, a great stallion from Hatra's fabled herd of whites, since before dawn so that its coat shone in the sun. On its back was a large red saddlecloth edged with silver with a silver horse's head in each corner, over which was a four-horned saddle made of red leather.

I certainly looked second-best in my repaired Roman leather cuirass, brown boots, tan leggings and white shirt, though at least my helmet sported a fresh crest of white goose feathers. For the entry into Palmyra Gallia and the Amazons all wore white horsehair crests in their helmets and white cloaks, though more to keep the sun from roasting their mail shirts than for ceremonial reasons.

Spartacus had no time for breakfast and paced up and down impatiently as we ate fruit, bread and cheese brought from Palmyra and washed it down with delicious wine.

'This is most excellent,' I remarked to Byrd.

'It is from Syria,' he said. 'I have agreement with the local vineyards.'

'Is there no end to your business interests, Byrd?' I said, raising my cup to him.

'I was a salesman before I became a scout,' he replied.

'You should have something to eat,' I said to Spartacus, who had drawn his sword and was inspecting the burnished blade closely for blemishes, 'and at least drink something. You will sweat buckets in this heat.'

He held his head close to the blade and looked along its length. 'I have no time, lord.'

'You look every inch a prince,' said Gallia, smiling as Spartacus sheathed his sword and then grabbed the shaft of the eagle that he had thrust into the ground. 'But Pacorus is right, you should eat something.'

So he sat beside me and gulped down some fare as around us the small army of onlookers gathered to follow our column into Palmyra.

The settlement seemed to grow every time I visited it, tents and corrals holding camels, donkeys and horses spreading out from the lush date palm forest that surrounded the great oasis in all directions. It was a veritable city and I knew that soon stone buildings would be dotting the landscape for Malik had told me that he intended to turn Palmyra into a great city like Dura when he became king. But that was in the future. Today we rode through a multitude of tents so that my nephew could claim his bride.

Word had reached Palmyra of our approach and a mile from the settlement we encountered great crowds of Agraci blocking the road and reducing our progress to a crawl. Spartacus was most annoyed and became angry when well wishers wanted to lay their hands on both him and his eagle, proclaiming that the latter was sent from the gods and was capable of granting wishes to those lucky enough to touch it. How bizarre are the thoughts of those whose existences are so miserable that they believe a piece of metal will transform their lives. Gallia sent forward a score of Amazons to rescue him from the throng, who placed themselves between the excitable people and Spartacus.

Half a mile from Palmyra two hundred black-robed warriors arrived to quicken our journey, using their spears to clear the road and striking down a handful of unfortunates who refused to get out of their way. Their commander rode up to me and put aside his black headdress.

'Lord Yasser, it is good to see you.'

He offered me his hand. 'And you, lord king.'

He placed his right palm on his chest and bowed his head to Gallia. 'Welcome Queen Gallia, lioness of the desert.'

Gallia took off her helmet and gave him a dazzlingly smile. 'I always rejoice when I see Haytham's greatest warrior.'

Yasser raised his hand to Byrd who was riding on the wagon behind us.

'I trust your leg is healing, Byrd.'

'Of a fashion,' he replied indifferently.

Spartacus interrupted our conversation, clearing his throat loudly and looking at me imploringly. Yasser fell in beside me and nodded at him.

'Is that the eagle we have heard so much about?'

'It is,' I answered.

'And he took it, the standard of the enemy?'

I nodded. 'He did. Another six fell into our hands.'

He looked at me in astonishment. 'Six?' He looked behind him. 'Where are they, still at Dura?'

'He give them away,' said Byrd.

'News has spread of your great victory over the Romans,' Yasser said admiringly, 'people say that you will now take a great army west to conquer Syria, Judea and even Egypt. They say that Rome quakes at the mere mention of your name.'

Gallia laughed aloud.

'People are wrong,' I said, 'I desire peace not conquest.'

More of Haytham's warriors lined the route to his tent, the cheers of those standing behind him making Spartacus smile as he and we made our way to the centre of Palmyra. Sweat was coursing down my face and neck as the temperature continued to rise and my nostrils filled with the pungent aroma of camels and animal dung coming from nearby corrals. At least the abundance of date palms offered welcome shade as we trotted into the royal enclosure and halted in front of Haytham's great tent.

Standing near the entrance was the king himself, his large frame and head swathed in black robes, sword and dagger at his hip, Malik beside him and at least a hundred equally fearsome warriors grouped behind them. Standing to one side, dressed in a blue robe and adorned with the fabulous jewellery her father had purchased for her, stood a radiant Rasha.

Haytham gave me a slight nod but otherwise showed no emotion. Spartacus beamed triumphantly at Rasha, rammed the butt spike of the eagle standard into the earth and then dismounted, handing his reins to a slave who ran forward to take them. Other slaves, bare-footed with shaven heads, came forward to take Remus and Epona as we too dismounted. Gallia embraced Haytham and I clasped his forearm before we stood beside him. He beckoned Spartacus to come forward.

My nephew plucked the eagle from the ground, took a few paces forward and then rammed it into the ground again in front of Haytham.

'Behold, great king, a Roman eagle, taken from the enemy on the field of battle and now delivered to you. I fulfil my quest.'

Haytham folded his muscular arms.

'It is smaller than I imagined.'

Spartacus' face drained of colour. 'Lord?'

Haytham observed him with his cold black eyes, clapped his hands together and then roared with laughter.

'Go and claim your prize, boy.'

Spartacus gave a cry of triumph and then ran over to Rasha, the two locking in a passionate embrace. Haytham's warriors whooped, whistled and cheered and Gallia smiled.

'Did you think he would do it, lord?' I asked Haytham.

'I have to admit that I thought it unlikely, but he has proved that he is worthy to marry my daughter. His name is famous now, and yours more so after your triumph over the Romans. What does Pacorus of Dura ask of the Parthian Empire that he has saved from foreign conquest?'

'What it cannot give,' I replied, 'the return of the friends who have fallen in its service.'

'I heard about Domitus. He was a great warrior.'

That night there was a great feast in Haytham's tent. Spartacus ate little, drank much, got very drunk and passed out. Malik and I carried him to his tent that was closely guarded to ensure he did not sneak over to where Rasha slept. Not that he would be going anywhere in his inebriated state. Gallia told Rasha that she and Spartacus could live in Dura after they were married, which Haytham insisted should take place within a month.

I sat with Haytham and Malik, who had been reunited with Jamal, and watched Spartacus take part in drinking competitions with the king's warriors, who had taken to this strapping, brave young man who was going to marry their princess.

Haytham had been disappointed that Byrd had not stayed for the feast but his wound had flared up and Noora had insisted on taking him back to their tent.

'How bad is the injury?' asked the king, stuffing a handful of rice and raisins into his mouth.

'Claudia has said he will not ride again,' answered Gallia.

Haytham was perplexed. 'Claudia?'

'Our eldest daughter,' I told him.

'Yes, of course. She is a physician?'

'She was tutored by Dobbai, lord,' I said, 'and has knowledge beyond her years.'

'It is said that sorceresses choose a disciple to pass on the secrets of their craft. I often wondered why Dobbai went to Dura. Perhaps she saw in your daughter a suitable candidate to inherit her skills.'

I laughed off his suggestion but the more I thought about it the more likely it appeared to be. Dobbai had helped deliver Claudia into the world and had been by her side for the first twelve years of her life. I had never questioned why Dobbai had made Dura her home until now. She had fled Ctesiphon following Sinatruces' death and made her way to Dura, but even before then she had taken an interest in my life, selecting the griffin to be my symbol and sending me the banner that followed me on campaign and hung in my palace. Had my victories and the prosperity of my kingdom been purchased at the expense of my eldest daughter's soul? I prayed it was not so.

426

Haytham seemed pleased enough that Spartacus was to be his future son-in-law, pleased that he had captured a Roman eagle, which fanned the flames of his fame, and pleased that the heir to one of Parthia's greatest kingdoms was going to marry his daughter. The day after we had arrived Haytham invited them both to share breakfast with us as we sat cross-legged in the king's tent. My nephew was bleary eyed and slightly subdued as a consequence of his indulgence the night before but Rasha was bursting with excitement and happiness.

I broke off a piece of warm pancake from the large metal dish placed in front of us and dipped it into a pot of honey as the two love birds sat down beside each other, Rasha grinning at Gallia.

'You are to be married as soon as possible,' Haytham suddenly announced. 'Rasha should be settled to curb her rebellious nature.'

I saw Gallia stiffen beside me but I politely nodded in agreement.

'And you will be married here, at Palmyra.'

I nearly choked on my pancake, taking a gulp of water to wash it down.

'You disapprove, Pacorus?' queried Haytham.

Spartacus was now grinning like a simpleton, unaware that as a Parthian prince Gafarn would want his marriage to take place in the Great Temple at Hatra.

'Not disapprove, lord,' I replied, choosing my words carefully, 'but Palmyra might present difficulties as a venue.'

'I don't see why,' remarked Spartacus, his love for Rasha having blinded him to the obvious.

'Well, for one thing,' I said, 'your parents will be expecting your marriage to take place at Hatra in front of the city's nobility as befitting your status as the king's son.'

'The king of the Agraci would not be welcome at Hatra,' stated Haytham, 'and I will not be an exile to my own daughter's wedding.'

'Perhaps Gafarn and Diana could come to Palmyra,' offered Malik.

'The rulers of Hatra would not foul their feet by stepping on Agraci territory,' said Haytham. 'Is this not so, Pacorus?'

'My brother and his wife treat people as they find them,' I stated, 'and your own daughter, Rasha, has been a guest in their palace at Hatra. But as Parthian rulers you are correct to say that they would not travel to Palmyra, though out of political necessity and not personal choice.'

'They could marry at Dura,' suggested Gallia.

It was an excellent idea. Haytham had visited the city many times and though his first visit had elicited widespread fear and alarm among the population, his subsequent trips to Dura had seen the city's hostility steadily abate and now no one batted an eyelid at his stays. Rasha had her own bedroom in the palace and Malik was treated as one of the city's own.

'Not a bad idea, father,' he remarked.

'It is a place where Agraci and Parthian mix without animosity, father,' added Rasha.

427

Haytham drew himself up and looked at the couple. 'Very well, you shall be married at Dura. Once again the wisdom of its queen has triumphed.'

He nodded at Gallia and slapped me on the back.

Spartacus left with us the next day, Haytham standing beside his daughter holding the eagle as he bade us farewell. Before our departure we visited Byrd and Noora to ensure he was settled back in his home. Outside the spacious goat hair tent a great group of agents and officials waited to speak to the man whose business interests had spread as far as Egypt and Cilicia.

'I am sorry about Byrd's leg, Noora,' I said.

'I am not, lord, for it means that he will always be by my side now. Your wife told me that he will not ride again. I am sorry for you but rejoice that it is so.'

I embraced her and kissed her on the cheek. 'No wonder Byrd is so successful with such a wise woman by his side.'

'And what of you, lord, what will you do now you are famous throughout the world for slaying Parthia's enemies?'

I sighed. 'Now, Noora, I would like to enjoy the thing that has so far eluded me in life.'

'What is that?'

'Peace.'

But the prospect of peace and quiet was a distant dream in the weeks following as Dura was filled with foreign guests. But before they arrived the legions returned to the city. I watched from outside the Palmyrene Gate as the cataphracts and horse archers stood on parade and Chrestus led the white-uniformed legionaries back to their camp. The horsemen had returned to their barracks and forts, having relieved the lords' men, leaving the camp a great empty space. But now it was filled as the serried ranks of the Durans and Exiles, preceded by their golden griffin and silver lion standards, marched past their king and queen.

The 'staff of victory', now festooned with silver discs recording the army's many triumphs, was carried immediately behind Chrestus, who now commanded both legions. I had a lump in my throat as I watched the men march past and searched in vain for a stocky, muscular man wearing a helmet with a white crest and clutching a cane in his hand.

Accompanying Chrestus and his legions were Peroz and his horse archers, now created an honorary prince of Hatra by Gafarn following his success at the Battle of Hatra and his participation in the subsequent campaign against Armenia. He had also been given a large amount of gold by Orodes, part of the reparations paid to the high king by Artavasdes, so that he returned to Dura not only garlanded by honours but also a rich young man. He galloped up to where I was sitting on Remus beside Gallia and could not stop smiling, largely because I had asked Roxanne to be present when her love returned. Peroz manoeuvred his horse beside hers as his standard bearer rode forward with the flag bearing the golden peacock and took up position immediately behind him, next to Zenobia carrying my griffin banner.

The return of the legions presaged good news for couriers arrived at Dura that day with reports that Khosrou, Musa and Phriapatius had won a great victory over the northern nomads, a battle in which Attai had been killed and his army scattered to the four winds. Khosrou sent the enemy leader's head to Orodes as a gift and then pursued what remained of the nomads back to the shores of the Aral Sea. It was a resounding triumph and brought much-needed peace to the eastern half of the empire. Orodes himself returned to Seleucia and paraded the prisoners we had taken at Carrhae through the streets of the battered city before sending them to Margiana as a gift for Khosrou. There they would live out the rest of their lives as slaves in a land a thousand miles from Roman Syria.

'And what of Syria?' asked Gafarn as he relaxed on the palace terrace following his arrival with Diana and young Pacorus in the days prior to the wedding of Spartacus and Rasha.

The gazebo that had been erected for Dobbai brought welcome relief from the sun because this particularly summer was proving unrelentingly hot and any shade was a precious commodity.

'What about it?' I replied.

Gafarn smiled at me mischievously. 'Before he left for Seleucia Orodes was talking about you leading a great expedition into Syria in retaliation for Rome's aggression against the empire. Surena thought it an excellent idea.'

A serving girl in a white gown and white sandals on her feet offered me a cup of fruit juice. 'He would, but I will tell you what I told him. Attacking Syria is a waste of time and effort. Antioch's walls are too thick and without being able to capture the city any campaign will end in failure.'

'You will tell Orodes that?' asked Diana, who smiled at a servant when she was offered a pastry and thanked the girl. Even after all these years of wearing Hatra's crown she still thought of herself as a simple serving girl.

'I will,' I said firmly.

'Even though you have siege engines with which to batter down the walls of Antioch?' said Gafarn.

'What is the point of capturing a city only to abandon it?' I replied. 'Unless Orodes has indicated that he wishes to conquer Syria and make it Parthian.'

Gafarn shook his head. 'He has given no intimation that he wishes to conquer Syria.'

'Just as well,' I said, 'for he would also have to conquer Judea, Egypt and the other Roman territories to the north and south of Syria.'

'Would that be so bad?' mused Gallia.

'What Gallia really wants is for me to march on Rome itself and burn it to the ground,' I said.

'A noble enterprise,' she replied.

'Alas, my friends,' I said, 'we have more mundane matters to attend to, though perhaps not less noble. How do the people of Hatra feel about their prince marrying an Agraci princess, Gafarn?'

'Having been liberated from the Armenians and Romans,' he replied, 'they are in a deliriously happy mood and are indifferent to whomever Spartacus chooses to make his wife.'

'The people are fickle,' reported Diana, 'and so are Hatra's great lords and their wives. When we became their rulers they complained behind our backs and made plots against us, saying that we were low-born and had brought bad luck on the city. Now they commission bards to write poems of interminable length that tell of how Gafarn is the greatest king that Hatra has ever had, they order musicians to create songs that extol his manly virtues and how the gods sent me to rule over them.'

'Diana does not like to play politics,' said Gafarn, 'but I have to say that our position is infinitely more agreeable than it was before we crushed the Armenians and you defeated the Romans and killed Crassus.'

'I did not kill Crassus,' I protested, 'Gallia did.'

'He deserved to die,' said my wife, 'my only regret is that he did not perish in the Silarus Valley twenty years ago.'

'Time has not diminished your wrath,' Gafarn said to her.

'Nor that of my sister, it seems,' I added.

Adeleh had not accompanied Gafarn and Diana to Dura, notwithstanding the recapture of Nisibus and the humbling of Armenia.

'Alas for Adeleh,' said Diana, 'the loss of Vata has filled her with bitterness against the world.'

'Against the world or just against me?' I asked.

'She is much influenced by her sister, Pacorus,' said Gafarn. 'While we sit here Aliyeh and Atrax are at Nisibus.'

'You must not be too harsh on Adeleh,' said Diana, as ever playing the role of peacemaker, 'the death of Vata was a terrible shock.'

'She is young and can remarry,' I remarked harshly.

But any dark thoughts were quickly dispelled by thoughts of the upcoming wedding. Haytham and Malik arrived with Rasha and their warriors pitched their tents in a huge circle immediately south of the city, followed two days later by Orodes and Axsen with Babylon's Royal Guard. It was fortunate that Haytham, his son and their men decided to camp in their tents because the palace quickly filled with royalty when Silaces and Surena also arrived to attend the wedding. Fortunately Surena did not bring his Sarmatians but I had to order the evacuation of the legionary camp to accommodate the various contingents that all the kings brought with them. The last to arrive were Nergal and Praxima with five hundred of Mesene's horse archers, who added an additional burden to the logistics of the wedding.

Spartacus and Rasha spent most of the days before their wedding hunting with Haytham, Malik and Peroz, allowing myself and the other Parthian kings to discuss matters of strategy. We met in the Citadel's headquarters building where I informed Orodes that I was standing down as lord high general.

'I have held the position twice and have fulfilled my duty to the empire,' I stated bluntly. 'It is time for another, younger man to assume the mantle.'

Orodes seemed unsurprised. 'Very well, my friend, if that is your wish. Rather than a younger man I had thought of promoting Phriapatius to the position. He has been your deputy, after all, and the appointment would help to heal any lingering divisions between the east and west of the empire.'

'Excellent idea,' I replied.

'I also intend to send forces into Syria next year,' he announced.

I saw Surena nodding in agreement but decided to pour cold water on the proposal. 'Not a good idea.'

'You surprise me, Pacorus, given your long-standing rivalry with the Romans,' remarked Orodes casually.

'It is because I have known them for so long that I would counsel against an invasion of Syria. Those Roman troops still in the province will shut themselves up in the towns and cities and wait for reinforcements, which will undoubtedly be despatched.'

Orodes rested his chin on his hands. 'You are correct in what you say, from a military point of view, but I must retaliate against Rome otherwise I will appear weak. Your victories have restored Parthian strength and now it is time to wield that strength.'

The rest of the meeting was given over to happier matters, Orodes informing me that Axsen was pregnant and he was sending me a thousand talents of gold in gratitude for my service to the empire. It was an unnecessary gesture but he was in a gracious mood and was rewarding those who had been loyal to him. We all congratulated him on his forthcoming fatherhood, and though Nergal was pleased for his friend I thought I detected a glint of sadness in his eyes. Dobbai had once told me that Praxima would never bear children and her words had, sadly, turned out to be prophetic.

'What is your opinion of Peroz?' Orodes suddenly asked me.

'A fine young man,' I replied.

'I have spoken to him a great deal during our recent campaign against the Armenians and have come to the same conclusion. He will make an excellent king.'

'Brave and loyal,' concurred Nergal.

'Humble as well,' said Gafarn.

'While I am basking in the glow of victory,' said Orodes, 'I have to think about the welfare of the empire, and that means ensuring loyal kingdoms. That is why I intend to make Peroz King of Sakastan.'

The throne of Sakastan had been vacant for many years since its ruler, Porus, had been killed in battle when he had sided with Narses and Mithridates, in what seemed another lifetime. Narses had subsequently assumed control of Sakastan but since his death at the Battle of Susa it had been ruled by Orodes, along with the other kingdoms that also had vacant thrones: Elymais and Persis, Narses' old kingdom. Silaces had now returned to Elymais as its king and obviously Orodes intended to fill the other two thrones as quickly as possible.

I made no immediate reply, prompting Orodes' brow to furrow. 'You do not approve?'

'It is a bold move,' I replied.

'Bold, how?'

'He is to marry Roxanne soon.'

'Ah, yes,' said Orodes, 'I have heard much about her.'

'Though not perhaps that she was formally a prostitute in this city.'

Nergal's eyes locked on Orodes to see what his reaction would be as Praxima had been a whore while a Roman slave. Surena looked unconcerned – he had been raised among the reed huts and marshes of the Ma'adan after all – while Gafarn had grown up a slave in Hatra's palace. Among us only Orodes and myself had been born into royalty, privilege and tradition.

Orodes smiled. 'If I have learned anything these past few years it is that nobility is not the preserve of kings and lords but can be found in the most unlikely places.'

'His father does not know he has chosen a whore to be his wife,' I reminded everyone.

'Former whore,' Gafarn corrected me.

'What?'

Gafarn smiled at me. 'Well, I assume that she no longer practises her former trade.'

'Very clever, Gafarn.'

He pointed at me. 'If I can tolerate my son marrying an Agraci girl then I am sure Phriapatius can bear his youngest son taking this Roxanne as his wife.'

'Especially as he will be ruling the kingdom adjacent to his own,' added Orodes.

So that was that, Spartacus would marry Rasha and Peroz would marry Roxanne.

'And that only leaves the matter of Persis to be decided,' said Orodes. 'As one of the largest kingdoms in the empire its throne cannot remain empty.' He looked at me. 'I had thought of making it a gift for my retiring lord high general.'

The prospect filled me with horror. 'I have a kingdom, my friend.'

'You could rule them both,' suggested Orodes.

'Pacorus, King of Persis and Dura. It has a nice ring about it,' smiled Gafarn.

'You would be the first among equals,' said Surena admiringly, 'a fitting reward, lord, for Parthia's greatest warlord.'

They all voiced their approval of his words but I held up my hands, my cheeks colouring with embarrassment.

'Orodes, my friend, though I esteem your wisdom greatly I cannot accept your most generous offer. Dura is my home and I have spent too long away from it already. I have had but fleeting glimpses of my daughters growing up and now wish only to stay in the kingdom I have come to love.'

'I understand,' said Orodes, 'though I have one last call on your service before you hang up your sword.'

'I cannot imagine a time when Pacorus of Dura will ever hang up his sword,' remarked Surena.

'Nor I,' added Nergal.

But in the days following, when Gallia, Diana and Praxima painted Rasha's hands and feet with henna to bring her luck and good health during her married life and Agraci and Parthian laughed together, had drunken fights and afterwards, bloody and bruised, embraced and pledged oaths of friendship, ran camel races and revelled in each other's company, I stood above the Palmyrene Gate, to gaze west into the desert. I looked beyond the black goat hair tents, and was gripped by a strong desire to remain at Dura. What was all the fighting and death for if not to be able to live in peace afterwards?

Rasha and Spartacus were married on a beautiful summer's day, Shamash having cleared the sky of every cloud and provided a gentle breeze to ease our discomfort. I stood with my friends and watched the girl who had been like a daughter to me become the wife of Spartacus. Diana cried tears of joy for she had been the one who had carried him as an infant when we had fled the Silarus Valley following the death of his parents.

Alcaeus, his wiry hair now thinning and showing grey, smiled and shook my hand as the couple walked back to the city to attend the feast that had been prepared in their honour. He had been the one who had delivered the son of Spartacus all those years ago.

'Do you remember that night?' I asked him as we watched the newlyweds walk towards the city gates surrounded by a great throng of well-wishers.

'Like it was yesterday. They would have been proud, Claudia and Spartacus. I wished they could have been here to see it.'

I sighed. 'There are lots I would have liked to have been here to see today. We have lost too many.'

He slapped me on the back. 'Come, we need to get some food in your stomach to stop you getting morose.'

If eating was a cure for depression then I must have been deliriously happy that night as the palace kitchens produced a seemingly endless supply of cooked eggs, chicken, goat, mutton and fish. Beer and wine flowed like floodwaters through a wadi and loosened everyone's tongues to such an extent that by the time the servants lit the oil lamps hanging from the ceiling and walls of the banqueting hall I had to shout to make myself heard.

433

Despite his fearsome appearance and reputation Haytham made great efforts to be civil to both Gafarn and Diana. He knew their history, of course, and knew that Gafarn was a Bedouin who had been captured as a small child and raised as a slave in Hatra's palace. The Agraci waged constant war on the Bedouin who inhabited the southern part of the Arabian Peninsular, and their mutual animosity was age old. A part of Haytham probably wished that his daughter was marrying the son of one of his lords, but as he informed me long ago she had seen a world beyond the black tents of the Agraci and longed for adventure.

At the wedding I had told the newlyweds that they could reside in Miriam's mansion. She had given it back to the crown after she had gone to live with Aaron and Rachel. This solved the immediate problem of where they would live but offered no long-term solution.

'Would the people accept an Agraci princess among them, or even an Agraci queen?' Haytham was relaxed and happy as he sat on the palace terrace the day after the wedding, but his question was in the minds of all of us.

Gafarn rubbed his neatly cropped beard and glanced at Diana. 'We all like Rasha, King Haytham, and she has been a guest at Hatra as you know.'

Haytham held up a hand to Gafarn. 'We all like Rasha, King Gafarn, your son most of all. But you know as well as I do that the people of your kingdom will not accept her as the wife of your heir, much less as their queen.'

'I fear it is so,' said Diana sadly.

'They can stay at Dura then,' I offered.

Haytham shook his head as a steward brought me Najya, the saker falcon that he had given me years ago, and she walked onto my arm.

'I blame Pacorus for all this,' he said.

Najya craned her neck as I stroked her under her beak. 'Me. Why?'

Haytham winked at Gallia. 'Before you came to this city the Agraci and Parthians were quite happy butchering each other, raiding each other's lands and swearing oaths of vengeance so that our sons and their sons would carry on the blood-letting. But then you came and offered the hand of friendship, and against my better judgement I took it.'

He pointed at Malik sitting beside Jamal flanked by Byrd and Noora. 'My son became your friend and served in your army. Your scout became my friend and now owns half of Syria and Egypt.'

'An exaggeration,' protested Byrd, grinning.

He held out a hand to Nergal and Praxima. 'The friends of Pacorus rule their own kingdoms from the great marshlands in the south,' he pointed at Surena, 'to the high mountains in the north.' He smiled at Orodes. 'And some have become rulers of half the world.'

'Pacorus turned me,' continued Haytham, 'from a warlord into a merchant and now my daughter has married a Parthian. I sometimes wonder if it is not Pacorus who in fact wields the greatest power. He has defeated Parthia's internal enemies, laid low the Armenians and Romans and made peace with the Agraci.'

'I have been most fortunate in the choice of my friends, lord,' I replied.

'And your sorceress,' he insisted, 'for though she has returned to the realm of the gods we must remember that she spent years in this very palace, weaving her magic.'

'Pity she is no longer with us, she could have created a kingdom out of the desert for Spartacus and Rasha to rule,' remarked Gafarn irreverently.

Haytham looked at Orodes. 'If you conquer Syria then my daughter and her husband can rule it from the palace in Antioch.'

I looked at Gallia and shook my head. Everyone was becoming obsessed with Syria, forgetting that the Romans would not relinquish it without a fight.

That afternoon I went hunting with Haytham and Orodes, Rajya bringing down a brace of buzzards and Haytham's own falcon bringing down three more. Orodes broached the subject of Agraci warriors joining his expedition into Syria and the king said that he himself would not go but Malik was free to partake if he so wished. The two of them clasped forearms on it but I said nothing.

Three days later, on a sunny morning, we said goodbye to our friends in the courtyard inside the Citadel. A company of cataphracts stood on parade and the route from the Citadel to the Palmyrene Gate was lined with legionaries to honour our guests' departure. Grooms held the reins of horses as we all gathered at the top of the palace steps and said our goodbyes.

I can see their faces now – Haytham, Malik, Jamal, Byrd, Noora, Surena, Nergal, Praxima, Gafarn, Diana, Orodes, Axsen and Gallia – all full of life and happy that the great time of trial was over. Haytham and Malik left first, their black-clad bodyguard trotting after them as they rode through the gates of the Citadel and down the city's main street to the sound of cheers and applause from the crowds that stood either side of the road.

Orodes and Axsen followed them, the dragon-skin armour of their bodyguard shimmering in the sun as they followed the high king and his pregnant wife back to Ctesiphon and its treasury full of Armenian gold. Surena embraced me and then Gallia, whose animosity towards him had finally died, and then rode form the Citadel with a score of his spearmen. At the gates he turned his horse, drew his sword and saluted me, or perhaps he was paying homage to the place where his dead wife had been one of the Amazons, before cantering into the city.

The six of us who remained, who had known each other since our time in Italy, stood in silence and looked at each other. There were few of us left now, the Companions who had escaped from the clutches of Crassus and made our home in Parthia, fewer than forty out of the one hundred and twenty that had taken ship from Italy.

I looked over to the granite memorial in the wall next to the gates that held the names of those Companions who had fallen and shivered. There was space enough for forty more names and I wondered whose would be the last to be carved in the stone.

We embraced our friends and watched them depart the Citadel and then Gallia walked to the stables to fetch Epona for her morning training session with the Amazons. I walked up the steps and turned to observe a scene that was played out every morning of every day. Legionaries patrolled the walls, sentries at the gates directed visitors to report to the guardroom and squires and stable hands carried out their mundane duties. The commander of the parade of cataphracts drew his sword and saluted me as he gave the order for his men to be dismissed. A breeze blew across the courtyard and ruffled the pennants on the end of each *kontus*. I caught a brief glimpse of a red griffin against a white background and then turned and walked back into the palace.

After he had returned to Ctesiphon Orodes sent a steady stream of couriers to Dura requesting that I send forces into Syria to throw the Romans off balance and prevent them from rebuilding their legions and launching a fresh invasion of Parthia. I wrote back informing him that I had excellent intelligence via Byrd's network of informers that not only were the Romans not preparing a fresh invasion of Parthia, but that there were hardly any Roman troops left in Syria. Around ten thousand legionaries, many wounded and without weapons, had escaped in the aftermath of Carrhae and now waited behind their walls for a Parthian invasion of Syria.

After a few weeks of Orodes' continual pestering I gave up and summoned Spandarat to the palace to inform him that I was authorising him and his lords to raid Syria. He was delighted and within a week had amassed nearly ten thousand horse archers, who promptly rode across Dura's northern frontier and spent three weeks plundering anything in their path and destroying property. I had warned Byrd of the impending invasion and he had alerted all his agents and allies in Syria, who took themselves off to Antioch and Damascus along with all their possessions.

Once the Romans realised that the great Parthian assault was nothing more than a band, albeit large, of plunderers, they despatched parties of horsemen to chase away Spandarat and his fellow robbers. They achieved this without much difficulty but Spandarat returned to Dura delighted with himself, boasting of bringing back wagons loaded with statues, marble and jewels that he had plundered. It was all very unedifying but I comforted myself with the thought that at least I had satisfied Orodes' wishes.

Life at Dura went on as before. The caravans transported goods from the east and the west and paid their tolls, the farmers worked the land and paid their lords their rents who in turn paid tribute to the crown, the treasury filled and the army drilled and prepared for the day that the Romans returned. Phriapatius was made lord high general of the empire at a grand ceremony at Ctesiphon where he met Roxanne for the first time. If he had any misgivings about his future daughter-in-law he did not make them known and treated her with great respect and affection. He could afford to be magnanimous as his family's star was in the ascendant. He himself held the highest military position within the empire and his youngest son was the king of neighbouring Sakastan. And so he and Peroz returned to Puta, his father's capital, where the former prostitute Roxanne became a Parthian queen.

The gathering at Ctesiphon was a happy occasion where I renewed my friendship with Khosrou and Musa. They were both old and grey now though Khosrou had lost none of his ruthlessness and delighted in telling me that he had sent the head of Attai to Orodes as a gift.

'I did not see it above the gates when I arrived,' he complained.

'It probably rotted in the sun,' I said.

'Just like the bodies of all the other nomads,' grinned Musa.

He linked arms with Gallia and began to lead her away. 'It is very remiss of Pacorus to keep you all to himself, my dear. Come with me and let me show you my bodyguard. They collect the scalps of the enemy and tie them to their lances. They will be diminished next to your beauty, of course.'

Gallia smiled girlishly at him. 'You flatter me, lord.'

Khosrou shook his head. 'He never changes. Queen Sholeh keeps him in check, rules him and his kingdom like a rod or iron.'

'I trust your wife, Queen Tara, is well, lord?'

Tara hardly ever left Merv, his capital. I had met her once, at Hatra when my father had assembled the other kings who were fighting Mithridates. Like Khosrou she had a hard countenance but was actually a thoughtful and charming woman.

'She's well but has little time for the conversations of kings. But what about you, Pacorus, will you lead this great expedition west that Orodes is planning?'

My heart sank. 'I hope not.'

My reply surprised him. 'You are Parthia's greatest warlord, the slayer of Narses, Mithridates, the Armenians and the Romans. It will be expected that you will lead the army that extends the empire to the shores of the Mediterranean.'

'Is that what Orodes has told you?' I asked with alarm.

He shrugged. 'Not in so many words, but Syria lies open like a whore's legs and Orodes wants to be the bull who has her.'

'What of the northern nomads?' I asked, changing the subject, 'are they now subdued?'

He gave me a world-weary look. 'For the moment. But they breed like cockroaches and will return to torment me. Of that I have no doubt.'

He cast me a sideways glance. 'You might be fighting in Gordyene first, though.'

The last time I had seen Surena was at the wedding of Spartacus and Rasha and afterwards relations between him and Orodes deteriorated markedly. Having been left out of the treaty negotiations between Parthia and Armenia, Surena had continued to unleash his Sarmatian mercenaries against Artavasdes' kingdom, burning villages and taking Armenians as slaves, those he did not impale that is. Artavasdes complained to Gafarn who sent remonstrations to Vanadzor, which resulted in Surena's horsemen launching raids into the Kingdom of Hatra itself. Atrax rode to Vanadzor to plead personally with Surena but the King of Gordyene would not be reasoned with and afterwards sent a great raiding party south to burn Irbil. Fortunately it was intercepted and turned back at the Shahar Chay River but it confirmed to Orodes that Surena had to be dealt with.

Soon after the gathering at Ctesiphon Orodes mustered an army and invaded Gordyene to topple Surena. The latter rode out of his capital and gave battle in the valley before Vanadzor, leading a frantic charge in an effort to kill Orodes. But the cataphracts of Susiana, Hatra and Media cut down Surena and his army dissolved. The man who had been my squire joined in the afterlife the wife whose death had broken his heart. I did not blame Orodes for dealing with Surena in the way he did. His actions earned him the respect of the empire's other kings and showed that he was prepared to act ruthlessly to protect his own and the empire's interests. But I was saddened by the death of Surena and believed that Parthia would miss such a capable commander.

Spartacus and Rasha lived happily at Dura and paid frequent visits to both Palmyra and Hatra. The people of my home city gave them a polite, if not rapturous reception every time they stayed with Gafarn and Diana and after a while came to accept Rasha. But Gafarn and his blood son Pacorus were the future of the kingdom. My part in the Battle of Hatra was glossed over and after a while forgotten altogether as Gafarn's reputation soared and he was credited with single-handedly defeating the Armenians and reducing their kingdom to a vassal state of Hatra.

And in the aftermath of Carrhae it had been Surena who had been proclaimed the battle's victor after having returned with the captured Roman eagles and thousands of prisoners. I did not object. Surena had been a great warlord and deserved to be remembered. And I was delighted that Hatra was restored to its position as one of the strongest kingdoms in the empire, a land made rich by the proceeds from the Silk Road and kept strong by its mighty army, which was substantially increased. The defences of Nisibus were greatly strengthened so never again would an enemy capture it, as was Assur and the towns in the west of the kingdom.

Vistaspa grew old and frail and so Lord Herneus became the general of Hatra's army and Pacorus became Prince of Nisibus and Armenia. His parents may have been outsiders but he had been born in the city and to the people and nobles of the kingdom he was pure Hatran and worthy to wear the crown, even if he would have an Armenian queen.

Artavasdes, eager to please his new overlords, made frequent visits to both Hatra and Ctesiphon and although Gafarn and Orodes always invited me to the banquets they gave in his honour, I always found an excuse not to attend. I did not like Artavasdes and could never forget that he and his father had made war on Parthia when the empire had been at its most vulnerable. And now Artavasdes was seemingly a friend of Parthia, though I did not trust him. The fact that he had offered his own daughter to ease his difficulties made me despise him even more but in this I was in the minority. The world was changing but I refused to change with it.

Chapter 20

Andromachus had been expecting their arrival, having been alerted that they had left Palmyra a week earlier by a courier pigeon sent by Byrd. They arrived as dusk was enveloping the earth, twenty-six black-clad horsemen led by a man with long black hair accompanied by a great hound running beside his horse. Andromachus ordered the gates of his villa to be closed as soon as his intimidating guests had entered the compound. The last thing he wanted was to arouse the suspicions of the authorities in Antioch and there were always prying eyes in the area that were only too willing to reveal what they had seen for money.

The large frame of their leader slid from his saddle. 'It is good to see you again, Andromachus.'

'The same, Prince Spartacus. I trust your journey was uneventful.'

Spartacus smiled. 'Do not worry. Since entering Syria we have avoided the main routes so as not to arouse suspicion.'

Andromachus looked at the rough-looking warriors who stood beside their mounts, swords at their hips and daggers tucked into their belts, their faces adorned with black tattoos. They looked like demons from the underworld and even a glimpse of them would have aroused suspicion but he said nothing. The dog, an ugly great beast with big jaws and long legs, sat by its master and studied him with evil eyes. It then emitted a low growl at him.

'Scarab, quiet!' snapped Spartacus.

As the guards at his own walled villa were all Agraci Andromachus recognised the score of black-robed warriors who were now being escorted to the stables where they would unsaddle their horses, but the half a dozen others who carried bows and two quivers each were not of his race. He nodded at them.

'They are Parthian, are they not? Soldiers from your uncle's army, perhaps?'

Spartacus half-smiled. 'Former soldiers in my uncle's army. King Pacorus would not approve of this undertaking, I think.'

Women lit torches in the compound as Andromachus showed the prince of the Agraci to his room in the villa, his men having been allocated a stable in which to sleep. Normally he would not have allowed this group of assassins to use his property as a base from which to launch their nefarious activities, but this angry young man was both the nephew of Pacorus of Dura and the son-in-law of Haytham himself, the most powerful men in the lands adjacent to Syria. It was common knowledge that the Parthians were massing their forces for an imminent invasion of Syria, which made the presence of Spartacus all the more perplexing.

'When my uncle invades Syria in the coming weeks all the owners of the villas in this area will seek refuge in Antioch,' he explained, stuffing a portion of roasted chicken into his mouth and tossing the malevolent hound at his feet another piece. 'I do not want my quarry escaping me a second time.'

440

The next day Andromachus used a dagger to draw a map in the earth of the nearby villa they were going to assault. The men under Spartacus' command stood in a circle and studied the position of the outbuildings, the gates that gave access to the villa and the residence itself that were traced on the ground.

'On the ground floor the atrium,' said a kneeling Andromachus, 'leads to a reception hall that gives access to the peristyle, from which you can access the kitchens, slave quarters, dining room, study and lounge. All the bedrooms are on the first floor.'

'How many slaves?' asked one of the Agraci.

'Thirty or forty,' replied Andromachus.

'That many?' queried Spartacus.

Andromachus stood. 'The owner has expensive tastes.'

'What about guards?' asked another man with a thick black beard.

Andromachus pointed his dagger at the gates in the perimeter wall. 'Always two on the watchtower at the gates and another two at the entrance to the villa itself. The guards are housed in a small barracks building beside the wall around fifty paces from the villa.'

'Numbers?' asked Spartacus.

'A score of legionaries at least.'

They left later that afternoon, a guide provided by Andromachus leading them through the thick woods that covered the hills of Daphne, the area where the rich and powerful citizens of Antioch escaped the stench and noise of the city to relax in their expensive villas sited in lush countryside where the endless number of streams and waterfalls fed expansive groves of laurel, walnut, fig and mulberry. They dismounted among a wood of bay trees and then posted guards and waited for night to fall. Spartacus and the guide crept to the edge of the trees to observe the white-walled villa enclosed within a circuit wall positioned in a great clearing on a gently sloping hillside. Two gates gave access to the compound and there was a wooden watchtower overhead that gave an uninterrupted view of the valley below. Spartacus noted the pair of guards above the gates and two more standing beneath them either side of the open gates. There were no people or carts on the single track that led to the villa's entrance.

When night fell two men were left to guard the horses while the others walked slowly through the wood to the edge of the trees. There was no moon and they all wore black so there was little chance of them being spotted, but there was also no wind and absolute stillness permeated the darkness. The snap of a broken branch would easily carry to the villa.

So they trod carefully and slowly as they inched in a long line towards the shut gates. Spartacus felt a tingle of excitement ripple through him and he gripped the hilt of his sword. All the men with him were accomplished killers, the Parthians being veterans of many of his uncle's campaigns and the Agraci having been hand-picked by Haytham himself for their ruthlessness. After what seemed like an age they halted fifty paces from the gates and knelt on the soft grass. Torches that flickered in the compound behind illuminated the watchtower and its occupants, making the task of the archers who now nocked arrows in their bowstrings much easier.

There was a quick succession of sharp twangs and hisses as the archers shot their arrows and then the others raced forward. Spartacus smiled to himself as he heard moans and saw the two guards collapse as half a dozen of his men rested their backs against the wall and then clasped their hands together to form a step in which others placed their feet, before being hoisted up and over the wall.

Within half a minute everyone except the archers and Scarab were over the wall. Once inside the compound Spartacus ordered the beam that was slotted into brackets on the back of the gates to be removed to let his dog and the bowmen enter. The latter were directed to find the barracks building and keep its occupants penned inside as two men were left to guard the gates and the rest headed for the villa.

They kicked in the ornate doors and then swept through the villa's ground floor, past wall decorations showing images of Aphrodite and Dionysus, the deities of love and fertility, to search for the slave quarters. The oil lamps illuminated their passage as they raced into rooms with swords drawn. They knocked over statues of gods and goddesses, the noise waking slaves who staggered, bleary-eyed, into their path.

In the compound shouts came from inside the oblong building with a tiled roof that housed the villa's tiny garrison. Seconds later the door opened and two legionaries in tunics carrying javelins ran out, to be shot by the archers who stood waiting for them. They fell to the ground and moaned as a third Roman armed with a *gladius* followed and was felled by an arrow in his belly. The door was slammed shut as two more arrows smashed into it.

The quiet was pierced by high-pitched screams as the Agraci began slaughtering the slaves. A few of the male servants grabbed knives and other kitchen utensils and attempted to fight off the invaders but were swiftly cut down by sword strikes. Women and young girls, terrified and huddling together, were quickly separated and sliced open with knives and swords. They fell to their knees and pleaded for their lives but these men were assassins chosen for their expertise at killing and they were only interested in getting their task done as speedily as possible. Mostly they stabbed and hacked at half-naked bodies, spraying the intricate mosaics with blood and gore, though occasionally they broke a slender young neck.

Spartacus raced up the stairs with four others following, Scarab bounding ahead of them all, and came to a pair of red doors decorated with gold leaf. Spartacus kicked at the doors to force them open and then he was inside the room that smelt of incense. A woman, a servant, lunged at him with a knife in her hand but her arm was severed at the wrist by an Agraci sword. She clutched her stump and sank to her knees, whimpering before being silenced as the man who had cut off her hand sheathed his sword and slit her throat with his dagger, kicking her body to the floor.

Another woman, middle aged, her voluptuous figure draped in a white silk gown, stood transfixed as Scarab leaped at her and knocked her to the floor before savaging her neck and shoulders in a frenzied attack. She squealed in pain and fear as the beast ripped at her flesh, Spartacus grabbing its thick, iron-studded collar to pull him off the prostrate woman. He ordered one of his men to haul the dog, its face covered in blood, away as he squatted beside the woman, her breathing shallow, blood oozing from her neck wound to mix on the floor with her oiled, curly black hair. Her eyes, wide and filled with terror, looked at the hulking figure staring down at her.

'Make sure every one else on this floor is dead,' he barked to those behind him before he turned to look at the woman whose life was ebbing away.

'Queen Aruna, we meet at long last.'

The mother of Mithridates made to speak but Spartacus placed a hand over her mouth.

'Do not speak; I have no interest in what you have to say. Bitch!

'I have come to repay a debt. You conspired to have my uncle and myself killed when we visited Antioch. Your treachery killed most of our escort and my friend, who died at the hands of your lover. Well, he too died and now you are about to join him in the pit of the abyss.'

Aruna's eyes flicked right and left in a desperate search for solace but there was none. She tried to lift herself up but her efforts were feeble as more and more of her lifeblood seeped from her body onto the floor. Spartacus stood up and took a last look at the dying woman who had once been the high queen of the Parthian Empire, before turning and leaving the room, calling his dog after him as he descended the stairs and walked outside.

His men had conducted a thorough search of the villa and all the outbuildings to ensure no one was left alive, the archers still covering the entrance of the barracks with their bows.

'Burn them out,' ordered Spartacus to the commander of his Agraci.

The archers shot arrows at the shutters that barred the windows and the door while the warriors collected dry wood from storerooms and hay from the stables and loaded them on two carts that were then doused with oil and set alight, before pushing them against the building. Within minutes the carts were ablaze and the flames were lapping round the building. As the fire took hold of the carts the legionaries inside the barracks charged from the building, preferring to take their chances against men rather than being roasted alive.

Two were immediately felled by arrows but the rest, armed with swords and holding shields in front of their bodies, charged at the Agraci warriors who faced them in a semi-circle. Coughing, their eyes smarting, the Romans fought bravely, jabbing the points of their short swords at the fleeting shapes of the warriors they faced. But they did not see the archers who had retreated a few paces and who now searched out targets illuminated against the blazing building. The Agraci teased and taunted the legionaries as the archers picked them off one by one, the last one being killed as he fell to the ground with an arrow in his thigh and the side of his head caved in by a series of sword blows.

'Time to go,' shouted Spartacus, alarmed that the flames might be seen from afar.

They ran out of the compound back to the trees where they collected their horses and rode back to the villa of Andromachus. The next day Spartacus and his party departed and headed southeast into the desert, away from Syria and towards Palmyra. Once there Spartacus would ride back to Dura to prepare for the great expedition into Syria that was being prepared by his uncle.

Chapter 21

Two years after the Battle of Carrhae I led forty thousand horsemen into Syria to satisfy Orodes' requests. I took Dura's horse archers, all my lords, seventeen thousand of their men and riders from Hatra, Babylon and Mesene on a great raid that achieved absolutely nothing. The Roman survivors of Carrhae shut themselves in Antioch and we burned and looted many Syrian villages and small towns whose inhabitants had mostly fled before us. Several times the Romans ventured forth from their strongholds and slaughtered small parties of our horsemen but when we pursued them they invariably retreated behind their stonewalls. I eventually ordered a general retreat back to Parthia and never set foot in Syria again.

I thought the whole affair folly as it showed the Romans that Parthian horsemen were not invincible but Orodes was delighted, believing that the Romans would not provoke Parthia again. I had my doubts but for a while both the eastern and western frontiers of the empire were secure and at peace.

Orodes should have enjoyed a long and prosperous reign but the gods had decided otherwise for the birth of his son had been accompanied by tragedy. Three days after she had given birth to the boy they named Phraates in honour of Orodes' father, Axsen had died.

Orodes had visibly aged before our eyes as grief gripped him with a cruel intensity. He gradually handed over much of his power to courtiers who had too much authority and like all small-minded and mediocre men coveted influence and wealth. Whether Orodes resented the son whose birth had robbed him of his wife I did not know, but the boy grew up in a Ctesiphon once again poisoned by intrigue and ambition and came to despise his father. Pale and thin, Phraates hid his emotions and presented a mask of aloofness and coldness to the world.

As time passed Orodes shut himself off from the world, shunning his old friends as sorrow consumed him while his son's resentment against his father grew. When he reached his sixteenth birthday Phraates had him murdered before declaring himself king of kings. Shock reverberated throughout Parthia to be quickly replaced by outrage that a good and just ruler had been murdered, but the advisers of Phraates were clever and knew that there was no enthusiasm for a civil war to topple the young high king. Letters were sent from Ctesiphon to the various capitals in the empire demanding allegiance to Phraates and it seemed as though Mithridates had returned to the world. Perhaps he had, the gods having sent back his rotten soul in the body of his nephew.

I ignored his demands for allegiance and requests for troops when, a year later, that young man whose company I had found so entertaining years ago in Syria invaded Parthia with an army of one hundred thousand men. Mark Antony decided not to march through Hatran territory but instead crossed the Euphrates at Zeugma and advanced north into Armenia where he found a warm reception from the treacherous Artavasdes, who offered support to his campaign. And so Mark Antony marched his army into northern Parthia together with thirteen thousand Armenian troops. But he lost his supplies, Artavasdes deserted him and Spartacus, now a king, destroyed his rearguard of ten thousand men. Antony was forced to retreat back to Zeugma, all the while being harried by swarms of Parthian horsemen. He lost a further thirty thousand men during this withdrawal before limping back into Syria where an Egyptian queen named Cleopatra joined him with money and clothes for his exhausted army. I heard that they were lovers and desired to rule the world, but ended up taking their own lives during a great Roman civil war in which a young man by the name of Augustus emerged victorious.

An end to all things

They are gone, all of them. Every Companion who had accompanied me from Italy was now dead, the only record of their existence being the names carved on the stone memorial in the Citadel. I am old now, a relic of a bygone age, a frail old man whose time has passed.

The Romans did not return to Parthia though they made many threats to do so. Phraates continued to rule the empire as high king but unlike Mithridates learned not to unnecessarily provoke the other kings of the empire. I never forgave him for the murder of his father, my friend. But he was always polite and deferential to me and I had neither the energy nor inclination to instigate a revolt against his rule, which in truth was no more tyrannical than other high kings. Phraates may have been ruthlessly cunning but he was also clever. He insisted on regular meetings of the Council of Kings at Esfahan, which I found personally tedious but were a useful venue where the rulers of the empire could vent their frustrations and get the ear of the high king. Phraates did what he wanted and ignored anything he disagreed with but gave the illusion that he was a benevolent high king who listened to his fellow rulers. After a while I stopped going to these bi-annual gatherings, giving as an excuse the pain in my leg.

It was not wholly untrue because as the years passed my leg became more and more troublesome and I was forced to rest it for days at a time. I had scars on my left arm, on my back and on my face but the arrow that had pierced my leg outside the walls of Dura had the most debilitating effect. It was during one such recuperative period, when I was sitting on the palace terrace with my feet up, that Strabo searched me out, a distraught look on his face that told me something was wrong.

'Remus is down.'

I hobbled to the stables to find my old stallion lying in his stall, his head lifting as he heard my voice.

'He can't get up,' said Strabo with a tremulous voice.

'What is the matter with him?' I whispered, already knowing the answer.

'Old age, majesty, nothing more, nothing less. Years of campaigning takes its toll on even the strongest stallion.'

I entered the stall and eased myself down to sit by him, gently stroking his neck. After the great raid into Syria I had no longer ridden Remus on long journeys and he had thrived in his semi-retirement. Tegha became my main warhorse. I still rode Remus, of course, taking him out every morning for a ride when I was at Dura, but as the time passed he developed stiffness in his joints. His stride became shorter, his movements slower and his flexibility much reduced. And now he had suddenly deteriorated rapidly.

As I talked to him and continued to stroke him he stopped trying to rise and seemed content to be in my company, snorting quietly and rolling his eye to look at me.

Gallia and my children came soon after, stroking his neck and kissing him on the head before leaving him for what they knew was the last time.

447

I stayed with him all that day and night, talking to him about the great victories he had taken part in and the thousands of miles we had travelled together. His breathing was calm and untroubled as the first rays of the dawn sun crept into his stall the next morning and he looked up at me one last time and then those big blue eyes closed and he exhaled. I held his head in my arms as his mighty heart stopped and tears ran down my face onto his white coat. The stall was illuminated by a bright yellow glow as Shamash embraced the soul of a mighty warhorse and carried it to heaven where he would wait until my time on earth was over.

I had seen death many times on the battlefield, witnessed the terrible injuries that arrows, lances and blades can inflict on flesh and bone, seen bellies ripped open and tasted the nauseating stench of blood and gore in my mouth, but the death of Remus affected me greatly. He had been my loyal companion for over thirty years and now he had been taken from me. It was a great loss but I realise now that life is about loss: the loss of parents, the loss of friends and, most of all, the loss of one's youth.

As the years passed I withdrew more and more from the affairs of the empire. Isabella came of age and married the son of King Peroz of Sakastan, who was a frequent visitor to Dura and brought his boy, a fine young man who had inherited the good looks of his mother. And so my second daughter left us and made her home at the other end of the empire. Shorty afterwards we also lost Eszter but her passing was a time of great sadness and privation and was accompanied by the death of Dura's queen.

A great pestilence came from China and swept through the empire like an army of demons from the underworld, striking down rich and poor alike. The epidemic decimated towns and cities and Dura was no exception. We heard of its approach and tried to take measures to prevent it reaching us, dismantling the pontoon bridges near the city and placing guards on the stone bridge further north to prevent trade caravans transiting through the kingdom. In this way we hoped to prevent anyone carrying the illness from entering Dura, but then word reached us that people in Palmyra were dying of the contagion and that it had entered Syria and Judea. And then, one morning as I sat in the throne room listening to Alcaeus reporting on how the bodies of those who had died of the disease were being disposed of, Gallia fell ill. Within hours she was confined to her bed as she was afflicted by a burning sensation in her head.

Alcaeus, ignoring the danger to his own health, attended her and administered medicines while Claudia spread charms around our bedroom and recanted spells to save her mother. I knew that it was all in vain as my wife's eyes became swollen and red and her voice hoarse. Coughing fits wracked her body and vomiting fits weakened her. I stayed with her day and night, wiping the sweat from her body as a burning fever coursed through her. The servants, those who still lived, were frightened by her appearance as her beautiful blonde hair fell out and the smell of death filled our bedroom. On the fifth day after she had fallen ill Gallia died as I cradled her in my arms. A week later Eszter also succumbed to the plague.

By the time the pestilence had passed it had claimed a third of Dura's citizens and hundreds of the army's soldiers. The city and trade slowly recovered but the army never did. I was still king but handed over the day-to-day affairs of the kingdom to Claudia, who had declared that she would marry no man and rejected the advances of a stream of suitors who made their way to the city, all intent on becoming the husband of the daughter of Pacorus of Dura. All their efforts were in vain and as the years passed they stopped coming and the sharp-tongued Claudia became Dura's ruler. She surrounded herself with mystics and sorcerers and gradually the army was reduced in size. The legionary camp was abandoned as the Durans and Exiles became mere shadows of their formers selves and eventually became nothing more than a city garrison. It was a sad end for two such prestigious fighting units but the regions around the kingdom were at peace and I was too old to lead them now. The cataphracts were similarly reduced to half their former strength and the horse archers numbered barely a dragon. They garrisoned the forts that dotted the kingdom but were more a force for maintaining order than fighting wars.

Not that there were any wars to fight because, despite Phraates' scheming and cruel nature, even he recognised that the empire would be best served by peaceful relations with its neighbours as opposed to eternal conflict. The young man who had defeated Mark Antony and his Egyptian queen became emperor of the whole Roman Empire. He was called Caesar Augustus. He promised peace in return for the eagles that we had captured at Carrhae being sent back to Rome.

In a surprising act of courtesy I received a letter from Phraates asking whether I would be amenable for the trophies to be surrendered to the Romans. After the battle they had been distributed among the great temples of the empire – at Hatra, Uruk, Babylon, Seleucia, Esfahan and Susa – so he could have ordered them to be sent to him at Ctesiphon without consulting me. I replied that I had no objection but reminded him that one of the eagles resided in Palmyra, having been given to Haytham by Spartacus. Haytham had died many years before, ironically peacefully in his tent, and his son, Malik, had also passed away. A cold, cunning individual named Fatih, meaning 'conqueror', who was actually not unlike Parthia's high king in character, though I neglected to mention that in my reply, now ruled the Agraci. But I did write that he was unlikely to surrender the eagle that the Agraci possessed. However, I had underestimated Phraates because he sent a courier back to Dura stating that he realised the Agraci had one of the eagles but this could be compensated for if I was willing to agree to the Romans being given the eagle that I had taken nearly fifty years ago and which resided in the Great Temple at Hatra.

'He well and truly duped you,' said Claudia scornfully as we sat on the palace terrace watching the sun go down in the west. 'He has poison in his veins. You should say no to his request.'

But I was old and tired and cared little for relics of a bygone age. 'To what end?'

Her eyes flashed with mischief. 'To annoy him, of course, and remind him that what he seeks to surrender cheaply was bought dearly with Parthian blood.'

I smiled at her. 'You get more like your mother every day. I will reply that I will authorise King Pacorus of Hatra sending my eagle to Ctesiphon.'

She sneered. 'Give me the letter once you have finished with it. I will attach a curse to it that will rot Phraates' innards.'

'You will do no such thing,' I rebuked her. 'It is my decision.'

'The Pacorus of old would have refused to bow down to the Romans.'

I smiled at her. 'And now I am old Pacorus and too frail to bow down to anyone, and in any case we have Romans living in Dura now.'

'That is entirely different,' she snapped in irritation.

But I was not to be swayed and so Phraates sent back the eagles and Parthia entered into a peace treaty with Rome. In the aftermath I received a very courteous letter from Caesar Augustus himself inviting me to Rome where I would be awarded the honour of addressing the Senate. I replied that though I was very touched by his kind invitation, I was now too old to make the long journey to Rome.

It was a most curious thing. I had spent my life either fighting Romans or making preparations to battle them but now we had them in Dura, merchants mostly, all making a handsome living from the trade that the city attracted. Some became wealthy and bought a mansion in the city, moving their families and slaves into Dura, though they adopted Parthian dress and after a while it was difficult to tell who was a native and who was a foreigner. No that it mattered; everyone was free to come and go as they wanted as long as they obeyed the law and paid their taxes.

Their wealth paled beside that of the man I had first known as a Cappadocian pot seller who had turned his hand to scouting. Byrd died one of the richest men in Parthia and Arabia, the owner of a vast transport system that used thousands of camels and mules to convey goods throughout the western part of the Parthian Empire, Agraci lands, Syria, Judea, Egypt, Cilicia and Cappadocia. He was courted by Roman governors, Egyptian pharaohs and Parthian kings but continued to live a simple life and had the appearance of a struggling travelling salesman to the day he died. I was at Palmyra when he suddenly fell ill and was taken to his tent. I held a sobbing Noora when he passed away. That was ten years ago now but it seems like yesterday.

Curiously, though I had been one of their most intractable foes, the Romans in Dura and Syria also sought my company. I received many invitations to be the guest of rich and powerful Romans but because it meant travelling far and wide I politely declined most of them. One

450

invitation I did accept was from the Roman governor of Syria, one Marcus Vipsanius Agrippa, a serious man with thick curly hair who had been instrumental in winning a great naval battle at a place called Actium that had secured the rule of his friend Caesar Augustus.

Claudia gave me two companies of cataphracts as an escort and the stables supplied a very docile mare for me to ride, not that I did much of that as my leg made sitting on a horse for long periods extremely painful. She also insisted that half a dozen squires attended me and gave strict instructions to the commander of the escort that I was to ride for only two hours at a time. But that journey to Syria was one of the happiest in my dotage. The cataphracts and their horses wore scale armour and pennants fluttered from every *kontus*. Every day the squires helped me into my leather cuirass and I wore my Roman helmet with a magnificent white goose feather crest once again, and at my hip I carried the *spatha* that had been gifted to me by Spartacus. And suddenly I was once more Pacorus of Dura as my griffin standard fluttered behind me and the sun glinted off whetted lance points. During the journey I thought I heard the steady tramp of thousands of hobnailed sandals on the sun-roasted earth behind me and on the horizon saw the fleeting shapes of black-clad scouts riding far ahead of the army led by Byrd and Malik. But then a gust of wind brought me back to reality and I saw my withered hands and felt the ache in my leg and knew that those days were long gone. Foolish old man.

Marcus Vipsanius Agrippa was a most excellent host, greeting me at the gates of Antioch and escorting me to the great palace in the city. If anything it had grown in size and was filled with more noise, though perhaps the truth was that I had diminished. He gave a great feast in my honour, to which all the nobles and their families were invited, and gave a most courteous speech stating that he was proud that I, the most famous man in the east, had accepted his invitation.

He may have been one of the most powerful men in the Roman Empire but his questions to me in the days afterwards were the same as those posed by all of his countrymen. What was Crassus like, was I the one who killed him at Carrhae and cut off his head, did I really ride a white stallion called Remus? I told him what I told them: Crassus was a most agreeable individual and in another time we may have been friends; no, I did not kill him, though I never told them that he had been killed by a woman, as that would have further sullied his reputation and that would have been unfair; and yes, my horse was called Remus. But most of all they wanted to know about Spartacus, the slave who had risen up and nearly toppled Rome itself. Most of them were not even born when he had been destroying Roman armies, or if they had would have been infants, and they were most curious to know everything about him. Talking with Agrippa and his officers I soon realised that the myth of Spartacus was very different from the reality. They had been told that he had been a giant who did not sleep and crept up on his foes in the dead of the night, that he stormed Nola with ten thousand men.

I shook my head. 'We bluffed our way in with a handful of horsemen.'

451

'It is well known that his wife was a witch who controlled the weather,' announced a young tribune. 'That is how he and his army escaped Crassus at Rhegium. She created a snow storm that blinded our soldiers.'

'There was snow,' I agreed, 'but it was courage and discipline that got his army out of Crassus' trap, not sorcery.'

'Some say that Spartacus escaped from the Silarus Valley and lived out the rest of his life as a bandit in Bruttium,' said another.

'He died fighting in the Silarus Valley,' I corrected him, 'and the day after I and thousands of others attended his cremation.'

I told them of how I had been rescued by Spartacus on the slopes of Mount Vesuvius and showed them the *spatha* that he had given me all those years ago. Agrippa held the weapon as though it was a religious icon possessed of supernatural powers, while the others stared at it in awe. I had to laugh.

'What was he like?' asked Agrippa.

It was a good question. One that I had been asked a thousand times. 'I believe that the gods earmark certain individuals for greatness, irrespective of their race or circumstances of their birth. Spartacus was one such individual.'

I saw their confused faces. 'I can see you are sceptical but consider this. How was it that an ordinary man, a slave no less, could revolt against Rome in its own land, raise an army of slaves – slaves, not soldiers – and lead them to victory after victory, if not with the help of the gods?'

Agrippa looked most thoughtful. 'Are you saying that he was a god?'

'No, but I believe that he was beloved of the gods and that helped him. He was also brave, intelligent and resourceful and had the ability to appraise both individuals and circumstances to his benefit.'

I enjoyed their company but also envied them their youth and the lives that lay ahead of them. For me such events were interludes in a long period of loneliness. I had seen my friends and wife die but often wondered if the gods had reserved the cruellest fate for me by keeping me alive and enduring the slow death of old age. My body became frail and a playground for aches and pains and my senses dulled. At night I lay on my bed and thought of Gallia and the times we had shared together, always falling asleep clutching the lock of her hair that hung around my neck. I prayed for death but it never came, and the next morning woke to endure another day without her.

My return to Dura was barely noticed, though I am sure that the six squires who had been tasked with looking after me were glad we were back from Syria. I returned the mare to the stables and went back to using the small cart pulled by a cantankerous mule for my regular morning trips from the Citadel, through the city and then south to a quiet spot a couple of miles south by the river, to sit beneath an old date palm. The palace carpenter built a seat under the tree that I could rest on and I spent most mornings watching the river flow south, invariably dozing off to the sounds of lapwings, herons and warblers.

452

Today was no different: a morning with the sun already warming the earth from a clear blue sky. There was much activity in the Citadel as Claudia was in the throne room authorising trade licences that had been agreed by the royal council, which sat each week in the headquarters building, now given over entirely to civil rather than military matters. Petitioners were standing at the top of the palace steps, waiting to be admitted. As a groom brought my cart to the foot of the palace steps I ambled through the group. One of them, a man in his mid-fifties with a full head of brown hair and a neatly cropped beard, dressed in a white silk tunic smiled and bowed his head to me. Out of courtesy I smiled back but he continued to smile and look at me so I went over to him.

'Do I know you?'

'No, sir, forgive me staring. We met once, a long time ago, but there is no reason you should remember me.'

Now my curiosity was aroused. 'I am old and unfortunately have no recollection of our meeting.'

Whoever he was he was obviously a man of some means for he wore soft leather boots on his feet and his white cloak was fixed to his left shoulder by a large silver brooch.

'It was a long time ago, sir, so there is no reason you should remember. I was one of a score of Roman soldiers, the sole survivors of a legion, who stood on a rise of ground near the town of Carrhae expecting to die when you saved us.'

That was over thirty-five years ago. I extended my bony hand to him. 'I am glad that you all survived.'

He took my hand. 'Only because of your intercession, sir, for which I am eternally in your debt.'

'What brings you to Dura?'

'I have a wine-selling business in Syria, sir,' he replied, 'and hope to establish a shop here in Dura.'

'Business is good?'

He nodded. 'It is, sir. Peace means trade and trade brings profits.'

It was not always so. 'What is your name?'

'Lucius Cato, sir.'

I stayed and chatted to him about the Battle of Carrhae until Claudia ordered the doors of the throne room to be opened to the petitioners. I escorted him inside to ensure he received his licence. As thanks he invited me to dine with him and his family that evening, a request I gladly accepted. Claudia was bemused by my support for this Roman merchant but she did not realise that to talk with someone who remembered me as a great warlord was heartening. Only someone who has outlived his or her usefulness would understand.

A stable hand helped me onto my cart and my faithful mule walked from the courtyard to transport me to my usual morning residence by the river. I glanced at the memorial to the Companions that had space for one more name as I left the Citadel. The city's main street was thronged with shoppers, travellers, sightseers, camels and mules loaded with goods and so it took me longer than usual to reach the Palmyrene Gate. Bored guards rested on their shields and others walked up and down on the gatehouse's battlements. They stood to attention when they recognised me and I raised a hand in acknowledgement, then looked up at the stone griffin that had stood guardian over my city for so many years.

Its head moved, I swear it did, in a gesture akin to a nod of recognition, as I passed under the arch and exited the city. I pulled on the reins to halt my mule and then looked back up at the statue. It was immobile. Of course it was. Foolish old man.

My old mule knew the route he had to take every day and once we had descended the gentle slope that led from the gates he headed off the road heaving with carts, wagons, camels, mules and travellers on foot and ambled south, towards the fields and date palms of the royal estates. Fed by irrigational canals that had been vastly improved by the engineering skills of Marcus Sutonius, they grew the crops and fed the cattle, pigs, sheep and goats that sustained the palace and the garrison, as well as producing a surplus that was sold in the city. Dozens of villages had sprung up inland of the Euphrates where farmers and their families prospered.

I sat on the cart as the mule trudged down the dusty track leading to my bench. When he stopped I alighted the cart, unstrapped him from his harness and then led him to the shade of the date palm. I never bothered to tether him because he was too lazy to attempt to escape, being content to remain by my side apart from the occasional amble down to the river's edge to drink.

I eased my creaking body down and rested my hand on my sword hilt. I don't know why I bothered to strap it on each day because I was far too old and frail to wield it. But then I had worn a sword since my teenage years and it was a link to my past, to a time when I had been a warlord and commander of armies. It was also a link to the man who had given me it and whose memory I still revered. I watched the waters flow past and heard the comforting sound of birds overhead. The tiring bustle of the city seemed far away as I watched a dragonfly hover above the blue waters of the Euphrates. The air was sweet and pure and the silence was having a most sleep-inducing effect and soon my eyelids were closing as I drifted into blessed slumber.

I awoke with a start. Something was wrong. The hairs on the back of my neck were standing up and my senses were heightened. I felt the same surge of tension and energy that I had experienced countless times on the eve of battle. I jumped up and drew my sword as the air was suddenly filled with the dull, melodious thud of marching feet. I swung round and saw a long column of soldiers approaching like a great black snake slithering across the terrain. But that ground was lush and rolling, a blanket of green as far as the eye could see. The river and date palms were gone. What madness was this?

I tightened the grip on my sword and saw that my hands were no longer covered with wrinkled skin and bulging veins but were smooth and strong. I stared at my left hand in disbelief.

'Sleeping on guard duty, Pacorus?'

I turned around and saw a man on a powerful brown horse, an individual with muscular shoulders beneath the mail shirt he was wearing, his face chiselled, his jaw line strong, his dark eyes unyielding. His hair was cropped short but he was no Roman. His lips broke into a broad grin.

'Has the cat got your tongue, King Pacorus of Dura?'

My sword fell to my side as I beheld the figure of Spartacus before me, who now slid off his horse and strode up to lock me in an iron embrace.

He pulled back and slapped me on the arm. 'Lord,' I whispered.

'It is good to see you, my friend.'

'Lord!' I shouted, before dropping my sword and embracing him in delirium.

'I hope you are going to give him back to me, little one,' another person said and I froze as I recognised the voice.

I turned to see a woman with hair as black as night dismount and walk towards me with a feline grace. Her full lips parted as she smiled and opened her arms to embrace me.

'Claudia.'

I felt tears welling up in my eyes to run down my face as I blubbered like a child. She held me close and kissed my wet cheeks.

'Why the tears, little one?'

'It has been so long, lady. I thought I would never see you again.'

My lord placed an arm around my shoulder. 'We never abandon our friends, Pacorus, you should know that.'

He vaulted into the saddle and helped his wife into hers as the vanguard of his army arrived, a great mass of men armed with javelins, wearing helmets and carrying Roman swords. They marched six abreast, rank upon rank filing past me and banging their javelins on the insides of their Roman shields as they did so. I saw long hair protruding from beneath the helmets and heard the chant, 'Parthian, Parthian,' and raised my hand to the Germans who acclaimed me.

A man with a long face, long hair and a beard sauntered up and offered his arm.

'We were beginning to think you would live forever,' he grinned as I clasped his forearm.

'We can't have you grabbing all the glory, Castus,' I replied.

'We will talk of that in camp tonight.'

I picked up my sword as I heard another familiar voice. 'I hope you've kept it sharp.'

I looked up to see Cannicus standing over me, with the hulking figure of Thumelicus beside him. I laughed out loud and threw my arms around them both.

'Never have I been so happy to see so many Germans.'

'Until tonight,' said Thumelicus before rejoining the ranks.

Next came thousands of Thracians led by a squat, dark-haired man with a scar down the right side of his face. He pointed at it as he passed me.

'I see you have a souvenir like mine.'

'Yours is deeper, I think, Akmon.'

The serried ranks continued to pass me as I placed my sword back in its scabbard and Spartacus and Claudia walked their horses forward to my side.

'Are you coming with us, Pacorus?' he asked.

I looked up at him. 'I have no horse, lord.'

'Do you not?' said Claudia, looking beyond the column of troops.

The horizon, previously empty, was suddenly filled with horsemen cresting a hill who then flooded the valley we were in and rode towards us. I saw a great white banner sporting a red design and then a rider with flowing blonde hair holding the reins of a white stallion that galloped beside her and a wave of pure joy swept through me. The riders slowed their horses to a trot and then halted as Gallia walked Epona and Remus through the parting ranks and brought my horse to me.

The tears came again as she gave me a dazzling smile, jumped down and threw herself into my arms.

'You did not think I would leave you, my love, did you?'

'Never,' I answered, my heart full of gladness.

I cupped her young face in my hands and stared into her blue eyes.

'Was it all a dream?'

'Life and death are but fleeting dreams, my love, but love is eternal.'

I hoisted myself into the saddle and once again felt the powerful frame of Remus beneath me. He snorted and flicked his tail and I leaned forward and patted his neck. Gallia mounted Epona and then we followed Spartacus and Claudia as they trotted forward beside his marching army. The other horsemen fell in behind us: Vagharsh carrying my banner, the grinning Nergal beside Praxima and Gafarn and Diana joining us with the mail-clad Amazons behind them. I shook hands with them all as we rode on.

Spartacus slowed his horse as we neared a man wearing a white transverse crest atop his helmet who was barking orders to the soldiers marching beside him. He struck one with his cane.

'No talking in the ranks. You're no longer slaves but soldiers, so act like it.'

Spartacus rode alongside him. 'Pacorus has joined us, Domitus.'

My friend turned and raised his cane to me. 'About time. We need someone to keep your horse boys under control.' He gave me a grin. 'We'll talk later, my old friend.'

Spartacus shook his head and smiled. 'Well, Pacorus, we must make haste if we are to get home.'

'Home, lord?'

Spartacus nodded. 'Yes, Pacorus, our objective. A land of peace. And freedom.'